$8.50
m

Heartlight

TOR BOOKS BY

MARION ZIMMER BRADLEY

Dark Satanic

The Inheritor

Witch Hill

Ghostlight

Witchlight

Gravelight

Heartlight

Heartlight

MARION ZIMMER BRADLEY

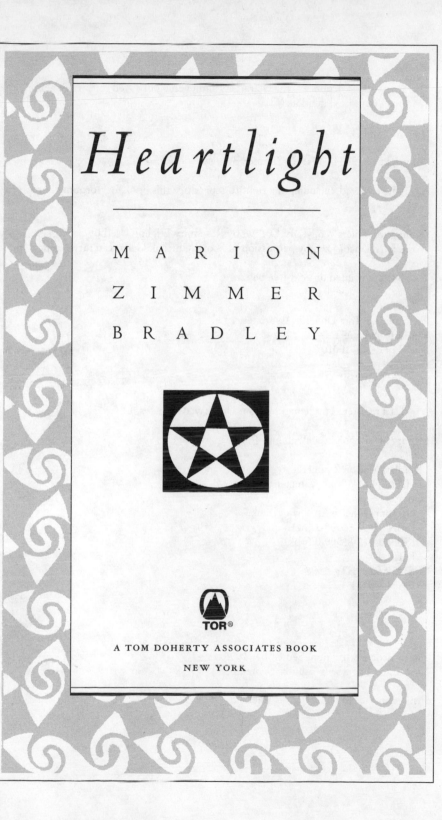

TOR®

A TOM DOHERTY ASSOCIATES BOOK

NEW YORK

HEARTLIGHT

A Tor Book
Published by Tom Doherty Associates, LLC
175 Fifth Avenue
New York, NY 10010

www.tor.com

Tor® is a registered trademark of Tom Doherty Associates, LLC.

Library of Congress Cataloging-in-Publication Data

Bradley, Marion Zimmer.
    Heartlight / Marion Zimmer Bradley.
        p.   cm.
    "A Tom Doherty Associates book."
    ISBN 0-312-86508-2 (hc)
    ISBN 0-312-86509-0 (pbk)
    I. Title.
PS3552.R228H39 1998
813'.54—dc21

                                                        98-23557
                                                        CIP

First Hardcover Edition: September 1998
First Trade Paperback Edition: September 1999

Printed in the United States of America

0 9 8 7 6 5 4 3 2

The author gratefully acknowledges the assistance of Sandy Ellison, Office of the Chancellor, University of California at Berkeley, for information about the campus and campus activities in the 1960s. Any inaccuracies which appear in the manuscript are, of course, my own.

I would also like to thank Rosemary Edghill, who has been instrumental in preparing this manuscript (as well as those of the three previous books in this series) for publication.

"Thus, this single most inflammatory and crucial document of the Third Reich had its origins in that strange twilight world where occultism and espionage meet, a world we will visit again and again in the course of this study."

—PETER LEVENDA,
UNHOLY ALLIANCE

AVALON OF THE HEART

Move along these shades
In gentleness of heart; with gentle hand
Touch—

—WILLIAM WORDSWORTH

DID I LOVE COLIN MACLAREN? IT'S AN ODD QUESTION, BUT I SUPPOSE IT IS one that the world would have to ask, assuming it knew anything about either of us—or, for that matter, cared. Certainly he has been the one constant in my life, outlasting jobs, residences, and even my beloved Peter.

I first met Colin when I was barely out of my teens, a young woman on her own for the first time in a world that has so changed over the last forty years that to a modern the 1960s might as well be a foreign country. It was a world where women knew their place, and kept to it for the most part—a world in which progress was inevitable and all change was for the best.

We—America, the Allies—had won, so we believed then, the war against evil not so very long ago. It was that war that shaped the lives of the boom generation, though the conflict I and my sisters grew up hearing about was not World War II, but Korea. At the time both of them seemed honorable wars and decisive victories for what in those days we called "our way of life," though as the years have passed, there have been arguments against both the justice and the finality, not only of those wars, but of Vietnam, the Gulf War, and the hundreds of smaller conflicts that have sprung up in every corner of the globe since.

I do not think we shall ever truly know what "the last good war" meant to us until the last soldier of that conflict is buried and the last of the unquiet dead exhumed from their graves.

Colin would say that knowing that you didn't know was the beginning of wisdom . . . Colin MacLaren, my teacher and my friend. He was one of those who had been tempered in that great conflict—changed as so many of those who were to become the parents of my own stormy generation were, but in Colin the war and its aftermath had bred a terrible, fierce, and demanding love, a love too vast to hold any one woman—or man either—as its focus.

Did I love Colin MacLaren? I truly no longer remember what I felt when I first saw him. But I do know that Colin MacLaren loved all mankind far too much ever to love me alone.

ONE

BERKELEY, CALIFORNIA, MONDAY, SEPTEMBER 5, 1960

All bright and glittering in the smokeless air,
Dear God! the very houses seem asleep;
And all that mighty heart is lying still!
　　　　　—WILLIAM WORDSWORTH

IN JANUARY OF THIS YEAR A MASSACHUSETTS SENATOR NAMED JOHN F. Kennedy announced that he was going to run for president of the United States. In February, the civil-rights protests that had torn the New South apart for the last four years escalated in Charlotte, North Carolina, and Elvis Presley—a white entertainer whose musical roots were in black "soul" music—received his first gold album.

In May, a U.S. pilot named Francis Gary Powers was shot down as he piloted his U-2 over Russia, sharply escalating the Cold War tension that held all Europe in the grip of a political winter, and the Queen of England's younger sister, Margaret, married Antony Armstrong-Jones in a wedding that captured the glamour-starved public imagination in a way that nothing had since Grace Kelly's fairy-tale wedding four years before.

1960. The year when the future itself was the New Frontier. But it was a frontier that was not without its Old World goblins. This was the year during which many in the world would awaken from their emotional paralysis and finally begin to total up the true cost of "the last good war"—the war before Korea, the war whose cost had been buried in the postwar economic boom. 1960 was the year that Adolph Eichman was finally arrested in Buenos Aires and taken to stand trial for his crimes in the embattled state of Israel. His trial would be broadcast worldwide, cementing the new medium's—television's—place on the New Frontier, making it an integral part of a world that could still believe in the global classroom and the global village.

1960. It was a year when the Great Powers continued to divest themselves of colonial possessions that seemed to belong to another time. A year that saw increased fighting in an area of the world still often miscalled the Belgian Congo, and a fledgling United Nations that was starting to flex its international muscle (while the Vatican and its newest Pope, John XXIII, claimed the same "right and duty" to intervene in foreign affairs for itself).

That summer, a thirteen-year-old government agency called the Central Intelligence Agency, which had been formed out of the remnants of the wartime OSS as a direct challenge to the FBI's increasing power, would begin the disastrously unsuccessful series of assassination attempts against foreign dictators—notably last year's new Caribbean strongman, Fidel Castro of Cuba—that would cause its fall from grace a quarter of a century later when the details of its various attempts were finally made public. At the Democratic National Convention, the popular and well-connected young senator from Massachusetts would choose a fifty-two-year-old Texan named Lyndon Baines Johnson as his running mate, and the Soviet Union would continue consolidating the gains of its infant space program.

It was a year of hope and despair; twelve months that saw the appetite for freedom spread like wildfire through Asia and the Middle East while Europe groaned beneath the weight of an Iron Curtain rung down upon it by allies turned to enemies. Like a phoenix from the ashes, the Russian Bear had risen up out of the cinders of the Allied victory to menace the nations of the West anew, armed with weapons that made a war too terrible for sane men to contemplate. Civilization stood poised on the brink of nuclear hellfire, and the world powers jockeyed for position in the new world order that was to come.

This was the world that Colin Niall MacLaren had returned to four years before—an exotic country that had created television and defeated polio, and had relegated Colin's war to the mists of the dead past. When he'd left Europe, he'd left behind a West Germany barely beginning to come to terms with the enormity of its crimes, but a West Germany no longer controlled by the Great Powers, a political landscape shattered and recast in no one's image over the nearly twenty years he'd been there.

He'd spent almost half his life in exile of one sort or another from the country of his birth. He'd been in Paris when the German army had marched in; a tall, lanky young man with piercing blue eyes beneath shaggy pale brows and the indefinable air of the eternal student about him. He was barely old enough to vote in the land of his birth, but at nineteen years of age Colin was already old enough to know that the war he was called to fight was not one that could be fought in an American uniform.

He'd spent the first half of his twenties running and hiding and killing, fighting for the Light against the Black Order that had manipulated an entire nation into doing its will. Friendships were brief and intense, made more piquant by the threat of torture and death that was a bitter fact of life for those who set their will in opposition to that of the Thousand-Year Reich.

When V-E Day had come in '45, Colin's war had in one sense only begun, for now that the German threat was ended, he was called upon to cleanse and to heal, to purify the battlefield just as a doctor sterilized the wounds of battle, so that the healing could be clean and the patient could rise up and go on with his life.

And at last, as with all tasks, there had come a time when that work, too, must be counted as done.

Coming back to Manhattan in the spring of 1956 had been like returning to an alien future for Colin MacLaren. There were skyscrapers everywhere he looked, and more under construction. The new UN Building dominated the East Fifties, and the friendly trolleys he remembered from his boyhood excursions into the City with his parents were long gone—along with the grassy verges on Park Avenue and the five-cent cup of coffee. Fortunately, Colin wasn't faced with the immediate need to find employment upon his demobilization—his back pay, courtesy of the U.S. Army, saw to that.

Almost at once, Colin had fled the city for the security of his boyhood home in Hyde Park. His Scots father had died when Colin had still been a boy, and his mother had died while Colin had been in Europe, but the old white farmhouse was still just as he'd remembered it. The house was the bulk of his mother's estate, but there was enough left over to pay property taxes and most of the bills for some years to come.

And so, for the first time in more years than he wanted to think about, Colin MacLaren found himself both at liberty and at leisure, without any demands on his time and no one attempting to kill him. The Hudson Valley was still as peaceful and welcoming as he recalled; he surrounded himself with his books and his music and learned once more to sleep without having to keep an ear cocked for a knocking at his door or the summoning midnight ring of the telephone. He was free. The world was at peace.

The quiet of the country healed something inside him that he hadn't known was injured, but after only a few months at home Colin realized that the bucolic countryside was no place for him, and so, after much thought, he'd sold the old place and gone south again, back to the bustling city in the spring of 1957.

There, he invested the proceeds from the sale of the house and the small family legacy in the purchase of a three-story apartment building on a side street in the East Twenties. It was divided into seven apartments; Colin left the management of it in his landlord's hands and moved into the vacant apartment on the top floor. The building was an investment that would—he hoped—provide him with both a roof over his head and a certain amount of income in the years to come, freeing him to continue his true work.

If he could only still be sure of what that was. Once not so very long ago it had seemed presumptuous to plan for a future that included old age, and afterward, his work had been clear-cut, and clearly set before him. Now everything had changed. For an Adept on the Right-Hand Path, dedicated to the Great Work of Transformation, his responsibility was to provide aid to those in need and succor to those others who were, as he was, pilgrims upon the Path. But the country he'd come home to was throwing itself headlong into the twenty-first century, intent on only what it could see and hear, smell and touch and taste. America in the fifth decade of the twentieth century seemed curiously indifferent—even numb—to the Unseen World that existed just beyond the grasp of these five senses.

That disinterest was not enough to make Colin despair—despair, in any case, was a sin, and Colin had seen things far worse in the last several years than the cheerful contentment of the American middle class. But it did make him wonder what his work in the world was to be, and if he had indeed made the right decision by coming home.

But knowledge of the future was in no man's gift, and so Colin set aside his own worries and concentrated upon the work before his hands, just as his teachers had taught him. Colin hated superstition with a passion; if not for the superstitious fears of the average German of three decades before, the whole nightmare machinery of the Nazi Party would never have gained its death-grip on European politics. He would fight superstition when and how he could, with the greatest weapon at his disposal: knowledge.

He signed a contract to give a series of lectures on folklore and the occult in one of Manhattan's numerous "universities without walls," and set about making his new accommodations into a true home. His few personal possessions were quickly reclaimed from storage, and bookshelves built and fitted to the walls. Slowly he adapted to the bustling beat of "cliff-dweller" life. He bought a typewriter and began producing articles for a number of small and arcane journals; their publication brought him a small but carefully-tended list of correspondents and—very occasionally—a cry for the sort of help Colin was uniquely qualified to provide.

But something was still missing, and as winter drizzled its way into spring once more, Colin took to the streets, trying to relearn what he thought of as "his" city on his long, rambling walks. The street that held his brownstone bordered (at least in a realtor's imagination) on the northern edge of Greenwich Village, and most evenings, after his other obligations were finished, Colin found himself walking the Village's twisted streets and byways.

He was looking for something, that much he knew, but whatever it was, he did not find it there—or at least, he did not recognize it if he did. More and more as the weeks passed, Colin realized that this was not the place that he belonged. He did not fit in here—not into this bustling New York, and certainly not among the scraggly poets and alienated philosophers in the coffeehouses of the modern Bohemia.

Colin instinctively disliked them and their rebellious culture even as he feared that the emotion he felt came not from what they were but from a lack within himself. The plaintive "folk" singers at places like Gerde's Folk City only made him remember how much he preferred the savagely constrained passions of opera to the almost atonal folk music that filled Folk City and venues like it.

But as he found himself—against all training—dismissing those youngsters who had never gone to war as a generation without discipline, he was finally disturbed enough by his feelings of anomie to share them with the only other exoteric member of his Order currently in America: Dr. Nathaniel Atheling.

It was a raw grey day, and the wind whipping in off the river cut like a knife The yellow-brick bulk of Bellevue Hospital looked unpleasantly animate, as though at any moment it might get up and walk. This far downtown, the Brooklyn Bridge, not the Empire State Building, dominated the skyline. Colin shivered as he hurried toward the glass doors marked ADMITTING.

Atheling had been a member of the Order's Lodge in Cairo, but Cairo had not been his home. He'd come to the United States immediately after the war; one of the stateless persons that the global conflict had created. Atheling had a medical background, making the transition easier—once he had requalified, he had taken a staff position at Bellevue.

As the rich and even the middle class continued forging inexorably uptown, Lower East Side hospitals like Bellevue bore more and more of the brunt of the poor and immigrant population's needs for physical as well as mental health care.

Like that of most men his age, Colin's childhood had been scarred by the Great Depression. Poverty was foreclosure and debt, clear-cut and easily recognizable. He didn't think of what he saw here as destitution, but he knew it made him uneasy. Odd to think of America as a country of the poor.

Dr. Nathaniel Atheling had a small office on the third floor of the main building. Colin found it without difficulty and knocked on the door.

Atheling was a spare, slender man, closer to fifty than to forty. His dark hair was several weeks late for a haircut, shot with early silver, and when he glanced up Colin could see that his eyes were a curious light amber color, nearly gold. The only thing at all out of the ordinary about his appearance was the scarab pendant in bright blue *faience* that hung from a silver chain about his neck, resting against his sober institutional necktie. He was seated behind a desk covered with paper.

"Ah. It's three o'clock. That means you must be Colin MacLaren," Atheling said. His voice held no trace of any accent, and only a careful precision hinted that English might not be his native tongue.

As Colin closed the door behind him, Atheling raised his right hand in what might have been a casual gesture. Certainly any of the Uninitiated who saw it would mistake it for such, as they were meant to: it was the Salute given from an Adept of a higher grade to one of a lower.

Reflexively Colin returned the salute, lower to higher, and sat down in the uncomfortable plastic chair on the other side of Atheling's desk.

"Forgive me for receiving you in these surroundings, Dr. MacLaren, but my days are long, and you had indicated that this was a matter of some . . . personal urgency."

"A neat way of putting it," Colin said. "And please, drop the title. Call me Colin. It's a Ph.D., not a medical degree. I don't really feel entitled."

"As you wish, Colin. Now, if you were one of my patients, I'd ask you to tell me what seems to be the trouble, and ask you to be honest, no matter how fantastic the events seem to you. And I suppose that's still as good a way as any to begin. . . ."

That meeting was the first of many—though Colin had gone first to Atheling as a Brother in the Order, he'd quickly found friendship as well as spiritual guidance and sound advice. It had been Nathaniel who had finally suggested that New York's nearly-familiar streets might not be what Colin really needed, and had suggested a course of sunshine and sea air, in a place as different from New York as Colin could find.

He'd also pointed out what Colin already knew: that in less than two years, Colin had managed to dig himself a cozy rut . . . or bunker—and it was mental comparisons like this that had convinced Colin that Nathaniel's advice was sound. He wasn't building to face the challenge of the future; he was retreating from it in confusion and perhaps even fear. He needed to get out into the world again; force himself to confront it as it was now and stop setting it against the backdrop of his memories.

The means were obvious. He was lecturing nearly every evening now, on wide-ranging subjects that followed his lifelong interests, and he always felt most at home at University. A long time ago—in a life that seemed now as if it had belonged to someone else—he'd even planned to make a career of teaching. Why not pick that place to reenter his interrupted life? On a college campus he'd be immersed in the tidal surge of the here and now, his daily life filled with youngsters whose eyes were fixed on the future.

It was a good solution, though it took a surprising amount of courage to implement. In the fall of '59, Colin finally nerved himself to take the first step.

Though Colin's academic credentials were a little rusty after ten years spent first with the Office of Strategic Services and then the Army of Occupation, they were still fairly attractive to prospective employers, and the lectures he gave, unorthodox though they were, were a point in his favor. In the end he was able to choose among several offers. Mindful of Nathaniel's advice to take something as far from what he was accustomed to as possible, he turned down offers from Columbia University and Boston College, and signed a contract with the University of California at Berkeley.

The reluctance that he felt as the date approached to leave his cozy apartment to its new tenant convinced him more than anything else that Nathaniel had been right; Colin needed more of a change of scene than New York had been able to give him. He needed to make a new start, in a new place.

California.

The silent campus—a vision in pale brick and prestressed concrete—had the ancient dreaming air of a sun-drenched Athenian city. The highest visible point in the brilliant Mediterranean-esque landscape that stretched before him was the campanile/clock-tower which added its quaint Graustarkian accent to the panorama of campus buildings that rose up beyond Sather Gate.

There was no traffic on Bancroft; the street scene was infused with that peculiar midmorning hush that Colin MacLaren had already learned was a distinctive feature of the San Francisco Bay Area. Only he mustn't call it the *San Francisco* Bay Area, Colin had also already learned, just as he mustn't call the city across the bay *Frisco*. It was "San Francisco"—everyone within a hundred miles simply called it "the City," just as if no other city existed—and the "Bay Area." If Colin meant to fit in here he'd do well to pick up the natives' habits of speech as soon as possible.

And he did mean to fit in here, Colin promised himself, into what pundits called the modern Lotos-Land, the Golden State. He was through with war in all its forms—hot war, cold war, forgotten war, undeclared war—and meant to turn his back on everything he'd learned from that most unforgiving of all teachers. As the gospel hymn said, he wasn't going to study war no more. Here he would shake off the ghosts of the past.

Here and now, his life would begin again.

Colin stood a moment longer on Telegraph Avenue staring at the lacy wrought iron gate of the main entrance to the University of California at Berkeley campus. Despite its placid appearance, there was an air of expectation about the campus, the sense of great things afoot.

Realizing he was in danger of loitering, Colin shrugged and took himself across the open space that separated him from Sather Gate. Signs informed him that something called Sproul Plaza was under construction, to be finished next year.

The campus was enormous, stretching for miles in every direction. Within its bounds were several stadia and athletic fields, a Greek Theater, and many of the most brilliant minds in the arts and sciences. Though he'd been a Berkeley resident for a little over a month, he'd been too occupied with tying up his affairs back East and settling into his rented bungalow to take a trip over to the campus. He'd been here last winter for a preliminary interview, but that had been in the depths of the California winter, and it had rained most of the time. Now he was seeing the university campus as it was meant to be seen—a canvas made of cement and stone for sunlight to paint upon. Though Tolman Hall—which housed the Psychology Department—was all the way across the campus on Hearst Avenue, Colin relished the walk through the quiet modern campus.

The sleek modern buildings in concrete and pale brick that he passed oddly evoked the air of a medieval university city while looking as if they were already at home in the future. Few students were in sight as Colin crossed the walk. Though Freshman Orientation began next week, as far as his body could tell, it was still high summer here. Colin had left his ancient trenchcoat back in his closet—he hadn't been able to bring himself to wear a topcoat, and his jacket felt uncomfortably warm, but something in his nature resisted appearing on campus in informal dress. After all, Colin assured himself, the chancellor and the board were known to be very conservative, and his future students would hardly respect him if he were dressed like a beatnik. Psychology was a field where one got enough odd looks anyway, without any need to cultivate personal eccentricity.

And despite his lack of a coat and hat, he was dressed more formally—in dark trousers, vest, tie, white shirt, and belted tweed jacket—than the few passers-by on the streets at midmorning. He wondered if he stood out, revealed as a transplanted Easterner by nothing more than his failure to wear a topcoat.

Colin smiled ruefully at the direction of his own thoughts. For so many years it had been almost second nature to efface himself; to go unnoticed, to deflect any but the most casual attention. He had begun to think that the habit had become a permanent part of his psyche, a characteristic that would remain a part of him through all the lives to come, long after the reason for it had been forgotten. But that was all it was now: habit, and not vital necessity.

Nathaniel had been right, as always. Time, the great healer, had healed him as well. There'd been a time, not so long past, that it would have been impossible for him to take this sort of innocent joy in any passing scene. A time when he had walked in the shadows cast by the Black Order, doing all that he could to bring Light to that Darkness—and always in danger of falling to that Darkness himself.

But thoughts of initiation and ancient magickal orders seemed oddly out of place here on the Berkeley campus. If anything seemed to belong to the world of rationality and sanity it was this place. Berkeley seemed filled with the American spirit—a kind of "can-do" wholesomeness that simply could not comprehend the shadowy half-world in which Colin's battles had been fought. And perhaps, in time, the memories would fade for him as well.

The following Monday was another brilliant cloudless day, and the morning sunlight found Colin in his new office, unpacking the cartons of books he'd carried up the steps from the trunk of his battered black Ford sedan—a recent purchase encouraged by his move to an area of the country where a car was a far more important part of life than it was in New York City.

The small office that was now his contained one battered metal desk and matching file cabinet, an ancient oak desk chair on squeaky rollers and a matching one that stood on four uneven legs, several metal bookshelves that edged the room, and one balky window with a dusty venetian blind. The walls were painted a glossy greenish beige that managed to clash with the worn brown linoleum tiles on the floor.

Colin had been assured that this furniture was only temporary—that better furniture was on order, and that in fact it was rumored that the entire department would be moving to better quarters soon, but Colin placed little credence in these hopeful reports. In his experience, there was little in this world or the next so permanent as a temporary situation.

But his current quarters weren't that bad, in Colin's opinion. Once his books were on the shelves, and he'd hung the bulletin board and a few pictures, the place would look as inviting as such places ever did. It was a place where he could do his work, and the students who came to him for help and guidance would be more interested in their own problems than in how his office was decorated.

Colin had spent the last several days filling out the endless reams of forms that academia seemed to require in order to sanction every action, meeting his new colleagues in the Psych Department, and orienting himself to the vast Berkeley campus. Registration was going on elsewhere on the campus, and classes would begin next Monday. Colin's fellow instructors had assured him that the worst of the confusion would be over by the end of September, when the late arrivals and the Drop/Adds had settled their schedules.

Colin's own schedule looked as if it would be equally busy, at least for the first two semesters. Parapsychology I and II and the Introduction to Psychology course (all the new hires were forced to teach it, or so Colin had been told) were already full. Add to that the usual load of extracurricular activities for which he'd be expected to stand as faculty advisor, and he wouldn't have any more time to brood. He'd be lucky if he had time to think.

"Hello—hello—hello! Anyone home?" a breezy voice called from the doorway.

Colin turned.

"Alison!" he cried delightedly.

Alison Margrave was a regal theatrical woman in her early sixties, a professional psychologist—and parapsychologist—and musician who was one of Colin's oldest friends. She was dressed in her usual flamboyant, gypsyish fashion, wearing a long red wool cape over her blouse and skirt. When she threw the cape over a chair, he could see that Alison was wearing one of her trademark shawls, a colorful weave of muted earth tones secured with a large silver brooch set with an enormous intaglio-cut amethyst. The stone matched the purple of the amethysts in the silver combs that held back her sweeping mane of white hair.

"Well, at least you're glad to see me!" she growled good-naturedly. "Almost a year, Colin, and not a blessed word from you—"

He'd meant to call her once he was settled in the Bay Area, but had kept letting mundane tasks get in his way.

"How did you find me?" Colin asked sheepishly. "I know I wrote you I'd be coming. . . ."

"And that was back in January, and by now I thought you'd probably gotten lost somewhere around Kansas and never gotten here at all," Alison teased. "Fortunately, I have my spies on campus. So I thought I'd see the late Colin MacLaren for myself—and bring you a sort of housewarming present." She advanced into the office and placed a small wrapped package on Colin's desk.

"I was going to call you this week," Colin protested, sitting down behind the desk and waving Alison to the other chair.

When she was seated—her eyes sparkling with youthful mischief despite her age— Colin began searching his pockets for his familiar companion, a battered old briar pipe. Once he'd located it and tapped the dottle into the battered metal wastebasket, he began rummaging for tobacco and matches.

"I was over here on business in any event," Alison said kindly, letting him off the hook. "So you needn't look so self-conscious, Colin. But I *did* want a chance to catch up on things. How have you been? It's been years since I've seen you in the flesh, you know."

Quick as a snapshot, a fierce vivid memory intruded itself on Colin's mind: the air was thick with incense, and he stood with four others before the high altar of a church whose roof had been thrown open to the sky by American bombers. His white robe was stiff with the embroidered signs of his Lodge and Grade, he wore the crown and breastplate of Adepthood, and in his hand he bore the silver stave entwined with emerald and scarlet serpents. All these things were mere display: the exoteric representation of his inward nature: Priest and Adept of the Path.

There, beneath the canopy of starry heaven, he and those others from every Order and Lodge that claimed the Light as its goal—most of whose mundane names he did not even know—worked as surgeons to cleanse the land of the dark taint that still lingered over its landscape like a poisonous fog.

The sharp memory faded, and he was back in his office at Berkeley with Alison. If she knew where his mind had gone in those brief seconds, she gave no sign, but Colin knew that the memories were there for her, too. That night had contained a moment of supreme self-sacrifice, an apotheosis that a man— or woman—might spend the rest of his life attempting to recapture.

There were times when Colin wondered if perhaps that one moment of battle as a warrior of the Light had not done him as much harm as his oversoul had suffered in generations of war against the Dark. The way and the goal of the Path was peace—but the fatal flaw of all their mortal kind was the delight they took in war.

"Colin?" Alison's voice jarred him rudely back to the here and now.

"I was just thinking about Berlin," he said.

Alison's face softened at the memory. "It was a long time ago, you know," she said gently.

No it wasn't! his heart cried silently. He could remember the date exactly: October 31, 1945. Fifteen years ago next month.

"You're right," he said aloud. "Sometimes it seems hard to believe this is the same world as that was," he added.

"It isn't," Alison said with a smile. "And thank the Light for that. We may not have slain the serpent, my dear, but we've certainly broken its back. It will be a long time before that particular ugliness rears its head again," she said positively.

"Let it be so," Colin said automatically. He shook himself loose from the ghosts of the past with an effort and smiled at Alison. Though she was not a member of his own Order, Alison was one of Colin's fellow Lightworkers, and knew as well as anyone did the peculiar ghosts that haunted him. "But tell me about yourself, Alison. What have you been doing?"

"Well," Alison began, as Colin tamped tobacco into his pipe, "you know I've got that old place—Greenhaven—over in San Francisco. I don't think

you've ever seen it—an old Victorian; you'll love it—it's just off Haight
Street by a few blocks and I can pick lemons right off the tree. I've even got
an herb garden now—you'll remember that was always my ambition. A few
years back I remodeled the old garage into a workspace; it's useful to have a
quiet place to meditate, now and again. Let me see: what else? I've been
teaching; both musically and otherwise—there are a few people out there
who are ready for something a bit stronger than parapsychology, so to speak.
And of course I consult—but these days, people are more likely to complain
of little green men than noisy spirits."

"Times change," Colin agreed, touching flame to tobacco and sucking his
pipe alight. "Ten years ago, I couldn't imagine that I'd ever be back on a college campus, let alone teaching."

"Wait until you have your first classroom full of students," Alison teased
him, laughing. "You'll understand why you came back to it, my boy! I
wouldn't give up teaching for all the kingdoms of the earth—but it's hard to
believe that either of us was ever as young as those students are!"

"I wonder if we ever were?" Colin mused somberly. Sometimes the great
gulf between what he had become and the innocents he was surrounded by
seemed almost too much to bridge.

Alison eyed him narrowly, cool appraisal in her warm grey eyes. "We were
all young once, Colin," she said gently, "just as we all age and die. And it is
our responsibility to see that our knowledge of the Great Work does not die
with us."

"I know, Alison," Colin said reluctantly.

She was telling him nothing he did not already know, and it was a situation that had concerned Colin ever since he had returned home. Every pilgrim on the Path, no matter how unfledged, had the responsibility to guide
others in the direction of the Light to the best of his ability. For someone like
Colin, who had followed the Path for many lifetimes, it was even more important that he find and teach his successor in the Great Work; another who
could take his place to stand among the Hosts of the Army of the Light.

To set someone's feet upon the Path was an awesome responsibility, one not
lightly entered into. But to find his *chela* and train him in his footsteps was
the ultimate test of an Adept, for there were many pitfalls along the way, and
failure meant a spoiled Adept, one who had tasted the seduction of power and
yet lacked the discipline to use it for Good. Such creatures, if they survived
the Abyss, came back to haunt their teachers with each turn of the Wheel:
dark wraiths who corrupted all that they meddled in.

Love was the only thing that made such a risk bearable, and in the secret
chambers of his heart, Colin MacLaren wondered if he were still capable of
such love, after the horrors he had witnessed. In all the years of this life he had
not yet met anyone that he felt called upon to teach—was there some lack in
himself that caused him to be so blind?

"There will be time," Alison said, reaching out and covering his hand with
her own as if she had followed the current of his thoughts—and perhaps she

had. The feeling of that warm contact was like a benediction, soothing his sense of guilt and of promises unkept. "Our Masters do not ask anything of us that we cannot accomplish through love and trust."

"I hope you're right," Colin said, slowly. He had never felt less capable of that dispassionate, powerful love that was the sword and buckler of those who warred for the Light.

Alison released his hand and got to her feet. "But I didn't come here to scold you, my dear—you certainly deserve better from me than that. I came to invite you to come over to Greenhaven for dinner some night soon. I'm an adequate cook, and afterward we might tour some of the local jazz clubs. There's more to North Beach than topless dancing, and you can't bury yourself in work every minute. There's quite a community of our fellow travelers here; you should get to know them."

"You're right, of course," Colin said, getting to his feet as well. As he did, his eye chanced on the box once more, and he picked it up. "And we'll make a firm date for dinner, just as soon as I know how busy my schedule's going to be. Now let me see what this is. I love presents," Colin added, as he tore off the gold paper and silver ribbon that covered the package.

"Oh . . . my. Alison, this is lovely."

"Functional, too," Alison said cheerily, her earlier somber mood vanished like San Francisco's famous morning fog. "You can hold down papers, open your mail, stab fellow faculty members in the back. . . ."

Colin turned the object over in his hands. It was a substantial piece. A sterling-silver sword pierced an anvil carved out of black jade, thrusting through the anvil into the white granite of the stone on which the anvil sat. Flecks of mica glittered against the pale stone, flashing in the sunlight.

The "sword" was removable, and was meant to be used as a letter opener; Colin slid it from its niche and inspected it critically.

"Excalibur?" he said quizzically, setting the paperweight down and sliding the letter opener back into its slot. "I hope you don't think I'll be needing *that* any time soon."

Alison laughed. "Those days are over and done with, thank the Light! But I have to dash—I've still got half a dozen errands to run and I have to be sure to be home before three. My newest pupil is coming for a music lesson and I'd hate to be late."

"Pupil?" Colin asked with interest.

"In every sense of the word," Alison said. "I've never felt such strength and dedication in one so young—he's only seventeen, but he's got the drive and discipline of someone three times his age. You'll remember his mother—she studied with me for a while, and thank heavens she remembered me when her boy came out with a poltergeist. She had him in a military school, of all places—well! It was an act of mercy to take him in; I gave him lessons, but even then there wasn't much I could teach him, and when the symphony offered him a position out here, I took him under my wing, as it were—to the great relief of his mother, I might add. You really must come to dinner soon,

Colin, so you can meet him—he's so brilliant that at times it's nearly frightening. I think the two of you will have a lot in common.

"His name's Simon. Simon Anstey."

After Alison had gone, Colin sat staring out the window for a long time, his relit pipe smoldering fragrantly between his teeth.

Simon Anstey. It was the first time Colin had heard the name, but some tolling echo of future memory made it resonate within his mind. Simon Anstey was someone who would matter to Colin in ways he could not yet imagine.

He sighed and shook his head. The future would unfold itself in its own good time—Colin was no psychic sensitive, able to rend the veil and peer into the Unseen World at will. The inspirations he received were only the faintest of echoes from the Akashic Records, meant only to warn, and, sometimes, to guide. He could not judge which this was to be, and in some small corner of his soul Colin feared that it might be a summons to renewed battle in the never-ending war for the Light.

The first weeks of the fall term passed swiftly, and Colin was soon caught up in the minutiae of scholastic life. Aside from a nagging tendency for his students to call him "Doctor" MacLaren, a title he disliked, he had no complaints to make. These children were not old enough to remember the Second World War and had even been too young to face the consequences of Korea; they seemed curiously unfledged, almost as if they wandered the halls of some waking dream.

He managed to keep only part of his promise to Alison—meeting her for a quick lunch in a downtown restaurant, and promising a visit to Greenhaven the next time—but Simon Anstey was away on tour, and so Colin missed the chance to meet Alison's dazzling pupil. Simon had soloed with the San Francisco Symphony by the time he was eight years old, and at twelve had already recorded five albums. When he had come to live with Alison, it was as much for her healing gifts as her musical ones, for Simon, at fifteen, was already dealing with pressures that most men did not face for another twenty years—as well as with a wayward curiosity that led him into little-frequented byways of the Unseen.

Alison spoke of him often, in ways that—were she a younger woman speaking about an older man—would have been easy to mistake for romantic love. But Alison Margrave had set that possibility aside in order to devote her energies to a professional career. In an era when most women still were married by twenty and mothers soon afterward, Alison Margrave had never married. She had always been a maverick, a loner, on guard against self-immolation disguised as social service. And in any case, Simon was young enough to be her grandson.

Alison had given Colin one of Simon's albums, a collection of Scarlatti concertos for harpsichord. When he played it, Colin had marveled at the pure brilliant sound those young fingers had evoked from one of Alison's antique instruments. The soaring rills of notes had echoed off the walls of the living room of Colin's little bungalow and streamed out over the Berkeley hills like a gust of starlight, making him catch his breath in wonder.

He'd listened to the record several times, trying to make up his mind about the musician who had produced such angelic sounds. The music was cold, mathematical, and nearly heartless, but surely that could be laid to the intention of the composer and the youth of the artist? The passions of childhood rarely ran as deep and true as those of their elders; the very young still believed that they would always be just as they were at that moment, heart-whole and immortal.

There was no reason for Colin to be so concerned about young Anstey. The boy was not his student, he was Alison's. And Alison Margrave was experienced and skeptical, unlikely to be wrong about her protégé's motives or capabilities—and certainly not overeager to take on the responsibilities of an apprentice. As a woman, she had sacrificed much for her art and her independence, and would not be eager to seem to be made a fool by unwise choices or impossible romantic attachments.

So Colin told himself, and was able to ascribe his nagging misgivings solely to a small twinge of professional jealousy. There would be time enough to judge Simon Anstey when he had met him.

The brief brilliant autumn passed through the East Bay in a series of crystalline days and increasingly chilly nights as the whole community held its breath—as it did every year—at the threat of fire from the dun brown, tinder-dry hills. Then at last the winter rains appeared, and as October became November the hillsides turned the brilliant emerald green of a Northern California winter.

The young president who had been elected that November seemed to have been born to lead the generation of innocents who filled Colin's classes. Though he kept no more than a weather eye on national policy and international politics, Colin could not suppress the feeling that the wrong candidate had won. His misgivings were nebulous, consisting mostly of the feeling that John Fitzgerald Kennedy was too young, too confident, to be able to deal with the jagged chessboard bequeathed him by the Cold War. Camelot's Crown Prince was too much the golden hero—despite his family heritage of bare-knuckle back-alley Boston politics and a father who had been a senator before him—to be able to go into the dark places and emerge unscathed.

But that, Colin told himself, was why presidents had advisors. His nervous fretting was only the anxiousness of an old polo pony ready to get back into the game. But Alison had been right: his task was over. That match was done.

Only each time he told himself that, some faint instinct told Colin that he was wrong. . . .

In late November, circumstances finally conspired to allow Colin to meet Simon Anstey.

The days were shorter now, hurrying into the dark half of the year, and more days than not the sun that had seemed so omnipresent when Colin had arrived in the Bay Area never showed its face at all. Veils of mist shrouded the Berkeley hills and wrapped the entire East Bay in a mask of grey gauze, making a New Yorker yearn for the bright blue days and pale clear sunshine of an Eastern winter.

Berkeley closed for several days around Thanksgiving, and Alison had demanded his presence for long enough to pay a proper visit to Greenhaven and see something more of the City than he'd been able to manage in his brief visits earlier in the year. So Colin had packed an overnight bag, taken his page of careful directions in hand, and turned the battered but dependable Ford (Colin had nicknamed it *la Bête Noire*, faithful beast of burden that it was) in the direction of the City by the Bay.

The new highway took him across the Oakland Bay Bridge, where the dependable Ford shuddered in the grip of winds severe enough that the local morning radio stations commonly posted "small car warnings" along with the usual weather and traffic reports. Though the Ford was in no danger, Colin was glad enough to get off the bridge and down onto the city streets. Less than an hour later, he was pulling *la Bête* into Alison's steeply tilted driveway.

Despite Alison's characterization of it as "an old barn," Greenhaven was a little brown-shingled Victorian with a pair of matched bay windows on either side of a recessed red-painted door. Warm golden light spilled through the leaded-glass fanlight above the lintel, as welcoming on this grey day as a glad "hello." As he cut the ignition, and the Ford's powerful engine stilled into silence, the door opened, and Alison stood framed in the doorway, wearing a long tartan hostess skirt and a ruffled white blouse.

"Colin! So you actually found your way here to us," she said in pleased tones. One of her white cats—Alison had several, as she'd had for almost as long as Colin had known her—wove back and forth about her ankles, shedding abundant white hairs on the gay red plaid.

"At times the outcome seemed to be in doubt," Colin commented. "I'd gotten used to navigating around the Village—but S.F. always throws me for a loop."

Alison laughed. "The City does take some getting used to," she said with proprietary pride. "But come in—Simon's here—his plane arrived early—and you know how much I've been wanting the two of you to meet."

Colin handed her the gift-wrapped bottle he'd bought and stepped inside, followed by Alison and the white cat. A sense of profound peace settled over him as soon as he crossed the threshold of her home: Alison worked with those of troubled spirit, and as a result, she kept her home rigorously cleared and shielded. Greenhaven was filled with the peace and joy of a dedicated holy place.

On either side of the ivory-painted foyer a broad white door led into a set of rooms separated by glass doors. Alison led him through to the set on the left. The front room contained a desk, couch, and file cabinets—Alison obviously used it for her consulting work—but the room behind it ran the full length of the house, with the back wall dominated by a huge picture window that looked out over the Bay. Today only the tips of the Golden Gate towers were visible through the mist, but Colin could tell that on a clear day the view from these windows would be stunning.

"The kitchen's on the other side; you can get out into the garden from there," Alison said. "Not that this is much of a day for outside explorations. I even built a fire in here." She gestured at the marble fireplace. "And here's Simon."

Colin had been watching his hostess. Now he turned to face the other occupant of the room.

Little Lord Byron on a scooter, was Colin's immediate, unkind assessment. Simon Anstey was the sort of youth the ancient Greeks might have written poems to—his curling black hair was theatrically long, brushing his collar in the back, framing a face beautiful enough to grace a *kylix.* He was standing in front of the small black marble fireplace in a pose that managed to look formal and natural at the same time, and a cut-crystal wineglass stood behind him on the mantle. He held another of Alison's white cats in his arms.

His dark blue eyes were so intense that their color was the first thing that one saw from across the room, and his strong features—hawk-nosed and high-cheekboned—added to the impression of maturity, giving young Anstey the look of eagles. He was wearing a black-and-white tweed sportcoat and dark slacks with a light blue turtleneck, adding to the Bohemian air about him.

But for all Anstey's professional poise, Colin could sense that the boy was nervous, keyed up. He wondered what Alison had told Anstey about the man he was to meet today. *Probably a lot of exaggerated twaddle,* Colin thought, and advanced into the room, his hand outstretched.

"Simon Anstey, isn't it? I've heard so much about you," Colin said warmly.

Simon gently deposited the cat upon the floor, then took Colin's hand and shook it. The cat, miffed, darted from the room on urgent business of its own.

Simon's grip was surprisingly strong, and Colin remembered again that the boy was already a professional pianist, with thousands of hours of practice behind that hearty grip. He'd glimpsed some of Alison's harpsichords across the hall when he'd come in, and wondered which of them Anstey had used for the Scarlatti he'd recorded.

"Professor MacLaren. I've heard so much about you from Dr. Margrave." Anstey's voice was low and strong, a trained voice to go with the trained hands. "I've looked forward very much to this meeting."

"As have I," Colin said warmly.

"Let me leave you two gentlemen to get acquainted while I check on the progress of dinner and put this bottle in to chill," Alison said. "I'll have to change before we go out, but I'll be switched if I'm going to try cooking dinner in high heels. Simon, why don't you fix Colin a drink?" she added. "I'll be back in a jif."

Alison had sworn she intended to take him to hear something called "The

Kingston Trio," at a nightclub with the improbable name of "The Hungry I" down in North Beach.

("As a psychologist, I find the name marvelously appropriate, Colin—the 'I'—the ego—is always hungry. But you'll love the place; you'll see," Alison had said over the phone.)

"Is there anything I can do to help?" Colin asked automatically, but Alison only laughed. She disappeared through the sliding glass doors and left Colin alone with her young pupil.

"Would you like a glass of wine, Dr. MacLaren?" Anstey asked courteously. "There's Scotch, if you prefer; I'm not quite sure what Dr. Margrave has in her drinks cabinet."

"Wine's fine—and it's 'Mister,' not 'Doctor,'" Colin said. "I'm only a Doctor of Psychology, and I'm afraid I'm old-fashioned enough to feel that the title should be reserved for the medical profession."

"As you say, Professor," Simon said with a smile. He moved toward the low table set in front of the enormous picture window—one of Alison's renovations to the hilltop Victorian, Colin was sure—to pour a second glass from the bottle there on the silver tray. He crossed the room to hand it to Colin, then indicated one of the two armless Danish Modern couches upholstered in olive linen that occupied the room. The spare sculptural lines of the modern furniture harmonized well with the room's graceful Victorian proportions.

Colin sipped at his wine, then drank deeper with appreciation. "An excellent vintage," he commented.

"Yes," Anstey said. "I brought Dr. Margrave back a case of it the last time I toured France."

Was it Colin's imagination, or was there a touch of belligerence in Anstey's voice, the attempt of a very young man to stake a claim to his own adulthood? He smiled at the thought, and strove to put young Anstey at his ease.

"It's a beautiful country, isn't it? Were you able to see much of Paris while you were there? I understand that traveling on business doesn't leave much time for sight-seeing."

"I saw a bit," Simon said, seeming to relax. He retrieved his own glass and sat down on the couch nearer the fire. "But a visit can't possibly compare with being able to live there. Dr. Margrave told me that you'd spent some time overseas?"

"I was there during the war," Colin answered, before he realized that there was no longer only one war. Was he getting stuck in his own past? "During World War II, I should say. After the surrender, I stayed on for a few years, working on projects of my own." Which was the best way to handle the time he'd spent with the army; some of the things he'd done with Department 23 couldn't be talked of, even a decade later.

"You must be glad to be home— or maybe not," Simon said, with his beguiling mixture of maturity and boyish enthusiasm. "But tell me—if I'm not being too presumptuous—Dr. Margrave tells me that you're also active in parapsychological circles?"

"Simon! You make Colin sound like a flight of china dishes," Alison teased, coming back into the room. Both men stood, and Simon hurried to retrieve her glass from the side-table and refill it with the excellent Burgundy.

"Now Alison, would you deprive me of the chance to expound upon my favorite subject? After all, I've spent the last two months dinning the basics of scientific method into the ears of my freshman class; it would be a relief to discuss the topic with someone who doesn't think 'parapsychology' is a synonym for 'elementary voodoo.' "

Both Simon and Alison laughed at the mild joke, and Alison said:

"Have you been able to get any fieldwork done? Simon and I had a fascinating case last year: a poltergeist right here in the city—remember that case up on Russian Hill, Simon?"

"How could I forget it?" Simon said with rueful humor, rubbing an imaginary bump on the side of his head. "After I took that Brodie down the stairs I was sore for a week—the last time I will underestimate the Unseen, even assuming I'd been inclined to do so in the first place."

The talk turned naturally to their mutual field of interest, and Colin discovered that Simon Anstey was already a dedicated researcher in the infant field of parapsychology, and also fascinated by the shadowy world of magick.

"If there is a world beyond the one we know, why shouldn't we be able to affect it just as we do the material one?" Simon asked over dinner. "The physical body affects the physical world—why shouldn't the subtle body affect the spiritual world?"

Greenhaven did not have a separate dining room—Alison having sacrificed that possibility to a larger music room—but the spacious Victorian kitchen had plenty of room for a lovely old rock maple farmhouse table that could have accommodated twice their number. Dressed up with white damask and a silver candlestick or two, the setting was quite elegant, even with the kitchen appliances hulking in the background. And Colin did have to admit that the location guaranteed that the food reached the table hot.

"Some of the ways we manage to affect our material world aren't something you'd want to expand to the spiritual realm. Look at soil erosion—strip mining—air pollution. Rachel Carson's written some pretty disturbing books. It would be nice to think that one reality, at least, was safe from that."

"That wasn't what I meant," Simon said impatiently, brushing aside Colin's objections. "There's so much we could learn, so much we could do, if we could put Magick on the same rational footing that Science is. Scientists don't shiver in terror every time they look through a microscope—they don't worry that they'll be struck down by jealous gods for every new insight into how the universe works—"

"But they do treat their material and their subject with the respect they deserve," Alison reminded her pupil. "The Unseen world is a dangerous place for the unprepared. But you're young yet, Simon. You have your whole life ahead of you. There will be plenty of time for your studies: lifetimes."

"I know, Alison," Simon said contritely.

But though he dropped the subject, and for the rest of the evening the talk turned on other things, Colin wondered about the ambition that had been so clearly revealed in Simon Anstey's self as he spoke of his aspirations. Too much passion was as dangerous to a would-be Adept as too little, and Simon had passion in full measure. Passion . . . and something more, something Colin had glimpsed in that brief instant before Alison had turned the subject.

Something dark.

Something dangerous.

TWO

BERKELEY, CALIFORNIA, OCTOBER 1961

My heart would hear her and beat,
Were it earth in an earthy bed;
My dust would hear her and beat;
Had I lain for a century dead;
—ALFRED, LORD TENNYSON

THE NEW YEAR BEGAN BADLY—THE UNITED STATES BROKE DIPLOMATIC ties to Cuba, and bitter fighting broke out—or resumed—in a number of places that had only been meaningless names on a map a few years before: Vietnam, Cambodia, Laos. There were Soviet incursions everywhere, it seemed, and the Communist superpower had managed to orbit and recover a cosmonaut, blazing the trail to its conquest of the ultimate high ground.

In Israel, the trial of newly-captured Nazi war criminal Adolph Eichman began in a chaos of news coverage and security precautions. The testimony awakened half-hidden memories for Colin MacLaren, and made him realize that the horrors of the Final Solution had not been conquered, but buried. Set aside, as if, like a fretful nightmare, ignoring them would make them disappear. Even its victims—those with the most personal stake in keeping those atrocities from ever happening again—were as reluctant to bring up the past as a burned child is to touch fire.

Eichman's trial changed that, though perhaps not enough. But it was enough to rouse Colin once more to the fear that the peaceful home-front years that America had enjoyed since the fall of the Reich had not been the healing sleep that follows great effort, but the drowsing coma that springs from a poisoned wound. His greatest fear—the one he lived with always—was that what the White Adepts had done had been too little, too late.

1961. The new West German chancellor, Konrad Adenauer, came to America to meet with her young president only days before an American general in

Germany was relieved of his command over fears of his ties to a new conservative organization, the John Birch Society. When Adenauer returned home, it was to form a coalition government that brought a temporary peace to defeated and partitioned Germany—a peace increasingly troubled by the Communist dictatorship in the East.

Was the East, just as the politicians had feared, the direction from which the new threat was to come? This year the Berlin Wall had gone up almost overnight, turning from rolls of barbed wire to a brick-and-cement cliff-face standing in the middle of a bleak dead zone. The phrase "Checkpoint Charlie" became common currency, and the Berlin Wall became a visible sign of the tension between Democratic and Communist Germany, East and West . . . just as a Russian ballet dancer named Rudolph Nureyev—who had defected as his troupe was performing in Paris—would come to be seen as a symbol of Eastern oppression and Western liberation.

Had the West smashed the Nazis only to allow their dark torch to be passed to the heirs of Stalin? Had the protean evil that Colin's Order fought simply found another form? Perhaps he—Alison—all of them—had been wrong in thinking that the great Dragon had been defeated. Perhaps they had only crushed the outer shell of the darkness without destroying its spirit, and now that spirit was roused once more to hunt for new disciples.

There was enough new evidence that he was right to render Colin MacLaren an increasingly troubled man, for he knew that the Material Plane—what most non-Adepts thought of as the Real World—was merely the reflection cast by the True Reality that existed on the Inner Planes.

As within, so without . . .

But not every battle on the Material Plane was a matter for an Adept to concern himself with, for spiritual evolution was a force as harsh and ruthless as the physical evolution practiced by Nature. Nations were sacrificed, whole races blotted out, in Spirit's quest for the Light. What Colin found cruel or unjust was not necessarily a sign of the Light's jeopardy, though such a philosophical view was never an excuse for those on the Path to countenance brutality. Certainty was a dangerous gift, and it had not been granted to him.

April was the cruelest month . . . an attempted countercoup by Cuban refugees who landed at the Bay of Pigs failed, and it began to seem—as the first civilian aircraft was hijacked to Havana a few weeks later—that newly Communist Cuba would be the pretext for the nuclear war that began to seem frighteningly inevitable. The death of United Nations' president, Dag Hammarskjöld, on a peace mission to the Congo, simply underscored how fragile the peace of the Cold War was, and the peace that a generation had fought for seemed more and more illusory as the year wore on.

That was the spring the Freedom Riders left Washington for Louisiana, a pilgrimage from which some would not return, as if in proof of Colin's fears that the war had come home and become a secret war, with battle lines yet to be drawn and a battlefield set in the hearts and minds of men and women.

It was a war in which Colin began to realize that he would have a part to play, though as yet he did not know what it was. . . .

* * *

Has it already been a year? Colin wondered to himself. *Yes, that and a little more.*

The windows of his hillside bungalow rattled demandingly each time a gust of wind struck them. Occasionally there was a dry rattle as pebbles and fallen leaves—mostly from the groves of eucalyptus that covered the hills— were dashed against the walls by the wind. The autumn color that Colin was used to from his Hudson Valley childhood was not a feature of October in the Bay Area; instead, in fall the natural world seemed simply to dim, to be transfigured by the winter rains from the gold and blue of summer into the silver and brilliant green of winter.

On this night, Colin found himself grateful to be tucked up snugly in his own living room with a favorite pipe and a glass of Scotch. The night had come early, and the scudding clouds played across the face of the waning moon. This night, of all the nights in the year, always made him uneasy.

It was Halloween.

There were many parties being held this Tuesday evening, both on campus and off, and he'd been eagerly invited to several of them by his student advisees, but somehow Colin hadn't felt like company this evening. Better to stay at home with his memories, and not inflict his company on those who would not understand. Tonight was a night for ghosts, and Colin had many.

Perhaps he was simply out of tune with the triviality of this so-American holiday, which turned what had once been a powerful and portentous night that marked a shift in the currents of the year into nothing but a light-minded excuse for revelry. Hours earlier, the neighborhood children— dressed as movie monsters and cartoon characters—had rung doorbells all along Colin's street begging sweets. As Colin gave them their treats—forestalling the threatened tricks—he wondered if any of their parents suspected that they were participating in the pallid and adulterated end of a grisly pagan custom.

Autumn bonfires had once been bone-fires; on this night, once upon a time, it had been believed that the dead returned to the living world, to be placated with food and blood and coaxed to return to their barrow-graves for another year's slumber. It was a night that still held power for those with hearts to feel it—power so strong that even the innocent and unwary were sometimes tangled in its unseen net.

What power was out there tonight, stalking the hills that surrounded the Bay? Colin wondered. He'd coasted through his classes that day almost unaware of his audience, so preoccupied was he by something at the very edge of perception—something more urgent even than the force of memory. He'd cut short his office hours—on Halloween, the students felt that there were more important calls on their time, in any event—and come home, where he'd prowled around the rooms of his little bungalow like a caged bear, trying to isolate the source of his unease.

All that came to his seeking attention were fragmentary images—cathedrals of evil constructed with pillars of light—that could belong as easily to the past as to the clouded present.

Easier, Colin told himself. In such an outpost of rationalism as the UCB campus, the peculiarly European perversions of the thirties and forties seemed like a bad dream, almost impossible to take seriously. Nathaniel had been right: he had needed to come here in order to let go of the past. What had been once would not be again—no matter how much current world events led him to fear the Shadow's renaissance.

But all of Colin's years of training also urged him not to lightly dismiss any intimation, no matter how ambiguous, of trouble. The unconscious mind was not verbal. It existed outside of time, in direct communication with the Unseen, and it did not use words to communicate with the conscious mind. If his unconscious was attempting to bring something to his conscious attention, it might be using images out of his memory that were linked to importance, or geographical location, or even to a particular type of disturbance.

But, though psychics were in tune with the future or the far-distant present, the reason most psychics—and Colin MacLaren was emphatically not one—tended to be so erratic in their public predictions was that they lacked the ability to correctly interpret the messages funneled to them by their preconscious minds. Colin's own sense of disturbance came from an Adept's training: there was a disruption on the Astral that was strong enough to intrude into the waking material world, but elusive enough that no amount of attentive concentration was enough to bring it fully out of the shadows into a place where his conscious mind could deal with it.

It was frustrating, and Colin could understand why many on the Path thought that an Adept must be psychic as well: it would be extremely comforting right now to have the ability to demand answers from the Unseen through his own inborn psychic powers. But in some previous life he had chosen to deny himself those abilities, and so Colin had no choice but simply to watch and wait.

It was after midnight—the older revelers who filled the streets, intent on mischief rather than candy, had finally departed for other localities or their beds, and the neighborhood was quiet once more except for the blustering of the wind. Colin had nearly decided that whatever the unrest was that had troubled him, he would not discover its source tonight, when he heard the sound of a car engine coming toward him through the wind.

There were few other residents along this dead-end street, and all of their houses were dark at this hour. Colin was unsurprised when he saw the shine of headlights sketch itself across the walls of his living room and heard the engine stutter to a stop outside his house. He walked to the door and opened it.

The night air was heavy with the promise of the rain that had held off all evening, and the lights of downtown gave a faintly green glow to the low cloud-cover. The car was unfamiliar—a gleaming late model with a scarlet finish that gleamed in the streetlight—but when the inside lights went on, Colin recognized the driver.

Jonathan Ashwell.

Slender, dark-haired, and intense, Ashwell was the highly-privileged son of East Coast old money; his full name was Jonathan Griswold Ashwell III, and his father was a U.S. Army general. Jonathan was the sort of student every teacher dreams of having—engaged, assertive, bright. And, unfortunately, young enough to believe that nothing bad could ever happen to him. He was one of Colin's student advisees, and, though ostensibly working toward a doctorate in psychology, Jonathan was fascinated by that science's distorting mirror, parapsychology. Colin had liked him at once, and so far he had been able to keep Jonathan's intellectual curiosity in the comparatively safe shallows of the Rhine experiments and similar research into the back alleyways of human cognition.

But something had happened to change that. Colin understood that at once, watching Jonathan bound up the steps two at a time, his face white and strained, his tie askew.

"Professor! Thank God you're here—I didn't know where else to go." He seemed almost hysterical, and Colin feared the worst. There were so many missteps a young man could make at this stage in his life. But it was not Jonathan's mistakes that had kept him up waiting so late.

"Come inside, Jonathan," Colin said, holding the screen door open. "I'm sure we can figure out something."

"No—you don't understand—she's in the car—"

For an instant Colin's blood went chill, and then he was sprinting down the steps of the house, past a surprised Jonathan Ashwell.

There was a girl in the passenger seat of the car. She was fair-haired, her light blond hair worn in a short pageboy, and—Colin guessed—fairly tall. She was also unconscious—or delirious—her head rolling from side to side against the back of the seat. Her lips moved silently, and her hands twitched in abortive gestures, as though she were dreaming an unheard conversation.

He took her wrist. Her skin was cold and clammy, the pulse faint and fast. He could see the rapid movement of her eyes beneath the closed eyelids, as though she were in deep REM sleep.

"I didn't know what to do," Jonathan said. "We were at this party, and suddenly Claire keeled over and started yelling."

"Don't you mean she yelled and keeled over?" Colin asked. He felt the girl's forehead. It was dewy with a chill sweat.

"No. Professor, I swear! Her eyes rolled up in her head and then she started saying all kinds of stuff."

Colin slapped the girl's face gently, trying to rouse her. "What kind of 'stuff'?" he asked absently.

"About—oh, I don't know—the city of the temple and the dragons in the earth—real sci-fi stuff," Jonathan said awkwardly. "That the dragon would rise up against the city of the temple and against the temple, that was it. And something about the path of the eclipse."

It did not sound like ravings to Colin—in fact it sounded oddly cogent— like prophecies still held by his own Order—but that might be mere coincidence. What was important now was finding out just what was the matter with Jonathan's girlfriend.

At that moment Claire's eyes opened, staring unfocusedly past Colin at something that only she could see. In the illumination from the streetlamp he could see that the pupils were wildly dilated, the iris only a pale silvery ring around the edge of the pupil.

"The Sun," she said in a hoarse distant voice. "The City on the Hill—Master— He's hanging on the tree and I won't—" Abruptly she jerked forward, trying to get out of the car. "I can't stand it," she muttered in a more normal voice. "Get out—get away. Stop it, stop it, *stop it!*"

"Be still," Colin commanded strongly. He suspected what her problem was, now. Claire bore certain signs that Colin had been trained long ago to look for, of a psychic Sensitive whose centers had somehow been forced open. Now she was defenseless, with no shield against an onslaught of sensory input from this world and the next. With the thumb of his right hand he sketched the seal of the pentagram upon her forehead, and had his suspicions confirmed when Claire fell back into her seat, limp.

A magickal seal would have had no effect on any mundane ailment, but it had worked here, giving Claire a momentary peace. Without knowing how the Kether chakra had been opened, he did not dare to try to close it, and it would take him time that Claire did not have to find out. She needed to be in a safe place until her centers could be closed once more.

While one of the basic tenets of parapsychology held that the psychic powers were not at all supernatural—being a gift that, though rare, was a normal part of the human sensory appartus—it was axiomatic that unless one were dealing with a strong Sensitive, forcing open the psychic centers of the mind would lead at most to a flurry of wild hunches and perhaps a few bad nightmares. Not to the sort of reaction Claire London was manifesting—unless she truly had not had any inkling of what she was.

Colin glanced back at the house. Take her inside? But no—if she was already open and unshielded, bringing her there could be the worst possible thing for her. Colin's wards were strong, but what lay inside them, though it was of the Light, was something too intense for the uninitiated to stand against. Taking her into the house would only make matters immeasurably worse.

Who did he know in the Bay Area who was equipped to handle this sort of crisis?

"Alison," Colin said aloud.

Greenhaven was a protected place, one dedicated to the Great Work, and Alison Margrave was rigorous and conscientious in her banishings. No force that Alison did not choose to admit could enter this place while its guardian lived. Claire would be safe there.

"Professor?" Jonathan's voice was frightened. "What did you do? What's wrong with Claire?"

"Don't worry, Jon, I think she'll be all right if we can get her the kind of help she needs. I'm going to take her to a friend I know. See if you can get her into the backseat; I'm going to go get my coat."

* * *

It was after two by the time they neared Greenhaven. He'd phoned Alison be-fore he'd left, but no one had answered the phone. There might be a dozen reasons for that, and Claire's trouble could not wait. If Alison was not there when they arrived, Colin could get inside Greenhaven anyway. Without that sanctuary, he feared Claire would die.

Blessedly, Jonathan had trusted him without question, and followed Colin's directions without hesitation even when they led him away from both the on-campus medical services and Kaiser Hospital. What he must have been thinking as Colin directed him across the Bay and into the foggy hills of San Francisco, Colin hesitated to guess, though he was in the boy's debt for his wholehearted compliance.

Though he renewed the Seal again and again, all during the journey, Claire kept breaking free of its benign influence. She raved and struggled, weeping and crying out against things Colin could not see. At times it took all of Colin's strength to restrain her, and he was grateful that he'd had the fore-sight to have Jonathan put her in the backseat—and to ride back there with her himself. If she'd been in front and able to grab the wheel, they'd proba-bly already have gone off the road more than once.

And as it was, Jonathan was completely terrified. Colin had tried to take his mind off Claire by questioning him in the lulls between her seizures. He learned that Claire London was nineteen, a nursing student attending school on a scholarship, and had been born and raised in Burlingame, which made her that rarest of all creatures, a native Californian. Jonathan didn't know her well, though he'd dated her a few times the previous year. He hadn't come to the party with her, though he'd met her there.

"It was just one of Toller's bashes, you know, Professor. A Halloween party; a couple of people done up as gypsies telling fortunes, Ouija boards—that kind of thing." His voice was bewildered. "Nothing happened to anyone else—not like that."

"Did Claire try the Ouija board?" Colin asked. The so-called game was said to be harmless, but in the wrong hands—innocent or otherwise—it pro-vided an undefended route into the unconscious mind as harmful, and poten-tially lethal, as an amateur's attempt to repair his television set with an icepick and a hammer.

"No," Jonathan said. "She hates that sort of thing. Says it's self-delusion. Parlor tricks. When she saw there was one there, she almost knocked it off the table."

"Hmn," Colin said. An interesting reaction from such a strong Sensitive.

Claire's head lay against his shoulder, her pale hair darkened to honey brown with sweat. Her skirt and sweater were soaked through; her body ex-uded the thick chemical scent of the sickroom and her pulse had a thready ra-pidity that Colin did not like to feel. He'd thought he had enough time to risk taking the girl to the safety that Alison could provide, but now he began to think he'd been overconfident.

It was a flaw his teachers had warned him about—with easy mastery of the Path came a brash impetuosity that could lead the Seeker into contests beyond anyone's strength. Failure tempered the spirit and taught conscientiousness and care, his Masters had told him, but Colin had never allowed himself to fail. Knowing even before he had been born into this life how high the stakes in his youthful battles would be, he had taken the risk in this incarnation of retaining the power and control that were normally the fruits of a long life of striving. As a result, the young Colin MacLaren had been sanguine in the face of hopeless odds . . . and was perhaps too optimistic now.

"Can't you hurry?" he asked, fresh tension in his voice.

Jonathan responded by stepping hard on the gas, and the sedan leaped forward into the fog.

It had rained on this side of the Bay, and the twisty streets of the Twin Peaks area were slippery. The car slewed back and forth on the road, and Colin heard a choked sound from Jonathan as the boy fought the wheel. He held his breath, but the car steadied, and the engine wailed as Jonathan downshifted to take the last hill.

"Hurry . . . hurry," Colin muttered under his breath. "There!"

Jonathan jammed on his brakes, flinging Colin and Claire both forward against the back of the bucket seats. He dragged the wheel around and gunned the engine, making the car buck and squeal as it lunged up the slanting driveway to Greenhaven.

Alison was waiting for them in the doorway. She reached the car almost before it stopped moving and yanked the passenger side door open.

"Simon told me you'd be coming," she said, as Colin climbed out of the backseat. "And he's rarely wrong about someone in trouble. What's wrong?"

"She's a Sensitive who's run into something more than she can handle, I think." Colin reached into the car and lifted Claire out.

She lay in his arms, limp with the long fight against her unseen demons. Alison clucked in dismay, and beckoned them to follow her. Colin carried Claire into the house, with Jonathan following behind like a worried duckling.

As soon as Colin stepped through the doorway, he felt peace and stillness descend over him; a nearly imperceptible cessation of the irritating background noise that was the minds and souls of dense-packed humanity resonating through the aethyr that surrounded them. Even Claire seemed eased by it.

"Upstairs," Alison said.

Between them, Colin and Jonathan carried the unconscious girl up to the guest room where Colin had stayed on his previous visits to Greenhaven. Simon was waiting there, wearing the cross, unworldly expression that came from an unexpected late night.

The vigil light was burning on the small altar in the corner—Colin guessed that the Elemental Symbols were Simon's, as Alison's Table of Hermes was larger and more formal, kept in the converted garage that she used as her Sanctuary—and the room smelled of cleansing incense.

"Lay her down on the bed," Alison directed.

Simon moved forward to help them, and soon enough, Claire London was stretched out on the bed. Though the Seal had long since faded, Claire was fairly quiet, protected by Greenhaven's shielding. Alison knelt beside her, peeling back an eyelid with the brisk efficiency of one who'd had much experience in tending an Adept's abandoned body while the soul journeyed far into the Astral Realms.

"She's been drugged," Alison said shortly. "I was afraid of that—it would take a whole coven to blast her this way through sheer Will. And she's very weak. Simon, get me my bag."

The young musician moved to obey.

"Drugged?" stammered Jonathan. He glanced from the small altar to Alison, his face a mask of questions—and faint, incredulous guilt.

"But she . . . All she— All she had to drink at the party was the punch, Professor. There was just a little vodka in it."

"She didn't smoke anything? Take some pills, maybe?" Colin asked, though the pep pills in vogue among the students anxious to be able to pull an all-night study marathon weren't likely to have this sort of effect, and neither were marijuana or hashish.

"No," Jonathan said uncertainly.

"Never mind," Alison said, as Simon returned with her doctor's bag. "I think I know what it is. It's dangerous, it's treacherous, and worst of all—it's perfectly legal."

She opened the bag and withdrew a hypodermic and a phial of clear fluid. "I'm going to give her a stimulant—as much as I dare—and then Simon and I will try to clear her channels and help her rebuild her natural shields. Is she one of yours, Colin?"

"I never saw her before tonight," Colin said with complete honesty.

"Too bad," Alison said. "This would work better if there were someone here that she knew to trust. I don't have the sense that she's a very trusting person—and why should she be?"

Alison tapped the syringe to clear it of air bubbles, then slid the needle into the soft skin of the inside of the elbow that Simon had already swabbed clean with alcohol. Slowly she slid the dose into the girl's vein.

"Professor, what's going on?" Jonathan demanded. "What are—"

Colin raised his hand for silence. "Quiet, Jonathan. I'll answer all your questions later, but right now, we need to give Alison and Simon quiet in which to work."

The two Adepts stood on each side of the single bed, their outstretched arms forming an interwoven bridge above Claire's supine body. With slow methodical brushing strokes they began working their way down her body, their hands always moving in the same direction, as though they brushed lint from a piece of velvet. They were doing for Claire what she could not do for herself: purging her higher centers of their inadvertent burden of psychic force, and allowing them to close and shield themselves once more.

Colin was no psychic, but years of training enabled him to imagine what they must be seeing: the network of conduits, like the branches of a tree, which made up the channels of energy comprising the Light Body. This ethe-

rial self, or Astral Body, was the component of the tripartite Self that clair-
voyants used to travel elsewhere in the physical realm and magicians used to
journey in the Overworld. It was the Astral Form, or double, that sometimes
survived death, wandering the Material Plane after the demise of the body
and the departure of the soul, giving rise to tales of ghosts and hauntings
from those who chanced to see it.

When they reached her toes, they began again at her head, their gestures
broader and more sweeping this time, sending the energy to dissipate into
the earth.

Beside him Jonathan watched, fascinated. Colin could tell that the boy was
responding to the currents of energy swirling through the room; he'd been
right in thinking that Jonathan Ashwell had an aptitude for more than book-
learning. Colin would have to be sure to steer the boy clear of table-tippers
and other occult quacks, lest he become one of those who founder in the shallows of the Unseen World, enthralled by flotsam.

At last Alison and Simon finished their work, wiping the last of the energy
from their hands. Simon looked drained, his face paper white with the effort
he had made. Alison, with the benefit of far more years of training and experience, seemed merely tired.

As if from nowhere, one of Alison's cats materialized and leaped up on the
bed, curling up against Claire's side and purring loudly as it settled down to
sleep.

"That's as much as I can do for her now, Colin; I only hope it's enough. I'll
come back and check on her in half an hour, though she should sleep straight
through till noon tomorrow, if we're lucky. Just now, I want to talk to you
and your young friend," Alison said meaningfully.

"Well, I'm for bed," Simon said, running a long elegant hand through his
tousled black curls. "I feel as if I could sleep until they blow the Last Trump."
Without another word, he brushed past the others and walked away.

Colin sighed, the nervous energy that had sustained him during the crisis
draining away now that everything was all right. It was always like this afterward: the danger-high, and then the low. Adrenaline was surely as much a
drug as heroin; did he somehow seek out situations like this to fill his need
for it?

"Come on, Jonathan. Claire should be all right, now. And I suppose I owe
you an explanation."

There was a fire burning in the fireplace of the long sitting room, and the
spicy scent of eucalyptus logs filled the room. Jonathan collapsed gratefully
into a chair, while Alison moved toward the drinks cabinet. Abruptly Colin
remembered something.

"Alison, what did you mean when you said, 'it's legal'? Do you know what
it was? What did Claire take?" Colin asked.

"I'm not completely sure, of course, but I believe she took—or was given
without her knowledge—something called *lysergic acid diethylamide*, a syn-
thetic ergot derivative that's been around since the forties. Sandoz makes it;

it's used in psychotherapy—in fact, I've used it on some of my patients, since it isn't a restricted drug. It affects the midbrain serotonin receptors—in essence, LSD throws open the doors of perception, short-circuiting the brain's censoring mechanisms."

She handed him two fingers of Scotch in a heavy crystal tumbler, and offered the same to Jonathan. Though he was several years below the legal drinking age, the boy accepted the glass gratefully, and Colin couldn't blame him. It seemed foolish that at eighteen an American was old enough to serve in the military but not to vote, drink alcohol, or sign a binding contract. Matters were arranged differently in Europe.

"A short-circuit . . . something that could be disastrous for a psychic sensitive," Colin mused.

"And Claire certainly reacted like one," Alison said. "The stuff is useful, but pernicious—any home chemist can whip up a batch; it's colorless, tasteless, and the dose is minuscule; I give it to my patients on a sugar cube, just so we can both keep track of it. It takes effect almost immediately and lasts for up to eighteen hours—and its effect is powerful, unpredictable. We'll have to hope that your Claire hasn't been scarred by her experience, but let's see what she has to say for herself when she wakes up."

"Is . . . is Claire a psychic?" Jonathan asked. "A clairvoyant? Can she see the future?"

Alison and Colin glanced at each other. Which of them should field this most elementary and troubling of all questions?

"Claire is certainly what we would term a 'Sensitive,' " Colin said at last, "in the simplest sense of being one who is 'sensitive' to a range of perceptions that come to her on a wavelength that most people are simply not equipped to perceive. As you'll remember from my lectures, between ten and twenty percent of all people are born with some sort of psychic faculty, which usually manifests itself in the form of hunches, lucky guesses, prophetic dreams, and the like. Some fraction of that number have a stronger gift—what used to be called 'Second Sight' and is now more formally known as clairvoyance and precognition. In them, the Sixth Sense is strong enough that they can manipulate it to some extent, choosing what events distant in space or time they wish to focus on.

"But there is another sort of clairvoyant, the Sensitive, who simply receives more-or-less constant perceptions of the Unseen World. These sensitives quickly learn to block out the flow of frightening unwanted information that no one else seems to perceive. Many of them pass their entire lives without realizing that they are among the gifted."

"Like Claire," Jonathan said. "But there's more to this than that, isn't there? Professor, I'd swear that Claire didn't know she was a whatchamacallit. She's the most practical, down-to-earth girl I know."

"Being psychic doesn't necessarily require a person to lose all common sense," Alison said with a smile. "Thousands of years ago, what was then called the Gift was a prerequisite for rulers and leaders. Civilization wouldn't

have lasted very long if they'd been nothing more than a bunch of colorful eccentrics."

"I suppose not," Jonathan said doubtfully. "But Dr. Margrave—if someone
is a sensitive, how do they find out about it? What is it like?"

"Now that's my cue for a very long lecture," Alison said. "Colin, could you
put some more wood on the fire?"

Colin got to his feet and went over to the hearth. The firebox was filled
with small logs, a mixture of pale soft eucalyptus wood, grey salt-soaked
driftwood, and solid ruddy splits of applewood. He set his drink on the man-
telpiece and added several chunks of apple to the fire, wielding the poker to
knock down the half-burned pieces and provide a good bed of coals for the
new wood. As he waited to be certain that the wood had caught, he glanced
toward the large picture window.

The curtains were drawn back from the glass, and Colin was unsurprised
to see that the sky was turning grey with predawn light. The world had survived another All Hallows Eve, and the Day of the Dead had dawned.

Behind him, Alison was explaining the fundamental beliefs of the Light to
Jonathan. "There is an energy that binds us all together—at the turn of the
century it was called the *aethyr,* though that term is rather out of date now.
This part of us—the Light Body—is what allows us, as a race, to do all those
things that are usually lumped under the heading of 'parapsychology and the
occult' on bookstore shelves."

Colin's thoughts turned away from the conversation and back to the girl
upstairs. The moment he'd seen her in Jonathan's car, he'd experienced a
bone-deep flash of recognition. He'd known this girl before, in some other
life.

Since he'd returned to the United States, Colin realized that he'd been
waiting, as if for orders. Claire London's arrival was as direct as a command:
the Lords of Karma required him to be about the business he had been dedicated to and had set this task in his way.

But though he had faced far more perilous tests than one young girl, for
the first time in his life Colin wondered if his will and his skill were equal to
the thing he meant to do. Was Claire the one who had been sent to him to
train, to shape, to guide? And if she was, what then?

Behind him, the fresh wood kindled strongly, sending new heat out into
the room. Colin turned away from the window, to where Alison and Jonathan
were sitting beside each other, talking intently.

"Once you accept that you are more than just a body—that you have a subtle body as well, with its own senses and needs—you've taken your first step
into a larger universe, and set your foot on a path whose passage can take you
many lifetimes."

Jonathan gazed at her, caught halfway between automatic rejection of such
an outlandish idea and a hopeful, hungry belief. Watching the two of them,
Colin was surprised to recognize in himself a sudden brief pang of envy. Alison found it so simple to speak of these things, to set a new seeker's feet upon

the Path. If she felt any of the misgivings or qualms that Colin felt about the danger and the responsibility inherent within her actions, she gave no sign.

But then, Alison was no stranger to teaching—Simon Anstey was only the latest of her many students; their lives like a garden of flowers that she had touched during her time on earth. Alison Margrave's was a life well spent, a life of service to the Light.

Could Colin truly say the same? He had fought great and terrible battles in the service of the Light, but an Adept's life should be the crowning work of his mind and heart, and Colin was not yet satisfied with what he had made of himself.

"If it was LSD that is responsible for what happened to Claire," he said into a lull in the conversation a few minutes later, "I'd like to know more about how she came to take it. You say that it takes effect fairly quickly, Alison—doesn't that mean she must have gotten it at the party she and Jonathan went to?"

"I guess so, Professor," Jonathan said slowly. "It was just, well, one of Toller's parties. Everyone knows what they're like. Claire did."

"Assume we don't," Alison said in ironic tones. "Just a minute. I'd better go check on the girl." She got to her feet, glass in hand, and headed for the stairs.

Jonathan turned in his seat, looking over his shoulder to where Colin stood.

"I guess I'm in a little bit over my head here tonight, eh, Professor?" he asked ruefully.

"You're doing fine," Colin told him. "A cool head in a crisis, and a willingness to follow orders intelligently, will do a lot toward taking you down any road you want to travel."

"This is the road I want to travel," Jonathan said strongly. "I know it sounds crazy, but it feels as if I'm coming home."

Not as crazy as you think it does, Colin thought with an inward smile. One of the fundamental tenets of the Light was the unending process of learning, as the Self returned to incarnation for life after life. Perhaps this was not the first life in which Jonathan Ashwell had pursued a deeper meaning to existence.

Alison returned. "Still sleeping. Pulse and respiration both good and strong; I think that when she wakes up tomorrow she'll be fine—at least physically. As for psychically . . ." Alison hesitated. "I suppose we'll deal with that when the time comes. Although the person I'd really like to deal with is whoever threw the party the two of you were at, since he seems to think that drugging his guests is funny."

"Nobody thinks you're to blame, Jonathan," Colin said reassuringly. "But anything you can tell us will be helpful."

Under Colin and Alison's patient questioning, a pattern began to emerge.

Toller Hasloch was the original BMOC—Big Man On Campus. He was twenty-two, a pre-law student from a well-to-do Baltimore family. He lived off campus in a rambling Victorian in an older section of town and threw frequent, famous parties. He was involved in a number of different clubs on campus of a less-than-respectable nature and had a reputation for both intellectual and physical daring.

Drugs—mostly marijuana and pills—were available at Toller's parties. Everyone knew it. But as far as Jonathan knew, no one had ever been forced to take them.

"If she was drugged, it had to be the punch," he said. "There was a big bowl; it was spiked with vodka, but everyone knew *that*. Claire knew, too—she usually doesn't drink, but she was drinking that night; I warned her about the booze and she just laughed at me. But a little liquor wouldn't do that to someone, would it? And if there was anything else in the punch, Toller was the one who put it in there," Jonathan added positively. "He likes to seem laid-back, but I don't think much goes on around him that he doesn't know about."

"How hard would this drug be to get?" Colin asked Alison.

"Not very," she admitted. "And it would be fairly simple to make, if you had access to a chemistry lab—or were dating a chemist."

"I take it that Mr. Hasloch fulfills at least one of the above criteria?" Colin asked Jonathan.

"Sure," Jonathan said uncertainly, beginning to be uneasy. "I mean . . . he can get all kinds of things," he said reluctantly. "At least, I've heard he can. I don't want to get him into trouble, Professor. . . ."

"He's already in trouble," Alison said darkly. "Assuming, of course, he's truly the one at fault. But for the sake of convenience, we'll assume that he is, that he got his hands on some LSD and thought he'd liven up his own Halloween party by providing some real—or realistic-seeming—ghosts and goblins. He's just lucky that Claire was the only one affected in that particular way—at least I hope so. And it's a good thing you didn't have any of whatever it was he spiked the punch with—at least, I'm assuming you didn't," Alison said. "LSD can have some pretty bizarre effects."

"No," Jonathan said gratefully. "I didn't drink any of the punch. I stuck to beer. That is—" he said, realizing what he'd said.

"Under the circumstances, I'd say your sins were minor," Colin said. "And forgiven."

"Sins," said a new voice from the doorway. "I suppose it's too much to hope that I've been committing any?"

Colin had been right when he'd guessed Claire London would be tall: five-eight or -nine, what Colin's Scots ancestors would have called "a braw strapping lassie." She was barefoot, her skirt and sweater slightly rumpled from having been slept in. She was holding to the doorframe for support as she ran her free hand through her short blond hair. Her mouth was set in a grim, suspicious line.

"We thought you'd sleep for several hours more," Alison said calmly.

"Why should I?" Claire snapped. "Did somebody slip me a Mickey? You, Johnny?" she added mockingly.

"You . . . got sick, Claire," Jonathan said feebly. "At Toller's party, remember? I was talking to you; by the punch bowl—you'd just gotten yourself another cup of punch, remember? We were both wondering where Toller was. . . ."

"No." The denial came too quickly, and Claire's edgy mockery was gone, leaving the naked fear beneath. "I don't remember anything, *because nothing happened.* Got it?"

Her eyes flicked sideways, toward Colin, and she stared at him with a look very like horror.

Yes, Colin realized with an irresistible flash of insight, they had known one another before. In life after life, since their first meeting in the halls of the ancient Temple of the Sun, in the City of the Temple when the man then known as Riveda first plotted the betrayal whose expiation had bound him to the Wheel of Rebirth ever since.

The jarring moment of transcendence faded, leaving Colin shaken with its power. "Everyone needs help sometimes, Miss London," he said, knowing these were somehow not the words he ought to be saying.

"Not me," Claire responded, still with that brittle gaiety. "Nobody looks out for me but me," she added warningly. "And I can take care of myself— God knows I've had to."

"How long have you been hearing voices, dear?" Alison said gently.

The response was as dramatic as if she had struck the younger woman. Claire's face went white, and she sagged at the knees. Jonathan sprang up out of his seat and just managed to catch her before she hit the floor.

"I'm not crazy," Claire muttered desperately as Jonathan half-carried her over to the couch. "I'm not crazy, I'm not, I'm not—"

"Listen to me, child," Alison said sharply. "All evidence this evening to the contrary, you are *not* losing your mind. I'm a licensed psychiatrist—you can take my word for it."

Claire London stared into Alison's eyes, seeming to actually see her surroundings for the first time. "You're . . . a doctor?" she said shakily. Tears welled up in her blue eyes, magnifying the still-dilated pupils.

"Licensed to shrink heads at reasonable hourly rates," Alison answered acerbically, "and, among my many other skills, I also play piano. But truly, Claire, you're among friends here. I don't think you're crazy—and neither does Colin."

Claire looked toward Colin. "Colin . . . MacLaren?" she asked. "I've heard about you. You're the new professor in the Psych Department—the one who believes in ghosts and tea leaves and all that nonsense. Some advocate," she groaned, leaning back against the couch and closing her eyes.

"I'll freely admit to believing in ghosts," Colin said, "and you can see tea leaves yourself in any bag of Lipton's. As for the rest—would you rather be thought gifted, or crazy?"

" 'Gifted' . . . don't you think that's a complete load of rot, Professor?" With the febrile energy that Alison said was a side effect of the LSD, Claire sat up and smiled at him coldly. There was a cynical edge to her voice, and her lips curved in a mocking smile. "Unseen worlds—mystic visions—you're going to want me to believe in little green men, next."

"Only if warranted," Colin said gravely. "And with sufficient proof. Claire, let us help you. I know that tonight has been a terrible shock for you, but you must understand that you've been given a great gift, use of senses that few people still retain access to. I know that it all seems overwhelming to you now, but believe me, you can learn to control these perceptions—consciously, rationally—"

"So much of everything," Claire whispered, slumping back and seeming to forget once more that they were there. "So much noise . . . going on and on and *on*. . . ."

"Claire," Alison said, reaching out to clasp the younger woman's wrist. "Come back to us. Nothing bad can harm you while you're in my house, no matter what you see. You've been given a drug that makes these things seem more upsetting than they are. It will wear off in a few hours. Try to be strong."

"No!" Claire pulled away from the touch with a scream. "You're going to die—I see you—he loved you and he killed you—you're dead and there's blood everywhere, blood, blood, blood—" Claire babbled, huddling blindly in the corner of the couch.

"You're seeing the future," Alison said reasonably. "Everyone dies, my dear, including cranky old musicians—just because you see it, doesn't mean you've caused it. Listen to me, Claire; I'm not dead. I'm right here, see? You can open your eyes and see me—"

Alison droned on soothingly, until at last, Claire effortfully opened her eyes again. Colin could see that the girl was exhausted; her face was sickly pale and there were dark circles beneath her eyes.

"How did you know?" she asked wonderingly.

"It was just a good guess," Alison admitted. "But I've known a lot of people like you. You aren't alone, Claire—you have to believe that. It's a rare gift, but it isn't unknown. Many people have possessed it down through history."

Claire stared into Alison's eyes, hopeful and reluctant all at once. Colin could see the moment her eyes clouded over; the moment when Claire rejected the idea of trusting Alison. She shook her head.

"If you won't believe her, believe me," Colin said. Now, at last, he found the words. "You know me, Claire—you've known me before—do you believe that I will always tell you the truth?"

He could see her frame the flip response and then hesitate over it. He watched as Claire struggled with herself; the stubbornness and innate honesty of her basic nature refusing to allow her to lightly dismiss his question.

"I . . . suppose you will," she said unwillingly. "You've got too much to lose if you don't," she added with a sneer.

Did she know how truly she spoke? Colin wondered. To an Adept of the

Light, a deliberate falsehood was the same act as physical self-injury; it was not something to be done lightly, if at all, and it always had damaging consequences, some extending beyond the gateways of this single life.

"I will never lie to you," Colin repeated firmly. "Will you believe me when I tell you that there's nothing sick or abnormal about you? You're sensitive to impressions that most people are not. To say that you're crazy because you see what you do would be like calling someone with extraordinarily acute hearing crazy because he can hear what most people cannot. But the psychic gift can best be said to correspond to a gift for music—it can take many forms, and it can be trained—or ignored."

"I'm tired," Claire said petulantly. "Alison said that somebody drugged me—oh, my God, it must have been something at the party, that son-of-a—"

"Claire!" Colin said sharply. "Don't try to evade this subject—it won't go away."

"Oh, yeah?" Claire muttered under her breath, and Colin repressed a smile. Frightened and emotionally damaged as she was, the girl had the spirit of a fighter.

"What happened to you tonight isn't something you can just pretend never happened. It has permanent consequences. I imagine you've been pretending not to see or hear a lot of things in your life. It will be much harder after tonight. Despite what you may believe, you have been reaching out with your Gift to the world around you. You've been given this ability for a reason, and it isn't something you can run from any longer."

The girl hesitated.

"Please, Claire," Colin said. "Trust me. Let me help you."

"Oh, all right," Claire said, sighing ungraciously. Though her voice was harsh, her eyes glittered with painful tears. "Do your worst, Professor. I guess I'm fresh out of choices."

BERKELEY, 1961

TRYING TO REMEMBER THE CHILD ONE ONCE WAS IS LIKE TRYING TO remember another lifetime—how much is truth, and how much hopeful imagination? I think there is something in all of us that chooses to forget; I think it would be too painful if we could really remember the hopes our younger self held for the future. I think every child expects the world to be reasonable, for events to have a kind of fairness and balance that is found only in fiction. As we age, we realize that life is otherwise. Some become bitter; others philosophical.

It is hard to remember the girl who first met Colin MacLaren almost four decades ago. I think she was an angry child; I know she had grown up hating the world because she thought it had lied to her. What she did not know—what it took her years to truly learn and believe—was that the world she lived in was a far different place from that of her mother and sisters, because she was born with the Sight.

The Sight places a heavy burden on those who possess it. For them, Space and Time are not absolutes; they see around corners and into the depths of the human heart. It is a cruel burden for a child to have to bear, and I rebelled passionately against it. By the time I was in my teens I had learned to show the world a cynical indifference, hurting others and pretending not to care when I was hurt. Lord knows why I chose nursing as a profession, feeling as I did then about people—in my own defense, I can only say that the career choice for women in those days was between nurse and librarian, and even then I rebelled at the thought of being stuck behind a dusty desk all day as the world passed me by.

I was at war with the world, and I intended to make it pay for all it had done to me.

But you cannot strike back at the world, only at the people in it. When I came into Colin's hands—through something greater than mere chance, I firmly believe—I was drowning in my own despair, perilously close to committing some act that would ruin my life beyond my modest power to mend it.

And the only person I was hurting was myself.

THREE

BERKELEY, NOVEMBER 3, 1961

*Why didst thou leave the trodden paths of men
Too soon, and with weak hands though mighty heart
Dare the unpastured dragon in his den?*
— PERCY BYSSHE SHELLEY

THAT FRIDAY, COLIN MACLAREN FINALLY MANAGED TO RUN HIS QUARRY TO earth.

He'd seen Claire London back to her dorm Wednesday morning, concocting a complicated tale of an all-night psychology experiment to satisfy the housemother's inquiries about her overnight absence. He thought he'd passed things off fairly well—he only wished he could be as confident about his handling of Claire herself. She was frightened, angry, argumentative—Colin wasn't sure he could even reach her, let alone teach her what she needed to know. And though he and Claire had been close through life after life, he had realized that this time Claire had not come to him as a disciple. The Path was not her way—in this life, the knowledge he could provide was merely a tool that Claire needed in order to make a journey of her own.

Which brought matters around to Toller Hasloch.

The first thing that Colin had done was to take advantage of his position to gain a look at the boy's file in the Registrar's office. Hasloch would be twenty-three in a few days; next year he'd have his Bachelor's degree, and according to his admission papers, planned on a legal career. From other papers in the file, it had not been difficult to ascertain his culpability in the matter of the drugged punch. A number of professors in Colin's department were experimenting with LSD. One of them had praised its effects to Colin highly, and further discreet questioning had elicited the information that he'd given Toller Hasloch samples of the drug to try at home only a few weeks ago. Horrifying as such irresponsibility was, the man had done nothing criminal—as Alison had said, LSD was as unregulated as aspirin.

Hasloch had means and opportunity—and, from all that Jonathan and others had said about him, motive.

Colin didn't want to spoil a promising future over what might only be juvenile high spirits, but neither did he want to see a repetition of what had happened at the Halloween party. The best thing, Colin felt, would be to speak informally with young Hasloch, and warn him that there must be no further pranks.

He spotted Hasloch as the boy entered Sproul Hall in the midst of a cluster of fellow students. The pale hair, worn neatly short and brushed straight back, stood out like a bright flag in the pale November sunlight. The boy was tidily and conservatively dressed—wearing a wheat-colored sweater with a white shirt and dark tie.

"Mr. Hasloch?"

The young man turned at the sound of his name, and Colin found himself staring into pale eyes on a level with his own.

"Professor MacLaren," Hasloch said. "I've been looking forward to meeting you."

There was a faint note of amusement in his voice, a disturbingly discordant note that raised warning hackles along Colin's spine. It was as if Hasloch had been looking for him, and not the reverse. *He's only a boy*, Colin told himself.

"I'd like to speak to you for a moment, if I might," Colin said steadily.

"Of course," Hasloch said easily. "But I am forgetting my manners." He laid his right hand over his breast and then slowly raised it to forehead level.

Colin stood rooted to the spot in shock. What Hasloch had just done was to acknowledge Colin in his grade as Adept of the Right-Hand Path—something that was hardly common knowledge on the Berkeley campus. And even if it were, it was amazingly unlikely that a boy in his twenties would have the information and training necessary to greet him as one Initiate to another.

By reflex Colin returned the Sign—higher to lower—and Hasloch smiled a cold, wolfish smile and turned away.

Colin followed him, feeling that he'd somehow conceded victory to an opponent before battle had been joined. Hasloch seated himself at one of the tables in the corner of the Student Union, and Colin followed suit.

"So, Professor, what did you wish to see me about?" Hasloch asked. "Surely you have not come as an emissary of your Order?"

For the moment, Colin let the remark pass; Hasloch was transparently baiting him. "It's regarding the refreshments you served at your Halloween party," he said, and Hasloch pursed his lips in an exaggerated moue of understanding. He did not appear in the least disturbed by the implication.

"You do realize that you could be expelled from school for what you did?" Colin pursued.

"A schoolboy prank," Hasloch murmured. "Something I have the impression you don't intend to censure . . . at least not through public channels."

"I will if you force me to," Colin said. "Don't underestimate the serious-ness with which I view your actions, Mr. Hasloch."

"Oh, I don't," the boy said easily. "But I think that you—or at least your Masters—don't take them as seriously as I do. Let us be frank, Professor. I know your beliefs, but you seem to be unaware of mine. I'd be more than happy to remedy your lapse. Who knows? We may be natural allies. Surely you don't identify your purpose with those of the slave races that surround you."

Colin recoiled in shock at hearing idiom he'd thought buried in the ruins of Berlin. Suddenly the past was not buried, the Dragon not slain. It was here before him, recalled to life in the person of this slender, pale, boy.

"You see?" Hasloch said, spreading his hands and smiling engagingly. "I'm being completely open with you. Those with whom I am, from time to time, in communication, have told me who you are—a great force for the Light." He kept his voice low, his expression neutral. None of the dozens of students who walked past their table would give the two of them a second glance.

"But there is more than one source of Light, Professor MacLaren. The illu-mination spread by the Thousand-Year Reich is not so easily eclipsed—but the flame of the candle is forgotten in the greater flame of the sun."

Colin struggled to conceal both his shock and his horror as he stared at the youth opposite him. Bright and deadly as a new-honed sword blade and cold as Alpine snow, Hasloch sat before him beneath the light of a California sun and claimed allegiance to a cult that Colin had believed safely defeated; its adher-ents dead or scattered, its unholy places sanctified. The Allied nations had mortgaged their futures and spent their strength to break the spine of the great serpent of National Socialism and the will of its black messiah, Adolf Hitler.

And this child's very existence told Colin beyond all doubt that they had failed.

"If that's your sun, I'd say it's already set," Colin said dismissively. "If you're claiming to be a Nazi, I'll remind you that your side lost—and as for your Secret Chiefs in exile, they're being run to earth one by one, or were you so busy studying that you missed the coverage of the Eichmann trial?"

"Professor MacLaren," Hasloch said chidingly. "What you see as destruc-tion the *Armanenschaft* sees merely as a purification; a refinement of our doc-trine of spiritual evolution to a higher level. The body of the Reich may lie in the ground, but the spirit survives, and *Germania's* eagle has become a phoenix. Where once we fought with tanks and machine guns, now we wage a battle of the spirit, allowing our work on the Outer Planes to shape the as-pect of the Inner. Your American Eagle is dying, Professor, and its successor will be the White Eagle of Thule, which will spread its wings over a Fourth Reich hewn from the never-ending ice. My allies are all the more powerful for that they work in secret—the nations of the world will not see the peace your countrymen sought in your lifetime or mine, Professor. If we must talk of current events, let me match your Eichmann with Secretary-General Ham-marskjöld, and his so-mysterious death in Africa. So much for this reborn League of Nations and its limp-wristed hopes for peace."

Hasloch's face glowed with a far from innocent enthusiasm; a fervor that Colin had hoped was eradicated from the Earth forever. In his secret heart he had always known that it was a wistful, a forlorn hope; the war of Light with Shadow was an eternal one. But this attempt—in this form—must be ended now, for the weapons mankind was now capable of wielding could unleash destruction on a scale heretofore only dreamed of by madmen and saints.

"Isn't it a bit grandiose of a college student to be claiming spiritual credit for international political assassinations?" Colin asked blightingly.

"Do I wander too far afield from receiving my slap on the wrist, Professor?" Hasloch asked silkily. "Let me tell you plainly then, that if you bring forward your accusations publicly, I shall be shocked and horrified, highly indignant—and some other fool will be made a scapegoat, will be found to take the blame—perhaps your precious Johnny Ashwell? I have powerful friends, Professor MacLaren; why spend your strength in tilting at windmills? A nation is an easy thing to destroy, if one approaches the matter properly. Nations have souls, just as men do, and both become husks when that soul dies within them. Your sun is on the wane, Herr Doktor Professor, while mine is rising. Why render the rest of your life a useless thing?"

No victory for the Light, no matter how seemingly insignificant, is wasted, Colin reminded himself. If he could do nothing else in all the years remaining to him, by simply failing to surrender to despair he would strengthen his brothers in arms.

"Surely," Colin said, keeping his voice even with an effort, "you are not suggesting that I join you?"

"Why not?" Hasloch said airily. "I am not so foolish as to deny that you have practical experience that I lack, in both the magickal and mundane senses. You have moved your playing pieces about the chessboard of Europe; there is something you can teach me about *Realpolitik*, I expect."

"If you know as much about me and my Order as you claim to," Colin retorted with asperity, "you'll know that such an offer isn't even a joke."

"Join us or die," Hasloch said simply, stretching out his hand as if in entreaty. He studied his own long elegant fingers for a moment and then withdrew his hand. "But if you will not, out of respect for your discipline and attainments—however misguided—I shall leave you in peace to become a footnote to history."

"Providing I extend to you the same courtesy?" Colin shot back. For all his formidable self-possession, Toller Hasloch was still a young man—hardly more than a boy—with all of youth's overconfidence. His dark soul was a creation of this century, without knowledge of previous lifetimes to bulwark it. No experienced member of the Black Order would have wasted his time in telling Colin so much of his plans.

"Give it up now, Mr. Hasloch. The Shadow doesn't reward its servants—it uses them up. If you know anything of what you claim, you know that as well. The same history that you say is on your side will bury you as it has so many others."

"I really believe we have nothing more to say to each other," Hasloch said, but this time the light tone in his voice was an audible effort. "But my offer of a truce still stands. I give you good day, Professor."

He got to his feet and walked away quickly. Colin watched him go, his whole being torn between horror . . . and pity.

A week passed. Colin sent a full report of the conversation to the Mother Lodge in Britain, for no hint of a Thulist renaissance was too slim to take lightly, and even a veneration of Nazi "ideals" was a symptom that must be watched carefully. But though his talk with Hasloch had chilled him to the bone, Colin needed proof of something more than youthful dabbling before he was willing to act. Arrogance and posturing were not enough to indict a man for, and beyond those, he had seen no hard evidence to support Hasloch's claims of being a member of an occult entity that had declared spiritual war upon the United States of America.

So matters had stood, until Jonathan Ashwell had come into his office late this afternoon.

"Jonathan, come in. Sit down. How are you doing?"

The lanky young student sidled into Colin's office, oddly ill at ease. Since the night of his unorthodox introduction to the Unseen World, Colin had been guiding his fledgling steps toward the Light. Jonathan was a voracious pupil, reading all that Colin gave him and pushing for more. Colin had already introduced him to the first of the simple exercises to ground and center, and to focus, that would begin to teach Jonathan to perceive and to control the Subtle Body. From this point, Jonathan's own Will would set the speed of his advancement.

But surely there was nothing in all Colin had taught him to occasion this level of unease?

"He's doing it again," Jonathan said. He held out a sheet of paper to Colin, as if offering him a poisonous snake.

Colin took the paper and spread it flat on his desk. It was professionally printed in red and black, typeset in ornate Gothic letters.

Toller Hasloch was throwing a birthday party for himself this evening— November 10th. A very special party, the invitation said, but that was only the part of the flyer that was printed in English. Sigils and talismans were scattered across the page—nasty ones, each the special summons of a prince or duke of Hell.

And twined among the sigils and the mundane wording, as if it were only decoration, was line upon line of blood-red runes. They were being used alphabetically, and Colin translated them with ease.

Hasloch invited his particular friends to come together on the anniversary of his birth to attend the Black Mass which Hasloch would be enacting in his own honor.

"I know it says it's just a birthday party, Professor—but it isn't. There's going to be a Black Mass. I've been asking around, seeing what I could find out for you, and Hasloch's got . . ." Jonathan's voice faltered as his imagination failed him. "He— They say he's a magician—that he does magickal rituals. People don't really do things like that any more, do they, Professor?"

"Far more than anyone believes, Jonathan. Which is unfortunate, in some cases." Automatically, Colin felt in his pockets for his pipe and began to fiddle with it.

To most of the twentieth century, the Black Mass was the stuff of cheap sensational novels, well larded with sex and blood. To the occult historian, it was something rather different—a rare, complex form of anticlerical protest, a ritual designed not to serve any worldly goal of enlightenment or enrichment, but to attack the Catholic Church while snatching some of the power of the great Adversary for itself.

Alison said she had attended one in Paris during the 1920s, and Colin was willing to bet that an actual Black Mass hadn't been performed since.

"But a *Black Mass*, Professor? Satanism?" Jonathan said incredulously.

"Probably not—at least I hope not," Colin said, puffing his pipe alight. "Most of what the popular press has labeled 'Black Masses' in this century have been the workings of one of the more scandalous and public of the Magickal Lodges, like Aleister Crowley's Ordo Templi Orientis, or one of the numerous offshoots of the Esoteric Order of the Golden Dawn."

Or the Thule Gesellschaft.

"Scandalous, but not quite Satanic," Colin said, soothing Jonathan's fears if not his own. "On the other hand, ritual magic, like prescription drugs, is much better left in the hands of trained professionals."

"But what are we going to do, Professor? He's invited me to the party— and I'd like to make sure he gets a taste of his own medicine, for what he did to Claire. . . ."

All at once Colin remembered Hasloch's lazy threat to make Jonathan the scapegoat if Colin attempted to have Hasloch's misdeeds punished.

"And that's why you're not going to go," Colin said firmly. "I want you to stay home tonight, safe inside your own dorm room. Don't go out for anything, no matter how tempting the excuse."

"But Professor—if I go, I could stop him." Jonathan looked confused.

"Believe me, Jonathan. If you want to ruin Hasloch's plans, there's nothing more damaging you can do than stay away."

It had taken him the better part of an hour to convince Jonathan that what he'd said was true—so much of magick was logical, but not plausible, operating with the same rigorous unreason usually found in fairy tales—but when Jonathan left, Colin was certain the boy would heed him and not go off halfcocked, his head full of cheap heroics, to offer himself up to Hasloch's plans.

Not that Colin thought that tonight's ceremony was being enacted for Jonathan's sole benefit. One's own birthday had a particular occult power, the moment of one's birth being also the moment in which all celestial influences were momentarily withdrawn, to be resummoned or barred at the will of the magician for the unfolding of another year.

And Hasloch's birthday was a particular unholy day in the German calendar . . . the date of Germany's capitulation in the First World War; the birthdate of Baron von Sebottendorf, founder of the Thule Gesellschaft. In 1939—the year Hasloch had been born—November 9 became the Night of Broken Glass . . . *Krystallnacht.*

In the tiny second bedroom of his bungalow that he used as his workroom, Colin MacLaren robed himself for battle. The winter rains had started right on schedule; and the dampness seeped through the walls, making everything in the room smell faintly musty. Rising above the smell of the wet were the biting scents of cedar and frankincense—cedar from the chest he had opened, frankincense from the folds of fabric packed inside.

The gold of the breastplate—a heavy plaque eight inches square set with twelve precious stones and inscribed with the Great Names—gleamed up at him from within the white folds of an embroidered linen shift.

It had been many years since he had donned the full vestments of his Order, but they had been packed carefully away against future need, and now, with slow reverence, he donned each element of the ritual robes.

What he must do was laid out clearly in his mind: locate Hasloch's magickal presence in the Astral Realm and banish it from that place. What did not exist in the Overworld had no force on the Plane of Being—once Colin had moved against Hasloch's Astral Temple, the boy's Black Mass would become a nasty piece of play-acting, nothing more. Its poisonous force would be gone.

An Adept could expect to wear his vestments only a handful of times in his life, only when he took part in one of the rare convocations of fellow Adepts that his Order called in time of greatest need. Certainly Colin ought not to need them simply to call the Light to mindfulness in the matter of Toller Hasloch's callow profanity.

But as a man might contemplate ascending a mountain which he lacked the power to master in reality, so Colin MacLaren contemplated his night's plans and felt only cold ashes where the flame of his Magician's Will had once burned. It was almost as if what Hasloch did tonight did not matter.

Even if the young magician were precisely what he claimed to be—the renaissance of the occult Nazi ideology that had destroyed a generation—how could Colin bring himself to care? He and his fellow soldiers of the Light had thought that they had shackled that great Evil forever; if it could be reborn from the very ashes of its defeat once, it could be reborn a hundred times, and no defeat could matter.

He knew that to go into battle bearing these feelings was treason against his Higher Self, and an almost certain guarantee of failure. But what was he to do? How could he command the certainty of Summer in the heart of Winter's ice—the ice that, for Hasloch, would be the stuff of the Second Coming of the Shadow?

The man that he had once been would not have had these doubts, these fears. But that man was gone, burned to ash in the fires of Berlin. Time had healed Colin. It had brought him wholeness of a sort, and peace. But all the time in the world would not make Colin the same man he once had been. He had counted on the strength of the man who had been the Sword of the Order, only to find that man gone, and himself alone in the vast mansion of time.

As if it were a mundane grace-note to his bleak thoughts, the front doorbell chimed. Colin ignored it. Among the oaths he had sworn was one to conceal the very existence of his Order. He could hardly answer the door in all the panoply of the Light and expect not to raise questions that he could not answer. A parapsychologist was an odd enough fish on the Berkeley campus—a working magician would be beyond the regents' ability to tolerate entirely.

But the doorbell continued ringing, a maddening, insistent two-toned chime that mixed with the heavy patter of the rain. Whoever was standing outside on the steps must be thoroughly soaked by now, continuing to ring despite the fact that they received no encouragement from the dark and silent bungalow.

Who could it be?

Reluctantly—but with a growing sense of urgency—Colin removed his habiliments and tossed them quickly into the brass-bound cedar chest. Grabbing up his wool plaid bathrobe—far too warm for the climate but retained out of sentimental feeling—and donning it hastily, Colin stepped from his study and closed the door.

The ringing doorbell had been replaced with a fainter—but equally determined—banging. Colin switched on the living room lights and opened the door. Rain hissed down, turning the night to silver. Claire London stood on the doorstep, looking like a drowned rat.

Her hair was plastered to her head. Mascara made faint dark smudges beneath her eyes, accenting their color and giving her a faintly demented look. Her camel-colored coat was drenched from shoulders to waist, and heavily water spotted below that.

"May I come in?" she asked. There was no trace in her voice of the urgency that must have impelled her here, or of any consciousness that she was standing unprotected in an icy winter's downpour.

Colin stood back to allow her to enter. Her loafers made a squelching sound as she stepped inside.

"I'm afraid I'm going to drip on your rug," she said, without any apology in her voice.

"Claire, what are you doing here?" Colin said. "Was it something that couldn't wait until office hours tomorrow? It seems a bit late for a social call. And on a night like this . . ."

"Who cares what kind of a night it is?" Claire snapped. "What I want to know is why you've decided to ignore me. It's been almost two weeks, and I haven't heard word one from you. Did you mean anything that you said that night? Or was it all hand-holding and head-patting?"

"Let me take your coat and get you something dry to put on," Colin said, placatingly. He could deal with the concerns that had brought Claire here once she was drier; she was risking pneumonia otherwise.

As she shrugged off her dripping coat, Colin turned up the heat and went in search of something for Claire to wear. The best he could come up with was an old wool fisherman's sweater, and he brought it back to the living room just as Claire was kicking off her sodden penny-loafers. She was wearing a jumper with a white blouse so wet now that it was nearly transparent.

"The bathroom's back that way," Colin said, handing her the sweater. "I'll put on the kettle."

While she was gone, Colin took the opportunity to dress again—bad enough, should it come to anyone's attention, that he had an undergraduate of the opposite sex in his house unchaperoned, without him being in his bathrobe as well.

When he returned, Claire was standing in front of the heater, holding her blouse out to the warmth. She'd rolled up the sleeves of the grey wool sweater as much as she could, but the sleeves still swam on her, and the hem of the sweater came down to mid-thigh. She was still wearing her slip beneath it.

"I suppose this will dry—or at least get less damp. I've never been so glad for Antron polyester in my life—if that jumper had been wool, it'd be ruined."

He was becoming used to her mercurial changes of mood by now; they were an attempt to shield herself from her own feelings, as much as from anyone else's.

"I did mean what I said at Alison's, Claire. It's just that I've . . ." *I've been busy*, Colin wanted to say, but in truth, he could have made the time if he'd wished to, as he had for Jonathan. His failure to follow up with Claire was simply more of that queer failure of nerve that he had experienced tonight, as if some inner heartlight had become extinguished without his noticing.

"Yeah," Claire said cynically. "But it isn't that. Well, it isn't all that," Claire emended. "It's—there's something else, too, more . . . oh, I don't know what to say!" She waved her blouse as if it were a toreador's cape.

"Just drape that over a chair," Colin said. "I'll make you a cup of tea."

"I'll make it," Claire said firmly. From the look on her face, she hadn't meant to say anything like that, but she gamely forged on. "If you'll show me where the kitchen is, at least. I never met a man yet who could even boil water."

Claire London knew her way around a kitchen, Colin decided a few minutes later. She'd unearthed his kettle, run the tap until the water was cold and filled it, and set it on the coils of the electric stove to heat.

She was the most decisively self-reliant person Colin had ever met; the sort of person who would stubbornly walk off the edge of a cliff rather than ask directions.

"You told me to follow my hunches," Claire said. "So I did. Which brings us to this." She shook loose tea into Colin's brown Rockingham teapot and poured the kettle's boiling contents over it. "Why am I here? Was it my idea, or yours?"

"Not mine," Colin admitted. "At least, I did not summon you on any conscious level. And without any great impetus, I don't think you'd have come out on such a wretched night, would you?"

Claire shook her head.

"So what does that leave? What sort of things does your Gift tell you?"

"How should I know?" Claire burst out crossly. "I don't want the damned—darned—thing in the first place. It's lucky, that's all I know—lucky for others."

Colin regarded her steadily. He could not force her to continue, and he did not want to coax her. When a psychic saw manifestation of his or her gift as a route to praise and attention, they would manufacture false information when the true intuition failed. Colin wanted Claire to listen to her inner self and tell the truth.

"I'm sorry, Claire. I'll explain what I can, but I'm not even a Sensitive, and every psychic has a different sort of, well, you might call it a knack. I can help you interpret your experiences, but I can't tell you in advance exactly what sort of experiences you'll have—or why."

Claire turned away and poured out the tea into two waiting mugs. Colin added milk and sugar to his, and reached for a glass jar on the counter. "Have a biscuit," he invited.

"A . . . ? Oh, a *cookie*," Claire said. She stirred sugar into her tea, then helped herself to a couple of pink-frosted sugar cookies from the bakery near the college. Colin waited, hoping she'd explain of her own accord.

"I've never been particularly lucky," she said, sipping her tea. "I'm not complaining, you understand—it's just that there are some people who're lucky—*and* they know it. I'm not like that. Never was."

"Go on," Colin said neutrally.

"But I'm lucky for other people, I've noticed. I'm always turning up in the nick of time with an extra safety pin, that sort of thing. I'll take a bus on a whim, just to ride around, and end up taking the seat next to someone who needs a shoulder to cry on. Whenever someone's in trouble, I just seem to be *attracted* to them somehow. Same now. But somehow, Professor, you don't look like someone in trouble."

"I might be," Colin admitted. With an inward sigh, he surrendered to the guiding hand of fate. "There's something I need to do, and I'm really not sure how to tackle it."

"Tell me about it," Claire said. "I'm good at solving problems—other people's problems, at least," she added.

"I'm afraid this might be out of your usual line," Colin began hesitantly. Claire was on the threshold of her life—a life that until now had not included the truths that Colin had lived with for longer than he could remember. How to begin, especially knowing that Claire was not bound to the Path in this life?

"Toller Hasloch is holding a Black Mass tonight," Colin said bluntly, "and I'm not sure what to do about it." As good an explanation as any, for something that both was and was not a crisis of faith.

Claire blinked, though she didn't seem as fazed by Colin's words as he might have expected. She thought matters over for a minute or so before she spoke.

"Why do you—I mean you particularly—have to do something about it? Satanism isn't illegal—at least, I don't think it is. 'Do whatever you want, so long as you don't do it in the street and scare the horses,' as the old saying goes."

"So long as no illegal acts are committed during the ceremony, I believe the matter comes under the Freedom of Conscience heading," Colin admitted. "Though if you're talking about Satanism, freedom to make a damned—and I use the word advisedly—fool of one's self is more to the point."

"Only you don't think Toller's joking," Claire said flatly. "Well, neither do I—though if he is, it's just as bad, since he has a well-deserved reputation for nasty jokes. You see," Claire said, brandishing a familiar flyer pulled from the sleeve of Colin's sweater, "I even have an invitation." She shrugged helplessly, unable to articulate what she felt. "Still, that begs the question—why you?"

"It's a complicated question, but I hope you'll forgive me if I have to give you a simple answer," Colin said. "It's my job."

Claire stared at him, cradling her cup of tea in her hands. Obviously, she expected more.

"A number of years ago, probably around the time you were being born, I was over in Europe, but not with the armed forces. I'd been a student at Oxford when Hitler invaded Poland in '39. I could have come home then, but my teachers asked me to stay, knowing I'd be needed. What isn't common knowledge—the Allies kept it pretty quiet, and in their place I imagine I would have, too—was that Herr Hitler didn't only see himself as a conqueror, but as a messiah. National Socialism was as much a cult as a political platform, and like any cult, it had its priests and its rituals."

"So you're saying Hitler was a black magician?" Claire said, trying hard to keep the incredulity out of her voice.

"Members of his inner circle undeniably were. They worked magick in places called Order Castles that were scattered all over Germany. Nazism denounced Christianity and set up a revisionist pagan cult in its place. The forces it called upon in those ceremonies used Adolf Hitler as an instrument of their will. Men can fight men—but only magick can fight magick."

He thought he would lose her then, and blessed Claire for the unexpected gift of belief when he needed it most. He knew this must sound like stark fantasy to her, and he could not reveal the details that would have helped convince her.

"So that's what you did in the war?" Claire asked, a little uncertainly. "You fought magick—with magick?"

"That's what I did," Colin said evenly. "It's not what I was trained to do, but in essence, by accepting the training I did, I also accepted the responsibility for seeing that it and similar disciplines are never used to harm.

"The great mass of humanity neither knows nor cares about magick—true magick, and not the Saturday Matinee Supernatural that many find so entertaining—and they have the right to keep things that way. To not be troubled by forces outside the scope of their daily lives, or manipulated by forces they have no way of resisting. When I find someone interfering in people's lives with magick in that fashion, it's my duty to stop them if I can—for their own sake, as well as for the lives they may harm."

"Is that what you're going to do with Toller?" Claire asked. "Stop him?"

"Yes," Colin said, suddenly sure of the direction in which his path now lay. "I am if you'll help me, Claire."

Her mother had always said that men wanted only one thing from women, and that went double for a rich man and a poor woman. The memories were irrelevant, in light of her current task, but as usual, Claire found it hard to get her mother's words out of her head. They were so much like the buzzing of a hornet that would alight to sting painfully the moment you forgot it.

It was still raining, and while she'd borrowed an umbrella from Professor MacLaren, her clothes were only half-dry. She shivered as she walked to the corner, the heavy weight of her purse banging against her hip. Toller's house was halfway down the block of the cross street, and she'd be chilled through by the time she got there. Still, it would add what the professor had called "artistic verisimilitude to an otherwise bald and unconvincing narrative," a line from something called "The Mikado." He'd promised to play it for her when this was over. He'd promised her a number of other things, all of which Claire warily filed in the category of "too good to be true."

Despite that—against every instinct and experience—she trusted Professor MacLaren absolutely. He radiated a sort of goodness—not the sappy, all-absolving infatuation of the worse forms of Christianity, but a sort of *demanding* kindness, a kindness that knew that goodness was possible, though hard, and that you were capable of it.

Faced with such belief, Claire's first instinct was to disappoint it somehow, to evade it and drop back into the anonymous herd. But she wasn't going to do that. Her self-respect wouldn't allow it. The professor believed she was worthwhile; she owed him more than she could easily put into words for his honesty and steadfastness. And besides that—on a very different level, but one that seemed pointed in the same direction—she felt that Toller Hasloch had gotten away with his pranks—too small a word, but it was all she had—for long enough.

What he was doing wasn't right. It was like the bigger, stronger bully beating up the younger schoolkids, just because he had the strength they lacked. As the suffering victim of bullying—from classmates, siblings, teachers, everyone who'd respond to her *differentness* with automatic malice—Claire hated bullies with the strongest passion at her command. If that was Toller's game, he deserved everything the world could dish out. And apparently one of the things the world could dish out was Colin MacLaren.

As she turned the corner, a gust of wind nearly wrestled the umbrella away from her, and as she turned, fighting with it, Claire's coat blew open and a blast of air cut across her ribs like an icy knife. She could no longer see the professor's car, parked halfway up the side street, but she knew he was there.

He'd assured her that once she'd found the room that he said *must* be hidden somewhere in Toller's house and signaled him as they'd arranged, he would be able to come to her aid at the right moment, and stop Toller Hasloch from doing . . . whatever he meant to do tonight.

A Black Mass . . . it sounded unbelievably medieval, and of course it didn't seem to be mentioned in her invitation. The fact that she'd received one at all brought her thoughts full circle, back to her mother's convictions about rich men and poor girls and the only thing men wanted.

Damn Mother and her sisters both. The little inner voice—the one that always caused her trouble, the one that dragged her into headlong collisions with other people's lives—was silent at the moment, but the memory of its insistence earlier this evening lingered like the aftermath of a dream. What would her family say about her throwing herself at Professor MacLaren that way? That a woman's first duty was to get married and settle down, and find some man to protect and provide for her, probably. Only she didn't think Professor MacLaren was willing to fall in with Mother's plans—nor did Claire think her mother would quite approve of a man on such easy terms with Satanism and parapsychology.

It was much safer to think about Toller Hasloch. Now *there* was a catch to delight a proud mama. . . .

Of course Toller had never been acutely interested in her, but somehow Claire had always found herself coming along to his bigger parties, usually brought by a friend of a friend, as these things went. This was the first time she'd gotten a personal invitation, and it wasn't hard for Claire to imagine why. After she'd fainted—or worse—under the influence of the spiked punch at his Halloween party, she'd become more interesting to someone like Toller Hasloch—assuming she could believe half the things about him that Professor Colin MacLaren had told her.

And despite experience and inclination, she could. She did. And she would do her best to provide the help that the professor had asked for.

Claire mounted the steps and rang the bell.

The person who answered the door was vaguely familiar to Claire from previous parties: a tall, older man with blazing blue eyes whose autocratic air didn't quite seem to fit him. He smiled when he saw Claire and gestured her inside.

"Come in, come in, come in! Welcome to Toller Hasloch's House of Fun— please make yourself right at home."

He reached for her umbrella, and Claire, not sure of what else to do, surrendered it to him. There was no reason to believe that everybody here was of sinister intent; Professor MacLaren had stressed that most of them were probably innocent bystanders, completely unaware of Toller's secret plans. Claire reminded herself of that firmly as she added her coat to the collection in the bulging hall closet and walked past the stairs and into the living room/dining room of the large white Victorian, clutching her purse tightly against her chest.

Miraculously, the old house had escaped the almost inevitable subdividing that had come with the trend to smaller families and the postwar urban flight of the last several decades. Half of the first floor was given over to two large rooms—the living room and the dining room or parlor—while the other side held kitchen, closets, foyer and stairs, and a small room that Toller used as a study. The two large rooms could be closed off from each other by oak sliding panels that were currently thrown open, making the two into one large room that was filled with local college students—a lot of people for a late party on a Thursday night when everyone had classes the next day. The record changer of the hi-fi set in the corner held a stack of current LPs, and the Chad Mitchell Trio was on the turntable, singing "John Birch Society."

Most of the kids had taken their shoes off and were dancing. Others wandered in and out of the kitchen, emerging with Cokes and bowls of chips. Several people greeted her, and she smiled and waved, though with newly honed suspicion, Claire realized how few of them were in any of her nursing classes. In fact, this seemed to be almost a different crowd even from the usual for Toller's parties—a lot of the people here were older than the average Berkeley student—she even saw one man with grey in his hair, standing to one side as if he were trying not to be noticed.

But then, she reminded herself, trying to be fair, Toller was a senior. He'd have his Bachelor's next fall. Why shouldn't he have older friends—she and Toller certainly didn't run in the same circles; how could she pretend to imagine she knew who his friends were?

Only if that were true—and it was—why his painstaking care to include her in his festivities, as though she were one of his circle . . . ?

Unless, as the professor seemed to think, Toller, too, knew what she had the power to become, and was courting her for it, seducing her slowly from the paths of sanity and common sense.

Tommyrot, Claire told herself roundly. She'd only taken the vodka punch because Mother had just called on one of her drunken vendettas to tell Claire what a disappointment she was. Everyone on campus knew that Claire was the original wet blanket when it came to booze. Toller couldn't have imagined she'd be having any when he'd slipped the LSD into the punch.

The crepe-paper Halloween decorations that had been in evidence the last time she'd been here had all been taken down, supplanted by a handmade banner wishing Toller a happy birthday. There was a brief, sickening moment in which the room seemed to shimmer and reel, caught between that moment and this, but then things steadied, and Claire knew where she was once more.

But the fact remained: he did take an interest in her.

Get a grip on yourself, girl. Everybody who drank that punch got Toller's Mickey Finn—it wasn't anything personal. If walking in the front door is enough to give you the heebie-jeebies, how are you ever going to handle the rest of it?

She'd find the strength. Claire squared her shoulders and walked into the nearest knot of partygoers.

*   *   *

It was easy to deceive them, Claire realized a few moments later. She wasn't that good a liar, but none of them were paying any particular attention. There was drinking—there always was, at Toller's parties—and once in a while Claire caught a whiff of a sweetish, burning scent that she thought was probably marijuana.

She didn't see Toller anywhere. That wasn't all that unusual, but Claire was grateful for it—she wasn't sure she could face him down as easily as she had his guests.

No one noticed when she ascended the staircase to the second floor. She'd been up here before, but the fact that this time she was on a clandestine mission of sorts made her jumpy.

Someone was coming out of the bathroom just as she got to the top of the stairs, and Claire ducked past them into the bathroom, closing the door behind her. Safe!

Her heart hammered as she gazed into the mirror. The face that looked back at her was white and scared, and she took several deep breaths. Everything would work out all right. It had to.

She splashed a little water on her face, hoping that no one else would come upstairs wanting to use the bathroom. Her damp clothes clung to her clammily, reminding her of where she'd been earlier tonight and why she'd come here. On a hunch she opened the medicine cabinet; there was the usual collection of bottles, but there seemed to be an awful lot of prescriptions. There was also a packet of cigarettes—Luckies—but when she took down the red-and-white packet only the first two cigarettes looked normal. The rest of the pack was filled with yellowish, hand-rolled cigarettes, their ends twisted shut. Claire sighed and put them back where she'd found them, losing all interest in investigating further. The more she found out about Toller Hasloch, the more she wanted to be somewhere else.

She groped for the tube of lipstick in her purse and slashed it across her lips. The pale pink gloss gave her a bit of color, making her seem more alive. There. Nothing to be afraid of.

Just a return to that dark ambiguous place inside her, the one filled with indefensible certainties. Where she knew things she could not know, where she was asked to do things beyond all reason. . . .

Claire London took another breath and stepped out of the bathroom, shifting her purse to the other shoulder.

The hallway was deserted, the doors closed. Closets—bedrooms—a library. The room filled with books smelled of incense, and the titles of the books behind the glass cases made her faintly uneasy, but she did not think that this was the place she sought. The professor had told her she'd know it when she found it, but had refused to tell her more than that. Claire sighed in frustration and continued searching, and a few minutes later—other than having disturbed a few necking couples—was no closer to finding what she was looking for than she had been before.

And where's Toller? He wasn't downstairs; he isn't here. . . .

She gazed dubiously at the steep narrow staircase that led into the attic. Searching the attic would take time, and be noticeable as well. Claire hesitated, trying to decide whether to risk it. But she had the feeling—faint, easy to ignore—that the attic did not contain what she was looking for.

Unless she'd missed something, the place she was looking for had to be down, not up.

It took her almost an hour to find it, by which time, Claire felt, Professor MacLaren, waiting in the car, must surely have given up on her. She was looking for a basement—it was the only place left for Toller to hide what she was looking for—and most California houses weren't built with them anymore, a consequence both of a high Bay Area water table and the frequent earthquakes that plagued the region.

There was no door to a basement in the kitchen; she hung around the area for several minutes, wondering what she could have overlooked. There was a big sheet cake on the kitchen table. Its surface was decorated with symbols that looked vaguely familiar to Claire; barred circles, odd cross-shapes, crude sharp-edged designs that almost (but not quite) looked like letters.

Two doors led out of the kitchen. The one by the stove let out into a pantry and the backyard. The other opened onto an uncomfortably narrow corridor that led into the study.

It was the only place she hadn't searched. But if she went barging in there and it was full of people, she was going to have to talk faster than she ever had in her life.

She didn't have time to hesitate; people were coming in and out of the kitchen all the time and someone was sure to ask her what she was doing. Claire slipped through the door and closed it behind her. There was no sound ahead, and she breathed a deep sigh of relief. The hallway was only a few feet long—more an architectural quirk of remodeling than an intentional space—and she quickly reached the other door.

Abandoned cups and bottles showed that this room too was in use. A fog of sweetish smoke hung in the air, its scent acrid and unfamiliar. Claire's glance darted around frantically, looking for a door on the east wall that could be the cellar door she sought.

There it was! A bookcase was pulled halfway across it, and Claire nearly wasted time moving it before she realized that the door opened outward, and there was no need. Fortunately, it was not locked. Claire eased it open and slipped through. Dusty wooden stairs led downward, and the staircase smelled powerfully of dampness. There was the chill bluish glow of fluorescent light coming from the basement. She skipped down the stairs, her purse bumping heavily against her side, nearly tripping and falling headfirst in her excitement.

She reached the bottom in a wave of apprehension that nearly made her ill. Directly ahead of her was a wall of shelves containing anonymous glass jars and boxes, and stacked on the uneven cement floor were wooden cases of beer and soda. Rain spangled the tiny window set high in the wall, level with the lawn above. The droplets glowed pale yellow in the light from the nearby streetlamp, and the window was clotted with cobwebs. There was nothing here.

Then she looked down, and saw a wide arc worn into the cement floor. It started at the center of the shelving and extended halfway across the floor. Claire walked over to the shelves, every instinct screaming that there was danger here, something vile—a monster out of her childhood, of the adult fears that had stalked her earliest girlhood.

When she touched the edge of the shelf, she could feel a handhold carved into its frame, and up close, she could see that the jars and boxes on this section of shelving were glued down. It slid open as she pulled it toward her, the rubber casters on the bottom providing the explanation of the marks she'd seen.

Claire pushed forward. A heavy velvet curtain was hung from the ceiling eighteen inches beyond the false front of the shelving. For a moment Claire struggled with pulling the shelves closed behind her while finding a way through the curtain, but she finally managed both.

The space on the other side of the curtain was out of a different world.

The three walls of the room were paneled in dark wood and the floor was covered with thick wool carpeting in a rich deep maroon. Directly opposite the curtained opening, there was a long heavy table completely draped in shimmering white cloth. But it was the object above the altar table that claimed all of Claire's attention, the last thing she would have expected to find under these circumstances: a wooden cross, about four feet high.

The cross itself was not inverted—somewhere in the back of Claire's mind was the thought that this would be too facile, too easy. It was the figure on the cross that was reversed.

The body was carved of ivory, or possibly just painted to look as if it was. It hung from a loop of cord above the crosspiece that was also looped about its left ankle, and whoever had fashioned this blasphemous piece of art had carefully depicted the way that the cords dug deep into the ankle. Only one leg was caught up in that fashion; the other was bent at the knee, throwing the twisted body into stark, tense relief. The body was carved all over with the same spiky symbols Claire had seen on the cake upstairs, and here again the artist had taken care to give the marks the look of cuts made into living flesh. But the greatest mutilation was to the figure's face. One eye had been completely torn away, and the left side of the face was awash with blood.

Claire felt as nauseated—as emotionally violated—as though she had unexpectedly come across a scene of actual torture. The whole room vibrated with a hideous secret delight that so stunned her that for a moment Claire, paralyzed with disgust and horror, forgot what she must do.

She fumbled at her purse, dropping it so that the contents spilled out across the rug. The walkie-talkie had been almost too big to fit inside; seeing it now reminded Claire of what she was here to do. She picked up the remote transmitter and switched it on.

"Hello? Hello?" There was no sound at all. She tried to remember what the professor had told her, then pulled up the antenna. "Hello?"

An encouraging hash of static rewarded her this time, and she pressed the Transmit button, hoping he could hear her. "Professor, I'm down in the basement. The door to it is in a room just off the kitchen. It's just what you said, and it's horrible—"

"Horrible?" an amused voice interrupted from behind her. "After all my hard work at decorating it—and on top of a full course load, too."

Claire, already keyed up, squeaked and dropped the walkie-talkie. It hit the rug with a dull thud, and the hiss of static stopped.

"If you wanted to come to my private party, Claire, why didn't you just say so?" Toller continued. "I would have been happy to issue you a personal invitation."

There was laughter at that remark. Toller was not alone. There were others with him—too many to easily count, perhaps a dozen—all wearing black robes with red tabards over them. Each tabard had a white circle over the chest, with one of the spiky designs in black. Toller's was the barred circle.

Unconsciously, Claire retreated from them, until her back was pressed against the altar table. It was a solid, immobile weight against her back.

"What—what—" she stammered, the combination of the horrible *feel* of the place and the shock of Toller's presence putting her fatally off balance.

"Poor Claire—suckered in by the Opposition already and nobody's told you the rules. I will: the Light has had its day, and the sun always sets. It is our time now—the time of the glorious, fertile Dark, and the unchanging stars!"

She heard a few mutters behind him, and somebody said, "Knock it off, Toller." Some of the people in the robes were her age and younger, and possibly not very serious about this, but Toller was serious enough for all of them. What the professor had told her she now heartily believed: there were some things so dangerous that they could not be approached even in play. Any dealings with them would always be real.

Toller darted forward and grabbed her, kicking the walkie-talkie away, and yanked hard on the front of her jumper. The zipper up the back split, and her blouse tore open. Buttons flew everywhere, and Claire made a sound of outrage.

"Come on," Toller called to the others. "What's she doing down here if she didn't want to play? She deserves what she gets—don't you, Claire?"

There was a hesitant mutter of agreement from the men behind him.

"*Damn* you, Toller Hasloch," Claire said with sincere intensity. Toller laughed and flung her to the ones waiting behind him. She was caught by the man who had opened the door upstairs, the one with the blazing blue eyes. He yanked the jumper down off her shoulders, and Claire felt the predatory intensity in the room jump.

She struggled, but there were too many of them—most of them more than a little drunk and all of them imbued with the ugly psychology of the mob. In moments she was stripped to her panties, bra, and garter belt, her nylons laddered by the struggle.

Toller tied her hands behind her back, and threw Claire up onto the altar.

She landed with a solid force, and while she lay there stunned, he grabbed her ankles and began to tie them as well. Despair seemed to seep out of the walls around her; it filled her like a cup, as sharp and sudden as physical pain—why waste energy in struggling when no success could come of it in the end? Claire lay limp, unable to control her shuddering as he tied her ankles together tightly. She was lying on her bound hands—her shoulders pulled awkwardly backward by the binding—and her body ached with cold, as though she were lying inside a walk-in freezer.

"We're going to try a little experiment, my friends and I," Toller said to her when he had finished. "We'll all concentrate on you—all twelve of us—and see if we can drive your soul out of your body. If we can, I'm afraid that the world will just think you've had another one of your spells, and this one—too bad!—will have been permanent. Of course, if we can't . . . well, the human mind isn't designed to stand up to that sort of pressure, is it?"

"You're a fraud," Claire flung at him through gritted teeth.

"I'm sure you wish that were true," Toller told her kindly. "But it isn't, and if you really thought it was, you'd never have come here. My apologies for the other night, by the way—I meant to have some fun and liven up my party, nothing more. It wasn't meant for you."

But you'd have taken advantage of it, wouldn't you, if Jonathan hadn't been there? She tried to remember that Professor MacLaren knew she was here, that there was at least some hope of rescue, but it was as if she were attempting to lift a weight beyond her strength. She could not manage to believe.

"Let me go," Claire said again. Tears welled up in her eyes, born of fury or fear or both.

"Don't be silly," Toller replied chidingly.

With a minimum of fuss, he and the others lit the candles scattered around the room, and then the dishes of incense that were placed on the shelf beneath the twisted cross. Silky blue smoke with a choking bitter odor began to stream up toward the ceiling, making the maimed face of the white figure seem almost alive. Claire closed her eyes and turned away, trying not to let herself know how scared she was.

Then Toller and his acolytes gathered around the altar and the silence became even more profound. Claire wanted to make some kind of smart remark, but a strange and powerful reluctance held her silent. They weren't just quiet—they were doing something, something she could feel the way she could feel the force of an incoming storm; as a pressure in her chest, in her head.

In her head.

It was like a painless headache, like a sensation for which there were no sensory referents. She did not like it, but she could not say that it was painful, or even unpleasant. But the thing that it represented terrified her—as much for the possibility that it would go on, as for the moment it shattered and became something uglier—and there did not seem to be anything she could do to resist it.

There is always something.

A calm certainty washed over her with gentle suddenness. It was the only thing she could feel beside the pressure. *Oh, dear God, help me*, Claire prayed awkwardly.

There was no discernible answer, but the crushing sense of fear lifted enough for an irreverent thought sparked by the music she'd heard earlier to surface. *Talk about a movement full of tools and cranks . . . I wonder if Toller knows that he looks terrific in a dress?*

The flare of speechless displeasure that greeted that thought made her groan. She could not see, and if it was simply because her eyes were closed then she could not find the strength to open them.

No, no, no . . . Claire chanted inside her mind, unable to form a coherent prayer and knowing, too, that the intent was enough. She was cold and half-naked and in desperate danger, but the knowledge that she was not alone was like an invisible shield. God saw, if no one else did. And even though Toller might kill her—

Just because you're stronger doesn't mean you're right, Hasloch.

She clung to that thought, as the roaring increased in her ears, and her hands and feet seemed chill and very far away.

Then, salvation.

"Toller Christian Hasloch, I charge you in the name of the Most High and Holy Name to abandon your errors of Darkness!"

Professor MacLaren's voice boomed out with the reassuring anger of the cop on the beat. The crushing pressure stopped, and Claire felt relief wash over her with a healing, numbing caress. He *had* come!

Once Claire had left, Colin waited in the car with the terrible patience that he'd learned on a hundred other cold and rainy nights thousands of miles away. At least tonight he didn't have to worry about whether his forged papers would pass a police check, and wonder whether he'd be greeting the dawn in a Gestapo cell. All he had to worry about was Claire.

She should be inside Hasloch's house by now, and when she found what they were looking for, all she had to do was call him on the other half of the radio set he'd given her. With a Sensitive acting for the Light already inside the bounds, none of Hasloch's magickal wards should be able to stand against an outside assault, and Colin would be able to tie whatever hoodoo the boy was using into a blue-ribbon knot.

He was fairly sure no one would prevent him from entering the house—he was a teacher at the college most of them attended; if worse came to worst, he'd just pull rank.

But where was Claire? He began to worry as the minutes stretched to an hour, then two. Why didn't she call?

It didn't occur to Colin that Claire might not fulfill her side of the bargain. Wary and tormented though she might be, Claire London had a natural will nearly as strong as that of a trained magician. When Claire said she'd do something, Colin knew she would not take back her given word lightly.

But there were so many pitfalls in her way—dangers that she might not

yet take seriously enough to guard herself from them The child barely believed in her own psychic sensitivity—to ask her to take so much more on
trust so quickly . . .

Needs must, when the devil drives, Colin quoted ironically to himself. He
could not work tonight's Operation without the aid of a Sensitive to get him
past the outer shields, and he could not put aside that work simply because it
endangered innocents. Many more would be endangered if it were allowed to
continue.

*The black phoenix of Nazism loose in the world once more . . . and this time, a
world with nuclear capability. What would the worshipers of the Eternal Night do
with the power of a newborn sun in their hands?*

The magnitude of the threat promised absolution for any extreme action,
but Colin knew that this too was a trap to maim the spirit. The end never justified the means. The means *shaped* the end, and so the Light was forever
barred from using the tools of the Dark to wage its war. Those who fought for
the Light must always know the danger, must always freely consent to risk
themselves in a battle that could never be anything but unequal.

*But how can any neophyte know the true nature of the peril before they face it? How
do I keep my own hands clean when I've chosen to sacrifice innocent men and women to
the goals I have chosen?*

There was only one hard unforgiving answer to that: Colin's hands were
not clean, and never would be. For so long as he fought for the Light, he must
do penance for his fight. Yet those who fought were needed as urgently as
those whose karma it was to stand aside.

The crackle of static on the transmitter/receiver was a welcome interruption from his own stark thoughts. Claire's voice erupted from it, sexless and
distorted.

*"Professor, I'm down in the basement. The door to it is in a room just off the kitchen.
It's just what you said, and it's horrible—"*

Abruptly the little device went dead, but Colin did not waste time trying
to raise Claire again. He was out of the car and running toward the house
through the rain, one hand clutched over the small revolver in his trenchcoat
pocket. A terrible fear possessed him, that he was risking more than he knew,
that to lose this fight—to lose Claire—would cost him all that he was. Even
as he realized the cost, he accepted it. He would not fail.

Once he was inside the house it cost him precious minutes to find the door to
the basement, but, like Claire, he had no trouble in unriddling the secret of
the false shelving that concealed the secret underground room. He could
smell the incense, chokingly thick.

When he pulled back the false shelving, the curtain swirled around him,
and Colin could feel the faint cheated snarl of the wards he had defeated ringing discordantly in his ears. His revolver was in his hand before he took his
bearings, blinking in the candlelit dimness, and the shock he felt at what he
saw was so great that for an instant he nearly fired at the nearest of the black-
robed, rune-blazoned worshipers.

It was as if he'd stepped into a past he never wanted to visit again.

There was the Rune-Christ hanging from the World Tree, his body covered with the symbols of ancient magic; a malign conflation of Odin and Lucifer. There were the *fylfot* banners, the *hakenkreutz* candlesticks and the sunwheel censers: the familiar trappings of the Black Temple before him were like a blow to the heart, symbols of the worship of a Lucifer who had never bowed to the will of Heaven, of a Grail that had never known the touch of the Christ.

Colin brandished his gun and roared out the first words that came into his mind and heart, rewarded by the sight of the robed and hooded figures that clustered around the altar scattering like the frightened sheep that most of them were. Claire lay on the altar, bound and half-naked, and she gazed at him with an expression in which relief and fierce triumph were mingled.

But though the others ran, Toller Hasloch stood firm. He faced Colin across Claire's body, his drawn face white and fanatical, colorless eyes glittering in the candlelight.

Carefully Colin slid the hammer back down and transferred the gun to his left hand.

Hasloch did not move as Colin walked over to the altar. A few quick cuts with a pocketknife freed Claire from her bonds, and Colin draped his trenchcoat around her shoulders. She slid off the altar, glaring blue murder at Hasloch, who seemed as immovable as the carven Rune-Christ.

Claire stepped away from the altar, never taking her eyes off Hasloch as she came to stand behind Colin.

The boy took a deep breath, assuming his cocky facade with an effort.

"Okay, Professor. The game is yours. You're more ingenious than I gave you credit for. No one will, of course, believe you—or Crazy Claire—if either of you chooses to talk."

Colin smiled bleakly. "Your youthful inexperience is showing, sonny boy. I'm not going to talk to anyone. I'm just going to pull your plug. I suggest you stay right where you are unless you actually want me to have to explain shooting you to somebody. Believe me, I take you seriously enough for that."

He raised his right hand in an ancient Sign, never letting the gun waver. Hasloch stared at the air where it had been drawn, the forced smile fading from his face.

The difference between Toller Hasloch and the average occult dabbler was that Hasloch's rituals *worked*. Toller Hasloch had Power, and most of the reason for that was the allies and servants his young Temple could claim on the Astral. Destroy it, and Hasloch's power was gone. Consecrate the place where the Astral Order Castle had stood, and Hasloch could not rebuild it without help that he was not likely to receive on the heels of his failure.

Hasloch's face went white as he realized what Colin was doing. One hand went to the ornate dagger at his waist, the other to the medallion that hung about his neck.

And the battle was joined.

For Colin MacLaren, without Astral Sight to guide him, the battle occurred in a double realm: that of the trained disciplined imagination, which forced the Will against the coiled Dragon of the ancient Darkness in the form of a shining White Eagle, and that of the mundane world, in which Colin held the revolver trained steadily on Toller Hasloch as the wail of police sirens—summoned by whom?—grew louder from the distance.

After each clash the Black Dragon tried to diminish itself; to transform into something small and ordinary and harmless, something that would be left alone. Each time the White Eagle refused to claim a victory that would allow even the weakest offspring of the Dragon to survive. And at last the shadows were all banished, and the White Light of the Eternal and Immutable Word roared through all the corners of the Desolation where the Black Tower had been.

When all hope of victory was gone, Hasloch fell back against his altar, tears of frightened rage coursing down his face. The skirl of a siren winding down in front of the house could be heard, very faintly, through the walls.

"I'll see you in jail for this!" he cried, his voice cracking. "You'll be dismissed from the university—you'll never teach again—"

"Your mother wears army boots," Claire snapped, her voice hoarse with anger. "It's two against one—and do you think people are going to take a gander at this movie set of yours and take anything you say *seriously*?"

"I believe the police are here," Colin said quietly. "Your friends in the robes must have panicked."

Even through the draperies and the false wall, the sound of shouts from the floor above could be heard.

"Hasloch, your friends are probably going to talk. It's up to Claire whether she chooses to press charges in relation to this evening's silliness, but if you'll take my advice, you'll get rid of your nasty little toys before the City of Berkeley comes up with a search warrant. The war may be over, son, but nobody likes a Nazi."

Hasloch simply glared, his face so white and furious that for a moment Colin actually thought he might suffer a seizure and fall dead right there. But he only dragged off his tabard and flung it down, then unbelted his dagger and pulled the robe off over his head. Beneath the robe he was wearing street clothes. The medallion gleamed against his red sweater for an instant before he scooped it beneath his shirt with shaking hands.

He averted his eyes from Colin and Claire with an effort that was almost physical and staggered away without a word, disappearing into the wings of the temple. Apparently there was a second entrance and exit to the cellar.

"What, no parting words?" Claire said with ragged cheer. "No threats of revenge?"

Her knees buckled and Colin put an arm around her shoulders, only then remembering that he still held the pistol. He shoved it quickly into his pocket. He had a permit for it, come to that, and there was still a number in Washington that he could call for backup, something that would probably annoy the chief of police no end. But it was much better if no one asked any questions, even if Colin did have answers ready.

"He'll probably phone me with them later tonight," Colin said. "Claire, you were wonderful—I wish I'd never subjected you to this—"

"Don't say that," the girl interrupted quickly, pulling the borrowed trenchcoat more tightly around herself. "My generation is the one that's always talking about saving the world, right? Well, for once I've managed to actually *do* something that made a difference, and that felt good. Sure, I was scared—heck, I was terrified. But it needed doing. And I'll do it again—if you'll let me."

She held out her hand.

"The Most High grant that something like this never needs doing again," Colin said. "But if it does, I'll call upon your promise, Claire—I swear it."

He clasped her hand and shook it, a solemn promise.

"And now I suppose we should go upstairs and talk to the police. Someone must have called them when the rest of Hasloch's coven bolted—I wonder what they think is going on here? I imagine they're having visions of decadent drug orgies; I wonder if the sworn word of a professor in the Psychology Department will carry any weight with them. Shall we go and see?"

Claire snickered, a muffled half-involuntary noise. "Oh, yeah. Certainly, Professor. And while we're explaining things, maybe somebody has a pair of shoes I can borrow to go with the trenchcoat."

The explanations required—to the Berkeley police, to the chancellor of the University, and to the head of Colin's department—were long and tedious, and Colin MacLaren celebrated Christmas with the addition of an official letter of censure to his personnel file.

It was a long time before he connected the evening and its aftermath with the information he gleaned from the newspapers four days later: President Kennedy had increased the number of military advisors that he was sending to a far-off place called Viet-Nam.

But twenty-four months and thirteen days after that November night, Colin did think about Toller Hasloch again.

BERKELEY, 1961

AND SO IT BEGAN, AS EASILY AS THAT. WHAT COLIN OFFERED ME WAS something I had been looking for all my life; it was nothing less than a lodestone to steer myself by.

It wasn't in any sense that Colin became my *guru*— how archaic that word seems now, though when I first met him it was years away from gaining general currency—since to both of our regrets, I never found it in my heart to follow the teachings to which I knew he had dedicated his life. It was more as if, if the world could contain a man like Colin MacLaren, it was a very different sort of world than the one in which I had previously believed—a world in which it was possible to build for the future, in which cause and effect were not the product of sadistic whimsy.

I believe that if I had not met Colin, I would never have met Peter, because the woman I was before Colin entered my life would simply never have believed that she deserved him. For so long I'd been living from day to day, simply surviving without suffering some new disaster, that having my affairs so easily set in order gave me a freedom that those born happy—and lucky—can hardly imagine. But suddenly the world was new, and I joined the rest of my generation in the unreasonable hope that progress was forever, and that peace was something we could achieve. How simple that faith was to embrace— and how strongly it would be tested in the years to come, both in our lives and in the history of our era.

FOUR

BERKELEY, 1962

Ah, for a heart less native to high Heaven,
A hooded eye, for jesses and restraint,
Or for a will accipitrine to pursue!
— FRANCIS THOMPSON

IN THE SPRING OF 1962 AN AMERICAN ORBITED THE EARTH FOR THE FIRST time. That autumn there were riots in Mississippi and federal troops in the streets. In summer a film goddess died, her short tragic life and self-destructive end serving almost as a template for all those who would come afterward, those focal points of their generation's dreams who would be consumed by love as the phoenix by the fire and lead the swift radiant lives of moths dancing with the flames.

That was the autumn that an entire nation looked into the fire: the October that the world stood on the verge of the nuclear hellfire that would write the last chapter in human history in a brief, bright, eclipse of the sun. There were Russian missiles ninety miles off the Florida coast. The Russians promised war.

And when it did not happen, the West breathed a shaken sigh of relief . . . and America looked to her young, invincible president to strike the last blow in the Cold War, as well as the first.

That was the year that Claire London married Peter Moffat.

"Colin, this is Peter." Claire presented her young man with shy pride, blushing as she did so. Peter had been a topic of conversation between Colin and Claire for several weeks now, and after a certain amount of insistence on Colin's part, Claire had agreed to bring Peter to meet him. An afternoon mixer given by a mutual friend provided the perfect opportunity for the two men to meet.

"I'm pleased to meet you, Professor," Peter said, holding out his hand.

"I hope I can get you to call me 'Colin,'" Colin said, taking Peter Moffat's hand. Peter's grip was firm and direct, and Colin found himself liking the young man very much.

Peter Moffat was a young man in his middle twenties, a few years older than Claire. He had light brown hair and hazel eyes, and radiated a steadiness of purpose that must be one of the reasons Claire was so attracted to him—at least if his Outer Self was any indication of the inner.

Having brought them together, Claire vanished in the direction of the bar. The party was mostly the younger faculty, the usual mavericks from the Drama and English Departments, wives, and older students.

"I hope I'm not telling tales out of school if I say that Claire thinks a lot of you," Colin observed, looking around the room.

"She thinks a lot of *you*," Peter corrected firmly. "You, and Dr. Margrave—you could have knocked me over with a feather when she told me she'd met Simon Anstey! I've got all of his albums. I used to play the piano—nothing like that, of course—"

The flow of small talk was interrupted by Claire's return. She carried three glasses awkwardly balanced between her hands, two sherries and a tall lemonade. Colin was mildly surprised when she handed the lemonade to Peter.

"I'm going on duty in a few hours," Peter explained, noting Colin's glance.

"Peter's with the Berkeley Police," Claire said. Her tone turned faintly chiding, "I *told* you, Colin."

"So you did," Colin admitted, smiling. "And I'm the first to admit that I have the most perniciously bad memory. So you plan on a career in law enforcement, Peter?"

"Well, sir—Colin—I'm still in uniform, but I'm taking the exams, and I hope to make detective in not too many years," Peter answered, looking toward Claire. "It's a hard life for an officer's wife—I won't deny that—and I'd be lying if I didn't admit that a lot of marriages don't last—"

"Peter!" Claire said, laughing and protesting at once.

"Are you two talking about marriage already?" Colin asked. He felt a faint pang. Not jealousy precisely; but marriage was such a big step, and Claire was so young. . . .

She's twenty years old, Colin reminded himself. *That's old enough to take charge of your life. When you were twenty, you'd already killed three men. Not that that's a fair analogy. . . .*

"I know what I want," Peter said firmly. "And it wouldn't be honest not to tell Claire so."

"He hasn't convinced me yet," Claire said, smiling, "but I have to admit he seems to be wearing me down."

Colin raised an eyebrow at her. In only a few months, Claire London had changed almost completely, a gawky cygnet becoming a self-assured swan. Under Colin's guidance and explanations she'd learned to trust the Gift that nature had given her, and by extension, to trust the people around her.

She'd taken eagerly to the simple mental disciplines he and Alison were able to teach her, and she'd gained confidence both in her ability to intervene successfully in the lives of others and in the rightness of doing so.

"I've told Peter everything—about myself," Claire added, though perhaps only Colin could have heard the qualifying hesitation in her voice.

"And how do you feel about that?" Colin asked, neutrally.

Peter laughed. "Well, it isn't something that I want to discuss with the boys down at the bar!" he said cheerfully, then sobered. "I know that this whole business of psychic powers sounds pretty much like Bunco Squad territory—"

"Sometimes it is," Colin agreed. "For as long as there have been psychics, there have been frauds—in fact, some people might say that the frauds came first. One of the things parapsychology—an emerging science, as I'll be one of the first to admit—tries to do is bring the study of these human abilities into the realm of the scientific method. I'm as interested as anybody in exposing the frauds that litter our field, but not at the price of issuing a blanket condemnation of anyone with paranormal abilities. Whew! That's quite a speech."

"But a good answer," Claire said. "Colin does as much to expose—oh, table-tippers and gypsy tea-leaf readers, and all those so-called mystics who prey upon the unwary, as—as *you* do, Peter!" she finished in a rush.

"That's my Claire," Peter said fondly. "But tell me, Professor—Colin—is there any way for someone like me to tell a psychic from a fraud? It isn't legal in Alameda County to foretell the future—at least for money—but there's lots of ways around the law for people who want to work that scam, and I can't bring Claire along with me to check them all out."

Claire wrinkled her nose. "You might as well read a good book as a pack of Tarot cards—it's all the same to me, Peter. *I* can't tell the future—I wish I could."

"There are certain obvious guidelines for separating the sheep from the goats," Colin said, "but the most obvious is one you already know: if a person has set himself up to make a living from his alleged psychic powers, it's almost a dead certainty that he's a fraud. Science understands very little about the psychic senses, but one thing that seems to be true is that these gifts are highly erratic, and rarely come when they're called."

"But what's *possible*?" Peter asked. "How can anyone tell the difference between, say, a fraud medium and, well, someone like Claire?"

"That's a difficult question," Colin said, "but if you'd like, I'll be happy to come down and talk to your department about it. I may have found a few ways of exposing a fake psychic that they haven't run into yet."

Peter grinned engagingly. "Wish me luck at getting them to go for it! Still, it can't hurt to mention it. Some of the guys, though, they aren't likely to think you're, well, on the square."

"And while my own assurances won't count for much, there is the fact that the state of California is trusting me with its children," Colin said. "But don't worry, Peter; my ego's strong enough to survive a few dents."

Colin saw a good deal of Peter Moffat after that. Peter still lived at home with his widowed mother, but Colin and Claire were both frequent visitors to the Moffat house, for Sunday dinner or simply to drop in for the evening.

And, slowly, Peter began bringing Colin the odd problems that cropped up in the borderlands of police work; those events that were not precisely criminal, or even illegal, merely . . . strange.

Claire proved to be an invaluable partner to Colin's investigations. She was sensitive to the presence of paranormal activity, and infallibly capable of recognizing the psychic gift in others. To Colin's secret relief, Peter was delighted with her competence and impressed with her abilities, and as the months passed it began to seem inevitable that the two of them would spend the rest of their lives together. . . .

It was a June wedding. Colin and Peter had attended Claire's graduation from nursing school only a few days before, and now many of the same people were gathered here.

The wedding was a quiet weekday affair held in the Lady Chapel of the Anglican Church that Claire and Peter both attended. The bride wore a sensible blue suit with a corsage of white roses and a pillbox hat with a scrap of veil; the groom was sober and conscientious in a blue serge suit, and both of them made their responses in quiet, firm voices.

She looks so happy, Colin thought prosaically, but didn't all brides look happy? Today he had given the bride away, in the archaic custom, and now Colin felt a great sense of peace, as of an obstacle gracefully negotiated. But the true work had been Claire's, and the impediments things he could not begin to guess at. None of Claire's family was at the wedding, for one thing — whether they had not been invited, or had simply refused to come, Colin did not know. Mrs. Moffat was sitting in the pew across the aisle from Colin in a pink flowered dress, beaming tearfully as she entrusted her only son into the care of another woman.

It had been a short engagement—Claire and Peter had met for the first time that December, barely six weeks after Colin had sent Claire to Toller Hasloch's birthday party. Those events seemed as if they'd taken place in another world, now. Hasloch had disappeared almost immediately, not even staying to finish out the semester. There'd been rumors and wild talk on campus, but without their focus, the gossip and speculations had eventually died away, as those whose lives Hasloch had touched found other—more wholesome interests. The old white Victorian still stood vacant with a FOR RENT sign in its yard, its basement now innocent and empty.

In the pew behind Colin, Jonathan Ashwell shifted self-consciously. For a while, he and Claire had seen a great deal of each other, but Claire had already been seeing Peter, and Jonathan had realized almost as soon as Colin did that

Claire felt only a sisterly affection for him. Claire had made up her mind only a little after Peter had, and now Colin wished them both all happiness.

Colin returned his attention to the front of the church, where Peter slipped a gleaming gold circlet on Claire's finger. A moment more, and the newlyweds turned to face the small congregation, matching rings twinkling on both their left hands.

It was done. Claire and Peter were bonded eternally to one another, a spiritual decision that man's laws, however gravely enacted, could not lightly set at naught. The organist played the recessional, and the congregation stood.

Young Mr. and Mrs. Moffat moved out of Colin's orbit for a time, but he was content to have it so. His commitment to teaching increased, and he found fulfillment in touching the lives of the children who passed through his care on their way to adulthood. Around him the world changed only a little each day, the gathering power of the events beneath the passage of the days invisible to those who lived through them.

1963 was the year that police in Birmingham, Alabama, turned dogs loose on civil rights marchers, just as their spiritual ancestors had unleashed them on the inhabitants of the European ghettos. President Kennedy demanded civil rights for all Americans in a speech before Congress, and, before the echoes of his speech were stilled, a black man named Medgar Evers was slaughtered for sharing the young president's dream, and would wait thirty years for justice. This was the year in which prayer left the public schools, when Camelot came to shadowed, still-divided Berlin, where President Kennedy announced that he, along with all who prayed for freedom, was a Berliner. It was the year that Martin Luther King had a dream.

And 118 days after Kennedy had stood unafraid in the Berlin sunlight and held out the hope of an end to Europe's long nightmare, the news came from Dallas.

What happened then ended the morning of America more completely than civil war and civil strife, two world wars, and half a dozen smaller brawls had ever hoped to do. The invincible innocence that America had carried like a torch into the postwar period was shattered forever. Like the Fisher King's unhealed wound, the destruction of Camelot would taint the American soul forever more.

It was November 1963.

It was a little after ten in the morning on Friday, November 22. Colin had finished his nine A.M. *Introduction to Psychology* class, and he was leaving Tolman Hall to walk across the campus to his office when he heard footsteps running through the corridor behind him. He turned around and saw Sylvia Eshleman running toward him. Her mascara was smeared like clown-wings across her cheeks; she was crying in an awful, gape-mouthed silence.

Dear God, Colin thought. *Someone has died.*

"He's been shot!" she sobbed, stopping in front of him. "The president's been shot in Dallas."

* * *

It was as if the Armageddon they'd all been braced for had come a year late. All through that terrible day and into the night the dead glassy eye of the television showed the commentators in Dallas and Washington, showed footage of Dealey Plaza and of the stunned, silent crowds. The president who had passed the torch to a new generation was dead—not in war, not by accident, but by the thoughtless bullet of an assassin.

People huddled together, not knowing what else to do. Everyone was stunned and desperate for news, as if each new bulletin might be a reprieve from the nightmare. Colin found himself in the Student Union, his face turned like all the others to the television in the corner, wishing that this news weren't true. Knowing that it was, and praying that the nation could find the strength to face it.

Claire found him there—he never afterward knew how—and came into his arms, weeping as if her heart would break.

"They've killed him," she repeated, over and over, as if no other words were needed. "They've killed President Kennedy."

The university canceled the rest of the day's classes an hour later. Colin knew that there were people he should see, words of comfort that he could offer, but first he had to see to Claire. He could feel her body shaking, resonating with the emotions of the people around her, emotions that ranged from shock, to disbelief, to grief, to rage.

"Let's go home, Claire," Colin said gently. "There's nothing you can do here."

They drove to the small apartment on Telegraph where she and Peter had made their first home. The phone was ringing as Claire let them in, and Colin crossed the room in one long stride and scooped the receiver out of its cradle.

"Claire? Claire?" Peter's voice was desperate.

"It's Colin, Peter. Claire's right here." He handed her the telephone and walked into the kitchen. Behind him he could hear the sound of Claire's responses, her voice hoarse but composed.

Where was the kettle? Colin puttered around the kitchen, letting the very normalcy of what he was doing soothe his frayed nerves. Here was the kettle, and the pot, and the sugar—but where was the tea?

"Let me do that." Claire came into the kitchen and took the kettle away from him. "Poor Peter—he's been trying to reach me all day. I left him a message, but I guess he didn't get it. We hardly see each other these days; he's working days and I'm working nights, but I'm sure everything will sort itself out soon."

She rattled on, talking much as she would to calm a troubled patient, as she filled the kettle and set it on the stove and took down the canister of loose tea.

"Peter's such a coffee hound that I've switched to bags; there's no point in brewing up a whole pot when there's only me to drink it. I think there's some cake in the icebox—good heavens, look at the time; are you sure you wouldn't rather have lunch?" She rubbed her eyes, and her shoulders sagged.

"I'm so tired. And I work again tonight, and after this, I know the Emergency Room's going to be a zoo. . . ." Her voice trailed off. "Oh, dear God . . ."

"Claire." Colin took her gently by the shoulders. "You have the strength to face this. It's a shock, but we'll all survive. There'll be a peaceful transfer of power—that's what this country's all about—Johnson will be sworn in as president."

Claire sighed, and smiled wanly. "I just want to know 'why?' That's what everybody wants to know, I guess. Why would anybody do something this horrible? What can they gain?"

Chaos. Chaos, and destruction, and ruin. . . .

And for just an instant Colin was elsewhere; in the vaults of memory, where the sword-bright image of Toller Hasloch smiled in confident cruelty. *We reshape the Inner Planes by reshaping the outer. . . .*

Had Hasloch been a member of a greater organization than he'd suspected?

1964 began with the new president's state of the union speech. Lyndon Baines Johnson declared a war on poverty—to distract the electorate, some said, from all the wars they were losing. More and more these days the evening news programs were talking about a war in Vietnam, a war that—if America lost it—would give Communism free reign over half the globe.

In Cuba, the American naval base at Guantánamo grew steadily more isolated; Fidel Castro had gone from cipher to clown to monster in the public mind, his scruffy, cigar-smoking image was iconized until it became nearly a trademark for Banana Republic Communism.

As if to divert America's attention from the dimming light of the American Dream, in February four English boys arrived in New York—a singing group called The Beatles. The teenagers who had bought 45s titled "Love Me Do" and "Please Please Me" flocked to the airport to meet the Fab Four in screaming thousands, and for the first time their parents heard the voices that would take six short years to blend the worlds of music and world events in a fashion from which neither would ever recover. Two days later America saw the faces that went with the voices on the *Ed Sullivan Show*, in a scene that would become an icon for a generation.

And as spring ripened into summer, the battle lines were drawn for a new war, this time between the generations. At last the dream of the protest singers had come true: music was politics. The children of the soldiers in the Last Good War, the generation that had been orphaned in Dallas, had identified their own generation's enemy, and this time the enemy was not over the sea or across a national border. This time the enemy lived in their own homes.

In California, 1964 was the first Endless Summer—in Mississippi it was Freedom Summer. And in the sultry days of summer a resolution was proposed in Washington by a president whose greatest offense was that he had survived—a resolution that was passed by Congress and began spreading its power through the fabric of American life as if it were a conscious retaliation against the brief hopeful candles of the idealistic Youthquake. The Gulf of Tonkin Resolution called for more troops to fight in the jungles of Southeast Asia, more troops to be committed to an unwinnable fight whose existence the American government would only admit to after another year had passed.

The bogeyman of a generation, Nikita Khrushchev, fell from power. Oswald was guilty and had acted alone (so the Warren Commission found), China had the Bomb, Vatican II had abolished the Latin Mass. Students everywhere had left the campus and taken to the streets, demanding that their voices be heard. All around them, the world changed, growing farther from certainties with each day.

And Thorne Blackburn arrived in San Francisco.

1965 began with another assassination—this time of black activist Malcolm X. Violence seemed entrenched on the American political scene, along with something called the Students for a Democratic Society. In March, protesters in Selma, Alabama, were attacked by state police, and in the crucible of August the Watts ghetto would erupt in hysterical, self-destructive violence. No one could be unaffected by the winds of change that blew with hurricane force through American society—least of all someone who taught on one of the most turbulent campuses in America.

"Kids today," Colin MacLaren said with a sigh.

"You're too young for that statement," Alison chided him gently. She and Colin were sitting on the terrace of Greenhaven, looking out over the sunlit city below—a city that had become world news as runaways from every corner of the globe flooded into the Haight-Ashbury district. They strained city services to the breaking point and proclaimed the birth of a new nation based on peace, love, and rock 'n' roll.

"Forty-five this last February," Colin reminded her with a sigh. Not an old man by any standard, but somehow the future he'd been planning to live in hadn't been here when he reached it. How could anyone who'd been present on V-E Day have predicted that this was what would happen to the unscathed industrial giant among the Allied Powers? And it had happened so fast . . . could anyone have predicted this frenzied self-destructive collapse on that day not so long ago when all the world was cheering?

No. But somewhere, out there, there were people who had worked toward it, and who now celebrated their dark victory. Since Kennedy's assassination, Colin read the daily papers with increasing dread, searching for the dead hand of the *Armanenschaft* in every new outbreak of chaos. Were its members behind these tides of social collapse—or was he the only one who saw the collapse? Perhaps these social upheavals were the pangs of a joyous birth instead. . . .

"Colin? Hello?" Alison broke into his thoughts, and Colin realized how far he'd drifted.

"Sorry, Alison. I was woolgathering," he admitted.

"You must have been!" she said, laughing. "But I'll do my best to anchor you to the Earth Plane. How's Claire?"

"She and Peter are both doing well—he's been promoted, and they're on the same shift most of the time, now. I saw her last week, and she told me she was thinking of listing with an agency and switching to temp work. I believe they're thinking of starting a family, once things settle down."

"What a waste," Alison said gently. "Don't frown at me so, Colin—I have to say it. You know as well as I do that a gift like Claire's is rare. And you also know that a woman with a husband doesn't have any freedom—any life—of her own. She's always looking after *him*."

"Someone has to," Colin offered diffidently. "We men are the most incapable of creatures, left to ourselves."

Alison snorted eloquently.

"And it was Claire's choice," Colin reminded his friend. "Both to marry, and to set aside the Path for this lifetime. She has other things to learn, and other ways of learning them."

"We never stop learning," Alison admitted. "And you're certainly doing well with young Ashwell—there may be something to that boy, with time. But I think you might have exercised more influence on Claire than you did, all but flinging her into Moffat's arms."

"There we must agree to disagree, Alison," Colin said firmly. "Claire is not my disciple; she has not come to me to have her feet set upon the Path once more. But we won't spoil such a lovely day with such an old argument. Tell me about Simon—what have you and he been doing? I've read your monograph, by the way; you must be very proud of your disciple. *A Natural History of the Poltergeist?* Ambitious."

Alison smiled as the gentle barb struck home. "Oh, Simon is a jewel! And his exoteric career is doing so well, too—I dread the thought of his music taking him completely away from me, though I suppose it will at some point. But we had a lovely time—in Ohio, of all places! Fascinating haunted house: poltergeists, mediumship, apportation, all the classic manifestations. Simon's working up my notes, but I'm not sure if we'll publish, at least not for a few years yet. The family involved has two young children, and the last thing they need right now is more publicity. But Simon will be here soon—why not ask him about it? You know he'd love to tell you all about it."

"And behold: speak the name, and the Disciple appears!" Simon cried genially, opening the garden's back gate and stepping through it. Now that he was of legal age and in control of the fortune he'd earned as a child, Simon had bought a condominium in one of the new high-rise buildings going up all over the Twin Peaks area, but he was still a frequent guest in Alison's house.

"Simon!" Alison rose to her feet to receive a kiss upon the cheek, and Colin rose also, to shake his hand. Simon had a powerful grip, but forbore to use it in petty contests of strength.

In the last several years Simon Anstey had changed from an intense, self-conscious, teenager to a graceful, self-possessed young man. He'd grown several inches and filled out through the chest and shoulders, fulfilling the early promise of physical power his body had held. Recently, Colin knew, Simon had tried his hand at conducting, in addition to composing and performing, and a conductor must have as much physical presence as any Olympic athlete.

"Colin— it's great to see you again; it's been far too long. I hear you've been—what's the phrase?—'assisting the police with their inquiries'?" He grinned impishly, and Colin found himself smiling in return.

"Something of the sort. The police often consult specialists, and Claire and I have been able to be of some help to them on a few occasions."

"Small potatoes," Simon said, not unkindly. He sat down at the table and accepted a glass of the white wine Alison was drinking. "The two of you ought to devote some time to the kind of two-legged jackals the police can't touch. I understand that the Rhodes Group makes rather a specialty of it."

"Simon," Alison said chidingly.

"Well, it's true, Alison. And you remember what happened in Ohio—the moment the first dish flew, the Kenyons were besieged by every sort of witch doctor, fake exorcist, ghostbreaker, and I don't know what. They came out of the woodwork, and none of them had any more occult power than that cat!"

Simon gestured at the white cat sunning itself on the stone wall. As if it had taken offense at his gesture, it leaped from the wall and vanished in a flirt of plumy tail.

"But they certainly wanted enough money for their services," Simon went on. "Thousands of dollars—for what boiled down to a few fake mystic passes and lighting a few sticks of incense. Someone should sic the Better Business Bureau on them! And there are people like them everywhere—here, in fact."

"Unfortunately," Colin said, "there aren't any regulating agencies for psychics, let alone for parapsychologists. It's a young field—something I constantly seem to be telling my students—which means that accrediting programs are few and far between."

"There's that place out in New York. Near where you used to live, Colin—you've heard of it?" Alison asked. She frowned, summoning the name into memory. "The Bidney Institute," she said. "They're affiliated with a small college; don't they offer a degree?"

"I know they offer a prize . . . one million dollars to the first person who can prove the existence of psychic powers. I don't think the prize is ever going to be claimed," Colin said.

"Amateur table-tippers with a steamer trunk full of juju," Simon sneered. "You can't quantify the occult and reduce it to a book full of charts and graphs."

"Maybe not," Colin said gently, more amused than otherwise by Simon's sulkiness. "But the occult isn't parapsychology, any more than parapsychology is the occult. It's the fact that people have gotten the two of them tangled together for so many years that's caused all the trouble. Now we finally have the chance to separate them."

"Oh, well spoken, Colin!" Alison applauded. "And if anyone can do it, I think you will."

Even Simon smiled, a little crookedly. "Good luck, Colin—you'll need it, especially these days. Ever hear of somebody named Thorne Blackburn?"

Thorne Blackburn, it seemed, was another low-rent messiah with a cult following who had invaded the Bay Area and set up shop in the Haight-Ashbury. He claimed, according to Simon, to be a god—among other things—and supported himself and his ragtag followers with public displays of magic.

"That's the disgusting thing," Simon said. "Apparently somewhere this jerk managed to get some real training. He didn't know what to do with it though, or maybe he just wanted to put on a show: it's all muddled up with stage illusionism and rock music. It's a carnival sideshow!"

"Everything is, lately." Alison sighed. "Lunacy may be the only logical response when our own government is firebombing women and children overseas. How did we come to this in twenty years?" she asked, the direction of her thoughts a despairing echo of Colin's own.

"You still believe that the U.S. government wears the white hats, don't you, Alison?" Simon said, with odd gentleness. "Us—Them—it's really all the same. Government is by its very nature corrupt."

"*If* that's true, we don't need to help it along," Alison said tartly, and the talk had turned to politics and then to less weighty matters.

Colin didn't think about Thorne Blackburn again for several days.

The school term had ended the month before, and Colin was teaching only one summer session this year, a three-week course on the history of the occult that started at the end of June. It was a graduate course, and Colin had pushed very hard for its inclusion in the curriculum, over the protests of the trustees.

Perhaps the incidence was on the rise, or perhaps knowing Claire was what had made him aware of it, but more and more, Colin realized that people with problems—problems which, though real, were outside the scope of conventional science—were being funneled into inappropriate treatment by professionals in psychology or medicine. Even with the best of intentions, these professionals were unable to treat the problems these people came to them to solve. It was psychiatry's fault as much as anyone's—psychiatry had gone from being a fashionable adjunct to being one of life's necessities since the fifties, as if not only the pursuit but the attainment of happiness had now become an inalienable right.

But psychiatry couldn't talk a poltergeist out of existence, any more than medical science could give its victim a pill to banish the symptoms of possession by a "noisy spirit." Not everybody who heard voices was suffering from a treatable psychological abnormality; not every report of telepathy or precognition was an indicator of a disturbed mental state—though the people who had been told all their lives that such things did not exist were likely to be understandably upset when the Unseen came barging into their lives.

If only the professionals who would see these people were willing to entertain the possibility of more explanations than the ones entombed in their
textbooks, much good could be done in the world. A summer lecture course
was a small beginning, but at least it was a beginning. And a number of those
signed up for his course might do great things with their lives, things that
might reconcile the painful breach that had been forced between Science and
Belief in this century.

Since he would be teaching over the summer, Colin had not closed up his offices and even kept to his regular office hours. The campus had been closed by
antiwar demonstrations for so much of the year that Colin felt that the students who were still here to get an education—as opposed to those whose
purpose seemed to be ending the war, for example—ought to get the chance
to see something of their professors. On the streets of America today, an entire generation was opting out of rationalism as a basis for their decisions, or
so it sometimes seemed to Colin. At least it was Sproul and Bancroft that had
been the usual focus of the students' attention, and not Tolman Hall.

The sword-in-stone letter opener that Alison had given him as an office-
warming present gleamed on the corner of his desk. There was a more prosaic
reason for Colin to keep office hours today. He was meeting Claire for
lunch—it was her day off—and it was easiest for her to meet with him on
campus, combining that with her errands at local shops.

He took a moment to breathe a silent prayer of thanks that Peter Moffat
had made detective before he might have had to take part in some of the
brawls the Berkeley campus had seen over the last year and a half. There'd
been no permanent injuries on either side, but Colin had found the passions
that ran so high on both sides deeply disturbing.

*This is how it starts, the road to fascism and genocide. You know that. This is how
it always starts, and then it ends, not with a bang, but with a whimper. . . .*

The sound of the knock at his door, though soft, was jarring.

"Professor? May I come in?" Jonathan Ashwell said.

The painfully clean-cut young student Colin had met four years before
was hard to discern in the man who—with unchanged deference—entered
Colin's office. The sportcoat and khakis had been replaced by tattered bell-
bottomed blue jeans sewn with daisies, flags, peace signs, and other symbols
Colin didn't even recognize. Jonathan was wearing a T-shirt that had once
been white, but now had been hand-tie-dyed in Day-Glo neon colors. Around
his neck he wore a number of seed-bead necklaces and medallions, and pinned
to his painted denim jacket was a small green button with the logo: "Vietnik."
There was an Army surplus backpack slung over one shoulder.

His hair was long now, straggling over his shoulders and accompanied by
the inevitable sideburns and mustache, and he was wearing a pair of wire-
rimmed glasses with octagonal lavender lenses. He was holding a slip of paper in his hand.

"Of course, Jonathan. What can I do for you?" Colin asked. He'd become
inured to student fashions long ago.

"Sign my drop-slip?" Jonathan said hesitantly, sliding the paper in his hand across the desk. "I've changed my mind. I'm dropping out."

As he came closer, Colin caught an almost overpowering whiff of strawberry; the rage for scented oils having kept pace with the penchant for smoking marijuana, which had an intense and distinctive scent.

"You're dropping the course?" Colin asked in bewilderment.

Jonathan had only one more semester to go before collecting his Master's and had already been accepted into the doctoral program. He'd been one of the most vocal supporters of Colin's desire to publicize what Colin called science's dark twin—the occult—and an endlessly inventive, questing mind.

"But why?" Colin asked.

"It's nothing to do with you, Professor," Jonathan said guiltily. "But it's, you know, like—"

Colin resisted the temptation to demand that the young man speak English; Jonathan was almost painfully sincere in his inarticulateness.

"I've just always known there was, like, something more. Something bigger. Something that would make sense out of this whole mixed-up crazy world, you know? And with what Alison said, about how we all have to be soldiers for the Light—but it's hard to be sure what to *do*, you know? But now I think I know."

And so once again Colin MacLaren heard the name of Thorne Blackburn. It seemed that Jonathan had attended an antiwar rally in Golden Gate Park a few weeks before, and Blackburn had been one of the speakers.

"And it was like . . . I'd been waiting all my life to hear what he had to say. I'm going to join his group and work with him to bring the New Aeon."

If Jonathan had been Colin's disciple, Colin might simply have forbidden him to do these things, but Jonathan had always been too passionate about finding his own answers to accept the discipline of a Magickal Lodge. He'd gone with grasshopper facility from one store of knowledge to the next, seeking, always seeking. . . .

And now his search had come to this.

"Jonathan, I'll sign your drop-slip if you really want me to, but I beg you to reconsider. You can't just abandon everything you've worked toward for years to follow some street-person who thinks he might have the Answer," Colin said, almost pleading.

"They followed Jesus," Jonathan said with the same apologetic serenity.

"Surely you're not comparing this . . . Thorne Blackburn to Jesus?" Colin demanded, scandalized.

"Why not?" Jonathan said. "Jesus didn't come to give us the Answer. He came to give us the questions. It's been two thousand years—why shouldn't someone else have more questions for us? But I know this comes as a shock, Professor. Why don't you come and meet him? You'll see what a great mind he has. I've told Thorne all about you, too, and he says he'd like to meet you."

I'll just bet, Colin thought to himself. His work with Claire had gained him a quiet but well-founded reputation as debunker, and one who did not suffer charlatans gladly.

"Look, Jonathan. I admit this comes as a bit of a shock to me, and it seems to be rather a sudden decision on your part. You've got at least another week before you need to drop these summer courses; why not give it a few more days and see what you think then?"

Jonathan's face lost its comfortable smile.

"I thought that you, at least, would understand, Professor MacLaren," he said, in hurt tones. "I know that you know there's more to the world than just this . . . military-industrial complex. And Thorne, he says it's time for the Old Aeon to end, for us to summon the Gods to earth once more and end the rift between us. And I can help him. It takes money to do the things he wants to do, and I've got my grandfather's trust fund—"

Colin listened in growing horror as Jonathan blithely outlined his plans to drop out of school and subsidize what he called an "underground newspaper," signing over his inheritance to do so. Only a fundamental belief in freedom and years of dealing with what sounded like similar blue-sky notions allowed Colin to remain silent.

He already realized that talking to Jonathan would do no good at all, but in the end, he wasn't even able to coax the young man to wait a few days before making such a life-changing decision, let alone keep him from dropping Colin's course. Unfortunately, Colin was in no sense standing *in loco parentis* to the young man—he had no right to withhold his consent in a matter that was, in essence, a formality. He signed the form, and allowed Jonathan to extract a promise from Colin to come to San Francisco to see Thorne Blackburn perform.

When Jonathan left, Colin suddenly felt very old.

Alison had said once in passing that these days San Francisco reminded her a bit of Berlin in the thirties, but were things really that bad? The fabled decadence of Berlin before the Nazis had taken power had been the fever of an infected wound. Was this country really in that much trouble?

It was embroiled in an unjust war that Colin could not support; its elected officials seemed to have become mountebanks and thieves overnight, and everything that Colin had once known would last forever was crumbling. Even in the wake of the Kennedy assassination, there had been a sort of tarnished hopefulness to the country that seemed antithetical to the sickness of the Third Reich and its would-be heirs . . . heirs who seemed to multiply every day. But somewhere in the last two decades America had lost the certainty that she was *right* and the will to act based on that knowledge.

Some might call that change maturity . . . but to Colin, it seemed very much more like decay.

Try not to borrow trouble, Colin counseled himself sternly. Trouble would find him in its own good time—he had dedicated his whole self to becoming an instrument of the Light, and if his merely human understanding sometimes did not comprehend the choices his Higher Self made, at least he knew enough to trust its decisions. This trust had led him to remain where he was, to go on teaching his classes when his heart told him to abandon his teaching and go looking for Hasloch's Masters down the scattered ratlines that the Third Reich had used to go to ground.

Perhaps one of the lives he touched here would make more difference to the future than anything he could do fighting the White Eagle of Thule. He could not *know*—he could only trust in the Light. But the Light did not make puppets or robots of its servants. The Adept's Will was always his own, his choices always his to make.

And so the question now was, should he intervene in Jonathan's decision, and if so, how much? Who was this Thorne Blackburn whose disciple Jonathan was so eager to become? Simon Anstey had spoken of him; Colin should call Simon later and try to gain his further impressions.

The name nagged at him, as if Colin should have heard it before, and finally the unresolved itch of it drove him to the pair of battered file cabinets that occupied the corner of his office. After only a little digging, he found a file with that name scrawled at the top in his own handwriting.

He'd received a letter from Thorne Blackburn.

Colin stared at the sheet of paper as though it were a communication from an alien planet. The return address was New Orleans. It was dated 1961, just after Colin had started at Berkeley. Blackburn was writing a letter in response to an article Colin had submitted to one of the esoteric journals, a preliminary inquiry into the question of whether the system of ley lines so well known in Britain might not in fact extend over the entire globe, and whether it might be possible to deduce the pattern both by extending the known leys, and by cross-checking those extrapolations with certain characteristic phenomena.

Blackburn's response—the letter was handwritten in an exquisite crabbed script, tiny and nearly impossible to read—was both enthusiastic and technical, and from certain references Blackburn made, Colin was reasonably sure that Simon had been right in assuming that the man had received at least some training. If Colin had replied to the letter, he'd kept no copy of the response, and wondered why he'd kept the letter at all.

Stuck to Blackburn's letter was another one. Colin glanced at the letterhead—it was from Nathaniel Atheling, dated the following year.

Nathaniel had left the hurly-burly of Manhattan for a private clinic somewhere in Massachusetts. He and Colin corresponded erratically, but the purpose of this particular letter was a business one. Nathaniel was letting Colin know, in his position as Exoteric Head of the Order in America, that one Douglas Thorne Blackburn, who had achieved the Sublime Grade of Master of the Temple at the Avalon Lodge in England, was not to be received or acknowledged as such by any of his brethren.

Why? Colin crumpled both of the letters together and began tearing them into strips. He had no business keeping a copy of such correspondence in the first place—he must have meant to respond to Nathaniel's letter and forgotten about it.

Or chosen not to. What was there to say, after all, unless he chose to take the unknown young man's part? If Blackburn had protested his expulsion from the Order, his protest had not succeeded.

Colin frowned, revising his mental picture of Thorne Blackburn from that

of a frivolous Pied Piper close to Jonathan's age to one of a dark and brooding
Svengali. Master of the Temple was not the highest grade it was possible to
attain, but it was one which took years of study to reach. He dropped the
shreds of paper into the wastebasket and sat back down at his desk, brooding.

"Colin?" Claire stood in the doorway. "What's wrong? I feel . . ."

"A bad mood and some bad news," Colin told her, banishing both with a
directed effort of will. "Claire. Come in. It's good to see you."

Claire Moffatt stepped into Colin's office. She was wearing a neat pantsuit
in sage green, and her fringed suede shoulder bag was large enough to contain enough items to meet most of life's emergencies. Her blond hair was
short and neat in a fashionable helmet cut, and—as always—she wore very
little makeup.

"I stuffed all my bags in the trunk," she said, smiling. "It's too nice a day
to be lumbered with bundles. But tell me what's happened. You look pretty
blue. It isn't Jonathan, is it?"

Fortunately, Colin was long used to the unnerving accuracy of Claire's
hunches.

"As a matter of fact, yes. He's dropping out of school. It seems he's found
a guru and decided to hand over his mind and his money." Colin couldn't
keep the bitterness out of his voice. "Someone named Thorne Blackburn."

"Now there's a coincidence," Claire said, her voice neutral. "You remember
Debbie Winwood? I went to school with her. We'd lost touch, but about six
months ago she turned up again. She's living with Blackburn over in San
Francisco."

"Good lord," Colin said inadequately. "Is he a friend of yours, Claire? I
have to admit I haven't heard much that's good about him."

He thought about the letter he'd received from Nathaniel Atheling.
While it tarnished Blackburn's reputation further, it really wasn't something
he could share with Claire. Despite their closeness, his oaths bound him still,
just as they would with any other person not of his Lodge.

Claire shrugged. "He's pretty . . . extreme, isn't he? But come on, let's go
to lunch. I'm starved."

Telegraph Avenue in June seemed a mirror twin of its counterpart in San
Francisco, but the experienced eye could discern differences between the two,
though the crowds of children thronging the streets seemed identically
dressed and the same scents of incense and patchouli hung in the air.

But in San Francisco the emphasis was on "feeding one's head" and "tune
in—turn on—drop out"; while here in Berkeley the emphasis was on social
change, from the SDS to the Black Panthers to people calling for a morato-
rium on the war.

Despite the fact that he shared many of their views, Colin distrusted the
young firebrands. Political activism could quickly turn to the sort of violence
that inevitably paved the way for a fascist state, as history had all too often
shown in recent years. Colin found himself walking past the banners and petitions as tense as if he watched a jumper balancing on a window ledge a

dozen stories above the street. The country stood at a crossroads of history—in which direction would Fate compel it?

Claire's choice of restaurant was one of the new ones tucked into a corner of an old building in what had until a few months ago been a run-down urban area. The words "It's A Beautiful Day" were painted on the window in an elaborate psychedelic lettering that Colin found almost impossible to read, and surrounded by painted symbols from all the world's religions.

But inside, the restaurant was bright and clean—if covered with posters for political rallies and rock concerts—and offered a menu of plain, old-fashioned standards, with some exotic additions like couscous and bean sprouts. The smell of baking bread came from behind the counter. Salvaged stained-glass windows hanging from the ceiling splintered the bright summer sunlight into a patchwork of rainbow hues.

"Say what you will about the decor," Claire said cheerfully, "the place is cheap, and two salaries don't seem to go any farther than one these days."

"How's Peter?" Colin asked on cue.

Claire shrugged, still smiling. "Working all kinds of hours. He says things are getting worse out on the streets—not just the runaways, or even the drugs, really. But drugs mean money, and that means organized crime, Peter says."

"I imagine he'd know if anyone did," Colin said. "It seems like half the kids on campus are high on something these days."

And particularly bad—from Colin's admittedly specialized point of view—was that the drugs they were choosing to abuse were some of the ones that had been in the arsenal of High Magick for centuries, to be used—cautiously and under the strictest of controls—to add power to the magician's work and lower the veils between the magician and the Infinite. Now the children seeking to cast off all established standards had seized upon the memoirs of those philosophical pioneers to use them as justification for their own experiments.

It was hard even now for Colin to feel that they were completely wrong in what they did. But he was convinced absolutely that what they did was dangerous.

"On drugs, on campus, and in the emergency rooms," Claire agreed. "There are some clinics around town that specialize in drug overdoses—well, that and VD," she said frankly. "That's how bad it's getting. Still, you've always said that each generation finds its own—'appalling forms of excess,' I believe your words were."

"Good heavens, I must have been in a foul mood that day," Colin said, smiling sheepishly. "I may be getting old, but the youth of today still strikes me as somehow . . . reckless."

"'Live fast, die young, and leave a pretty corpse,'" Claire quoted flippantly. "At least, if the Bomb lets you—leave a corpse, I mean. But how did we ever get onto such a depressing subject on such a pretty day? Let's find something nicer to talk about."

"All right," Colin said. "I saw Alison the other day. She and Simon are back from their jaunt back East—"

The two friends kept their conversation turned to lighter subjects for a few minutes, but as soon as the waitress—a cheerful young woman in tie-dyed overalls— had taken their orders and left them, the conversation turned inevitably back to Thorne Blackburn once more.

"I've only met him a couple of times when I was visiting Debbie, and I guess he isn't that much crazier than some of these other antiwar demonstrators," Claire said. "But Jonathan dropping out to go live at the *Voice of Truth?*" Her voice was bewildered and disapproving. "It's an underground paper, sort of a—well, a bully pulpit; Thorne writes most of it himself and it all seems to be about astrology and Tarot cards and that sort of thing. Well, that and Thorne Blackburn's philosophy and politics. Debbie keeps trying to give me copies of the thing—they hand it out free, or you pay whatever you like—but I'll admit I've never read one." She took a bite of her salad, which was filled with chunks of fresh chicken and exotic greens, all in a wonderful herbed vinegar dressing.

"Dropping out a semester before graduation is bad enough," Colin answered, still thinking of Jonathan, "but it isn't only that. As far as I could gather, Jonathan intends to sign over his trust fund to the Master as well. Granted, Jonathan's a big boy now, and it's his money, and he's got a right to do as he likes with it—"

"But you think he ought to be a little more careful with it—and if he's planning to underwrite the *Voice of Truth*, so do I," Claire said. "I honestly don't like the sound of this at all. Why don't we pay a visit to Thorne Blackburn and see what you make of him? I'm sure if I give Debbie a call she can get us into the Presence."

FIVE

SAN FRANCISCO, CALIFORNIA, JUNE 1965

As I in hoary winter's night stood shivering in the snow,
Surprised I was with sudden heat which made my heart to glow;
And lifting up a fearful eye to view what fire was near,
A pretty Babe all burning bright did in the air appear.
— ROBERT SOUTHWELL

THE AUDITORIUM IN THE FILMORE DISTRICT HAD FIRST BEEN A VAUDEVILLE house and then a movie palace. It had fallen on hard times and lain derelict for some years, until a shift in the tastes—not to mention the age—of the audience interested in live music had made its reopening economically possible. That the building was undoubtedly in violation of a hundred building code standards was a matter of indifference to the young audience—some teenaged runaways, some Bay Area locals with steady jobs—that filled its shabby moth-eaten seats nightly.

In the place of the movie posters of yesteryear, the outside of the auditorium was plastered with bright, eye-hurting placards advertising upcoming performances. The bands had names out of Disney cartoons and dope dreams. The psychedelic iconography that accompanied them was as precisely surreal as a Windsor McCay illustration, a sort of post-Apocalyptic Art Nouveau manqué.

The time was a little after nine o'clock. The show was supposed to have begun at 7:30, with Blackburn scheduled to come on at nine, but apparently several of the bands who were supposed to appear had been late coming in or had run long, and when Colin and Claire arrived, Blackburn had not even arrived at the auditorium yet.

They could hear the music even at the box office outside, and when they entered the auditorium itself, the sound became a solid wall, filling the space as if it were a thing with form and weight. The air-conditioning had fought the good fight and lost; the air was close and sweltering, charged with the scents of tobacco, unwashed bodies, and drugs. The stage was lit intermittently by flashing strobes and spotlights with colored gels over the lenses, their colored beams in constant motion. Scenes that seemed to have no connection to the music were projected on the screen behind the musicians, bathing them in a shifting sea of form and color.

The effect was as disorienting as a bomb blast, and Colin stopped dead, senses reeling. He felt Claire clutch at his hand, whether to save him or herself, he wasn't certain.

On stage, five long-haired boys in velvet coats were playing, the distorted, amplified sound assaulting its listeners like a physical force. The guitars they carried looked like child's drawings, flat and brightly colored, and the amplified sound of the drums echoed through the crowded auditorium like gunshots.

"Loud!" Claire shouted in his ear, and Colin nodded.

The crowd was packed into the old vaudeville palace as tightly as the hordes in a Cairo bazaar, sweltering in the still air. Despite that, there were a few seats empty at the back, and once he'd gotten his bearings, Colin moved toward two of them, Claire in tow. Once he was seated, he took the opportunity to look around the auditorium.

The balcony was blocked off as too rickety to support the weight of occupants; despite that, it was filled with listeners who shouted and clapped and danced along with the amplified sounds of music played so loud that the battering of drums and basses shook plaster dust from the walls and ceiling throughout the performance.

But despite the unfamiliarity of his surroundings, Colin could tell that there was a sense of joyous anticipation in the air, a sort of Christmas morning expectancy, as though what was to come was wonderful, was worthy, was all those things that had been absent from the world for far too long. Here was the answer to the black mood that had possessed him so often of late, the refutation of the sense of decay and despair.

He hadn't gotten old, Colin MacLaren realized with a sudden rueful awakening. He'd gotten tired.

When was it precisely that he had lost his way into this sense of joy? When had life become something to get through with as few mistakes as possible, instead of a glorious adventure to savor? The Path taught that its disciples must risk their lives as well as save them; when had he lost sight of that eternal truth?

"It's just going to get louder," Claire warned, squeezing Colin's hand to make sure he heard her over the wash of raw noise.

"I'll survive," Colin promised her.

The music was hardly the point, Colin was beginning to realize. Like some Dionysian cult of old, the audience howled itself into ecstacy, battered by the music and primed by expectation and the experience of a hundred previous concerts. The band surged into a new number, and the audience roared enthusiastically and began to clap, whether in time with the wailing, distorted noise of the electric guitars, or simply as a commentary, Colin couldn't tell. He could not follow the audience on their journey, but at last he began to understand where it was they were going—on the path toward the Unconquerable Sun followed by the seekers in every generation.

But in this generation it was as if the trailblazers had determined that this time no one was to be left behind when the journey was made. All must go. The doors of perception would be opened to all.

Two hours later Colin's insight was unchanged, though his temper was less sanguine and his head ached from the constant battering of sheer noise and the psychedelic light show that accompanied it. Blackburn had still not made an appearance, and there was little to distinguish the sounds the performers made onstage from those made by construction workers with jackhammers, at least in Colin MacLaren's opinion. His throat and lungs ached from the harsh smoke that hung like a blue pall in the sweltering air. If he felt lightheaded just from breathing, he could only imagine what those actually smoking the stuff felt.

The performers on stage fell silent amid disappointed shouts from the crowd. The musicians unplugged their guitars and wandered off the stage and a sheer scrim dropped between the drumset on its platform and the apron.

All the lights went out.

In the darkness, the wail of a single amplified flute could be heard, and against it, the sound of a voice chanting Aeschylus' "Hymn to the Sun" in flawless classical Greek.

Then a bright red spotlight snapped on, illuminating a figure in a fantastic costume: a long black tailcoat over a tie-dyed T-shirt, blue jeans sewn with rhinestones, and a shiny top hat displaying the Uraeus disk flanked by glittering cobras.

"Dudes and chicks—Epopts and Illuminati: The Magister Ludens of the New Aeon, Thorne Blackburn!"

Thorne Blackburn turned out to be younger than Colin had thought he would be—a young man barely out of his teens, maybe even Claire's age. Long blond curls spilled over his shoulders, making him look like a cross between General Custer and a dimestore Jesus. His eyes were blue enough to retain their color even under the harsh theatrical lighting.

What Blackburn gave the crowd that night was an unholy mésalliance of genuine Mystery School teachings, parlor tricks, Beat poetry, and pop history—promising his hearers that by thinking good thoughts they could play St. George to a military-industrial dragon of international greed and corruption. The claims he made for his personal history and occult teachings were too outrageous for any sane person to take seriously, and in general his audience seemed to take Blackburn's remarks in the spirit of entertainment. His patter had the well-oiled ease of the stage illusionist's, and Colin was possibly the only one who noticed that in the space of five minutes Blackburn had made his audience quiet and attentive as he quickly explained about the four essential elements that were also the four pillars of creation.

But no matter how debased his pied and emended liturgy, what Blackburn did here had power; Colin could feel it. It was foolishness—sloppy, undisciplined, madness, like handing a flamethrower to a baby. But Blackburn made it work. Colin felt the potency he summoned—and beside him, Claire did, too, shivering uncertainly and clutching at his hand as if for reassurance.

"—so that as you become a part of the Universal, boys and girls, the Universe becomes a part of you. So let's invite the Universe to the party!"

While Blackburn had been speaking, other figures, garbed in long hooded robes, had entered the stage. Four of them bore the familiar Tools of the magician—sword and paten, wand and cup—and two of the others carried a lighted candle and a censer that put out a thick fog of smoke, the smoke changing colors as the images of the light show hit it.

Quickly—the man was as aware as any performer of how easy it was to lose the attention of an audience—Blackburn summoned the Elements: earth, water, air, and fire. His amplified voice boomed out over the crowd, and mixed into his sideshow patter were the great Names that Colin had sworn to keep secret, tossed casually against the ears of the hoi polloi like pearls onto a seashore.

Lord of Light, he knows what he's doing, was Colin's first horrified thought. This was no form of magick he had ever seen—it was magick without form, without ritual, a casual elemental summoning of the primal forces of creation, through nothing more than the strength of Blackburn's charisma. It was power summoned without wards, without barriers, without limits, power called with only love to build a bridge, as if between equals.

Outrage, irritation, and shock momentarily threatened to overwhelm him, but Colin kept his temper. He'd known before he'd come that Blackburn had some magickal training, after all, and people weren't banished from the White Orders without good reason. Like so many before him, Blackburn had obviously decided to turn the use of the Great Secrets that he'd been taught to mundane ends—and, as with those before him, the Order's greatest defense was simply to take no notice of him, protecting the Secrets by misdirection.

As quickly as he had caught the audience's attention, Blackburn released it, leaving his viewers euphoric in the quick titillation of a brush with the Unseen. He took the candle from one of his acolytes, and then the stage blacked out once more, leaving Blackburn's face lit from below by the golden flame of the candle.

"The New Aeon is coming," Blackburn intoned. And blew out the candle.

The darkness was almost immediately replaced by worklights on the stage, and the audience settled down, pleasurably keyed-up, for the headline act. Colin caught Claire's eye, and she nodded toward the edge of the stage. Blackburn would be coming off there. The two of them got to their feet and began moving toward the aisle.

Well, now he'd seen the man, Colin told himself. But oddly enough, the more information he gained, the less he knew what to think.

Claire led Colin through the door that led to the backstage. The crowded area was filled with people and equipment, but Blackburn was instantly recognizable—by the hat, if nothing more. He was surrounded by a coterie of what Colin assumed to be self-styled acolytes and well-wishers, and he was relieved to see that Jonathan wasn't among them.

Blackburn looked up and saw Colin, and in the younger man's narrowed eyes and sudden suspicious expression—the suspicion with which everyone under thirty seemed to regard everyone over thirty these days—Colin saw a reflection of how out of place he must look here among the tie-dye and denim.

Fortunately Deborah Winwood had been one of the acolytes in the hooded robes who had carried the props on stage. When she saw Claire, she squealed and flung her arms around the taller woman. Blackburn's expression changed to one of puzzled disinterest, and he turned away to speak to another of his followers.

"Claire! I hoped you'd come," Debbie said. "You look so . . . straight," she added, as if only just now seeing Claire for the first time.

"I *am* straight," Claire said, smiling. "Square, too. Debbie, this is Colin MacLaren; I've told you about him."

Deborah Winwood was one of those breathtakingly lovely women who had given rise to the cliché of the "California Girl." Her long blond hair was parted in the middle and hung in two shining straight wings down the sides of her face, and she stared at Colin, hazel doe-eyes wide, until he wondered what Claire could possibly have told the girl to put that expression on her face.

"Pleased to meet you," Debbie said lamely, in a soft voice.

She'd been about to say more, but the band on stage—a local favorite which had been greeting its audience rowdily for the past several minutes—suddenly began to play. Though they were insulated from the band by a thick wall—and were now behind the amplifiers, at any rate—Debbie shrugged apologetically, as if conversation had now become impossible instead of merely difficult. She beckoned to them to follow, and Claire and Colin stumbled after her through the half-light of the cluttered backstage area in Blackburn's direction.

"Thorne, look!" Debbie said, when she was within range. "Claire came—the one I asked you to get the tickets for?—and she brought her friend, um, Colin?"

She'd raised her voice to be heard over the band, and for a moment Colin didn't think Blackburn had heard, but then he turned away from the man he'd been talking to. He had already shed the top hat and tailcoat, and was dressed now in the nearly universal youth culture costume of jeans (if jeweled) and T-shirt.

"I'm Colin MacLaren," Colin said, holding out his hand.

At the same time, Debbie said: "Thorne, this is Claire—"

For a moment Blackburn looked surprised; Colin had been right about his age—the man was in his early twenties, if that—which meant he'd accrued an impressive store of magickal credentials for someone his age. But he obviously decided to be amiable, even if only for Debbie's sake.

Blackburn laughed and took Colin's hand. "City or Feds?" he asked cheerfully.

It took Colin a moment to untangle this, not quite sure for a moment if he'd heard Blackburn correctly over the din. "No. I'm not a policeman." *Not of this world, at any rate.* "I'm on faculty at Berkeley. I believe you know one of my students—Jonathan Ashwell."

Blackburn still looked puzzled, though he obviously placed the name. "You're here because of Johnnie? What's he said, then?"

There was something not quite native about Blackburn's English; a certain working-class undertone that would have marked him as British even if Colin hadn't already known that about him.

"He said you were the hope of the New Age," Colin said baldly.

Another man might have tried to soft-pedal such an unequivocal statement. Blackburn merely grinned wider.

"I have come to lead you into a new era, where the great separation of the beginning of Time shall be healed; wherein heart and hand, mind and body shall all be as one," he intoned fulsomely, bowing in a theatrical fashion.

"I'd be interested to hear how you plan to do it," Colin said tartly. "Jonathan said—"

"Johnnie's a credulous fool, looking for a Messiah," Blackburn answered amiably. "I'll give him better than that. I'll give him a mind of his own before I'm through."

The band stopped playing.

"Thorne is almost three hundred years old," Colin overheard Debbie explaining to Claire in the sudden lull. "He used to be, like, this great French magician, Count Cagliostro, or something."

Colin glanced back at Blackburn, who had heard the exchange.

"Is this what you tell them?" Colin said, unable to keep the reproach out of his voice.

"I tell them a lot of things," Blackburn said ambiguously. "If you want to hear more, why don't you come back to our place with us? There's a party."

He turned away, motioning to Colin and the others to follow, and went out through the door—propped open with a cinderblock—that led into the alley. Behind them, the music began again.

The warm summer air felt almost chilly after the sweltering stuffiness of the auditorium. The song—muted to a bearable level by the walls of the old movie palace —became a fitting backdrop to the tawdry glamour of the alleyway. The alley walls were papered with posters for acts and events, and a Volkswagen minibus was parked halfway up the alley, lights on and engine running. "Just follow us," Blackburn said over his shoulder as he trotted back to the minibus.

"Thorne says you can come back with us! I'll show you where to go." Debbie had pulled off the cheap satin robe she'd worn on stages and stood looking at them hopefully.

Colin shrugged infinitesimally, catching Claire's eye. He'd come to see the so-called Magister Ludens, and the chance to observe him on his home turf was not to be missed.

On the way to the car, Debbie kept up a steady stream of chatter. Debbie Winwood seemed to be convinced that Claire, at least, had come to join the Master's crusade, and was telling her everything Debbie felt that Claire needed to know. By the time Colin had gotten back to the auditorium, he'd already learned that Thorne Blackburn was either the Comte de Cagliostro or his reincarnation, that he had been sired by an angelic being summoned into a magick circle by the wizard Merlin, and that he had possession of the Philosopher's Stone which granted physical immortality.

Fortunately, Colin had been able to park the Ford nearby, but he was still a little surprised to find the others still waiting for him out in front of the auditorium. There was no mistaking their vehicle—the side panels were painted with what appeared to be the logo of Blackburn's underground newspaper, suitably embellished with flowers, stars, and rainbows.

As soon as Colin pulled up behind it, the bus took off, and he was forced to follow at a breakneck pace through the streets of the Filmore District. Whoever was driving the bus was doing so with either consummate skill or reckless disregard—Colin wasn't sure which, even as he exerted all his skill to keep up with them.

As he drove, Debbie continued to chatter amiably, at one moment explaining how happy all of them were living together in a communal apartment, and at the next, providing Colin with driving directions a heartbeat too late to do him any useful good. If he hadn't known the van's approximate destination, he would have lost sight of it a dozen times, yet despite that, he did not believe that the others were deliberately trying to lose him. They were much too trusting for that. Trusting. An odd assessment to make of a group to which, scant hours before, he had imputed only the lowest of motives.

And there did remain the fact that Thorne Blackburn had been banished from Colin's own Order, not something that could happen to a wholly innocent man. Yet now, having met Blackburn and the others, he was not certain that Blackburn was wholly guilty either.

It would have been easier to dismiss the claims—and Blackburn himself—if Colin had not already seen the man and one of his peculiar rituals. An intelligence and power radiated from the young Magus that didn't match the image of the psychic frauds and bunco artists that both he and Claire were familiar with.

The bus finally stopped—as precipitously as it had started—double-parked on a slanting side street that overlooked the Panhandle section of Golden Gate Park. In city blocks it was not that far from Greenhaven, but it might as well have been in another world. The street was lined with a row of seedy Victorians long since converted to apartments, their first floors hosting a variety of marginal businesses all now closed for the night. Despite the lateness of the hour, there were people still on the street, all wearing the bright fantastic clothes of the hippie movement.

All four doors of the minibus opened and its occupants began to exit; apparently they planned to leave the bus parked where it was. Colin looked up and down the street. There was no other parking in sight, and street parking in San Francisco at any time was notoriously difficult.

"I'm afraid I'm going to risk the ticket," Colin said to his passengers as he pulled in behind the bus. "It's almost midnight; if anybody wants to move their car tonight, I'm sure they'll honk." And he didn't want to miss this opportunity to satisfy his curiosity—if that was really the right word—about Blackburn and his coterie. Shutting off the engine, he followed the two women into the building the others had entered.

Colin could hear the music even before the door was flung open; despite the fact that there had been nearly a dozen people in the minibus, there were more already in the apartment, along with the ever-present haze of drug smoke.

The noise level went up sharply as Blackburn entered the apartment; everyone was talking at once, and in the background, the acid-laced music of the Doors played on. Unnoticed by anyone, Colin and Claire followed Debbie into the room.

The apartment was one of those rambling spaces so beloved of San Francisco residents, its interior proportions left oddly unbalanced by the conversion from private home to apartments. A bay window overlooked the street and the green space beyond. The apartment was furnished in a thrift-shop jumble of mismatched pieces: a sagging couch, sheets tacked up over most of the windows in lieu of curtains, posters covering the cracked unpainted walls. If Blackburn was going after Jonathan Ashwell for his money, it was obviously the first time he'd tried something like that; the offices and living space of the *Voice of Truth* looked as if its inhabitants were surviving on handouts.

There was a tang of incense in the air as well as the riper smell of marijuana, and books were piled everywhere, along with piles of what Colin guessed must be unsold copies of the newspaper.

"I'm going to have to be fumigated before I go home," Claire muttered. "I can just imagine what Peter will think if I show up smelling like this."

As they entered the main room, a small child came running down the hall through the crowd of people, shouting Blackburn's name. Blackburn scooped it up into his arms and hugged the child fiercely, then shifted the child to one arm and accepted a beer from a dark-haired woman who had not been at the performance. Blackburn's preaching seemed to attract more women than men, but that was hardly uncommon in any cult with a charismatic male leader.

"This is my son Pilgrim," Blackburn said, turning to Colin with the child in his arms.

Colin had assumed the child was female until Blackburn had spoken. Pilgrim looked to be about four or five; his eyes were the same startling vivid color as his father's, but almost green rather than a true blue. His black hair was long and flowing, and he wore a tie-dyed T-shirt, several bead necklaces, and a pair of jeans that had been lovingly embroidered with a pattern of vines and flowers. There was a blue star drawn on his forehead and daisies painted on each cheek.

"Oh," said Colin politely. "I didn't realize you were married, Mr. Blackburn."

"I'm not," Blackburn said calmly. "Why should I enslave women under an archaic religious or legal code? Until we reinvent marriage to suit the demands of the New Aeon, I refuse to practice it."

He gazed challengingly at Colin, obviously expecting a disapproving response.

"I suppose that's between you and the young lady," Colin said evenly. "Or ladies, as the case may be," he added.

" 'An it harm none, do as ye will'—so said the sage of Thelema. But come on, crash with us for a while." Blackburn made a gesture that seemed to take in the entire apartment. "Ask anybody anything. You don't look like the sort of people who usually come to hear the truth, but I'll be happy to tell it to you."

"*A* truth, anyway," a tall man in the corner drawled. He was dressed like a cartoon cowboy, down to the wide suede chaps that covered his jeans.

Blackburn turned toward him, smiling sunnily. "They're *all* true, Tex; every single one. All things are true, even false things." He walked off, deeper into the apartment, with Pilgrim staring back over his shoulder.

"An interesting philosophy," Claire said, settling cautiously into a chair whose stuffing was leaking out of the top.

"Everything Thorne does is interesting," the man Blackburn had addressed as Tex answered. He was older than most of the other people Colin had seen here tonight. He had a deep Texas drawl and looked to be somewhere in his thirties. "That's because he's a conduit of the Aeonic Current that will reunite the world of Gods and Men. If we aren't all bombed out of existence first. Can I get you something to drink, ma'am? We've got ice tea— t'isn't anything funny in it, you know, Thorne don't hold with that, nohow."

Claire glanced over his shoulder, to where the young dark-haired woman who had given Blackburn the beer was rolling joints from a sandwich bag full of grass on the coffee table in front of her. Claire's raised eyebrow was eloquent.

Tex glanced in the direction of her gaze and grinned. "Oh, well, ma'am, I'd guess they know what they're smoking, wouldn't you? That's different."

"I suppose you're right," Claire said reluctantly, though not as if she believed it.

"We were at the auditorium this evening. Can you tell us anything about what Mr. Blackburn was trying to accomplish tonight on stage? It was fascinating," Colin said.

"That was some *tay atra sack ray*," Tex said, his drawl mangling the French to the point that it took Colin a moment to figure out just what he'd said. *Théâtre sacré.* Sacred theater.

"The first duty of the magician is to enact sacred theater," Blackburn said, coming back into the room. He'd showered and changed, and now was wearing a garishly patterned dashiki over faded bell-bottoms. His damp hair was held back with a strip of buckskin and his feet were bare. He draped an arm companionably around Tex's shoulders. "All the world's a stage, an' all that."

"But what purpose does it serve?" Claire asked, looking up at Blackburn. "Is it serious or not? The audience thinks it's all for fun."

"'He who has eyes to see, let him hear,'" Blackburn misquoted cryptically.

Though he didn't seem eager to promote his philosophy, Blackburn sat down on the floor at Claire's feet and began to talk about the work he was doing in San Francisco. It all sounded like arrant moonshine to Colin, all the more so for containing a number of unlikely assertions: such as that Blackburn was over two centuries old, of nonhuman parentage, and come as a savior to bring about a golden age for mankind. Claire listened to all of this with commendable gravity.

As for Jonathan and his intention of donating all his money to the *Voice of Truth,* Blackburn continued to point out, when challenged, that anyone who wished was free to follow him or not as they chose, and that all of them held their property in common.

"The trouble with pure Communism is that it's inefficient for a large-scale economy. We have to dismantle the nation-states and recreate society on the tribal level before we can truly say we have buried the evils of Capitalism," Blackburn said sagely.

Looking around, Colin had to admit that he didn't see any particular evidence of wealth, though he supposed it was just barely possible that Blackburn had a large bank account stashed somewhere. Neither, beyond the doting attention of his women, was Blackburn being treated with the exaggerated deference that marked the leader of one of those insidious mind-control cults that were springing up all over the place like mushrooms after rain.

In fact, Blackburn was a very slippery fellow altogether. Beneath all the glib patter there was a hint of something real—though what it might be remained as baffling to Colin now as it had been before he'd met Blackburn. And though the man was unfailingly polite, Colin could not escape the feeling that somehow Blackburn was laughing at him, like the Trickster-god Coyote laughing at the moon.

"But I've taken up enough of your time," Colin said finally. He could see that Claire had been bravely stifling yawns for the last half-hour or so, and in any event Colin didn't think he'd learn anything more this evening. It was late, and by now most of the others had drifted off to bed, though two young dark-haired women—alike enough to be twins—remained, sitting unselfconsciously beside Blackburn on the floor.

"Come again—we're always here, except when we've left. And don't worry about Johnnie, Colin—I promise I'll make an unbeliever out of him before I'm done," Blackburn said cheerily.

And with that ambiguous promise, Colin would have to content himself, he supposed.

Blackburn got to his feet, and—flanked by the girls, whose names Colin hadn't learned—showed the two visitors down the steps to the door that opened on the street.

"Do come and see us again, Claire," Blackburn said at the door. "And do bring your husband next time."

"Is that supposed to impress me?" Claire responded with some asperity. "Would you like to guess his name and weight as well?"

Blackburn smiled. "You're wearing a ring; it wasn't a tough guess. His name's Peter, by the way, but maybe you'd better not bring him. Cops don't approve of our little family for some reason."

He closed the door. Claire stared at it for a moment, a baffled expression on her face, and then it cleared.

"Of course. Debbie told him about Peter. I must have mentioned him when I was talking to her."

Colin was looking up the street toward his car. Even from here he could see the white banner of a parking ticket fluttering on his windshield, though the VW bus parked right in front of him didn't seem to be similarly flagged.

"It's the first rule of the psychic fraud," he agreed slowly. "Always have a good intelligence network. But Blackburn doesn't strike me as your usual sort of fraud. What did you think of him, Claire? Honestly?"

"I'm not sure." Claire's voice was troubled and thoughtful. "He's charming, of course. *And* knows it. And he doesn't seem to be an out-and-out charlatan, for what that's worth. He seems to be doing *something*, though I'll be blessed if I can figure out exactly what."

JUNE 1965

WHAT IS THERE LEFT TO SAY ABOUT THORNE BLACKBURN, NOW THAT A quarter of a century has already passed its judgment? When I met him, it was as what my generation still called "a young matron," happily married and happy with myself for the first time—so to a certain extent, I was insulated from Thorne's indisputable charisma, about which so much—fair and otherwise—has been written.

He charmed everyone he met—even Colin, though I know it went much against Colin's instincts. I think he did it because Thorne loved tricks and pranks of all kinds, though there was very little malice in him; his delight in his own jokes stemmed more from an appreciation of their technical difficulty than from any distress they may have caused.

It was hard to stay angry with Thorne at the worst of times; he loved to tease, and eventually you would realize you were simply *tired* of being exasperated with him—and it was too much trouble to stay mad, anyway.

The dark side of that charm was that Thorne Blackburn listened as little to good advice as he did to anything else. He was convinced that once other people understood his philosophy they would agree with it, and nothing Colin or I could say would ever change his mind.

I've always been a very prosaic person—I suppose it is the inevitable result of the Gift that seems to run in my bloodline: when so much that seems strange and wonderful to other people comes so easily to you, you tend to become very matter-of-fact about everything. The only thing that ever truly astounded me was discovering that people were willing to take me on trust and believe in my sanity: once I had accepted that gift, nothing else that the world had to offer was ever quite so surprising.

And so perhaps I was not as surprised by Thorne and what he was trying to accomplish as perhaps I should have been. It is only looking back across a gulf of years that I realize how extraordinary his ambitions were, even for the time he lived in. At the time—that vivid, turbulent time—what he was doing seemed as if it were only one more wonder in an era crammed full of wonders. But Thorne wanted more than to amuse, dazzle, and delight.

Thorne Blackburn meant to change the world.

SIX

BERKELEY, OCTOBER 1966

The blood-red blossom of war with a heart of fire.
—ALFRED, LORD TENNYSON

THROUGH THE AUTUMN OF '65 AND THE FOLLOWING SPRING, THE EMBAT-
tled university administration, increasingly under fire from all sides, began
responding to the unceasing attacks on its authority by wave after wave of
draconian measures directed against the only group over which it had any
semblance of control: the faculty.

The message Colin MacLaren received was clear: stop teaching Berkeley
students mumbo-jumbo. Toe the line. Preach the status quo. But even if he
had been no more than a conventional academic, Colin would not have been
able to do that. His students were hungry for a meaning that would replace
the conventional piety of their parents' generation. They searched for it in
drugs, in politics, in mysticism of every shade and stripe. When they asked
Colin his opinion, there was little he could offer them but his honesty—
something that brought him increasingly into conflict with the trustees of
the university.

The Vietnam War appalled him, even as it forced a generation to choose
between the letter of the law and the spirit of a country. As the Outer Planes
were the reflection of the Inner, Colin could not refrain from that fight. He
fought, as he always had, for the Spirit.

The visit from General Jonathan Griswold Ashwell II had not improved
matters. Just as he had said he would, Jonathan had dropped out of
school and gone to live in Thorne Blackburn's commune in San Francisco.
Jonathan's father had come to Colin's office at the beginning of the fall term

demanding that Colin—Jonathan's teacher and advisor—produce his son at once. When Colin's answers had not satisfied him, the general had gone to the president of the college.

Colin had called Thorne to warn him.

The two men had continued to meet after that first night, and looking back on that first evening—odd as it had been—Colin sometimes thought nostalgically of it as the last island of peace in a life grown increasingly turbulent and free of signposts.

He deplored what Thorne was doing, of course: the *Voice of Truth* was a hopeless farrago of New Age jargon, Eastern philosophy, metaphysics, Mystery School teachings, and Thorne's own brand of peculiar edification. Thorne preached the gospel of High Magick at every opportunity—a magick without limits, without the safeguards that Colin had been taught were absolutely necessary to its practice. Reckless endangerment—as the Order had charged—indeed.

But despite his disapproval of all that Thorne stood for, Colin could not help but like the man himself, and hope that maturity would temper the young Magus' youthful exuberance. For his part, Thorne recognized in Colin a like mind, one for whom he did not have to explain his concepts, only justify them. It was an odd friendship, built on differences, and one with surprisingly strong bonds.

The phone rang late in the day, summoning Colin MacLaren's attention from the pile of papers before him. The paperwork seemed to increase with every year; after five years at Berkeley, he was no longer teaching introductory courses, but the advanced students seemed to generate as much in the way of paper, if not more.

"MacLaren," Colin said curtly into the phone.

"Colin? It's Thorne," a familiar voice said cheerfully.

"Thorne? What can I do for you?" Colin asked cautiously. After his last appearance on the Berkeley campus, Thorne Blackburn was persona non grata within its gates.

"Well," Thorne said amiably, "this is my one phone call. So I was kind of hoping you'd come down and bail me out."

"Which station?" Colin said, reaching for a pad and pencil.

Colin reached the station house ninety minutes later. This was hardly the first time Thorne Blackburn had been arrested, even in the few months Colin had known him, but so far he had not been convicted of any offense that carried with it a jail term.

This time might be different. Thorne had been arrested for assaulting a police officer at an antiwar demonstration earlier today. Though a bail bondsman—as planned—had been waiting at the station to help demonstrators effect their release, Thorne hadn't been able to arrange bail.

The inside of the station smelled like disinfectant and tear gas; the combination made Colin's nose prickle. Once he'd explained what he'd come for, the paperwork was quickly completed, and after a few minutes Thorne was brought out.

His appearance was startling. Dried blood from a split lip was smeared across his jaw and throat, and his shirt—decorated with the Stars and Stripes, and thus a red flag to the riot police—was ripped at the shoulder and missing most of its buttons.

"Good Lord," Colin said mildly.

Thorne grinned cockily and winced. "Fell getting into the van," he said, with a mocking glance at the officer behind him. The man's face was set in a rigid mask of distaste, making Colin wonder for a brief, shocked moment what he might have done if Colin weren't here as witness.

"Well, let's get you out of here," Colin said harshly. "Are we free to go?" he asked.

"Sure, buddy. He's all yours."

A short stop to recover the rest of Thorne's personal effects—including the broken remnants of a picket sign with a photo of LBJ on it—and they were in the outside air once more.

"My camera. They broke my camera," Thorne groaned, holding the battered remains of what had once been a Leica cupped in his hands as they walked toward his car. He was limping slightly. Colin wasn't surprised that Thorne had brought a camera to the rally—Thorne was an enthusiastic amateur photographer, and liked to document everything. "Maybe I can at least save the film."

"What really happened?" Colin asked suspiciously. While he was no stranger to institutionalized brutality, it was odd and unsettling to realize that the practice was so entrenched in America that even its victims were matter-of-fact about it. When had America become a police state?

"You sure you really want to know?" Thorne asked. "Oh, before I forget—here's your money back." He tucked the shattered camera tenderly into his knapsack and then dug into his wallet to pull out a wad of twenties, holding them out to Colin.

At Colin's blank expression he laughed. "So why did I call you when I had the money for my bail? Just a little matter of having to *pay* my bail before I could get my hands on it. They do that all the time. It's harassment, but it's legal. They want us off the streets; that's no secret."

"Perhaps if you weren't so antagonistic . . ." Colin took the money and folded it into his pocket.

"Like we were last fall, when the Angels came down on us and the cops just stood back and watched? Wake *up,* Colin—there's a war on for the soul of America, and it's being fought in the streets. Which side are you on?"

It was a question Colin had answered long ago: he was pledged to serve the Light. Only when he had made that pledge, the world had been a simpler place. Today, he was not certain that any of the sides he could identify were of the Light, if things like this could happen here in America.

"I suppose you're convinced there have to be sides?" Colin asked, temporizing. "And know which one's right?" They'd reached the car; Colin opened the passenger door and Thorne climbed in.

"Hell, yes!" Thorne burst out. "If a bunch of guys who can't even vote yet are frying babies under orders over in 'Nam, what am I supposed to do—sit back and say that napalm is an instrument of national policy? They're the bad guys—they want to turn the United States of Amerika-with-a-K into a police state so they can skim off the profits. Lockheed and Dow Chemical are hand in hand with the Pentagon—you can't sit this one out, man! It's a rat race, and the rats are winning. You have to take a stand—you're on the Berkeley faculty; if you speak out, it would count for a lot."

In fact Colin had already spoken out, but political activism was the least of the things that Thorne advocated, and much of his philosophy Colin could not agree with.

"I don't want to argue with you now, Thorne," Colin said, starting the engine. While he honored his friend's political views—and honored the American tradition of dissent as well—what he could not stomach was the cavalier way Thorne squandered his birthright and training to make a mockery of the things Colin held most dear.

"You don't want to argue with me *ever,*" Thorne complained. "Not down in the trenches where it counts. Damn it, you didn't even tell me you were one of us."

Colin flicked his glance sideways, and saw Thorne make that same curious half-salute that Toller Hasloch had made years before. With an effort of will, he forced himself to ignore it. None of the Order was ever to acknowledge the Initiate it had cast out.

"I'm not one of you, Thorne," Colin said evenly. "Whatever it is that you think you are. Now. Where shall I take you? Back to my place?"

"The Bellflower Clinic over on College," Thorne said unexpectedly. "Claire's there. Kate's with her; we were supposed to meet back there after I got out of jail, anyway." Like many experienced activists, Thorne expected—in fact, actively sought—to be arrested each time he participated in a demonstration.

"Katie's preg, so I didn't want her out in the streets today. Good thing, too. The pigs were vicious."

Colin wondered why Thorne hadn't called Claire to bail him out if she was already involved with the demonstrators, then decided he must not want to implicate her. Asking a policeman's wife to come and bail out a hippie peacenik was something that might be embarrassing for Peter. Thorne's sense of tact surfaced at the oddest moments.

"Congratulations. I don't suppose you two would think of getting married," Colin said in a tone of resignation.

"Why should I marry Kate in particular?" Thorne seemed honestly surprised. "I—ouch," he said, squirming around in the seat.

"Are you sure you don't need a hospital?" Colin said.

"Claire's a nurse," Thorne reminded him.

There was silence for a while as Colin drove toward the free clinic on College.

"You can't just assume the government is the good guys forever," Thorne said after a few minutes. "You've already been presented with the evidence. You have a responsibility—"

"You're a fine one to lecture me on responsibility," Colin said in exasperation. "You claim to have the ultimate secrets of life and death—and you're prostituting those arts to make yourself into a media circus. No one takes you seriously, Thorne—haven't you noticed? For all that you claim to venerate it, you're turning the occult into a sideshow, a joke."

"People remember jokes, Colin," Thorne answered. "Nobody listens these days unless you've got clowns and dancing girls. I'd rather give birth to a living tradition than be curator to the mummy of a dead one."

Is that what you think of us? Colin thought. Was that what Jonathan had thought—why he'd gone to follow Thorne instead of setting his feet upon the Path?

"Come on, Colin," Thorne said coaxingly, when Colin said nothing. "Join us. Or oppose us. But do *something.* Do you really want to spend the rest of your life being the psychic advisor to the Berkeley Bunco Squad, unfrocking table-tippers for fun and profit? You're protecting people who don't deserve protection. If they're gullible, fleece them."

Thorne's words struck uncomfortably close to home, raising the specter of the Thule Group once more in Colin's mind. Toller Hasloch had been the first to say there was a war on for the soul of America, and Colin believed that more deeply than Thorne could ever know. But he knew that if he spoke of his fears, Thorne would dismiss them as Old Aeon, not worth anyone's trouble. Sometimes the young could be as blind as the old.

"Social Darwinism doesn't make a very good match with antiwar protest," Colin said irritably. "There are a lot of problems in this country, but its business is still to protect the weak and ensure justice for all. I don't think I'm prepared to toss out two hundred years of the Constitution and the Bill of Rights just because you say the government is corrupt."

"Isn't it?" Thorne asked cryptically. "You ought to check for yourself. Keep up with your old war buddies a little more, my friend."

Colin didn't bother to pursue the remark: he was too exasperated. Fortunately, they arrived at their destination before either of them had time to say anything more.

The Bellflower Clinic was one of the new so-called free clinics, which existed to provide basic medical care to an ever-growing rootless population of love children and transients. Patients paid whatever they could afford—or didn't pay at all—and operating expenses were covered by grants and donations. Claire volunteered her time here for a few hours each week.

Blessing his luck, Colin found a parking space behind the clinic. Before Thorne could even get the door open, Katherine Jourdemayne came running through the back door toward him.

Thorne had said Katherine was expecting a child, but her figure was still as slim and girlish as ever. She flung her arms around Thorne and hugged him fiercely, as though she'd never expected to see him again. Thorne winced, but did not push her away.

"Are you going to be all right?" Colin asked, coming around to Thorne's side of the car.

Thorne was leaning on Katherine. Claire, who had followed Katherine more slowly, reached them now and inspected Thorne's face critically.

"Hello, Colin. Hello Thorne. The victor home from the wars, I see," she said tartly. "Does it hurt much?"

Thorne smiled his lopsided grin at her. "You know what they say, Claire."

"Well, come inside," Claire Moffatt said. "We'll get you cleaned up." She glanced questioningly at Colin.

"I think I'll head on back to the campus. I've had enough excitement for one day," he said. And if he stayed, he was sure to argue with Thorne again, an argument neither of them could win.

But as he drove back toward the campus, Thorne's words would not leave his mind. *Was* he doing all that he could—and should—be doing to further the Light in this world? Though he took pleasure in teaching, he was not teaching the things he had been taught. He assisted those who were already on the Path. He did not place their feet there.

But how could that be wrong? Colin knew—no one better—that there were shades and degrees of rightness, but a sense of his own lack was a far cry from embracing Thorne's accusation that he was doing nothing.

There were no easy answers, Colin thought as he sat down at his desk again and contemplated his paperwork. The silver sword paperweight gleamed from atop a stack of files. No easy answers—and no quick ones. Impatience was one of the surest routes into the Shadow.

He pulled out his pipe and fiddled with it for a few moments. Once it was well alight, he picked up the paper at the top of the stack and began to read.

It was hard to believe he'd lived here for five years, Colin thought idly, walking up the steps of his bungalow a few hours later. The paperwork had been held at bay for another week or so—there were times when he thought that the university would be just as happy if he never taught a single student, so long as the paperwork was all in order. And every year it seemed to increase.

Five years—long enough to put down roots, to come to love the Berkeley Hills and to begin to understand its citizens' passionate worship of San Francisco. He was building a sound career in academia, with life insurance, a pension plan, and all the rest. It was security, of a sort. But was this really the shape he wanted his life to take?

Colin pulled the car into his driveway and parked. There were no easy answers, Colin reminded himself yet again. And nothing that had to be dealt with urgently. There was no need for him to take any action in haste.

He walked into the house, pausing to retrieve his mail from the box beside the door. There was a long cream-colored envelope from the Rhodes Group. They wanted him to come to work for them—a friend of Claire's consulted for them already, and Colin had met one of the directors at a seminar a few years before.

It was a tempting proposition, but he wouldn't reach nearly as many people pursuing pure research for the Rhodes Group as he did teaching parapsychology at Berkeley. And mainstream acceptance of parapsychology was more likely to be achieved by academic affiliations than through a small though well-respected consultancy.

If he weren't just deluding himself that this was even possible. What difference was there between "psychic" and "superstitious" in the public mind? Colin shook his head, feeling suddenly bone-weary. He put the letter aside to answer later.

There were the usual litter of bills and solicitations in the rest of the mail, along with a personal letter and one from the university.

He took the two envelopes into the kitchen and set them on the counter, looking around for the teakettle. The housekeeper had been here today, with the result that the kitchen was formidably neat and Colin couldn't find anything. Eventually he located what he wanted and turned back to the letters.

The one from Berkeley was from the dean of faculty's office. Colin tore the heavy envelope open, wondering why it hadn't come in the interoffice mail.

He scanned the dense academese through once, then reread it more slowly.

It was a Notice of Intent to Censure. He was being condemned for his radical (read: antiwar) activities as well as for teaching materials and presenting views in his courses that ran counter to the expressed position of the board—whatever that might be this week—as well as potentially undermining the character of the students to whom the university stood *in loco parentis*.

It seemed that General Ashwell's labors had borne fruit at last. There was to be a hearing, at which Colin would be given the opportunity to respond to these charges. Depending on the outcome of the hearing, the letter he held in his hands would be placed in his personnel file . . . or not. The date of the hearing was next Wednesday, which gave him precious little time to prepare a case.

The insistent whistling of the teakettle brought Colin back to the here and now. He crumpled the letter angrily into a ball and flung it into the trash, but such a gesture did not affect the facts. He supposed that tomorrow he'd have to start asking around and find out what one did in these cases. The last complaint that had gone into his file hadn't been conducted with quite this much ceremony.

Trying to focus on the immediate, Colin poured his tea and took it into the living room to drink. It was only then that he remembered the other letter and had to go back into the kitchen to retrieve it.

It was from Nathaniel Atheling. Colin's heart sank as he opened it, already half-certain of what he would find. The Seal of the Lodge was embossed in bright gold at the top of the folded sheet of vellum, and beneath it a few brief words in Atheling's ornate Spencerian script.

Colin was called to London, to attend a meeting of the Inner Order.

Such meetings were rarely convened; the last one had been over twenty years ago. The Lodges worked independently and quietly, without either the internal politics or the empire-building of some of the more public White Orders. For the Visible Head of the Order to send out a summons of this sort meant that matters were grave indeed. There was no question but that he must go at once.

Colin picked up the phone and began to dial. Two days later, he was in London, the summons from the dead forgotten.

They met in a quiet, old-fashioned hotel nestled into a side street in Piccadilly. They came from all over Europe and the Far East, these scattered men and women who were closer to Colin than his own blood family had ever been. He had not seen many of them in twenty-five years, and others whom he had hoped to see were sadly absent. There were perhaps twenty people in the room, all of them exoteric Masters or Adepts of the higher Grades—Master of the Inner Temple and above—and Colin was disturbed to see that he was among the youngest there. Their membership had slowly dwindled over the years.

The postwar world moved too fast—few these days were drawn to a Path that required years of study and dedication for little visible repayment. Those who sought such enlightenment today were far more likely to seek it in hallucinogens, which granted at least the illusion of power.

But it was power without control and insight without wisdom; a path to enlightenment that only led—for most—to confusion and disenchantment.

Though his own life's work was toward enlightenment and an end to superstition, Colin wondered—not for the first time—if he ought to actively— openly—teach the disciplines of the Path. Certainly he had earned the right, yet there were so many pitfalls involved in choosing to actively impart the teachings. The question was always not what could he do, but what *should* he do? To teach meant to risk much, especially in these troubled times. And if his parapsychological investigations caused the university to censure him, only imagine what recruiting a magickal Lodge would cause them to do.

A familiar figure worked its way across the crowded room, seeking him out.

"Colin. I'm glad you could make it," Nathaniel Atheling said, as if there had been any doubt that Colin MacLaren would obey *this* summons.

The psychiatrist was as correct and nondescript as ever in proper English tweeds; the only unexpected note was the antique scarab of blue faience that hung—as always—about his neck.

"I wish it could have been under happier circumstances," Colin responded, shaking his old friend's hand in greeting. He glanced around the room. "Is everyone here?"

"So far as I know," Atheling responded gravely.

The Order's members operated in the old tradition of secrecy and isolation less from fear of persecution in these more liberal times than from the desire to be free of distractions from listening to the still voice of the Light. It was a rare event for the Order to communicate with its members, much less gather them all together.

And together they were so few.

The door to the inner room of the suite opened, and the last member of their gathering entered.

The present Visible Head of the Order was a grey-haired woman with piercing blue eyes. Colin had met her once, what seemed a very long time ago. She was known to the world as Dame Ellen Lindsey.

Dame Ellen was in her early sixties, and walked only with great effort, using two heavy black canes. She was dressed somberly in unrelieved black, with no mark of rank or distinction about her.

"My friends," she said, lowering herself heavily into a chair. "I greet you all in the name of the Unconquered Sun, and apologize for taking you away from your mundane lives. But there is a matter that I must place before you all, and make it the Order's business, though I have waited—perhaps too long—to do so."

For almost two hours then Dame Ellen spoke, giving them names and places, dates and facts, and slowly, a chilling story began to emerge. Colin had known some of it beforehand—he lived in California, where nut-cults proliferated, and he'd been in the forefront of the fight against the Black Orders—but even so, the entire picture was more disturbing than even he could have surmised.

The occult forces that the Order had fought so desperately a quarter of a century before had not been destroyed, as they had once thought. Like some hideous destructive insect, the Black Orders, by whatever exoteric name they chose to be known, had hidden themselves within the body of their most implacable opponent, and now were emerging in strength once more.

From the very first days of the Third Reich, a clique high within the American government had sympathized with its goals, holding the country aloof from the European war during its early months and refusing to bomb certain targets once America had been forced to fight. And when it became apparent that the Axis Powers' fall was inevitable, those same individuals stood ready with money, false passports, false identities, to aid the Nazi executioners for their own political—and personal—enrichment.

"You can't just assume the government is the good guys forever," Thorne Blackburn had said to him. And now those words came back to haunt Colin as he listened to Dame Ellen.

Thousands of members of the SS were smuggled out of Germany and into new identities elsewhere in the world by members of the U.S. government. Some of the greatest human assets of the fallen Reich, such as Reinhard Gehlen and Wernher von Braun, simply changed masters: Spymaster Gehlen to run the CIA operation that provided Russian intelligence to his new American overlords—and to mastermind the architecture of the Cold War itself under the auspices of new intelligence chief Allen Dulles—and von Braun to oversee the space program that was created as a challenge to perceived Soviet dominance of space.

Gehlen's straw dog of an attack on the West by the Warsaw Pact nations effectively kept Western political analysts from paying sufficient attention to defeated Germany. While postwar America's attention was elsewhere, organizations such as *Odessa,* the largest of the underground Nazi escape organizations, had been busy rescuing and relocating its members in safe havens worldwide . . . and regaining lost political and economic power. Power that it was now preparing to exercise.

"Now you know as much as I of the threat we face: the same threat as always, only this time so cleverly disguised that I do not know if we can count on any help at all from the mundane world. To convince them of the reality of this danger could well do as much damage as the Shadow Orders themselves would, and we no longer know who in any government is friend, and who is foe.

"I cannot choose a specific course of action for you, or attempt to direct your True Wills in this matter, but we must conclude," Dame Ellen said, in her dry, practical way, "that neither the Third Reich nor the Thule Society and its platform of genocide, racial superiority, and directed evolution has been as conclusively defeated as we had once thought them to be. While their members have scattered, we now have every reason to believe that the Shadow Orders are nearly as strong as they were before the war. We believe that they are recruiting and rebuilding a new organization worldwide, though under a variety of new guises.

"We do not expect this to lead to a conventional war any time in the near future: we must grant our great enemy that it is smart enough to learn from its mistakes. Those I have dared to consult believe that this time the Black Order's grasp at power will take the form of subversion, a slow attempt to remold the governments of the Great Powers in their ideological image."

"But that isn't possible!" someone whose face Colin couldn't see protested. By his accent he was American, as Colin was.

Dame Ellen did not censure him. Instead, the lines that pain and weariness had carved into her aristocratic features seemed to deepen, as if she contemplated a grief too terrible to bear.

"Perhaps not all at once; perhaps never if we are careful and vigilant and do what work we can. But the enemy is capable of waging his war on every front at once, and our resources are few. I will direct the members' attention to the founding of an extremely public organization in San Francisco, California, in April of this year. It calls itself the Church of Satan, and while it does not seem to have any overt ties with the Shadow Orders, the fact that it exists at all is a disturbing harbinger of things to come."

Colin had heard of it—the press had given it extensive play at the time, and its founder, Anton LaVey, was a master of self-promotion. At the time he'd thought it merely silly; hearing it spoken of here, he wondered if his perceptions had been so coarsened that Evil could seem amusing to him.

There was complete silence in the room now, the silence of men and women who had given their whole hearts and souls to a Herculean task that had been nearly beyond their strength, only to see that now they must somehow find the will to do it all again.

"I thank you for your attention and commend you for your vigilance. And

I pray that each of you will win those battles the Light sends you, for the sake of all humanity. Go with the Light."

As she struggled up out of the chair, a woman whose name Colin did not know—a striking redhead with long coltish legs and a runway model's slimness—was there to help Dame Ellen to her feet. The younger woman helped the older through the inner door, and it closed behind them with a firm click.

They were dismissed back to their own lives.

But lives in which their own subjective senses of threat and peril had now been directed and magnified a thousandfold, for the temple that Colin had smashed five years ago had not been an isolated nastiness, as Colin had prayed. Hasloch had been right. Thorne had spoken the truth.

It had been a harbinger of things to come.

His return to the United States less than forty-eight hours later left Colin MacLaren feeling exhausted and disoriented. Most of that time had been spent in the air: the interminable Atlantic crossing to JFK Airport in New York, then a brief layover and almost eight hours more to San Francisco International. And once he reclaimed his car he faced another two hours' drive home.

It was October, and so it was raining; the veils of fog so dense over the headlands that the Pan Am flight had almost been forced to divert to another airport. When he'd come down the steps onto the rain-slick tarmac and headed for the terminal, the damp chill of San Francisco had settled over his shoulders like a heavy cloak, and in just that short walk his face was chill and numb.

By the time he reclaimed his car, it was already getting dark. Fortunately the engine started without incident, and soon Colin was driving across the Oakland Bay Bridge toward home.

In the dark, the other cars on the highway seemed like faceless threatening animals, and Colin's mind turned wearily upon the same fruitless paths. What was he to do about what Dame Ellen had told them? He still had a few contacts from the old days; perhaps he should call someone, investigate to see what corroboration he could dredge up. . . .

No. The intuition was so sharp and clear-cut that it was impossible to mistake for mere wishful thinking. He had left the Service without ever suspecting it was riddled with double agents and traitors bent on undoing everything he had worked so hard to accomplish, and thus his cover had been perfect. If there was anyone within its ranks still watching him, let them believe he was still blind. A political confrontation was not within his brief.

But now more than ever it was important to be firm in his beliefs; not to compromise, no matter how tempting the offer. Compromise was a slippery slope that led step by reasonable step into darkness and damnation.

When Colin reached the bungalow it was already after seven. He opened the door to the ringing of a telephone—hopeless, insistent. He dropped his suitcase to the rug and rushed over to it, leaving the front door still hanging open.

"MacLaren," he said—slightly breathlessly—into the receiver.

"Colin! Oh, thank God; I wasn't sure if you'd gotten back yet. Can you come to the clinic? We have an emergency," Claire said.

Claire did not ask for help lightly, and the word "emergency" was not often found in her vocabulary. Weary as he was, Colin turned around, got back in his car, and drove to the Bellflower Clinic.

He could hear the screams from the front door; a harsh sound neither human nor animal, but almost machinelike in its monotonous ululation.

"Colin!" Maria said with relief, getting to her feet and coming around the end of the receptionist's desk to him. Maria was a pretty, petite *chicana* who was one of the clinic's few full-time paid staff.

"Thank heaven Claire was able to reach you. Come on."

Colin followed her almost at a run as she hurried into the back of the clinic, toward the examination rooms. As he did, the mechanical screaming got louder.

"He's been here since six o'clock this evening. We don't know what to do with him, and Claire said you'd have some idea. In here," Maria said. "And I only said I'd stay until you got here, so I'm getting out of here. I don't want to see anything like that ever again!"

Colin opened the door.

At one point, this had been one of the clinic's standard examination rooms, with a table, cabinets for supplies, and posters on the walls that explained the symptoms of the most common social diseases and the commonest forms of birth control. But that was before some force had taken the entire contents of the room and shredded them as if it were an enormous Mixmaster.

The examination table had been reduced to kindling, the cabinets battered into a twisted mass. The posters had been shredded, and tiny pieces of paper, like insanely festive confetti, were scattered about the room like snow.

There was a young man crouched in the corner, naked except for a pair of boxer shorts. His arms were wrapped around himself, and he rocked back and forth, his face expressionless as he screamed. His face and body were sheened with the sweat of his exertion, but he gave no sign that he knew what he was doing.

Claire was standing in the opposite corner of the room. She was wearing her white nursing uniform with a blue cardigan over it, but her starched white cap was missing and her normally neat hair was in disarray.

Colin stepped into the room as Maria retreated back to her desk. He glanced at his watch. It was 9:30, already half an hour past the clinic's usual closing time.

"Colin," Claire said. Her blue eyes had heavy shadows beneath them. "I thought you'd be back today." She took a deep breath, as if even speech was exhausting. She had to raise her voice to be heard over the screaming.

"He should be in a hospital," Colin said, nodding at the crouching man. "Bad trip?"

"We think so. Some kind of a voodoo cocktail with Lord knows what in it; an honest tab of windowpane would be a godsend in comparison. His friends dropped him here earlier this evening—just put him out of the car in front of the clinic and drove off. He managed to make it inside and tell us that his name is James Rudbeck and that he's from Virginia, but we couldn't get anything more out of him. We brought him in the back and started to examine him, and I guess we found out why his friends dumped him.

"He did this."

Colin looked around the room again. He didn't think that any amount of physical strength could have accomplished the destruction he saw here.

"With his mind?" Colin said. Almost unconsciously he had ruled out magick as the source of this disturbance. It would have to be black magic, to cause such harm. Evil had a distinctive signature, and he felt no trace of it here.

"Yes. Every time we try to do anything for him he throws another fit; can you imagine what would happen in a hospital emergency room if that happened? At least we haven't got much in the way of fancy equipment here. But we haven't been able to get any tranquilizers into him, or even a saline IV, and that isn't good.

"Jimmy? Can you hear me?" Claire crossed the room and crouched down in front of the rocking man. She spoke gently, but did not touch him. "Jimmy, it's Claire. Can you hear me? You're safe now. Nothing bad is going to happen to you. You took some drugs—do you remember that? And you're having a bad trip, but it will be over soon. There's nothing to be afraid of—"

She tried for almost ten minutes, coaxing gently, but without any result. Whatever Rudbeck was seeing within his own mind, whatever had wrenched open the doors of perception to let him reach—and to make him defend himself with—the untapped wells of psychic power inside himself, it was still very much in possession of him.

And even if psychic powers were only manifest in ten percent of the population, and if even only one percent of those had a truly stellar level of power, that still meant hundreds—thousands—of people in California alone with this level of ability. Training could never reach all of them. But mind-expanding drugs could, and did.

Claire sighed, getting to her feet. As she did, she swayed forward, off balance with exhaustion and the awkwardness of her position. As she put out her hand to steady herself against the wall, her wrist brushed Rudbeck's shoulder.

The contents of the room exploded into life.

Colin didn't need to see it begin to know what was happening. All the hairs on his body stood straight out with the sudden charge that filled the room. Before he had even decided to move, he'd reached Claire and yanked her to her feet. As the first of the heavy pieces of wood hit the walls, Colin shoved Claire through the door to the examining room and slammed it behind him.

The rattle of debris against the door was like the impact of machine-gun fire.

"And besides," Claire said, as though finishing a sentence, "he does that every time somebody touches him." She looked hopefully at Colin. "Know any good exorcists?"

"I used to be a fairly good one myself," Colin said, "but that isn't what that boy needs. There's nothing of the occult here, only the power of the mind."

"'Just' the parapsychological," Claire said wearily. "Whatever that word means. I don't think I know anymore. I do know that Jimmy Rudbeck needs help . . . and if we can't touch him, we can't treat him."

"Claire. Any luck?" Dr. David Soule, the senior member of the staff, came around the corner. His face fell as he heard the battering of the psychic vortex against the closed door. "I guess not. Are you our expert consultant?" he asked hopefully.

"I'm Colin MacLaren," Colin said. "And I don't know how much of an expert I am. I'd say that you were more of an expert than I am, except I'm not sure that's true in this particular case."

Dr. Soule sighed. "Professor MacLaren, since I stated working here I have seen the dead walk, pigs fly, and a number of things that I would have relegated to the realm of nursery rhymes not two years ago. Nothing in all of God's creation can possibly surprise me anymore. But how do I treat someone I can't touch? For bad trips like Rudbeck's we try to support the patient—give a vitamin shot and maybe a mild sedative, replace fluids, provide a quiet environment for reentry if we can. But we can't do any of that here. I've seen people die of self-induced exhaustion before. I hate to say this, but you're our last hope."

As Dr. Soule spoke, the sounds from within the room—other than the robotic screaming, which had almost managed to vanish from Colin's consciousness—stopped.

Claire sighed, straightening her shoulders with an effort. "There's my cue, I suppose," she said. She opened the door cautiously. All was quiet. She stepped inside.

"Let me think for a moment," Colin said. "Mind if I smoke?"

"Go ahead—although as a medical man, I feel duty-bound to advise you to quit. Personally, I'm planning to let overwork kill me," Dr. Soule said with gallows humor.

Colin retrieved his pipe from a pocket and began to fill it. Tobacco, like alcohol, was a poison—he knew that cigarettes weren't called "coffin-nails" for no reason. Still, his mind was still half-addled by the long flight, and the tobacco would help him think.

He set the bowl of his pipe alight and smoked in silence for several minutes, mind working furiously.

"Tell me," Colin said suddenly. "Have you any idea of Rudbeck's religion? I think I may have a few ideas."

Dr. Soule frowned. "When we went through his wallet, we found a card for one of the campus Christian Fellowships, and he was wearing a cross when he was brought in, if that's any help to you."

"Hm'n," Colin said, thinking.

James Rudbeck wasn't possessed by any supernatural entity. A believing Christian, and a devout one, whatever he'd taken had opened some deep-rooted psychic center in his mind and made it a channel for Rudbeck's darkest fears. It was these he lashed out against, not anything in the material world, but that was small consolation to those who were trying to help him. An exorcism would be of little help in dispelling the force that was destroying him—a force within his own mind, mundane as his own muscles, wielded by some part of his *self*.

But perhaps, if the boy *believed* it would work. . . .

It took all three of them about half an hour to clear the room of debris. Colin had feared that it might not be possible, but Rudbeck seemed to take no notice of anything except of being touched, and all three of them were careful to avoid that. By the time they were finished, there wasn't so much as a scrap of paper left in the room.

"Now what?" said Dr. Soule.

"Now I'm going to see if I can convince him to stop harming himself. Emptying the room may buy a little time for that," Colin said, "but make no mistake: I believe that Rudbeck can be just as dangerous when he doesn't have something to throw."

"Do you want me there, Colin?" Claire asked.

"I'm afraid so," Colin said. "I hate to ask you—"

"It's my job," Claire said firmly, just as Colin had said to her several years before. "If there's any way I can help, I have to go."

Colin nodded, and motioned for Dr. Soule to step back. And then he opened the door to the room again.

Jimmy Rudbeck was still crouched in the corner. His face was sunken in, the skull beneath the skin showing blatantly. Whatever drug he'd taken should be wearing off by now, but that was no guarantee that Jimmy Rudbeck would come down. There were some bad trips that didn't end. His screams were softer now, only a rusty whistling through his dry throat. He was failing visibly.

If only Colin and Claire could manage to reach him, to help him tell the real from the illusory, that might be enough.

They reached the center of the room.

"James Rudbeck," Colin said commandingly. "I charge you in the name of the Living God to hear me."

No response.

"I order the powers of Darkness to depart from you and to leave you in peace. I order it in the Name of the Most High, in whose presence Darkness cannot remain."

Colin knelt down in front of Rudbeck and clasped him gently by the shoulders to still his rocking.

"Colin," Claire said, her voice strained.

He felt it, too; the charge of energy that had come just before the room exploded the last time. But this time there was nothing within reach to throw;

only the force itself. Colin could feel it pressing on his skin like the anticipation of a storm magnified a thousandfold.

"The Light will always defeat the Darkness. You know that this is true."

He could feel Claire's presence behind him, but her gift was in a far different realm than James Rudbeck's, and it could not match Rudbeck's in strength. Colin felt a painful spark of discharge energy as Claire put her hand on his shoulder, but he dared not allow himself to be distracted. With all his strength, he *willed* Rudbeck to believe, to hear him and trust him.

Even if he was no longer certain of his own faith.

Even if he could not believe that the Light would always triumph over the Darkness.

The energy in the room was a painful pressure now, something only instants away from turning on all three of them.

"Jimmy, it's Claire. You have to let go. You have to let us help you. There's nothing to be afraid of here. I promise you," she said from behind Colin's shoulder.

The tuneless whispered howling stopped.

". . . monsters . . ." the boy said. His eyes flickered, as if he were trying to look away from some inward vista.

"The Light will always defeat the Darkness," Colin said firmly. "You know that it's true. Remember what you know. Say the prayer, Jimmy. 'The Lord is my Shepherd, I shall not want—'"

The boy's eyes flickered once more, then closed. He took a ragged breath.

"'Yea, though I walk through the valley of the shadow of death—'" Colin said, willing Rudbeck to join him. The boy's lips moved along with Colin's words, and slowly the storm he had conjured faded away, dissipating like fog in the sun.

"'Surely goodness and mercy shall follow me all the days of my life—'"

And James Rudbeck slumped forward into Colin's arms in boneless unconsciousness.

Half an hour later there was no sign—save the emptiness of the room—that anything had ever happened there. An ambulance had come to take Rudbeck to the hospital for further treatment, and there was every likelihood that he would remember nothing of what had happened—or at any rate, little enough beyond a resolution not to experiment again with recreational drugs.

As they watched the ambulance pull away, Claire turned to him suddenly with the air of someone who has remembered something.

"Colin? What happened at the hearing?"

The hearing. The disciplinary hearing precipitated by his so-called radicalism. The trip to England and all that had come of it had driven the university problems completely out of his mind, and somehow now, after all that had happened, he could not manage to still think of it as very important. Colin shook his head.

"I'm afraid they had to proceed without me. No doubt I'll be notified of their decision in their own good time," he answered.

* * *

But apparently the hearing had been more significant than Colin had thought, and his absence from it had created an unfavorable impression, especially when no explanation of his absence was forthcoming upon his return. An emergency, Colin had said to the colleagues he had gotten to take his classes, and when he returned, he left it at that.

But in the next several days following his return, Colin was summoned to meetings with the head of the Psychology Department, the dean of faculty, the dean of students, and even the president of the university. The message in each of these meetings was the same: drop the parapsychology courses, toe the party line, conform, submit, agree. . . .

And Colin found himself unable to do it.

More to the point, he didn't *wish* to do what they so plainly wanted him to. After what he had learned in London, their concerns seemed petty, somehow; fools dancing on the edge of the Abyss, unaware of the peril they were in, in a world where the sacred cause of human freedom was guttering on the edge of extinction.

He was not, himself, certain of what to do. That power corrupted had always been tacitly understood of those who chose public life, but sheltering and exploiting war criminals went far beyond simple nepotism or self-enrichment. It was betrayal on a cosmic scale, the nihilistic worship of the great god Expediency, reducing the victors to the same moral level as those they had defeated. It was like some horror movie come to life, where friends and allies were transformed into inhuman monsters . . . and no one knew until it was too late.

Simon had been right. Thorne had been right. Everyone had been right. The United States government—or some powerful faction of it—was so unspeakably corrupt that it was feeding upon itself in a cannibalistic orgy, destroying the very ideals it had been created to protect.

As much as they served the Darkness, Colin was sworn to oppose them, but what could one man do against the inertia of the government? Some of the children he taught preached revolution, but Colin knew from bitter experience that a revolution would not save them. It would only produce the chaos that would allow a dictatorship to take explicit control.

Colin thought briefly of Thorne, and the people Thorne called his sacred clowns. Could turning the streets into a circus actually be what was needed? Or was what was needed, as it had always been, no harder—and no easier— than men of good will keeping faith?

He could not *know.* Ultimate certainty was reserved to the Light Itself, not to mortal, fallible men. Colin could only *hope,* and act in accordance with his own conscience.

He thought again of James Rudbeck, trapped and terrified by the unleashed power of his own mind. Of Claire as he had first known her, hostile and tormented by a gift for whose existence there was no room in the conventional worldview.

These were his people. These were the ones he must find, and reach, and teach. Each soul he could save from fear was a blow against the Darkness. This was his new war, and now he must find the field on which it was to be fought. And he had been his own master for far too long to continue to devote half his life to something he couldn't respect.

"I have to say that I'm delighted to see you here, Dr. MacLaren," the man behind the desk said.

The Rhodes Group had spacious offices on the fifteenth floor of one of the anonymous new office buildings that had begun to infest the financial district of San Francisco. Anyone entering the foyer would be forgiven for believing that this, too, was some high-level think tank, or perhaps an international financial firm, teak office suite and English-accented receptionist included. And, in a manner of speaking, this *was* a research organization.

The Rhodes Group was a for-profit foundation dedicated to study and investigation of the paranormal in all its guises. It investigated mediums and haunted houses, tested self-proclaimed psychics, and correlated reports from all over the world about advances in the field of parapsychology. Its research library was internationally famous and it held a contract as a government consultant in the field of the paranormal, but the majority of the group's support came from the individuals and organizations to whom it provided its services, those individuals whose lives had somehow been touched by the uncanny, and who now needed expert counsel.

"I'm delighted to be here, Mr. Davenant," Colin responded.

"Please. Call me Michael," Michael Davenant responded. He was a few years younger than Colin, with the darkly brilliant good looks that were a hallmark of his Irish ancestry.

Behind him, through the wall of glass that formed the outside wall of the office, Colin could see the entire sweep of the City spread out before him like the proverbial land of dreams. It was a sunny, late spring day, the start of the long rainless stretch that made up three seasons of the California year.

"And I'm Colin."

Davenant smiled. "Colin, then. As you've probably guessed, the reason I've asked you back here today is to offer you the position. It would be a great asset to us to have a field researcher with your reputation working with the group, and frankly, I deem it lucky that you're willing to consider us. The board was favorably impressed with your CV . . . and fully sympathizes with your decision to leave Berkeley."

"Thank you. Although you could say that it was as much Berkeley's decision as it was mine."

His resignation from the university had been a relief all around. They didn't want a parapsychologist on their staff, and Colin was more and more impatient with the time he was forced to devote to the disciplines that a hundred other men could teach as well. Once he'd made the decision to leave, he'd toyed with the idea of simply returning to New York, but he'd managed to put down roots in the six years he'd lived here, and had made friends he would miss. And it was California that was the center of the Occult Renaissance, from the Church of Satan that Lady Ellen had spoken of . . .

To Thorne Blackburn.

"Well, you may find we're a more liberal master than the university. No one here cares what a man's politics are, and as for an interest in the paranormal, that's why we're here," Davenant said.

Colin had received the full tour of the facility on his previous visit. It was an impressive facility, including interview rooms and two laboratories which could be used for everything from remote viewing experiments to astral travel. He'd be able to devote more time to his parapsychological interests, and the Rhodes Group considered cooperation with the Bay Area police departments as good PR, so they would have no objections to his continuing to make himself available to law enforcement agencies.

"I suppose that all there is left to do is make certain that you still want the job," Davenant said.

"Yes, I think so. It should be an interesting association," Colin said. Working with the Rhodes Group was only an interim solution, of course, to keep him in the game while he took his bearings.

But it would be an intriguing one.

The rest of the formalities managed to consume a couple of hours, and then Davenant had insisted on taking Colin out to lunch at the Galley in the Alley down on Maiden Lane. Despite its overly quaint conceit—the front of the restaurant was built in the shape of a galleon's prow, complete with buxom mermaid figurehead—the food was good, and Davenant exerted himself to be amusing.

Afterward, Colin took advantage of the combination of leisure and a beautiful day to walk around the City. Between Dame Ellen's revelations and the letter of censure from UC Berkeley, he'd withdrawn into a routine of work and research, the better not to have to confront these concerns.

Colin realized that he hadn't seen much of any of his friends since his visit to London last October. Katherine was due to have the baby—he only hoped Claire had persuaded her to go to a hospital, instead of having the baby at home in the middle of a magickal ritual, as the young couple seemed to intend. Finding out was reason enough for a visit.

And from such innocent, nearly unconscious decisions, the future is woven.

Colin took the cable car for the first leg of his journey—it was jammed as always, and he rode standing on the outside, handing his fare in to the conductor over the heads of his fellow passengers. The motorman rang the bell in the rhythmic double-clangs that were a worldwide aural symbol of the City by the Bay as the cable car proceeded at its magisterial eight miles per hour through the colorful residential district of the most cosmopolitan city on earth.

San Francisco is a city made to be savored at a walking pace, and walking had always been one of Colin's great recreations. The closer he got to the Hashbury, the more crowded the streets were. Spare change was a constant request, and Colin gave what he could. The runaway population was reaching alarming numbers; the tally increased with each passing month, and many of the children fell into the hands of shadowy Fagins who turned their bright futures into a dark one of prostitution and hard drugs.

What was it they were seeking? Why did they come in their hundreds? Were their lives so empty and unhappy that they would come hundreds of miles in pursuit of a dream?

You might as well ask when people had become desperate to keep what they had, rather than confident that more would always be there, Colin thought bleakly. It was easier now to understand the frenzy that drove this postwar generation in its twin quests for political power and transcendence. The unconscious mind always knows what the conscious does not even suspect, and on some level, these children realized they were the last defenders of the Golden Age, and that if they did not win here, the loss was for all time.

Thorne would, of course, say such a notion was Old Aeon thinking, that the Golden Age of Gods and Men could be summoned at any time, no matter what had gone before.

And for the first time, Colin began to wish that Thorne was right and his own Lodge was wrong.

SEVEN

SAN FRANCISCO, APRIL 1967

But I will wear my heart upon my sleeve
For daws to peck at: I am not what I am.
—WILLIAM SHAKESPEARE, *Othello*

THORNE BLACKBURN'S STAR HAD RISEN DRAMATICALLY IN THE LAST SEVeral months; his public rituals now drew sizeable crowds. He'd attracted the attention of the national press, anxious to harvest new fodder from the Age of Aquarius, and stories about him—distorted almost to gibberish—had appeared in both *Time* and *Newsweek*. High Magick was being merchandized as if it were rock music, turned into a quaint sideshow that the rest of the world could pass by. And Thorne, with his outrageous claims—no, *demands* for belief—was in the forefront of that movement, shaping it, catering to it, for reasons Colin could not understand.

The *Voice of Truth* occupied the whole of the Victorian now, and it was no longer white. The house had been repainted in bright acid colors, exuberant as a comic book. Its ground floor apartment had been turned into what the hippies called a "head shop"—it sold the *Voice of Truth* as well as underground comics (or "comix" as they were now labeled), black lights, and lessidentifiable paraphernalia. There was an office of sorts for the newspaper in the shop's back room that also contained the press off which it was run, and the smell of printer's ink mingled with the scent of incense and pot in the air of the shop.

People gazed at Colin curiously as he entered, but no one stopped or questioned him as he made his way through the crowded aisle.

Possibly he didn't look as much like a policeman as he had the first time he'd seen Thorne. Or perhaps Thorne's messianic roadshow attracted all kinds. Thorne, in his way, was a refutation of the fear that the twentieth century had lost its battle with the Shadow. Even if the New Aeon he preached seemed to be nothing other than Chaos come again, it was a hopeful chaos.

"Colin!" Katherine Jourdemayne greeted Colin warmly. A tiny baby was looped into a sling made of Indian-print fabric that Katherine wore, bandolier-style, across her bosom. "Did you come to see Truth? Isn't she the most perfect baby? Pilgrim adores her."

The boy—he must be seven by now—regarded Colin gravely, his hands covered with the chalk he was using to draw on the wall. Colin had never found out who Pilgrim's mother was—Katherine had never claimed him as hers—and thought it would probably be futile to ask. Thorne seemed to treat all of his liaisons and their products with equal fondness, and certainly Colin had never seen anything approaching jealousy among the ones he knew about.

Colin admired the baby for a few minutes, taking care to give equal attention to Pilgrim. (Why wasn't the boy in school? He was afraid to ask.) The formalities over, Colin asked after Thorne.

"Oh, he'll be back soon," Katherine said. "Things are really starting to happen for us now. But c'mon upstairs—I'll make us a cup of tea while we wait. C'mon, Pil, let's go see Auntie Irene."

The apartment was occupied as always. Thorne's star might be on the rise, but the apartment was as shabby as it had ever been. Colin had discovered that Thorne held a more or less permanent house party for anyone who cared to come, and Colin had never been able to keep track of those who came and went. Its current occupants were scattered about the living room, and Pilgrim ran to the woman sitting on the floor—she had bright red hair and wore a spangled scarf tied over it in a gypsy fashion.

"There's a little love," the woman said. "Come to Irene." Her accent was English, and she gave her name the three-syllable pronunciation common in Europe. She scooped the little boy into her lap and handed him a deck of Tarot cards.

Colin followed Katherine into the kitchen. As Katherine puttered among the tea things—the baby seeming to be perfectly content in her strange cradle—she explained to Colin that Thorne's latest plan was to use magick to end the Vietnam War.

"—in Washington; we're planning to go to the Pentagon and beam love-thoughts at them until they become incapable of bombing anyone. Thorne wants to get all the magicians in the Bay Area working together on this; he says that only when the enlightened take social as well as spiritual responsibility can the Great Work proceed without interruption. But Anstey's been really trying to bring him down—"

"Anstey?" Colin asked in bewilderment. "*Simon* Anstey?"

"He wants us to stop what we're doing," Katherine said, stirring her tea slowly. "He's been saying that all Thorne wants is money. That's so *stupid*, Colin! Anstey's got more money than Thorne does—"

"Money, and position, and a positively sheeplike devotion to his own consequence," Thorne Blackburn said, walking into the kitchen. He set the camera he was carrying down on the table, grabbed Katherine's teacup and drained it at a gulp, and then leaned over to kiss her and nuzzle Truth, still holding an armful of papers.

"Hi, Colin. If you've got any influence with Anstey or the city council, it'd be really groovy if you used it." He flopped down into a kitchen chair and dropped the papers onto the table, then plucked the baby out of her makeshift cradle.

"What's the problem?" Colin asked.

"City council's denied us a permit to assemble . . . again. And Anstey did an op-ed piece in the *Chronicle*—which isn't as bad as what he's saying in person." Thorne sighed, and for the first time since Colin had known him, looked truly tired.

"He's just jealous," Katherine Jourdemayne said loyally.

"He's saying that I'm running a mind-control cult; of course, Anstey's so square he thinks rock ought to be banned. . . ." Thorne said. He glanced at Colin provocatively; Thorne knew that Colin and Simon were acquainted; Colin made no secret of it.

"Haven't you said that everyone should be free to express themselves?" Colin asked. He could not imagine what had set Thorne and Simon on a collision course. The two men lived—almost literally—in different worlds.

"Yeah, but—Jesus, not when they disagree with me," Thorne said reasonably. "Anstey's into the occult up to his forty-dollar haircut—and *he's* got the nerve to call *me* a cult-running phony? Just because he's Alison Margrave's anointed successor and has spent half his life chasing ghosts around the haunted houses of Europe gives him *no* basis for judging me or my work."

The baby, awakened by Thorne's vehemence, began to fuss. Thorne joggled her in his arms, trying to quiet her. "But you'll show them all, won't you, sweetheart? You won't just hear about the New Aeon—you'll live there, won't you?"

"Oh, give her here, Thorne, I think she's hungry," Katherine said, sounding like every young mother since the beginning of time. Thorne relinquished the baby, and Katherine pulled down the neckline of her peasant blouse to give the child access to her breast.

Thorne got up and walked over to the refrigerator and pulled out two beers, popping both bottlecaps and setting one in front of Colin.

"I'm glad you came," he said. "There's something I want to ask you about. Ed Sull—"

The sound of shouting from down in the street interrupted him, and Thorne ran to the living room window to look out. Colin followed, more curious than worried—until he recognized the voice.

"Blackburn!" Simon Anstey shouted. "Come out here, you libelous fraud—I'll sue, damn you!"

The rest of what Simon had to say was lost in the jeering of the street people gathering around. Colin looked out the window. He could see Simon's

Mercedes standing in the street, and Simon himself standing on the sidewalk. Simon was dressed in a turtleneck and a dark suit. The contrast between him and Thorne's tatterdemalion acolytes couldn't be more marked.

"Hey, Anstey!" Thorne's voice was gleeful as he leaned out the open window. "Want a drink?" He tilted the beer bottle out into space, pouring carefully. There was a roar of rage from below.

"Thorne, for God's sake!" Colin said, managing to grab the bottle away from him before it was quite empty. He dragged Thorne away from the window. "This isn't going to solve anything!"

"If he's mad now, wait until he sees the *Voice of Truth.* We're doing a cover story on him," Thorne said, laughing happily. "Simon Anstey: New Age Ninny or Old Aeon Fraud?"

In the street below, there was the sound of a car door slamming and the roar of the Mercedes' high-powered engine as Simon gunned it and drove away.

"This is not worthy of you," Colin said to Thorne.

Thorne regarded him brightly.

"Exactly whose idea of a messiah am I supposed to be, Colin? His? Yours? Or mine?"

"—and I'm afraid it's only going to get worse, my dear," Alison Margrave said sadly.

The two friends were sitting out on Greenhaven's terrace, enjoying the fine (though still cool) May weather and the sense of being suspended high above the city, like a pair of hawks hovering among the clouds. It was Saturday, and Colin had finally accepted Alison's standing invitation to visit, repairing a lapse of months.

Alison had warmly applauded Colin's decision to leave Berkeley and join the Rhodes Group, and Colin supposed he ought to be thinking about finding a place on this side of the Bay, but he was by nature a packrat and hated the thought of moving. But after the small talk and pleasantries, the discussion had turned, as it inevitably did, to magick and its practitioners.

"Compared to the troubles we see on the streets these days, I don't suppose a battle between two magicians is anything much, and Lord knows being seen by the mundane world and treated by the press as nothing but a pack of kooks is not a new experience for any of us—except maybe Simon—but it's the people he and Blackburn draw in after them that I'm worried about. Blackburn's playing pretty rough, and I'm afraid Simon will be tempted to strike back in the same way that Blackburn is attacking him."

The quarrel between the two men had begun with Blackburn's antiwar rituals. When Simon had attacked them for being both dangerous and frivolous, Thorne had counterattacked by pointing out that Simon, by reason of his deferment, was in no danger of being drafted, something that was more dangerous to more people than any magick Thorne could ever perform.

"Surely Thorne isn't working magick against Simon?" Colin asked.

But he knew, with a sinking feeling deep inside him, that it would be perfectly in character for Thorne to do such a thing. *I wish to know in order to serve . . .* That was the credo that Thorne had rejected.

"Well, he's said he is, of course. And *something* certainly rattled the doors and windows around here a few nights ago. If it was Blackburn's doing, I'd say he's got a pretty impressive string of firecrackers at his disposal," Alison said. "Fortunately my wards held."

This was more evidence—not that Colin had needed it—that Thorne had rejected the rules which bound the Adepts of the Right-Hand Path, the Adepts for whom magickal power was only a by-product of the Path of Self-Knowledge. If not Black, Thorne's approach was certainly Grey.

"Of course Simon is absolutely livid," Alison went on. "I've told him that the best course is simply to ignore it. I dare say I've taught him enough about shielding himself and his home and possessions that Simon shouldn't have a thing to worry about, any more than I do. But Simon doesn't always take my advice," she finished, sighing.

"And Thorne has never taken anyone's advice at all," Colin said ruefully. "He certainly won't listen to anything I have to say. Maybe Claire can make him see reason; he's always been fond of her."

But Claire had no more success than Colin had in changing Thorne Blackburn's mind. Colin had the sense that Thorne was simply baiting Simon, mocking him because—at least to Thorne—Simon Anstey represented both the mundane and the magickal Establishment. Thorne was doing his best to make Simon an object of public ridicule as a form of sympathetic magic, and Simon was determined to run Thorne out of the Bay Area. Neither Thorne nor Simon would break off the feud. It had become increasingly personal and bitter, at least on Simon's side, and it was polarizing the Bay Area occult community.

Those who were members of more traditional Magickal Orders—the Ordo Templi Orientis, the Golden Dawn, the Builders of the Adytum, the Rosicrucian Fellowship in America—had taken this opportunity to flock to Simon Anstey's banner. Thorne had made too many enemies among traditional occultists with his breezy, publicity-seeking style and grandiose claims for the Old Guard to be able to resist the temptation to strike back at him now.

Thorne's supporters were mostly drawn from among his own growing band of followers, and from the membership of the increasing number of new Wiccan and Neo-Pagan groups that were springing up everywhere like mushrooms after rain. These new groups had few ties to traditional occultism, condemning it as monotheistic and patriarchal. Their credo—"an ye harm none, do what thou wilt"—captured perfectly the spirit of the Age of Aquarius, and like Thorne, they, too, wished to remove magick from the Temples and set it loose in the streets.

The dispute even made the pages of the *Examiner* with an article that cast Simon in the role of a noted parapsychologist exposing a depraved charlatan. Certainly Thorne didn't make as favorable an impression as Simon did on members of the Establishment—in fact, he sounded very much like a crank by the time the reporter was through with him. But Thorne had other avenues of attack than the Establishment press, and he used them all.

At any other time, Colin would have considered this a tempest in a teapot. Now, he regarded it as a symptom of a graver divisiveness: the factions of the Light embroiled in petty quarrels at a time when their cooperation was most needed.

Which side are you on? Thorne had asked him once. Now Colin wondered the same thing about the young magician. Which did Thorne serve: the Light or the Dark? Did even he know?

June 1967. Colin had found an apartment in North Beach and had moved across the Bay a few weeks before. He was now working with the Rhodes Group full-time. Most of it was fairly routine—if the investigation of hauntings and possession could ever be said to be routine—and the majority of the cases presented to him so far had boasted distinctly mundane solutions. Those which had not had been easily explicable through misunderstood but truly mundane causes had been the rare but hardly supernatural manifestations of common (for lack of a better word) psychic powers—telepathy, precognition, telekinesis, clairvoyance—though many came with occult trappings attached.

Most people who discovered themselves to be in the tiny psychic minority of mankind turned to the occult for the explanation of their seemingly irrational abilities. They had little choice, since Religion and Science had both failed them—Religion by consigning their gifts to the realm of devil-worship and Science by denying that they existed at all.

It was no wonder that the majority of psychics were neurotic, as they attempted to reconcile the evidence of their senses with the teachings of their culture. Though Colin disagreed with Thorne's platform of revealing all the Great Secrets, surely there was some middle ground of psychic education, so that normal, conservative people didn't have to choose between the Devil and madness when confronted with the Unknown?

The flyer stuffed into the door of Colin's apartment—and most of the rest of the ones on the block—announced a Love Magick Be-In Against the War in Golden Gate Park, to be held Saturday, June 17. Thorne had apparently finally received his long-sought permit to assemble, despite all of Simon's efforts to the contrary. Colin didn't expect Simon to attend, but Thorne would almost certainly use the occasion to crow about his victory. Watching Thorne and Simon quarrel irritated him almost beyond reason, so Colin had no plans to go, and he'd thought Claire would stay away as well. Then just last night, Claire had phoned him from Berkeley, saying she was coming to the Be-In after all.

"It's just a feeling, Colin—and probably indigestion at that. But I feel as if I might be able to do some good if I'm there. I'm planning to bring Peter along for moral support."

Claire was not often wrong in her hunches, and Colin had grown to trust them unquestioningly.

"Then I'll meet you there. How bad can it be, after all?" he said.

The sky glowed a deep faience blue, with a few tiny white clouds radiant with the sunlight that passed through them. The temperature was in the high seventies, and the air was clear.

The Be-In had attracted the usual collection of street people: mimes, face painters, belly dancers, jugglers, wandering musicians, bubble-pipe blowers. Copies of the *Voice of Truth* were being hawked, and someone was selling helium balloons. Several of the balloons had already escaped, tangling in the trees or riding the ocean winds high above the city. An outdoor stage—empty of people but already set up with a drum set and amplifiers—made a loose focal point for the crowd that had gathered.

They wore granny dresses and bell-bottoms, dashikis, crocheted halter tops, denim skirts, bright vests, and fringed leathers. They wore peace symbols and granny glasses in candy store tints; love beads and slogan buttons in all the colors of the rainbow. Their hair was almost universally long, men and women alike, hanging straight and shining down their backs, sometimes pulled back into a long tail. They were barefoot and sandaled, carrying backpacks and shoulder bags and their children. They'd come for the music, or the politics, or just for Thorne, this peaceable tribe that would soon—for one brief, shining moment—be known as the Woodstock Nation—a nation which, like the kingdom of Camelot, would dissolve in the very moment of its realization, leaving its exiled children to yearn for it forever after.

But today their losses were all in the future.

"Claire!" Colin said with relief, glad to recognize at least one familiar face. "Where's Peter? I thought he'd be coming with you."

"He was called in to work a case at the last minute," Claire said. "He said he'd be along when he could, but I'm not counting on it, mind." She smiled.

Her ensemble made no concession to the thrift-shop look of counterculture fashion, and she stood out from the crowd almost as much as Colin did. Claire was wearing a short-sleeved pantsuit in chocolate brown with inserts of hot pink and bright yellow. Her purse and boots were white patent leather, and her white button earrings matched the wide white frames of the sunglasses she wore against the summer sunshine.

"I'm glad I found you," Claire said. "This place is really a zoo, isn't it? Not much chance of a private word."

"I stopped by the house earlier, but Tex told me that the others had already come over here. I'd hoped to get a chance to talk to Thorne alone before all this started," Colin said.

"You think he's going to make another attack on Simon," Claire guessed.

"It doesn't take psychic powers to predict that," Colin said, grimacing. "And, yes, I'd hoped I could talk Thorne into being reasonable. He'll never get mainstream acceptance for his ideas if he keeps attacking the Establishment at every turn."

"And even if he doesn't want acceptance," Claire said, "I don't think Alison can talk Simon out of a lawsuit against those pieces in the *Voice of Truth* much longer. And with Thorne's arrest record, it's hard to see him winning the case."

Colin sighed. "That young man is too stubborn for his own good."

"Which one?" Claire asked with a wicked smile.

Thorne's extended family was easy enough to spot; while Colin and Claire had been talking, they'd driven the Mystery Schoolbus up as close as possible to the stage and were unloading more equipment from it.

The Mystery Schoolbus had started life as an ordinary yellow school bus, before it had somehow wound up in Thorne's hands. He'd gutted the bus, converting it to a combination of a motor home and a rolling church, and it had become a Bay Area landmark in the months since its acquisition. The outside of the bus was now covered in a mural-cum-collage that was in a constant state of flux. Today the sunlight glinted brightly off of a shower of glitter stars painted across the dark-blue backdrop of the front right fender. Colin could see Pilgrim running around among the adults, waving a bubble wand. He was covered in multihued body paint and not much else, and had feathers braided into his long black hair.

Colin and Claire headed in that direction. Katherine was standing off to one side, balancing her daughter on her hip.

"How's Truth?" Claire asked, stopping to admire the baby.

Truth Jourdemayne was three months old now, the lace cap and terrycloth romper she wore oddly conventional when contrasted with her mother's tie-dyed overalls and T-shirt.

"She's growing so fast," Katherine said. "The last time Caro was here she couldn't believe how big she'd gotten. I'm so lucky to have her."

Caroline was Katherine's twin sister. She'd been at the *Voice of Truth* the first night Colin and Claire had gone there, but she was not a member of Thorne's group. She had a degree in library science and worked at a library back East.

"Do you know where Thorne is, Katherine?" Colin asked. Maybe Thorne, in the midst of his own success, would agree at least to stop baiting Simon and let the quarrel die of its own accord.

"He's got to be somewhere around here," Katherine said, frowning thoughtfully. "He's been working on a new ritual ever since the tide turned at the equinox. He calls it Opening the Way. He was going to try part of it out today."

Just like Thorne, to test in public what most magicians would try out in strict privacy.

"He might be back behind the bus," Katherine suggested.

"We'll try there," Claire said.

Thorne was, in fact, behind the bus. He was standing on a battered footlocker, photographing the festival with another in a series of the battered cameras that accompanied him everywhere he went. He was wearing faded jeans and worn sandals, and several strands of love beads gleamed against his bare chest. Jonathan Ashwell—similarly dressed—was standing beside him.

Both men grinned when they saw them.

"Claire! And Colin—how's the ghost business these days?"

"As ever," Colin said.

"Gotta go," Jonathan said, ducking his head. He was still self-conscious around Colin on the rare occasions when they met, as if he suspected Colin might still be angry about his departure from Berkeley. "Nice seeing you, Professor. Claire."

"And what about you?" Claire said, when Jonathan had gone. "*Ed Sullivan?* I watched it the night Debbie said to, but I didn't see you."

"You should have been in the studio audience, baby." Thorne grinned at her. "I'm doing the *Dating Game* next week: 'Bachelor Number One: when immanetizing the eschaton, do you prefer to use (a) Love under Will (b) Vatican City or (c) a nuclear warhead?'"

Claire snorted. "They'll probably throw out the tape from that, too."

"I wouldn't be surprised," Thorne said. "It's so much fun to jerk the pigs' chains, I wonder why anyone ever does anything else?" He stepped down off the trunk. "C'mon over here. I want to get a picture of you two. A commemorative."

He led Colin and Claire a few yards away from the bus, so that he could position them against a stand of trees.

"The end of the month I'm taking off on a gig that nobody can censor," Thorne went on, as he adjusted the focus. "Anstey may have queered my pitch here, but I still think that solidarity is going to save us. Nothing is stronger than magick! And nothing can stand in the face of magick!"

As he spoke, Thorne clicked and wound the camera, snapping several pictures.

"There," he said with satisfaction. "You have now entered immortality."

"What kind of solidarity are you planning?" Colin asked warily. He hoped he didn't sound as dubious as he felt.

"I'm going to become a god," Thorne said happily. "And get everyone to worship me. There's no reason the Great Work of Transformation needs to be limited to the subtle body—that's just Old Aeon crap. The Universal Mystery Tour will bring the Great Work to the attention of more people than ever before. I will transform that fame into money and power and use them to reshape the world."

"Thorne—" Colin began, but Thorne's mercurial attention had been summoned elsewhere. "Hey! There's Irene! Gotta go!" He slung the camera around his neck and took off at a run.

Colin sighed sharply.

"Why does he always have to do his best to sound like a raving lunatic?" Claire asked plaintively. "I talked to Johnny Ashwell last week—the Universal Mystery Tour is just a couple of rock bands going on tour, and they've asked Thorne to come along. There isn't anything in that about . . . gods."

"Nobody ever got television coverage by being reasonable, moderate, and serious," Colin said. "And Thorne seems to be in the entertainment business, for better or for worse. I'd give a great deal to know what Ed Sullivan made of him."

"Well, we know what he made of the *Ed Sullivan Show*," Claire said succinctly. "Hash."

"I'm going to go look for him," Colin decided, almost against his better judgment. He still wanted to talk to Thorne; if—as he'd implied—he was giving up on his plan to unite the Magickal Lodges and Bay Area New Age groups in political activism, perhaps Colin could persuade Thorne to settle with Simon as well. And if Thorne would drop his "sacred clown" persona for a few moments, perhaps Colin could even explain to him why unity among the forces of the Light now was so important.

But Thorne seemed to possess an amazing ability not to be found, no matter how hard Colin looked for him. Meanwhile, the stage where the presentations—including Thorne's—would take place was being decorated with bunting, papier-mâché masks, and posters, including some that said "Speed Kills!" with a skull above crossed hypodermics. Brightly colored banners—pink, yellow, purple, acid green—with hand-painted designs billowed gently in the cool breeze at all four corners of the stage. The whole spectacle had the bright unreality of an illustration from a book of fairy tales.

But the world in which it existed was grimly real.

Where was Thorne? He couldn't simply have vanished. For one thing, he needed to get into costume—Colin would not grant him the dignity of calling what Thorne wore ritual robes—but Colin feared that if he waited until Thorne returned to the bus there would not be enough time to talk to him, and Thorne was much too excited after a ritual for there to be any possibility of a conversation then.

While Colin had been searching, one of the bands performing at Thorne's "Be-In"—the name painted on the drumset was "Narzain Kui"—took the stage. Colin had been heading for the bus, but when Narzain Kui began to play, the crowd closed in around the stage, drawn like iron filings to a powerful magnet. Their mass trapped Colin where he was, and he ground his teeth in frustration.

The raw noise of their first number hit him like a wall of water, but after a moment or so Colin discovered that he could actually make out the words.

> They made a promise they don't understand
> Now they've gone to a strange foreign land
> Pick up your gun and follow the band
> And find yourself killing for killers—

The song was apparently well-known to the audience; they responded to it as if it were an anthem, and Colin felt a tingling on his skin as the energy level around him soared. The lead guitarist responded with a break that howled like feedback before the band headed into the second verse.

Killing for killers—it isn't your fight
Come rage against the dying of the light—

Colin had the sense of an inexorable, powerful beast, only half-aware, but simmering with righteous rage. *"Wading through blood—do you know what is right—"* It was as if the children around him believed that music could substitute for political activism—and God help the country if they ever realized differently.

When you find yourself killing for killers—

At the end of the second verse the band headed into an extended bridge, and Thorne climbed up on the stage, moving carefully because of his costume. Colin was momentarily nonplussed, jarred from the music's violent spell.

Thorne was wearing the robes of an Adept; the robes he had been entitled to as a member of the Inner Order. If that had been all, matters would have been bad enough, but he'd made some additions to his costume. Over his shoulders he wore a sort of fur capelet—Colin thought it might be wolf fur—and on his head he wore an antler crown with the sun-disk set in the middle. He'd doused himself liberally with glitter, and it shook loose from the costume in a constant gentle sprinkling. Now that his expressed desire to work together with the other Magickal Orders in the Bay Area had been defeated by his own flamboyance, Colin had hoped that Thorne would modify his behavior.

No such luck.

The bridge ended. The lead guitarist gestured toward a second microphone, grinning, and now Thorne was singing, too.

Dying light makes it darker every day—

If Thorne had wanted to alienate any of the occultists who'd remained sympathetic to his cause, he was off to a great start.

Get down on your knees remember how to pray—

"Good heavens," Claire said, rising up on tiptoe to shout in Colin's ear. "What's he got up as?"

Just follow orders that old-fashioned way—

Colin didn't wonder how she'd found him; Claire had that knack.

"Something he has no right to be, ever again," Colin answered, raising his voice as well to be heard over the band.

And find yourself killing for killers—

Narzain Kui hammered into the end of the song; by now most of the audience was singing—or chanting—along with them.

> *Killing for killers—It doesn't stop there*
> *Killing for killers—The war's everywhere*
> *Killing for killers—Just do what is right*
> *Or find yourself killing for killers—*

The audience was cheering by the time the song was over; Thorne hugged the lead guitarist and the cheers got louder. The band remained on stage as Thorne waited for things to quiet down a little. When they did, he lifted his microphone from its stand and whipped the cord back and forth.

"Hey-y-y-y, Epopts and Illuminati," Thorne crooned. "Who wants to change the world?"

"*We do!*" the audience screamed back. The drummer hit a lick and there was a feedback squeal.

Thorne took the energy from the music and built on it, goading the crowd into a frenzy that Colin was afraid would turn them into a mindless mob. Was that what he had in mind—was that the wellspring his rituals came from?

In the cheering all around him, Colin now heard the howling of the Beast.

"Look, Colin—isn't that Simon Anstey?" Claire said suddenly, a worried tone in her voice.

Colin tore his gaze away from the stage and saw Simon. He felt a faint pang of relief—whatever Simon was here for, it would abort the monstrous birth that Thorne was engineering.

Simon was dressed in a dark business suit, and looked even more out of place here than Colin or Claire. He was pushing his way determinedly through the crowd toward Thorne, and there were two U.S. marshals with him.

Thorne had seen him, too. He lowered his arms reluctantly and tried to take control of the situation.

"Well, look who's here. It's Simon Anstey, well-known concert pianist and arbiter of truth. Come down here to give all us hippies music lessons, Simon?"

The keyed-up crowd laughed, parting reluctantly for Simon as he moved toward the stage. Colin and Claire were shoved backward by those making room for him; both of them could feel the incipient violence in the bodies around them.

"This is one time that you aren't going to get what you want by ignoring everyone else, Blackburn! You and your scraggly hippies can just pack up and get out of here," Simon shouted.

"I've got a permit," Thorne drawled in his most irritating voice. He mugged for the crowd, and they laughed.

Simon sneered. "Well, *I've* got a restraining order. You're a public nuisance, Blackburn, and I'm shutting you down."

Simon stood in front of the stage, waving the document. He threw it at Thorne's feet. Thorne looked stunned, as if he had not expected this.

"What do you want, Anstey?" he finally asked.

"I've come to expose you for what you are, Blackburn—a fraud! A clown! An insult to the very teachings you claim to impart!" Simon shouted.

"Well, then—by all means do it!" Thorne said into the microphone in front of him. His amplified voice boomed out from the speakers at the sides of the stage. He stepped back, tossing the microphone down to Simon.

Simon had the sense—or showmanship equal to Thorne's—not to use it; that would have brought the whole affair down to the level of two stand-up comics trying to upstage one another. He tossed the microphone back onto the stage; it hit with a thump and an electronic howl. One of the members of the band jumped to yank the microphone jack out of the amplifier.

"Give up and go home, Blackburn—nobody wants you here," Simon said. "Personally, I'm sick and tired of you parading your ego and your ridiculous claims to power! Aren't there enough frauds in the world preying on the helpless? The sad part is that anyone believes you and your con game," Simon said.

Thorne turned away from Simon to face out over the audience.

"If you want a con game, Anstey, for my money it's this Path that you— and Colin MacLaren—" Thorne added, looking directly toward where Colin stood in the crowd "—and all the rest of you black-robed white light monks keep trying to push on anyone looking for answers. Your Path is a con game, Simon *Magus,* a delusion put up by generations of old men in white night-gowns to keep their adherents from trying to make a difference in the real world! And it ends here!" Thorne shouted, flinging his arms out in a theatrical gesture.

There were some shouts of agreement, but most of the audience stirred uneasily. Without the microphone, all of them couldn't hear what was happening on stage, and the presence of the marshals made them uneasy. Colin could feel the violence in the air like the promise of a storm.

"Well, the only difference your followers make is to your bank account, Blackburn!" Simon snarled. "They give you everything they have, and what do they get for it? Nothing!"

"At least they get the chance to judge for themselves," Thorne shot back. "All you want is for them to follow you instead of me— isn't the concert hall applause enough anymore?"

"All right, Mr. Blackburn. You're going to have to come along with us," one of the marshals said, stepping up onto the stage.

Colin could see by the expression on Simon's face that he hadn't meant things to go quite this far. "I've got to stop this before Thorne starts a riot," Colin said to Claire. He began pushing his way closer toward the stage.

The crowd, roused to the edge of hysteria by Thorne only moments before, was becoming increasingly agitated by the disruption, and there were growing catcalls directed at Simon.

"Judge for themselves? That's rich!" Simon shouted. "What can they judge when all you're giving them is lies and tricks and empty promises? *I'm* not the one telling people that I'm the son of a god!"

"Looks like you think actions speak louder than words," Thorne cooed mockingly into another microphone.

Laughter.

Thorne backed away from the marshal who was climbing up on the stage. By now Colin had reached the edge of the platform, and was working his way around to the steps.

"Yes," said Simon doggedly from below, "I do. If you've got the godlike powers you claim, Blackburn, why not make the restraining order go away? Turn me into a frog? Something?"

The day that had been so bright only moments ago was dimming, clouding over as clouds came boiling in off the San Gabriel Mountains to shroud the day in dim light that looked as if it had been filtered through soft cheesecloth.

"I try never to improve on Nature's handiwork," Thorne snapped. The marshal reached him, and there was a brief struggle as Thorne tried to shake him off. The man pulled out his cuffs. Colin climbed up on stage and headed toward him. In another moment the crowd would rush the stage, and people would get hurt.

"There's no need for this," Colin said quietly to the officer. "If this is a legitimate restraining order, I'm sure Mr. Blackburn will comply."

"*Et tu,* Colin?" Thorne said, staring at Colin over the marshal's shoulder. The marshal stepped back without cuffing Thorne.

"Don't start trying to overawe me; I've had a classical education, too," Colin said sharply. He was more irritated—and yes, frightened—than he'd thought by Thorne's parading of the robes he no longer had the right to wear and his easy appropriation of the energy of the mob.

"Simon, what did you think you were accomplishing here?" Colin demanded, turning away and looking down at Simon Anstey.

"I'm tired of watching this *mountebank* ruin everything Alison and I are working for!" Simon shot back, climbing up on the stage as well. "How can parapsychology be accepted as a legitimate field of research while he's turning the occult into a sideshow?"

"It *is* a sideshow," Thorne said quietly, stepping away from the marshal. "That's the point."

"No," said Colin, abruptly goaded beyond endurance. "It's what each of us makes it. You could have made it into something good, something fine—you could have been the gateway through which new seekers could approach the Ancient Mysteries—"

"Ancient boondoggle!" Thorne shouted, lunging toward the front of the stage again. His horned crown was wildly askew, and Thorne wrenched it off and flung it out into the crowd. "Give in—give up—*submit*—Forget it! Mankind has the power of the gods, and it's time it was used to do more than spin prayer wheels—"

"Either shut your face and pack it in or you're going out of here in cuffs. Mike! Get these people moving!" the marshal on stage barked.

Thorne shrugged, seeming to surrender all at once. He started to pull off his robes. Thorne looked at Colin.

"You attack everything I believe in," Colin said, answering the unspoken plea, "and then expect to trade on the very qualities you despise the moment you get into trouble. I can't help you this time, Thorne."

"Go on, then," Thorne said. "Go on back to your precious, safe, tame, white light. Only you're wrong about it being a Path—it's a dead end. Come on, boys and girls," Thorne called to the audience, holding out his hands for their attention. "Today the pigs win—tomorrow we win. Let's all go quietly; they're scared enough of us as it is."

It was only later that Colin realized why Claire's Gift had sent her to the festival that day. She had not come for Thorne Blackburn.

She'd come for him.

JUNE 1967

THORNE AND COLIN SAW VERY LITTLE OF EACH OTHER AFTER THAT DAY. IT was as if Thorne had given up on Colin and decided he was no longer worth his time—and in practical terms, their paths had diverged to the point that Colin could no longer overlook the things Thorne was advocating.

A few weeks after the fight in the park, Simon got at least part of his wish. Thorne left on the Universal Mystery Tour—a six-week extravaganza of peace, rock and roll, and magick—both stage illusionism and the truer sort. After that, Thorne was truly a national celebrity, as that time understood the word—and so, being Thorne, he decided to disappear almost completely from public life. He'd managed—somehow—to amass a sizeable personal fortune, and used part of it to purchase an estate in upstate New York called Shadow's Gate.

After that June day in the park, I never saw Thorne Blackburn alive again. But before I received word of his death, I was to experience a far more personal bereavement. . . .

EIGHT

BERKELEY, MONDAY, SEPTEMBER 16, 1968

He is secure, and now can never mourn
A heart grown cold, a head grown grey in vain.
—PERCY BYSSHE SHELLEY

1968 WAS A YEAR DEFINED BY VIOLENCE AND DEATH. BEFORE IT WAS OVER, two assassinations had forever changed the tone of American political life: Martin Luther King, Jr. and Senator Robert F. Kennedy. The two men were killed barely eight weeks apart, and in the wake of the second murder, the riots at the Democratic National Convention in Chicago took on a surreal, apocalyptic importance: seen by the Right as an extension of the animal savagery that had coopted the political process, and by the Left as a confirmation of the view that America had become a brutal police state.

The trial of the Chicago Seven that followed became a media circus; a carnival sideshow where Image cast out Truth and Justice was not blind, but mad. . . .

They'd bought the little stucco bungalow four years ago, when Peter had been promoted. They'd been so happy the day they'd finally moved in—a real home at last. Sometimes it seemed to Claire that she could still feel that joy, as if it had been recorded by the very bones of the house and echoed, like old music, through its rooms.

She'd been determined to make their home everything her own had never been; sometimes Peter laughed at her for the fierceness of that determination, but his mother never did. Elisabeth Moffat understood her daughter-in-law with that wordless communion that makes two strangers heartfelt friends in the space of an instant. She had made a place for Claire in her heart and her family with a simple grace that Claire often felt was the single greatest miracle she had ever been gifted with. Under her mother-in-law's tutelage, the little tract house had become a home. For two, and, perhaps, someday—for three.

Claire knew that Peter wanted a family; she had held back from the idea, afraid that she would only recreate her own childhood hell for a child of her own. It had been a long time before that fear had quieted, and Claire knew that it would never really go away. But with Peter and his mother to help her, she had slowly become confident—if not of her success at motherhood, at least that her mistakes would not be intolerable ones. That spring, she had begun to try to become pregnant.

The dreams had started then.

At first she thought they were simple anxiety. In the wake of his break with Thorne, Colin had gone back to the East Coast. A friend had offered him a position with Selkie Press, a publishing house that specialized in parapsychological and occult subjects, and Colin, increasingly at odds with the Rhodes Group's policy of conciliation and concealment, had accepted the offer.

But while Claire knew that she would miss Colin—as a friend, and one who understood her faults far better than Peter ever would—she did not think that she was so dependent upon him as to be sunk in terror by his absence. He was, after all, only a phone call away.

Yet she still dreamed.

They began as simply hints—a disquiet spilling over into her other dreams. Later came the images—of herself, running through fog, crying out for the return of . . . something. There was loss in those dreams, loss deep and wounding.

She knew what it was.

Each time the knowledge surfaced, Claire rejected it. It was not true. It was some sick, inverted wish fulfillment. Or just this once, her Gift was playing her false, tainted because *she* was tainted by the unearned guilt of her childhood upbringing.

In her heart she knew that none of these explanations was true. The dream continued, month after month, until half a year had passed. She told no one, but in her mind the unheld conversations echoed. *Claire, why didn't you tell me?* Colin's voice.

And her own, in answer: *How could I? If I tell no one, I can still hope that I'm wrong. And if I tell you, I have to tell him, or it becomes a secret that I'm keeping from him, and I cannot bear that. Who can I tell, without telling him?*

No one.

When she was still very young, Claire had become an expert at dissembling; hiding the unwanted truths far away and presenting an unruffled, cream-smooth face to the world. Now she resurrected all the skills she thought she no longer had need of, using them to bury the truth deep and pretend that everything was normal. And she managed to fool even herself, except when she dreamed.

When her dreams woke her, Claire would slip quietly from their conjugal bed, huddling in the kitchen over a cup of tea and trying to imagine how to keep Peter safe. She could not warn him. There was nothing to warn him *about*—only her frightening sense of loss. She had known the work he did before they married. She had always known that it was dangerous, and that he loved it too much to easily give it up. Telling him that she was afraid would not armor him against the danger. It would only be a useless cruelty.

And so Claire kept her own counsel, her mind partitioned into shapeless dread and willful ignorance.

Until one day she could be ignorant no longer.

It was September 16, a Monday. Peter was working the evening shift, three to eight. Claire was home, fixing dinner, to the sounds of *Rowan and Martin's Laugh-In* in the background.

For the last several years she had listed with a temporary agency—there was always work for someone with an RN degree who was willing to fill in here and there—but once the meaning of her premonitory dreams had become unmistakable, she'd worked less and less. She'd begun dreading having to leave the house for any reason, as if the act of staying home could provide some sort of bulwark against what was to come.

Most of the time she kept busy, but lately, each night around seven o'clock, she began to watch the time. And when eight o'clock had come and gone she breathed a prayer of thanksgiving, even though Peter would not be home for another hour. At eight o'clock his shift was over, and Peter was safe for another day. She could go on with her life then, and by the time he arrived home she could greet him as if nothing were amiss.

It was 8:45. She was in the kitchen, cooking dinner. She'd shifted her schedule to match his, so they ate at quite a continental hour. There was a ham baking in the oven; Peter's favorite. It would be years to come before she could smell ham without feeling nauseated.

She was filling a saucepan at the tap and turned to place it on the stove. And then, in an instant, her world fell away.

She was lying on the ground, in the dark. Above her, she could see the bright lights of the convenience store a few blocks from their house.

There was no pain. Only cold, and wet, and a vast calm, knowing that death had come, and that now everything stopped.

"Peter!"

The sound the saucepan made as it hit the linoleum brought Claire back to the world. There was water all over the floor, but she did not stop to mop it up. She grabbed her car keys and ran for the door.

She knew where he was. She would have known even if the ties that bound them hadn't drawn her to the little shopping plaza less than fifteen minutes from their house. She had no memory of the drive, only of the moment when she turned the corner and saw the two patrol cars parked in the lot.

"Hey, lady —oh, Jesus, it's Claire—honey, don't—" The words went by her meaninglessly; she tore at the hands restraining her until they let her go.

They'd covered Peter with a blanket out of the back of one of the patrol units; impatient, she pulled it away, kneeling beside him. The ground was slippery and wet, and just then she didn't understand why. Why had they covered his face?

"Peter?" Claire whispered. She reached for his hand, her fingers closing over the pulse-point in an automatic nurse's gesture. But she was too late. The hand was cold and lifeless in hers. He was already gone.

It isn't fair. It isn't fair—he wasn't even on duty. How could somebody shoot him when he wasn't even on duty. . . .

Nothing mattered then. Later they would tell her the whole story—a hold-up, a sawed-off shotgun. They would assure her that Peter's death had been merciful, painless, and quick. They would tell her that her husband died a hero. None of that mattered now. All that mattered was the realization that with her husband dead, she must be the one to go and tell his mother.

One of the uniformed officers drove Claire to Mrs. Moffat's house. He'd wanted to drive her home, but Claire had been firm. She felt an urgent need to tell this news at once, as if by waiting it could somehow become worse. She knew that her calmness was an illusion wrought by paralyzing emotional trauma. She knew that it might be kinder to wait, to break the news to Mrs. Moffat in daylight. But in some part of Claire's heart the irrational conviction survived that somehow Peter's death was not real, that Elisabeth Moffat would have some secret magic that could make the bad news go away.

The car pulled into the driveway.

"Claire, why don't you wait here and—"

"Don't be silly, Steve," Claire said. Her words had the blunt cruelty of shock. "It won't get any easier for me if I don't hear the words. I already know that Peter's dead."

She yanked open the door and swung out of the car.

Peter's mother knew before Claire said a word. What member of a policeman's family would think anything else, when a uniformed officer appeared at her door in the middle of the night?

Only later did it occur to Claire that she must have looked like the Angel of Death herself. She'd wiped off the worst of the blood on the drive over, but her legs were still smeared with it.

Steve said everything that was proper, but Claire could tell that he was grateful when his partner pulled up at the curb a few minutes later and he could leave. She knew that he could imagine too vividly that it could have been him lying in that parking lot. It could have been any of them.

"I'm so sorry. Oh, Claire, my dear girl, I'd hoped this would never happen to you," Elisabeth Moffat said.

Why are you so worried? Claire wondered, faintly puzzled. *Peter is dead. There's nothing more we can do. There's nothing to worry about.* And deep inside, she felt a sense of relief that the waiting was over, and pride that Peter had never known what it was she waited for, all those long weeks.

"It's all right," she said meaninglessly. Unheeded tears rose up in her eyes; for a moment she could not understand why her vision had blurred, then she blinked them away. "Why don't I make us a nice cup of tea? And then I suppose we need to think about what to do."

Not that it mattered. Not that anything mattered, or would matter again for a very long time.

The funeral was the following Monday, and in defiance of everything seemly, it was a beautiful day. The sky was cloudlessly blue, the sunlight was golden, and the air was summer-hot. The gravestones and tall monuments were brilliantly white.

The department turned out in force for the funeral, of course. Peter had been well liked. The minister from their church conducted the service; there was no need for Peter to be laid to rest by the words of strangers who had never known him.

Colin had come, thank God. Claire did not think she could have stood it otherwise. Elisabeth was steadfast, calm and composed, but now she had buried both her men, husband and son, and the strain of it etched stark lines into her face. Elisabeth Moffat had always seemed an incorruptible rock, but she seemed to have aged twenty years overnight, and Claire feared for her well-being. For herself, she feared nothing. She did not think she would feel anything, ever again. That part of her had died with Peter, killed as surely as a summer rose withered in an early frost.

Some part of her knew that she would live past this moment, that time, if nothing else, would numb the insistent pain of this amputation and teach her to find life good again. And so she would—even in the shock of her first grief Claire knew that—but the reckless merry part of her that Peter had opened to joy was gone forever.

"Claire."

The graveside service was over, and everyone else was gone, but Claire couldn't bring herself to leave. Terrible as this moment was, she clung to it, because when it was over, her life without Peter would begin.

"Colin. A fine hello this is," she managed to say.

"I wasn't expecting dancing girls, all things considered. I know it sounds trite and superficial, but if there's anything I can do—"

"Not unless you can resurrect the dead," Claire shot back before she could stop herself. "I'm sorry, Colin. That was unworthy. This isn't your fault. It isn't anybody's fault—except that little bastard with the shotgun, and they've picked him up." She rubbed her eyes tiredly. They were dry, but only because she had cried so much already. "So there's a happy ending after all, isn't there?"

"I don't think anyone can claim to be that detached," Colin said. He put an arm around her shoulder. "And anyone who tries to tell you that this is all for the best is a coward and a sadist."

Claire rubbed at her eyes. "I suppose I ought to cry, but I'm just too tired. Everything seems so pointless, somehow. I know its just shock, but—" She shook her head.

They turned and began to walk back to the car.

" 'But' nothing," Colin said firmly. "You've suffered a grave loss. Take the time to grieve before trying to get on with things. Peter was a good man. We will all miss him."

"But it didn't help, did it, Colin? Being good, or . . . anything. He still died, didn't he? So what's the point? What's the point of doing anything?"

Colin had no answers for her.

NINE

NEW YORK, WEDNESDAY, APRIL 30, 1969

Dark house, by which once more I stand
Here in the long unlovely street,
Doors, where my heart was used to beat
So quickly, waiting for a hand.
—ALFRED, LORD TENNYSON

"THE SUN! COMES THE SUN! BY OAK AND ASH AND THORN, THE SUN! COMES THE sun!"

He was in some kind of temple, but he had never seen its like. Not dedicated to the Light, nor yet tainted by service to the Great Dragon. Not Black, not White—but Grey, grey as mist. . . .

"The sun is coming up from the South!" cried the red-robed woman. "I call thee: Abraxas, Metatron, Uranos—"

The ancient Names echoed through the temple. Twelve great stones set in a ring, and where the thirteenth should have been a great oak, its bark grey with weather and age. The trunk split, and out of it stepped a Horned Man.

There was a woman clothed in the sun; she stepped from the shadow of the red-robed Caller to greet the Lord of the Oak. "Come, the Opener of the Way," she said.

"By Abbadon! Meggido! Typhon! Set!" cried the red-robed woman. "Open now, open now the Way!"

But instead the Serpent raised its head, coiling over the three of them, dragging them down into the Great Darkness as the church bells rang.

And rang . . . and rang. . . .

Ringing . . .

His hand found the cold plastic of the receiver and lifted.

"Colin? Colin, is that you? Please, Colin, are you there?"

The words spilling out of the telephone in the dark were frantic, mixing disorientingly with the dispelling mists of sleep in Colin MacLaren's mind.

"Yes, yes I'm here. Give me a minute."

He sat up, still clutching the receiver, and groped for the switch on his bedside lamp. Outside the window he could hear the hiss of traffic on the rainy streets outside his first floor right apartment. April in New York meant inclement weather, and a proper spring storm was battering at the windows of the old brownstone. The lights shining from the street made each separate droplet on the glass into a tiny crystal prism.

Finally he found the switch and turned on the light. Instantly the room shrank to its daylight contours and he felt more awake.

"Colin—" the voice keened through the open line, and finally he recognized it.

"Caroline? Caro, is that you?"

Caroline Jourdemayne was Katherine's twin sister; she worked as a librarian in a little town called Rock Creek far up the Hudson in Amsterdam County.

"Yes! Oh, Colin—I didn't know who else to call, and— There are police everywhere, and I don't know what to do. There's been a terrible accident—"

"Calm down, Caroline. Of course I'll come. I'll be there as soon as I can. Where are you?"

"Thorne's place. Shadow's Gate. It's in Shadowkill—you just take the Taconic north to Dutchess, then take 43 to 13. Please hurry, Colin!" He could hear the tears in Caroline's voice, the terror that she tried so hard to hold at bay.

"Caroline, what's—" Colin started to say. But the line went dead.

A peal of thunder echoed through the sky, and the lights flickered; reason enough for the connection to have been broken without him needing to think up any darker explanation for it. Fortunately the service was still fine at this end. Colin sighed, rubbing the sleep out of his eyes. He pulled the phone over to him and dialed another number. He glanced at his watch. *Three* A.M. Colin groaned quietly, listening to the distant ringing through the receiver. A hellish hour at which to have to awaken someone.

But his fears were groundless; Claire wasn't home. When her mother-in-law's death—of a stroke—had come only weeks after Peter's murder, Claire had wanted a complete change of scene, and had accepted Colin's suggestion of a move to New York. He'd been worried, when the double tragedy had struck, that Claire would not survive it. Her initial flight from everything she'd known, the violent rejection of her old life and all connected with it, could have been the start of a downward spiral, but Claire had pulled herself together and painstakingly rebuilt her life again. Never, even in her darkest moments, had she rejected the promptings of the Gift that infallibly led her to the side of people in trouble.

Colin sighed again, then got up to dress. He would have liked to have had her with him, but she was working as a private duty nurse these days and spent many nights away from home. He'd phone her again from the road if opportunity presented itself, otherwise, he could phone from Shadow's Gate.

* * *

Cornby's Garage, where Colin kept his car, was just around the corner, and the walk finished the job of waking him. By three-thirty he was on the road, heading north.

He'd never been to Shadow's Gate, Thorne's magickal Elysium, before. Their friendship had cooled a great deal since that day in the park, but the terms on which he and Thorne had separated hardly mattered. Caroline had appealed to him for help, and she would have all the help Colin had to give.

He called again from the road. The phone lines were still down at the house, and Claire still wasn't home—and even if she had been, it was a bit over two hours from Manhattan to Shadowkill. By the time she could get here, the crisis would be over, so Colin hoped. He dreaded to think what he'd find by the time he reached Shadow's Gate.

All that he knew of Thorne's current activities came from seeing Thorne on *Johnny Carson* last fall along with millions of other Americans. Thorne had been wearing a silver headband set with moonstones, a pair of python-skin jeans, and sunglasses which he'd refused to remove all the time he was on. He'd talked about purchasing a magickal retreat, where he and his followers hoped to engage in cutting-edge research into the nature of human reality.

Whatever exploitation Thorne was engaged in these days, it seemed to be doing well for him. He'd looked sleek and prosperous, a far cry from the scruffy and far-out idealist that Colin had met in what now seemed like another lifetime.

The sky was lightening with the first rays of dawn by the time he reached Shadow's Gate, and the storm had blown over, leaving the sky scrubbed and clear, filled with the last faint stars of morning. The gatehouse of Thorne's estate was already barricaded by state and local police, two cars drawn across the entrance, lights flashing.

"Sorry, mister. Nobody's allowed in." The state trooper, faceless beneath his broad-brimmed hat, leaned into Colin's car.

"My name is Colin MacLaren," Colin said. "I'm a friend of the family." Fortunately, Colin had continued to work with the police when he'd relocated to New York; he pulled out Martin Becket's card and offered it to the patrolman.

"You can check my bona fides with Martin, if you like. His home number's on the back." Detective Lieutenant Becket headed up NYPD's informal Occult Crimes Unit, and he and Colin had worked together more than once.

"May I take this for a moment, sir?" The statie's manner was a little more respectful. He walked away, and returned with a quiet man in a grey suit and hat who might as well have been wearing the letters "FBI" embroidered on his suit pocket. Colin's heart sank. What kind of trouble had Thorne gotten himself into now? Drugs?

But Caroline had known Thorne from his San Francisco days, and a simple drug bust would not have prompted such a frantic phone call.

"Dr. MacLaren," he said. "I'm Special Agent Cheshire. What can we do for you today?"

"You can let me in," Colin said, beginning to become irritated. He plucked Becket's card from Cheshire's fingers. "A friend of mine called and asked me to come here. She said there was some trouble, and it looks as if there is. What's going on?"

"And who would that be?" Cheshire asked, ignoring Colin's questions.

Colin debated telling him. The man had no right to question him—or, at least, Colin had a right not to answer—but stonewalling Special Agent Cheshire wouldn't get Colin into Shadow's Gate.

"A friend of mine, Caroline Jourdemayne. She called me about two hours ago, but we were cut off by the storm. Is she all right, Mr. Cheshire? She seemed to be pretty upset."

The agent smiled thinly. "An officer will drive you up to the house, Dr. MacLaren."

Colin didn't bother to argue. He got out of his car and climbed into the back of a Dutchess County Sheriff's car. The car pulled away smoothly, passing through the mock-*Neuschwanstein* ornament of the gatehouse, and heading up the long drive. Shadow's Gate was set at the back of a hundred-acre parcel, and it was almost a mile to the house.

"It's good to see you here, Mr. MacLaren," the sheriff's deputy said. "You won't remember me, but my name is Lockridge. Frank Lockridge. I was at an interdepartmental inservice about Satanism and cult crimes that you spoke at down in the city about eight months ago? It's been a real help—especially since *he* moved in up here. I don't know who whistled you up this time, Professor, but I'm damn glad to have you here."

"Could you tell me what's going on here? If the FBI doesn't mind, of course," Colin said.

Colin could see Frank Lockridge grimace in the rearview mirror. "Once the Fibbies get into a case, that's usually the end of it. They think this son-of-a-bitch Blackburn was mixed up with the Weathermen, and that's all they care about."

"'Was'?" Colin seized upon the word.

"Definitely past tense, for my money. They've been waiting for dawn to search the woods, but they aren't going to find him. He's run far and fast, and I can't say I blame him. That, or he's dead."

Thorne dead. No wonder Caroline had sounded so upset on the phone, if that were true. Colin knew that Caroline Jourdemayne had loved Thorne nearly as much as her twin did, but had been unwilling to follow him as blindly. His death would devastate her.

Colin pieced the story together from his own knowledge as well as from what Frank Lockridge told him on the long drive up to the house.

The Dutchess County Sheriff's department had been first on the scene, a little after two o'clock this morning. There'd been a call for an ambulance, which had taken away one Katherine Jourdemayne, pronounced dead on the scene by the medical examiner, autopsy pending. According to Deputy Lockridge, the whole house had reeked of incense, pot, and worse, and there was evidence that a Satanic ritual had been in progress at the time the girl died.

The authorities very much wished to question Katherine's lover, Thorne Blackburn, but no one could find him. Meanwhile, everyone in the house was being held as material witnesses to the crime, if crime it truly was.

Colin wanted to ask Lockridge a question, but just then the car came over the rise, and he caught his first glimpse of Shadow's Gate.

The sprawling Victorian, made of red brick and the pale local stone, had much the same look of a fairy-tale castle as the gatehouse had. Three cone-roofed towers set with long narrow windows rose up from the corners of the rambling structure, and clustered around the front door were more emergency vehicles. The surrounding grounds were covered with storm detritus, and Colin could see the white scars of downed trees all across the grounds and into the forest beyond. The echoes of some force greater than the storm still echoed over these hills.

"And none of those kids'll give us the time of day. They keep yammering on about First Amendment rights—dammit, this is a murder investigation!"

Katherine dead, Thorne missing. And the police willing to believe it's murder because of Thorne's reputation, and the FBI involved because of . . . the Weather Underground? That's ridiculous!

"How did Miss Jourdemayne die?" Colin asked, voice even. Thorne had never used any safeguards in his rituals, and now the retribution had come.

"Drugs, probably. That's what the ME said." Lockridge shrugged. "Stark naked, and not a mark on her that I saw. *Hippies.*"

The contempt in his voice was indictment enough.

The survivors of Thorne's band—already that seemed the right word to use—had been gathered in the dining room. Other than the wan light of dawn streaming in through the windows, the only illumination in the room was provided by candles: the power was out at Shadow's Gate.

He saw Jonathan Ashwell, still in his ritual robes, stroking the back of a weeping woman. Since the last time Colin had seen him, Jonathan had grown a beard; it was dark and bushy, and with his long hair, it gave him a passing resemblance to the mad monk Rasputin. About half of those gathered in the room were still wearing their ritual robes, and of the rest, some were in pajamas, some in street clothes. Caroline, wearing a sensible pantsuit and aviator-frame glasses, looked as if she had come from another world. Several of the women were holding crying babies, and young children clung to the adults' legs and whimpered. Most of the women, and some of the men, were crying, sobbing unashamedly as children. How could anyone think that Thorne Blackburn was a fugitive, when here in this room was all the evidence of his death that anyone should ever need?

With the grieving survivors surrounding him, the anguish of the tragedy was overpowering. Sternly, Colin forced himself to concentrate, to shut out the emotions that filled this room, the sea of agony through which the officers walked as if it didn't exist.

"Colin!" Caroline said, coming over to him. There were dark circles under her eyes, and she'd been crying for so long her eyes were swollen and dry. She threw her arms around him—a young woman who had suffered the most intimate of all bereavements, the loss of a twin, desperate for comfort.

For a moment he simply held her as her body shook with unsheddable tears. Then she pushed herself away.

"Caroline?" Colin asked. He needed to know what had happened here. She shook her head, as if no matter what he said, she had no answer.

"Caroline, where's Thorne?"

Her eyes focused on him then, fathomless wells of pain. "I don't know. They were all in the temple. I helped both of them get ready for the ritual. And . . . Katherine's dead," she finished, as if it were a new discovery.

"I know," Colin said gently.

Colin could feel the seething currents of violence that eddied beneath every action in this room. Thorne had not been well liked in Shadowkill, and he'd never done well with authority at the best of times. With a pang of memory, Colin thought back to that day in Golden Gate Park. Two years ago. A lifetime for Thorne Blackburn.

The deputy standing in the doorway glared at Colin. "And who the hell let you in here?"

"MacLaren's our big city voodoo expert," Deputy Lockridge said mildly, defusing the scene as much as he could. "Let me see if I can find Detective Hodge and see what he wants done, Mr. MacLaren." He walked away quickly.

Colin spared a useless wish that Claire were here. Somehow she always had the ability to calm tense situations just by her presence. He could use a little of that calm now.

"It's no use," Caroline said quietly, in a voice made rough by weeping. "They hate him too much. He made fools of them and now they're going to destroy everything he ever worked for. It's finished. The New Aeon is dead."

A redhead in a red robe, her heavy makeup running down her face in black tear-streaks, came over and put her arms around Caroline.

"Now hush, lovey. Kate's gone on to a better place, you know that. And Thorne . . . don't you grieve for him. He's free. No one can hurt him now." Colin recognized Irene Avalon from Thorne's San Francisco days. She looked at Colin beseechingly. "Make them let us go, Colin," she begged. "We haven't done anything. And there are children here." She pointed at the corner where a black-haired toddler slept on a folded blanket, clutching a battered teddy bear to her cheek.

"Get your hands off me!"

Colin turned toward the familiar voice in time to see a uniformed officer shove Jonathan Ashwell back into a chair. Colin could just imagine what he looked like to the officer, between the long hair and the ritual robes. *Just another wild-eyed loonie, right, boys?* Colin thought derisively.

"Just cool your heels, sonny-boy," a uniformed officer said.

"You Nazi Neanderthal," Jonathan snarled. "You've got no right to hold us here. You're tearing the house apart—where's your warrant? '*Miranda*' was ratified three years ago!"

"I'll see what I can do," Colin said to Irene. He walked over to Jonathan.

"Suspicion of a crime in progress, longhair," the officer snarled at Jonathan. "And I'll '*Miranda*' your ass, you little—"

"Back off, pig, or I'll have you up on charges faster than you can say 'ACLU,' " Jonathan snarled. The mingled anger and grief with which he regarded the policeman did nothing to make him look any saner.

"Jonathan," Colin said quietly. "Can you tell me what's going on?"

"Hey," the uniformed officer said. "The lieutenant doesn't want these guys talking to each other."

"Arrest me, pork rind," Jonathan sneered.

The officer started for him; Colin hastily interposed his body between them.

"Jonathan, shut up. Officer, I'm Colin MacLaren; I'm a consultant to the New York City Police Department. This young man is one of my former students. I'd appreciate the opportunity to talk to him."

Colin had told no lies, but he had subtly managed to convey the notion that he had been called in by the police. He saw the uniformed officer relax and step back.

"Sure. Take him on into the kitchen. There's coffee there."

Colin took Jonathan's arm and led him through into the house's old Victorian kitchen. It had obviously become a base of operations for the police; there were several cardboard boxes on the kitchen table, filled with Styrofoam coffee cups bearing the logo of a deli down in Shadowkill. Colin sorted through until he found two that were full, and handed one to Jonathan.

"Now. Quickly, as we may not have much time. Tell me what happened here, Jonathan. I have to know before I can help."

"Thorne's gone."

The last time Colin had seen such a look of blank bewilderment in someone's eyes it had been in the eyes of the refugees in the DP camps after the War. He pushed the memory aside.

"Gone where, Jonathan?"

"Gone." Jonathan shrugged helplessly, much as Caroline had done. "Kate's dead," he added, as if this were news.

"Tell me what happened," Colin said.

He was unprepared for Jonathan's answer.

"No."

Colin stared at him in disbelief.

"I can't. You aren't Sealed to the Circle. I can't tell you what happened. You're not one of us."

"For God's sake, Jonathan," Colin burst out, before he could stop himself, "this is serious!" *And I would have given the same answer, if our positions had been reversed.*

"So is the Work," Jonathan said wearily. With a gallant effort, he pulled himself together. "Do you think I don't know what's going to happen when we tell the police that? If they're going to hold us as material witnesses, we don't have any Miranda rights—not to an attorney, and not to a trial. It isn't going to be pretty, but we haven't got any choice. But I'll tell you what I can.

Maybe Caroline can tell you more—she isn't one of us. Not Sealed to the Circle, at least, but I know she believes in what Thorne's doing. Anyway, we were doing a working tonight, during a big storm. Something . . . went wrong."

Colin waited, but Jonathan was obviously finished talking.

"That's all you have to say?" Colin said, striving to keep the incredulousness out of his voice. "'Something went wrong'?"

"Kate's dead," Jonathan repeated, as if the thought kept suddenly occurring to him. "And Thorne's . . ." There was an almost unbearable hesitation. "Thorne's gone."

"Gone where?" Run away? Colin couldn't believe it. He could believe that Thorne might have killed Katherine Jourdemayne with malice aforethought sooner than that he had fled the scene of even the worst mishap in fear. Thorne was utterly fearless, and fiercely loyal. He would never abandon his followers. Never.

"Gone." Incredibly, there was a note of amusement in Jonathan's voice. "Just . . . gone, Colin, and no one will ever find him." His voice broke, and he struggled for self-control. "And Kate's dead. Oh, God, we were trying a new mix; Thorne said it would keep her 'there.' But she must have taken too much. He was always on her about that. . . ."

He put his hand over his face, and his next words were muffled. "And now the cops're looking for a scapegoat. And it's going to be us. And it doesn't matter. Because he's gone."

"Gone." That was the word all of them had used, Irene and Caroline, and Jonathan. *Gone.* Not dead, not fleeing. Just . . . gone.

"Where did he go?" Colin demanded. "Jonathan, if you know, you have to tell me. Thorne needs a lawyer—protection—"

Protection from the police. Colin could not now even remember the moment in which that last innocence had died and he'd come to understand that even the guiltless were punished in this brave new America.

This time Jonathan laughed. "Oh, Colin, you don't get it, do you? *Thorne never left the Temple.*" He slumped into one of the kitchen chairs and leaned on the table, resting his head on his folded arms. "They will never find him."

The sentence had the finality of an epitaph. And despite Colin's pleas, Jonathan would say nothing else.

It was another hour before Colin managed to see Lieutenant Hodge. He'd gained permission for a couple of the women to go upstairs—under police escort—and bring down things for the infants and children, and Caroline and Irene had moved into the kitchen, producing fresh coffee and a scratch breakfast for everyone. Caroline Jourdemayne was thoroughly respectable—a spinster librarian—and she used that respectability like a weapon, forcing the officers to acknowledge her.

But the situation was still tense. No one had been arrested yet, but that could happen at any moment. And Pilgrim and two other children were missing, no one knew where.

"Dr. MacLaren. I'm Lieutenant Hodge."

Lieutenant Hodge was a few years younger than Colin, but already comfortably entrenched in middle age. He was fair and balding, as so many natives of this area of the country were, and he wore a rumpled trenchcoat over a grey suit.

"Lieutenant," Colin said.

"Deputy Lockridge thinks you're pretty groovy," Hodge said. "But what I want to know is, what are you doing here?"

He was, Colin reflected, getting pretty tired of answering that question.

"I'm a friend of Caroline Jourdemayne," he said again. "She called me and asked me to come. I came. I don't want to intrude on your show, Lieutenant," he added, "but I may be able to help. I have a certain amount of experience in this area, as Lieutenant Becket and a number of other people can tell you."

"Do tell," Lieutenant Hodge rasped, sounding irritable and tired. "And suppose you tell me what your 'experience' tells you."

It was a setup question, since all Colin had seen was the dining room. He hadn't gone into the Temple or even seriously questioned any of the members of Thorne's Circle other than Jonathan.

"Well, first of all," Colin said, "these people aren't Satanists. As far as I know, they aren't worshiping any deity at all, least of all the Christian Devil. Blackburn's Temple—where, I gather, Katherine Jourdemayne died, probably of an accidental drug overdose—is a place where Blackburn and his followers practiced ritual magic, which is, at its simplest, a collection of consciousness-altering techniques derived from experimental psychology. This being the case, I wouldn't expect to see any animal sacrifices or blood offerings—as are typical of *voudoun,* for example. And I'd be very surprised to see any Christian iconography at all, let alone any desecration of the Cross or the Host."

If Hodge didn't stare at him in slack-jawed amazement, he did at least regard Colin with something closer to respect.

"Well, aren't you the little expert? Why don't you and me take a little walk?" Hodge flicked on his flashlight and indicated the door. "Frank, me and the Professor are going for a walk—keep Cheshire off my back, would you?"

Lieutenant Hodge led Colin through the shadowy halls of Shadow's Gate, stopping outside a room that was garishly lit with battery lamps. The double doors had been ripped from the hinges, and even the metal of the hinges was pulled and distorted.

"That wasn't us," Hodge said, noting the direction of Colin's gaze. "The doors were like this when we arrived. They're in here." Hodge stepped through the doorway.

Following him, Colin could see the doors lying just inside the doorway, as though whatever force had ripped them free had let them fall almost immediately.

The room was round, thirty feet in diameter and almost twice that in height. Heaven only knew what this room had originally been. The ceiling had been painted—long before Thorne had owned the place—with the signs of the Zodiac, gold against blue. Below its dome there was a band of stained-glass windows, some of them open. Watermarks stained the walls below. Around the edge of the black-and-white marble floor, gigantic papier-mâché figures of the Egyptian gods alternated with banners in red, black, white, and grey—at least they had, before some force had flung the statues about the room as if they were ninepins and ripped the banners from the walls.

Colin stared around himself, searching for familiar landmarks of the Inner Tradition in vain. There was no Table of Hermes. The edge of the circle had been marked by candles, but whatever force had ripped the doors off their hinges had dashed the candles against the walls as well. Colin could see six from where he stood, and thought there must be more.

This was like no Temple, Light or Dark, that he had ever seen. The four banners were not hung at the cardinal points, nor were they of the cardinal colors, nor were the Four Tools or the Four Elements represented anywhere. These banners had the figures of animals: the red banner had the figure of a white horse, the black banner had a red stag, and so on.

Nor was the double-cube altar present, though there was a low couch in the center of the floor, directly beneath the apex of the dome. The couch was covered with animal furs and pine boughs, now in disarray. Their green scent warred with the heavy bitter scent of frankincense and another odor Colin couldn't quite place.

What had these children been doing? What sort of magick had Thorne been working here—and what had he summoned? Colin felt no sense of presence here in Thorne's Temple, but without Claire he couldn't be sure. If only he had some idea of what they'd been doing. . . .

A cold sense of failure settled heavily over him. He should have made it his business to know. Who was he sent to protect, if not innocents such as these? He'd been distracted by the more obvious threat of the Thule cult reborn. Only now, when it was too late, did he realize that there had been a more subtle, less glamorous battle to fight—one well within his power. But his pride had blinded him, dismissing what Thorne did as childish mummery, without content.

And so it had come to this.

"Dear Lord." Colin sighed. "Forgive me, all of you. . . ." Arrogance was the shadow-self of competence; though the easy mastery he had once possessed had faded with the fires of youth, the hubris had remained.

Never again.

Never again would he turn away from a battle because it was too small, too insignificant, the adversary too harmless. Never again would he set conditions to his participation in the fight. He had thought that Thorne's maverick magick did not matter, and he had been wrong.

Everything mattered. Each moment of inattention brought the Shadow closer. Each tiny compromise, irrelevant in itself, diminished the Light.

Colin set those painful thoughts aside for later contemplation. He was here now. He must do what he could for the living.

There were two swords lying on the floor, as though they had been carelessly tossed aside. He walked over to them, looking down.

"Don't touch those," Hodge said sharply. "We still have to dust for finger-prints."

"Good luck," Colin said absently. The only fingerprints Hodge was likely to find were those of the children here in the house, and that would hardly be of help to him. Neither of these blades had been used to kill.

Both swords were custom-forged ritual blades, their steel etched with runes. The black-hilted sword had silver furnishings and a spherical moon-stone pommel; the white hilt had a gold haft and quillons, with a carnelian cube for the pommel weight. Colin straightened up, looking around.

"Did you find a book?" he asked.

"A book?" Hodge said suspiciously. "What kind of a book?"

"This would be . . ." Colin closed his eyes and thought, trying to put his description in words they'd understand. "A handwritten book, possibly fairly large, but elaborately bound in any case." The design of Thorne's Temple told him that much about the magician's style: flamboyant, as Thorne himself had been. "It would contain a number of diagrams. It might not be in English."

Every magician Colin had ever known kept a magickal workbook, and if he could find Thorne's, it might give him a clue to what had happened here.

"Sid! You seen a book here?" Hodge barked.

One of the crime-scene technicians straightened up; he had been pho-tographing one of the fallen statues. "This whole place is full of books, Leo," he said disgustedly. "They got a whole library full."

"Something handwritten—like a trick book," Hodge said. Sid shrugged.

"We'll look for it, Doc," he said to Colin. "So. These guys weren't Sa-tanists?"

"No," Colin said absently, looking around the room. *I'm not sure what they were, but it wasn't that.* "I can tell you that much right now. Their rituals would have been something more like . . . are you a Mason, by any chance, Lieutenant?"

Hodge stared at him suspiciously, obviously not intending to answer the question.

"At any rate, these rituals certainly wouldn't have involved any unwilling participants, so if you're hoping to close the books on any missing children, Lieutenant, I'm afraid you're going to have to look elsewhere."

"The only missing child I'm interested in is Blackburn," Hodge growled. "And those three kids. All this . . . stuff wouldn't happen to tell you where any of them are, would it, Doc?"

Colin sighed inwardly, giving up on the hope of getting the Lieutenant to call him "Mr." or even "Colin." He thought about what Jonathan and the others had said about Thorne.

He's gone.

He never left the Temple.

"I'm sorry," Colin said. "I haven't the faintest idea. For what it's worth, I hope you find them all, Lieutenant."

"Oh, we'll find them, all right," Hodge said.

Two of the children were located an hour later, when a deputy heard them crying—they'd shut themselves into a cupboard upstairs when the commotion had started, and then couldn't get out. Nine-year-old Pilgrim, Thorne's son by an unknown mother, was found in the woods behind the house after a five-day absence. The area had been searched several times before, without success, so it was believed that Pilgrim had received adult assistance in his disappearance—Pilgrim refused to tell them where he'd been. The boy was turned over to the child protective services to join the rest of the children from Shadow's Gate.

And though there were roadblocks on every main road in Dutchess County for a week, and the entire area was combed with dogs and helicopters, Thorne Blackburn was never found.

Colin did what he could to help the surviving members of Thorne's Circle, goaded by a combination of nebulous guilt and outrage at the way they were treated. The murder/disappearance at Shadow's Gate quickly became a media circus, and like the ancient Roman circuses which it so closely resembled, sacrificial victims were required.

Irene Avalon, Jonathan Ashwell, Deborah Winwood, and the rest of the active members of the Circle of Truth—who were already being held as material witnesses—were formally arrested on May 3 on a smorgasbord of charges, including drug dealing and conspiracy to commit a felony.

It was a witch hunt, pure and simple: the Establishment against the hippies. Without Thorne to protect them, his followers were easy prey. Those who had not been arrested were turned out of the mansion and the site "sealed," but that didn't keep the estate from being overrun by looters and curiosity seekers who stripped it nearly bare before the authorities would consent to the expensive necessity of posting a twenty-four-hour guard over the estate.

"There's so little I can do, Caroline," Colin said sadly.

It was late July, and the fan turning lazily overhead brought the scent of simmering asphalt from the street outside. They were sitting in a booth in a diner outside the county courthouse in Poughkeepsie. Caroline had come to file another in what seemed to be an unending series of petitions; Katherine Jourdemayne was dead, but Katherine's daughter lived, and Caroline was desperately trying to gain custody of her.

Hovering over them both was the grim memory of Deborah Winwood's suicide six weeks before. Despite her lawyer's best efforts, Deborah had been declared an unfit mother, and her baby girl had been taken away from her. The prosecution took her death soon after as a vindication of its judgment, but Colin's heart ached for the despair that had prompted Deborah to take her own life. It seemed a final mockery that the charges against the Shadowkill Twelve had been dropped just a week later.

"At least Johnnie's dad sprang for a good lawyer," Caroline said with a sigh.

General Jonathan Griswold Ashwell II held the same opinion of his son as he did of his country: mine, right or wrong. He'd had the money and clout to get the charges against his son dropped, and the grudging but rock-ribbed sense of fair play to insist that Jonathan's codefendants be treated in the same way that Jonathan had been. Conspiracy charges had been dropped, and bail had finally been set. It was likely that the drug charges would be quietly dropped before the cases came to trial.

"How are you doing?" Colin asked.

Caroline sipped her coffee. "As well as can be expected. That poor baby! She cries and clings to me every time they let me see her—" Her voice roughened and she stopped. When she spoke again, her voice was deliberately cheerful, with a bravery that came near to breaking Colin's heart.

"But thank God for birth certificates. They can't deny that Kate was my sister or that Truth is her daughter. I'm Truth's closest living relative, they have to grant me custody, don't they, no matter what that damned psychiatrist says? I swear to you, if he whines one more time about the advantages of Truth having a home with a father *and* a mother—if I would just give her up for adoption. As if single women weren't out there raising children every day—" She stopped herself again and took another sip of coffee.

"Sorry. Sorry. But you see, don't you, how very careful I have to be? Respectability is all I have going for me. I've sworn myself blue-faced assuring them that I never had anything to do with the commune, or . . . him. And I've got to keep it that way. One reefer, and that's all it would take. I'd never see Truth again. And she's all I have left, of either of them."

"I understand," Colin said quietly. "And as I've told you, if there is anything that Claire or I can do, for either of you . . ."

"You've already done so much, both of you. I'm sure I'd have gone mad without a shoulder to cry on these past few weeks. That just makes what I need to say so much harder."

Colin waited.

"Stay away." Caroline stared at her plate, her sandwich nearly untouched. "And tell the others, the rest of the Circle, if you talk to them. Stay away. I can't afford . . . any appearance of impropriety, if you follow. Not if I'm to get Truth."

Colin smiled to himself grimly. Guilt by association, the terror-tactic of the fascist state. Here in sixties America, alive and well. He was not offended. Caroline was right—even the most respectable parapsychologist was too outré for the connection to do her any good.

He reached across the table and patted her hand. "It's all right, Caroline. I understand, and Claire will, too. Thorne has already been tried in the court of public opinion and found guilty. The only thing you can do is open up as much distance between yourself, and him, and various fellow travelers as you can."

"It's so unfair," Caroline whispered huskily. "They just want to crucify him for telling them they could be free. And he was right. Wasn't he?"

Colin had no answer for her.

JULY 1969

LOOKING BACK UPON IT FROM ACROSS THE BRIDGE OF YEARS, I THINK THAT 1969 was the year that the battle lines were really drawn. Thorne's disappearance in May was, in a weird way, almost a sort of prelude to the Tate–LaBianca murders that August. After that, the Age of Aquarius was firmly intertwined in the public mind with insanity, torture, and murder. . . .

In October, one of Thorne's dreams was realized when a quarter of a million people marched against death in Washington D.C., forming a circle around the Pentagon, chanting and holding hands, attempting to destroy the war machine through pure love. If Thorne had been alive to lead them, I wonder—would it have worked?

In a strange way, his death hardened Colin—I think he always felt personally responsible for what happened at Shadow's Gate, even though the Almighty Himself could not have changed Thorne's mind once he'd decided to do something. But after that terrible night, Colin focused more and more on insulating innocents from the kiss of the Unseen, as if somehow that could redeem those who had died at Shadow's Gate.

All around us through those dark months, events seemed to conspire to hold up a mirror to our dreams and nightmares, showing us how much we had changed in ten short years. Within twenty-four hours of Neil Armstrong's walk upon the moon—something that should have been a glorious landmark in human history—the horror of Chappaquiddick had pushed *Apollo 11* off the front pages. Somehow, unfairly, it seemed worse that a

Kennedy had done this thing, as though somehow the family that we'd pinned our national hopes to had betrayed us—as if they had held the soul of America in their keeping and had failed some trust.

I think it was that sense of betrayal that sent my generation to Woodstock in such passionate numbers, as if now that all hope of regaining Camelot was truly gone, we needed a new dream to sustain us. Woodstock became a myth even while it was happening, and the myth grew in splendor until, the following year, Abbie Hoffman could claim citizenship in the Woodstock Nation.

In some way, Thorne was one of the lucky ones—he did not live to see it. I know that he would have seen then what I only thought of years later—that the apotheosis of a generation was also its end, the moment when the best and the brightest among us abandoned us and themselves, setting the stage for what was to follow.

They'd given their hearts to a dream, you see, and the dream had died. The Woodstock Nation was a dream, and no one could live there. Or if they could, it was, like Neverland, a country of the young, and Time is the one thing that no one can argue with. Time passed for my generation as it had for our parents, driving us out of the Nation. When we discovered that our own hearts had betrayed us, we were abandoned in a world that had no more dreams.

Without a dream to light your way, the world is a very dark place.

TEN

NEW YORK, AUTUMN 1972

O! never say that I was false of heart,
Though absence seem'd my flame to qualify.
—WILLIAM SHAKESPEARE

NEW YORK SEEMED TO GROW DARKER AND DIRTIER EVERY YEAR, COLIN MacLaren thought to himself in resignation. He knew better than to ascribe that dour observation to anything other than the passing of years; he was two years past the half-century mark, the point at which any man must stop and consider his life.

For most of his early life his inner sight had been dazzled by the enormity of the battle in which the Light was engaged, but the passing of years had reminded him that the generalship of that great struggle was not his, nor had it ever truly been. Slowly he had learned to concentrate on those battles within the reach of his hand. It was not his to build the cathedral, nor to tear it down; only to repair what other hands had made, so that the hands to come after could take up such work in their turn.

And when he was not called to that Labor, Colin did his other work—a small, undramatic, and purely mundane striving to enlighten the great mass of people.

Selkie Press was a small, independent publisher of occult books—teetering, like all such presses, on the verge of bankruptcy. It was dedicated to collecting and reprinting important material in the field of magick and the supernatural. Under Colin's editorship, a number of classics of parapsychological research had been brought back into print, as well as more esoteric items of interest to a small yet dedicated readership.

Last year Selkie Press had reprinted Margrave and Anstey's *The Natural History of the Poltergeist,* Taverner's *Ha'ants, Spooks, and Fetchmen,* and a number of extracts from a medieval Spanish grimoire called *La Tesoraria del Oro.*

In Colin's opinion the grimoire was a thoroughly dangerous book, and he saw no reason to make its potential available to the world at large. He'd edited the press's version of *La Tesoraria* rigorously and without a single qualm. There was a middle ground between censorship and utter irresponsibility, and there was certain information which Colin would not freely dispense any more than he would give a baby a loaded gun. Responsible stewardship was the first commandment of his Lodge, and Colin kept the faith.

As Thorne Blackburn had not.

Reflexively, Colin put the old pain from him. Thorne was dead and the world had moved on, much as if what had happened at Shadow's Gate had ended the morning of the Aquarian Age in one fell stroke of night. These days, it seemed impossible that anyone had ever seriously thought that they could reshape the material world with magick.

The hard brilliant light that was such a feature of a New York autumn gilded the brick walls of the buildings across the back courtyard and turned the tiny scrap of sky he could see a deep Egyptian blue. This time of year always made Colin feel restless, as though he were late in setting out upon a journey.

Perhaps he was.

Sighing, Colin set the book he was reading—a biography of a pioneer in the field of parapsychology that Selkie was thinking of reprinting—down on the desk in his tiny back bedroom office. He missed the view from the top floor, but the first floor had been the only apartment vacant when he'd decided to move back East, and Colin had hated the thought of evicting a tenant for nothing more than a whim. And the first-floor apartment had its compensations—there was a fireplace in the living room.

He gave the book a farewell pat and dismissed it from his mind. He had a couple of weeks before his report on it was due to Alan, and another engagement for this evening.

The Sorcery Shoppe was located in the east Thirties, just off Sixth Avenue (like all true New Yorkers, Colin had never been able to adjust to its rechristening as the Avenue of the Americas, even after thirty years). The brisk walk uptown from his apartment reminded him of how much he still loved the city, despite its many flaws. The great occultist Dion Fortune had once written that in the major population centers, one could see Civilization as it would be twenty years in the future.

If that were so, then the future was a place in which only the strong would survive. New York's population had nearly doubled since the fifties; the grace notes to daily living that cities such as San Francisco still retained were being hammered out of Baghdad on the Hudson beneath the heavy hand of progress. Colin tried to imagine the streets around him in another twenty years' time and could not manage it. *Our vision always fails in the homely things, not the great.* His first teacher had told him that.

The Shoppe stood out among its neighbors, a bright peacock among a flock of dingy commercial establishments. It was that rarest of beasts, a store catering to the occult and New Age that predated the Age of Aquarius. While its stock consisted primarily of books—many of them Selkie Press titles—it also sold herbs, candles, and other oddments.

The building in which the Sorcery Shoppe was housed was over a century old and had begun its life, long ago, as a pharmacy and soda fountain. All that remained from that long-ago incarnation was the pressed tin ceiling (now painted black), the parquet marble floor, and the long mirror that filled all one side of the shop. Now greenish and corroded with age, the mirror served as a backdrop to jar-filled shelves of dried herbs, causing the unwary to startle when they caught a glimpse of themselves in the ravaged mirror beyond the jars. The storefront was painted bright red and dotted with black-and-yellow cabalistic symbols, and a black banner with silver letters hanging from a flagpole over the door proclaimed the shop's name.

As Colin approached, he could see that the display window was, as always, draped in black velvet, and bestrewn with the most lurid of the Sorcery Shoppe's merchandise: illuminated crystal balls, star-tipped Wizard Wands, dried bats, human skulls, and other lurid Hollywood paraphernalia.

As its name suggested, the Sorcery Shoppe happily catered to the more sensational aspects of magick, serving as the crossroads for most of Manhattan's esoteric community no matter their Path or inclination, but alongside its amulets and voodoo-doll kits, it carried serious scholarly books impossible to find elsewhere, and hosted lectures given by authorities in their various fields. Colin himself had lectured here on a number of occasions.

Today, however, he had not come to lecture, but rather to hear a lecture given by John Cannon, a notorious popularizer of the occult in the Hans Holtzer vein. Unfortunately, there was a certain amount of meat to Cannon's books—sound research and extensive quotations from public domain sources—but Cannon's books, for all the facts they contained, were not meant to teach. They were meant to entertain and titillate, producing in their readers the same sort of pleasurable fear that a child experienced in walking past a "haunted" house.

Tonight, the subject was Black Witchcraft. John Cannon claimed to have firsthand knowledge of an operating black coven.

Colin knew that most self-styled witches—or, as they preferred to be known these days, *Wiccans*—practiced a harmless form of Nature-worship established by the Englishman Gerald B. Gardner. Even though their practices had more ties to the Hashbury than to Hell, their attempts to "reclaim" their traditional designations of "witch" and "coven" only led to them becoming confused by the public with LaVey-style Satanism (which also used these terms for its practices).

Fortunately, most of the modern "White" Witches that Colin had met were quiet, reserved, and decidedly publicity-shy, so that public conflicts rarely arose. Still, it was important to draw the distinction between White and Black Witchcraft in the public mind, lest innocent people be harmed.

As Colin entered the shop, the usual reek assaulted his nose, the mingled scents of frankincense and dust and pot that made up the place's distinctive fragrance. He stopped at the register and bought a ticket to the lecture. There was a large bulletin board beside the cash register; Colin stopped to glance over the postings. Most of them, as usual, were the typical farrago of ads by astrologers and self-proclaimed descendants of recently founded ancient priesthoods, but one or two items were of interest.

In addition to the large color poster advertising tonight's speaker—a glossy full-color 11 x 17 poster with a studio portrait of the speaker, who looked more like an insurance agent than an intrepid explorer of the dark underbelly of magick—there were two that caught his interest. One was silkscreened in shades of green and purple, with stars and unicorns and a Moon-crowned Goddess of suspiciously Art Nouveau aspect. Its design owed more than a little to the acid art he was familiar with from the Bay Area, and seemed to be proclaiming the formation of the Earthrite Temple of Pagan Witchcraft, sponsored by Coven Tree.

Colin smiled at the gentle play on words. He knew some of the members of Coven Tree; they were harmless dilettantes, interested in feminism and spiritual self-expression, though some of those attracted to them might not be. He made a note to keep a weather eye on them and turned to the other.

In comparison to the first, it was crude; a black-and-white Xerox of a press-typed original. It announced that applications were being taken for a study group on the Blackburn Work. Serious inquiries only, and a familiarity with the Work was essential, the notice said. The contact address was a post office box in Queens.

Colin gazed at it, frowning, his mind thousands of miles away as he tucked his ticket into his vest pocket.

There'd been a flurry of interest in Thorne Blackburn just after the Shadow's Gate mess; *Time* had done a cover story on his disappearance and Katherine Jourdemayne's death. Though no trace of his body had been found in three years of searching, Colin had no doubt that Thorne was dead. Apparently death had catapulted him into some strange American immortality usually reserved for dead rock stars, at least judging by this advertisement.

Colin shrugged, turning away and heading for the lecture room in the back of the store. The Sorcery Shoppe's lectures were notorious for their late starts, and in fact, when he arrived in the lecture room, Colin was the first one there.

He glanced around. The Shoppe's back room was also used by a Magickal Lodge active in the New York area; the equipment from their last ritual were stacked carefully in the corner, looking like nothing more fantastic than worn and dusty theatrical props.

Was this all that magick was? It was easy to think so; to doubt, to give in and accept what everyone said—that magick was no more than self-hypnosis in fancy dress.

But Colin's entire life had been dedicated to the belief that the sum of humanity was so much more than a simple empirical assessment of quantity and duration. To deny the realm of the spirit was to deny half of all Creation: even if magick were reduced to nothing more than passionate *belief,* such passion was a force that could build cathedrals out of nothing and carve empires out of wilderness. Yet Cannon's books were the only glimpse some people ever got of a world outside their own, and the viewpoint he presented made it easy to dismiss magick as a Faustian exercise in self-delusive smoke and mirrors: self-important, foolish . . . and harmless, in the long run.

The nineteenth century had been like one long chess game between Spirit and Substance, played out in the echoing aftermath of the French Revolution and the defeat of Napoleon's imperial ambitions, and the scars of the Rationalists' misguided reforms still shaped the modern world. If the Age of Reason that had swept through the West at the end of the eighteenth century had committed any great crime, it was this: that in shutting out superstition and fanaticism, the Rationalists had attempted to reduce the whole of God's creation to something that could be measured in a balance.

On one side, Darwin and Freud, proclaiming mankind nothing more than a computer made out of meat, assembled by random chance and a blind watchmaker.

And on the other side, Mathers, Case, Waite, Fortune, Crowley . . . the magnificent irrationality of Helena Blavatsky, fighting against the Rationalist's cold equations, working desperately in a world that thought them ludicrous eccentrics or even criminal lunatics to keep the glorious medieval panoply of High Sorcery from being swept away, so that the tools of that alchemy by which animals become angels would not be lost.

It was a battle without malice, without enemies, as oblivious as that of the seed to take root and flower; a battle that continued to this very day.

That would be fought here, again, tonight.

The room had started to fill as Colin stood lost in his own thoughts. As he'd suspected, the audience was substantially the same as that for his own lectures: young and upwardly mobile gypsies of the spirit, with a small scattering of veteran dilettantes and seasoned seekers.

There was a good turnout; John Cannon was apparently a popular speaker. Colin took his place on an uncomfortable metal chair in the front row and turned his attention to the podium. It was decorated with a poster similar to the one out in front, proclaiming John Cannon as the author of *The Devil in America, The True Story of Witchcraft,* and *Voodoo in the Modern World,* as well as of several other equally sensational titles.

When the room was fairly full, a man wearing dark slacks, sportcoat, and a black turtleneck—gaunt, and much taller than Colin had suspected from the photograph—entered the room. John Cannon had the stooped carriage of a file clerk. Except for his imposing height, he would blend easily into any crowd; a good attribute for an investigative reporter to have. He was carrying a sheaf of papers as he ascended to the podium, and spent a few minutes arranging them as he stood there, waiting for the audience to settle.

"Good evening, folks. I'm John Cannon—my friends call me Jock. In the past few years I've poked my nose into quite a few dark corners of the world, and seen a few things that would make your hair stand on end." He ran a hand through his sandy brown hair and smiled self-deprecatingly. Cannon had a confident resonant voice—he was obviously a practiced public speaker.

"I've chased ghosts in England, devils in Haiti, and demons in New Orleans. I thought I'd seen just about everything, but I was wrong. Tonight I'm here to talk to you about Black Magick—not as something safely tucked away in a history book, but right here, right now. In New York City, today, right this minute, there are people forming covens and worshiping the Devil. It's no joke. These people are deadly serious—and I do mean deadly."

For the next hour John Cannon spun his audience tales of his experiences in his practiced raconteur fashion, telling of how he'd penetrated a dark occult underworld that existed right beneath their very noses—a world of orgiastic sex, dangerous drugs, and deliberate blasphemy.

"These people have absolutely no scruples whatsoever. They will use any method to achieve their sensual self-gratification, whether it be old-fashioned strong-arm techniques, or . . . Black Magick."

He spoke of the occult powers that the black covens could wield to steal a man's mind, to bend the will, to hurt or even kill. It was pure *Rosemary's Baby* stuff, but as far as Colin could tell, Cannon never quite stooped to out-and-out fabrication. There was always a grain of truth in even his most lurid writings, and so there must be something to this.

But your viewpoint depended on your perspective. By Cannon's wide-ranging definition of Black Magick, Colin MacLaren's own Lodge and its ancient sacred trust was a part of that same recondite occult conspiracy that seemed—from Cannon's description—to be on the verge of taking over Manhattan at this very moment. Left to Cannon to describe, the activities of even the whitest Witchcraft would take on an unholy tinge.

When Cannon finished, there was a scatter of pleased applause, and a few people came to the podium to get autographs or to ask questions. Colin dawdled until the traffic jam in front of the door had eased, then got up to go. He had no particular desire to meet John Cannon.

"Colin MacLaren!" Someone behind him had called out his name, and Colin stopped, turning to see who it was.

Cannon hurried up to him. "It is—You *are* Colin MacLaren, aren't you? The ghosthunter?"

Any residual sympathy Colin might have felt for the writer evaporated with his easy use of the dated, pejorative term. But he answered, cordially enough:

"I'm Colin MacLaren. That was an interesting talk you gave back there."

"Years of practice," Cannon said candidly. "But I think I've really struck gold this time. This stuff is real—these people are actually out there, and they're as serious about this hoodoo as you or I about the pennant race."

"I don't follow sports, Mr. Cannon," Colin said, hoping he didn't sound too disparaging. "But what can I do for you?"

"Well, you know a writer's always looking for his next book," Cannon said. "And I think I've got a doozy. So I was wondering if I could interview you. Let me give you my card—"

"Me?" Colin was horrified, and thought, absurdly, about how Claire would laugh to see his expression. "I'm sure I'd be of very little interest to you." Automatically he took the proffered card and tucked it into his jacket pocket without looking.

Cannon finally seemed to notice Colin's coolness.

"Well, that is . . . Naturally I'm familiar with your work, Dr. MacLaren, and I certainly wouldn't dream of doing anything to, ah, *sensationalize* the work you're doing—"

"As a ghosthunter?" Colin asked, and Cannon had the grace to wince.

"Sorry if I put your back up. I'm afraid I've fallen into the habits of my profession, Prof—"

Colin held up a minatory hand. "Please, Mr. Cannon. My doctorate in psychology was a long time ago, and I no longer teach. Just plain 'Mister' is good enough for me."

"Mr. MacLaren, then. But I was serious when I said I admired you. That article you did for *Police Journal* about ten years back on the commonest sorts of psychic frauds—I freely admit that it was a great inspiration to me. Sort of got me into the field, so to speak."

Colin remembered that John Cannon's first book had been an overview—and debunking—of fraud mediums. There were several, Colin knew, whom Cannon had researched but not included, because he could find no way of exposing them.

"I'm glad my life has not been wasted," Colin said dryly. "But you'll understand my confusion, Mr. Cannon. Why would you want to interview me?"

"Thorne Blackburn," Cannon said quickly. "You knew him, didn't you? I've talked to some people, and your name came up a few times. After I'm done with the current book, I'd like to do one on him, you see, and—"

"Thorne Blackburn?" Colin said blankly. "Forgive me, Mr. Cannon, but unless you're planning to solve his mysterious disappearance—and, frankly, it's pretty clear to me that the man's dead—I can't see what appeal your book will have. Nobody outside of a rather specialized field even remembers him."

"Now there you're wrong," Cannon said, warming to his subject. "Everybody's interested in Blackburn—look over here."

He led Colin to a section of bookshelf in the center aisle of the store. Neatly typed labels on the front of each shelf said "Golden Dawn," "Crowley," "Kabbalah," "Regardie," "Blackburn." There were four or five different titles in the Blackburn section and several copies of each, ranging from crude pamphlets to a gaudily produced small-press volume bound in black leather and stamped in red and gold foil. The spine of the book said *The Opening of the Way*.

Colin reached to take the book down and hesitated, letting his hand fall to his side once more. He'd looked at some of Thorne's writing just after the accident, and had found it an amalgam of blasphemy and wishful thinking more suitable to a pulp novel.

"Even if there is the interest that you say, Mr. Cannon, I'm not so sure that a popular book on Thorne Blackburn is such a good idea. What he was trying to do—whatever it was—got two people killed. Putting that material into the hands of the general public might be considered a bit irresponsible."

"Oh, pish," Cannon said, lightly dismissing Colin's objection. "You don't really believe in all this hoodoo, do you?" He smiled briefly at his own joke. "We aren't talking poltergeists here; this is a bunch of people who think that if they click their heels together three times and say, 'There's no place like home,' something's going to happen. Besides, Blackburn's stuff is already in print, as you see. I just want to humanize it a little, that's all. Make it accessible. Give people an idea of the man behind the myth."

"Mr. Cannon," Colin said. "A moment ago you called this hoodoo, and from your lecture tonight you seem to be hell-bent—and I use the term advisedly—on involving yourself with a lot of pretty unsavory people. I'm not interested in arguing the legitimacy of any of this with you, but without even entering into the realm of the supernatural, let me remind you how fiercely people will defend their beliefs when they feel them threatened . . . no matter how outré you feel their beliefs to be."

"I can defend myself," Cannon said, patting a pocket as if he held some sort of weapon there.

Colin shook his head. "I'm certain that you believe that, Mr. Cannon, just as I'm certain that the forces that you are trifling with—if you're so unlucky as to run into the genuine article—are dangerous beyond your wildest dreams. And completely without a sense of humor, when it comes to investigative journalism."

"You talk a pretty good line, Professor," Cannon said. "I don't suppose you'd like to back it up with some names, places, dates? Something I can check out?"

Colin sighed, feeling suddenly tired. "No, Mr. Cannon, I wouldn't." He felt in his pocket for his wallet and withdrew one of his cards, holding it out to the younger man. "But I strongly advise you to give up this project of yours, and forget about Blackburn as well. You haven't the right attitude for it. But there's no way I can force you, so . . . please. Here's my card. If you ever feel that you're in over your head, call me, at any hour of the day or night. I'll do my best to help you."

Cannon took the card, inspecting it closely. All it contained was Colin's name, address, and phone number. The writer shrugged and thrust the card into a jacket pocket.

"Sure, Mr. MacLaren, thanks," he said in a tone that made Colin certain he would throw out the card as soon as he got home. "Thanks for the tip. And maybe I'll give you a call in a few months, and we can work on that Blackburn thing together. Call it something like *King of the Witches,* eh?"

Without waiting for a reply, he strode jauntily off.

It was hard to imagine who'd be more offended by such a title, Thorne or the witches, Colin mused as he gazed after the departing writer. He'd say a prayer for John Cannon tonight. The man was playing with fire.

Hellfire.

The lecture had started at six, so it was dark by the time Colin left the shop. Wan streetlights at the end of each block did little to illuminate its middle, but Colin was not worried. The evening was mild, and the hour was still early. Possibly he'd arrive home ready to tackle the galley proofs for a few hours more before bed.

As he rounded the corner, a man in a dark blue trench coat brushed past him, hurrying up the street. He wore no hat, and as he passed beneath the streetlight, it flashed brightly off his flaxen hair.

Colin stopped and stared after him before continuing on his way, somehow suddenly uneasy. When he was within a block or so of home, he finally traced the source of his disquiet. The chance-met pedestrian had reminded him, somehow, of Toller Hasloch.

He had not thought of the boy in years, and so Colin took the connection advanced by his unconscious mind seriously. Instead of returning to the manuscript when he reached his apartment, he went to his bedroom and opened the closet door. In the back of the closet hung a long tunic of heavy cream linen and a pair of loose-fitting pants of the same material. He changed into them, then reached for the items piled atop the chest in which his robes were stored—a large flat pillow, a low wooden stool, and a small oil lamp.

He set the pillow on the floor, and, using the stool as a low table, set out the lamp and a packet of matches beside it. He checked to be sure the lamp— a simple clay shape, purchased on one of his passes through the Near East— was filled, and then sank down to the floor in a lotus position with an ease that belied his years.

Lighting the lamp, Colin let his eyes fix on its brilliant light. His Lodge did not invoke the elements to aid them, as Alison Margrave's did; rather, Colin had been taught to make his appeal directly to the Light itself, the Light which held the elements and all Creation within itself. Colin gazed into the Light, allowing the Light to gaze into him as he breathed slowly in and out in the Yogic discipline of "no mind."

He did not permit his mind to drift; rather, he emptied it completely, so that it could become a more perfect reflection of the One Mind upon which was built the foundations of the world. It was one of the first disciplines that the Adept was taught, the one upon which all of the others were based, and it was both a tool and an end in itself. He released all Self and all desire, and waited, like a blank page, for the touch of the scrivener.

Hours later, the oil lamp flickered out and Colin stirred, closing his eyes and stretching after the long immobility. He put away his equipment and checked the time: nearly midnight.

It could have been Toller Hasloch that he'd seen in the street, but whether it had been or not did not matter now. It had been a warning.

People like John Cannon existed to be protected. No matter how strenuously they put themselves in harm's way, it was Colin's job—and that of those like him—to see that they never came to any. The words he had said to Claire when he'd first explained himself to her, many years ago, came back to him now: *"The great mass of humanity has the right to not be troubled by forces outside the scope of their daily lives, or manipulated by forces they have no way of resisting. When I find someone interfering in people's lives with Black Magick, it's my duty to stop them if I can. It's my job."*

John Cannon was hunting for a black coven. No doubt he'd already run into an example or two; there were a lot of would-be Satanists out there, filled with a collegiate desire to shock and impress the mundane world. Most of them were pretty harmless, never rising above extortion and a little forced sex from its female acolytes, leaving their members sadder but wiser overall. If that sort of thing was what Cannon faced, the man was quite right: he could take care of himself.

But Colin did not think it was. Call it a hunch, a whim, or even a genuine communication from the Inner Planes. He was certain that bigger game prowled the forest of the night; something darker and altogether more proficient than the hobbyists who made up the clientele of places like the Sorcery Shoppe. For their own sakes, as well as for the sake of those lives they might harm, Colin must stop them.

All that he had to do was find them—before John Cannon paid the ultimate price.

A fortnight later, Colin was less sanguine. As he knew from his own experience, the only time a cell—which was how he must look at the thing, after all—became vulnerable was when it communicated with outside groups. If this black coven were not recruiting or making some other sort of mundane contact with outsiders, it might take Colin years to find them. A Black Lodge might be easy enough to track down in the Overlight—though the hunt was insanely dangerous—but locating its Astral Temple gave no clue to its temporary location. Finding their real-world location required real-world means.

Unfortunately, Colin could not hunt them in person. His meeting with Jock Cannon had shown him that he was too well known to risk impersonating a gullible Seeker, and because of what he was, it was impossible for him to pretend to his quarry that he was instead a more experienced practitioner of the Black Arts.

For this hunt, he'd need help.

"Nothing." Claire's succinct assessment as she slid into the booth opposite him made Colin sigh.

They were meeting at an all-night coffee shop up near Columbus Circle, far enough from either of their homes so that if they *were* under surveillance, there was a good chance their stalkers might miss them.

His wartime habits had come back to Colin with frightening ease, as though the war were not thirty years ago, but yesterday. He'd taught them all, painstakingly, to Claire: how to follow, and how to see if you were followed. How to lose a pursuer. How to tell whether your home or office had been searched. How to leave a message for a confederate. How to run, and when, and what to do if you could not run.

It all seemed silly—theatrical, somehow, without even the shadow of a present threat to justify it. But Colin knew they would not always be as lucky as they had been a decade ago in Berkeley, when Toller Hasloch, boy Nazi, had tipped his hand so grandiloquently. So often the Shadow only manifested itself unequivocally in the moment it was about to strike.

"You're sure of that?" Colin asked. Claire pulled a wry face.

"I'm certain," Claire said.

The waitress came over to take their orders, and after she'd left, Claire resumed her story. Colin reached for his pipe and began to fill it.

"I didn't Sense a blessed thing. The so-called Inner Grotto of the Court of Typhon isn't anything much. Some drugs, I think, and probably a lot of group sex. Nasty enough, but not what we're looking for. They've got an Enemies List, all right, and members are encouraged to add to it, but as far as I can tell, they couldn't raise enough Power to blow out a candle. They've got a very fancy setup, though—apparently one of their members is a theatrical set designer—Mr. Cannon's going to have a field day when he gets around to them."

"And they were our most promising lead." Colin sighed and struck a match. He puffed his pipe alight, giving the gesture all his concentration.

The waitress brought their orders—an omelette for Colin, a hamburger for Claire. Claire tucked into her food with good appetite.

Colin was glad to see her looking so well—he would never have involved her in this dangerous game if he had not thought she was psychologically whole. It was a little over four years now since Peter's death; perhaps enough time had passed that Claire could finally gain enough distance from it to be willing to take emotional chances again. Lately, she'd been taking classes in small business management and was thinking about finding a career outside of nursing. Considering the dangerous state of the city hospitals, it was a move that Colin heartily endorsed.

"What now, Colin?" Claire paused with a french fry halfway to her mouth. "I'm getting pretty good at this wide-eyed innocent act, and I'm not crying quits, but . . ."

"Actually, I'm wondering if we're going about this in completely the wrong way. We've been going after the coven and running up against a dead end. We might have better luck if we started at the other end and worked backward."

"You mean, start with the victims . . . or so-called victims, anyway? Like that woman from Minnesota who wrote that book about how she suddenly remembered she'd been a Satanic High Priestess?" Claire's lip curled in scorn.

"Not quite," Colin corrected with a smile. "We know from Cannon's lecture that the group we're looking for is operating somewhere in the New York area, and it's probably up to the traditional scare tactics to consolidate its power. We just need to find out who they're using them on."

"A tall order," Claire said. "Frightened people don't talk—they're too scared."

"No," Colin agreed. "But they look for protection. And if the conventional safeguards fail them, they're likely to fall back on instinct, even superstition."

"Organized religion, you mean," Claire supplied teasingly. Colin smiled sheepishly.

"Well, yes. And since these days even the Catholic Church won't perform an exorcism without some pretty hard evidence, those poor souls who find themselves victimized by the forces of Darkness frequently find themselves appealing to their parish priest—or local rabbi—in vain."

"Which throws them right into the laps of the occult con artists. Fee-charging lay exorcists, bogus psychics, and all that sort of unscrupulous two-legged shark. But Colin, you know as well as I do how many of those creeps are out there. As fast as we close one down, another pops up. How are you going to check every single one of them, and their clients as well?"

"I'm not," Colin sad, gesturing to the waitress for the bill. "I'm going to check out the sharks who were scared away by a bigger shark."

ELEVEN

NEW YORK, TUESDAY, DECEMBER 20, 1972

Tell me where is fancy bred.
Or in the heart or in the head?
How begot, how nourished?
—WILLIAM SHAKESPEARE

IT WAS THE EVE OF THE WINTER SOLSTICE, AND THE ROOM WAS DARK EVEN at midday. It was the living room of an apartment on West 8th Street just off Broadway, a neighborhood that had been poor not many years before but was now steadily becoming more fashionable.

The chamber was almost a parody of the popular conception of the occultist's Sanctum Sanctorum. The floor was painted with a Seal of Solomon copied out of the *Grimoirum Verum,* with additional arcane symbols added around the edges for effect. The walls were covered in purple crushed velvet and held plaques representing the signs of the Zodiac, a phrenological map of the human head, a poster depicting the path of kundalini energy, a drawing of the Tree of Life, and several blowups of Tarot cards. The ceiling was draped with dense swags of multicolored fishnet, into which had been thrust a number of objects that had apparently caught the occupant's fancy: a baby doll, stuffed animals, a hand mirror, some Mardi Gras masks, and several of the small mirrored fishing floats colloquially known as "witch balls." The windows were hung with black velvet drapes, and the panes were covered with stained-glass Contact paper, making the room murky even in the brightest daylight.

Colin sat on the edge of a black plush couch, holding a cup of coffee untasted in his hands. Across from him, in a high, elaborately-carved chair, sat Lucille Thibodeaux.

Colin had been hunting Lucille for several weeks, though he hadn't realized it until three days ago. She was the shark he'd been looking for: the woman who had put John Cannon on the trail of the black coven, and who might yet provide Colin with a lead to their location.

Madame Lucille made her living as a bogus voudoun priestess, catering to a largely white and totally credulous clientele that felt that something so alien to their experience was by definition superior to anything more familiar. For the right price, Madame Lucille changed bad luck to good, crafted love charms, lifted curses, and relayed messages from the dead, all without any more success than could be chalked up to coincidence and a little trickery.

The first time Colin had seen Lucille had been several years ago, when he'd been extracting an old friend, newly widowed, from the rapacious clutches of the phony medium. Then, he hadn't been sure how old she was. Then, she'd been a beautiful exotic young woman, dressed in a theatrical gypsy fashion and wearing armloads of bargain-counter jewelry.

Today she looked every year of her age and more. Her old-ivory skin now had a sallow greyish undertone, and she hadn't bothered to put on makeup to see him. She'd greeted him at the door in a pink chenille bathrobe, conducting him into her sitting room with what seemed a laborious parody of her former charm. In the harsh light of day, she had the gaunt, raddled aspect of a cancer victim. Even the *tignon* wrapped around her head looked faintly dingy.

"What you want wid Lucille, hahn? I tell you before, M'sieur, I doan' fix curses no more, me." Lucille spoke—when she remembered—with a fetching French accent. But when she was upset or afraid, her native inflections—a thick and almost unintelligible Acadian *patois*—overwhelmed her speech.

She was very afraid now.

"Lucille nobody special, *cher*. Lots worse people out dere. I jus' give dem what dey ask for, me. You are a ver' bad man, M'sieur, to bodder me so."

"Now, Lucille, you know I'm not upset with you this time. I want to help you. Help me, and I *can* help you." All of them, Colin thought resignedly, protested their innocence even before they were accused, almost as if they couldn't help themselves. And since Lucille had urged this meeting, her protestations were doubly ridiculous.

The Creole woman sipped at her coffee. Her hands shook, rattling the cup against the saucer, and beads of perspiration dotted her forehead despite the winter weather outside.

"I should never 'ave talk to dat man," she said fiercely. She shook her head, and her earrings flashed below her white *tignon*. "He was poison, dat one — poison for Lucille."

"You spoke to John Cannon, you told me that over the phone," Colin prompted. He already knew some of Lucille's story, both from others he'd talked to in the past several days and from the conversation he'd had with Lucille to set up this meeting.

"He pay me to," she said simply. "He say he want to do a book about my life, so dat I get famous an' be on television an' all. An' he want to know about de dark forces dat I do battle wid, and dose who worship dem. An' so I tell him about dat, too."

"But they found out that you'd talked—told Cannon about them," Colin prompted her. He could afford no mistakes, nor to leave any question unasked. He suspected that Lucille would be too frightened to meet with him twice. And if what she'd hinted at was true, Cannon was in more immediate danger than Colin had suspected.

"Dat girl, she tell dem, I t'ink. She crazy in de head, her! She say she want to get free of dem, and den she go running back to dem again, I bet!"

Slowly Colin coaxed the whole story out of her, verifying each statement carefully as he went. It had begun months before Cannon's lecture at the Sorcery Shoppe, when a woman named Sandra Jacquet came to Lucille, wanting protection.

"An' she doan' tell me from what, her, not at firs', so I give her dis charm to wear an' charge her fifty dollar, an' de nex' week she come back to me an' say, it work not so good, an' dere dese t'ing in her apartment, an' can I come an' exorcise de place. So I do dis t'ing—a good job; de ingredient, dey cos' me forty dollar. It take me t'ree hour, an she say it a good t'ink she fin' me before somet'ing worse happen. But den I start having . . . de bad dream."

"Is this the girl?" Colin asked, pulling a small photo out of his pocket.

Lucille took the photo in trembling hands and peered at it in the room's dim light. "Dat her, I t'ink. Where she at now, her?"

Colin put the photo back into his pocket without answering. He did not think that it would help Lucille's composure to know that her client was currently an unclaimed body in the city morgue. The pieces of her dismembered and mutilated body—most of them, anyway—had been found stuffed into garbage bags and scattered over most of a city block.

It was lucky—if that was truly the word—that the occult symbols that had been branded and carved into her both before and after death had caused Lieutenant Martin Becket of the Occult Crimes Unit to call Colin in on the case. Just as it was fortunate that the police had been able to get a fairly recent photo of Sandra, because it had been impossible to take an ID photo from what they found of the corpse.

"Tell me about Sandra, Lucille. Why did she come to you? What did she want—exactly?"

"I don' know how she fin' me, M'sieu, but she wan' what dey all do. She want Lucille to lift de hoodoo. An' at first', everyt'ing work out jus' fine."

Which meant, Colin understood, that Sandra Jacquet was rich, and more than willing to pay—lavishly—for protection, without inquiring too closely into her mentor's bona fides. At least at first. But after a few unsuccessful "purification" sessions, Sandra had become unsatisfied with the results for which she was paying. And, finding that her usual tricks were not satisfying her wealthy and openhanded client, Madame Lucille made her first mistake. She did an afternoon's research at the New York Public Library and decided that what was needed to lift Sandra Jacquet's curse was a séance.

It took Lucille almost two weeks to talk Sandra into it, but the girl was terrified—and, Colin gathered, the nebulous problems she was experiencing were getting worse—so Sandra Jacquet finally succumbed to Lucille's coaxing and parted with the $300 that the faux psychic said was required to buy the necessary materials for the ritual.

In fact, Lucille had pocketed the bulk of the money as usual, and spent only a few dollars on colored candles, oregano, and a Ouija board from FAO Schwarz. But something she had not counted on had happened at the "séance"; something terrible enough to drive Lucille away from her plump half-plucked pigeon. Madame Lucille wouldn't—or couldn't—tell Colin what had happened that April night, but her hands shook and her voice quivered as she recounted the moment at which the planchette had taken on a cold life of its own beneath her fingertips.

She broke off her narrative at that point, taking a cigarette out of the onyx box on her coffee table and lighting it with shaking fingers.

"An' what it say den, nobody know about Lucille but her! So den I t'ink . . ." There was a long pause. Lucille sucked smoke into her lungs and blew it out in a harsh exhalation.

"I t'ink maybe dis girl, she too much trouble to keep aroun', her." Lucille shrugged.

After that, Colin gathered, Lucille had refused to take Sandra's calls or to see her when Sandra came to the apartment. And eventually, to Lucille's great relief, Sandra had stopped calling. Colin wondered if she had stopped because she was dead, or whether she had found some other equally helpless rescuer.

"But de dreams don' stop, M'sieu. An I dream Mam'selle Jacquet, she dead but still alive some'ow, alive an' in torment. An den I hear of dis man, an' I t'ink maybe he can help me because he know all about de hoodoo an' stuff."

Colin knew this wasn't the reason she'd agreed to speak to Cannon—this part of the tale was a pretty story made up for Colin's benefit. Undoubtedly, Madame Lucille had contacted Jock Cannon out of sheer avarice. Cannon paid for his interviews, Colin knew that much by now. And after all, by the time she'd talked to him, the night of the séance had then been several weeks in the past, and nothing more of a truly inexplicable nature had happened since. Most people in those circumstances, Colin knew from sad experience, would rather simply concoct a soothing explanation to cover the uncanny events, and would even forget about them in time, rather than continue to live with awareness of the uncanny.

In any event, when Lucille had been interviewed by Cannon, while she'd told him perhaps more than had actually occurred in the Sandra Jacquet case, she had also passed on to him with reasonable fidelity all the names and details—few though they probably were—that Sandra had confided to her. And after that, things had gotten worse for her.

And for Cannon, who, like any good journalist, was out to confirm his facts by tracking them back to the source—Sandra Jacquet's killers.

"What did you tell him?" Colin pressed.

Lucille lit a second cigarette from the stub of the first. The predominantly reddish light shining through the fake stained glass darkened her skin with the illusion of health, but Colin knew better. Lucille Thibodeaux was dying, as surely as if she'd been poisoned.

"No. Dat mistake I don' make twice. No more do dose name pass my lips."

"You told John Cannon. You knew he was a journalist when you talked to him; you knew that he was going to write about them." *And lecture about them. It may already be too late for me to save him.* "What you told him won't remain a secret."

"Yes, it will," Lucille said bleakly. "Dey kill me, *cher.* Dey kill M'sieu Cannon too, I bet."

"If I can find them, I'll make sure that they don't hurt you anymore, Lucille, either of you. I swear it. But you have to tell me what Sandra Jacquet told you," Colin pressed.

"She dead now, hahn?" Lucille guessed.

"You don't have to die," Colin said, evading an answer. "I can help you— if you'll help me first. Tell me who they are."

Lucille hesitated, then shook her head. "Lucille got sins enough on her soul so dat when she die she go straight to de bad place. Dat poison-man Cannon, he on my conscience. I won't have you dere as well, M'sieu."

No matter what he said, Colin could not budge her, and finally he gave up.

"All right. There's little I can do for you if you won't tell me who is attacking you. I can give you the name of a priest. He's a good man. He won't laugh at you, Lucille, and they can't touch you on consecrated ground."

To Colin's shock, the Creole woman laughed; a harsh, smoke-roughened bark.

"So de Church going to save Lucille? What de pries' gone say to me—dat Lucille get down on her knees an' come to Jesus an' be saved, hahn? I don' t'ink so, M'sieu. It too late for dat—God, he dead, an' only de Devil is left. An' de Devil goan' get Lucille in de end."

She stared broodingly toward the darkened windows for a minute, then got to her feet. "I t'ank you for coming, M'sieu, but I do a wrong t'ing to let you. Dere ain' not'ing no living man can do for Lucille Thibodeaux in dis life no more, so you bes' be go now, before dey see you an' put a hurt on you, too." Her voice was firm.

Reluctantly, Colin got to his feet. "I'll pray for you," he told her, knowing that such action would be too little, too late. He dug for his wallet. "At least get out of town; if you leave the area, they may not be able to track you down. Do you need money? I can—"

Lucille waved the offer away. "Dere no'ting more you can do for me, M'sieu MacLaren. Bes' you go now, hahn?"

A few moments later, Colin stood on the street in the dull light of a December afternoon. He glanced up at the window of the second-floor apartment. Behind the shrouded window, Lucille Thibodeaux waited for death with the bleak fatalism of a trapped animal.

He would pray for her as he had promised, though he did not think it would save her. But there were others whom his intervention might yet help.

* * *

Colin was a pack rat and tended to save every scrap of paper that fell into his hands. It had taken him several hours to find Jock's business card, which he'd tossed into the drawer where such pieces of paper tended to accumulate. The phone was answered by a woman who admitted that it was the Cannon residence; she asked his name, a faint wariness discernible beneath the polite tones. A moment later Jock Cannon came on the line.

"Mr. Cannon? This is Colin MacLaren; we met several months ago, at the Sorcery Shoppe?"

"I remember you, Mr. MacLaren." Cannon's voice was weary.

"You'll forgive my presumption in tracking you down, but the last time we spoke you were preparing a book on Black Witchcraft."

"Hold on." Cannon's voice was suddenly sharp. "I want to take this call in the den."

There were a few moments of shuffling around, while Cannon picked up in the den and told Bess—the woman Colin had first spoken to—to hang up the other phone. Then Cannon came back on the line.

"Perhaps you'd like to state the nature of your business, Mr. MacLaren?" Cannon said coolly.

"I've just been speaking to a woman named Lucille Thibodeaux," Colin answered candidly. "What she told me worried me a great deal."

"Ah . . ." Cannon gave a long sigh. "Is she all right?" he asked hesitantly.

"She's dying," Colin said bluntly. "Her client—whom I presume she mentioned when you interviewed her?—is already dead. Murdered."

There was a pause from the other end of the line. "How did she die?" Cannon asked hesitantly.

"Badly," Colin said, refusing to elaborate. "These people mean business. Lucille's convinced she's next—and if you're planning to publish an exposé about them, so are you."

"I'm a big boy now, Mr. MacLaren. It's been quite a few years since I've been intimidated by schoolyard threats," Cannon answered.

Colin sighed inwardly. He recognized graveyard bravado when he heard it. Cannon must already be under attack.

"Do they know where you live, Mr. Cannon? Have you been having any . . . peculiar troubles?" Colin asked gently.

"How do I know you're not one of them, wanting to find out what I know?" Cannon snapped, his voice suddenly flat with suspicion.

"Come now, Mr. Cannon," Colin said. "Of course I want to know what you know, but I'm the one who warned you against getting involved in the first place, remember? I just want to help you. The best thing might be if you abandoned your project, and—"

"Too late." Cannon's voice was ugly with triumph. "I turned the final draft of *Witchcraft: Its Power in the World Today* in last week—it's at the publisher's now."

There was a brief moment of silence.

"They already know that, of course." Cannon said. "They've got a terrific intelligence network. I've actually been to one of their filthy rituals. A Father Mansell tried to recruit me, get me to withdraw the book. He put on a good show, but it's all just hoodoo. That's all. Coincidence, intimidation—" His voice faltered and died, and there was a long silence. "Help me," Cannon whispered.

Colin checked his watch. "You're near Gramercy Park, right? I can be there in less than an hour; I'd like to bring along a—"

"No—don't come here," Cannon said quickly. "I don't want Bess upset any more than she has been so far, and I don't—I don't want them to see you here," he finished raggedly.

There was another pause while Cannon gathered his wits. "I have to drop by Blackcock—my publisher—to see Jamie about the book tomorrow. I'll come by your place afterward. I need to talk to you. Maybe if I withdraw it the way they want . . ."

"That would probably be a very good idea," Colin said. "At least let me see the manuscript. I understand that you name names—well, these kind of people are usually terrified of exposure, and with good reason. I have a few friends in the police who might be able to make their lives pretty hot—and take the heat off you."

"I . . . I suppose so," Cannon said, obviously more rattled by the minute. "I need to think about this. It isn't that I take them seriously, of course—it's just strong-arm techniques and scare tactics. . . ."

"There's no 'just' about it, Mr. Cannon," Colin said forcefully. "Please don't make the mistake of thinking these people won't make good on their threats. If what I believe is true, they've already killed once."

"I'm not going to turn tail," Cannon said, abruptly changing tack again. "But we can talk about it tomorrow. Still . . ."

Colin waited, but Cannon said nothing more.

"Mr. Cannon?" he finally said.

"Oh." Cannon sounded as if he'd been roused from a doze. "Well, thanks for calling, Mr. MacLaren," he said in a bright, false voice. "I appreciate your interest."

"Come and see me," Colin said urgently. "Or I can meet you up at Blackcock. What time are you meeting your editor?"

There was a bitter laugh at the other end of the phone. "You think I'll tell you that? I'm not that much of a greenhorn. Tell you what, MacLaren: I'll call you tomorrow. Maybe we'll have lunch."

"Mr. Cannon—" Colin began desperately. "Jock—"

"Thanks so much for calling, Professor," Cannon interrupted. There was the click of a receiver being replaced in its cradle, and then the buzz of a dial tone.

Colin stared at the telephone in exasperation and pity. He only hoped that Cannon *would* call him tomorrow—and even more than that, he hoped Cannon would withdraw his manuscript about the black covens. The "good-faith" gesture might be enough to save his life.

It might.

* * *

The call he waited for didn't come. All through the day Colin waited, while he debated the wisdom of calling Cannon's wife, or his publisher, and reluctantly dismissed both notions. By the Oaths that bound him, he could not force his help on someone who did not wish it. He prayed that the call he waited for would come. When the telephone rang at four o'clock, Colin lunged for it anxiously.

"Yes?"

"Colin?" The voice was faintly familiar. "It's Michael Davenant."

"Michael," Colin said warmly, hiding his disappointment that the call had not been what he'd wished. "How has life been treating you?"

"Oh, I can't complain. You heard that we lost our funding?"

"No." Even through his worry about Cannon, Colin was shocked. The Rhodes Group had been privately funded and owed a good deal of its viability to government contracts.

"Afraid so. The Sharon Tate thing hit us pretty hard out here—that and the Blackburn murders were a sort of one-two punch. Frankly, when the government contracts dried up, the group couldn't make a go of it in the private sector."

"I'm sorry to hear that," Colin said honestly. "How are you doing these days?"

"Oh, not too badly. There's always room for a good administrator. But I ran across something the other day that I thought might interest you, and I thought I'd buy you a drink and tell you about it."

"With all due curiosity expressed," Colin said, "I *am* a bit tied up here in New York."

Davenant laughed. "Oh, silly of me; I should have mentioned. I'm in New York, staying at the Warwick. Come on by—I guarantee it'll be worth your while."

Colin glanced at his watch. He tried to convince himself that Cannon still might call, and failed.

"It's four o'clock now," Colin said. He mistrusted his own eagerness to involve himself with Cannon's problem—he needed to step back from it if he could. Meeting Michael would be a heaven-sent distraction. "How about if I meet you at six-thirty? We'll have time for a drink or two before dinner. I know a nice little Italian place only a few blocks away from where you're staying."

"Great," Davenant said. "I'll see you then."

The bar at the Warwick was like something out of a lost world: dark and intimate, with a faintly shabby coziness. It seemed to belong more to the fifties than to the seventies. Colin located Davenant at a corner table and quickly moved to join him.

Part of Colin's mind was still occupied with Cannon, but he'd called Claire to phone-sit while he was out. She knew where Colin was, and Colin put more faith in Claire's ability than his own to keep a frightened, distrait caller on the line long enough to elicit some hard information. Her years spent manning various crisis hot lines had honed her inbred people skills to the point that nobody remained a stranger to Claire Moffat for long.

"You're looking well," Davenant said when he arrived. "The publishing life agrees with you, though it's a pity to lose your services in the field."

"I do keep my hand in here and there," Colin admitted.

Davenant smiled. "I was hoping you were. So many folks burn out, you know—get religion, or just lose their taste for ambiguity. I'm glad you're still in the fight."

"So to speak," Colin said.

They ordered drinks, and chatted of current events—the Watergate break-in, Nixon's reelection, the war—until they came. After they'd both tasted their drinks—the Warwick poured an excellent selection of single-malts—Davenant finally broached the subject of their meeting.

"I've already told you that the Rhodes Group is disbanding, but of course there's still the matter of the company's assets to dispose of. The research library—not to mention the records of our cases—constitutes a significant resource. And it would be a pity if all that data were to be lost."

"It certainly would," Colin agreed. "I suppose you'll be donating it to a library or university?"

"Donating!" Davenant laughed. "You've been out of the business world too long, Colin. I've spent the last eight months looking for a *buyer* at the express direction of the board."

"I suppose so," Colin said noncommittally. He was always depressed when commerce got in the way of pure research. "Any luck?"

"Fortunately, yes. The library was broken up—most of it went to Duke, of course—but I'm happy to say I've found the perfect home for our case files."

"Didn't you have some confidentiality issues there?" Colin asked. "Some of those case files have some pretty hot stuff in them."

"Oh, well, of course. Naturally all the government files were turned over to the Central Intelligence Agency—something called Project Star Gate has taken over our work in-house over there, but you didn't hear it from me. As for the rest, real names have been deleted, and most of our clients signed partial waivers back in the beginning anyway. The only real problem was in finding a suitable recipient, and fortunately, I have success to report. We ended up selling the material lock, stock, and ectoplasm to the Bidney Institute, right here in your backyard."

"Not quite my backyard, Michael—Glastonbury is a good ways up the river. But close enough, I suppose," Colin said.

"Which brings me to what I wanted to pass along to you. While I was up there closing the deal, I happened to hear that they're looking for a new director, since Newland's retiring next year. I suppose you're familiar with the terms of the funding bequest?"

Coincidentally enough, the book Colin was reading for Selkie Press was on the life of Margaret Beresford Bidney. "As a matter of fact, yes. The institute is associated with the college, but it manages and administers its own funding, including that million-dollar prize."

"For just as long, I gather, as the good doctor can keep the money out of the sticky fingers of the college trustees. Well, now that he's decided to retire, the college is putting real pressure on the institute to wind down and assimilate with Taghkanic."

"Which would, of course, give Taghkanic control of the Bidney bequest?" asked Colin, out of familiarity with the intricacies of both internal politics and academic feuds.

"Precisely. The institute won't have much hope of remaining an independent entity if they can't search out a qualified director. While of course the college doesn't have any actual control over who the institute chooses, if the institute makes a really bad appointment, the college can always withdraw its support and leave them without accreditation."

"Who picks the new director?"

"The outgoing director and the institute's board of directors. Frankly, I think Newland's on Taghkanic's side, the way he's conducting his job search. Or maybe he just doesn't want to get caught in the middle."

"I can understand his feelings." Colin considered the matter. "Well, I can hardly walk in and propose myself for the job. To be frank, I'm pretty happy with Selkie Press and my consulting work. Still, if the institute is going on the block, I'd at least like to take a look at it before it's gone."

"That's the spirit," Davenant said enthusiastically. "And speaking of spirits—"

The conversation turned to parapsychology, and rambled through the field of mutual friends and acquaintances. Soon the venue was moved to Colin's "little restaurant around the corner," where both men did full justice to the table d'hôte. It was only at the end of the meal, over brandy and cigarettes, that Davenant returned, briefly, to the subject of the Rhodes Group library.

"It was a near thing, and even if the institute is going to go under next year when Newland resigns, I'm still glad they got the records—they'll just roll over into the Taghkanic Library, and you know how colleges are about letting go of anything once they've got their hands on it. Anyway, I had a job of persuading the board, because Hasloch, Morehouse, and Rand were frankly offering more money, but—"

"Hasloch?" It wasn't a common name, and Colin felt a chill strike straight to his heart, as though he'd unwarily breathed in a deep lungful of arctic air. There were no coincidences—all his experience and training had taught him that. Michael had called today—and Colin had accepted his invitation—for a reason, and now he knew what it was. Suddenly, without any need for temporal proof, Colin knew the enemy he faced.

"Toller Hasloch," Davenant said. "Hotshot legal beagle: used to be Hasloch, Hasloch, and Morehouse before Hasloch's father died last year and one of the senior associates got promoted. Apparently they were bidding for a client who didn't want to be named—I can't imagine what interest a New York law firm would have in parapsychology."

For an instant the cozy restaurant was gone, and Colin stood in the basement in Berkeley, looking up at the blasphemous inverted figure hanging from the cross.

"Neither can I," Colin said evenly.

The talk moved on, but the mood of the evening had been clouded, and when Davenant pleaded an early flight on the morrow, Colin was almost eager to let him go.

He decided to walk at least partway home, in hope of finding an off-duty cab, and went a few blocks out of his way to inspect the big tree at Rockefeller Center. It towered brilliantly over the plaza, its colored lights casting a sort of a magic glow over its surroundings in token of the greater Light that this season celebrated. The air had that almost-minty bite that spoke of snow, but even four days before Christmas, any flurries they got weren't likely to stick.

Colin felt his heavy mood lighten a little and was even moved to purchase a copy of the *Times* from a kiosk at the edge of the plaza. Claire always accused him of burying his head in his work and paying little attention to current events.

Perhaps he had, but he couldn't imagine how even the most scrupulous attention to world events could have warned him about the reappearance of Toller Hasloch in his life. The boy had been so young . . . Colin had always hoped that the fright he'd given him had been enough to turn him away from the Shadow, but in his heart, he'd always know it hadn't been.

Almost absentmindedly, Colin reached toward his pocket, feeling for the weight of a gun that wasn't there.

It was half past eleven when Colin let himself into the apartment. Claire was fast asleep, wrapped in a quilt and curled up in Colin's big leather easy chair. The phone was nestled in her lap like a sleeping cat.

As Colin shut the door, she roused.

"Oh, Colin." She looked at her watch. "You're back early."

"I don't suppose I even need to ask if there were any calls?" Colin said, taking off his ancient topcoat and tossing it over a chair, dropping the newspaper on top of it.

"Not unless you count an opinion poll and somebody trying to sell you the *New York Times,*" Claire said, setting the telephone back on its table and unwinding herself from the quilt. "Oh, and a wrong number—but I think they figured that out for themselves; they hung up in the middle of a sentence." She got to her feet and stretched. "How was your dinner?" She paused, and looked at him closely. "Colin, you don't look well."

"I got some disturbing news tonight. You remember Toller Hasloch?"

"Ugh." Claire made a face. "How could I ever forget? Such a *charming* man—and *such* a way with the ladies. Don't tell me you ran into him tonight, Colin. I'd been hoping he was dead."

"Not quite. Apparently he's practicing law in New York now . . . and his law firm was one of those bidding on the Rhodes Group library."

"Brrr." Claire gave a not-entirely-theatrical shiver. "Well, I hope you aren't going to tell me he got it. Tea? I think I could use a cup before hearing all the gory details." Claire strode off to the kitchen, and in a few moments Colin heard her moving around between stove and refrigerator.

He wandered around the room, flipping on a few more lights, and then picked up the paper. He skimmed through it—*Apollo 17* was still heading for Earth without incident, the Watergate conspirators were moving closer to trial— and tossed it aside. Its contents seemed to have no bearing on his life.

By then Claire had returned, carrying a large tray. Colin moved a pile of papers and she set it down, using a large ottoman as a makeshift table. There was a plate of Christmas cookies on the tray, and Colin raised an eyebrow.

"Oh, you know how it goes," Claire said. "This time of year you can hardly escape a few Christmas cookies. Last week I got *two* fruitcakes, so I squirreled one away here for emergencies."

"Or at least for whatever emergencies can be addressed by a serving of fruitcake," Colin said, selecting a cookie for himself.

"You'd be surprised," Claire said placidly. "Most of life's crises can be settled with a good meal, a stiff drink, and a hot bath. Toller Hasloch, however, does not fall into this category. So he's practicing law in New York? I wish I'd known before I moved here, then. But what does he want with a bunch of books? He never struck me as much of a reader, somehow."

"Not the reference library, but the case histories," Colin said. "And in any event, he didn't get it."

"There must be more to things to put that look on your face. What else?"

"I think," Colin said slowly, "that he's practicing a little more than law. But if he is, what he's doing is very well hidden. In the last six weeks I think you and I have hit up every single Left-Hand practitioner in Manhattan and the boroughs, not to mention selected locations in Westchester and Long Island, and we haven't heard of anything even remotely similar to that bad patch back in Berkeley."

"*Thule Gesellschaft.*" Claire pronounced the word as if it were the name of a loathsome disease. "You'd think we'd have gotten a *hint* if he were up to his old tricks."

"You would, wouldn't you?" said Colin musingly. "I suppose that means he isn't, but that's something I'm not willing to take on faith. As soon as this John Cannon thing is settled, I'm going to make it my business to deal with Hasloch personally. I may not be allowed by my oaths to interfere in the lives and destinies of ordinary people, but perhaps an exception can be made for Hasloch."

"Why don't you ask Can . . ." Claire's voice drifted away as she sat with a teacup poised halfway to her mouth. Her eyes had taken on a faraway look. "Cold. So cold. Oh, Colin, why didn't you tell me?"

"Claire?" Colin said, very softly.

"They've gotten Lucille," Claire said. Though her voice was still her own, her *manner* of speaking had changed, until Colin could almost visualize John Cannon sitting in front of him. "Colin, you've got to save—" Her voice broke off. "Save . . ."

Claire stopped and blinked, her eyes focusing. "Save what?" she asked in her normal voice. "Did I just nod off here?"

"Not quite," Colin said. "I think someone was using you to deliver a message." *Someone who passed through the wards I have set about this place as if they didn't exist.*

Claire looked around the room vaguely, as though searching for the messenger in the corners of the ceiling. "There's no one here now," she pronounced decisively. She drained her tea and glanced at her watch again. "Will it keep, do you think, or should I try to call it back?"

Colin hesitated. "Let me make a phone call, first."

Cannon did not answer his phone, and after Colin had let it ring thirty times, he knew that no one would. *"They've gotten Lucille—"* the voice had said. He tried both of Madame Lucille's numbers as well, but no one answered there, either. He hoped she had taken his advice to leave New York, but knew in his heart that she hadn't.

"I think you'd better see what you can raise," he said grimly. There was only one force he knew of that could pass through the wards an Adept set about himself—that of the pure spirit in the lands of Death.

"Nothing." Forty minutes later, Claire shook her head decisively. She set the shewstone aside, rewrapping it carefully as she did so. "I'm sorry."

"You did your best," Colin said. "I'm sorry to have kept you so long. I'll call you a taxi—I don't want you riding the subway at this hour."

"And what about you?" Claire demanded suspiciously. She found her answer in Colin's expression. "Not without me you don't, buster."

At two o'clock in the morning, all the windows of the buildings lining Gramercy Park were dark.

Colin wasn't entirely certain of why he had come. There was nothing he could do here, and he certainly couldn't go banging on Cannon's door in the middle of the night, demanding to know if he were all right. Cannon had not asked him to intervene. Colin's hands were, in a sense, tied.

"Anything?" he asked hopefully.

Claire shook her head. "Just the usual residual nastiness you'll find on any city street. What are you going to do, Colin?"

Colin sighed, shaking his head wearily. "The only thing I can do—wait for a new day and start over. Tomorrow morning—well, later today—I'll see what his publisher can tell me. I wonder if Jock kept his final appointment?"

He'd only been asleep for a few hours when the phone rang.

"MacLaren."

"Colin? Turn on the radio to that news station," Claire said. "Quick."

Colin sat up and quickly activated the clock-radio beside his bed. He kept the radio alarm tuned to 1010 WINS; in seconds the abrasive tones of twenty-four-hour news radio filled the bedroom.

"—and noted popularizer John Cannon, dead today at age forty-nine.

Cannon, the author of several books on the occult such as *The Devil in America*—"

Colin raised the phone to his ear again. "I heard," he said tersely. *Rest easy, John Cannon. You will be avenged.*

"When I got home this morning I just couldn't sleep. There was a bit in the morning paper, too, just a squib on the Obits page. They're calling it a heart attack. I'll hope that's true. But I can't shake this feeling—sort of a vague nagging, nothing concrete enough to act on—that there's someplace I need to be. So I guess my work for today is to wander around and see if I strike into it."

"Good luck," Colin said. "I'll give you a call this evening and we can compare notes. I'm going to see if John Cannon kept his last appointment."

As he was dressing to go over to Blackcock, another phone call came. This one was from Alan Daggonet, the owner of Selkie Press, reminding him that there was a production meeting scheduled for this morning.

Reluctantly, Colin headed uptown to Alan Daggonet's brownstone. His visit to Blackcock would have to wait a few hours.

After the meeting, Daggonet took him aside.

"I'm afraid it's not good news, Colin, but I wouldn't be doing you any service by holding it back. You know we've been in trouble financially for several years now. . . ."

"Is this a pink slip, Alan?" Colin asked quietly.

Alan Daggonet was the scion of an old New York family, and Selkie Press had been his pet project for almost twenty-five years. But recession and inflation combined had conspired to put book publishing out of the financial reach of even a rich man, and Colin had been expecting news of this sort for months.

"Oh, Lord no!" Alan said, appalled. "At Christmas? I'm not quite that much of a Scrooge! No, we can make payroll for a few months yet, but come January I'm going to be putting the press on the market. Not that I think there's the possibility of a buyer, but disposing of the inventory may defray some of our debts. And most of our authors are dead, so there *is* the backlist on the asset side of the ledger. But I'm afraid that we're done for. Barring a miracle, of course."

Colin sighed, trying to take an interest in the problem, though his thoughts were largely elsewhere.

"What about the books I'm working on now?" he asked.

Daggonet shrugged. "Anything that's already in production, fine, but nothing new. We'll need to get together in January after I've talked with the lawyers, but I wanted to give you as much warning as possible."

"I appreciate it," Colin said. He shook Daggonet's hand. "My best to Barry."

"You'll have to come by the place for a drink," Daggonet said. His voice was hollow. Alan Daggonet was a gentle man, and hated to be the bearer of bad news.

"Sure," Colin said. "And do try to have a Merry Christmas, Alan."

* * *

So. Perhaps I should look into that Taghkanic thing Michael mentioned after all, Colin thought to himself as he reached the street. He'd always known that Selkie Press wasn't something meant to last forever, but getting his walking papers so abruptly was still something of a shock. Still, he was willing to bet he didn't feel half as bad about things as Daggonet did.

And Colin had much bigger fish to fry at the moment.

By now it was nearly noon, and Colin's stomach was reminding him that he'd missed breakfast. He was on York Avenue in the upper eighties; hardly an area in which he was likely to find an open pizza joint. Still, there ought to be a coffee shop somewhere in the area where he could snatch a quick bite.

He was just crossing Park Avenue when he felt a sudden *tugging,* as precipitously as if someone were plucking at his coat. He glanced around, trying to see what had summoned his attention.

Across the street, he saw a building of professional suites nestled between two old dowagers of apartment buildings. It stood out sharply to his schooled perception, as though it was illuminated by a separate light.

When the traffic light changed, he crossed the street and inspected the building's entryway more closely. None of the names on the brass plates—Clinton, Wynitch, Barnes—were particularly familiar to him, though Wynitch woke a vague spark of recognition in his mind. Oh yes. An ugly little scandal a few years ago, when a boy he was treating committed suicide.

Someone in there needs help. Of this, Colin was quite certain.

But not now. Not yet. He had another errand to run first.

Blackcock Books' offices were located on the sunny side of Park Avenue South, down in the thirties. Though small by the standards of older publishing firms, their offices still took up an entire floor of their building, including a stylish foyer containing the company logo, executed in brushed aluminum and mounted on the fabric-covered wall behind the receptionist's desk. A tinsel-cloaked Christmas tree stood in the corner of the foyer, testament to the season.

Blackcock published paperback originals exclusively; it was one of the publishing houses that had sprung up like mushrooms in the last thirty years to handle what had been (at the time) a new, low-cost format that no one had really thought would ever endure. But these days, over half of all new books weren't even published in hardcover anymore, but only in the cheap disposable paperback format. Only one of John Cannon's vast and varied output—*The Occult History of the New World*—had ever seen hardcover publication, and it hadn't been Blackcock that had published it.

Several of his other books, however, made up a lurid display on the wall behind the chair where Colin MacLaren was sitting.

He had identified himself to the receptionist and asked to speak to James Melford. As he'd surmised, the next person he saw was not Melford, but a pretty young woman in a very short skirt who introduced herself as Peggy Kane and identified herself as James Melford's assistant. She, too, asked his business, but when Colin told her that his business was private, she had accepted that with a good grace and disappeared once more.

He'd been waiting now for more than an hour, and was wondering if they simply hoped he'd go away, when Ms. Kane returned again. Colin followed her through the door into the Blackcock offices.

This close to the holiday, most of the staff was on vacation, and the bareness of the desks in the little cubicles along the hallway reflected that fact. But despite the barrenness of the office, it had a slovenly, unkempt look that went far beyond the normal chaos of editorial offices. Potted plants had been hastily righted, but the dirt spilled when they'd been overturned had only been hastily and sketchily tidied.

It was a calculated risk, Colin knew, to come to Cannon's publisher on such an outlandish mission as this. But Cannon's last manuscript, like a literary Typhoid Mary, would continue to spread death and destruction in its wake so long as the black coven was trying to suppress it.

Ms. Kane stopped outside a door and knocked perfunctorily before opening the door and ushering Colin inside.

James Melford was a man in his early forties. His curly light brown hair—worn long in the fashion of a man who was late for a haircut—curled over the collar of his striped Oxford shirt. His jacket was tossed over the back of his chair, and the room was filled with boxed manuscripts and other publishing ephemera, including two framed awards and something that looked like a comic-strip spaceship cast in bronze. Its display stand had been cracked—Colin was willing to bet recently. The sense of derangement in this office was, if possible, even stronger than that in the hall outside. He stood when Colin arrived.

"Mr. MacLaren. How are you? You're a friend of Jock's, aren't you? I remember him mentioning you to me a few months ago. I don't know quite how to bring this up, but—"

"I know that Cannon's dead," Colin said. "And how he died. In a way that's why I'm here. Mr. Melford, I've come to see you about John Cannon's last book—"

He was entirely unprepared for Melford's reaction.

"*Get out!*" James Melford roared, rising to his feet.

It took Colin several tense minutes to convince Cannon's editor that he was not a minion of the black coven that had been harassing Cannon—and had broken into Blackcock's offices just last night in search of the publisher's copy of the manuscript.

Unfortunately, that was the only thing that Colin managed to convince Jamie Melford of, and by the time he left the office half an hour later, he wasn't completely sure that Melford didn't believe that Colin was, if not somehow connected to the group that had murdered Cannon, at the very least an unwitting dupe of their schemes. He had certainly not convinced Melford to either suppress the manuscript or to let him have a look at it.

Still, perhaps the seeds he had sown here today would bear wholesome fruit in the future. And at least he now knew how determined the black coven was. Murder by magick was one thing—a wholly physical break-in was quite another, and in one sense, far more menacing.

For a moment, Colin wondered what secret they could have that they would have revealed to an outsider—John Cannon—and yet still go to such lengths to protect. Colin himself, oddly, had more reason to wish to suppress such a book as *Witchcraft: Its Power in the World Today* than they did. Based on his recollection of Cannon's lecture, the manuscript undoubtedly provided a detailed occult workbook for the mentally unbalanced.

"Would you give a baby a loaded gun?" Colin had asked Jamie Melford in their interview, but he knew that Melford had not grasped the analogy. Melford was an editor, a man whose business was books—yet at one and the same time he could believe that there was nothing more powerful than the written word and that written words could do no harm. Colin prayed that Melford would never discover differently—though he had failed to protect Cannon, Colin vowed he would not fail twice. Even without gaining access to the manuscript, Colin still had one lead.

The so-called black coven Colin was after was composed of Satanists, not witches. He could only hope these Satanists were highly traditional in their practices—if they were, they had very particular requirements for the practice of their Black Art, including that their conventicle be led by a Catholic priest. And Cannon had mentioned a Father Mansell.

A quick call to the diocesan offices netted him the information that there was a Father Walter Mansell, but that he had been *laicized*—defrocked, in the old terminology—over ten years before, and thus the diocese no longer kept track of him.

Colin hesitated for a long moment, then dialed a second number.

"Can I help you?" The familiar voice was efficient, neutral, and crisp.

"I'd like to speak to Father Godwin, please," Colin told the housekeeper.

"Who is calling, please?" Now the voice was decidedly cooler, betraying an undertone of an accent. English was not Frau Keppler's first language, and her devotion to Godwin was intense. Few callers got past her dedicated protection of his privacy.

"This is Colin MacLaren," Colin said. He switched to an accentless German. "How are you, Inge?"

"Very well, thank you, Herr Doktor." Her voice warmed slightly, taking on a note half prim, half playful. "You are playing a very dangerous game these days, *nicht wahr?*"

Colin did not waste time wondering how she knew what he'd been up to. Frau Keppler's intelligence-gathering service was still one of the best he'd ever seen.

"I'm afraid so. Will it be possible to speak to the good father?"

"He has not been well, lately. But if you must see him, be so good as to come around four. I believe he can give you a few minutes then."

TWELVE

NEW YORK, FRIDAY, DECEMBER 23, 1972

As an unperfect actor on the stage,
Who with his fear is put beside his part,
Or some fierce thing replete with too much rage,
Whose strength's abundance weakens his own heart
— WILLIAM SHAKESPEARE

FATHER ADALHARD GODWIN LIVED IN AN IMPOSING BROWNSTONE IN THE East Fifties. The building had been the gift of a grateful client, and Father Godwin, who took his vows of poverty, chastity, and obedience with absolute seriousness, had donated the property to the Church. In turn he had been granted a lifetime tenancy. Since his retirement fifteen years ago at the age of eighty, he'd lived here, compiling the notes for a book he would never write.

Colin presented himself on the steps of the brownstone at precisely four o'clock. Frau Keppler inspected him through the peephole for almost a minute before she relented enough to open the door and let him in. She guarded her charge with the maternal ferocity of a lioness, and did not feel that Colin was a good influence on Father Godwin.

Colin stepped into the hallway and waited as Frau Keppler bolted the door behind him. It slid back into place with the sound of a bank vault closing— the door was sheathed on both sides with thick steel plates against the enemies Godwin had made in the course of a long and turbulent life.

The young man in the dark suit and clerical collar—as much a fixture of the house in the east fifties as Frau Keppler herself—watched Colin with a fixed, pale-eyed stare until he had satisfied himself, then withdrew through the doorway and closed the door behind him. Colin had made many visits to this house in his life. The identity of the young man in the foyer changed frequently, but Colin had never exchanged a word with any of them. He'd never even heard any of them speak.

Frau Keppler conducted Colin to the ornate elevator at the far end of the hall and slid its telescoping bronze gates closed. The small cage made its slow progress four floors closer to the angels, stopping at the top floor. Frau Keppler slid the doors open and stepped out.

"You will not tire him?"

"I would not have come at all, Inge, if the matter weren't urgent. You know that."

She sighed, giving up. "He is in the solarium," she said.

What had once been an open patio on the top floor of the building had since been glassed in with thick, triple-paned windows. Even on this bitter December day, the room was tropically hot, and the pale winter light turned golden as it shone through the shelves and tables covered with plants. Colin could almost feel the pulse of vegetable life here in this place.

"I take such pleasure in watching the plants grow. There's such reassurance to be found in nursing them from cutting to bloom, each always the same, according to its nature; each blossom producing more of its own kind . . ."

"Hello, Adalhard," Colin said.

The old man got slowly to his feet—Colin knew better than to help him—and turned around, wiping his earth-stained hands on his apron. His skin had the porcelain translucency of age, and his thick white hair was still cut in a military brush.

"Ah. It is bad tidings when you come to see me, my stormcrow. Which of my fallen angels concerns you?"

"I'm not even sure—" Colin began.

"Tut." Father Godwin held up a minatory finger. "Let us not fence, you and I. We both know what you have come for. But I will give you a few moments to gather your resources. Youngsters your age have no stamina," he added with a twinkle in his eye.

Father Godwin crossed to the intercom and pressed a button. "Sherry and biscuits in the solarium, if you would, Mrs. Keppler," he said, and turned back to his guest.

"It becomes awkward. I hardly know how to address my dear housekeeper these days. Is she a 'Mrs.'? Or must I stoop to calling her 'Miz' as the liberationists would have us do? It is a larger problem than mine, of course, and will not be solved in my lifetime, but once more Holy Mother Church is being asked why it is that women cannot administer the sacraments." He lowered himself into a chair with a sigh. "And of course we have no good answer for them, since we must all restrict ourselves to the domain of the strictly rational." Father Godwin snorted derisively. "If we were all rational beings in a materialistic world, what need would men have for the Church, or She for them?" he asked. "Or the Good Lord for any of us?"

For eighteen years Father Godwin had been an exorcist, one of less than two dozen men worldwide empowered by the pope to perform the Ritual of Exorcism for the Catholic Church. Calls for his services had come from all over the world. If the case satisfied the Vatican's strict requirements for intervention, Father Godwin had interposed himself between an embattled soul and the blackest forces of Hell itself.

An exorcism could take months—even years—to complete, and the work destroyed its instruments quickly, taking their health, their strength, and their sanity. At last Father Godwin's superiors had forbidden him the work, but in his retirement he had found another way to continue the fight.

"Men always have need of the Light," Colin said.

Father Godwin nodded. "Most of all when they least think so. Ah, Mrs. Keppler. Here you are with something to tempt our palates."

"The doctor says you should not drink," Frau Keppler said, whisking a white linen cloth over a table with one hand and then setting the tray carefully upon it. Working methodically, she emptied the tray of a decanter half-filled with ruby liquid, glasses, and a plate of cookies that smelled as if they were still warm from the oven.

"When the doctor has reached my advanced age," Father Godwin said with some spirit, "I shall be delighted to entertain his suggestions. Until then, we must presume that what I have eaten for the past ninety-five years will not kill me in the ninety-sixth."

Frau Keppler sniffed audibly.

"Go on, go on," Father Godwin said, taking a linen napkin from the table and waving it at his housekeeper as if she were a wayward crow. "And tell Donald that he might smile more if he took a glass of wine occasionally."

Frau Keppler left.

"I ought not to tease her—or that terribly serious young man who has come to learn all that I can teach him before he must walk these dark roads alone. I shall have to apologize to the Lord when I speak with Him this evening."

"I'm sure it's good for them," Colin said mildly, pouring two glasses of sherry and handing one to Father Godwin.

"Ah, yes . . . certainty. One of the cleverest pathways to damnation," Godwin said softly. "No man can know with certainty what is best for another, yet God has called us to be the shepherds of His people and to choose their path. . . ."

His voice subsided, and he sat silently for some minutes, his sherry untasted. Colin was about to attempt to attract his attention when Father Godwin roused and lifted his glass.

"One of the penalties of a long life, Colin. So many memories—and so much experience that each choice becomes a dilemma. But you did not come today to hear a lecture upon the horrors of age. You've come about a spoiled priest, have you not?"

Father Godwin still used the older term for a laicized member of the Roman Catholic clergy. Many who left the priesthood left the Church as well, but Father Godwin never gave up hope of returning them to the fold. He had made these men his special vocation in his retirement, watching over them as tenderly as a mother hen over her chicks—though some of those he watched over would have cursed his name had they known of his concern.

"Yes. A Father Walter Mansell," Colin said. "I was hoping you could give me some information about him. His name came up in rather . . . odd circumstances."

Father Godwin chuckled dryly. "You should give up trying to spare my feelings, Colin. Walter is a Satan-worshiper. He was excommunicated for it, as well as laicized. Even after Vatican II, the Church retains some standards, though She makes many foolish compromises. I pray for him every night, that poor dear tormented soul." There was no irony at all in Father Godwin's words.

"May he find the Light," Colin agreed quietly.

Father Godwin gathered himself together with a sigh. "But you won't have come to tax me with my failures. I was his counselor before he left the priesthood, did you know? This was some few years after my retirement, but the bishop kindly allows me to keep my hand in. I think His Grace and I both suspected the direction that Walter's curiosity would take. And so it became necessary to . . . do what was done."

"The Church excommunicated Walter Mansell for heresy?"

"The Cathar heresy, to be precise; an old and pernicious one, but there's a dance in the old girl yet, as the actress said to the bishop. You'll be familiar with it, of course. It holds that Satan is coequal with God, and is the supreme ruler of the Material Realm." Godwin sighed, as if suddenly weary. "Now, tell me what your interest is in him."

"A friend of mine has died," Colin said. "He mentioned Mansell's name as if he might be involved with the Black Order my friend was investigating. I don't know if he is—or even if it's the same group that I have reason to believe has ended the lives of three people in the last year—but I do know that I want to talk to him."

Father Godwin shook his head sadly. "Oh, Walter, I warned you. And instead I seem to have flung you directly into their embrace."

"You can't blame yourself," Colin said. Father Godwin glared at him, his normally mild brown eyes suddenly blazing.

"Indeed I can, young man! It were better that Walter had died than that he should become such a tool of the Enemy. Nights when I cannot sleep, I wonder if I take too much refuge in the law. Knowing what he would become once he'd left us, it might have been better if I had killed him myself."

Colin was no Catholic, but in many ways the Light that he served and the Roman Church held similar views. "He can still repent," Colin argued reflexively. "So long as he lives, there is hope."

"Ah, yes. An excellent rebuke, Teacher. Pride and despair together in one beguiling spiritual fault. But there are times when it is so hard to stand by and let Evil be done. It is a cold consolation to know that one is preventing a greater Evil by one's own inaction."

"It is the hardest lesson," Colin agreed. The two men sat together for a moment in silence.

"But you will be wanting to talk to Walter," Father Godwin said staunchly.

"He is living in Brooklyn now, I believe. Would you ring for Mrs. Keppler? She will know which of my Liber Negri I need."

Mrs. Keppler brought the ledger quickly—and fixed Colin with a meaningful glare. Colin raised a hand in token that he would cut the visit as short as he could. Father Godwin might have the vitality of a man twenty years his junior, but he was still a very old man.

The Liber Negri were the records Father Godwin kept of his fallen angels, as he called them. The pages were inscribed in an exquisite copperplate Latin, the color of the ink showing that the entries had been made over the course of many years. He turned the pages quickly, obviously certain of what he was looking for.

"Here we are. Walter Mansell. He lives in Flatbush. If you have a pencil, Colin, I will give you the address."

Colin returned home, where half an hour spent with his atlases enabled Colin to pinpoint Mansell's precise location and give himself some idea of the layout of the streets surrounding the building. He was planning to tweak the tiger's tail, and there was no room in such a plan for surprises. When he was certain of where he was going, he went around to Cornby's Garage to pick up his transportation.

The Black Beast had died two years before, at the end of a long life of faithful service. Colin had hesitated over a new car, but all the new models had looked too low-slung and gleaming for his tastes, and he couldn't imagine fitting his lanky frame into the front seat of one of those tiny imports.

He'd compromised—far too close to the side of self-restraint, according to Claire—on an anonymous Ford van, bought secondhand. It was painted gas-chamber green and came pre-dented, but there was enough room in the driver's seat for Colin's long legs. A van had a number of other advantages as well, not the least of which was its cargo capacity.

By six o'clock he was on the FDR Drive, heading south toward the Brooklyn Bridge.

Ocean Parkway cut straight through Brooklyn on its flight toward Coney Island. Along both sides of the parkway stood brownstones and the classic C-shaped redbrick Brooklyn apartment houses. Generations of immigrants from every part of Europe had come to Brooklyn, leaving their legacy in nicknames that ranged from Little Sicily to Little Odessa. Once Brooklyn had been a thousand segregated neighborhoods, from Park Slope to Borough Park and beyond.

Flatbush was an area of comfortable middle-class homes and apartments. Though once entirely Jewish, its population was changing as the old neighborhoods evolved with the influx of new tenants. Today it was no longer so easy to make an assumption about a person's religion by knowing their address.

Case in point.

Colin parked at the end of Mansell's street. There was a synagogue at one end and a yeshiva at the other, but they were both dark at this time of night, and on a Wednesday evening traffic was not particularly heavy. Colin eased the green van into the last available space on the street—someone must have just pulled out, because he could see the dark bulk of a double-parked car halfway up the street: a big black sedan.

Colin did not think he would have to lie to Mansell—the unvarnished truth should be a shocking enough impact to gain him the man's cooperation, or at least the information he sought.

He climbed out of the van and locked the door, handling the key carefully with his gloved hands. It was a brilliantly clear night, and the air was already startlingly cold; his breath made dense clouds on the evening air. Colin glanced around warily, but the street was empty, and he walked up the sidewalk toward Mansell's apartment, going over in his mind what he would say to the man.

If Mansell was indeed a member of the same black coven that had murdered Sandra Jacquet, the lead detective on the case would be able to call him in for questioning. And if Colin's past experience was any judge, this would draw the whole coven out into the open, allowing Colin to neutralize them before they could do any further harm.

It would still, however, leave the problem of Toller Hasloch. . . .

Colin stopped as the door to the apartment building opened. The double-parked sedan—a Mercedes—stood at the curb. It made Colin automatically think of a doctor seeing a patient, although most doctors had stopped making house calls years before.

Most New York apartments were constructed with an "airlock" as part of the lobby: two doors, an inner and an outer, that provided both security and insulation. The space considerations that controlled every facet of city life frequently reduced the space between those doors to awkward dimensions, necessitating callers' backing out through the outer door.

The man on the steps faced precisely this problem. At first all Colin could see was the light of the streetlamp falling on his black cashmere topcoat and a sleek helmet of flaxen-fair hair. Then he turned, starting down the three steps to the double-parked Mercedes.

The shock of recognition was like a shout in a silent world. But—somehow—it was not as startling as it should have been. It was as if Colin were an actor following a script he had read long ago, and on some level he already knew what was to come and who he was to meet here.

Indeed, in some sense he had been born, he had come here, only to meet this man.

The fair man stopped in the act of crossing the sidewalk to his waiting vehicle, and turned back toward Colin. Colin could not see his eyes, but he knew what color they would be: a grey so pale it was almost colorless, as cold and hungry as the winter sea.

"Why, it's dear old Professor MacLaren," Toller Hasloch said gaily. "What an unexpected privilege it is to see you again."

The years from twenty-three to thirty-four had been generous to Hasloch. His hair, though it brushed his shoulders in the current style, was no unkempt hippie mass, but an expensive Sassoon cut. His black polo coat was open over a double-breasted pin-striped suit with extravagant lapels; the silk pocket-square and fashionably wide tie were a bright Peter Max print and the deeply cuffed bell-bottoms broke over gleaming boots with high stacked heels.

"I wouldn't call it a privilege in your position," Colin said. "Still, I suppose tastes differ. You've done well for yourself, haven't you? I see you've sold out to the Establishment."

Hasloch smiled, an expression as cold and false as the man himself.

"Professor MacLaren, I never intended to challenge the Establishment. I have always intended to suborn it, and then place it in service to the eternal Reich. It's remarkably easy once you've begun, so I find."

"It sounds like a full-time job," Colin commented calmly. "I suppose I had better let you get back to it."

"We'll meet again," Hasloch vowed. He turned to go, then stopped. "I suppose I ought to be coy in the best movie villain fashion and ask if you've read any good books lately, but you strike me as such an unlikely candidate for the role of James Bond that I can't bring myself to do it. I should mention, though, that if you're looking for Walter, I'm afraid he's out. But do feel more than welcome to call another day."

He knows about the manuscript. He's baiting you. Don't react, Colin told himself.

"Yes," Hasloch said, as if Colin had spoken. "I'm in this John Cannon business up to the eyes. Walter's one of mine. Every single one of those pathetic anti-Church reactionaries is mine—and there's nothing that you, with your precious White Light scruples, can do about it.

"It's quite amusing, really. They think they're rebelling, but they're still celebrating the Big Lie of the Jew-inspired Roman Church, even in their trivial blasphemies."

"I do wonder why you put up with it," Colin said commiseratingly.

Hasloch threw back his head and laughed.

"Because there's *power* there, my dear monk! Anywhere there is fear or hatred there is power that feeds the Aeonic Current. But acquit me of being anything so inconsequential as a Satanist—this is simply another mask for me, a diversion until the time for masks is over. And do go on with your pathetic and useless crusade," Hasloch said amiably. "You've put so many obstacles in your own way, you'll never prevail."

In one thing, Colin thought to himself grimly, Hasloch had not changed. He still talked too much, though in one sense he was right—the actions which Colin could take and remain of the Light were much more circumscribed than those available to the Shadow. To lose patience with that fact, to use the methods of the Serpent, was to fall to the Shadow and become its tool, witting or not.

"And do have a Merry Christmas, Professor." Hasloch turned away and climbed into his car. A moment later it was moving quietly up the street, white clouds of steam billowing from its exhaust.

Colin watched until the car was out of sight, and then went up the steps to ring Mansell's bell. There was no answer, not that he had truly expected any. The encounter he had been drawn to here in Brooklyn had been with Hasloch, not with Mansell. And a challenge had been offered—and answered.

The odds seemed insurmountable, the contest unwinnable, but all of Colin's life had been spent waging just such a war. The first victory must be over the Self, to gain the tools for all that followed. It was a battle that must constantly be refought, but each time he conquered his own impatience and despair, something far greater than himself had won a victory, and Colin became stronger.

And so as it had been, it must be now.

Colin walked slowly back to his van. His first stratagem had been blocked; there was no point in approaching Mansell now. He would try another approach.

Preoccupied with his thoughts—any day which included Alan Daggonet, Father Godwin, and Toller Hasloch had to be considered an exceptionally full one—Colin nearly forgot that there was one last task for him to perform.

"Claire? It's Colin. I'm sorry it's late, but I just got in. Did you manage to track down that hunch of yours? No? Well, then, there's a doctor's office on Park in the Eighties that I think might be the place you're looking for. Maybe you should see if they need a temp. . . ."

Friday, December 23, was cold and bright. Colin's destination was One Police Plaza, where Lieutenant Martin Becket and the Occult Crimes Unit had a small office tucked away in a corner of the sprawling maze of police headquarters.

The building was located near city hall in what had been, almost a century before, the heart of Manhattan. In the years since, the city had spread, its center moving uptown with the skyscrapers that lined Madison, Fifth, and Sixth, and with the great public spaces such as Rockefeller Center that had been created half a hundred blocks north. Downtown—its concrete canyons in shadow on even the brightest summer day—had been left to the wizards of Wall Street and to various municipal offices, such as the one its inmates called, with varying degrees of affection, the Puzzle Palace.

A uniformed policewoman ushered Colin to Becket's door and tapped on the glass. Becket looked up, waved at Colin through the glass, and the woman withdrew.

Colin opened the door and went in.

Detective Lieutenant Martin Becket, like most of his real-life brethren, was a middle-aged sedentary man with a receding hairline and a chain-smoking habit he tried intermittently to break. He had a wife, three kids, and a house in Queens. Only the .38 revolver in the black shoulder holster that he wore—visible, as his blue plaid sport coat was hung on the coat tree that teetered in the corner of the office—and the gold shield clipped to his belt distinguished him from thousands of other office workers in a thousand anonymous office buildings all over Manhattan.

"Merry Christmas, Colin! Nice of you to drop by," he said, waving Colin to a chair. "I suppose it's too much to hope for that you've come to crack my big case?"

"Sorry," Colin said, moving a pile of reports off the chair and seating himself in it.

Becket fired up another Camel and offered Colin the pack. Colin waved it aside; he'd managed to wean himself down to an occasional pipe, and lately he was starting to think he should give even that up.

"So. You didn't come in just to pass the time of day," Becket said. "There's a limit to how long I'm going to be able to sit on this Jacquet thing—though the holiday helps—and if the ME's office ever lets some of the details slip to the press, I'd better be ready with the perp's head on a platter or the mayor's office is going to be asking for mine."

The Occult Crimes Unit was only a small part of Becket's workload. It was primarily for information sharing and resource development, and the possibility for negative publicity ensured that it kept a very low profile. The Sandra Jacquet murder, however, might just be the one that blew the lid off the unit once and for all, and Becket was justifiably worried about the repercussions.

"Then I've got some good news and some bad news for you, Marty," Colin said. "The good news is, I've got a pretty good idea of who killed her—it's a group—and I've got the name and address of one of them. The bad news is, I haven't got a blessed shred of proof. One of the people who could make the connection died two days ago of allegedly natural causes, and I don't think Lucille Thibodeaux will testify."

"Neither do I," Becket said dryly. "They fished her out of the river this morning—suicide, the coroner's office says. I'd flagged her file, so they gave me a call."

"Poor soul," Colin said softly.

"You said you had a name for me?" Becket asked.

"Walter Mansell, currently living in Flatbush. He's in the phone book, but I'll give you his address. He's a defrocked Catholic priest. I checked with a friend of mine in the diocese: he was also excommunicated for heresy."

"Sounds like a model citizen so far. Not many people go to the trouble of getting themselves excommunicated these days," Becket commented. "So how do you connect him up with Jacquet?"

"John Cannon mentioned the name in a phone call to me the night before he died," Colin said. "According to Lucille, she was pretty forthcoming with Cannon when he interviewed her, and passed on names that Sandra had given her. Cannon said that Mansell had tried to recruit him for the group when he got in touch with them."

"So Thibodeaux—who's dead—dropped the dime on Mansell to Cannon—who's also dead. Nice. But it isn't," Becket sighed, "anything we can go within twenty blocks of the DA with. Still, it's always good to make new friends. I'll keep an eye out for our friend Walter."

"While you're opening new dossiers, try this: before he died, Cannon turned in his finished book about Satanism in New York to his editor, Jamie Melford of Blackcock Books. When I spoke to Cannon, he implied that he was receiving threats and pressure to withdraw the book. Melford's office was broken into and vandalized after Cannon's death and his copy of the manuscript stolen. It looks like Melford's starting to get the same treatment that Cannon got."

"Did he swear out a complaint?" Becket asked, suddenly more alert.

"He said the police were in about the break-in. I doubt he knows anything about Mansell, unless Cannon used his name in the book." But if he had, Cannon would know he'd be opening himself to an action for libel, and the old pro would have been too cautious for that.

Unless, of course, he'd named names as a form of *insurance,* expecting to be able to go back and delete them later.

"I hope you're going to tell me you've stayed away from Mansell," Becket said, lighting another Camel from the stub of the first.

"I haven't spoken to him," Colin said truthfully. He thought about Toller Hasloch, but said nothing. He had no proof, other than Hasloch's own word, that he was involved with the Satanists . . . and he would have to be far more foolish than he was to trust Hasloch's word even for the fact that the sun would rise tomorrow.

"Well, it's a start, anyway. I'll shoot Mansell's name down to Files and see what comes back. If he's got any priors—including littering—we can pull him in and see what we get with a fishing expedition. It'd be nice if we had the contents of Jacquet's apartment to work from, but somebody torched it the night she disappeared. Arson."

Colin sighed, getting to his feet. "I'm sorry I couldn't be more help."

"Well," Becket said, "at least now we know all these folks are connected. If there do have to be a bunch of kooks out there pretending they're witches, it helps that they all know each other."

THIRTEEN

NEW YORK, DECEMBER 24, 1972

I have owed to them,
In hours of weariness, sensations sweet,
Felt in the blood, and felt along the heart;
And passing even into my purer mind,
With tranquil restoration:
—WILLIAM WORDSWORTH

CLAIRE MOFFAT SAT BEHIND THE RECEPTIONIST'S DESK IN DR. MARIAN Clinton's office, as band-box perfect as the day she'd graduated from nursing school—which was more years ago than a woman was supposed to like to remember, these days. She fanned herself idly with an empty manila folder; Marian Clinton kept her office uncomfortably warm, although Claire supposed that all the women who undressed in her examining room throughout the day were grateful for the heat.

It was too bad none of them were here to appreciate it—Dr. Clinton had been forced to cancel her morning appointments when one of her patients had gone into labor early, and Claire was alone in the office. She spared a moment's sympathy for the new arrival, afflicted with a December 24 birthday. Oh, well. There were worse fates than to be born happy, healthy, and wanted.

She tried not to wonder what she was doing here. On the surface, the answer was simple enough: the temporary agency she listed with had placed her here when she'd called them yesterday and said she was available to work today. On another level, Claire was here because Colin had called her last night and asked her to find some way to be at this address today. There were times when that RN came in very handy—a nursing degree was almost as good as a passport for getting you into odd places at short notice.

And on the deepest level of all, she was here because for years she had made herself the hands of a Power that moved through the world, and done its bidding without asking why. She did not know what happened to those whose lives she touched, or why she was drawn to them and not to any of the others who suffered daily in the world. She could not believe that some were more deserving of succor than others. In Claire's belief, all who suffered were equally worthy of aid—and the question of why some received it and some did not had troubled her ever since she had committed her heart to this path.

Why should Peter have died and his killer lived on in jail? Why should her Gift not have been able to save the man she'd loved so deeply? What Purpose directed her Gift as it did, and to what end?

There was no answer, nor did she expect one, but Claire was too much a child of her generation to feel that blind submission and unquestioning acceptance could ever be a virtue. She might never receive an answer to her questions, but she certainly wasn't going to beat herself up over the fact that she asked them.

And despite the fact that it had been Colin who had directed her here, Claire had the odd sense that she would have been drawn here anyway, compelled here by the cryptic force that so influenced her reality.

It was early afternoon. Dr. Clinton had come back from the hospital, and Claire had just ushered Dr. Clinton's one o'clock into the examining room when Claire heard what sounded like heartbroken weeping coming from the hallway outside the office. She was already heading for the door—propped open with a brick to afford her some relief from the heat—when she realized that the sound she heard so clearly was not audible to anyone else.

She opened the door and saw a slender woman a few inches shorter than she was standing in the hall, hesitating between the door to Dr. Clinton's office and that of Alexander Wynitch across the way. The woman's dark hair was cut short and topped with a snow-spangled tartan tam. She was wearing a Navy peacoat barely shorter than her skirt and a pair of brown leather boots, and as Claire watched, she took a hesitant step toward Wynitch's door.

Claire wrinkled her nose: Wynitch was one of the pseudo-professionals who infested the field of psychology, and Claire was willing to bet that any certification the man possessed had come out of a box of Cracker Jack.

"Were you looking for Dr. Clinton's office?" Claire asked hopefully.

The woman spun around and stared at Claire with a wild expression on her face, and Claire felt an uprush of instinctive sympathy. She did not know whether this was the woman she had been sent to aid, but this was certainly a woman in need of her help.

Speaking soothingly, she got the stranger to come into Dr. Clinton's waiting room and drink a cup of water from the cooler. It took all her professional composure not to react when the woman introduced herself: Barbara Melford.

And Colin told me that Cannon's editor was named Jamie Melford! This can't *be a coincidence.*

Because there were no coincidences—Colin had told her that, often enough. Those were words he lived by—no coincidences, only a Pattern too vast for them to see, whose weave they could make or mar of their own will.

Under a little gentle coaxing, Barbara Melford told Claire a confused story of fighting with her mother-in-law, of doing things she could not account for, of feeling that she was losing her mind, that made Claire's heart ache with informed sympathy. Barbara's mother-in-law was set on having her see Mr. Wynitch, and Claire was equally set that she should not.

She did not want to say anything that would make her sound eccentric— by the look of her, Barbara Melford had just about had her fill of strangeness. She did not know precisely what she said, only that she convinced Barbara to see Dr. Clinton before she did anything else.

And then, using all her guile, Claire extracted a promise from Barbara to come with her to see Colin after Dr. Clinton's office closed for the day.

She was glad that she had when Barbara came walking out of Dr. Clinton's consulting room a few minutes later, as stiff-legged and glassy-eyed as if she'd just been given a death sentence. Claire called out to her as she passed, but Barbara didn't really seem to hear her.

Don't push. An inner urging kept Claire seated as Barbara mechanically collected her coat and hat and sleepwalked out of the office. After working so hard to get the job, Claire couldn't simply walk—or run—out in the middle of it.

She's agreed to meet me in front of Lord & Taylor's at three—I hope she remembers, Claire fretted. But that matter had been taken out of her hands.

Barbara *had* remembered—or at least, some good angel had brought her to their rendezvous at the appointed time. The sidewalk was choked with tourists come to view Lord & Taylor's famous Christmas windows, but Barbara stood staring out into the street, looking like a lost child.

With the firm decisiveness learned from years of nursing, Claire took charge of Barbara Melford and got them both into a cab. Barbara sat silent throughout the short cab ride downtown, as if she were hoarding her strength for one last effort soon to come.

When the two women arrived at Colin's apartment, Claire discovered that things stood much as she'd guessed they did. Barbara Melford was the wife of Cannon's editor and suffering persecution of her own to bring pressure on her husband. As Claire brewed tea and sliced the fruitcake she had brought over only a few days ago—Colin had a pernicious sweet tooth, and she was glad to see that there was some of it left—Barbara explained everything that had begun when Cannon had brought the manuscript to Jamie, including the fact that Dr. Clinton had told her that she was being poisoned with ergot—probably by someone very close to her.

Claire felt herself recoil in revulsion. Ever since she'd fallen victim to that cup of spiked punch at Toller Hasloch's party, the thought of someone being drugged against their knowledge or will had held a special terror for her.

Colin, bless him, took everything in his stride, and even managed to work a little old-fashioned charm on Barbara, though the indications that she had been a victim of the black coven for months—even years—were dark indeed.

But that means they can't be after Barbara because she's Jamie Melford's wife—or does it? Could they have targeted Barbara for some other reason that has nothing to do with the manuscript? How could they have known that Melford would be the book's publisher—or even that Cannon planned to write it? Either way, it's horrible—horrible! That poor woman . . .

"Jamie!" Barbara gasped, wild-eyed. "Could they be doing anything to Jamie?"

Claire simply stared at her. From what Colin had told her last night, the fact that Jamie Melford was already the black coven's target was so obvious that Barbara's cry could only have been a rhetorical question.

Colin gestured her toward the phone. Barbara clutched at it as if it were a lifeline, her hands shaking as she dialed. Claire set down her teacup and got to her feet, ready to do what she could to help Barbara. No useful purpose would be served by a fit of hysterics, but frightened, endangered people rarely thought that clearly.

But Barbara Melford did not have hysterics. Whatever she heard at the other end of the line caused the heavy receiver to fall from her nerveless fingers as she simply stood there, numb and white with shock.

The three of them reached the Melfords' apartment less than twenty minutes later—armed, Claire thought to herself, for bear. Jamie Melford was not there—and worse, it was clear that wherever he was, he was in the hands of the black coven.

The malice—no, the *evil*—that Claire felt radiating from the very walls nearly did her in. It was as though something foul were being forced down her throat, and her stomach revolted spectacularly, leaving her nauseated and shaking.

But the empty rooms yielded nothing—nothing, that was, except proof that Melford's own mother was a member of the black coven, and had been for years.

What a ghastly coincidence, if you could even call it that. No wonder they've seemed to be one step ahead of us all along, with a spy in the house of John Cannon's closest friend.

And now they were moving openly against Jamie Melford—and neither Colin nor Claire had the faintest idea of where their Temple was.

It was nearly eight o'clock when the three of them left the Melfords' Upper West Side apartment. Their only chance to save Jamie Melford's life—and soul—lay in Claire's erratic scrying abilities.

Claire had been fortunate to be taught scrying by Alison Margrave. Alison had worked patiently with her for months under Colin's aegis, guiding Claire to discover the techniques that unlocked her Gift. Every psychic was different, using items as disparate as fire and water, a deck of Tarot cards, or an astrological chart, to unlock clairvoyant powers, but scrying was one of the fundamental disciplines that all psychics stumbled into eventually. Claire had been trained in one of the oldest methods: that of the *shewstone*. The mincral crystal was a heavy weight in the pocket of her coat as Colin drove down the East River Drive.

It was Christmas Eve and the traffic was heavy. Each time the van became stopped in traffic Claire winced as the tension inside it took a sharp upswing. She could almost hear Colin grinding his teeth in frustration.

But Jamie Melford was not dead. Claire clung to that tottering certainty. She could not sense him at all, and had only the most wavering sense of *place,* but she clung to the conviction that he lived as desperately as his wife did. She could not bear to think that he had fallen into that Night which was eternal, but the clues revealed by Claire's scrying were so muddled and few: explosions, alarm sirens . . .

Thanks to Martin Becket, they'd been able to restrict their searching to only those areas where blasting was going on tonight—an emergency, indeed, to make men work on Christmas Eve, but the bank that had the advertising slogan "The city never sleeps" certainly had the right of it—New York was a twenty-four-hour town.

The first site they tried was on Second Avenue, over on the East Side. They wasted forty minutes checking out a several-block area—uselessly—before heading downtown once more.

"Hurry. Please . . . hurry," Barbara Melford whispered under her breath.

Colin turned off the East River Drive onto Houston Street, and within moments they were lost in the twisting maze of Greenwich Village streets. When she heard the dull *crump* of explosions, Claire felt a pang of relief so strong it made her giddy.

"Well, there's the blasting," she said. "Now all we have to find is the firehouse." *Or whatever other source there might be for the sirens I heard . . .*

"That way!" Barbara said suddenly, pointing off to the left. Colin looked at her strangely, but followed her directions without comment.

This was one of the oldest sections of New York, and many of the streets retained their original cobblestones. Claire rolled down the passenger-side window as the van drove slowly through the streets, straining her senses to search for the black coven's hideout. The night air was sharp, with the mintiness of fresh snow on the air. She breathed deeply, trying to banish the nauseated faintness that had dogged her ever since the apartment, but she felt as if there was a tide of liquid garbage rising around her, and waves of sickness seemed to steal the oxygen from her lungs.

As if from a great distance, she could hear Colin asking her to take the wheel. Barely conscious, Claire slid across the seat, but changing position seemed to make the sickness worse. It was horrible—like drowning, like dying—watching the faint clean light of life and air dim out far above.

Suddenly, Colin placed a hand on her shoulder, speaking to her sharply. She tried to rally, but she could feel herself greying out. . . .

"Barbara, can you drive?"

The intent that coiled around them was like nothing he had felt in many,

many years—Colin could well understand why a Sensitive was swooning just from exposure to it. There was a peculiar immediacy to the Evil that manifested through human intervention; something far more frightening than the sheer inhumanity of the Shadow. All men were born with a spark of the Light, and the deliberate destruction of that part of themselves was what gave their actions this extraordinary taint of ghastliness.

He blessed the foresight that had caused Claire to place so many vital items into the emergency kit that she'd packed in Colin's apartment, and he blessed his own prudence, that had made him store his ritual dress here in the back of the van—they'd be needing the biggest of big guns here tonight. He opened the door and got out of the van, walking around to the back and climbing in again.

Barbara crawled over Claire across the bench seat and managed to navigate the van into a parking space along the curb. All up and down Houston Street, faceless warehouses presented indistinguishable unblinking facades. Any of them might be the hiding place they sought, and time was running out.

Carefully, using a box of wooden matches that had never been used for any other purpose, Colin lit two tapers which had been blessed by a cooperative priest. As soon as the flames began to burn steadily, the crushing weight of the evil all around them lifted slightly in the presence of the holy light. He placed one of the candles in Barbara's hand, and kept the other for himself.

As the consecrated light shone down on her, Claire began to revive. By the time Colin had settled his heavy jeweled breastplate into place and began to tie on the complicated folds of his cap, Claire was sitting up again, bent forward and breathing deeply.

"Good girl," Colin said encouragingly. He pulled the hood of his plain outer robe up, allowing it to hide most of the ornate ritual finery beneath, and picked up the long wrapped bundle that would be his most formidable weapon in the struggle here tonight. "Let's go."

Colin strode up the block, holding his consecrated flame high, as if it were a torch. All around him, the air vibrated to silent shouting, and the icy wind off the Hudson River dragged at his clothes, making the long bundle he carried awkward and unwieldy. He was uncomfortably aware that the two tiny flames were all that stood between the three of them and suffocation in the sea of Darkness that surrounded them. While the force being raised here tonight by the black coven might not have the potency to actually kill them, Colin had enough experience of the world to know that there were many things worse than death.

Claire was reeling along beside him almost as if she were drunk, moaning to herself painfully with each breath. Barbara was following behind, sheer nerves making her babble like a standup comic. She held the candle low against her body and sheltered from the wind with her free hand.

"Quiet!" Colin barked at last. "Let her concentrate!"

Barbara fell silent in midword, and Colin spared a moment of sympathy for her, but he could hardly afford more, as beleaguered as they were.

"This one," Claire whispered, lurching to a stop in front of one door that could not be differentiated from any of the others that lined the midnight street. "No . . . I'm not. I don't—"

"No, it's this one," Barbara said definitively, sounding a little puzzled that neither of them realized what was obvious to her. With the fearlessness of ignorance, she walked up to a door a few feet away and grabbed the handle, only to release it with a startled cry. She tore off her mitten, staring at the hand beneath as though she expected to see something horrible.

"It must have been just . . . a shock. But it felt as if it were . . . hot?" she said, bewildered.

So Barbara Melford is a Sensitive, too, Colin thought to himself.

It would explain much about this whole affair, including why Barbara had fought so stubbornly for so many years to hold onto Jamie, even with all the forces of Hell arrayed against her. Many people fought and died for the Light without ever understanding that they were in a war at all; if not for this encounter, Barbara Melford would have been such a person. Colin vowed that if they all survived this night, Barbara would strive in ignorance no longer.

"Get back, Barbara," Colin said gently. He handed Claire the bundle that he carried. "Let me handle this. You take care of her." He thrust the reeling Claire at Barbara, and turned to the door.

He felt nothing when he reached for the handle—for once he blessed his lack of the Gift—but on the other hand, the door didn't move, either. It was locked.

He supposed it had been too much to hope for that the door would have been open, but Colin had brought his skeleton keys with him for just such a circumstance, and fortunately the lock was an old one that one of his blanks was likely to fit. He found the right master for it at just the moment when his ungloved fingers seemed about to go completely numb in the cutting river wind.

He kicked open the unlocked door and took his candle back from Claire.

"In normal circumstances, I'd say ladies first, but I think this is a special case." He strode into the filthy building, and heard Claire and Barbara hurrying after him.

On the fourth floor the smell of frankincense and asafetida seeping out from around the door was all the evidence he needed. There was a sickly sweet tang to the smoke that made his head spin—there was hashish in that incense, the black magician's quick and dangerous method of opening the higher chakras.

"Give me that," he said to Claire, taking the wrapped parcel from her hands. He shook the sword free of its protection; the Seal of Solomon set into the quillons seemed to blaze like the sun in the dimness of the dingy loft.

Then he took one step back and kicked the door in.

The darkness seemed to roll out through the opening like ink diffusing through water. Colin heard Claire cry out with real revulsion in the moment before he ran forward into the gloomy haze. Jamie Melford was here somewhere, and their prisoner. God grant that he was still alive—and sane.

When Colin crossed the threshold, he could see that the coven was gathered in the next room, crouched about its altar and the naked bound form of Jamie Melford that lay before it. The room was filled with a cold damp mist that stank of the herbs burning on the brazier, but—weirdly—the smoke stopped at the perimeter of the circle marked out in charcoal on the floor in the center of the room.

The Satanists did not move. The lines of power were as visible in that room as if they had been drawn on the ground and the walls in chalk, and the force of the black coven's focused intention was a solid weight and reality.

Colin sweated and shook like a man in the grip of a malarial fever, but his Will, too, was unwavering as he forced himself forward, toward the edge of the circle. He could feel the Darkness and the Powers of Hell gathering around, summoned by pain, desperation, and fear, and it seemed as if dark and shadowy figures shifted slowly about the periphery of the circle, anxious for the climax of the rite enacted within. The weapon in his hands vibrated like a living thing; it was an act of determination to hold onto it.

"In the name of God! In the name of the Lords of Karma and the forces of Nature! In the name of the Fatherhood of God, the motherhood of Nature and the brotherhood of Man, I scatter your forces!" Gritting his teeth, he brought the sword down across the edge of the circle, calling upon those Forces by Whose leave he operated.

When his sword came down, there was a great soundless shout, and suddenly the swarming monkeylike shadows at the circle's edge turned toward Colin, crowding toward him. The coven members, shocked from their trance, screamed and thrashed like victims of electric shock, and suddenly the silent loft was filled with the sounds of gabbling voices.

The most important thing is to move fast once you've made up your mind. The voice of Colin's first teacher spoke quietly in the back of his mind. *If you wait to see what effect you've had on the Darkness, it may be the last thing you see.*

Colin strode through the screaming gasping bodies thrashing about the floor, and shoved over the double-cube altar. The black candles atop it—soft and misshapen because they were not made of honest wax—rolled stickily across the floor, and Colin grimaced with disgust as he stamped them out.

"I spit upon the uncleanliness of the Pit. I spit on those who make unclean those things that God has ordained to the use of man!" Colin roared.

He kicked over the brazier of incense, scuffing through the mess to extinguish the embers of charcoal. He heard a shriek behind him as Barbara ran forward looking for Jamie. He paused for an instant and watched, light-headed, as she reached him.

"Colin! He's got a knife!" Claire shrieked.

Colin spun around. A big man came shambling toward him, his lank black hair falling into his eyes. There was an inverted cross branded into his chest—an old scar—and in his hand he held the double-edged knife from the altar.

The years between Colin's combat training and this moment melted away in an instant. Hardly thinking, Colin flung down the sword and plucked up the skirts of his robes like a dowager preparing to waltz.

The French called it *la savatte;* In Thailand it was known as kick-boxing. Americans, with a fine disregard for attribution, called it and every form of combat like it kung-fu. As the man charged, Colin pivoted on his other foot and lashed out.

His leg traveled through a short arc to connect with the black priest's chin. The shock of contact telegraphed through Colin's bones; he felt the crunch and the sudden sickening slackness as the man's lifeless body dropped to the floor. Suddenly the lights came on; Colin could hear the sound of the switches being flicked in another room.

"Barbara," Colin said, taking a deep breath. The sound of his own voice brought home to him how tired he was, and leftover adrenaline made his hands shake. "Run round to the firehouse and call the police—see if they can find Lieutenant Martin Becket; he works out of Manhattan South, and this is his case as much as it's anyone's. We'll need some police here—and an ambulance."

Colin hoped that self-defense would be explanation enough for what he'd done. The coven's priest—it was probably Walter Mansell—and God above knew how many more were dead here, and the survivors were in profound shock.

Barbara left, running. Colin heard her footsteps echoing down the stairs as he knelt beside the body of the man who had attacked him and gently closed his eyes, murmuring the words of absolution. One of Father Godwin's fallen angels had come home at last.

In the distance, he could hear the sound of a siren wailing.

It was a little after five, and the sky was beginning to lighten with Christmas dawn when Colin stopped the van outside the Melfords' apartment and went around to the back to open the door. Jamie and Barbara climbed out, looking tousled and exhausted, like sleepy children who had been lost in the woods.

"I don't know how we can ever thank you," Jamie Melford said awkwardly. "Not just for saving my life, but for everything."

"I think you know how you can repay me," Colin said.

"The Cannon manuscript," Jamie said, embarrassed. "I'll messenger it over to you first thing . . . uh, next year. I think that Bess will agree you can make any changes you want."

"There's that of course," Colin said. "But more to the point, I hope you'll stay in touch. Barbara's a Sensitive, you know, and we need people like both of you. Though this has been quite a battle, the war goes on."

The war goes on. The words resonated in Colin's mind as he drove southward. Claire was asleep in the seat beside him, and it took him several minutes of shaking before he could rouse her enough to get her to her feet and started in the direction of her apartment door. He waited outside until he saw the light go on in her window, then drove off toward home.

What had happened here tonight should have made him feel good. The Ungodly had been routed; the soul of poor John Cannon had been put to rest.

The power of the black coven had been decisively broken; it would never trouble anyone again.

But Toller Hasloch had not been there tonight, and Colin was betting that Martin Becket's investigation would find nothing to connect Hasloch to Mansell and his crew. Hasloch would simply move on to new villainies. To the seduction of new innocents.

Colin tried to tell himself that if Hasloch had been spared, it was to a higher purpose. The Oaths he had sworn so eagerly once upon a time had made him no more than an obedient tool in the hands of the Lords of Karma. Those bonds had been eased briefly, many years before, but what he considered doing now was an unsanctioned and unlawful thing. *Thy Will, not mine,* he prayed, and for the first time, found the words hollow.

He had lost the detachment that allowed those who follow the Great Laws to walk among men and guide only, never compel. Perhaps he had lost it earlier tonight, when he killed Mansell. Perhaps he had lost it years ago, and had not truly known his loss until he had once more been confronted by Hasloch's particular brand of evil.

And what good did such resignation do him, if it freed men like Hasloch to do more harm? He tried to tell himself that the evil that Hasloch did would overtake him in time; that it was not for Colin to judge or to sentence, but to be a mindful Instrument of the Light. But he could not keep himself from thinking that this was willful blindness, not resignation—and as great an abuse of his Oaths as active harm would be.

How could he live with himself when he uncovered the next evidence of Hasloch's malicious spirit, and knew, gazing upon the pain and the devastation, that he might have prevented all that he saw? People had died tonight—people whose lives Hasloch had touched and twisted, making them into a profane work of art for his own idle amusement. Hasloch had boasted of the accomplishment. . . .

In vain Colin reminded himself that the urge to intervene for a Higher Good was the greatest temptation the Shadow could present men with. He reminded himself that to use the methods of the Serpent was to become its tool; that the purpose of the war he fought was not to win, but to endure. But the harm Hasloch would yet do in the world was an unendurable knowledge. And Colin had the power to end that harm. . . .

Let it be so. A great weight seemed to settle upon Colin's shoulders; a weight almost too great to be borne. He had no choice; knowledge was the first corruption of innocence, and there had been no other choice for him but to embrace that corruption. He would take upon his own soul the weight of this disobedience, expiating in a future life the harm he chose freely to do here today . . . so that Toller Hasloch would do no more.

"Good morning, Toller," Colin MacLaren said.

Cloaked in that invisibility which a warrior of the Light could summon in time of greatest need, Colin had walked into the building unnoticed, just as the sun was rising over the Park on Christmas morning. The locks of

Hasloch's Central Park South apartment were good, but Colin MacLaren had been given decades to hone his lockpicking skills.

Hasloch came out when he head the front door open; now he stood in the center of the living room, looking tousle-headed and sleepy in the bottom half of his pajamas. His expression sharpened when he saw Colin, however, and he made as if to retreat into the bedroom.

"Don't move," Colin said, and showed Hasloch the pistol in his hand.

Hasloch stared at it in unbelief, as if he did not understand what he was seeing. "You're going to shoot me?" he said blankly.

"I'm going to do far worse to you," Colin assured him honestly, "but I'll shoot if I have to. Now be a good boy and come over here, or I *will* shoot you now."

On some irrational level, Hasloch still counted on Colin's goodness, or perhaps he realized that what Colin did here today might be a greater victory for the Shadow than any Hasloch could claim for himself. At any rate, he came docilely enough, and soon Colin had bound him to a heavy chair with the roll of duct tape he carried.

"And now you shoot, and I become just another casualty of city life, is that it? I expected better of you, Professor," Hasloch said, a teasing note in his voice even in this most extreme of all circumstances.

"Did you?" said Colin. *I expected better of myself.* "You should have known better than to tweak my nose quite that openly, boyo. I've always had an appalling temper."

"Yes. But when I saw you coming up the street that night I couldn't resist. I did so want to see what would happen; you were so cross with me the last time we'd met. I had a call from Father Mansell last night, you know. He said he'd call again when he was finished with the current operation, but do you know, I expect that I'm not going to hear from him. You broke my toys, didn't you, Professor?"

Colin did not answer. It was the greatest effort of his existence to simply stand there and not throttle the life out of Toller Hasloch where he sat, helpless and bound.

"Ah, well, I was nearly done with them anyway," Hasloch continued easily. "I'd learned as much as they had to teach me, and what I've learned, I intend to put to good use."

"No," Colin said sadly. "You won't." He cut a short strip of tape and used it to gag Hasloch; he didn't want him shouting out and attracting unwanted attention when he realized what was to come.

Staring down into the face of the bound man before him, Colin saw the moment when fear entered Hasloch's eyes; the moment at which the boy—and even at thirty, Colin could not refrain from thinking of the younger man as a boy—realized that his attacker was insane, or serious, or both. That harm could actually befall him here in his own apartment, on this day dedicated to the celebration of the birth of the Prince of Peace.

Hasloch began to struggle wildly, but Colin had chosen a heavy chair and used most of the roll of tape to secure his prisoner. All Hasloch could do was fling his head from side to side, making frantic grunting noises through the gag. He began to sweat, his hair darkening as it dampened, spraying fine droplets of salt into the air as he thrashed.

Colin stepped behind him as he struggled, and stopped his head between both hands. Hasloch's skin seemed to burn his palms, and all at once Colin could feel Hasloch's fear and anger, more sharp and intimate than imagination could paint them. He could feel the metallic taste of the other man's terror in his own mouth, and his own heart beat panickily fast with the sickening horror of a nightmare come true. But he would not allow even pity to deter him from what he meant to do here today.

The Astral Body was the part of his Self that each Adept sent into the Overworld to do his bidding, transferring his consciousness into it as he did so. Hasloch was proficient enough to have experience of sending his Astral Body forth—Colin knew this because he was able to detach it from his physical Self with ease, and pull Hasloch's Astral Double with him into the Overworld.

Separating the physical body and its Double—sometimes called the *Doppelgänger*—was something comparatively easy for the trained Adept to master, but only the most advanced Adept could separate Soul and Double in the same manner that his less-advanced brethren could sunder the Astral and Physical forms. And Colin was betting that Hasloch wasn't as advanced as that.

This close to the Prime Plane, their surroundings were shadows of the real world, weirdly radiant and stripped of color. This was the place where duration and cause were nullified; the realm to which ordinary people ascended, in ignorance, in their dreams. This was the place from which psychics drew their clairvoyant images of places far removed in space and time.

Hasloch staggered back out of Colin's grasp, and then realized that he was free. His body had been bound to the chair in the world below, but Colin had not yet bound his Double.

Because he was a magician—no matter how tainted—in this place Hasloch wore the robes which were the outer manifestation of his magickal self. His robes were much as Colin had seen them years before, only here the Rune was graven upon a silver disc over his heart, and it writhed and shifted oddly. Upon his forehead was bound the fylfot cross incised into a gold disk, and swept back along his temples were branching antlers carved of ivory and gold. And instead of a dagger at his belt, Hasloch carried the red-hilted Sword of Sacrifice, whose blade seemed to be metal and Darkness and the coiling Dragon which was the flaw that lived at the heart of Creation all at once.

Colin wore the robes and breastplate of his Order. Upon his brow was bound the ancient phylactery that sealed him to the Eternal Law and upon his finger was the ring that symbolized his knowledge. Here on the Astral he and Hasloch were equals, though Colin had perhaps a slight edge, through his longer training and experience.

It took Hasloch a moment to realize that he was free and armed; in that same instant, Colin reached toward him with the Sword that he had expected to find in his own hands, and found himself weaponless. He recovered quickly, snatching barehanded at the Runesword's quillons, but by that time Hasloch had recouped slightly, wrenching the blade away and stumbling backward. The Sword of Sacrifice hissed as it moved, cutting through the congruent objects of the Lower Astral as though they were a tissue-paper backdrop.

He would not win his battle here; Colin retreated deeper into the Astral, to the place that occultists called the Realm of Intention—where thoughts and expectations took physical form, and the Will became a physical weapon. Permanent structures could be created here: the thought forms that most Lodges used to build their Astral Temples were fixed things in this place, objectively perceptible to any well-schooled traveler in these realms.

Likewise, the ruins of such Temples existed, crumbling away to nothingness when their acolytes no longer reinforced them with meditation and magick. How long these holy places endured once they were no longer tended depended on how much energy had been put into their original construction—and of course, some were revitalized by new Adepts who stumbled upon the wellspring of this tradition or that and traced it back to its primal source.

Distance was mutable here; Colin's arrival bought him close to the outer precincts of the Temple of the Sun. Around it, the city of the Temple spread its ghostly facsimile. Though it was thousands of years dead, a few Adepts of the Temple had survived the drowning of their City, and in their longing for their lost homeland, those exiled Adepts had created a simulacrum of the City of the Temple that had endured to this day in the Realm of Intention.

Within that severe and beautiful space Colin could see the faint shapes of his brethren at their work and see their disturbance as they sensed his presence, unannounced and unhallowed.

Then Hasloch followed him, bringing with him his bond to his own unholy places. Colin caught a confused glimpse of a black cathedral whose pillars were pure Darkness, and for an instant, just as if he were any innocent ephemeral entity, his soul was swept by a pang of fervent and absolute terror.

It was the terror of the rational man faced with the madman; the bottomless horror of the victim when he realizes the scope of the evil which has marked him as its prey. It was hopelessness and despair and unreasoning panic, all the dark emotions distilled into one searing whiplash of agony that coursed across Colin's nerves as if they had suddenly been laid bare.

Then the two Places, Light and Shadow, flew apart through the emblematic laws of the Astral, and Colin and Hasloch stood in a place equidistant from both and prepared for battle.

Today Colin acted without the Order's sanction, and the Order's weapons were denied to him—but even so, there were some weapons which Colin wielded in his own right. From the storehouse of memory he drew forth a shining golden chain, and flung it up, stretched between his two hands, to counter Hasloch's first blow.

Hasloch did not speak—either unable to do so in this aspect or fearing the distraction it would bring. He attacked tirelessly, wielding the Sword of Sacrifice with fatal skill. If he struck Colin with that blade . . .

He would do to Colin what Colin intended to do to him, only for Colin, there would someday be another life, another incarnation.

And it was not Colin's intention that Hasloch should ever live again.

At last the weighted chain in Colin's hands did as he had intended it to— it tangled in the guards of the Runesword and jerked the weapon from Hasloch's hands. Colin flung them both away—Sword and Chain together, Will and Discipline, and they disappeared into the misty Overlight.

Hasloch was weaker now—in stripping him of the Sword, Colin had divided him from much of his Will. Now Colin struck Hasloch about the head until the Black Adept's knees buckled, and Colin threw him to the ground, placing his foot on the back of Hasloch's neck to keep him from rising to his feet again. From his will he summoned fetters with which to bind Hasloch. Though the chains he invoked would not last beyond his departure from the Overlight, they would hold Hasloch for as long as required.

Victory. But a temporary thing, over one individual alone. Only Colin's Will now kept their Astral Bodies here on the Astral Plane; and when they fell back into the Plane of Manifestation, Hasloch—with all his temporal power and inventive ability to harm—would be untouched, until that unknown day when the Lords of Karma should choose to act.

The battle had tired him; he could not remain much longer in the Overlight. Colin uttered a heartfelt prayer that he could somehow be spared what he was about to do. He could still walk away, leave Hasloch's harmful potential unchecked, though if he did, he did not think he could live with himself any longer. But there was no mercy to be found anywhere in the vast Intention that surrounded them both.

So be it. *Into Thy hands . . .* Colin appealed again, and took the next step in his crime.

Hasloch was very weak—that, or he had simply stopped resisting, depending upon the fundamental charity of the Light to preserve him from extinction. In his dimished state, the silver cord that bound his wandering Double to its earthly host was obvious, leading away from his body and disappearing into the mists.

Sever it, and Hasloch would not be able to reunite the two parts of himself: Body and Double. Each would dwindle and die, cloven from the other— and if Colin also bound Hasloch's Spirit here in the Overlight, it would never be reborn again on earth.

He took the cord of Hasloch's life in his two hands.

Here Colin held all that Toller Hasloch was and all that he had been, life after life, back to the beginning of Time when the Wheel of their fates had first been set in motion. Held thus, his past lives should be visible to Colin like a string of pearls . . . but there was nothing there.

There was no sheaf of lives lying side by side like the pages of a book, waiting for any who had the understanding to read them out. There was only —

A darkness and a howling. He was borne upon a shadowy wind, drawn through Space and Time by the rite being worked here tonight—a ritual that would compel formless spirit into corporeal flesh, would give the incorporeality of the Dream a physical body.

Like a restless spirit Colin was drawn down through the Astral, to the edge of the Material Plane, but the sight he saw in the World of Form was one that had not been real for many years. In this moment of crisis, of inattention, he had been drawn back through Time to an oddly familiar place and moment: to the moment when the sorcerers of the Thule Gesellschaft *worked to incarnate the spirit of the Reich itself; to fashion the leader who would follow Hitler and consolidate the Nazi victory. . . .*

Or avenge its defeat.

Ingolstadt, Bavaria.

Colin watched, helpless and horrified, as the tiny spark of intention was shaped: the spirit of an age, a soul as young as the century, owing nothing to elder civilizations and older laws. It would be cruel, this child, and ruthless: the blond beast, the Superman that Nietzsche and his acolytes had prophesied, that Hitler had invoked and dreamed of.

Somewhere on the planet, a child conceived for this purpose was being born to house this inhuman spirit, and Colin MacLaren remembered the date exactly: it was November 9, 1938. The rite was timed to coincide with the SS demonstrations in Germany.

Krystallnacht.

The Magus raised his hands. The spirit flew to its destination, and Toller Hasloch was born in a country across the sea, a country that would not enter the war with Germany for three more years.

When the first staccato peal of machine-gun fire stuttered out, Colin remembered the rest of what had taken place here tonight. With doubled attention, he both watched and was his younger self—eighteen this year, nineteen next spring, if he lived—run into the Temple, a hooded mask pulled over his face.

He and his comrades wrecked the Temple, pulling over everything they could, flinging down pieces of the consecrated Host among the implements of magick in an attempt to wreck the ritual. They hadn't even known what was being done here tonight, only that it was important to the infant Ahnenerße—*and fortunately so secret an undertaking that there were only half a dozen SA guards here on the estate.*

Colin watched his younger self set fire to the Temple draperies and flee in the confusion. A dozen of them had come on this raid, and after tonight only three had been left alive.

When he'd gotten back to the Lodge, Colin had demanded to take the oath that would make him the Sword of the Order. He had already taken his first oaths, but not his most binding ones; those he would take after tonight were nearly as terrible as the evil they sought to combat.

And look where that Oath has brought me, *Colin thought bleakly. The past faded as suddenly as it had been summoned, and Colin realized that his hands were empty. The cord of Hasloch's life that he had held between them was torn and severed.*

Let it be so. *With an instant's thought he summoned up the Sign that would permit the chains that bound Hasloch to endure in the Overlight until the memory of Man had passed away, trapping Toller Hasloch's spirit here forever, sealed away from the Wheel and the eternal cycle of rebirth.*

Toller Hasloch had been destroyed, for now and for Ever, as surely and completely as though he had never been born.

The apartment seemed icy when Colin opened his eyes. Automatically he checked his watch. Less than ten minutes had passed since he'd opened the front door. Hasloch was still breathing, but Colin knew that now it was only an automatic reflex.

He was shaken to the core of his being by what he had learned. Hasloch was not a mortal soul, a spark begotten of the Light, but a *Zeitgeist* given human form. Colin was not certain what effect his binding would have upon an artificial soul. Would the chains he had forged hold such a creature?

Had they even been necessary at all?

It is done past all undoing, Colin told himself brutally. *Now all that remains is to see that no innocents are harmed by what I have done here.*

Working quickly, Colin unbound Hasloch from the chair and dragged him back into the bedroom, wadding the tape up in his pocket and replacing the chair in its place in the living room.

It wasn't enough to fool an experienced police officer if foul play was suspected, but now the apartment wouldn't immediately scream "murder scene" when the body was discovered.

The body.

Colin suddenly felt every one of his fifty-two years and more. More than anything the outside world could bestow, he realized, he had always valued his good opinion of himself, and today he had lost it forever. He had perverted the teachings that had been entrusted to him. He had used them to kill.

He did not question why he felt it so necessary to cover his tracks—to get away with murder when all his Order's training had been that an individual should accept full responsibility for the consequences of his actions.

But half an hour's work had rendered the apartment once more much as he had found it, and at a little past six in the morning, Colin MacLaren exited the building on Central Park South as silently and unnoticed as he had entered.

He caught a cab at Columbus Circle—the van had been safely garaged hours ago—and rode downtown through the awakening city. He still felt numbed by what he had done, and his imagination painted for him the picture of Toller Hasloch, half-naked in his cold and lonely bed, as his heart slowed . . . slowed . . . stopped.

And all because Colin MacLaren had set his own judgment above that of the Law which he served, acting on his own Will instead of at the urging of the Lords of Karma. He felt soiled, unclean, and ill. He wanted nothing more than a drink and the comfort of his own bed, though no matter what he did, he could not elude his own condemnation.

He was so wrapped up in his own bleak thoughts that Colin didn't even notice that the lights were on in his apartment until Claire opened the door.

"Colin! Where have you been?" She flung herself into his arms, holding him tightly.

He could not imagine what she was doing here, when he'd left her at the door to her own apartment less than two hours before.

"I was so worried—I thought something had happened to you, too!" she said.

It took a moment for the sense of her words to penetrate the fog that seemed to veil Colin's wits, and at first they only confused him. Something *had* happened to him. Something terrible.

"Has Jamie . . . ?" he began.

"No!" Claire said fiercely. "It's Simon—there's been an accident—he's been hurt.

"He's dying," Claire added raggedly.

FOURTEEN

SAN FRANCISCO, JANUARY 1973

Some random truths he can impart,—
The harvest of a quiet eye,
That broods and sleeps on his own heart.
—WILLIAM WORDSWORTH

THE HARSH, DRUGGED BREATHING OF THE MAN IN THE BED WAS THE loudest sound in the room. Colin sat in the uncomfortable chair beside the bed, watching Simon sleep.

His face was swathed in bandages, both eyes covered. Just after the accident, the doctors had been sure he'd lose his sight. Now they thought they'd be able to save at least the right eye, but Simon Anstey would never again be cover-model handsome.

Disfigurement was bad, and blindness would have been worse, but it was not the most terrible injury that Simon had sustained in the accident.

Automatically, Colin's gaze strayed to Simon's left hand. It, too, was swathed in bandages, held immobile in a brace to keep him from flexing it.

The doctors had wanted to amputate, but Simon would not give them permission. He'd been hysterical—Colin could well imagine the scene—refusing opiates, refusing to let the doctors touch him unless they would promise to leave his hand alone. If he had not been a fixture in the Bay Area community for so many years they might not have listened to him, but everyone in that emergency room had known Simon Anstey, who soloed with the San Francisco Symphony and taught at the conservatory.

He'd held them off until Alison had gotten there, and only after he'd extracted her promise to help him did he allow the doctors to begin their work. And Alison had kept her promise, fighting the doctors until they had given in, refusing to consider the possibility of amputation.

They had worked miracles, but though Simon's hand was intact, no one thought he would ever use it again. The bones of two fingers were crushed, the delicate nerves destroyed. Though someday he might lift a cup to his lips with his left hand, it was unthinkable that he would ever regain the fine control over it that a concert musician required. His career—his *life*—was over.

He was twenty-nine years old.

This is my fault. Though he knew it smacked of hubris, Colin could not shake that conviction. Somehow, he thought, if he had been stronger, if he had not surrendered to temptation to act without sanction . . .

If that is so, then this, too, is part of your punishment, Colin had told himself inexorably.

The door to the hospital room opened.

"How is he?" Alison said in a whisper.

"Still sleeping," Colin answered softly. Alison tiptoed into the room and seated herself in a chair on the other side of the bed. She was haggard and drawn, looking every day of her seventy-four years even in the soft January light.

"If only I'd been with him," she said.

"Then you'd be dead, too, just like the girl who *was* with him," Colin pointed out.

"Damn all drunk drivers to hell," Alison said with quiet venom. The driver who had killed Simon's passenger and ended his performing life had walked away from the collision without a scratch, as drunk drivers almost always did. At least the culpability was clearly his—Simon had been sitting, stopped at a red light—but no legal judgment could repair what he'd destroyed.

Simon began to stir restlessly, fighting his way up through the morphine. Automatically, Colin sketched a Blessing in the space between them, hoping to gain a few more moments of peace for Simon.

"Alison?" Simon's voice was slurred. He plucked at the covers with his free hand.

"I'm here, Simon." She took his right hand gently, lifting it to her cheek.

"My hand. Don't let them take . . ."

"It's all right, Simon. I won't let them operate," Alison said soothingly.

He began to thrash restlessly, obviously in terrible pain but unable to remember why. For one whose psychic centers had been opened by training, the loss of self-control that came with narcotics was equivalent to going to bed with all the doors and windows of the house unlocked and open. Anything might walk in—and wreak untold havoc while the house's true occupant lay helpless to prevent it.

"I will play again!" he muttered. "No matter what. . . . I will—I will—"

"You'd better ring for the nurse," Alison said to Colin. "Simon. Hush, my darling. It's all right."

Colin finally located the call button—it was pinned to the pillow on the right side, where Simon's good hand was—when the nurse came in, already holding a syringe. With brisk efficiency she pressed it through the intravenous tubing that led into Simon's arm, and almost instantly he subsided into a troubled sleep again.

"Dr. Margrave," she said, once her patient had quieted. "How are you to-day?"

Alison gave her a tired smile. "As well as can be expected, I suppose the saying is, Rhonda. Is there any news?"

"Dr. Kiley is going to change the bandages on his face tomorrow; if everything looks good he's going to leave the left eye uncovered, which should help Simon stay awake." She smiled with professional encouragement. "I gave him some Valium just now; he's been insisting that he doesn't want anything at all, so he and Dr. Kiley compromised on a mild tranquilizer."

No trained Adept, Colin knew, would willingly submit to the impairment of his faculties that drugs brought, preferring to trust to the disciplined Will to overcome the pain. And a hospital room was by its very nature a public space, nearly impossible to consecrate and Seal in any meaningful fashion, though both he and Alison had erected what Wards they could.

"I know that everyone here is doing the best for him that they possibly can," Alison said raggedly.

"He has a tremendous will to heal," Rhonda said encouragingly. "That's the most important thing."

But when the damage to the physical body was so great; when the pain continued for so long . . .

Claire arrived half an hour later to spell them, and Colin took Alison out to a nearby restaurant, making sure she ate and doing what he could to lighten her mood. Despite Colin's efforts, it was a melancholy meal, each of them lost in his own unspoken thoughts. The early winter dark was falling by the time Colin drove Alison back to Greenhaven.

"Both of you look pretty whipped." Claire was there to greet them, having left the hospital at the end of visiting hours. She'd already made plans to stay out here for a while, both to keep Alison company, and to help Simon as much as she could.

Alison gave her a tired smile, stepping inside. "It kills me to see him like this. Such a . . . waste." Tears glittered in her grey eyes.

"I suppose there's no hope at all . . . ?" Claire asked tentatively.

She led them back to the parlor, where a cheery fire was adding light and color to the room. The drapes were drawn against the night, making the room seem intimate and cozy. Alison had redecorated it since the last time Colin had been here; it was now aggressively modern in burnt orange and plum, the stark Danish Modern replaced by a couple of sleek leather sofas.

"They still want to amputate," Alison said, as if that were a full explanation. "I spoke to the staff neurologist a few days ago; he said there was no nerve function in the fingers, and that even if the nerves had been intact after the crash, the swelling of the tissues around them would probably have crushed them by now. And if blood poisoning sets in, Simon could lose a lot more than two fingers."

"He does keep saying that he'll get the use of his hand back," Claire pointed out.

"I don't think so," Alison said simply.

"What a terrible loss," Claire said softly. "Poor Simon."

"Don't let him hear you say that," Colin warned gently. "He'd rise up from his sickbed and smite you as Sampson smote the Philistines."

"With the jawbone of an ass?" Claire grinned wanly and went over to fix them all drinks.

Though Claire was two years older than Simon, Colin had once cherished vague hopes that the two of them might make a match, and had not wholly abandoned them. Certainly they could understand one another in the fashion those not touched by the Gift could never master.

Alison stared into the fire, a haunted expression on her face. "I think—in a way—that this accident might have been a blessing in disguise for Simon," she said.

Both of the others stared at her in shock. This was the last thing they'd expected to hear from the woman who had all-but-raised Simon.

Alison sighed harshly. She turned away from the fire and reached for a malachite box on the coffee table. She took out a cigarette, and Colin lit it for her. Claire handed Alison her drink.

"For the last couple of years . . ." Alison began, and stopped, shaking her head. "Well, actually, it goes back further than that. Simon has always been . . . adventurous."

"Adventurous?" Claire said blankly.

From her expression it seemed an inadequate condemnation, but Colin understood exactly what Alison meant. "Adventurous" meant that Simon had turned aside from the practices and exercises his teacher had set him and had gone exploring the paths of power by himself.

"He . . . oh, hell, Claire, you know what Black Magick is. Simon played around with it a bit as a boy, before I caught him at it and gave him merry hell. I thought I'd set him right; the stuff's as bad as hard drugs, and just as seductive. But somewhere—" Alison broke off to sip at her drink, wincing as if it were medicine. Her cigarette made lazy blue spirals up toward the ceiling.

"You know how easy everything's ever been for Simon. Not that he hasn't had to work at his music, but his work's always paid off. There's never been anything he wanted that he didn't—eventually—get." She ran a hand through her hair. "You might say he's never lived in an irrational universe.

"So when I wasn't looking, he came up with this theory that while the practices of the Left-Hand Path were dangerous, they could be performed safely, so long as it was by a trained Adept taking proper precautions."

Colin stared at her in horror. "You know that's not true."

"Oh, yes. But it sounds so plausible, doesn't it? And look at the rewards: absolute power over the Material Plane, the resolution of all obstacles, the destruction of old age—the ability to heal the sick, to raise the dead. . . ." Alison smiled bitterly. "Only we aren't meant to have that power. We're not gods—we don't have access to the Formless Uncreated from which all Manifestation flows. The power to perform all these lovely parlor tricks has to come from somewhere, and for the sons of Adam and the daughters of Eve it comes from blood—from stealing the life energy of others."

"From murder," Claire said flatly.

"Animal sacrifice, usually, but yes. And from torture before the sacrifice, to raise the power to its ultimate expression."

"And Simon was doing this?" Colin asked, incredulous. "Really doing it?"

"He did it once," Alison said. "Years ago. One of my cats. When I caught him, I told him that if he ever did that again, I'd—" She broke off and laughed bitterly. "I told him I'd cut off his left hand."

Claire flinched, as if trying to ward off the image. "But that was years ago, Alison," she said hopefully. "And you didn't mean it."

"I did mean it, Claire, and he knew it, so—as I thought—he dropped the stuff. And then a couple of years ago he brought it all up again, just hypothetically this time, thank god. I could see what was happening, where he was going with this, but there was nothing I could do to talk him out of it. He kept saying that the Left-Hand practices had been barred from our use through nothing more than superstitious ignorance, and the time for that was over. I only hope that this tragedy, well, makes him take stock of his life and look inward. But you know, I've wondered sometimes lately if he might not be right? The world seems like such a dark place these days. . . ." She sighed.

"To turn to the Dark is never right," Colin said firmly. He felt like a hypocrite as he said it, even though he knew he was telling only the truth. He simply hadn't known, when he was first taught this Rule that he must live by, how hard it was, and how overwhelming the temptations to surrender could be.

He wondered what Simon's temptations had been, and which of his friends and mentors had failed him most. *We are all each other's caretakers,* Colin reflected. He did not think he had been a good one, so far.

Looking back at his life, all Colin could see were halfhearted attempts at stewardship, as though it were something he had been only playing at until he could return to his rightful work. But stewardship *was* his rightful work. The sanguine glamour that had been cast over his early life had been meant to fade and leave him as he had been before. Only when he had renounced the power, he had not been able to set aside the memories. To go on, to do what he had been meant to do, he must renounce the memories as well, and set that part of himself to slumber, for the sake of those whose lives he touched.

"Alison, you know there are things we are forbidden to do. It's the Code we live by, and no one ever said it was easy. All of Simon's arguments sound reasonable, but that's hardly the point at issue here. We already know that appropriating the Shadow's methods can only lead to disaster—you and I both have absolute proof of that. The means creates the end—to reach an impeccable goal we can only use the most impeccable tools."

"And so we diddle around with peashooters while the Enemy has the heavy artillery," Alison said bitterly. "And we lose people like Simon every day." She stubbed out her cigarette in the ashtray. "It isn't fair, is it?"

"No," Colin agreed. "But that's the way it is."

Toller Hasloch hovered, an unshared secret, over the conversation. Now Colin had seen the full extent of what damage those ghosts of the past could do, but right now the important thing was not to salve his own wounds, but to lend strength where he could, so that others did not suffer the same pain of separation from the Light that he had brought on himself.

Two weeks later Simon was transferred to a long-term care facility. He was walking—with help—and the long process of reconstructing the left side of his face had begun. Though the eye itself was intact, the sight in his left eye was badly compromised, and he suffered blinding headaches unless the damaged eye was kept covered. But his determination to be what he had been before the accident was unwavering, and almost frightening in its intensity.

"I will play again," he said to his visitors.

The left side of his face was exposed now, crossed with livid red scars awaiting the hand of the plastic surgeon. He wore a patch over his left eye. The blackness of unshaven stubble over the scarred half of his face and neck, along with his half-shaven scalp, gave him a particularly brutish look, though some of the effect was offset by the fact that he was wearing his own clothes at last.

His room at the rehabilitation clinic looked more like a bedroom in a luxurious hotel than like a sickroom. It had a panoramic view of the City, and there was even a fireplace. But the bed was outfitted with side rails and a call button, and all the pathways around the room were wide enough to allow the passage of a wheelchair.

"Simon, there are other—" Alison began.

"'Other things to do with your life than play!'" Simon mocked angrily. "Why, I could *teach*—or conduct—or compose. So Colin had been kind enough to tell me, the witless hypocrite! He's a eunuch lecturing a whole man on the joys of chastity—"

"Simon!" Claire said, shocked.

Alison had said that Simon was being difficult, but until now Claire hadn't known quite how difficult "difficult" was.

"Yes, *Simon*," Simon jeered. "And I'll tell you—both of you—what I told him: I do not intend to lie down and seek the consolations to be found in groveling submission to the ineffable Will of God. That was never my way, and I don't intend to take it up now. Why are we given power, if not to use it?"

"You know the answer to that," Claire said quietly.

"I know the answer your loving God would have me choose," Simon snarled, "but—"

He broke off, stiffening in his chair. His head jerked to the side and he twitched spasmodically, as if an electric current were running through him. His lips were curled back from his teeth in a snarl that forced beads of blood through the surface of his half-healed scars.

"Get the nurse!" Claire barked, jumping up from her chair and running over to him. "Simon—Simon, can you hear me?" The muscles under her hands were rigid, and Simon did not answer.

In a few more seconds—though it seemed an eternity—the seizure had passed. Simon slumped against Claire, panting raggedly.

"Mr. Anstey!" the floor nurse said, coming in just ahead of Alison.

"All . . . right. I'm all right now," Simon said, his voice barely a whisper.

"He had another one of those spasms," Claire said. Simon's face was slick with mingled sweat and blood. She plucked the silk handkerchief from the breast pocket of his dressing gown and blotted his forehead with it. The lid of his good eye drooped with exhaustion.

"I think that you ought to get back into bed," the nurse told Simon. "The doctor has written you a prescription for—"

"No drugs," Simon said breathlessly.

"If they'll help you heal, you should take them," Alison said. Her face was twisted with the pain she felt for him. "The faster you heal, the less need you'll have for them."

"Let me help you get him into bed," Claire said to the nurse. It helped that they knew here that she was an RN; it made the staff more willing to rely on her.

Between the two of them, Claire and the floor nurse quickly muscled Simon into bed and out of his dressing gown. He wasn't able to be of much help—the wracking nerve spasm had left him weak—but the two of them got him tucked in easily.

"Mr. Anstey, you really should—"

"Go away," Simon said tiredly.

Claire understood why he was so unwilling to accept any of the painkillers the staff wished to give him. She herself rarely took anything stronger than aspirin, and never drank anything stronger than the occasional glass of wine. Both Alison and Colin had offered to erect the Wards that Simon was still too weak to build, but he had angrily rejected their help—calling it pennies to a blind beggar's cup—and they could not act without his permission.

But it was a hard row to hoe, relying on your own strength alone, and Claire's heart wept for him. She took his good hand in both of her own. "Rest now, Simon," she said gently. "I'll watch with you."

"You're a good girl, Claire," Simon said. His fingers flexed momentarily about her own as he fell down into unguarded sleep.

When Claire was certain he'd gone deep enough not to be pulled back into wakefulness by any lingering twinges, she tucked his hand under the covers and got to her feet, tracing the Seal of Man on his forehead with a light touch. She shook her head ruefully, gazing at Alison.

"I wouldn't want to be in charge of his treatment," she said in a low voice. "He's the worst sort of patient to have: bright, stubborn, and half-right."

The description, as she'd hoped it would, brought a smile to Alison's face.

"I know that Colin had to go back East, but you'll stay with us awhile, won't you, Claire?" Alison said, almost pleading. "I think Simon might listen to you. We've quarreled so much this past year that I think he's just got the idea that I'm opposed to anything he wants to do, and I'm not." There was a faint quiver in the older woman's voice.

"Well, if he thinks I'm going to go along with those crack-brained ideas of his about using magick to heal himself, he's in for a rude awakening," Claire said firmly. "It's foolish, and it's wrong."

"You're right, my dear," Alison said, sounding more like her old self, "but you have no idea how stubborn Simon can be."

"I've known a few stubborn men in my life," Claire said, with a faint smile. "And however bad Simon is, he can't be half as stubborn as Colin."

FIFTEEN

GLASTONBURY, NEW YORK, FEBRUARY 1973

He sought,
For his lost heart was tender, things to love,
But found them not, alas! nor was there aught
The world contains, the which he could approve.
— PERCY BYSSHE SHELLEY

THIS MIGHT NOT HAVE BEEN A GOOD IDEA, COLIN ADMITTED TO HIMSELF AS HE drove north along the Taconic Parkway. But staying in San Francisco and browbeating a helpless invalid—and Simon Anstey was still very close to being that, no matter how sharp his tongue—was not a useful course of action either, and Colin had barely been able to have a civil conversation with Simon any time in the last two weeks.

John Cannon's last book, *Witchcraft: Its Power in the World Today,* had been edited and returned to Jamie Melford—along with a basic reading list, so that he and Barbara could begin to understand the strange world they'd been thrust into.

Colin had been more than a little disturbed at the material contained in the manuscript. Now, rituals and techniques that had been closely guarded secrets for centuries—and had been at least hard to find in Thorne Blackburn's heyday—were, through popularizers such as John Cannon, available to anyone with a dollar bill. And the easier they were to find, the more frivolously they would be used, with disaster the inevitable result.

The Path was not a thing to be entered onto lightly out of a rainy day's boredom; nor were its paths to power suitable to every individual's state of mind, even in a democracy where—in theory—all persons were created equal. Far too many people were driven into the magickal underworld not by any inborn craving for the answers there, but because conventional science had failed to provide them any answers when their lives were interrupted by the Unseen. The only thing that could truly help these people was to open the closed minds of the physical sciences, and that could only be done by offering them proof on their own terms.

And that was the heart of the reason why Colin was making his journey north to the Taghkanic College Campus, and the Margaret Beresford Bidney Memorial Psychic Science Research Laboratory.

The college's nearest neighbors were the town of Glastonbury and a small artist's colony; Colin visited them both involuntarily before he finally found the campus. A recent snowfall—winter was harder here, north of NYC— made the roads treacherous, and some of the smaller roads hadn't been plowed at all. After ending up in the center of Glastonbury for the second time, Colin got back onto the main road and this time found the turnoff for Leyden Road. This time he crossed over the railroad tracks—the point at which he'd turned back last time—and made it all the way to the college. He felt an unreasonable sense of triumph as he passed between the fieldstone posts and beneath the wrought-iron gateway that said "Taghkanic College."

Even in the depths of winter, the college had a stark Victorian prettiness. Brick walkways, swept clean of snow, crossed the lawns between the black, winter-bare trees; when the trees were in bloom the campus must be dazzling. It was as if Colin had stepped two centuries back in time; the college stood like something preserved in Arctic ice, an echo of another age. He drove slowly past the red brick buildings and the clumps of anonymous students moving between them, looking for his destination. Dr. Newland had told him that the laboratory was impossible to miss . . .

. . . and he'd been perfectly right, Colin decided a few moments later, standing beside his parked van and staring up at the snow-dusted structure with something like awe.

The effect was very much as if someone had plunked down a Greek temple among a group of log cabins. The building's shallow porch was supported by seven Doric columns, and above them, in bronze letters weeping verdigris into the porous white marble were the words: MARGARET BERESFORD BIDNEY MEMORIAL PSYCHIC SCIENCE RESEARCH INSTITUTE. The relief above the name depicted classical themes: Helios, Pandora, Prometheus; all examples of mankind reaching for the power of the gods.

It was a pity, Colin reflected, that all those tales ended in tragedy, but the Greeks weren't much on happy endings to begin with. Colin climbed the shallow steps and stepped onto the porch. The stone above the bronze entryway was carved with the quotation from Joel 2:28: "Your old men shall dream dreams; your young men shall see visions." Colin pulled open the door and walked in.

He found himself inside a small rotunda, as if this were truly the temple its form mimicked. The marble beneath his feet was inlaid in an elaborate knot, and the domed glass roof filled the room with light. The elaborate bronze clockface set into the wall opposite the door told him that he was only a few minutes late for his appointment.

The receptionist was obviously one of the students who attended the college; she had a pile of textbooks beside her elbow, but she looked up alertly when Colin entered. Oversized aviator glasses with wire frames gave her the look of a helpful dragonfly.

"Hi; I'm Leonie. Nesbit?" she added, as if she weren't quite sure. "Can I help you?"

"I'm Colin MacLaren. I have a two o'clock appointment with Dr. Newland, but I'm afraid I'm a little late—"

"Oh, Dr. MacLaren! Yes, Dr. Newland is expecting you. Go right through that archway and all the way down the hall—it's the door at the end." She pointed over her shoulder.

Colin went in the direction she indicated, past a row of white doors with names beside them that led into office cubicles. At the end of the hallway there was a cross corridor, and just before it an open area, with file cabinets, a couple of vacant secretarial desks, and a coffeepot and refrigerator.

The place seemed oddly deserted; even the coffeepot was empty. Straight ahead was the door that Leonie had mentioned; set into it in severe bronze letters were the words: *Dr. Reynard Newland, Director.* Colin knocked, then opened the door.

Dr. Newland was sitting behind a massive rosewood desk in an office that was almost a stereotypical recreation of the study of an Oxford don. The windows on the left side of the office looked out on a screen of snow-covered pines through which could be seen some of the other campus buildings. Built-in bookshelves set into oak-paneled walls were filled with a variety of exquisite and well-loved books, and there was a tall glass cabinet filled with curios along the other wall. There was a coffee table and a set of club chairs in the far corner for more relaxed seating, and the jewel-tones of an antique Persian carpet glowed upon the floor.

Dr. Newland was in his mid-seventies, Colin guessed, and the ill-health that was the reason for his retirement had given his skin a waxy pallor. But he was cheerful enough as he rose from his seat behind the desk and motioned Colin to a chair.

"Sit down, Dr. MacLaren. You look rather frazzled—not too much trouble finding the college, I hope?"

"Not after I'd exhausted every other possibility," Colin agreed, smiling. "I'm sorry I'm late."

"Oh, not at all. I was just catching up on my professional reading; the place practically runs itself." Dr. Newland gestured toward a familiar pile of professional journals lying on the corner of his desk. "But I'm overlooking the niceties. Would you care for a cup of coffee? Tea?"

"Tea, but I wouldn't want to put you to any trouble," Colin demurred. Dr. Newland had already buzzed for Leonie, and there was a short pause while he gave her directions and sent her off again.

As Michael Davenant had predicted, Dr. Newland had been eager to interview someone of Colin's caliber regarding the upcoming vacancy. Unfortunately, as Davenant had further suggested, Dr. Newland was rather inclined to take the college's view of matters.

"It's sad, really—the whole Bidney endowment sitting here, all tied up by the institute, while the college goes begging for funds. The trustees won't accept federal money; no, the college still operates on the terms of its 1714 charter, and it is funded entirely by private contributions. But these days . . . "

Colin knew that liberal arts colleges all across the country were closing, unable to keep tuition costs low enough to attract students.

"But surely, turning over Miss Bidney's bequest to the college isn't the answer?" Colin said tactfully. "I'd think that the presence of the institute could be a major asset to Taghkanic. Very few places offer a degree program in Parapsychology these days, you know."

"Very true," Dr. Newland said doubtfully. "But it all seems rather pointless, somehow. What are they to do with their degrees once we've awarded them? Psychic phenomena simply cannot be quantified; it merely devolves into smoke and mirrors. The scientific method is anathema to the manifestation of the Unseen World."

"I don't believe that's completely true," Colin said slowly, unwilling to offend his host. "Certainly psychic phenomena haven't necessarily consistently demonstrated a cause-and-effect relationship under laboratory conditions in the past, but it's possible that this is simply through our own ignorance of the number of variables involved. And human subjects introduce human error— what if you were attempting to prove the existence of perfect pitch, and 99.999 percent of your test group were tone-deaf? You'd need a much larger statistical pool to even begin to isolate the thing you wished to study."

As Colin paused, there was a knock at the door, and Leonie entered, carrying an enormous silver tray. Staggering a little under the weight, she set it carefully down on the table in the corner, smiled cheerfully at the two men, and flitted out again.

There was another pause in the conversation as Colin and Dr. Newland moved to the less formal seating in the corner.

"Good heavens," Colin said mildly, gazing down at the tray. It held macaroons and sliced cake in addition to the tea things. "I wasn't expecting this."

"I have always held that a proper English tea is a civilizing influence," Dr. Newland said firmly, "and I will admit, I am pleased to be entertaining a fellow tea-drinker. Will you pour?"

It was not the most bizarre circumstance Colin had ever experienced—to discover that whether or not he got the job he'd come to interview for hinged not on his qualifications, but on his preference for tea over coffee—and he was no believer in accident at the best of times. Though he possessed no psychic gifts, Colin began to believe that he had been foredestined to take Dr. Newland's place.

As they chatted over tea and cakes, Colin found that Reynard Newland was a parapsychologist of the old school. His interests lay almost exclusively with ghosts—that most subjective of psychic phenomena—and he took very little interest in quantifiable talents such as clairvoyance and psychokinesis. Needless to say, Dr. Newland's worldview did not even admit of the possibility of nonhuman noncorporeal entities, and Colin was wise enough not to raise the question. But it became tragically easy to see how the Bidney Institute had dwindled over the last few decades to simply an extension of Dr. Newland's avocation, and why the college considered it to be moribund—overfunded—deadwood.

"But surely it would be very difficult for the college to simply assume the Bidney endowment?" Colin asked a little while later.

"Oh, dear me, no, young man. Taghkanic has always been the residuary legatee for the bequest. In the event that the Bidney Prize were to be awarded, the endowment fund would certainly have to be liquidated to pay it out, and in the event that the institute can no longer support itself afterward, any balance of funds is to be paid to the college."

Margaret Bidney's entire fortune had been willed to fund research into the psychic sciences—incidentally creating the Bidney Institute—but her will also made proviso for a prize of one million dollars to be awarded to the individual who conclusively provided absolute and verifiable proof of paranormal abilities. Though competitors had been attempting to attain it for over half a century, the prize had never been claimed.

"I don't suppose you consider the possibility of someone winning the prize very likely?" Colin asked diffidently.

"Oh, my, no," Dr. Newland said, smiling gently. "When I came here back in the thirties, I'll admit that I was all on fire with the thought that someone might come in and claim the prize at any moment, revolutionizing the world of science as we then knew it—and certainly a week didn't seem to pass without someone trying for it. But the criteria for its bestowal are so very strict—this is one of the reasons why the institute keeps a stage illusionist on retainer—that no one has ever managed to claim it."

"A magician is a very wise idea," Colin agreed.

"Oh, Miss Bidney wasn't at all softheaded—I had the privilege of meeting her once, as a young man—though naturally people tend to equate a belief in the Spirit World with gullibility. Anyone who successfully claims the prize will have earned it indeed."

By the time that Colin signed the contract that made him director of the Bidney Institute a few weeks later, he felt that he'd worked as hard as any of those hopeful contestants for the million-dollar prize.

Though in one sense he felt that it was preordained that he become the institute's new director, in another, there were a large number of people to convince. The institute's board of directors, for one, and the president of Taghkanic College, for another. Neither was easy, for opposite reasons.

Next, there was all the minutiae of relocation to attend to, though fortunately he'd wound up his involvement with Selkie Press right on schedule, and Alan had even found a buyer for his backlist—Blackcock Books, spurred by the success of John Cannon's postmortem bestseller, had decided to take a strong position in New Age titles.

Fortunately, Colin was lucky enough to obtain a lease on an old Colonial-period farmhouse out on Greyangels Road. It was only about a half-hour drive from the institute—at least in good weather. The place had a peace and solitude that reminded him of the house he'd grown up in, and the view from the bedroom windows—of the apple orchard and the river beyond was breathtaking. He'd moved into the farmhouse in time to enjoy the full glory of a Hudson Valley summer, finding to his relief—since there was no possi-bility of installing an air conditioner with the house's wiring in the state it was—that the proximity of the river tempered the heat and the humidity to something closer to the northern California summers he'd been spoiled by.

He'd be taking over the directorship in September. At the moment the in-stitute followed Taghkanic's academic year, one of the many things Colin in-tended to change. There was no reason for that, just as there was no reason for all of the institute's staff to be accredited teachers and members of the Taghkanic faculty. The more Colin reviewed conditions at the institute, the more he found things that he wanted to alter. Fortunately—despite the board of directors of the institute and the trustees of the college—the director had sweeping powers to define the institute's mandate, and Colin intended to ex-ercise them in full.

Even while he was settling in to his new job, Colin kept up with the news from San Francisco, and little of it was good.

Simon had been sent home at last, though a long series of operations was still scheduled for his hand and eye. He was walking—even driving—with-out particular difficulty, and had even accepted a post as guest conductor at the symphony for the 1974–75 season.

But Alison reported that he was as determined as ever to play again, and was willing to go to any lengths—and for Simon, that meant magick—to re-gain his full abilities as a musician. She had all but severed her relationship with him, and made sure that the local occult community knew of her dis-pleasure. Once Simon would have been crushed by that, but now—according to Claire, who'd remained Colin's faithful correspondent—he'd simply laughed and marked Alison's behavior down to the timidity of old age. Claire was still staying with Alison, but by now she'd lost all hope of being able to intervene with Simon and was planning to return East.

Colin had debated the wisdom of interceding himself, attempting to awaken Simon to the spiritual danger he was in, but from the first time they'd met, he and Simon had always tended to clash. It would be too easy for Colin's intervention simply to antagonize Simon and drive him further down the reckless path he was following.

In the end, Colin had written Simon a careful, formally-worded letter, lay-ing out the arguments against Simon's present course of action with scrupu-lous disinterest, though his own psyche still smarted from the aftereffects of his own disastrous choice.

He'd received no reply, but Colin made a solemn vow not to give up on Simon, though it might be years before Simon was ready to listen to him. In the meantime, he threw himself wholeheartedly into the work of the institute.

I'll never get used to these blessed monkey suits, Colin thought resignedly, cautiously tugging his bow tie into shape in the blotchy bathroom mirror. But the invitation had specified formal dress, and Colin had already learned that since the nearby artist's colony was capable of putting on the style on occasion, the college followed suit.

The party tonight would be at President Quiller's house, and the occasion was the formal announcement of Colin's appointment and his introduction to college society.

He wasn't looking forward to this. But politics seemed to be a function of every human endeavor, and he knew perfectly well that his appointment was not popular with the elements of the administration that had hoped to see the institute dismantled at Dr. Newland's retirement.

While Colin sympathized intellectually with the college's administrative plight, he thought that the administration should be focusing on the good the institute could do for the college. Properly run, the parapsychology program could certainly generate a respectable amount of revenue through student tuitions alone. And its value to the college in terms of research and prestige could hardly be overestimated.

All he needed to do, Colin thought wryly, was sell them on that.

President Quiller's house was on campus, an exuberant example of Riverboat Gothic built almost a hundred years ago on a bluff overlooking the Hudson. Light streamed out through the mansion's windows, glittering in deep scarlets and greens. There was a gravel drive in front with several other cars parked in it, and Colin pulled his new Volvo in at the end of them. He'd had to replace the van—dependable though it was—simply because he'd be doing a lot more driving here, and under worse conditions. And because, much though he deplored it, he'd have to live up to certain expectations of behavior suitable to the Bidney Institute director.

Though sunset came early here in the Hudson Valley, there was still enough light when Colin arrived to give him a breathtaking view of the river, the far bank reduced to a black silhouette against the shining sky. After a moment's appreciation, he turned to the house.

Leonie Nesbit opened the front door as he ascended the steps. She was wearing a velvet pantsuit in a dark jewel print with an extravagantly ruffled blouse.

"Doctor MacLaren!" she chirped excitedly. "Come in!"

"About half the guests are here now," she said, ushering Colin into the main parlor. "Dr. Quiller is having the college for cocktails and then just department heads and the institute for dinner, so you can get to meet them."

And then the college will have the institute for breakfast, Colin finished sardon-
ically. Well, he would do the best he could to smooth things over, though he
knew it would be a task of months, perhaps years. A great work, but one he
felt equal to.

"Colin!" Dr. Newland's greeting was filled with genuine warmth. "Come
in, dear boy, and meet everyone. Harold—President Quiller—is here somewhere . . . at least, I'm sure I saw him just a few minutes ago. . . . "

At fifty-three, Colin reflected, there were fewer and fewer people who were
entitled to address him as "dear boy," but Dr. Newland had that privilege if
anyone did. Leonie tactfully dropped back, and Colin allowed himself to be
conducted by Dr. Newland in search of their host.

But President Quiller did not seem to be anywhere in the front of the
house, and after a few moments of fruitless searching, Dr. Newland conducted Colin over to a small group of people.

"I suppose I should at least introduce you to *someone,* dear boy; Lee Chapman—John Dexter—Miriam Gardner—Morgan Ives," Dr. Newland said,
introducing the two men and two women. "All my respected colleagues. But
let me leave you to get acquainted and I'll see if I can find Harold. I know
he'll be anxious to meet you."

If there's anything left after the lions are finished, Colin thought, surveying the
group. These four people were most of the current staff of the institute, and
this was the first time Colin had been given the chance to meet them.

Of the four of them, only Morgan Ives and John Dexter looked really comfortable in formal dress. Morgan wore her quilted satin maxiskirt and pleated
gold lamé peasant blouse with the slapdash eccentricity of a diva, and her
wrists were weighted with bracelets until she had the look of a woman
chained.

"Colin MacLaren," she said in greeting, extending her hand. The bracelets
clinked. Her nails were long and blunt-tipped, lacquered a deep arterial red.
"How charming to meet you. I'm certain we shall deal splendidly together."

"Cut it out, Morgan. MacLaren eats table-tippers like you for breakfast,"
Dexter said amiably. His hands were thrust deep into the pockets of the
tuxedo that he wore as easily as if it were a business suit. For some reason, he
looked oddly familiar to Colin.

"I never tipped a table in my life, Dexxy," Morgan snapped, withdrawing
her hand and glaring at him.

"Maybe not—but you fall for every single person who does," Dexter said,
before turning back to Colin. "John Dexter. I've followed your debunking
work with great interest."

Suddenly Colin realized why Dexter had seemed so familiar. "Have I the
honor of addressing Theophrastus the Great?" he asked.

"Ah. You've heard of me?" Dexter said, pleased.

"I had the opportunity to watch you work once at the Magic Castle. I've
never seen more artful closeup work," Colin answered honestly.

"The classic stage illusions are fun," Dexter said, "but essentially the audience knows it's being fooled and doesn't really care how. Closeup, they've got no choice but to care." He produced a coin from nowhere and walked it across the back of his fingers, grinning engagingly.

"I see you've met Newland's pet magician in a previous life," Lee Chapman said ungraciously, "though professional bully might be closer to the mark. Once our Mr. Dexter has finished what he calls 'making sure they're not cheating,' my psychics are so demoralized they can't possibly demonstrate their powers."

"Possibly because they haven't got any to begin with," Dexter responded, with an irritability that suggested that this was a feud of long standing. He flipped the coin up into the air and it vanished. "In all my years practicing the Art, I've never seen—"

"Gentlemen," Miriam Gardner said, firmly enough to silence both of them. "There's no point in trying to scare him off—like it or not, he's our new boss. So let's be nice to him." She smiled at Colin a little nervously.

Miriam Gardner was somewhere on the far side of forty, partridge-plump and short. She was wearing a dress in a trying shade of bronze that looked as if she had run it up out of a set of old brocade curtains, and her short-cropped hair was hennaed an unconvincing shade of red. She reminded Colin very much of a forest creature caught far from cover, blinking confusedly in the light of oncoming headlights.

"Well, then, he'll hear all of our nonsense soon enough," Chapman said with ponderous jocularity—and more generosity than Colin had expected of him. "I'm willing to bury the hatchet for tonight."

"I'm looking forward to talking to each of you individually about the future of the institute," Colin said. "Though I doubt that what any of you will have to say is nonsense, Mr. Chapman."

Chapman's field was telepathy and remote viewing, while Ives was interested in mediumship as it related to personality survivals and transfers— ghosts, in mundane parlance. Gardner seemed primarily to be a folklorist, from what Colin was able to glean from the records kept at the institute.

"It's *all* nonsense," Dexter assured him with the blithe confidence of the devout unbeliever. "Let's talk about something else. Oh, here's Lion; Lion, come meet our newest victim—"

Colin had just begun to exchange pleasantries with Professor Lionel Welling—Lion to his friends—when he felt a ripple around him, rather like the reaction of a school of fish to the approach of a shark.

"Ah, Dr. MacLaren," Harold Quiller said, appearing at last. "There you are. I've so looked forward to meeting you."

President Quiller moved toward Colin in much the fashion of an ocean liner cutting off a tugboat. From the corner of his eye, Colin could see that the institute staff had vanished with the ease of long practice.

Colin had met Quiller previously, during the interviewing process; the man was a born politician, and had gone after the Bidney money with the single-minded rapacity of a seventeenth-century corsair after a Mughal trea-

sure ship. That Colin had achieved his appointment over Quiller's own candidate—a man who had championed the notion of a series of "pass-throughs"
from the institute's budget to the college's—the Taghkanic president considered to be a setback, nothing more.

Their conversation this evening had more in common with a fencing
match than with any real exchange of information. What Quiller wanted
tonight was assurances that Colin would take his cue from the administration; Colin was prepared to offer no such promises. After several minutes,
Quiller surrendered the field, and wished Colin a long and happy future at
the institute. As he walked off, Colin had the relieved feeling of one who had
baited a tiger and gotten away with it.

"Score one for the new boy," Dexter said, sotto voce, appearing again. "You
look like a man who needs a drink." He held out a plastic cup containing an
amber liquid, no ice.

Colin smiled, a little grimly. He might have won the skirmish, but it
looked like it was going to be a long war. He accepted the drink gratefully.
Scotch. Either it was a lucky guess, or Dexter had done his homework.

With the obligatory clash with Quiller out of the way, Colin made it his
business to meet most of the faculty of Taghkanic. Many of those Colin met,
such as Professors Auben Rhys and Lionel Welling of the Drama Department, were perfectly amiable, but there were others who were as coolly antagonistic as the college president.

Along the way, he cemented his impression that academics the universe
over had more similarities than differences. If he closed his eyes, Colin could
imagine he was back on the Berkeley campus a dozen years ago—and since
Taghkanic was a liberal arts college, most of the political convictions weren't
much different from those of Berkeley in the sixties, either.

"I don't care *what* you say, Lion," Selena Purcifer said resentfully. "The library's book budget has been cut again, just so a bunch of crackpots can chase
UFOs. I don't particularly find that a cause for celebration."

"Now Purcy," Lion Welling said pacifically, "the one has nothing to do
with the other. Everybody's budget's been cut. It's the nature of the beast."

Colin turned away before they could catch him eavesdropping. Selena Purcifer was the Library Director, and one of the people he particularly hoped to
win over to his cause. If the Bidney Institute now possessed the Rhodes
Group's case files, it would be an enormous job of cataloguing to get the material ready for the public, and he'd need to work closely with the library
staff. Possibly there was a way to arrange a pass-through of Bidney money to
the library without opening the floodgates to a wholesale looting of the institute. But that, too, was a problem to be approached in the future.

He was glad enough to be pulled into another conversation, and doubly relieved that it had nothing to do with either the college or the institute. Finally the reception was over, and President Quiller's guests filed in to dinner.

While there were isolated moments of shoptalk and upcoming events of
the fall term around the table, most of the talk at dinner was about current

events, particularly the Watergate trial, which was still dragging on. The hearings had been televised since May, and had held a sort of perverse fascination for Colin; he'd watched them whenever he could.

Predictably, the staff of a liberal arts college unanimously condemned Nixon and his activities, but to Colin's mild surprise, none of them probed any deeper, or asked how such things could ever have happened. Corruption and moral indifference on such a scale could not be an isolated incident, nor did it flourish in a vacuum, but none of the people at the table asked the vital questions: who, and how, and how long.

It was as if none of them wanted to believe that the Watergate scandal could be the result of anything more than one man's evil, easily blotted out with an impeachment. The discussion left Colin feeling unspeakably depressed, as though he were listening in on the self-important chatter of young children. But these were the people who were shaping the minds of the next generation.

Thorne was right; Simon was right; even—God help me—Toller Hasloch was right, may his soul find peace in its imprisonment. In the only way that really matters, we lost the war. We were fighting for the American way of life—the four freedoms— and they simply don't exist in this country anymore.

And each year, it takes a greater effort to remain blind to that fact. . . .

GLASTONBURY,
SEPTEMBER 1979

FOR THE NEXT SEVERAL YEARS COLIN AND I SOMEHOW SAW MUCH LESS OF each other. It was as if he were shutting the world out, though on the surface he had thrown himself more into the world than ever, at the turbulent Bidney Institute in upstate New York. Perhaps in some way Simon's accident had injured Colin as well, and made him a dark and desperate man, though I think something must have happened to him even before that.

Whatever it was, Colin never spoke of it, in that way that we left so many things between us unsaid. But after that terrible Christmas when Simon was crippled, he was very much changed. It was as if in fighting for the institute's survival, Colin was fighting for his own life as well.

But slowly his hard work brought success. He hired new staff, both exploiting the assets that Dr. Newland had left him and drawing on his old Rhodes Group contacts. Within a few short years the institute developed the reputation for sympathetic but tough study of matters touching upon the Unseen World. God help the researcher whom Colin caught faking his results—and nothing could help the psychic who tried to fool him.

When he confronted psychic frauds was the only time I ever saw Colin really lose his temper—not with the cold, furious, sense of purpose I had known him to exhibit so often, but with a roaring Scots rage that thundered like a summons to judgment. There were few people who could stand up to him under those circumstances, and none of the sort that John Dexter so happily called "table-tippers," in which category John included not only fake mediums and bogus Spiritualists but every form of psychic con and fraud. I do believe that sometimes he deliberately sought those people out and encouraged them to apply to the institute, just for the joy of watching Colin read them out of the book.

Poor John. Wherever he is now, I wish him eager audiences, and an inspiration that never fades. He was a gallant, fearless soul, taken from us far too soon.

But that is an old sorrow, and he was certainly there for the first years of Colin's regime—and I use the term advisedly—acerbic court jester to the reigning lion.

From the first, Colin had a very definite view of what the institute should be and how he could achieve his vision. He insisted on the strictest code of standards and ethics from all the members of the institute, and even taught a course on occult ethics himself, making it mandatory for all freshmen who wished to enter the parapsychology program. You did not study Parapsychology at Taghkanic without a solid understanding of what Colin MacLaren considered right and wrong.

What sin he was trying to expiate through this I never knew. It would have been impertinent of me to ask, and unnecessary besides—Colin was always harder on himself than any outsider could ever have been.

Years passed, and what we asked out of life changed imperceptibly, month by passing month, so that it was only years later that each of us awoke to find ourselves on pathways that I imagine he had looked to follow as little as I had. Had Colin ever expected to be attempting to prescribe the morals of a generation? Yet what was he doing at the Bidney Institute, if not that?

And as for me . . .

In 1976 I was thirty-five. In her thirties, a woman finally escapes the shadow of her childhood and the inevitability of her family's expectations of her into her own adulthood, becoming at last a person of her own creation.

Though I had severed ties with my own family long ago, and my adopted family was dead, I carried as much emotional baggage with me as anyone else my age did. More than anything, I think, I had never felt entitled to my own happiness, but 1976 was the year that I finally grew up, and realized that no one was standing in the way of my fulfillment but me.

For many years my dream had been to own a bookstore, and in that year I opened Inquire Within in Glastonbury, New York.

I'd decided a long time ago that the sort of bookstore I wanted was called in those days an "occult bookstore," but I also knew that I didn't want it to be anything like the Sorcery Shoppe, with its jarsful of dried bats and mummified frogs. I wanted a bookstore that could also be a refuge for seekers as troubled as I had once been.

It was the worst time in twenty years to start a small business—inflation rates were through the roof and money was tight—but I had my savings and Peter's insurance and I was determined not to wait any longer to do what I had dreamed of for so long.

You might say that I chose Glastonbury to be near Colin—and that might

be so, for he badly needed friends in those years, but as much as it might have
been for that reason, my choice of location was a pragmatic business decision.
On the most basic level, I couldn't possibly have afforded to open an "occult
bookstore" in Manhattan—I would have gone broke in a New York minute,
as the saying goes. I needed a place where the rents were low but I still had a
built-in clientele, and Glastonbury seemed tailor-made for my ambitions.

What better place than a town near a college that offered a doctorate in
Parapsychology? I located an empty store; Colin drafted my labor force from
among his students, and in short order, Inquire Within was open for business.

And I was lucky; the store thrived, and soon I found myself up to my nose
in wholesale catalogues, confronting an array of products whose existence I
had never even suspected. My favorites were the aerosol cans of *Hex Be
Gone*-brand spray incense and the All-In-One Witch Kits, which guaranteed
that they contained everything you needed to become a witch and cast a spell.

Needless to say, neither object found its way into Inquire Within, though
I did stock a small selection of harmless oils, teas, and incenses. But most of
all, I stocked books, because what I wanted to provide at Inquire Within was
knowledge. Never before—or since, in my opinion—was there such a need
for it.

By the 1970s, spirituality had become a part of the women's movement,
divorced almost completely from its magickal antecedents. Wicca, which in
the beginning most people had considered the little sister of Satanism, had
prospered as an Earth Religion that owed no debt to Christianity, and which
paved the way for other forms of Neo-Paganism.

It was Goddess worship, not magick, that most of my customers were interested in. Though they weren't adverse to casting spells, their magick was
of the simplest sort. If you had asked any of them to calculate planetary hours
or to cast a horoscope to determine the governing angel for their rituals, they
would simply have laughed: American efficiency was finally being applied to
magick, with admittedly peculiar results.

Though I was never tempted to give up my own faith, I still saw the fem-
inist witches' covens and Goddess healing circles as a good thing, a necessary
counterbalance to the deeply materialistic currents that were beginning to reshape daily life. Yuppies were replacing yippies, and those who had been on
the barricades a few years before were laying away their idealism in lavender
and turning to the brutal business of making a living.

At least, most of them were.

And then, of course, there was Hunter Greyson. . . .

SIXTEEN

GLASTONBURY, NEW YORK, SEPTEMBER 1979

How can thine heart be full of the spring?
A thousand summers are over and dead.
What hast thou found in the spring to follow?
What hast thou found in thine heart to sing?
—ALGERNON CHARLES SWINBURNE

COLIN KNEW HIS INSIGHT HAD BEEN RIGHT—EACH YEAR IT TOOK MORE effort to ignore the fundamental corruption of the American soul. But it also seemed that the nation was willing to make that effort.

By the end of the seventies, the citizens of the Woodstock Nation had, for the most part, gone quietly off to brokerages and law firms, exchanged hash pipes for coke spoons, and geared up for a decade-long consumer orgy that would lose its frenetic momentum only with Black Tuesday and the spread of AIDS.

The last of the sixties idealism had died an ugly death in the Watergate courtrooms, and the grotesque, self-interested end of the Vietnam War in 1975 had put the stone upon its grave. Two failed assassination attempts upon Nixon's appointed successor, Gerald Ford, less than three weeks apart elicited laughter and jokes when a scant decade before they would have roused horror. It was as if the nation, like a lover betrayed too often, simply refused to care any longer.

The jingoistic fervor of the Bicentennial festivities in 1976 rang curiously hollow, filled more with a plaintive nostalgia for what once had been than with the spirit of a real celebration of nationhood. That fall, in desperation, the nation elected a largely unqualified fifty-two-year-old Georgia farmer without big-league political experience, the youngest presidential candidate since Kennedy, to the highest office in the land. Gerald Ford, who had once served on the Warren Commission, and who would be known forever as "the man who pardoned Nixon," disappeared from the political scene without a trace. Jimmy Carter would follow him into political obscurity one term later, having pardoned the draft dodgers, given away the Panama Canal, received a Pope on American soil, and provided the nation with a 23% inflation rate.

People wanted to believe in something—they were desperate for truths—but on every side they were presented with the dangers of faith. The Reverend Jim Jones led his People's Temple followers into death in a mass suicide in Guyana, and in Iran, the return of the Ayatollah Khomeini to power led to theocratic totalitarianism and the seizure of the American embassy in Tehran. Sixty-three Americans were held hostage by "students," and all America's military-industrial clout was not enough to bring them home.

And worst of all, everything seemed to be some kind of unfunny joke.

I wonder if I'm getting too old for this? Colin MacLaren wondered to himself. It was a rhetorical question; he'd never felt more vital, more in control of his destiny. After six years the institute was on a firm footing at last, the first wave of the new doctoral program was about to graduate, and Taghkanic had even backed off a bit in its eternal attempt to annex the institute's operating budget. With President Quiller's retirement last year, a new period of harmonious cooperation seemed to have dawned for the Bidney Institute.

He glanced around his office. For a moment, his gaze lingered on cherished mementoes: a picture of the front of Claire's bookstore; a photo of Barbara and Jamie Melford with their two children, John Colin and Margaret Claire; an old photo of Colin standing in front of his college at Oxford; another of him standing with Claire in Golden Gate Park. Moments snatched out of the rushing current of time, now forever inviolate. Enough such moments, and the shape of a life was marked out for all to see.

The interoffice phone buzzed; Colin plucked the receiver deftly out of a nest formed by stacks of journals and raised it to his ear.

"Colin, you told me to buzz you at one-forty-five," his secretary said. "You've got *Welcome to the Twilight Zone* at two."

"Thanks, Christie. I'll be there," he answered, a smile in his voice.

The Lookerman Auditorium was almost a quarter full when Colin entered. It was a grandly rococo building, named for the college's founder, Jurgen Lookerman, and looked like a Viennese opera house in miniature; a fact that the Drama Department found ideal for the staging of its various productions throughout the year.

Today a podium with microphone had been placed at the center edge of the half-round stage. Several dozen students, a significant fraction of Taghkanic's student body, were waiting for him—this year, for a miracle, all down in front instead of hiding in the shadows at the back of the auditorium. As Colin took the stage, he saw Dylan and Cassie and several others that he recognized from summer interviews.

To attend the Taghkanic's degree-track parapsychology classes (all taught by staff of the Bidney Institute), a student had to have taken *Introduction to Oc-*

cult Ethics during their freshman year and have had a personal interview with Colin before the start of their sophomore year. Fortunately this summer's interviews had been profitable, turning up two particularly promising candidates.

Dylan Palmer was frank about his interest in ghosts—and equally frank about his desire to integrate this rowdy and disreputable stepchild of parapsychology into a classical scientific framework. His eventual ambition was to teach, and Colin thought he'd be good at it. Though he was barely twenty, Dylan's open-minded willingness to *know* made him a good candidate for survival in a field where cherished theories could be disproved in a heartbeat and researchers frequently had to resign themselves to a lifetime's equivocation.

Cassilda Chandler, on the other hand, was outspokenly mystical—an "old soul," some of Colin's counterparts would have called her. She wanted all the tools that science could arm her with, but her interest lay in discovering the extent of the Unseen World by any means she could employ. Cassie was very much the sort of student that Colin wanted the institute's Taghkanic-sponsored degree program to attract: young questioning minds that he could guide past the many pitfalls that the study of the Unseen World entailed.

Colin knew that if the institute were to move into the twenty-first century, he was going to have to find and train the next generation of parapsychology researchers himself, and so, in a sense, he was actively recruiting students to the degree program. In order to avoid answering the same questions over and over individually, Colin had arranged to add this lecture to the Orientation Week schedule. Though anyone was welcome to attend, his usual audience was incoming freshmen and a few curious sophomores.

"Good afternoon. My name is Colin MacLaren, and I'm the director of the Margaret Beresford Bidney Memorial Institute for Psychic Research."

Scattered laughter at the institute's full unwieldy name.

"I know that many of you will be curious about what we do here, and in the course of your enrollment here at Taghkanic, many of you will participate in the institute's research as volunteers, while some of you will choose to make parapsychology your field of study. Perhaps some of you will have chosen Taghkanic for just that reason.

"I'd like to begin by mentioning what the institute is *not*—it is not in the business of promulgating any particular creed or doctrine, nor is it engaged in the practice of any form of religion. Parapsychology is a young science—"

As he went on with the introductory lecture—covering only the most rudimentary outline of the subject—Colin allowed his gaze to roam over his audience. They were universally long-haired and denim-clad, some listening raptly, some already trying to come up with embarrassing questions to trap him with later.

As he continued, explaining that parapsychology was not something supernatural, but in fact a normal—though rare—part of the natural world, he noticed that someone else had come in. He—Colin was guessing about the newcomer's gender—was wearing a white buckskin jacket that glowed almost supernaturally in the gloom of the back of the auditorium. As Colin glanced at him, he felt a sudden flash of *akashic* memory; a sense of recognition. Here was one whom he'd known once, and would know again.

He put the distraction from him firmly. If the two of them were meant to know one another, they would not be able to avoid doing so—it was not for Colin to force the Unseen Hand or tell others the truths they had chosen to put aside in this life. He spoke for another fifteen minutes, and then opened the floor to questions.

"You've said that parapsychology isn't the occult," a girl sitting in the front row said. "But aren't you studying the occult?"

"In part," Colin said. "What we today refer to as 'the occult' preceded the development of parapsychology by several thousand years, just as church exorcism preceded a knowledge of mental illness. The word 'occult' only means 'hidden'; it comes from the same Latin root as 'oculist,' and physicians still speak of testing for 'occult' blood and mean nothing magical by it, I assure you. Much of what we today dismiss as folklore and magick came into existence when people misapplied cause and effect relationships or misinterpreted what they saw in the natural world. One of the goals of the Bidney Institute's work is to separate the wheat from the chaff, and to decide what part of this inheritance has value to the modern world."

"Professor MacLaren?" A boy this time, almost painfully neat in corduroy jacket, creased jeans, and Hush Puppies. "Do you mean that there *is* magic?"

"I'm afraid I have to beg the question, as we first have to define 'magic.' If you mean the rabbit-from-a-hat, stage illusionism variety, it's alive and well, but it's not something we teach at Taghkanic or study at the institute. If you mean comic-book hocus-pocus, then I'd have to say I've never seen any."

"What about the art of making changes to the nature of reality in accordance with the will?" a new voice asked. "Do you believe in magick-with-a-K, Dr. MacLaren?"

It was the young man at the back of the auditorium, and he'd quoted the classical definition of true magick as proposed by the great twentieth-century magician Aleister Crowley.

"If that is how you define magic," Colin answered honestly, "then, yes, I do believe in magic. Come down and sit in the front, please; I don't like to shout. What's your name?"

"Hunter Greyson," the young man said, moving down to the front of the auditorium. His pale hair was just past shoulder length. "I'm a transfer from SUNY New Paltz."

"Next time, don't be late," Colin cautioned, and went on to the next question.

There were no more surprises in the question-and-answer period, and it wound up right on schedule. The usual students hung back to ask one last question; predictably enough, Hunter Greyson was among them, though he waited until all the others had drifted away.

"I was hoping you could help me out," Greyson said. "I wanted to take some of the advanced courses, but they said over at registration that I had to have your signature."

Greyson smiled winningly. He had an easy charm, and the particular sort of confidence that sprang from a young lifetime's experience of being able to talk his way into—or out of—anything.

The ghosts of knowledge he should not have stirred beneath the surface of his mind—which of Colin's beloved dead stood before him now in new flesh? "They were right," Colin said.

He took the list of courses from the boy's hand and scanned it. "You do need my signature. You also need a personal interview with me and a passing grade in *Occult Ethics and Practices.*"

There was a pause as Colin saw Hunter Greyson digest both this information and his manner and retrench accordingly.

"Well, I'm a transfer student, so I haven't taken the course yet. I'm pretty well read, though; if I can't test out of it I was hoping I could maybe take it along with the others . . . ?"

The next batch of students was already filing into the auditorium. During Orientation Week, the scheduling in Lookerman was tight.

"I have a meeting at three, Mr. Greyson, and we're not wanted here. Why don't you walk over to my office with me and we can finish our discussion?"

"SUNY New Paltz is a state school. I take it Taghkanic wasn't your first choice college?" Colin asked.

Early September was still summer in the Hudson Valley, with the sultry days of Indian summer lying in wait. But the air had an agreeable bite to it, and the apple trees that dotted the campus were heavy with ripening fruit.

"It was. But Taghkanic's expensive, and it gives preference to New York State students, and my grades weren't exactly . . . " the boy shrugged.

"Mr. Greyson," Colin began. Now was as good a time as any to discourage Hunter Greyson from his attraction to the parapsychology courses. He was a charming young man, and Colin distrusted that charm even as he felt its pull: such charming young men were likely also to be heartless manipulators, and additional power was the last thing that would be good for them—or for anyone else.

"Call me Grey." Again the flash of the irrepressible smile.

"All right. Grey. I'll tell you right out: I honestly don't think you have what it takes to make it on our parapsych track, and your attempt to maneuver your way around the requirements as if they were meant for everyone but you doesn't impress me favorably."

Grey stared at him as if he could not believe what he was hearing. But it was not so easy as all that to step back into one's place in each life: Colin would not let the boy trade on a friendship they'd shared before his birth.

"But . . . That's *it?* If I have to wait a whole year before starting the Bidney courses I'll be a year behind! You aren't being fair! You didn't even look at my qualifications—" Grey yelped.

"You should have gotten in touch with Taghkanic sooner to find out what the requirements were," Colin said implacably. "One of them is *Introduction to Occult Ethics.* I'll be looking forward to seeing you there. Good afternoon."

* * *

"I wonder if you might reconsider the Hunter Greyson case?" Eden Romney said a few days later.

The new Taghkanic president made it a point to lunch weekly with Colin in the faculty dining room—assuring them both, she had said with a smile, at least one civilized meal per week. The Bidney Institute was the original 800-pound gorilla; it had the potential to make every sort of flashy trouble for the university, and Dr. Romney was insistent on keeping up-to-date with developments there.

"I didn't know there was a Hunter Greyson case," Colin said evenly.

Truth to tell, Colin's conscience had been poking him since his summary dismissal of Hunter Greyson earlier in the week. A freewheeling attitude toward rules and requirements didn't necessarily indicate that Greyson was not meant to take the Path once more, nor that he wouldn't be a good student.

Dr. Romney shook her head. "Well, it isn't as if there are parents involved, thank God—technically, there's an aunt somewhere out West, but practically speaking, Hunter Greyson's been on his own since he was sixteen. You know we hand out very few scholarships here—"

"Good Lord," Colin said, surprised. "Don't tell me that Greyson's here on a scholarship?" He remembered the boy mentioning that the school was expensive, but he'd thought nothing of it: everyone did.

"Scholarship, work-study, and a few loans; the Finance Office had the devil's own time making it work. But we were glad to be able to get him—you should see his list of credits and publications."

"I see," said Colin, who didn't. He was saved from having to add to that by the arrival of their lunches, brought over by a student waitress from the dumbwaiter in the corner. The area reserved for the faculty's use was on the second floor of Taghkanic's cafeteria building, and doubled as the faculty lounge.

"Perhaps you'd like to fill me in," he said, once the plates had been set out. Today's hot entrée was roast beef; Colin sniffed the steam rising from his plate appreciatively. "Greyson mentioned that his grades weren't particularly good, so I'll admit I'm puzzled about the scholarship," he said, after taking a bite.

Romney sipped at her wine—a faculty privilege—and considered her words before answering.

"Well, the GREs and SATs weren't anything special, but he graduated high school at sixteen with Emancipated Minor status and has amassed quite a CV since then. Published a number of scholarly articles in academic journals and an underground comic book—about Carl Jung, of all people—appeared in dinner theater in San Francisco, did some commercial art: quite a number of different things, really; I haven't told you the half of them. Apparently he's finally focused his interests toward aiming for some sort of art-therapy credential based on his own theories. He's working on a book about them; I've seen the first few chapters, and if the rest of the book lives up to them, I think it could be rather brilliant."

"And he wants to take the Bidney courses," Colin said.

"It's one of the reasons that he chose us," Dr. Romney pointed out.

"And after I told him he had to follow the rules like everyone else, he came to you."

Dr. Romney looked startled; Colin was startled himself by the amount of rancor in his voice. It was a transgression against all he had ever been taught to let knowledge gained of a soul in a previous life prejudice one against them in this. And if anything, his prejudice was in favor of Greyson—not against. Why was he judging the boy so harshly?

"I'm sorry, Eden. That was completely uncalled for. I apologize," Colin said.

"Well, I'd be a liar if I didn't admit that sometimes the kids can get on our nerves. But for the record, it was his advisor, Professor Rhys, who spoke to me about it, and I thought I'd see why you turned him down."

Fear.

Colin was honest enough with himself to be able to admit that. When he looked at Hunter Greyson he saw not the boy's potential for greatness but the potential for sheer disaster. He saw Simon Anstey. He saw Thorne Blackburn. He saw every other brilliant adventurer who'd flown too near the sun.

He saw Grey's death long ago across the sea, himself unable to save him. *Oh, Michael—*

"I'll give Auben a call and see about setting up an interview with Greyson," Colin said, still feeling that terrible reluctance to let the boy into his life. "I'm not making any promises until after I've reviewed his file and spoken to him, but at this point I won't rule anything out."

"Thanks, Colin. I appreciate you taking the time to look into this."

What in heaven's name is wrong with me? Colin wondered, staring around his office. He toyed with the cold pipe between his fingers, tapping its charred bowl against the thick file in front of him.

As Eden had promised, Hunter Greyson's credentials—especially for an incoming college sophomore—were impressive. Impressive enough to have warranted at least a first look instead of a summary dismissal. He hadn't let his emotions take control of him that way in years—and certainly not in such a surreptitious fashion.

His first intuition had been correct: it was fear that motivated his actions. But fear of what? If Grey should choose the Path once more and fall victim to its many perils, that would be a tragedy, true, but nothing that could not be repaired by another turn of the Wheel. Yet Colin had been afraid—and for himself, not for Hunter Greyson. If Colin should take on the responsibility of teaching him—and if, then, Grey should fail . . .

What would that say about Colin? The outward was the reflection of the inward: if he could not make anything that was not marred . . .

Then it's just as well to know it, Colin told himself brutally. *And to address the matter while there is still time.*

There was a knock at the door. Greyson had learned to be prompt, if nothing else.

"Come in," Colin said.

Hunter Greyson sidled through the door. He was dressed with scrupulous normalcy in tie and blazer, as though going for a job interview.

Or reporting to his parole officer, Colin thought caustically. The tone of his thoughts made him feel guilty; he had less reason than before to think badly of Hunter Greyson.

"You'd wanted to see me, sir?" Grey said.

"Sit down," Colin said, wondering how to begin the interview. After he'd spoken with Dr. Romney, he'd spoken to Grey's faculty advisor, Professor Rhys of the Drama Department, and reviewed Grey's original transfer application. But the Hunter Greyson he really needed to know about wasn't in any of those things.

"A number of members of the faculty have spoken on your behalf," Colin began.

Grey stood up, suddenly angry. "And so you're seeing me because they blackmailed you into it. Forget that."

"Sit *down.*" Colin rarely raised his voice in anger, but he had a commanding presence when he chose to use it. Grey sat, his gaze fixed firmly on the gleaming silver hilt of the sword-in-stone paperweight balanced precariously atop a pile of journals.

"No one blackmails me. Not the college administration, and not you, Mr. Greyson, so relax." Colin, following the direction of his gaze, picked it up and moved it to a safer location. "The Bidney Institute is world famous in its field, which means it's a lodestone for crackpots, cranks, fanatics, and freaks. I have no desire to admit students to the curriculum who will be seeing UFOs or announcing that they're possessed by the devil half a semester later. Now, your application to the college looks very promising, so why don't we start at the beginning, and you can tell me why it is that you wanted to come to the Bidney Institute and what you expect to do here?"

If Grey didn't exactly squirm in his chair, Colin could see the effort he made not to fidget.

"I think I may have given you the wrong idea about me," Grey said with painful care. "I'm not particularly interested in parapsychology, except to lay a groundwork for my other studies. You can spend till Doomsday trying to prove its reality to the mundane world, and someone like the Amazing Randi is always going to come along and cast doubt on your results by duplicating them through stage illusionism—as if there wasn't more than one way to skin a cat. With all due respect—and believe me, I do understand why what the Bidney Institute does is necessary—I'm just not interested in saying my ABCs over and over until the end of time. We know these abilities exist. We know how to develop them. It's time to move on to what comes next."

Colin felt himself warm to Grey's sincerity, and this time, he did not suppress the feeling.

"Taking that as a given, Grey, what *can* we do for you? If you're not interested in parapsychological investigation or research, what do you want from us?"

Grey hesitated, obviously mulling over in his head whether he wanted to tell Colin the truth. Finally he spoke.

"I'm interested in studying magick."

It must have taken a certain amount of nerve to say that, especially to someone he couldn't believe to be a sympathetic audience.

"You know that we don't offer courses in magick here," Colin said gently.

"No," Grey said quickly, "but I can study both Theater Arts and Psychology here, and that's a start toward what I want to do out in the real world. And the Bidney Collection is one of the best accumulations of books on the occult available to the public. For the rest, I know I'd have to work on my own—I joined an OTO Encampment out in California, but they made me leave when they found out I wasn't eighteen." Grey shrugged. "I thought you might help me."

It wasn't sponsorship into one of the private Magickal Lodges that Hunter Greyson was talking about—Colin would have been surprised if the boy, for all his well-traveled sophistication, suspected that such things existed . . . at least in this life.

"Why me?" Colin asked.

"The truth?" Grey countered warily.

"Ideally."

"Well . . . I could find you. And you're not a nut like LaVey, or a fraud like—well, you know. And I didn't want to have to start by swearing a lot of oaths and making a lot of promises before I knew what was going on. I mean, a lot of these modern so-called secret societies are just an excuse for some loser to feel like God, and that'd just be a waste of time for me."

"So you're only willing to follow the principles of a Magickal Order providing it meets your standards?" Colin asked.

"Well . . . would you follow principles that didn't?" Grey asked reasonably. Colin could not help smiling.

"And what is your ultimate goal?" Colin asked. "Why study magick at all? I know you've already done your basic reading, and have a little experience if you were a member of the Ordo Templi Orientis. So it all comes down to 'why'?"

"Because there *are* answers," Grey said earnestly, leaning forward. "Why should humankind be such a complex, evolved, self-aware creature if we're only supposed to live seventy years and die? What is it for? What are *we* for? I don't believe we ought to just ignore questions like that. I want to know the truth—but the sciences say it isn't possible to study something like this. Philosophy's self-referential and morally bankrupt—and religion only wants us to accept the status quo. So what does that leave? We have to gather our own information and make our own decisions—but we also have to accept that ethical behavior has a basis in objective reality. That just leaves magick."

It was impossible not to be engaged by Grey's fervor.

"Very well." Colin pulled open the drawer to his desk and rummaged through the papers there. "Here's a reading list—let me know which ones you've already read, and prepare me written reports on all of them—as long as you like, but fifteen hundred words minimum. I'll sign your admission into the advanced courses—*Practices and Ethics* is still a prerequisite, and if I don't see you there every single session, you'll get an 'F' for *all* your parapsychology courses. Do you agree?"

"Yes, sir," Grey said meekly. But his eyes were shining.

Colin looked out over the heads of his latest freshmen class—had he ever been so young? It seemed that they got younger as the world turned darker, and while his students in the dawn of the sixties had spoken of changing the world, at the end of the seventies, students spoke of finding a place in the world as it was, as if change were no longer possible.

"Professor MacLaren?" A hand went up in the back—Jeremy, a good student but cautious. "Could you tell us—in your opinion—what it's all *for?* I mean, supposing you can prove that psychic powers exist, everybody still isn't going to have them. So what practical use could they have?"

It was a common question, for which Colin had a practiced answer. For a moment his mind wandered—to his contemporaries, to those other students whose lives he had touched through the years. To Grey, who in his senior year remained an endless challenge to authority. He thought of the sacrifices two generations had made, the losses both had suffered in trying to realize their dreams. Was it all for this—that the world should end neither with a bang nor a whimper, but with some slow inexorable dwindling, impossible to mark?

February second fell on a Monday, and the New Year had come in with a bitter black cold that did not fall as snow, but sheathed every stem and branch with a brilliant coating of dense ice. Colin had been director of the institute for eight years now, and was beginning to look toward the day when he'd hand the institute off to someone else. But not yet. He still had more to do here.

Colin drove carefully along the slippery roads. It would not do to put the car in a ditch and be late for his own surprise party.

He was, of course, not supposed to know, though half a dozen clearer heads had warned him clandestinely—including Christie, who knew her boss's temperament well enough to know that surprise parties worked out better when the victim cooperated. Since he'd known what was afoot, it had been easy to collaborate in all the runaround errands designed to keep him from getting home too soon.

Sixty-one this year. I hope they haven't tried to put a candle on for every year— they'll burn the house down, Colin thought whimsically. He'd done his best to avoid this sort of observance of his birthday—a date of interest, now, to no one but himself—but since it was inescapable, he found himself actually looking forward to it. *You're turning into a foolish old man, Colin MacLaren.*

He turned onto Greyangels Road and could now see the farmhouse in the distance. All the windows were dark, but nothing could disguise the wealth of tire tracks leading up the empty drive.

I wonder where they parked? Colin thought to himself, before deciding that it was probably down in the old orchard. The apple orchard behind the house was long past its fruiting days, though it still produced blossoms in spring and a few apples in the fall, and the ground was hard-frozen enough to allow the easy passage of even Eden's 4WD Jeep. He spared a hope that Grey'd had the sense to hitch a ride with someone else—a motorcycle wasn't safe on these winter roads, though Grey rode his year-round in most weather, with a fine disregard for his personal safety.

Colin pulled in to the top of the gravel drive and stopped. Leaving the motor running, he got out to drag open the doors of the woodshed-cum-garage before getting back into the car and driving it inside. The wide wood planks of the floor testified to the building's earlier incarnation as a stables and carriage house.

Several cords of wood—a winter's supply—were stacked along the side wall, and along the back were a wheelbarrow and various gardening implements, the grace notes of country life. Fortunately Greyangels' owner, Ted Zacharias, took care of what groundskeeping the place required. Colin was no gardener and had never had any ambitions in that direction, though Claire, who had an apartment in Glastonbury, came out and fussed over his flowers occasionally. She'd offered him a kitten from Poltergeist's latest litter, but Colin had not accepted; cats were at far more risk in the country from foxes and weasels than in the city, though it was never a good idea to let a pet animal roam.

Running her own bookstore agreed with her; Colin had to admit he hadn't seen Claire this happy since Peter had died. He only wished he could say as much for himself.

In this second half of his life, a cloud seemed to have settled over him, as if he were somehow in exile through accident or unwise choice. Since Simon's accident—and Hasloch's murder—Colin felt as though he'd lost touch with something fine and meaningful, but dared not go in search of it lest he do some unimaginable unwitting harm. Slowly his life had come to be ruled by that fear, a dark spectator whose presence colored his every action.

First, do no harm. The injunction that formed the basis of the Hippocratic Oath was a good one for any meddler, Colin thought to himself encouragingly, and nothing to be ashamed of.

And now he'd better get inside, before his guests decided he'd gotten lost on the way to the house.

"For he's a jolly good fellow—which nobody can deny!" The raucous, friendly chorus—led by Grey and his girlfriend on their guitars—rang from the walls of the old farmhouse. A substantial fire blazed on the hearth, and marshmallows and chestnuts were laid by for later toasting.

All Colin's friends were there—even John Dexter, whose unexpected and

baffling illness had forced his retirement from the Bidney staff the year before.

"And a happy Groundhog Day to you, Colin, and the hope of many more,"
Dexter said, coming over to stand at Colin's side.

His skin was sallow and almost reptilian, hanging from his gaunt frame in
folds and covered with the livid bruising that was the result not of blows but
of tiny spontaneous hemorrhages throughout his body. His doctors frankly
measured Dexter's future in months, and constant tremors in his hands had
rendered him incapable of performing his beloved sleight-of-hand illusions,
but he was unfeignedly merry as he joined the revelry.

"And to you as well," Colin said automatically.

"Don't be naive and sentimental," Dexter said. "Or I'll worry more than I
do now about leaving the institute in your hands. I'll be lucky if I see July
Fourth, let alone next Groundhog Day."

"I wish there was something I could do," Colin said.

"Just keep the faith healers off me," Dexter said. "I'll go out as I came in,
and I'm too old to start believing in hoodoo. Leave the mumbo to Jumbo has
always been my motto."

"And you a magician," Colin joked gently. It hurt him to see his friend this
way, but in the face of Dexter's steadfast refusal to consider what was now beginning to be called Alternative Medicine, his friends had no choice but to
respect his wishes.

"How's my successor doing?" Dexter asked.

"Quite well," Colin assured him. Maskelyne Devant—the professional
name of a man whose birth name was Houdin, and whose parents had oblivi-
ously christened him Henry Harrison—had been Dex's handpicked successor, and the two men were as different as night and day.

Devant's performing tastes ran to smoke and mirrors—the gaudy, Vegas-
style illusions of much of modern magic—and he carried his "man of mystery" persona with him offstage as well as on, something that irritated Colin
more on some days than others. But Devant was just as hard-nosed and unforgiving as Dexter had been, and had already exposed a number of *soi-disant*
"psychics" whose trickery had fooled Colin's researchers.

Without revealing the secrets of the Brotherhood, Devant also did several
seminars each year at Taghkanic on the more basic forms of bait-and-switch,
which was the central principle of most psychic fraud, as well as of stage illusionism.

"He's a good man," Dexter said. "And now, if you'll excuse me, I'm going
to get a slice of that cake before Claire gives it all away." Leaning heavily on
his cane, Dexter moved slowly toward the table set up at the far end of the
room.

"Happy Birthday, Colin." Eden said, handing him a slender, gold-wrapped
box.

"Good heavens. A gold watch already?" Colin joked.

"Not quite. And it's from me, not the college—I have no intention of
opening the 'official gift from the administration' can of worms again."

"Very wise." They both abominated in-group politics, but Eden had less opportunity to steer clear of it than he did. Colin tore off the paper to reveal a silver Cross pen. It was engraved along the barrel. *Success and Fortune: 2/2/81.*

"I'll treasure it," Colin said. Eden smiled.

"And now I do have to dash," she said. "Bobby would appreciate it if I put in an appearance at home occasionally, and I have yards of paperwork backed up." She held out her hand and Colin shook it formally. "Happy Birthday, Colin."

"Thank you." He watched as Eden made her way through the crowd toward the kitchen door—it was a more direct route to the orchard.

"For God's sake, man, don't just stand here—enjoy yourself!" Morgan Ives, flamboyant as ever and more than a few sheets to the wind—Colin smelled the sharpness of bourbon on her breath—leaned against him confidentially, taking his arm. "Come have a drink."

Colin allowed himself to be drawn toward the table. There was a small pile of presents—something he'd unsuccessfully tried to discourage—Claire's huge cut-glass punch bowl with its nonalcoholic contents (a wedding gift, Colin recalled, and something whose employment had baffled her for years), a copper wash-boiler filled with ice and champagne bottles, and a huge chocolate sheet-cake with white icing and a representation of the institute on it in pale blue.

He'd already blown out the single candle, and the cake was being disemboweled for the guests. The gathering was fairly evenly split between teachers, members of the institute, and students. Dylan and Cassie were here, along with Grey and half a dozen other kids, including Grey's latest girlfriend, Winter.

"Here you are, Colin," Claire said, handing him a large slice of cake on a paper plate. I brought you a present—you don't have to worry; it's cookies," she said, nodding toward the large box wrapped in gold paper that sat beside the cake.

"You spoil me," Colin said, accepting the plate and picking up his fork. He looked with mock-apprehension toward the rest of the parcels. "Any idea what else there is?"

"Well, Jamie sent books, but he always does. It's a big box—I put them in the kitchen. And there are a lot of cards, but—" Claire lowered her voice conspiratorially "—I think one of your students knitted you a muffler."

Colin rolled his eyes in silence. "Well, at least it isn't a Fair Isle sweater." He took a bite of cake.

"Hey, Ramsey—you coming out to the Lake later?"

A lull in the conversation around him brought Janelle's words to Colin clearly, and if he had not been looking in the direction of Grey and his friends, he would have missed what came next.

"How's the spring play coming?" Winter asked, too quickly and too loudly for the words to be anything but a hasty change of subject. The others around Grey spoke up quickly, covering the moment, but Colin had seen the look of guilty complicity among the five of them, as clearly as if they'd shouted it aloud.

He glanced away, not wanting to let them know he'd heard, and said something offhand to Claire. When he looked back a few seconds later, he caught Grey watching him expressionlessly.

To follow the Path required the kindness of the surgeon, the clarity of the general, and the willingness to stand aside while innocents endured the suffering they had chosen for themselves before their entry into this life.

Faced with the need to intervene once more, Colin was not certain he still had the strength. The shameful guilt of his one irresistible impulse to act against the Law was still with him. He prayed that never again would he face such a moment of hubris and false mercy as that had been—it was the sort of failure that could destroy not only lives but souls.

But he had taken on that burden willingly, though the guilt remained—and it seemed, as the years passed, that the pain had itself become a kind of temptation, a lure to renounce all responsibility, to reject the possibility of doing good out of fear of doing harm. It was a temptation to which he dared not surrender.

"Claire, do you ever hear anything about Nuclear Lake?"

Janelle had mentioned "The Lake," and for residents of Amsterdam County, there was only one: Nuclear Lake.

On maps, its name was Haelvemaen—Half Moon—Lake, and it was on a small parcel of private land tucked into a corner of Huyghe State Park. Some sort of private research group had used the area, and since its departure, Nuclear Lake had collected the usual assortment of unlikely local folktales about itself. The property had been unoccupied for about ten years, give or take a few; sporadically the college attempted to buy the acreage for its own use, but so far without success.

"Not much," Claire said slowly. As she mused, she reached out and rubbed Monsignor under the chin. The dignified black-and-white tom immediately flopped over on his back, purring, while Poltergeist, a white queen, remained more aloof.

The shop smelled pleasantly of cinnamon and sandalwood, and radiated a sense of serene peace. Inquire Within had been such a good idea that Colin couldn't imagine how he'd ever gotten along without it. Claire's bookstore provided a perfect nonconfrontational meeting place for those curious about the Unseen. It provided answers for those with questions, a way for them to meet one another, and a place to go before their troubles became too grave. And Claire was in her element, providing tea and no-nonsense advice to anyone who needed it.

At least twice a month, Claire made it her business to cook dinner for him in her little apartment above Inquire Within, apparently on the theory that without her he might starve. While that was not entirely true, it was true that without Claire's home-cooking he'd get pretty tired of TV dinners and diner food. Colin was no cook and had never claimed to be.

"It's a preferred make-out spot, of course, because the park rangers don't patrol it and the sheriff's deputies don't get up there much either, so I hear. Why?"

Because they all looked so guilty. . . .

"I'm wondering if you've heard anything 'odd' about it. Odd in our particular line, of course," Colin said.

He picked up one of the Tarot decks piled on the counter beside the register in hopes of tempting patrons and turned it over in his hands. Pride had always been his besetting sin, and he'd been proud of the communion he'd forged with his students. Knowledge of that pride vexed him nearly as much as worry about what these students had gotten up to.

"Not about Nuclear Lake in particular, really," Claire answered thoughtfully. "The local coven goes up there, I think. Going down to the river's too dangerous and probably too public for them, and the lake is, after all, reputed to be a place of power," Claire finished dryly, picking up Monsignor. She gestured at her bookshelves with a free hand.

"I'm not an expert, but my stock is. There isn't much folklore about Amsterdam County other than the Grey Angels—and you'll find them up in Columbia and down in Dutchess as well—and I don't think I've seen anything at all about Nuclear Lake."

Colin frowned. Students played pranks and pushed the rules—those things had been true even when Colin was a student. Drugs, illegal as ever, were still a part of college life, as were freewheeling sex, bootlegged music tapes, and ghost-written term papers. But Colin couldn't believe that those kids would have looked so *guilty* about any of those things, Grey particularly.

And around me of all people! Colin thought, amused at how much the notion pricked his vanity.

"You're thinking again," Claire accused him. She went through the curtain to get her keys, and Poltergeist appeared as if by magic, trotting toward the sound and miaouing. She knew that the jingle of keys led to the sound of the can-opener, when Claire took the cats upstairs for the night.

The space that Claire had rented for Inquire Within was actually almost square, but a brick wall down the center of the space divided it nearly in half. The landlord had been willing to knock it down, but Claire had chosen to keep it, adding a second drywall partition that sectioned the left side of the store off into two storage rooms, one of which was also used for discussion groups. Though Claire sold herbs, she could not bear the thought of her stock being tampered with or contaminated in any way, and so kept it under lock and key.

"Ready?" Claire asked.

"So tell me," Claire said later. "What are you worried about Grey getting up to? Group sex? Orgies? Satanic rites?"

Colin stared down into an after-dinner cup of coffee, as though he were a psychic and could see answers there.

"I wish I knew. The five of them are doing *something*—and try as I might, I can't imagine what."

"Well, no one's ever accused you of a lack of imagination before," Claire observed, setting the cake plate down on the table. "Maybe it's just too much imagination this time. Why don't you ask him?"

"Ask him what?" Colin sighed. "I don't even know how to frame the question. If it was something Grey wanted me to know about—or didn't care if I knew—he would have told me. Lord knows he's told me about enough other things: rehanging the Lookerman portrait from the library, tampering with the key sheet on the physics exam, putting the brandy in the coffee urn. . . . "

"Not to mention smoking the Christian Prayer Fellowship out of the Student Union with asafetida and petitioning for permission to found *Students for Satan*," Claire said, "although *that* was perfectly legal, just silly. Colin, I think you're worrying too much. But if you like, I'll go up to Nuclear Lake and take a look around."

Colin sighed again. He knew what Claire was offering, and what they both worried about—that Grey's irrepressible curiosity would lead him down the same dark path that Simon Anstey seemed to be following. If Grey was meddling in Black Magick, Claire's Gift would pick that up immediately.

"It feels too much like spying," Colin said, "but the real reason I'm going to turn you down is that if it isn't outright Ungodliness—or even something mundane, like selling drugs—"

"Not Grey!" Claire protested.

"Oh, I don't mean he's the local pusher, but grass is illegal, too, even if most of the students smoke it. It comes from somewhere, and if that's what he's up to you'd have no way of telling. And I think it's probably something like that; drugs are one of the Paths to Power, after all."

"But you don't encourage that at all, Colin; it's dangerous. And Grey looks up to you. He'd do what you said."

"Oh, I suppose that generally he thinks I know what I'm talking about, which is more than he grants most of his professors. But as for blind obedience . . . "

"No," both of them agreed in chorus.

"I'll just go up and take a look around myself," Colin said. "If I don't find anything, probably there isn't anything to find, and I can just forget the whole thing."

He prayed he could forget the whole thing.

Though the poets would have it otherwise, February, not April, was the cruelest month in Amsterdam County. The day dedicated to the little God of Love—later a Catholic saint—was bitterly cold, and a sudden heavy snowfall a few days before had made travel a difficult proposition. The eight inches of snow that had fallen was powdery and dunelike due to the still-bitter cold, but where the plows had shifted it the snow had melted and refrozen itself into crusty knolls that formed impassable barriers to traffic. And on the un-plowed roads, a shifting coat of snow concealed an inch or two of pack ice.

The weather was probably the reason that Colin had chosen today for his expedition to Nuclear Lake—that, and the fact that the weekend gave him a whole free day. It wasn't likely that he'd be disturbed. Only a fool would try these back roads in a car, but Colin had possessed the foresight to borrow a friend's Range Rover for his expedition, and the 4WD vehicle took the snow-bound track in its stride.

Soon the lake—its snow-covered, frozen surface only discernible by the cat-tail growth that rimmed it—was in sight, with the building beyond it. Colin pulled up in a place he guessed to have once been the parking lot and got out.

The heavy snow deadened even the sounds that he would normally have heard this far out in the country, save for the faint tinkling of ice-bound tree branches and the occasional hiss as a snowmass slid to the ground. The wind off the river lifted veils of snow from the ground and carried them for a few feet before they dropped. The sky was a pale blue, and reflection from the snow washed out all the colors around him, giving the world an ethereality that contributed to the dreamlike quality of the moment.

The front door of the building opened easily to one of Colin's skeleton keys, and a quick search of the building revealed nothing more nefarious than a few discarded wine bottles and a mattress someone had dragged into a cor-ner of one of the offices for the obvious purpose.

But Colin knew there was more than this to the place, and when he found the stairway leading down into the basement he wasn't surprised.

There was enough light from the windows along the south wall to make the contents of the room dimly visible in the afternoon light, though Colin was glad enough that he'd thought to bring a flashlight. The basement was all one large room, thirty feet by about twice that. The sinks along the win-dowed wall and the complicated sockets drilled into the cinderblock above them were indication that this had once been some kind of laboratory, but all the original furniture had been long since removed. Its current tenants had put up a set of brick-and-board bookcases in the corner, and brought down a couple of footlockers, a table, and some folding chairs.

In contrast to the rooms above, this space was painstakingly clean. The cement-slab floor had been scrubbed until it shone, then painted with a com-plex multicolored design that covered an area almost twenty feet across. Three tall jar-candles were set at the points of a triangle just inside the outer rim, which had nine candles spaced evenly around it. There was a thirteenth candle set between the inner and outer rings just at the foot of the stairs: car-dinal North.

Colin stared down at it, the hackles on the back of his neck rising. Some-how he wasn't surprised at what he found when he got there. On some level he'd been expecting it.

The circle-within-a-circle was common to most of the forms of magick that he knew, but the elaborate asymmetrical figure within it was nothing he knew. Reflexively, he looked over his shoulder, knowing what he would find.

On the wall behind him another symbol was painted. The black paint had run slightly, the drips giving the glyph the look of something in motion.

In the north . . . the North Gate. The gate through which the members of the Circle send their spirits to the Overlight.

Somehow Colin had hoped that the Aquarian Frontier would lose its fascination with Thorne Blackburn and his works, but it never had. In the thirteen years since Thorne's death in 1969, those attracted to the tainted exploitive wellspring of the Blackburn Work had been a steady—and slowly increasing—number. More books had been written on the Work since his death than Thorne could have imagined in his wildest dreams, their writers enchanted by the black romance of a magickal system which permitted its practitioners to use people for their own ends as if they were cattle . . . or fodder.

But the end did not—could never—sanctify the means. That was why the Light proscribed such interference in the lives and destinies of the Unawakened. Colin wondered how many of Thorne's postmortem followers had paid the same price that Thorne and the Circle of Truth had for their reckless disregard of the ancient Laws—Laws as easy to disregard as those of the physical world, and just as unforgiving.

Colin turned his back to the North Gate and took a step forward, until his feet nearly touched the edge of the outer ring. He studied the design beneath his feet—the crude attempt to duplicate, using color, what was described in the books as seven Gates, laid one on top of the next, first to last. The last time he'd seen these shapes they'd been silver, not paint. *And two people were dead, and the rest irredeemably scarred. I will never forgive you for that, Thorne—never.*

"I knew you'd come," Hunter Greyson said at his back.

"Why didn't you tell me what you were doing?" Colin asked, not turning around.

"You wouldn't have liked it."

Grey walked around from behind him, casually stepping into the painted sigil and across it. He lit the propane lantern sitting on the table, and the room was filled with a hissing and a blue-white light.

"You're right. I wouldn't have. And you knew the reasons why, or you would never have taken such pains to conceal it." The strongest emotion Colin was aware of at that moment was outraged pride; that the student he'd invested so much time in had callously discounted his warnings. Paradoxically, it was the selfishness of the emotion that allowed him to transcend it.

He'd fallen prey to this sensation of outrage before, but Colin knew now that it was misplaced pride. And he would not let pride blind him again.

"I knew you'd find out. Five people can't keep a secret, and I figured you'd see our Circle on the Astral eventually, even if nothing else busted us."

Though Grey was doing his best to act as if he didn't care, Colin could tell he was upset and fighting not to show it. The shoulders of his fringed leather jacket were dark with melted snow, and the legs of his jeans were wet. He must have hiked here from Taghkanic.

"So you've gotten as far as that?" Colin asked, trying not to sound incredulous. The Astral Temple—the work of a group of Initiates concentrating together on a single image—was fairly advanced ritual work for a group of neophytes.

"We've been working together for about a year. I really thought you'd find out before now." There was no triumph in Grey's voice, though his hair and his clothes gave him a casual resemblance to a haughty Elflands courtier.

A year! This was no casual dabbling, then. Colin pushed his emotions away with a surgeon's discipline, working to keep his mind clear for the questions he must ask, for both their sakes.

"I wasn't looking for something like this from you, Grey. I thought I'd given you a better basic grounding than this . . . " *dangerous trash,* Colin's mind supplied, but he kept his mouth shut.

"You gave me the background, but magick evolves. In the twentieth century, for the first time in thousands of years, it's possible to study and question what we do and why we do it. To develop new methods, to restore our knowledge of old ones. To bring back everything that was lost when Atlantis fell. . . . "

"Some things should stay lost," Colin said unequivocally. "In the name of the Light, Grey, who taught you this?"

Grey shrugged, the mute adolescent resistance reminding Colin of how young the boy was.

"I bought some books. I didn't start out to do this, but I liked what Blackburn was saying, and it made sense to me." He looked up at Colin, and the older man could see the hope plain on Grey's face. "If you could only see what I've seen . . . the Blackburn Work is about reconciliation—nobody's perfect, as the saying goes, but somewhere in the world there's always something to supply what we lack. And with enough iterations of Balance we obtain the leverage with which to act consciously, and not just in blind reaction to whether something is White or Black. And through *that* action, we obtain the power to open the Gate Between the Worlds, and reconcile the worlds of Men and Gods, supplying our ultimate lack."

The honest idealism, the sincerity, in Grey's voice tempted Colin to agree with him that what he was doing was right. But the bright promises the Blackburn work made were only a gilded mask over the foulest of realities.

"You're talking about hastening the action of entropy," Colin told him curtly.

The ultimate goal of entropy—if a mindless force could be said to have a goal—was the redaction of all forces to homeostatic equity, reversing the separation of all things and their opposites that had transpired at the beginning of time.

"I'm talking about supplying our lack and perfecting our Selves," Grey said. "It's the goal of the Great Work, isn't it?"

"You know that it is. And you know as well that this is *not* the Great Work, but a treacherous shortcut leading to a dead end. Blackburn's rituals are Black Magick of the worst sort—the sort cloaked in good intentions. He believed that the tools of the Shadow could be used in the service of the Light, and he was wrong. Power always—ultimately—corrupts."

"You're saying that the Light has no power," Grey pointed out. He looked down, fiddling with the fringe on his jacket in a way that betrayed his nervousness more than he would have wanted to admit.

"That's Jesuitical logic and you know it," Colin answered. He could hear the anger in his own voice and wished it weren't there. "I'm saying that the Light has built-in safeguards against the misuse of power that the Shadow—and the Blackburn Work—does not. Thorne was the most arrogant man I ever knew—" *saving present company, alas* "—and he refused to believe that the Laws of the Path could ever apply to him."

"You knew Thorne Blackburn?" Grey asked, looking up. The expression on his face and his tone of voice both suggested incredulity.

"Yes," Colin said shortly. He refused to feed Grey's obvious hero-worship with any tales of the "great man." What Grey had managed already, without outside help, was bad enough. "And maybe you'll believe me when I tell you that this so-called Blackburn Work is flawed, dangerous, and ultimately useless."

"You don't know that," Grey said stubbornly.

"You must think that one of us is pretty stupid," Colin snapped. "How many ways do I have to say it? *These rituals are dangerous.*"

"We're being careful," Grey persisted.

"*You*—yes, maybe. When things go wrong, *you* might notice before it's quite too late and get yourself out of harm's way. But what about your friends? Or do you just mean to sacrifice them to your ambitions?" His change of tactic had scored off the younger man—Grey looked visibly upset now.

"It isn't like that! Why do you have to keep painting everything in terms of black and white?" Grey cried passionately.

"Because they are," Colin heard himself say inexorably. The next words were on the tip of his tongue: to issue Grey an ultimatum—to threaten him with expulsion from the institute's program—to demand immediate compliance.

But that wouldn't work. If Grey did not abandon the Shadow freely and in full knowledge, he would not have abandoned it at all, no matter what his actions were.

"But we can talk about that somewhere else," Colin said, more gently. "Just don't tell me you rode your bike out here today; I don't think my heart can stand the strain."

"I walked," Grey said, relief at the change of subject plain in his voice. "Well, I hitched a ride as far as the turnoff with Ramsey; he was going down into Rhinebeck."

And how were you planning to get back? Colin found himself thinking with the unromantic sensibility of age. But youth never worried about "getting back" or any other form of retreat and retrenchment. Youth was immortal.

"Well, let me give you a ride back to the college. Make no mistake,

Grey—we *are* going to talk about this again. I disapprove very strongly, but you knew that when you decided to start down this road. There's no point in the two of us standing here shouting like action movie heroes and one of us walking home in the snow."

It was an anticlimactic end to an emotional confrontation, and Grey's face showed a certain disappointment.

"Aren't you going to deliver an ultimatum?" he demanded. "Wave a flaming sword? Banish me?"

"What good would that do?" Colin answered.

As much as Colin yearned to grab Hunter Greyson by the scruff of the neck and shake all the nonsense out of him in the weeks that followed, he restrained himself. Grey couldn't—or wouldn't—articulate to Colin just what drew him to the Blackburn Work, leaving Colin with the muddled sense of the Blackburnites as a self-appointed Occult Police, interfering in other people's lives in order to redress their subjective perceptions of a Balance that was out of whack.

The other members of the Circle—Janelle Baker, Ramsey Miller, Grey's girlfriend Winter, and, much to Colin's dismay, Cassilda Chandler, the student for whom he'd had such high hopes—were probably only drawn into the Blackburn Work through friendship. None of them except Cassie was taking any of the parapsych courses, though Winter had audited a few of Colin's lectures after she'd begun to date Grey.

Because the stakes were so high, Colin reviewed the material that Grey had followed but the picture he formed of the Blackburn Work didn't become much clearer than the one he'd held that day at Nuclear Lake.

When Colin had known him, Thorne had stressed gnosis through ritual and enlightenment through direct communion with Outer Plane entities—about as safe for novices as sticking a wet finger into a light socket, and about as informative. But Thorne had never cared about safety and had stressed apotheosis through misinformation. The combination made the Blackburn rituals devastatingly perilous when they worked at all—which they often didn't. Much of Thorne's writing, including the final rituals of the Opening of the Way, had been lost in the chaos following his death. Possibly the key to his philosophy had been lost there as well.

But stop Grey's preoccupation with the Work, and Colin did not think that any of the others would continue with the Circle. Colin found himself with grounds for hoping that this infatuation with Blackburnism would burn itself out in the way of any puppy love. All he had to do was win Grey back to the Light, and the matter would end there.

Colin was certain of it.

As winter melted into spring, Grey began to relax and become more forthcoming again. He would be graduating this spring, but he was expecting to go on to his Master's for the teaching certificate he wanted. The scholarship money would stop when he took his BA, but there were a couple of TA positions he could fill to take up that slack, and Colin was expecting to have Grey in his summer lecture series as well.

I can win him back for the Light. It was a thought that came to Colin more and more as the days lengthened. He was certain of his victory, given time.

Spring break ran from the 12th to the 18th that April. On the 19th, Grey wasn't in class.

Cassilda was. Colin stopped her as she was leaving.

"Have you seen Grey today?" he asked without preamble.

Cassie shrugged and did not meet his gaze. The white streak dyed into the front of her short dark hair gave her a more-than-passing resemblance to a Pekinese.

"I guess he had some things to do?" she muttered unconvincingly. She glanced up at Colin with a stubborn blankness on her face. "Maybe you should ask him."

Before Colin could say anything further, Cassie slithered away and hurried off down the hall.

Now what was that all about? Colin wondered to himself. He debated the wisdom of searching for his absent student—would it strain things between them further? Would Grey consider it meddling?—but set those thoughts aside. Even though they were only cautiously on terms lately, Grey would not miss one of Colin's lectures except for an emergency; not a scant six weeks before graduation.

Several hours later he found Grey in an off-campus hangout, drinking coffee in a back booth.

"Mind if I join you?" Colin said.

Grey looked up at him hazily. His face was haggard with the effect of too little sleep and intense emotion.

"Colin," he said, sounding surprised, as if they had not seen each other only last week. "Yeah. Sure."

Colin sat down and ordered coffee for himself.

"You look like hell. When did you eat last?" he demanded. *Why do the old always say the same useless things to the young, despite our best intentions?*

"She didn't come back," Grey said bleakly.

There had only been one "she" in Grey's life for many months: Winter Musgrave. They'd seemed like the perfect couple; the uncrowned king and queen of Taghkanic; the prankster troubadour and his high-spirited noble lady. The two of them were closer than many old married couples Colin knew, and it had been a surprise for Colin to learn, in casual conversation with Professor Rhys, that Winter had gone home for spring break rather than spend it in Glastonbury with Grey.

"And?" Colin prompted gently.

"She didn't come back!" Grey repeated impatiently. He picked up his coffee and stared into it as if he'd never seen it before.

"There has to be more to it than that," Colin said. He refrained from the obvious question—whether she was hurt; whether she was sick. Reasonably or not, Grey had obviously already ruled out these possibilities.

And Colin realized that—unconsciously—he had as well. Cassie's behavior earlier—as if she were in possession of a guilty secret—was part of the reason. That, and the way Grey was acting. Whether Colin liked it or not, Winter and Cassie and Grey had all been working magick together, and the ties that bound them were stronger than any ordinary ones of love or society.

"We were going to get married," Grey said quietly. He set his coffee aside and ran his hands through his hair, pulling it out of its customary ponytail. The freed strands hung forward around his face, veiling his expression. "I asked her to marry me. I thought she'd come back."

The phone rang, pulling Colin out of fitful sleep. He reached out in the darkness, still half adrift in time.

"Hello?"

"Colin?"

The dream refused to let him go; with the odd insistence of dreams Colin was certain that it was Thorne Blackburn at the other end of the line, calling from jail once more. Then his mind cleared, the last veils of sleep lifting.

"Grey?" Hunter Greyson hadn't been in class all week, and Colin had been more worried than he cared to admit. "Where are you?"

"I'm in jail." Grey's voice was flat, tightly controlled.

The eerie conflation of dream and reality banished the last sleep-fed confusion from Colin's mind.

"In jail? What happened?"

"I don't know. It's some place out on the North Shore. Long Island. They're going to set bail in the morning, but I don't have any money." A long pause. "I didn't know who else to call."

Colin could imagine the effort that confession had cost him—Grey was as proud as Lucifer, and Colin feared it would lead him to similar disaster.

"Don't worry," Colin said. "I'll be there. Let me talk to the sergeant." He glanced at the bedside clock. It was almost two A.M., and somehow this night seemed to elide into all the other late-night emergency calls of Colin's life, calls made by men and women now dead, while only he survived.

He got the particulars from the desk sergeant; Grey had been picked up for trespass and disorderly conduct on the grounds of a local residence, and the owner was pressing charges.

The owner's name was Kenneth Musgrave.

When Colin heard that, his heart sank. What had happened to Winter?

He found no answer to the question in Ramapahoag.

Grey arrived at the arraignment, where, after a short discussion with the judge, he pleaded guilty to the charge of wilful trespass—a misdemeanor. The fine was set, and Grey went off to the court clerk. Colin joined him there.

"Thanks for coming," Grey said. His voice was rough with lack of sleep, and his face had the haggard look of the emotionally battered.

"It's not a problem," Colin said gently. The dilemma seemed something more substantial than a fight with a girlfriend—what in God's name had Grey done that Winter's family should have had him charged with trespassing?

But he didn't ask; he simply paid Grey's fine and got them out of there.

They had to stop and pick up Grey's bike, which had been impounded when he was arrested. There was another fine to pay there. Grey was uncharacteristically docile—still in shock, Colin supposed. There were a number of more tactful ways of breaking off an engagement than getting your fiancé arrested.

"You're riding back with me," Colin said firmly, as Grey took the bike by the bars. "We can put that in the back of the car, but you're not safe on the road." With the backseat folded down in Colin's now venerable station wagon there was just enough room to fit Grey's bike lying on its side.

"I suppose I owe you an explanation," Grey said, as soon as the car was moving. "But I guess you're going to have to chalk this one up to the ol' instant karma. Sort of in the 'there are things man was not meant to meddle with' line."

"Is that what you think happened here?" Colin asked in his most neutral tones. Most people were willing to talk if given a little nondirective encouragement, and Colin doubted that Hunter Greyson was any different.

"She wouldn't see me," Grey said numbly, as if he couldn't believe it. "She wouldn't come out. Her old man called the police." His mouth twisted in a bitter sneer. "She always said they wouldn't like me. She was right."

That was all the information Grey would provide—because, Colin realized after they'd stopped in Tarrytown for a late breakfast, there simply wasn't any more information for him *to* provide. Winter Musgrave had gone home for spring break and never come back to Taghkanic. When Grey had gone to see her, her father'd had him arrested.

"We loved each other," Grey said, answering unspoken questions. "She wouldn't do this."

But Colin noticed that he spoke of Winter in the past tense, as if a part of him already knew that what they'd shared was over.

Could what you were doing at Nuclear Lake have frightened her that much? Colin wondered. But it would be too cruel to ask the question now, and it was one that Grey would ask himself soon enough—soon, and for the rest of his life. Whether, in the end, Winter came back or not.

It was midafternoon by the time they reached the house in Glastonbury that Grey shared with several other Taghkanic students. "I don't think you should be alone," Colin said.

"What do you think I'm going to do, slit my wrists?" Grey snapped, bridling. "I just want to get some sleep."

He shoved open the passenger side door and stood at the back, waiting for Colin to open the hatch. When the two of them had wrestled the cycle out of the back, Grey hauled it upright and prepared to wheel it off the street.

"It's going to take me a couple of days to get the money together to pay you back," Grey said with sullen determination.

"Don't worry about it," Colin said. *I'm worried about you, Grey.*

Grey shrugged, as inarticulate as Colin had ever seen him. Flamboyant, theatrical, self-assured . . . at the moment Hunter Greyson was none of those things.

"Thanks—for everything," Grey said awkwardly, and turned away, walking the motorcycle toward the back of the house.

It wasn't over. Colin wasn't surprised when Claire came to his door several hours later—in fact, though it was well after midnight, he was still fully dressed.

"Nuclear Lake?" Colin asked.

Claire nodded.

"I won't ask how you knew—as for how I did, it certainly didn't require psychic powers. Cassie was down at Inquire Within with Janelle most of the afternoon, both of them weeping their eyes out," Claire said.

Colin grimaced, his gaze intent upon the road. The turnoff to Nuclear Lake was hard to find at the best of times, let alone in the darkest part of an overcast night.

"I wish I knew what had happened," Colin said. "All of it, and not just what Grey was willing to tell me—or knew himself."

"*That* would make a nice change," Claire agreed darkly. "But—please hurry, Colin."

"I've just got to—ah, here's the turn."

The road that had been easily passable in a Range Rover in February was a much dicier prospect in an automobile in April's treacherous mud, and several times Colin feared that the Volvo would simply stick. But he finally gained the comparatively firm ground of the lakeside, and the car's headlights shone full on the front of the laboratory . . . and on Grey's motorbike, parked outside.

Colin sighed, although he'd expected nothing else. He stopped the car and Claire darted out, running for the back of the building—she'd been more upset than she'd let on. Colin swore under his breath and followed her, leaving the car running with the brake on so that they would at least have the headlights to mark their way.

The back door to the building was propped open with a brick, and when Colin reached it he realized why Claire had been so upset. He could already smell the smoke.

"Claire!" he shouted, dragging out his flashlight.

* * *

When Colin reached the top of the stairs, he could see flames, and the air was hazy with smoke.

"Grey—don't!" Claire's voice.

When Colin reached the bottom of the stairs, he could smell the reek of acetone mixing with the smell of burning. The acetylene lantern with its pressurized chamber of fuel was hissing away brightly in the corner, and Colin winced; acetone was flammable. He looked around. Claire was standing in the corner, unhurt. But this entire basement could go up like a torch at any moment, and take Grey—and both of them—with it.

"'I'll break my staff—bury it certain fathoms in the earth—and deeper than did ever plummet sound—I'll drown—*burn*—my book!'" Grey shouted. He had a five-gallon can of acetone in his hands, and was slopping it about the painted sigil that made up the Floor of the Temple. The caustic liquid pooled on the cement floor, and where it did the outlines of the brightly painted figure began to soften and blur.

Colin wasn't sure that Grey knew he had an audience at all; he tossed the can aside and went back to the smoldering pile of books. The bookcase had been smashed, and the books on it ripped to shreds, piled atop the splintered boards in one of the footlockers. There was broken glass on the floor from the smashed jar-candles; the card table and its chairs had been knocked over, and one of the footlockers stood open.

"Grey!" Colin shouted.

Grey turned to Colin. "Hi, Colin," he said, as mildly though they were meeting on any city street, though his eyes were red with tears and his voice was hoarse with shouting. "I didn't see you guys come in."

"Grey, I know you're upset," Claire began.

"Of *course* I'm upset," Grey told her in a voice of faintly exasperated patience. "Everything I've ever believed in has gone to hell." He reached into his pocket and came out with a lighter in his hand. When he flicked it the flame erupted in a long jet.

"Don't do this," Colin said.

"So I figured I'd just bag it," Grey said, as if Colin hadn't spoken.

He tossed the lighter over his shoulder; it hit the inside of the footlocker's lid and slid down it, still burning. There was a faint huff as whatever he'd poured into the footlocker ignited and began to burn with a sickly bluish flame, consuming Grey's books, his magickal journals, all of his ritual paraphernalia.

"That's it. I'm done," Grey said, walking toward them.

"Come on," Claire said, grabbing him by the arm and pulling him quickly toward the staircase.

The acetone might ignite at any moment, or the three of them might be lucky. Neither Colin nor Claire had been moved to bring a fire extinguisher, and Colin wasn't sure he'd have used it if he had—there were already enough volatile chemicals down here.

They were lucky. Claire got Grey into the clearer air of the ground floor without incident, and Colin followed them outside. He left the back door propped open, in the faint hope that the vapors from the solvent Grey had slopped around would dissipate instead of igniting.

Standing at the back of the building, they could see the light shining out through the row of low windows; the leaping orange of the burning books, and the steady white of the acetylene lamp. The room was filling with black smoke; Colin could see it streaming up through the flames.

"What were you doing?" Claire scolded, all but shaking him.

"It's all over," Grey said again. "Everything's finished."

"Come on," Colin said, putting a hand on Claire's shoulder. "It could still blow up."

"My bike," Grey said, when Claire began leading him toward the car.

"Get it later," Colin told him curtly. He was in no mood for the lengthy process of wrestling Grey's bike into the back of the Volvo just now.

"I'll ride it back."

"No you won't," Claire told him fiercely. "Grey, you could have been *killed* in there tonight—and we won't even mention the fact that arson's a crime. What if there's an explosion? What if the fire spreads?" she scolded.

"Frankly, Scarlett—" Grey began.

"Oh, get in the car!" Claire said, yanking open the door and shoving him toward it.

Colin knew that much of her ruthlessness was sheer relief that nothing worse had happened, and at least it seemed to be having a practical effect on Grey, since he did what she told him.

By the time they reached Greyangels, Grey's teeth were chattering, and he was hugging himself through the fringed leather jacket.

"Build up the fire," Colin told Claire as he shut off the ignition. "I'll get something hot into him."

They went about their business with the ease of long practice. Claire led Grey inside and wrapped him in the afghan from the couch, and settled him in the chair in front of the fire.

As she worked with matches and tinder—Colin always left a fire laid in the grate, for just such occasions as these—he went on into the kitchen and lit the range. Finding a small saucepan, he half-filled it with cider from the local mill, then added a generous dollop of unpasteurized honey. As it was heating, he rummaged about the pantry just off the kitchen until he found a bottle of brandy. It wasn't Colin's preferred drink, but someone had given him a bottle and—pack rat that he was—he'd tucked it away in a corner for future use. Now he poured several ounces of it into a cup and added the steaming cider. No matter what had happened out at Nuclear Lake tonight, it had been a serious ordeal for Grey, and appropriate measures must be taken.

When he came back into the living room, Claire had the fire going and was sitting on the hassock, holding Grey's hand and talking to him.

"Here. Drink this," Colin said, handing him the cup.

Grey took it without comment.

"I'd better go back out there and make sure the fire hasn't spread," Colin said. "Will you two be all right here?"

I think I can hold my own," Claire said. Grey shook his head slightly, a gesture that might mean anything, and pulled the afghan tighter around himself.

Colin picked up the fire extinguisher from beside the front door and drove back to Nuclear Lake.

He could smell the tang of smoke in the air when he got out of the car, but there was no sign of a blaze. When he reached the back of the building, the basement windows were dark, and cool to the touch.

Odd . . . and interesting. The footlocker was right under this one, and I've only been gone half an hour, if that. The stuff should still be burning.

But when he shone his flashlight in through the window, the panes were clear, not smoke-darkened, and there was no sign of a fire.

Curiouser and curiouser, said Alice, Colin thought to himself. He retraced his steps to the back door—still propped open—hesitated, and went inside.

The basement was full of acrid smoke—but not as much smoke as there ought to have been. Colin descended the stairs warily, ready for anything.

The basement floor was covered with a gritty ash that hadn't been there before, but the glyph was still visible, blurred from the acetone; apparently it had not ignited. The lantern in the corner had shattered, leaving a scorch mark on the wall, and pieces of blackened glass were scattered around it in a fan pattern. Colin swept his flashlight back and forth; this might be an investigation better done in daylight, but he was here now.

The candles were spread pools of melted wax that had pooled around the broken blackened jars. Colin bent over and touched the blobby white mass of wax. It was still faintly soft, as though it had only cooled recently. That was strange enough, but what Colin saw when he reached the footlocker convinced him that the Uncanny had been here in this place.

The footlocker was almost unrecognizable, its metal walls warped and twisted, half-charred by a fantastic heat. What it had held had been reduced to greasy ash and a few small blobs of metal—including the pine planks, which should have taken hours to burn.

Grey had left the other footlocker closed, and had done nothing to it that Colin had seen, but there were scorch marks all over the outside, and when Colin cautiously flipped it open, all that it held was a thick grey-black ash.

But the insides of the second trunk weren't even scorched.

Colin let the lid fall back down. It hit with a hollow sound, and a dust of ash as fine as talc puffed out around the edges of its lock.

Colin walked back to the center of what had been the Floor of the Temple. The half-dissolved paint was slightly greasy under his shoe soles.

As Colin knew from his reluctant studies, there were seven Gates and four

Summonings for the Initiate to master in the early stages of the Blackburn Work; the Summonings were four of the six rituals involved in Laying the Floor of the Temple, and involved the Elemental Powers: Earth, Wind, Ocean, and Fire. A Blackburn Circle could—at least in theory—call on any of the Elemental Kings to manifest, though that was a dangerous proposition at best.

It looked—at least from the damage done here tonight—as though Grey had indeed summoned one of them: Salamander, Prince of Fire. He'd said he would burn his books, and he'd kept his word. Colin shuddered at the thought of the power that had been so casually unleashed here.

No, not casually. *Deliberately*—the power of the Adept's will fueled by strong emotion—misery and rage—drawing its power from man's animal nature as the Blackburn Work taught. Furious and grief-stricken, Grey had known precisely what he was doing: he'd summoned Fire without any attempt to balance it, and this had been the result. No wonder the boy was dead on his feet, if that was what he'd been doing.

But Fire was gone now, and the woods were in no danger of burning. He'd better get back before Claire started to worry.

Colin drove back to the farmhouse in a contemplative frame of mind. Grey plainly blamed the Blackburn Work for his break with Winter—or blamed it for not getting her back for him, which amounted to the same thing in the end. If what Colin had seen here tonight was any indication, Grey had chosen to make a clean break with the Work.

That might be a foundation we can build on. Colin shut the thought out of his mind—it was too pragmatic to truly appeal to his sense of himself—but he could not deny its allure. He had wanted Grey to renounce the Blackburn Work, and now, for all intents and purposes, he had.

It was only later that Colin realized how much more Grey had given up that night.

He'd given up everything.

SEVENTEEN

SAN FRANCISCO, WEDNESDAY, MARCH 16, 1983

Even here prowess has its due rewards, there are
tears shed for things even here and mortality touches the heart.
—VIRGIL, *Aeneid*

ON A WINDY DAY IN MARCH, IN THE CITY BY THE BAY, ALISON MARGRAVE'S friends gathered in a chapel on a hill to pay their last respects and to see her to her final resting place.

While Alison had been granted a long and peaceful life—she'd turned eighty-four this January—and a quick and peaceful death, Colin was once again reminded forcefully of something he had already known: that no day was a good day to die. Alison's death was like the removal of some invisible protection from his own mortality, forcing him to acknowledge what he'd thought he understood long before: that someday, fewer years from now than he had already lived, he must leave this life behind.

Claire sat beside him in the chapel, weeping with silent unreconciled bitterness. Alison had been like a parent to her, and this fresh loss reopened old scars.

Alison had requested that her ashes be scattered on Mount Tamalpais, and those she had known throughout her long life had gathered here in this eccentric nondenominational chapel to witness the fulfillment of her last request.

At least one of Alison's own was here to conduct this last farewell. Colin glanced back toward the podium, where Kathleen Carmody stood. She and her husband had been members of Alison's Lodge since their introduction to the Path many years ago. Today Kathleen was dressed all in white—a long open robe over a more mundane turtleneck and pants—but the large gold ankh pendant she wore was all she needed as indication of her standing.

She spoke of her years of friendship with Alison, of the many people seeking the Light whom Alison had helped in all her long life—a life in which the knowledge of the mystic arts had gone from being a secret shared by an elite few, to the common currency and public property of the flower children, to the trivial stuff of comic book entertainment.

As the century—and the millennium—drew toward their ends, it seemed to Colin that mankind had withdrawn from the spiritual in the same way that the burned child spurned the fire. Today's world did not so much assert that nothing existed outside the material world of the five senses as it insisted that nothing was more important than that world and its potential wealth.

Meanwhile, as if in some subtle corollary, crimes became more terrible. Only last September seven people near Chicago had died from taking what seemed to be randomly-poisoned Tylenol, and international affairs seemed ever more complicated and ghastly. Vietnam had been a simple little war fought for simple ends compared to current entanglements in Libya and Nicaragua, and in response to its worldly confusion, America was greedily returning to its enchanted political sleep of the 1950s.

Only the world had grown too wide for that, Colin realized. And this slumber might well become a terminal coma, as the psychic rot at the root of its nation–soul continued to fester. Something was terribly wrong in the world: anyone could see that. But what was harder to see was what could be—what must be—done to change things for the better. . . .

Conscious that he was letting his mind wander, Colin forced his attention back to Kathleen. As he focused on her, she suddenly stopped speaking, staring toward the back of the sanctuary with a stunned expression. It was impossible not to look, and so Colin did.

Simon Anstey stood in the doorway of the chapel.

The scars of his terrible maiming had faded with the years, but Simon still wore the black eyepatch over his left eye and both hands were gloved. He wore a black suit and tie, and looked formidably formal—as if he wore not a simple suit but the most potent armor.

Colin did not need psychic powers to feel the ripple of distress that passed through the congregation at Simon's arrival. Colin supposed that mourning should cancel all feuds, but Alison had known her health was frail ever since the first stroke in 1972. If she had wanted Simon here at her memorial, she would have left explicit instructions to that effect.

"How dare he come here?" Claire said in an outraged whisper.

"He loved her too," Colin said. But was that really true, considering how much Simon had gone against Alison's wishes and pleas?

Claire half-rose from her seat, and Colin put a restraining hand on her arm.

"No," Colin said quietly. "He's probably counting on someone to cause a scene."

At the moment when the whispers of embarrassment might have broken into words, Simon moved, striding down the aisle, taking command of the space with the easy competence he still retained from his performing days. In all things save the use of his hand and eye, Simon seemed recovered from that traumatic accident of years ago.

At least physically . . .

The Path was no pastel sugar-coated confection of rainbows and moon beams whose white-robed Adepts drifted through this life dispensing homilies like a television hero. To be an agent of the Higher Power meant much more than taking on the chains of manifestation long beyond one's required span. It meant the possibility of the sort of failure that could destroy not only lives but souls. It was just this dilemma that drove many Adepts to refuse the fearful burden of action when it was offered—and to steadfastly withhold action could also be a sin.

Thus, the first act of the Adept must be to call the fires of Karma into his own life, to burn away the merely human imperfections that lay there. This was the test that Simon had failed. He had summoned up the cleansing fire, but when the accident had taken his skill from him, he had refused to see it as the act of Karma that it was, and saw it instead as a flaw in the plans of the Lords of Light.

But there are no accidents in this life. Simon was taught that much as any of us who walk the Path were. Only he could not bear to remember it—to take responsibility for his own maiming.

Ignoring the consternation around him—though he surely heard it and must have expected it—Simon stepped up to the podium. Kathleen stepped back—or recoiled—ceding him the space.

"I have come to say good-bye to Alison Margrave, the woman who gave me life, more so than any mother," Simon began. His rich, full, voice filled the room, casting them all irresistibly in the role of audience.

"When I first met Alison Margrave I was a child . . . a prodigy whose gift was a curse, insofar as it alienated me from those who surrounded me. Alison took me into her home and her heart and helped me to understand what I was . . . *all* that I was. Because in addition to being both healer and musician, Alison was more—she was Priestess.

"For many of you, such an old-fashioned word conjures up lurid New Age images of young women playing at being witches, but Alison was a priestess in the older—I may say, oldest—sense. She was a guide and a refuge for the troubled, bringing the Higher Learning within their reach and setting their feet upon the Path. She did much good in the world, and that is what we— what I—will remember here today as we say good-bye: not the rigid insistence on cleaving to an archaic standard of practice that darkened her last years—"

He can't leave it alone, even here, Colin thought. That left-handed slam at Alison's rejection of him was something that everyone here today would recognize. Undoubtedly her judgment of him still rankled: Simon's ego was Luciferian in its arrogance.

"Good-bye and Godspeed, Alison Margrave. We will meet again," Simon finished.

With an actor's sure intuition, he stepped from the stage just as the consternation among the gathering was about to break out into audibility. As quickly as he had come, Simon made his way through the doors at the back of the chapel and was gone.

His appearance had cast a bad, dangerous glamour over the whole memorial, though others spoke after him, and even when those closest to Alison went to scatter her ashes to the turbulent spring winds, a troubling sensation lingered in their minds. And the sense of Simon's presence hovered over the gathering that followed as well.

San Francisco had a long tradition of wakes—Janis Joplin's had been held here, in the city that she loved best—and Alison's was in the grand tradition. It was held at Greenhaven; the old house flung open to allow all who had known Alison to say one last good-bye. Next week the house would go on the market, its sale to benefit distant heirs, and Colin wondered who would be the next person to call these rooms home.

Colin had been away from the Bay Area for nearly fifteen years, and even when he had been living here back in the sixties, he had never been a part of what had since become "the New Age community." For many years, his mission had been to help those who had no previous experience with the Unseen, and it was their needs upon which much of his work with the Bidney Institute had been focused.

Perhaps it was time now to change.

Without conscious volition, his mind strayed back to Hunter Greyson. It was almost a year now since Grey had vanished.

After that April night at Nuclear Lake, Grey had been withdrawn, but Colin had marked that down to the loss of Winter, something from which Grey would surely recover, given time. In his heart Colin had begun to hope that in this life Grey would be the disciple he'd sought, the one who would take all that Colin had learned in this life and carry it forward, taking up part of the burden Colin could not yet himself renounce, the burden of the Great Work. He had hinted as much, and Grey had seemed to welcome the challenge.

Grey had left Taghkanic a few weeks later, at the end of the school year. When he had not returned for the summer lecture series, Colin had been concerned, but not yet worried, marking it down to Grey's need for solitude and healing.

But Grey had neither called nor written over the summer, and he had not returned to campus in the fall. He had vanished. Even his school records were gone. Somehow, Colin had failed him.

Failure was something an Initiate of the Light must learn to accept with grace—though true failures were rare. What the world saw as failure, the Initiate saw as a postponement, sometimes to a future lifetime, it was true, but what was to be, would be. Even so, Colin wished he had been able to give Grey what he had needed, for the sake of the dear friend Grey had been to him before this life, and for the sacrifices that friend had made.

But he had not. He had not acted in the case of Hunter Greyson, and so had lost him, for good or ill. Now the problem of Simon Anstey was before him—Simon whom he had known almost from childhood—and Colin prayed he would know what to do, and when to do it.

Filled with his own solemn thoughts, Colin wandered through the house. There were recordings of Alison's keyboard work playing over the sound sys tem, and the rooms were filled with people who had come to say good-bye. Every strata of San Francisco society was present, from formidable profes- sional women in severely tailored suits, to late-blooming flower children in tie-dye and denim. Mercifully, Simon had not made an appearance here, though it was almost as if he were present, so much was he upon the minds of those who gathered here.

Colin's attention was caught by one long-haired young man with eyes of a startling forest green, who looked much too young to have ever known Ali- son. Colin was wondering how they could have met, when he focused on the woman standing next to the boy.

"Cassie!" Colin crossed the room to greet her.

"Professor MacLaren!" she said, unfeignedly pleased. "Frodo, this is Colin MacLaren—he was one of my teachers back East. Professor, this is Frodo Frederick."

A small gold pendant flashed at her throat; Colin recognized, with resig- nation, the North Gate sigil that many Blackburnites wore. Grey's apostasy had not ended Cassie's involvement in the Work after all. Colin said nothing.

Frodo was wearing the more common silver pentacle of the Pagan and Witch. "It's a pleasure to meet you, sir, but I'm sorry that it has to be on such a somber occasion." He held out his hand.

Colin shook it. The boy had beautiful manners, he thought—and chided himself mentally for thinking anything of the sort. That sort of thinking was the mark of a crotchety old age, and Colin was far from ready to embrace such a thing.

"So am I. Had you known Alison long?"

"All my life." The boy grinned. "Well, since I was twelve, anyway. She caught me climbing the wall into her garden, and I thought for sure she was going to make a big fuss, but she didn't. She just gave me some cookies, and told me that any time I wanted to see her garden, all I had to do was come around to the front door and ask. And when I was leaving, she asked if I liked to read, and suggested that if I did, there were a couple of authors I might like."

"Madeline L'Engle was one of them, I remember. And when I got older, she had some other authors for me. I'm going to miss her," Frodo said sadly.

"We're all going to miss her," Colin agreed. In some ways, Alison had been the still point around which the entire Bay Area New Age Community had revolved. The West Coast was traditionally a breeding ground for kooks and nut-cultists of every description: who would it be who set the tone for the Lightworkers now?

"So, how are you enjoying the real world?" Colin asked Cassie, trying to lighten the subject.

She grimaced. "You know the old saying: for this I spent four years in college? But I'm glad to run into you here, Professor. I was going to write to you and ask—do you hear anything from Grey? I wrote him at the Glastonbury address, but all my letters came back marked 'Moved, No Forwarding.'"

"I'm sorry," Colin said, and saw her face crumple in a disappointment that she tried hard to conceal.

When Grey had not returned to Taghkanic in the fall, Colin had sought him in the Overworld within the limits of the Law he served. He had found that Grey was alive and physically whole, but no more than that. He had not raised the matter with Claire, for fear that she would not understand . . . or would understand too well. Like it or not, Colin had been shut out of Hunter Greyson's life for good or ill.

"I'd been wondering if he kept up with any of his old friends," he said, trying not to hope.

"No." Cassie's response was quick and comprehensive. If she was still studying the Blackburn Work, Colin imagined she'd looked for Grey even harder than he had. Her eyes glistened, brimming with tears. "Oh, well."

Frodo put an arm around her shoulders; a gesture that seemed to hold more of comfort than possessiveness.

"You knew Simon Anstey, didn't you?" Frodo asked Colin, changing the subject.

"For many years," Colin answered, a little warily.

"Do you think he'd listen to you?" Frodo asked. His manner seemed composed of equal parts determination and embarrassment.

"Frodo, don't," Cassie pleaded.

"Somebody has to," Frodo said stubbornly. "Anstey, he's . . . he's doing some really bad things."

It was the very banality of Frodo's words that convinced Colin that the boy was serious. People who were inventing horrors took care to make their words as vivid, dramatic, and compelling as possible. Those who had looked upon the actual face of Evil were usually reduced to insipid generalities.

"Tell me," Colin said quietly.

"He's . . . they say he's . . . sacrificing animals. Taking their life force and adding it to his own, so that the nerve grafts the doctors are doing on his fingers now will take, and he'll get the use of that hand back," Frodo said in a rush.

"Have you seen him do this?" Colin asked. The most serious crime an Adept could commit against the Light was to *take*—to take the life and soul of another to feed his own power. Colin could not afford to take Frodo's words lightly.

Frodo passed a hand over his face, as if trying to blot out his own words. "No. And nobody I know has, either. But you hear things; San Francisco is really a small town, especially when it comes to anyone who's into what Alison was into. And Simon's quick enough to tell the rest of us that we're cowards and idiots, and he's the only one who understands the full true secrets of magick." Frodo didn't sound bitter—only tired and a little afraid.

"Yes, that sounds like Simon . . . unfortunately," Colin agreed.

There were certain practices that the Light strictly forbade—it was the basis of Colin's long-ago break with Thorne, his quarrel with Grey. To manipulate the material world for personal gain through the use of the Art was one; to use the Art to sway the minds of the Unawakened for one's own end was another. These were the things that the Blackburn Work had in common with the Left-Hand Path, but apparently Simon Anstey had gone even further into the Kingdom of the Shadow, into those practices which could not be justified by even the most tolerant apologist.

"The blood is the life" wasn't simply a phrase from a classic horror novel; to an Adept it was the simple—literal—truth. This was the secret meaning behind the blood sacrifice, and why it had been held in such abhorrence by all civilized cultures. The power a Black Adept gained in this way could be used to heal the body, to hold back the ravages of age, even to raise the dead—but each use, each sacrifice, separated the Black Adept more irreversibly from communion with the Light.

Colin knew that Simon had dabbled in blood sacrifice as a child—if he had returned, in desperation, to those old habits to gain the power he felt he needed . . .

Suddenly Colin *felt*—rather than heard—the sound of a deep chime that seemed to resonate within his chest. It was the vibration of the great Bell which hung in the Temple of his Order, though its physical manifestation had ended centuries in the past. That Bell rang only in moments of greatest need, or to signal the blackest peril. Colin had not heard it for many years.

Was it tolling for Simon? The peril to his soul was great, and it was possible that now at last it was time for Colin to intervene. He had held off from meddling in Grey's life until it was too late—perhaps this was a sign that he must not make the same mistake twice.

He glanced around the room, seeing members of a dozen different Magickal Lodges mingling freely with Witches and Pagans and Blackburnites. It had taken Alison's death to overcome the barriers that kept them apart . . . and it came to Colin suddenly, borne upon the impetus of the Astral Bell, that they must not be allowed to fall back into the paths of divisiveness. Opposition to the Shadow was not a simple matter of tilting at windmills in darkness: it was the creation of a Positive Energy to supplant the Negative. They must look for their common ground, not focus upon their differences.

Perhaps if Colin had concentrated on what the Blackburn Work shared with the Light . . . but no. That was the path of equivocation that Simon had followed down into the darkness of the Left-Hand Path, and now he had reached its deepest shadows.

The way to save Simon was not to follow him.

Abruptly Colin realized what that Bell had signaled. His work at the Bidney Institute was done, and another chapter of his life was about to begin— here.

For one man, working with a whole heart, is a more effective reproach to evil than the half-hearted actions of a million men. So mote it be.

EIGHTEEN

SAN FRANCISCO, MONDAY, JANUARY 9, 1984

But, for the unquiet heart and brain
A use in measured language lies;
The sad mechanic exercise,
Like dull narcotics, numbing pain.
— ALFRED, LORD TENNYSON

CLAIRE MOFFAT SAT BEHIND THE BOOKSTORE COUNTER, READING HER textbook, a good cup of fresh-brewed tea steaming at her elbow. Monsignor watched her gravely, amber eyes glowing. Poltergeist was asleep on a shelf somehere in the back of the store.

Claire loved the early morning, before the Haight was really awake. It seemed at that time of day that the city belonged to her alone, and despite the raw January chill—and the open door leading to the street—the inside of the Ancient Mysteries Bookshop was cozy and inviting.

Relocating cross-country once more hadn't been as difficult as she'd thought it might be—and Colin had asked so little of her in this life compared to what he had done for her that she had been glad to repay him in this small way. She'd succeeded in finding a good manager for Inquire Within without much difficulty, and in a college town she'd had no trouble renting the apartment above the store.

As for Colin . . .

It seemed impossible that he should have been able to wind up his affairs as quickly as he had. He'd not only had the responsibility of finding someone who could take over his classes at Taghkanic, but someone to helm the Bidney Institute as well. Claire was glad to see it accomplished so smoothly; Colin had been good for the institute, but he was not at heart an administrator, and Claire had to admit that Miles Godwin was a perfect successor. And Miles was a young man—barely thirty. Now that Colin had recrafted the institute in his own image, Miles—brisk, efficient, unflappable Miles—could run it right into the next century.

Now Colin was—officially—on sabbatical from Taghkanic. In fact, he was lecturing at San Francisco State this winter, dividing his time between that and the bookstore.

The Ancient Mysteries Bookstore had been founded in 1979, but it had been failing for the usual reasons that plagued small business when Claire had found it for Colin on a preliminary trip West last summer. Colin had invested some money—becoming part-owner—and taken over the management a few months ago. His plan was to make the store something of a community center, and so far the idea had worked admirably. Now more than ever before, there was a free exchange of ideas and goals among the Lightworkers of the Bay Area.

To Claire's mild surprise, Colin had even accepted Cassie Chandler's presence without demur, though Cassie was working with a group called Circle of Fire, a Blackburn Workgroup operating in the East Bay. *How Thorne would laugh if he knew! He hated dogma, and they've taken his work and made it into a set of regulations that have to be followed precisely. If there was anything that could bring him back from the dead, it would be that. . . .*

It was ironic that where Thorne Blackburn had once tried and failed, Colin had succeeded with the Ancient Mysteries Bookshop. Colin had asked her to manage the place, and had hired several of the local members of the occult community as additional staff, as he did not wish to tie himself down to being in the store on a regular schedule. Claire worked in the store on Mondays and Fridays, as her schedule of classes permitted.

She'd worried that returning to the places she'd known with Peter would bring her pain, but to her surprise—and regret—the pain was not as overpowering as she'd feared. Peter was with the angels now, and Claire could go on with her life without an overwhelming burden of grief. But she'd been concerned about facing a familiar landscape with too much time on her hands, and so she'd arranged to work toward a degree in psychology at San Francisco State. Most of the credits that had earned Claire her RN could still be transferred, even at this late date. She'd started last fall and was already well embarked on earning a master's degree in psychology.

Claire was a little surprised at how much pleasure the coursework gave her. The world had changed a great deal in the quarter of a century since she'd entered nursing school. Most women expected to have careers now, even after marriage, and nobody thought of them as emotionally-stunted man-haters. The change had been so gradual that only in looking back could it be seen at all.

I suppose all change is like that. Gradual. Who would have thought, in those days that Colin and I were visiting Thorne on this very block, that we'd be back here and running an occult bookstore that has more in common with the old Voice of Truth *than not?*

She shook her head fondly. Life, in the words of the philosopher, was not only stranger than they imaged, it was also stranger than they *could* imagine.

At that moment, Claire felt the familiar summons to mindfulness. A slender, dark-haired woman had paused at the display of lurid secondhand paperbacks that were racked outside the front of the store. She hesitated over them for a moment, her whole aspect that of someone who is searching for something unknown, then made her selection and walked into the store, holding the book out before her as if it were radioactive.

She was obviously a professional woman, slightly out of place in this bohemian neighborhood. Her short dark hair was cut in a practical bob, and her pale grey suit, with the small "good" gold brooch on the lapel, was pure "Dress for Success." Someone less likely to pick up one of the tattered two-bit paperbacks sitting out in front of the bookstore was hard to imagine, though the woman had the faintly wild-eyed look of one whose life had recently been disturbed by a brush with the Unseen. For some reason the sight of her struck a chord of recognition in Claire's mind, though it was too faint to follow up.

Claire glimpsed the title as she set it down: *Those Incredible Poltergeists.* One of Jock Cannon's books, God rest his soul.

"That's not at all a bad book," Claire said gently.

"I don't know much about it," the stranger said gruffly. "Is this book—er—reliable?"

Bingo, Claire thought to herself. Her visitor looked to be in her late twenties, old enough—just possibly—to be the mother of a child poltergeist, but somehow Claire did not get the sense that this was that sort of problem.

"I'm out of the Margrave and Anstey monograph just now, but this—" Claire picked up a copy of Dion Fortune's *Psychic Self Defense* and tendered it toward the stranger "—is very common-sensical."

The woman recoiled faintly at the sight of the cover, which even Claire had to admit was nearly as sensational as that of the tattered paperback. She set the book back down on the counter. Obviously, her customer wasn't yet quite desperate enough to grasp at any straw, as yet.

"I have Nandor Fodor's *On the Trail of the Poltergeist,* too—if you want to wade through a lot of psychoanalytical twaddle," she offered, and saw the woman's face relax at a name she recognized.

"I'll take that one," she said. Relief lightened her voice to a husky contralto.

Claire's subjective hunch had been right: this woman was either a psychologist or psychiatrist. She went into the back room to find a copy—Colin had sold the last one the day before, and they only managed to keep the out-of-print volume in stock by buying up used copies.

When Claire came back the woman was looking through one of the books on reincarnation, an expression of distaste on her face, much as if she'd caught one of the church elders dancing naked in the street. When Claire handed her the Fodor, the woman all-but-flung payment at Claire for the two books and rushed out without another word.

Claire picked up the book she'd been leafing through. *Twenty Cases Suggestive of Reincarnation,* the title read, by another credentialed psychologist. Claire looked after the woman, a troubled frown on her face. She knew that they would meet again. She only hoped that it wouldn't be too late for either of them.

"Hey, Claire—have you heard? Greenhaven's been sold . . . again!"

April was a month filled with sunshowers and blustery winds; not even the canopy over the street was enough to save the sale table books from damage. Frodo was sorting through them, trying to decide which ones were too damaged to sell.

So that's who that woman was. She had no proof, but in her heart Claire had no doubt that the young woman who'd come to the store to get information on poltergeists was the same one who had come to take over Greenhaven. And this one, Claire hoped, would stay.

Greenhaven had been sold three times since Alison's death a year ago March, but the house had seemed unable to find its match. Tenants never seemed to stay more than a few months—or, in the case of Kathleen Carmody's sister, Betty, *weeks*—before the house was back on the market.

I wonder if Alison is restless?

Alison Margrave had died without naming a successor. After Simon's accident, and his gradual turning away from the Path, Alison had repudiated him formally, severing the magickal link of master and *chela* that bound them. It had been too late for her to find someone else to carry on after her; she had died unhappy, unfulfilled.

"Hey, Claire?" Frodo said.

"Hm? I was just wondering if this one would last. Do you know who it is?" *Have you found your successor, Alison? Is she the one?*

"Um . . . my dad heard from the realtor, but he didn't get a lot of details. A doctor, I think. I heard she'd be moving in there in May."

"Well, she'll get our best weather, then," Claire said peaceably. *Maybe she'll stay.*

As they talked the bookstore filled with its usual Monday visitors. Far from discouraging what other retailers called "museum shoppers"—people who treated stores like museums, with contents that could be viewed but not purchased—Colin and Claire welcomed them for the sake of strengthening the flourishing occult community here in San Francisco.

And just in time, Claire mused, *if Simon's back in town and Greenhaven has a new tenant.*

As if to illustrate the truth of her words, the day seemed to darken as a figure appeared in the doorway. Claire looked up, and felt the shock of recognition as a hammerblow to the heart.

Speak of the devil and hear the sound of his wings. . . .

Claire had not seen Simon since the day of Alison's funeral, and then not closely. The scars were white and sunken now, though he still wore the eyepatch. His hair had gone prematurely grey, making him look much older than his forty-one years, and there were harsh lines bracketing his mouth.

He hesitated in the doorway, as if he were uncertain whether he should go in or not, but then he realized Claire had seen him. Almost reflexively his shoulders straightened, and he strode into the bookstore like an actor taking the stage.

"Claire. I'd heard you and Colin had come back," Simon said in his deep resonant voice.

"That's right," Claire said, forcing herself to be calm. "I see you're back as well."

She wished she didn't feel so very much like a mouse that had attracted the attention of a large hungry cat. The thought brought with it the memory of the persistent rumors that had gathered around Simon in the years since his accident—dark, unpleasant rumors of torture and blood magick, almost impossible for Claire to reconcile with the memory of the daredevil boy she'd once known.

"Poor Claire," Simon said mockingly. "Did you tiptoe home thinking that I'd gone for good? San Francisco is my home, too—and I'll not be driven out."

"Nobody's trying to drive you out, Simon," Claire said reasonably. "And as for my motives in coming back, I honestly didn't give you a thought."

Simon laughed. "I can hardly believe that, when you took such pains to preach your gospel of praiseworthy submission to me while I lay helpless. I should have realized that you wouldn't give up so easily."

"Which way do you want it, Simon?" Claire snapped, feeling her temper fray. "Did I come back hoping you were gone, or was I supposed to be hoping to find you here? You can't have it both ways."

Everyone in the bookstore was watching them. Claire gritted her teeth.

"Can't I?" Simon purred. "But I've told you that nothing is impossible to the trained will. I warn you, Claire, if you think to take up where you left off in '73, you will find me a worthier opponent this time. I will not hold with your continued meddling interference in my destiny—nor Colin's. I assume that now that he's back he intends to tilt once more at the windmills of virtue? Does he still hold his narrow-minded, racist views on the colors of magick?"

"Did you come here to deliver a warning or just to posture?" Claire demanded, getting to her feet. "If Colin MacLaren were to interfere in *my* life, I would get down on my knees and thank God for my good fortune! Like any bully you can't stand being wrong—black, green, or purple, that wickedness you're dabbling in is *Evil*."

Her plain speaking didn't seem to faze Simon. In fact, he looked rather pleased at the reaction he'd gotten out of her.

"I had such high hopes for you once, my dear. But I see you've given in entirely to that sanctimonious old fraud. I believe the expression is 'blinded by the Light.' There is no difference between Black and White Magick—only the Will of the trained Adept acting upon the Material World. All else is antique superstition. I would have thought that you, at least, would have put it behind you, though perhaps I should not expect as much from a tired old man."

Claire gasped, literally stricken speechless by the effrontery of Simon's statement. He had changed in the ten years since his injury—even with seeing him at the memorial service, she had not realized how much until this moment. The constant pain he was in had forged a darkness, a hardness in his spirit that frightened her more than she would allow herself to know.

She realized she dared not let this go on; she was shaking with rage, and at any moment, she might say something that she regretted. "Simon," Claire said evenly, "you are a damned fool, with the emphasis on *damned.*" She got to her feet and walked back to the storeroom on trembling legs.

"—if I'd stayed another moment I'd have picked up my Psychology text and brained him with it," Claire said ruefully. "And a pretty bit of gossip *that* would have made."

The two friends were met over tea in the living room of Colin's cramped and cluttered apartment, one of four in a remodeled Victorian a few blocks from the bookstore. It bore, Claire thought, a certain family resemblance to every place Colin had ever lived: a jackdaw's nest of books and papers, strewn about in no appreciable pattern. Despite the fact that he had been here since the end of October, half-unpacked cartons of books and papers were still scattered about every room.

"I'm afraid that no matter where Simon is, there's going to be gossip," Colin said. "But you handled that as well as anyone could have."

"Well, I just wish he'd go away!" Claire snapped. "Don't you?" The paperweight that Alison had given Colin stood on a windowsill, its silver sword gleaming in the sun. Claire's eyes were drawn toward it. If she'd had it yesterday, she'd probably have flung it at Simon. Her fingers itched in anticipation of its weight. She'd *like* to throw something at Simon. . . .

"No," said Colin unexpectedly. "I hope he stays."

"But Colin," Claire protested, startled. "You can't think he'll listen to you! You didn't hear him yesterday—he hates you."

"I think he's afraid of me," Colin corrected gently. "But no matter how deranged Simon has become—and I think that anyone who chooses to embrace the Shadow is certainly mad in a sense—he knows that I would never hurt him. So there's something else he's afraid of."

"Afraid that you can help him?" Claire suggested eagerly. She'd heard of the condition in her classes: since the human mind hated change and uncertainty above all other things, people would often reject help—and hope—choosing to suffer rather than to accept the possibility of change.

"*Can* you help him, Colin?"

"I hope so," Colin said, seeing his hope reflected on Claire's face. "But I must resign myself to the fact that in this situation, I am only an instrument of the Light, intervening at its good pleasure." And he did not know yet whether he would be permitted to interfere with Simon's self-chosen destruction at all.

Was this Simon's test—or his?

But Simon, grave though his problems were, was not their only concern that spring.

Truth was the common currency of the New Age; truth and honesty were the only tools Lightworkers had to build a common language with the mundane world outside their own fraternity. In the materialistic eighties, the search for spiritual truths came with a hefty price tag attached. With money to be had, the frauds and exploiters gathered like sharks, and Colin battled those threats with fierce defensiveness. Any force which devalued truth, which made the followers of New Age doctrines seem that they were attempting to cheat their mundane brethren, was something that attacked the principles of solidarity that Colin worked toward.

That was one of the reasons Colin had agreed to allow a local Spiritualist group to meet at the store once a month. Personally he found their doctrine puerile and essentially unconvincing, as well as far outside what was, in the last quarter of the twentieth century, the mainstream of occult thought. But it was no use to complain that people drank the dirty water if there was no possibility of their getting clean. Better a Spiritualist Church, which allowed people free access to what purported to be the spirits of their departed friends and relatives, than a storefront "psychic" who would charge them hundreds of dollars for a collection of vaudeville mentalist tricks.

He had given the Spiritualists fair warning that he would unmask any frauds he found among the mediums who exercised their gift at the bookstore. *But Heaven defend me from the "well-meaning" self-professed "psychic," whose sincere self-delusions cause so much grief to those who believe in them and follow their advice in medical and financial matters. Sometimes I wonder which is worse: honest unbelieving greed, or self-aggrandizing self-delusion. . . .*

Colin finished arranging the chairs around the table and debated whether he should set up the fan. It was warm for the beginning of May, and once the curtain cutting the back room off from the shop was drawn, the room would have no ventilation. It would probably get pretty warm back here.

Let it. The séances—there were usually two or three mediums each time—would probably not run more than a couple of hours. It was a weeknight, after all, and things didn't usually get started until after seven.

"Colin?" He heard the jingle of the front door and Claire's voice. A moment later she poked her head through the half-drawn curtain.

"That looks nice." She had a brown bag in one arm and a white bakery box dangling from the other hand. "We were out of coffee, so I stopped at the corner market up the block and got some, and then I decided to stop at the bakery. I know Kathleen usually brings something, but the cookies looked so good. . . ."

"Let me help," Colin said, coming forward to take the unwieldy box from her.

"You stay out of those until afterward," Claire scolded fondly. "Come on. You can help me set up the coffee urn."

To avoid distraction for the mediums, the table that would hold the coffee urn and the desserts for afterward had been set up in the stockroom. Unlike Claire's store back in Glastonbury, the Ancient Mysteries Bookshop sold only new and used occult books, so there were no herbs and oils back here to worry about—just a bunch of half-open cartons and untidy piles of secondhand books from book searches and used bookstores, organized (more or less) on a number of rickety bookshelves.

Claire carried her bag of groceries into the back; when this had been a private home, this section had been the kitchen, and there was a sink here. The percolator—a large one, with a thirty-cup capacity—stood beside the sink, waiting. Claire tucked the quart of milk into the tiny dorm-sized refrigerator under the counter, and then rummaged around until she found the can opener and attacked the tin of coffee.

"Rainbow said the new tenants are all moved in to Alison's house—I suppose we're going to have to stop calling it that eventually, but it *is* hard—as of last week. Not a family; a woman and her sister. The woman is some kind of counselor—I think she stopped into the shop a few months back, but I couldn't say for sure—she's running a practice out of the house. The sister's a music student at the conservatory. Rainbow said she'll be bringing the younger sister with her tonight, so we'll get to meet her."

"Is the girl interested in Spiritualism?" Colin asked curiously. It wasn't a path that attracted many young people, at least in urban areas like the San Francisco Bay Area.

"No," Claire admitted, "But she's young, and curious, and interested in making new friends. Apparently she's already made quite a hit with Frodo."

"Well, that's a point in her favor, certainly," Colin said. He picked up the heavy percolator filled with water and carried it over to the table. They'd plug it in later, just before the first medium began to sit. "I'm looking forward—"

The doorbell chimed.

"Someone must be here. I'll get it," Claire said, wiping her hands clean on a towel.

"Colin, this is Emily Barnes. Her sister Leslie has just bought Greenhaven," Claire said.

Emily Barnes was a tall slender teenager with the grace of a black swan. The way she held herself bespoke years of training in classical dance, but Claire had said she was studying music. Rainbow and Frodo were with her, along with a couple of the other local Wiccans.

"I'm pleased to meet you, Emily. I'm Colin MacLaren." He held out his hand, and Emily took it, with the caution of one whose art was concentrated in her hands. He shook it gently, and saw her relax.

"Hello," Emily said shyly. The light of an old soul shone from her dark eyes, but Colin did not sense any Call to awaken it.

Emily's eyes flickered from Colin to Claire, and widened slightly at the sight of the store. "Wow! You've got more books than my sister does."

"We try to sell them," Colin said, smiling. "But they keep piling up." Another knot of people gathered at the door, and Colin moved away to open it.

Kathleen Carmody entered with another woman—apparently the other medium for tonight's séance.

Colin had known Kathleen and Edward for a long time, having come into their lives on an occasion when a legacy from a distant relative had brought with it a good deal more trouble than anyone could have expected. It was then that Kathleen had discovered her gifts as a psychic, and she and Edward had gone on to work closely with Alison in the last years of the older woman's life.

"Hello, Colin. This is Rhonda Quentin."

Ms. Quentin wore a voluminous Egyptian-print caftan and a great deal of jewelry, including a six-inch-long quartz crystal pendant carved artificially into a point. Her eyelids were painted a deep bruise-purple from lashes to browline. She was several years older than Kathleen—in her late fifties, Colin would hazard.

"Ah, you are the friend of whom Kathleen has told me so much," Ms. Quentin declaimed in a throaty voice. "I see that you are an old soul, who has trod the Path through many more lives than this. But your aura seems somehow clouded—" She put her hand to her forehead in a theatrical gesture.

Colin pegged her as a harmless crank—who might even actually be psychic. That particular ability, like a gift for singing or sharp eyesight, carried with it no particular guarantee of mental stability or even common sense.

"I'm pleased to meet you, Ms. Quentin. All legitimate followers of the Path are welcome here," Colin said tactfully. He turned away to greet another guest, and out of the corner of his eye saw Kathleen turn to Rhonda Quentin and begin whispering to her.

Kathleen worked first, sliding quickly and untheatrically into a trance state and reaching those on the "other side" whose message she had to convey. To Colin's surprise, there was a message for Emily Barnes from her grandmother, but it was something essentially harmless, and the girl did not seem upset by it.

Kathleen worked in a very modern style; though she asked the sitters for quiet and to place their hands upon the table, she did not dim the lights nor engage in any prayers or exhortations. She also dispensed with the embarrassingly-implausible spirit guides that characterized both previous generations of mediums and that New Age phenomenon, the "channeler."

While it was true that "spirit guides" were only another mask for the self—the ritual magician often encouraged the division of his personality into various magickal "personas" which could perform the tasks he set them without the additional burden of twentieth-century rationalism—it was one that had led to much ridicule and misunderstanding over the years.

When her turn came, however, Ms. Quentin proved to be a medium in the grand old tradition. She'd arrived carrying a large carpetbag, out of which she drew a large pillar candle and a heavy brass ashtray into which she placed several pieces of cone incense.

"It clears the vibrations, my dears. So much unhappiness in this world is due to blocked or clogged auras," she pronounced grandly.

About half the people here tonight were older women, with short permed hair and strings of beads around their necks. They nodded, agreeing with her, while the younger ones— and even in her late forties, Kathleen Carmody was one of them—looked pained and politely noncommittal.

Colin glanced at Claire. She had the expression of a woman who has bitten into a very sour lemon and is doing her best not to show it.

So she suspects as much as I do, Colin thought wryly. *Well, let's see if Ms. Quentin has anything novel in her bag of tricks.*

For several minutes the older medium bustled about the table, rearranging her audience for "proper energonic flow." Colin wasn't surprised to have been seated as far away from her as possible, with Claire a couple of seats to his right. Kathleen must have warned the woman that Colin didn't tolerate frauds here; he hoped she'd heeded the warning.

The medium lit the candle and the incense, then turned out all the lights, requested everyone to clasp hands tightly, and led the group in several rather Christian prayers.

This didn't go down too well with the Wiccans there; Rainbow looked rather embarrassed, Frodo determinedly polite, and Emily Barnes looked actively stricken, much as if she'd been suddenly called upon to handle live snakes. In the eighties, "freedom *of* religion" seemed to have become "freedom *from* religion" for many people; the girl might well never have been in a synagogue, mosque, temple, or church in her entire life.

Ms. Quentin entered trance with a great deal of moaning and head-rolling, and then produced a spirit guide named Yellow Bear.

Moving slowly, Colin brought the hands of the people on either side of him toward each other. When Ms. Quentin had asked them all to clasp hands, he'd kept his hands close together in front of him, precisely so he could do this.

Without demur, the people on either side of him clasped hands, their whole attention caught by the dialogue between Ms. Quentin and Yellow Bear that was taking place at the top of the table. Moving as noiselessly as possible, Colin crept, crouching, to the back of the room—and waited.

As he'd expected, soon Ms. Quentin began to emit faintly glowing streams of ectoplasm, that material every good medium was supposed to be able to generate at will from her own body, in order to form actual shapes of the dear departed. Ms. Quentin was putting on quite a show, and Colin could feel the level of tension in the room rise expectantly.

He turned on the lights.

Ms. Quentin screamed.

In the glare of the harsh overhead florescents, a length of sheer fabric daubed with luminous paint could plainly be seen. It was suspended in the air by an ingenious mechanism composed of thin bamboo strips which Ms. Quentin held between her toes.

"She's a fake!" Emily Barnes burst out, and then began to giggle in nervous relief. Several of the others joined her.

The lattice of bamboo strips clattered to the floor. In the open carpetbag beside Ms. Quentin's chair, Colin glimpsed the rest of the paraphernalia of the fraud psychic: several different bells, a clicker, a length of rope, and a small stoppered bottle containing a fine granulated powder.

Ms. Quentin burst into tears. "No! You don't understand! It's real! It's all real!"

"Oh, Ronnie," Kathleen Carmody said reproachfully. "I *trusted* you!"

"Why don't we all go get something to drink?" Frodo suggested, practical and businesslike. He put a hand under Emily's elbow, steering her toward the other room. Most of the others, as embarrassed to have witnessed the bogus medium's unveiling as she'd been to be exposed, followed them.

Claire moved to the head of the table, to where Ms. Quentin crouched, weeping, her hands over her eyes.

"There, there, dear," Claire said, motherly and practical. "You must have known you'd be caught sooner or later. Here's my hankie. Now put on your shoes, and have a nice cup of coffee. And I think you ought to apologize to all these people."

"I didn't do anything wrong," Ms. Quentin said belligerently, still weeping. Her mascara made muddy tracks down cheeks soft and seamed with age, and wiping at it with Claire's soft linen pocket square only made matters worse. "The Astral Plane is real—it *is*—but people aren't content with that. They want signs and wonders."

"But you can't give them to them, you know," Claire said, still soothingly. "Not by trickery. It's wrong. Not everyone is a materializing medium, and you must never pretend to carry messages from Beyond that you haven't received. Who knows what mischief you might do? Come on now; why don't you wash up and put on some fresh lipstick? You'll feel ever so much better."

Ms. Quentin nodded, and Claire put an arm around her shoulders to help her to her feet. But just as she straightened, the woman's knees buckled under her, and Claire sagged under her weight.

Colin rushed to help.

"She's out cold—and she's not faking," Claire decided, as Colin helped lower her to the floor again. "Best to let her come around naturally—I'll go get a blanket."

Colin took off his jacket and bundled it into a pillow to place beneath her head. As he did, he realized that behind closed lids, the medium's eyes were darting back and forth, as if she were deep in REM-sleep. He took her hand, disturbed.

"Don't—" the voice that forced itself from Ms. Quentin's throat was hoarse and masculine, oddly familiar. "Don't—"

Colin leaned forward. Was she dreaming? Faking? Or was this a true trance?

"Don't let me—" The voice broke off, and there was a confusion of sound, as though several people were talking at once.

"Who are you?" Colin asked. "What do you want?"

Ms. Quentin's eyelids fluttered; she awoke as if she'd been asleep.

"What?" she said, struggling to get up. "What's going on?"

Though she'd certainly been faking earlier, what had come after she fainted—of which she had no memory—was undoubtedly genuine. Ms. Quentin belonged to that class of psychics who had genuine powers but resorted to trickery on those all-too-frequent occasions when the Gift would not present itself. Colin would not be foolish enough to disregard her message, mystifying as it was.

It was a cry for help—but from whom?

A couple of weeks later Claire was replacing the books on one of the high shelves. Most of the browsers at the bookshop had the usual tendency to replace the books wherever was convenient, rather than where they belonged, and after a few weeks of that, it was difficult to find anything. The weather had settled into the endless string of fair temperate days that marks a California summer, and the air this close to the ceiling was stifling. It was a relief when she heard Colin summoning her from the front of the store.

"Claire? I think this must be the lady you mentioned to me."

Claire hurried down the ladder and came out to the desk. A dark-haired woman was standing in front of the counter, talking to Colin. She bore a certain resemblance to Emily Barnes, but where Emily possessed the gawky ethereality of youth, this woman was definitely a grown-up. Claire recognized her from their previous meeting.

"Dr. Barnes, is it?" Colin asked. "I heard that you had moved into a house which once belonged to our dear friend Alison Margrave."

Claire saw how Leslie Barnes shied away from the mention of Alison's name, as though it held no good associations for her.

"The book you gave me on poltergeists contained the only sensible thing I've ever read about them. I came back to see if you had anything else," Leslie said to Claire.

"I'll start you with the Anstey and Margrave monograph," Claire answered. They'd been out of it, she remembered, the last time Dr. Barnes had called, but that had been back in January.

She went to get the book, since she'd just been handling it, and when she came back, they spoke for a few minutes about the séance the previous week, and the fake psychic that Colin had exposed. But that wasn't what Dr. Barnes had come to the bookstore to hear, and Claire knew it.

"It's none of my business," Claire began hesitantly, "but I hope that your interest in poltergeists does not indicate that . . ." She glanced toward Colin. "How shall I say this?"

Colin, bless him, had just the right words. "What Claire is trying to say is that at one time we knew your new house well, and it's no secret that ever since Alison's death there have been disturbances reported there. I'd hoped that when you and your sister moved in—a psychologist and a musician—that there would be no more disturbances. I knew that Alison would be unhappy with anyone living in the house who did not share her interests—"

"But that's impossible!" Dr. Barnes burst out vehemently. "You *can't* believe that! The dead—if they survive—why would they still be interested in what happens to what they left behind?"

Because there is unfinished business here, Claire thought, but did not voice the thought aloud.

"I hardly know what to say to you. I don't have any idea how much you know about these things . . ." Claire began.

"Nothing," Dr. Barnes said flatly.

And abruptly Claire remembered why it was that Leslie Barnes had looked so familiar, even when they were meeting for the first time. "I find that hard to believe," she said, as gently as she could. "Not if you are open-minded enough to investigate a poltergeist—and forgive me, Dr. Barnes; I don't think much of the *Enquirer,* but there must have been something to that story they printed last year. Let me—"

"Claire." Colin's voice was quietly firm. "She came to us for books, not for unasked advice."

Claire blinked at Colin in mild surprise. It was unlike him to withhold help, but for some reason, he did not wish her to offer. She thought about the newspaper story. If it was to be believed, Leslie Barnes, then a school psychologist in Sacramento, had experienced a vision that led police to the notorious "Pigtail Killer." No wonder she had wanted to move as far away from that as possible. How horrible that would be, to find one's self in the mind of a serial killer. . . .

"Oh, please," Leslie Barnes burst out. "If you know anything at all about this business, I'm at my wit's end! I was just thinking that I needed all the help I could get!" She looked from one to the other of them pleadingly.

Claire glanced at Colin. He would not act—but he would not stop her from acting, either.

"Has there been any poltergeist activity in the house itself?" Claire asked.

Leslie Barnes took a deep ragged breath, and it all came tumbling out— the crank calls that had begun while she and Emily were still living in Berkeley—the disconnected doorbell that rang when there was no one there and continued to ring after she'd ripped it out of the wall—the troubled nightmares that had plagued both her and Emily, of a blood-drenched howling man. . . .

In such company, the poltergeist phenomena were almost innocuous, but it was obvious that Leslie Barnes was terrified at the thought that the psychic flashes that had begun so suddenly had not simply vanished, but taken on a new and more terrifying manifestation.

"Take these home and read them," Claire said, holding out two books, the monograph and the book Alison had written by herself. "And if you like, I can come over this evening and try to see what's going on in your house."

"Are you a medium, too?" Dr. Barnes said, abrupt suspicion and open hostility in her voice. Claire kept her face still, knowing what was going through the younger woman's mind. Like many of her own patients, Leslie Barnes knew that she desperately needed help, but was deeply wary of accepting any.

Claire shook her head, searching for the words that would soothe the other woman's fears. "I've had a little experience, nothing more. I'm not sure I can find out anything, but I do know the house, and I could try."

"Oh, Colin, how could we *not* help her?" Claire demanded as soon as Dr. Barnes had left. "You saw—that poor woman was at the end of her tether! What if—if Alison has chosen her—if she's the one—"

"She's strong enough to handle it," Colin said with that calm conviction that was sometimes his most irritating trait.

"And you think she's *chosen* to scare herself blue with a poltergeist, I suppose," Claire said tartly.

"Possibly not," Colin admitted. "But I do know that she's chosen to date Simon Anstey."

Could that possibly be true? Claire wondered as she walked up the hill to the house later that day. While Colin would certainly not have said such a thing if it were not so, it was nearly impossible to believe.

Claire had known Simon for a bit over twenty years now, and she had never seen him with anything less than a stunningly dazzling woman, the sort of international trophies men of riches and fame tended to collect as a way of keeping score. While Leslie Barnes was certainly pretty enough, she wasn't in that class, nor, Claire knew intuitively, did she desire to be.

Perhaps, scarred as he is, he does not wish to have to compete with a whole man for a more beautiful woman's attention. Even as she framed the thought, Claire discarded it. Such a course of action would have required a certain reasonable humility from Simon, and as far as she had seen, supreme arrogance was still his key character trait.

Claire shook her head at the unconscious assumptions her thoughts betrayed—as if an accident of beauty truly were a woman's only desirable trait. It was possible that Simon had simply lost interest in what he could so easily gain, and was looking, as he matured, for a woman who could be his intellectual match. Whatever his reasons, Simon was not wooing Leslie Barnes because of feelings of inadequacy. But what *were* his reasons?

Claire mounted the front steps of the house.

It has been twenty-three years since I first entered this house.

For a moment time folded in on itself, and it was not a sultry May evening, but a bleak November night. Claire stood in the front hall, looking toward light and warmth, and fearing them both from the roots of her soul.

"Sins . . . I suppose it's too much to hope for that I've been committing any?"

Those long-past words echoed through her mind. What a long way she had come in just one lifetime!

And others still had as far to travel. . . .

Leslie answered the door, looking elegantly casual in white linen slacks and a sleeveless pale blue turtleneck sweater. The combination suited her dark beauty perfectly. She welcomed Claire into the house, and as the two women lingered over a cup of tea in the kitchen, becoming Claire and Leslie to each other, Claire told Leslie a little of her own beliefs and encouraged Leslie to talk about her experiences.

She listened as Leslie told her of the horror of seeing Juanita Garcia dead in a drainage ditch—first in a vision, then when she led the police to the scene of the crime. She'd moved to Berkeley to escape the notoriety she gained from the case, and had fallen into what sounded as if it had been a disastrous relationship with the brother of the detective on the Pigtail Killer case. Joel Beckworth was one of those draconian rationalists whose only defense against the Unknown was to ridicule it, and Leslie seemed only relieved that she'd managed to make a break with him—over buying Greenhaven, of all things.

Apparently there'd been some poltergeist phenomena involved in the breakup. Oddly enough, Leslie was treating a classical poltergeist—a teenaged girl—at the same time she was experiencing her own troubles, but flying wineglasses and Kleenex boxes, whatever the cause, worried her far less than the ceaseless ringing of the doorbell and telephone.

"And there's never anyone there—and the phone rings when it's off the hook as well as on, and disconnecting the doorbell only inconveniences the—the living," Leslie said raggedly.

The incidents of clairvoyance were increasing as well—Nick Beckworth was more pragmatic than his lawyer brother, and had called her several times for advice on cases, including a recent child abduction.

"And the poor woman was half-mad with worry, but this time the child was safe and well—off with her father. Only what if she hadn't been, and I'd seen that?" Leslie demanded.

"It must have been very frightening," Claire said gently. *Are you the one, Leslie? Will you take up the work Alison had to leave unfinished?*

Leslie smiled with sudden wicked humor. "Bravo. Perfect nondirective counseling technique."

Claire had laughed, and admitted that she was taking psychology classes at SF State, and working as a counselor as well. Talk turned to the subject of Alison Margrave. While Leslie could not dismiss the evidence of her own senses, acknowledging one's own psychic gifts was a far cry from accepting the whole world of the Unseen. The possible reality of after-death survival baffled her—it seemed too extreme, too unreal.

Claire told Leslie a little about Alison—wanting neither to prejudice her against what was happening here in the house by telling her too much, nor wishing to tell Leslie things which she was obviously not ready to hear. While it was true that Leslie Barnes was a psychic, she was a highly reluctant one.

But that's how it always is, isn't it? It's only in movies or bad books that people greet the appearance of the Sixth Sense with delight. It's a frightening thing. But Leslie needs to be pushed on as fast as she'll go. What's happening here seems so pointed. What if it isn't *Alison who's behind all these goings-on—the flying crockery, the phone, the doorbell?*

And if it was not, what other power had the strength and the determination to pass the barriers of this house which had been dedicated to the Light for more than half a century? Claire only hoped that Leslie wouldn't be able to pick up her growing unease.

"There's something wrong with the garage, too," Leslie was saying, "but the house was always a—a haven. Until this morning. A Wedgewood plate—it's a family heirloom; it was my grandmother's—came flying down off the wall like a, a—like a flying saucer!" Leslie giggled nervously.

"May I see the office?" Claire asked. *Alison—if it is you—what in the name of Heaven are you doing?*

Claire paused at the door of Alison's study. She felt nothing beyond the quiet and peace that she had always associated with Alison's home, though it was strange to see new furniture—an old, battered wooden desk, a chair and table, and an endearingly kitschy cuckoo clock—in Alison's quiet office.

It is Leslie's office now. We must all let Alison go, Claire reminded herself.

After first asking permission, she picked up the ornamental plate, which was still where it had fallen this morning. She braced herself, but she felt nothing.

"I don't sense anything wrong with it," she said mildly, "and I think I'd know if there was any actual infesting energy. . . ."

She did her best to explain as much as she could, but she could sense Leslie's growing tension as she did, and finally dropped the subject. Colin would not thank her for making an enemy of Leslie—and it would be a damned bad turn to do the woman herself, when she was reaching out to them for help.

"You said there had been disturbances in other parts of the house—could I see the window that won't stay shut?" Claire asked.

As they stepped out into the hall again, Leslie's younger sister had begun to practice, and great crashing chords echoed from the walls, much as they had when Alison was in her prime.

Leslie led her up the stairs, showing her (to Claire's secret amusement; Leslie was so gravely solemn about the whole thing) the pentagrams inscribed beneath every window and above every door.

"I set the wards on this house myself," Claire said, "when Alison was in the hospital after her first big stroke."

The one that had come almost a year after Simon's accident. She remembered sitting in the hospital with Alison as she had sat with Simon, and Alison's determination then that Simon should not have Greenhaven. It was only then that Claire had realized how deep into the Shadow Simon must have gone, to set Alison against him so unyieldingly.

Somehow, it was no surprise to discover that the window that Leslie complained would not stay shut was the one in Simon's old room. Now it was Emily's room—Claire could feel that it was occupied, even if Leslie had not told her—but without the usual litter of teenage occupation. Emily Barnes, it seemed, was as compulsively neat as other girls her age were messy. Claire placed her hand on the sill, trying to sense what had passed this threshold, but once more there was nothing.

"The window is certainly unguarded," she said. "But I don't have the sense that there is anything wrong here. It's neutral, if anything. But you said something about a cat?"

"A white cat. Frodo said it was Alison's cat," Leslie answered, a little defensively.

"See? It's not my cat. It's nothing to do with me." Claire filled in mentally. She smiled a little. How it must annoy Leslie to find herself presenting such a classic textbook case of denial! *But if one could control one's instinctive reaction to things, it wouldn't be instinctive, I suppose. Still . . .*

"Alison always had white cats," Claire explained. "Once one got out before she could neuter it, and she gave me one of the kittens. Mehitabel was the first pet I'd ever had, and I've had cats ever since. I know that Alison had half a dozen cats at one time, but when she knew she was failing, she found homes for most of them. . . ." But Claire already doubted that the white cat plaguing Leslie was one of Alison's legacies gone feral. She could check with Kathleen Carmody to be sure, but it wasn't likely Kathleen had failed to discharge her final obligation to her friend.

"I can reestablish the wards. Of course, ideally, the whole house should be cleansed and resealed, and you should do it yourself. It will be much more effective that way."

"And that would keep the cat out?" Leslie said dubiously.

Claire had to admit that it probably would—assuming the animal wasn't simply an opportunistic stray after all—but declared that it seemed like overkill to her. She had a sense that there was something about the cat that Leslie had not mentioned yet—something that she had been skating closer to each time she'd brought herself to discuss what was happening here in the house.

"I think this particular cat met a messy end," Leslie said reluctantly.

Bingo! Poor Leslie—what can possibly be happening here?

Leslie led Claire back downstairs—Emily was still practicing, this time a piece that Claire recognized, something by Mussorgsky—and out into the garden.

Rainbow and Emily had been working in it almost every weekend, and it was beginning to flourish once more, losing the mangy, moth-eaten look it had possessed after Alison's death. Leslie crossed the open space, leading Claire toward the little garage that Alison had remodeled into a workroom when she'd started operating with a group once more. Kathleen's sister Betty had talked about there being something dreadful out here, but she'd never gotten around to asking either Claire or Colin for help.

And so Claire was completely unprepared for what she felt when she stepped over the threshold.

Cold . . . darkness . . . hunger and despair. A pain so vast, so wracking, that utter foulness from which the healthy soul would have recoiled in horror became unnoticeable, became a tool, became the profane medium in which some mad artist worked. . . .

"There is certainly something very wrong in here," Claire said faintly, trying to block out that wordless howl of despair that filled her senses. "I don't know what it is, but it's horrible—horrible!"

Leslie said something. Her cheerful, unconcerned voice grated on Claire's abraded nerves—couldn't she feel the horror of this place? Horror accomplished—and horror yet to come. The walls vibrated with a child's terror, and the smell of blood was everywhere, as if Claire herself were bathed in it. . . .

Claire turned and pushed blindly past Leslie. Reaching the open air of the garden was like being able to breathe once more: Claire sucked in deep lungfuls of the herb-scented air and hoped she wouldn't faint. She felt as nauseated as if she had bathed in—had *drunk*—raw sewage.

How could this have happened? How could Alison's lovely dedicated Sanctuary have been so profaned? Certainly Betty had not done it, nor either of the other two families that had tried to live here. Claire thought of the man who had died, the young mother who had committed suicide here. This was what they'd felt in their last moments, she was sure of it. She could not believe that this aura, the disturbances at Greenhaven, were anything to do with Alison— no matter how angry she was, Alison could not do this to innocents.

But Simon could. It was Simon who had killed one of Alison's cats years before, Simon who now preached the gospel of black magic, blood sacrifice, and the purging of society of those with no value to it.

Claire said something—she did not know what—to Leslie, and the other woman took her arm and led her back toward the kitchen.

Did Leslie know what Simon had become? Claire searched her face anxiously, but saw no sign of such terrible knowledge there.

Over another cup of tea, Claire did her best to explain about Simon to Leslie, but saw to her growing dismay that every word she spoke had somehow been countered by Simon beforehand. Leslie would not hear a word against him, nor would she even agree that there was such a thing as Black Magick, as if the discipline that could produce such undoubted effects could not have its means twisted to evil ends.

The whole history of Claire's generation was a refutation of that—if further refutation was needed—and Claire felt increasingly frustrated at her inability to persuade Leslie Barnes of something that was as obvious to her as summer sunlight and the city that surrounded them. Simon had become a black magician, and if Simon was dating Leslie, then he would draw her into his works sooner or later. . . .

"I'm sorry, Claire," Leslie said at last. "I know you mean to be helpful—"

The most damning phrase in the English language, Claire thought wryly.

"But I simply can't believe any of this that you're telling me. Reincarnation—blood sacrifice—Black Magick—I have enough trouble believing in the ghosts of cats. . . ."

Too much, too fast—but oh, Leslie, can't you see that there is no time to waste? Claire realized that all she could do now was salvage what she could of her relationship with Leslie Barnes, but with her nerves still jumping from immersion in that psychic cesspit, she couldn't tell how effective her counsel was. She said soothing, placating things, and urged Leslie to speak further of the problems that plagued the house with Colin. There was no one Claire trusted more, and she was certain that Colin could get Leslie to give a fair hearing to his warnings.

If only it was not already too late.

* * *

"You don't look happy," was Colin's mild comment, when Claire walked back into the bookstore. It was almost eight; he'd stayed open to wait for her, but the store was empty of customers at this hour of a Friday night.

"I made a hash of things—I'm just lucky Leslie didn't throw me out on my ear! Oh, the house is clean enough—somebody scraped out the ward to Simon's old room, but I'm willing to bet that no evil's entered there, so I left it open. But the Sanctuary . . ."

Claire sat down on the stepladder, realizing she was still shaking at the thought. "Colin, it's horrible! No wonder Betty left and those other people died—I don't think any sane person could bear to remain in that room. Despair—and pain—and terror—" Suddenly, inexplicably, Claire found herself weeping.

"There, now, my girl," Colin said, coming from behind the desk and putting an arm around her. He handed her a handkerchief. "We'll set it right, don't you worry."

He waited until she regained a little self-possession. "Do you think it poses any active harm to the Barneses?" Colin asked.

"N-no," Claire said slowly, dabbing at her eyes with Colin's handkerchief. It smelled of tobacco and the incense Colin used when he meditated, scents Claire realized she had long associated with him. She thought hard, reluctantly casting her mind back to the terrible moment when she'd crossed the threshold of Alison's debased Sanctuary and confronted what could only have come from an Adept. An Adept of the Light who had fallen into the ways of the Shadow—an Adept whose dark power sprang from the perversion and destruction of that which his soul still held as good.

Simon.

"I don't think it will do them any harm, so long as neither of them spends too much time in the Sanctuary—and they think that it *smells* bad," Claire added, unable to keep a faint note of indignation out of her voice.

Colin chuckled. "Our ancestors didn't refer to the stench of evil and the odor of sanctity out of mere empty convention. For most people, stimulus from the Unseen is perceived as coming from one of the ordinary five senses—and I'm afraid that what we sometimes call morality has been rather arbitrarily assigned to the sense of smell."

"Laugh if you will," Claire grumbled, slowly regaining her mental equilibrium. "You didn't have to wade through that stuff!"

"No," Colin agreed, suddenly solemn. "Not yet."

"It *was* Simon," Claire insisted. "And on my way up to the house I was wondering—you'll think it very unreconstructed of me, Colin, but I was wondering what a man like Simon could possibly see in a woman like Leslie. She's so far from being his usual type. And I'm wondering—you know that Frodo mentioned she'd had the locks changed—what if Simon's professed interest in Leslie is in order to continue to have access to the Sanctuary? I'm not much on predicting the future, but I'm willing to bet that at least part of the horror I sensed there hasn't happened yet. There was a child—"

"Emily?" Colin asked quickly.

"No. Younger. But there was something strange about her, as if . . . oh, I don't know. As if she were only pretending to be a child. I know it's ridiculous. . . ."

"Psychic flashes often are, when we don't quite understand them," Colin reminded her. "But there's time to puzzle this one out, I think. And now, it's late and you look all in; let's lock up the place and go home."

"And maybe a good night's sleep will give me some idea of what to do about Simon—besides strangle him," Claire said. "Leslie's besotted with him past all reason. I can tell that already, even if she can't!" *Just as Alison had been, in her way. Unable to see the darkness in her protégé, until it was too late. . . .*

"The best thing you can do is continue to be a good friend to her," Colin said solemnly, "and we'll trust the Light to show us the way to best intervene in Simon's life before he can do more harm."

Closing up the store for the night was quickly done, and a few minutes later they stood outside the shop, savoring the moment when the Grey Lady of Cities—San Francisco—lets go of the last spark of twilight and drapes herself in the cloak of night.

"I almost forgot," Colin said, patting the breast pocket of the suit he invariably wore. "I meant to ask if you'd come to the symphony with me next Friday." He extricated two tickets from his pocket and flourished them like a banner. "I picked them up yesterday morning from the box office. It should be interesting," Colin added with a twinkle in his eye. "Simon's conducting."

NINETEEN

SAN FRANCISCO, FRIDAY, JUNE I, 1984

And all man's Babylons strive but to impart
The grandeurs of his Babylonian heart.
— FRANCIS THOMPSON

THE OPENING NIGHT OF THE SAN FRANCISCO SYMPHONY'S SUMMER PRO-gram was jammed with concertgoers in furs and diamonds and long glitter-ing gowns—regardless of how badly suited to the season. Every music lover in SF and the Peninsula, it seemed, had turned out to see Simon Anstey take the podium for his first public appearance in twelve years.

Colin could find no fault with the performance; Simon was every bit as brilliant a conductor as he had been a performer, and here the maimed hand formed no obstacle to his interpretation of the music. The audience was on Simon's side from the first downbeat, and by the intermission were as ecstatic as any rock fans.

"Well, he certainly *seems* well enough," Claire said as they were rising to their feet at the interval.

"How disapproving you sound!" Colin joked, trying to kid her out of her pensive mood. Ever since she'd visited Leslie's house and sensed the evil in the Sanctuary, Claire had been brooding over Simon. Was it a sense of lost op-portunities that depressed her so—he and Alison had always rather hoped an attachment would form there—or did she feel threatened by Simon's temp-tation and fall? Heaven knew that there were pitfalls for all who opened their awareness to the Path; perhaps Claire feared her own temptation, whatever form it might take.

"Come on, why don't we take a turn around the outside? It'd be a shame not to get a good look at some of those outfits," he said encouragingly.

Whatever the cause of Claire's dark mood, Colin saw in her the frailty he himself had fallen prey to—the overwhelming need to cast aside the detachment that ruled those upon the Path and take matters into one's own hands.

"Oh, look!" he heard a familiar voice say. "There's Colin and Claire!"

It was Emily and her older sister, Leslie. Colin sensed that Leslie would have preferred not to approach them, but Emily seemed oblivious to any emotional undercurrents and simply wished to introduce her sister to some of her new friends.

As the four of them made polite conversation, Colin learned that Simon was teaching Emily—a good sign, since it might mean that Simon had abandoned his dream of a comeback. But when he said as much, Emily was quick to defend her tutor's performing skills, and Colin realized that Simon had not abandoned his dangerous ambition after all.

The discussion might have escalated into an undignified squabble about Simon—though at his age, Colin had no intention of letting a teenaged girl pick a fight with him—but then, unexpectedly, Simon himself appeared.

Though it was unprecedented for the conductor to roam the halls during a performance, Simon had obviously been squiring Emily and Leslie about. He looked surprised—and, for an instant, *glad*—to see Colin and Claire, but almost instantly his manner hardened, and he tried to draw Colin into saying something that would turn Leslie and Emily against him.

"Colin. I'd forgotten you were a music lover. Or did you come to find out the extent of my disability?"

Colin returned a noncommittal answer, but Simon refused to let the matter drop. He persisted until Claire, as Colin had feared she would, took his remarks to heart.

"Why do you think I wish you anything but the best?" she protested, genuinely hurt. "It was for your own sake that I warned you against certain methods—"

"Wait till you are where I am before you judge my methods, Claire!" Simon snarled. A few minutes later he found an excuse to take the Barneses away with him.

Claire looked at Colin with troubled eyes, and he patted her arm in wordless reassurance. *Though I'm not sure I have any to give. He's obviously got designs on both the Barnes women—but for what, I wonder? Emily obviously isn't interested in anything beyond her music, and Leslie seems scared stiff of the Uncanny.* "Come on. Let's go get a drink before the bell rings," Colin said.

The Bay Area pagans celebrated the Summer Solstice with a picnic up on Mount Tamalpais toward the end of June, and apparently Frodo managed to quarrel disastrously with his lady fair sometime that day.

He was nearly useless in the bookshop the following Monday, putting books on the wrong shelves, forgetting what he'd been sent to the storeroom for as soon as he'd gone. His usual sunny cheerfulness was replaced with the stricken quiet of one who has suffered a mortal wound. Cassie Chandler stopped by the store that evening and bore him off with her in an act of merciful charity.

But though Colin had suggested that Frodo take a few days off, he was back at the store the next morning.

"It helps to have something to do," he told Colin. "But when I see Emmie playing Trilby to that son-of-a-bitch's Svengali, I could just—" Frodo sighed.

"Is it really that bad, Frodo?" Colin asked.

"Bad enough," Frodo answered. "'Yes, Simon,' 'No, Simon,' 'Oh-yes-I'll-do-just-as-you-say, Simon,'—it makes me sick to see how he's exploiting her, stifling her growth as an artist. That man has an ego the size of the Trans-Am Pyramid *and* the box it came in."

Colin smiled faintly. "The box it came in" was the local name for the BankAmerica Building, an ugly black glass skyscraper more suited to New York or Houston than to Baghdad-by-the-Bay.

Frodo shrugged in wordless disgust. "But nobody can get through to her. Anstey's got her brainwashed, making her think she's got to practice all the time and avoid contamination from us *hoi-polloi*."

"She'll get over it," Colin said soothingly.

"How? He's quick enough to despise what that accident did to him—and quick enough to play off it when it will get him what he wants. He's practically living at Greenhaven now," Frodo said.

"I don't think you're being entirely fair to Simon," Colin said. Frodo snorted eloquently and went to unpack books in the back of the store. The cats, disturbed by his arrival, wandered out to the front in search of quieter company.

The midsummer air was like milk, and the white Mediterranean light bleached the buildings along the street into a mosaic of pale walls and dense shadows.

It was nearly noon when Leslie Barnes came through the front door of the shop. She moved warily, obviously on the lookout for Claire, but whether she hoped or dreaded to find her, Colin didn't think Leslie herself knew. At last she seemed to come to a decision and approached the desk where Colin sat.

But whatever force had brought her back to the bookshop, it seemed that she could not bring herself to speak of it, and they chatted for several minutes about Poltergeist and Monsignor. The big black cat was brazenly affectionate, as usual, and when Leslie finally brought herself to broach the subject of her visit, for a moment Colin thought that she was still addressing the big neutered tom.

"We seem to have this cat," she said. "Or maybe we don't. Emily keeps saying it's hurt—in the garage—but there's never any blood anywhere . . . I saw that, too. Once. Everyone talks about Alison's white cats—but there's something nobody's telling me." She closed her mouth tightly, as if to keep herself from saying anything more.

She's coming to you for help. Don't fail her, Colin told himself.

"I don't like to say anything, because I didn't see it myself," he began carefully, "but one of the reasons that Alison disinherited Simon was—forgive me, Leslie, for telling you something you won't want to hear—was because he had taken one of her cats and ritually murdered it. Claire told you that Simon was dabbling in Black Magick, didn't she?"

"Yes, but—" Leslie looked faintly greenish. "I didn't know she meant . . . that. Why would he do such a thing?"

"I can't tell you," Colin said honestly. "It was not an act of wanton cruelty—though I'm not sure that makes it any better—but the willful destruction of another living being to a deliberate magickal end."

It seemed to Colin that Simon had already set his Seal upon her aura. He saw the moment when Leslie's mind slid away from the horror of it, cloaking what Simon had done in that facile and deadly rationalization of the twentieth century: justifying what had been done as the pursuit of pure knowledge for its own sake.

"I can't think of a better reason for investigating parapsychological events than pure curiosity," Leslie said stubbornly, making the novice's common conflation of psychism and magick.

Simon was obviously meddling in Leslie's life with the techniques of the Left-Hand Path. If matters had progressed as far as Colin feared, it would be too dangerous to allow Leslie to continue in her Unawakened state. Breathing a prayer of apology for what he was about to do, Colin spoke.

"There is only one acceptable motive for any investigation, scientific or otherwise, and this is the only motive acceptable on the Path: *I desire to know in order to serve.*"

Leslie blinked, as though she were being called to awaken from a deep sleep. She was not consciously aware of the inner knowledge that she possessed, but now that Colin had called her Higher Self to mindfulness, her instincts should take over and lead her quickly to the Path once again. And to her destiny.

When she left the bookstore, Colin watched after her, troubled. He had a feeling he had not experienced in many years—the sense of sending a young warrior into battle against almost insurmountable odds.

As July sweltered on into August, the Overlight was turbulent with the reflections of Simon's dark work, though Colin could gain little further Earthplane insight into his plans or knowledge of what effect—if any—his call to mindfulness had had on Simon's chosen consort and Alison's chosen successor. After conducting his series of concerts, Simon had gone on to teach a Master Class at the conservatory—Emily Barnes was in it—before disappearing on an extended business trip at the beginning of August.

Cassie Chandler—who played with an early music consort, and thus was privy to much of the music-world gossip—said that Simon had flown to Chicago to talk to Lewis Heysermann, the world-famous conductor, about scheduling Simon's return to the stage.

Her voice had been studiously neutral as she relayed the information, but Colin was horrified. He was not a professional musician himself, but he had known many over the years. If Simon was expecting to perform in public within a year, he had either lost what was left of his sanity, or he had reason to believe that he would be back at the height of his power soon.

And there was no natural way for him to be so. . . .

The second week of August, Colin awoke to the sounds of crashing thunder; a raging storm powerful enough to rattle the windows and doors of the Victorian. He fought his way up out of sleep, and only then realized that there was no earthly storm at all.

His body ached as though he'd been sleeping in chains; the effect of the sweltering summer weather, which might allow oblivion but didn't allow rest.

He switched on the lamp. It was only a few hours past midnight; he'd fallen asleep on the couch in the living room, and the window fan still desultorily flipped the edges of some papers as it rotated past them. Outside the open windows, the star-choked sky shone cloudlessly over a city parched with unseasonable heat, but in Colin's mind the storm still resounded.

What had awakened him? He looked around the room, drawing his cotton bathrobe more securely closed and getting to his feet. He ran a hand over his greying hair and grimaced in annoyance. Whatever it was, it had made no incursion into his conscious mind—and this was no hour at which to awaken Claire and see if she had sensed anything herself.

As he was making himself a cup of tea—Colin's universal panacea for those things which could not be cured but must be endured—the phone rang. Colin picked it up at once.

"MacLaren here."

"Did somebody already call you?" Joe Schiafardi sounded faintly suspicious.

"I couldn't sleep," Colin said. "It's the heat. What's up?"

Joe Schiafardi was one of Colin's contacts on the SFPD. He'd been a friend of Alison's. Colin did not know how deep that friendship had run, nor did he wish to pry, but back when all this had started, Colin had asked Schiafardi to keep an eye on Leslie and the house, and—as far as he could, within the bounds of professional ethics—let Colin know if anything happened.

"I just called to tell you that Dr. Barnes had a break-in about an hour ago. Some loony with a wrecking maul came in and smashed the sister's harpischord to matchwood. We chased him off before he could get started on the other stuff, though. Both the women are okay, although they're pretty shook up."

"Thank God," Colin said quietly. Had he been foolish to stay so far out of things, trusting to Leslie to call him when the need was greatest?

"Say it twice, brother. Funny thing is, we can't figure out how the hairball got in. The whole house was still locked up tight as a drum when we got there."

"That's . . . interesting," Colin said slowly. It wasn't interesting, of course; it was terrible, confirming the Otherworldly nature of the attack. There could be only one source. But why would Simon lash out so at Leslie and Emily?

"I'm glad I amuse you." Schiafardi's voice was sour.

"No." Colin collected himself. "Of course you don't. It's just that this is such a shock."

"Not as much of one as some skel is going to have when I catch up with him." Schiafardi's voice held grim promise. "Jesus, Colin—you should'a seen that place. It looked like somebody's put the thing in a blender and then poured it out again."

Colin sighed. "I just hope you catch him, Joe." *I wish this had been done by a person that you could catch.*

"Don't worry; this one we're putting in overtime on. Dr. Barnes has helped us out a couple of times, and I guess we owe her one."

After a last brief exchange of pleasantries, Schiafardi hung up—there was still the paperwork to do on the break-in.

Colin went back to the kitchen and rescued his tea from the teabag. It was stronger than he liked, but he drank it anyway, hoping for clarity, and wished for his pipe, though it had been years now since he'd smoked. Still, he missed the company it had been as he wrestled with some elaborate problem.

Further sleep would be impossible. He dressed, then decided to walk over to the bookstore. He could use the walk to order his thoughts, and the city streets would have to be cooler than his apartment.

Though Colin was a supremely urban soul, there was something in him that loved the quiet that could only be found in the city's unused hours. He supposed he'd learned the habit during the war; strange to think that those events which were still so immediate in his memories were now more than forty years in the past. He was sixty-four this year and soon—not this year, nor even next, but soon—it would be time to leave this life behind and go on to the next turn of the Great Wheel.

The odd, pleasant melancholy stayed with him as he opened the bookstore. It was nearly six by now, but the only other light on the street was the diner up the block. He went into the back and put the water in the kitchenette on to boil. Claire would be here soon, and normally he'd leave such tasks to her, but if her night had been anything like his own, she would need an immediate restorative.

He was right. Claire came dragging into the shop at seven-thirty, looking rumpled and puffy-eyed, though her Madras skirt and crisp blouse were bandbox-neat, as usual.

"I thought I'd be first in. Is that tea I see?" she said hopefully.

Colin handed her the cup, and Claire drained it in a few swallows.

"That's better. Oh, dear, I feel as if I slept inside a kettledrum while the orchestra was playing. There was a terrible ruckus on the Inner Planes last night; I spent most of my night with my hands over my ears, figuratively speaking. I think it was the same energy that I stirred up over at Alison's

Sanctuary a while back—I would have called you, but I thought one of us should get some sleep," Claire said, a little enviously.

"It actually managed to wake me," Colin admitted, "though if it hadn't, Joe Schiafardi would have. He called to tell me there was a disturbance up at the Barnes house last night."

"Disturbance?" Claire said warily.

"Something turned that harpischord of Alison's that Simon lent Emily into kindling," Colin said bluntly. And since none of the windows or doors was forced or even unlocked, three guesses as to the cause."

Grief etched itself on Claire's face, showing Colin what she would look like when she was old. "Simon. But what is he *doing?*" Claire demanded with weary anger. "He isn't even here in the City! I'd better go and see—"

Colin held up a hand. "Wait. It would be better if she asked you to intervene. Leslie's understandably touchy about things as they stand, and if she were to suspect that either of us has been keeping a weather eye on her . . ."

He watched as Claire struggled with her impulse to help and finally sighed. "I suppose you're right," she admitted. "Lord! Was I ever that prickly?"

"That much and more," Colin assured her, smiling. "That's not to say that I don't want you to go, only to have a good obvious harmless reason for going—and when you do, I want you to turn the place inside out and find out exactly what we're dealing with here. Maybe it isn't Simon after all."

Claire grinned back. "Shame on you, Colin, teasing a helpless woman this way. For a moment, I almost thought you were going to go with a hands-off policy! I'm going to go pour myself another cup of tea—and I suppose you haven't had anything in the way of breakfast?"

Meekly, Colin admitted that he had not.

"Well, the diner's just up the block. Why don't we go there for breakfast? And then we can come back here and see what the day brings."

Frodo called around nine A.M. to let Colin know that an emergency had arisen and he wouldn't be able to come into the store that day. Fortunately he and Emily had made up their estrangement earlier this week; it wasn't hard to guess the nature of Frodo's "emergency."

The heat was brutal and very few people seemed to be in a book-buying mood. Even the bookstore's regulars stayed away, influenced by the strange oppressiveness that seemed to hang over the city. Claire was on edge, searching for the pretext that would let her go to Leslie.

Finally, a few minutes before five, Frodo called again—he was taking Emily home with him for supper and was worried about Leslie being all alone in the house so soon after the assault. Would Claire go up and see if she was okay, he asked?

"Of course," Claire said, so calmly that Colin smiled to hear it. "I'll just get my purse and leave Colin to lock up. It won't take me twenty minutes."

The shadows were already blue and slanting when Claire reached Greenhaven. The walk—Claire didn't keep a car in the City, and Greenhaven was just up the hill—had given her plenty of time to regret her decision to sim ply come without calling ahead. She was not at all sure of her welcome, after the way she and Leslie had parted. But when Leslie opened the door, she only seemed a little surprised, and invited Claire into the kitchen.

The atmosphere in the house was different. Claire noticed it at once. It had been cleared since the last time she was in it—Simon would have taught Leslie how to do it, but its new atmosphere was not the one of calm peace that Claire had always associated with Alison's house. Though superficially quiet, the house was edgy, charged, and if Simon had helped Leslie to clear the house, he had certainly not set up barriers against himself. Leslie must be en couraged to reseal the house herself, or last night's violence would only re turn, worse each time, feeding on itself as it escalated out of control.

Leslie, too, had changed greatly in the month since Claire had last seen her. Claire could sense the power that enfolded her now, but it was curiously pas sive—as if it slumbered unnoticed within her, awaiting its summons.

But if it did slumber, it seemed to be the only thing that did. Leslie her self looked as if she had not slept well in weeks, or were ill with some wast ing disease. There was more wrong here than one world-class fright and a sleepless night.

Alison, how could you let this happen to her?

But Claire said nothing, and soon the two women were drinking tall glasses of iced herbal tea in Leslie's spacious kitchen. The house was blessedly cool—situated at the top of the hill, its wide windows caught every breeze; it had been built in an era when architects could not rely on technology to rem edy their failings. As they lingered over the cold drinks, Claire made a few tentative expressions of conventional sympathy for Leslie's calamity, and as she had hoped, that was enough to bring Leslie's real concern to the surface.

"Sometimes I feel this house isn't mine at all. It's still Alison's—and she's trying to run my life!"

Despite their previous conversations, Leslie obviously expected Claire to pooh-pooh the notion, but Claire gave it serious thought. Alison had pos sessed the perfectionism and temper of the professional musician, and she'd probably been rough enough on the house's last several tenants—if indeed it had been she influencing them, and not that horror in the Sanctuary. But in her wildest dreams Claire could not imagine Alison being as cruel and vin dictive as the power that was tormenting Leslie.

"That would have been the last thing Alison would want," Claire said. "I expect that you and Simon banished the house together at the Solstice, but Simon . . . might not have known that the Sanct— That the garage needed anything more than the ordinary routine clearing." She spoke gently, trying to lead Leslie to the understanding that Alison had chosen her to continue Alison's unfinished work—without, if possible, saying anything against Si mon.

"Now you're making me feel guilty for not being able to protect my house against—against violence!" Leslie burst out in angry fear.

It took all of Claire's tact to soothe her down again, without allowing

Leslie simply to go back to pretending that nothing out of the ordinary was wrong. At last Claire suggested that they go have a look at the music room—a room full of toothpicks that had once been a harpsichord would be a great cure for a woman in denial.

And the reminder did seem to have the effect that Claire hoped for. Leslie stood quietly in the middle of the room, her face pensive.

Claire came and stood beside her, bracing herself for what must surely come. Cautiously, she opened herself to the atmosphere in the room, probing, searching. . . .

Pain. Terror. And RAGE—*a cheated fury that was as far beyond human as a blow-torch is beyond a candle . . .*

Claire opened her eyes with a gasp. It was only the echo of the force that had been here, not the force itself—the psychic equivalent of footprints in a muddy flowerbed. The imprint would fade with time, though a Sensitive would always be able to detect it if the room were not cleared.

But it was not Simon, as Claire had expected. The force that had ravened here was inhuman—not as a cat is, but as a stone is; something of a different order of creation entirely.

It was not Simon.

In her relief and worry, Claire tried to explain what she'd sensed here, but only succeeded in confusing Leslie once more.

"Are you talking about black magic?" Leslie asked. "Satan? The devil?"

"I don't believe in Satan," Claire said. *At least, not as Milton's fallen angel; Christ's demonic twin. Colin says that he has faced demons—but I haven't, and that's nothing to be bothering this poor woman with just now.* "But the force in this room was so completely inhuman that I haven't any handy way to describe it. If it was generated by a human mind, it would have had to come directly from the id; the part that is buried far below rational thought and operates purely upon instinct. And *that* is a more terrifying thought than any classical Satan out of a medieval grimoire!"

She felt Leslie's panic recede as Claire told her what she needed to hear. She thought that Leslie could be brought to do what must be done here so long as it could be made to seem reasonable, a part of the mechanistic world of explicit cause and effect. Though Simon must be harrying her somehow along the Path—for Leslie was far more accepting of the paranormal than she had been even three months before—she was still fighting against full acceptance of the new world that Simon and her own Gifts were unveiling to her.

There were few things more terrifying to the average person than the discovery of their profound vulnerability to the forces of magick: Black, White, or Grey. Magick was a force that solid walls could not stop, that simple will-power could not thwart. It could suborn the gatekeepers of the human ego and gain unrestricted access to the unconscious mind. It was not thwarted by time or distance, and paid no heed to the logical sequence of cause and effect.

Without an understanding of the fundamental laws which governed the world of the Unseen, most people's first encounter with magick seemed as if they had suddenly entered an evil funhouse where effect preceded cause and time ran not even backward but inside-out; where absolutes no longer existed and reason was forced to submit to a logic that had no basis in common sense. No wonder their instant impulsive response was usually denial and terror—it was as if reality itself were challenged, and with it, all their life's experience.

But just as Claire began to relax, she felt a power gather itself here in this room, pushing at the barriers between the World of Form and the Unseen World, seeking the weakest point at which to break through.

Claire.

No—not now, Claire pleaded, but the force took no heed. It rushed in with the frustrated haste of something that has long been trying to make itself heard and dares not miss any opportunity.

"Claire! Oh, Claire—my darling girl . . ."

"Alison?" Claire whispered aloud. How could Alison still be trapped here, when she had known that her duty was to go toward the Light?

"How could he do this? My house was always a temple of healing—"

"She is not happy," Claire said aloud, for Leslie's benefit. *Alison, how can I help you? Tell me what keeps you here.*

"I stayed because I had no inheritor . . . until now. Now she is ready to take up my fight. I will help her all that I can, but when the Tide turns it will be time for me to go. There is one charge that I lay upon you and not her: tell Simon that I forgive him everything—what he took from me I would have given him gladly. Tell him, Claire! You must!"

"Very well. I will tell him. When I can." There was a disorienting, almost nauseating, sense of dislocation as the charged atmosphere trickled away. Alison was gone, and with her, the taint of inhuman violence vanished as well.

Claire turned to Leslie. "Nothing further to be done in here," she said brusquely. "Let's look at the rest of the house."

It was after eleven when Claire left. She'd given the house as good a going-over as Colin could have asked—and she thought she'd managed to rebuild her relationship with Leslie, as well.

She and Leslie had blessed the major trouble spot, the garage—once Alison's Sanctuary—together. Leslie had taken to the tools of the Path easily, though she had shied away from performing the operation herself. Despite that, Claire had felt Leslie's fledgling power as a bright beacon in the Overlight.

But for the first time that Claire could remember, the use of her Gift had exhausted her, left her feeling drained—as if, deprived of some natural well-spring upon which it could feed, it had turned upon Claire's substance and devoured that, instead. She hadn't gone half a block when she began to wish that she'd brought her car instead of walking up from the bookshop; she could not remember the last time she'd felt so tired.

She stumbled, catching herself against a nearby lamppost and realized that she'd been staggering across the sidewalk like a drunk in her exhaustion.

No more of that, Claire told herself sternly. *I'll just rest a minute here.* She could go back to the house and call a cab, of course, but it would take one at least half an hour to arrive and Claire was reluctant to disturb Leslie further. She leaned against the lamppost, belatedly realizing, as she saw the flare of headlights that meant a car was coming up the hill, that she was in the clichéd pose of the streetwalker. She felt a combination of horror and hilarity as the car slowed, then stopped.

"Claire? Are you all right?"

"Colin!" Relief banished all previous thoughts.

"I came to see if you were still up here. I thought you might like a lift home."

In the illumination of the Volvo's dome light, Claire could see how worried he was.

"I was just leaving," Claire explained, "but am I ever glad to see you. I don't think I could have walked another step."

Colin reached over and opened the passenger door; Claire sank gratefully into the leather upholstery, closing her eyes. Colin drove on, and the inside of the car seemed to whirl giddily around her.

"I ought to tell you what happened tonight," she said, almost mumbling.

"Tell me tomorrow—unless it won't keep?"

"There's some time," Claire said, already half asleep. "Until the Tide turns."

The Tide that Alison had spoken of to Claire was the Tide of the Year. Magicians believed that the four great turning points of the year were the solstices and the equinoxes, the still points at which the Great Cycle shifted emphasis and direction.

The vernal equinox was a rising tide, rushing upward into the summer solstice, but the autumnal equinox was a falling tide, slipping down into the winter darkness. Any well-trained magician planning an operation involving the Left-Hand Path would be likely to choose that date for his working. When Alison had spoken of leaving with the turning Tide, it was the autumnal equinox that she meant; the date upon which the Sun moved into Libra. September 21 was a little over six weeks away, and Colin and Claire both hoped to be ready for anything that day might bring.

Frodo was now seeing Emily regularly; apparently Simon had stopped interfering there. He had passed on to Colin the news that Simon had borrowed the garage just after his return from Chicago—and locked it.

It's a luxury to have so much time to prepare, Colin thought in an idle moment. Though the affair was as serious as any Colin had ever been engaged on, this time the battle would not be a last-minute scramble. This time Colin had a good idea of both the date and the place. Alison's Sanctuary. September 21.

From his explorations in the Overlight, Colin knew that Simon had not yet taken the last step on his path to damnation. Animal sacrifice was one thing; the extinction of a human life—no matter how mean—a far graver matter. If Colin had sensed that Simon had taken such a step, Colin would have called upon his Order at once to deal with him; necromancy, like plague, spread its contagion swiftly if it were not excised.

But Simon had not yet committed the ultimate obscenity, and Colin meant to prevent him if he could. He would have one chance: at the moment of the turning Tide itself, Simon's higher self would be free of the Shadow he had called into it and would be able to hear Colin. Colin could use that moment to call him back to the Light if it lay within mortal power, but the timing must be exquisite, exact. And there would be no second chance, for either of them.

And so, as the year faded toward the equinox, Colin made his preparations just as Simon made his, and called into himself all the authority of the Light.

And tried not to dread, with all his unaccustomed heart, the use that the Light would choose to make of him.

The day of the autumnal equinox dawned clear and warm, and Colin rose with the sun to greet it. He had fasted since sunset the previous night and had eaten only lightly during the previous fortnight, taking no form of animal protein. He spent the morning in meditation, trying to empty himself of all desire and to make himself a pure tool of the Light.

Though he did not have Claire's gift of Sight, it was as if he could sense Simon's working like a baleful thunderhead just beyond the horizon. He had consulted an ephemeris: Simon would time the climax of his ritual for 5:14 this afternoon, the moment when the Sun moved into the Zodiacal house of Libra, the Balance. He had only to hold himself in readiness for the summons to battle.

It was afternoon when the call he had been awaiting came; unsurprised, Colin rose from the lotus seat before his altar and picked up the phone.

"MacLaren here."

"Colin!" It was Leslie Barnes. "Something terrible has happened—" Her voice was distorted almost beyond recognition by hysteria.

"I think you'd better come over, Leslie," Colin said, willing her to be calm. He gave her directions, hoping she was still collected enough to take them in—from the sound of things, she was finally unable to ignore the truth about what Simon had become, and it was tearing her apart.

While he waited for her to arrive, Colin brewed tea. There was still time before the ritual, and Leslie Barnes was his strongest ally in this fight. Simon loved both her and her sister, so, by the implacable Laws of the Left-Hand Path, he drew his greatest power from harming them. Conversely, Simon was vulnerable to their power, but Leslie was the only one of the sisters with the will and the discipline to strike back at him in love.

But it must be her will, her decision. If she could not do what was needed, Colin must face Simon alone.

A few minutes later, Leslie arrived at the house. Terror had aged her twenty years in a matter of hours and made her pale coral lipstick into a garish slash across a face gone clown white with terror.

She was nearly babbling as she spilled out the ugly fears she had lived with for weeks: that inside the passionate artist she loved was a grotesque and ruthless slayer who would use and kill with neither thought nor remorse. She told Colin that Simon had kidnapped the developmentally-impaired young daughter of one of her patients and meant to kill the child.

Leslie no longer had any difficulty believing that Simon meant to sacrifice little Chrissy Hamilton; Colin led her gently to the deeper truth of the atrocity—that the sacrifice Simon meant to make would not be that child, though he did plan to use her in his ritual, but instead would be something dear to him: Leslie's sister Emily.

Art for art, skill for skill, life for life—destroying Emily, a skilled musician, would return Simon's own skill to him, but at an unspeakable price to both his soul and hers. To be used to feed a Black Adept's power crippled those souls preyed upon beyond their power to restore themselves. Each life a Black Adept touched was frozen as it was at the moment of death: blighted, stillborn.

"What can we do?" Leslie asked at last in a tear-ravaged voice. "How can we stop him?" She looked up at Colin, hope and resolution shining from her dark eyes.

"Come with me," Colin said.

They arrived at Greenhaven at a little before five. Colin was careful to park on the street; everything inside the house's boundary-line would be affected by Simon's workings. The laws of magick were as logical and unreasonable as those of a computer program, and arbitrary lines drawn on a map stored in a building twenty miles away were as compelling to the forces Simon worked with as a concrete wall would be to a physical force. Humans, who could pass those intangible boundaries with ease, did so at their peril.

As soon as Colin set foot on the house's grounds he knew he had been right to be so careful. The dark energies operating here were like a slow rising tide. Not the psychic cesspit that Claire had described, but a chill inexorable summoning, easily perceptible to another magician—even one without the Gift.

Colin gasped for breath, and each forward step was a struggle. His heart was a sharp hot pain in his chest, but he thrust aside all thought of his own safety. *I will put on the armor of Light*—

But the Darkness that Simon had set as his *tyler* was too strong—a thing of venom and poison that assaulted the senses with its foulness. Colin felt himself begin to fail, as his heart stuttered under the impact of its hate. The real world of the herb garden that surrounded him and Leslie was shrouded from his sight—caught up in the maelstrom as he was, Colin stumbled forward on instinct alone.

"*Begone, begone, BE YE GONE!*" Leslie's voice, vibrant and demanding, seemed to echo inside his head—she gestured, and drops of Light rained from her fingertips, striking the Darkness and banishing it back to the realm from which it had been evoked. Once more Colin could sense the green life that surrounded them.

The austere and majestic pride of a parent filled him at Leslie's action. Though she was young upon the Path, she would grow strong and straight and true to the armies of Light.

If she lived past today.

They had reached the door of the Sanctuary. Leslie touched the knob and drew back without turning it, believing, as Colin well knew, that the door was still locked, as it had been all month. But Colin knew that for Simon's ritual to proceed, certain conditions must be met, and they did not include the security of a locked door. When Colin put his hand on the knob, it turned freely, and the door opened.

He sketched a Sign in the air to breach the Wards, and it was answered with a crackle of Astral Flame. Behind him, he heard Leslie whimper.

Inside the studio the air was thick with incense, and Simon stood within that diagram which is the six-pointed star drawn with but a single line.

Chrissy Hamilton lay upon the double-cube altar, still wearing her mundane clothes, but Simon and Emily were both garbed in ritual dress—Simon, naked beneath the Black Adept's red cloak, and Emily, as his Sacred Harlot, seated upon a stool in a white gown that left her breasts bare. They did not react to the breaching of their Temple, but Emily was in trance and Colin did not think that Simon's mind was in this world at all.

Simon reached for the knife that lay upon the altar.

"In the name of Almighty God and the Light into Whose Presence I first brought you, Simon, Pilgrim, Magister, servant of God—I say *no!*" Colin shouted with all of his strength. In his state of heightened awareness, Colin could feel the forces of heaven grinding unstoppably forward like great millstones.

At last Simon reacted to their presence. His face contorted with a fury from which everything human had long been banished, and he clutched the Red Knife as if it were a weapon.

Lords of Light, if it is Your will to take me in this way, let it be so. What I give up today, I surrender freely; let it be used for the Light.

Again, Colin made the Sign. Its very presence in this room was enough to cause Simon exquisite physical pain, debased as his nature was now: it paralyzed him, allowing Colin to cross the space between them and step into the circle chalked upon the floor.

The seconds in which he had to work were trickling away. With one great gesture he kicked over the altar, and the sound of his boot against the wood resounded like a strike upon a great drumhead. The burning incense jumped from the dish and smoldered in a sticky spill upon the cement floor, and Colin crushed the lamp beneath his foot, extinguishing its flame.

Simon leaped up, the knife flashing in his hand as he rushed forward. Colin did not move, calling out to Simon's True Self in that terrible moment with all the force he possessed.

Simon Anstey, remember who you are!

He felt the Power descend upon him: once more, in this bright instant,

Colin MacLaren became the Sword of the Order. Simon struck with the knife, but it fell away from Colin's chest without penetrating. Colin made the Sign for the third time—and felt a great silence spread around him as the Still Point of the Equinox was reached.

And now there were two Simon Ansteys here in the room: the gibbering, blood-soaked creature of rage and pain and appetite, and the merely human man who had been tempted beyond his strength—but who had not killed.

"I was mad. Surely I was mad," Simon said in a numb, dazed voice. "What have I done—what will I do?" He looked toward Colin with agonized eyes, and in the secret chambers of his heart Colin wept for the boy he had once known.

"Simon! Oh, my love—" Leslie cried, reaching for him.

But Colin held her back. Simon had not chosen. Those who walked in the Shadow might be honestly pained by their own actions—but still choose to commit them.

"Simon, you stand at the crossroads. If you hope to walk in the Light again, there is still a sacrifice to be made," Colin told him. "What will you sacrifice, and what will you do with the power which must be dispelled from this place?" Colin moved his hand, and the ghostly Astral Lightning followed his gesture. For an instant, the gates of memory opened to Colin MacLaren.

So had he stood, once, in a Temple that had been ashes for ten thousand years, and listened as these words were said to him. He had been offered redemption and had spurned it in the dust, and he had been tied to the Wheel ever since, expiating that arrogance.

Just as Simon would be, if Colin could not save him now.

He felt a crushing pain grow in his chest. The power in the room built, and the Wheels of Time slid forward. In a moment all would be lost—they would all go on, forward through Time, and Simon would find some other way to commit his crime.

"Quickly, Simon!" Colin said urgently. "Time is running out! Choose darkness or light—and be forever bound by your choice!" *Remember that you are a being of Light, that you chose this destiny for yourself. Remember—and be proud.*

Simon drew a deep breath, and Colin felt the agony in his own chest.

"I will not—" Simon said hoarsely. "I renounce the Darkness forever—my power—and what I could have been. I renounce it forever, and that power I give to Emily—"

He rose from his beastlike crouch and kissed Emily gently upon the lips, then turned to the altar before which the child still lay.

Colin felt Time slip from his grasp, moving onward into the Waning Tide, and with it went all the Panoply of the Light. All of them within these walls were merely human once more, not angels or archetypes.

The child sat up and began to cry for her mother, human understanding flooding her eyes at last.

"And lest I be tempted again—" Simon raised his damaged hand, and brought it down upon the edge of the overturned altar. Colin felt as well as heard the sickening crunch as fragile bone gave way, and Simon wept as waves of uncontrollable agony jolted through his body. His skill was lost for-ever. There would be no second miracle for Simon Anstey.

"Emily—" he gasped, sinking to his knees. "You—shall be my hands. . . ."

Leslie ran to him, and this time Colin did not stop her. Simon's choice was made. The Light had won its victory.

He did not hear her cry out to him as sagged to his knees.

TWENTY

SAN FRANCISCO, 1985

Be near me when my light is low,
When the blood creeps, and the nerves prick
And tingle; and the heart is sick,
And all the wheels of Being slow.
— ALFRED, LORD TENNYSON

SIMON AND LESLIE WERE MARRIED THE MOMENT SIMON GOT OUT OF THE hospital, then had traveled for several months. While he and Leslie were gone, Emily's commitment to Frodo deepened, and it became tacitly understood that they, too, would eventually marry. The thought of Simon and Frodo as brothers-in-law caused Claire a great deal of quite amusement, a distraction she sorely needed in the weeks that followed.

Colin's battle with the Shadow had wasted him as if it were a high fever, and through the dark winter months he was nearly frail, moving with the stiff caution of the aged. Knowledge of his own mortality was constantly with him like an old well-loved friend. He recovered his old energy more slowly than he liked, and Claire fussed over him like a nervous mother hen.

He had said he would make any sacrifice to gain the redemption of Simon's soul, but like every man, when he spoke he had not believed that the Powers Above would accept what he had so freely offered. Slowly, as the weeks of slow recuperation passed, Colin came to realize that the battle for Simon's soul might well have been the last such battle he would ever fight. He was in his late sixties, and while the trained Will of the Adept only grew stronger with age and study, the physical stamina—the energy, the *vril*—required for some acts of magick could vanish overnight, blighted as by a killing frost, leaving the Adept as powerless as an ordinary man.

But if the Lords of Karma had taken his power at last, so be it. He would hold himself obedient to Their Will, and strive to conduct himself, always, in the Light. If he were to be only a spectator to the Great Battle in these last years of his life, he would strive to learn all he could from watching the workings of the Lords of Karma upon this plane.

Though some of those lessons were bitter ones.

The world went on, moving faster and faster, as though it, too, were eager for the millennium. While Colin slowly mended, the year ended on a bizarre grace note, where a man called Bernhard Goetz opened fire upon his young attackers in a New York subway—and the world cheered.

The love of violence was in the air. Everywhere, war seemed not only possible, but inevitable, and Colin awoke one morning with the sudden understanding that it was not only men who were mortal . . . dreams were mortal as well. Dreams could die.

Thirty years ago they'd all lived in a wonderful dream . . . the fantasy that governments waged war, that people, left alone, would choose peace. But in the last three decades, as the world had slowly darkened and the violence of the great wars of the past had decayed into constant acts of random violence, the dreamers slowly realized that they'd been wrong all those years ago. There would always be war, because war came from the people. Not from the government, or the military, or the industrialists. War began with the stick, the thrown bottle, the firebomb. War began with a riot in the street . . . *your* street. And war would not be extinguished until the last human being was dead.

But just as eternal war seemed inevitable, there came some fugitive rays of hope. In the spring of 1985 the Soviet Union began to soften its eternal opposition to the West. With the appointment of Mikhail Gorbachev as premier, the unremitting winter of the Cold War seemed at last to be ready for its own spring. That autumn, the Soviet premier and the American president met, and the world held its breath.

And then, as if some dark force were mocking their hopes, the second half of the eighties began with the death of another dream: the space shuttle *Challenger* exploded, killing all seven astronauts aboard.

They were black, white, Asian . . . men, women—and one special woman named Christa McAuliffe. The explosion tore the heart out of an America that refused any longer to invest its soul in leaders; of an America that had grown to distrust promises and only believed in deeds. An America that had learned to believe that promises were lies.

Colin thought of that, as he watched Ronald Reagan offer words of expertly-crafted commiseration to a grieving nation—topspin from a president hypocritical enough to have publicly honored Nazi dead only six months before. It made Colin angry in a dull, quiet way: nearly four decades had passed since V-E Day, and this was to have been the world in which all men were free.

But the victory that Colin had waited for—that clear-cut, shining moment—had never really come. It was always just one more fight away, somewhere in the glittering future.

Wearily the nation bound up its wounds and went on. When the scandal that the newspapers, with a fine sense of history, called variously "Irangate" and "Contragate" erupted that fall, Colin didn't even bother to follow the coverage on CNN.

What did it matter? They would learn nothing new from it. America's leaders were corrupt—the country had known that since Watergate, since Chicago, since Kent State. It would take two years to bring home indictments against Colonel Oliver North and his coconspirators, and in his heart Colin knew that the judgment did not matter.

By the late spring—six months after his collapse—Colin had resumed most of his regular activities, though he had little heart for them. Emily and Frodo married in a Wiccan ceremony held in Mount Tamalpais Park, with Cassilda Chandler officiating. During his convalescence, Colin had sold his interest in the Ancient Mysteries Bookshop to Cassie, and she and Claire managed it together. He'd set the price deliberately low: his real estate investments brought in an income sufficient to his needs, and Colin was not a greedy man.

Cassie was fulfilling her early promise as an occultist and teacher. Though the path she followed through the Light was far from Colin's own, he could find it within himself to be joyful that she was on the journey.

And slowly it began to seem, now, that every worldly loss was balanced by a gain, in a subtle playing-out of some great chess match. The Russians withdrew from Afghanistan, bringing a measure of peace to that oft-disputed country, but at the same time the U.S. was taking the first steps toward an armed clash with Iran. The Chinese massacred students demonstrating for freedom in Tiananmen Square, but in Poland, the worker's union known as Solidarity was providing the first substantial challenge to Russian communism since the end of World War II. Two and a half years after the *Challenger* disaster, the *Discovery* launched successfully—and deaths from AIDS topped fifty thousand a year, as many as were killed in a single holiday weekend by drunk drivers.

Weeks turned to months, months to years. And on November 9, 1989, the Berlin Wall came down.

Colin watched it, alone, in his apartment. The men and women who could have known what this moment meant to him were all dead, or scattered beyond any hope of recall. None of his present circle of friends, dear though he held them, could have understood. Not even Claire.

We won. This means we won.

As a young man, Colin had thought he was a realist—now, having reached the threshold of his seventies, he was beginning to understand what the word really meant. To be a realist, one needed a certain perspective.

It was night in Berlin, the live televised image carried to him by far-distant cameras. Gone were the days when film had to be flown out of the war zone and developed for the six o'clock news—"and now, the news"—gone the days when news was a voice carried by transatlantic cable to the parlor radio—"This is London calling." Now the minicam and the satellite uplink brought the events into homes all over the world at the moment they happened—the announcers sounding giddy and drunk with the enormity of what they were watching, the Berliners in ordinary clothes, carrying sledgehammers and spray cans to smash and deface the Wall that had scarred two postwar generations.

This shows that we've won. A battle, at least, if not the war. And so long as the war continues, there is hope.

It was a block party on an unimaginable scale; an entire city turning out to rejoice in freedom in the shadow of the Brandenburg Gate and the symbol of Cold War oppression. Soon Checkpoint Charlie would be no more than a legend, fast becoming a myth. And future generations would never understand that tyranny had once had a visible face.

Perhaps it is better that way, Colin thought. He watched the distant images of the night from a room where sunlight still streamed through the windows. It seemed, as the years passed, that he understood himself better than before, and with more emotional distance he could be saddened by the passionate follies of his animal nature, but no longer surprised by them. *Perhaps the best thing to do with victories is to forget them.* He raised his glass of wine and silently toasted the television screen.

There was a new emotion growing in his chest, something that had been unfamiliar to him for many years. A fierce, pure hope, a stainless joy. He had looked too long into the Darkness, counting up its victories as if they were his own. But the Light won its victories as well, and they were just as real.

He watched the broadcast a while longer, as it cut back and forth between live footage and talking heads in the studio. At last, the channel switched to other coverage and Colin turned it off. He sat quietly on his couch for almost an hour, basking in this rediscovered sense of grace, then picked up the phone and dialed a familiar number.

"Nathaniel? This is Colin. Give me work."

SAN FRANCISCO, 1990

IT WAS ONLY IN LOOKING BACK ACROSS THE EIGHTIES THAT I REALIZE HOW complacent I became. For a few terrible months after Simon's redemption, I thought I had lost Colin—if not forever, then at least for the rest of this life. But as he grew stronger, my fears eased. I realized that the dark shadow that had haunted Colin's life during his Taghkanic years seemed to have lifted. For the first time since I had known him—and how many years that was, now!— Colin seemed content to live in the moment, taking each day as it came.

It was true that he had sold Cassie his interest in the bookstore and spent more and more time away from it, but I paid no attention to that. It was as if I believed that all those things which had been so much a part of Colin's life for so long had simply . . . stopped.

I realize now that it was because I was the one who wished them to stop. Fortune had brought me a full life, and I had no desire to "rock the boat." Cassie Chandler's strength and energy took much of the burden of running the bookstore from my shoulders—a good thing, since by then I'd taken the degree in psychology that I'd worked toward for so long and was working as a counselor at a local Planned Parenthood Clinic.

I found great contentment in helping those whose lives I touched through the bookstore and the clinic, and there was nothing more—so I thought— that I wanted out of life. Shortly after Frodo married Emily—with Simon giving away the bride, something I thought I'd never see—Frodo and Cassie began running a coven together.

But it was Emily's wedding that was the beginning of the end of my emotional hibernation, though its effect did not bear fruit for months afterward. The wedding was a large—though not formal—affair, and so naturally her mother was there.

It was easy—with the 20/20 hindsight that characterizes our attention to other people's problems—to see the tension there was between Leslie and her mother. The elder Mrs. Barnes's approval of Leslie's marriage to a wealthy, important man—and Leslie's barely controlled fury at it—could have been funny, if it had not struck so close to home. Inevitably, seeing the Barneses together—so angry and so polite—made me think of my own family. I had not spoken to any of them for over a quarter of a century.

I think if Peter's mother had lived, I might have sought reconciliation with them, for my estrangement had always troubled Elizabeth and I would have done nearly anything to please her. As it was, I stayed away, refusing to return to any part of the life I'd had before Peter's death, and the suspended relationship was like an old wound that scars over but never really heals. I did not know what happened to my mother and my sisters over the years and I told myself I did not care, even though Colin had told me often enough that the first duty of those who walk in the Light was to seek clarity within.

For if we do not, that clarity will seek us out, with painful results.

To this day I don't know how Gail found me. But my eldest sister had always possessed a maddening persistence in going after what she wanted, especially when she thought she might cause someone else pain through it, and I suppose that honest, law-abiding citizens aren't particularly hard to find. So I picked up the bookshop phone one day in 1987 with no sense of foreboding whatever.

"Ancient Mysteries Bookshop," I said.

"Is this Claire London?" an unfamiliar voice said.

If the events of Emily's wedding had not been working their way through the back of my mind, I would probably have simply hung up the phone. Instead, I answered honestly.

"I no longer use that name," I said carefully. "I am Claire Moffat now."

"I don't care what you call yourself," she said, and now, with an absolute thrill of horror, I recognized Gail's voice. "Mother's dead. I thought you'd like to know."

Why? was the only thought in my mind. For a strange disjointed moment, the only thing I could think of was that she'd told me so that I would no longer worry that someday Mother might simply reappear in my life, but Gail had never been that kind.

"When is the service?" I found myself asking. Ah, the things that courtesy will lead us to!

She gave me a date and time and told me she would send directions, and then hung up before I could collect my scattered wits enough to ask her how Mother had died. When the directions came—to the bookstore, of course; I had enough instinct for self preservation not to give Gail my home address—I was certain I would not go. It was Cassie who convinced me I must.

"Better go and make sure she's dead," she said with gallows humor. I suppose I was not the only person in America who had ever been estranged from their family, but one's own problems always seem unique.

But good things come at the most unexpected times. I met my cousin, Rowan Moorcock, at my mother's funeral.

I was a nervous wreck by the day of the funeral. Thank heavens Colin had kept his driver's license—he had to drive me to Petaluma, and once we got there I begged him not to come in with me. It seemed so important then that these two streams of my life not cross. I suppose I must have seemed half-demented, but he was very patient with me. To this day, I do not know how I found the physical courage to mount the steps of the funeral parlor and walk inside.

Gail pounced on me the moment I entered the room reserved for the London party and dragged me up to the coffin to pay my "last respects." It was hard to reconcile the *thing* inside—wasted by age and alcohol, and, as Gail wasted no time in telling me now that she could see my reaction, cancer—with the monster who had stalked my childhood and adolescence.

I turned away from the coffin, and would probably have run from the room if someone else hadn't come up to me at that moment.

"Claire?"

The speaker was a plump woman in her fifties, her hair a bright artificial gold. With a certain amount of disbelief, I recognized my middle sister Janet beneath the mask of adulthood.

"Hello, Janet." I desperately wanted to flee this terrible place—I, who had faced demons and Satanists and creatures beyond all human understanding.

She hugged me. It was as if we had never met—two strangers playing the part of fond siblings without acknowledgment of our past—and dragged me away from Gail and over to another knot of mourners.

"And this is Uncle Clarence—you were named for him," Janet told me.

I simply stared. It had never occurred to me—never!—that Mother had any relatives, or would have wished to acknowledge them in any way. She had always cut herself and her children off from the world, a tiny, self-contained unit of torment.

Uncle Clarence introduced me to his grandson—my cousin—Justin Moorcock, and to Justin's daughter, Rowan.

She must have been somewhere in her early teens, and had that glowing farmgirl healthiness that is often more compelling than beauty. Her long hair was a lovely rich red-gold, braided and pinned up atop her head, giving her something of the look of a Saxon princess. She stared at everything around her with a sort of trapped terrorized look I knew from personal experience; the look of one trying to hold on to their concentration and their sanity in the midst of a raging tumult.

"Hello, Rowan," I said, holding out my hand to her.

Her fingers were icy cold, and I found myself drawing on strength I didn't know I possessed, willing it into her. My heart lifted as I saw her face relax.

At that point we were all seated for the service. I remember nothing of what happened then, only Rowan clinging to me as if I could save her from drowning.

Afterward, the mourners were ushered out to the waiting limousines, to accompany the coffin to the cemetery. Of course there was no place for me—Gail had seen to that, vindictive to the last—but with Rowan clinging to me like grim death, she couldn't just tell me to leave.

It was my newfound Uncle Clarence—in every way his sister's opposite—who suggested that Rowan could ride with me to the cemetery. And so poor Colin found himself drafted into the funeral procession, with Rowan leaning over the backseat, her head on my shoulder, the whole way there.

At the end, when Rowan was reluctantly separated from me by her father, she clung to me as if I was an old friend. In one sense it was true; instinctively I knew that we shared that Gift which makes strangers as close as sisters, bound together by that cursed blessing of seeing what others cannot.

"You'll come and visit us, won't you, Cousin Claire?" Rowan asked me, as if she were far younger than her years. "Won't you?"

Of course I said yes. And had I known then what would come of that promise, my answer would have been just the same.

TWENTY-ONE

SHADOWKILL, NEW YORK, MARCH 1990

Most true it is that I have look'd on truth
Askance and strangely; but, by all above,
These blenches gave my heart another youth,
And worse essays prov'd thee my best of love.
— WILLIAM SHAKESPEARE

IT WAS TWO O'CLOCK, AND COLIN HAD HOPED TO MAKE BOSTON BEFORE the start of the rush-hour traffic, but instead he found himself making a detour.

Claire had been against the idea of him driving across country—at *his* age, she'd said, with some tart comments about second childhoods and people with histories of heart disease. But Colin was well aware, these days, of the limits of his strength, and knew that he did not have many more years like this one left to him. He'd wanted to revisit old familiar places while there was still time.

And more than that, he'd wanted the time to take stock. After Simon's rescue, Colin had once more retreated from the search that would have brought him a disciple, yet Alison Margrave's posthumous distress had been a keen lesson to him of his own need to find a student who could learn what he had to teach—and soon.

But who?

Hunter Greyson had been the most promising candidate Colin had seen in decades, and Grey had thrown his future away and vanished. Frodo Fredricks was committed to the Wiccan Path. None of the young men who drifted in and out of the bookstore had the determination, the discipline, and the calling to embrace Colin's Path.

Yet what a tragedy it would be if he should die with a successor untrained, without the repayment that every Adept must make for the teaching he him-self had been given.

And Colin, in his life, had had many teachers. . . .

Though he'd been here only once, twenty years ago, Colin found his way without difficulty to the little village of Shadowkill—an archetypal Hudson River town, with rambling Victorian mansions grouped around a picture-perfect town park. He drove past the war memorial and down County 13—Main Street—to the place where Main Street formed a T with Old Patent Grant Road.

To Shadow's Gate.

The gatehouse was straight ahead, but the entrance was blocked by the running fence that edged Old Patent Grant Road. NO TRESPASSING signs were posted every few feet, but this section of the fence—and the building beyond it—was heavily defaced with graffiti, and someone had made a half-hearted attempt to spray-paint the North Gate Sigil in the center of the road.

Thorne Blackburn was still remembered.

Colin pulled his car over to the side of the road and stopped, staring through the windshield at the miniature castle. The gatehouse building formed an arch across the drive. even from here Colin could see that the iron gates within that arch were chained and padlocked shut, the drive scoured of gravel and choked with weeds from two decades of neglect. The property was deserted, left to rot while the miles of red tape surrounding it and its gone-but-not-definitely-dead owner slowly unfurled, and Thorne Blackburn's long-suffering lawyers filed petitions and disbursed tax payments. If not for that, Shadow's Gate and its hundred-acre wood would have been sold off years ago.

It was unlikely that any of Thorne's half-dozen surviving children—all il-legitimate—could lay claim to the estate. Except for Katherine Jourde-mayne's girl, they had all vanished into the foster-care system and might not even know, today, who their father had been.

If he had not repudiated Thorne, would the outcome have been any differ-ent? Could he have kept the boy from heading so far down that dark path—or at least prevented the deaths?

Colin opened the door and climbed out, pulling up the collar of his coat against the icy March wind. There was no sound of traffic; only the sound of the wind through the ice-covered tree branches. He crossed the road and leaned upon the fence. Why had he come here? What did he hope to find?

Absolution?

The house itself was a mile or so away, invisible from the road. As far as the eye could see there was nothing but desolation, rust, and neglect. Thorne was gone, along with the flower-children of the Aquarian Summerland in which he had flourished. All that remained was the fact of what he had tried to do, and those disciples who still endeavored to complete his work.

At least Thorne has *disciples,* Colin thought, unable to resist making the rue-ful observation.

Facing Thorne's memory across the gulf of years Colin wondered—had what Thorne tried to do been so very wrong? It was no longer possible to remember exactly what that had been—or to summon the moral certainty that had allowed him to fashion such easy judgments.

It seemed so easy now to say that humanity had taken the wrong path. To say that mankind had needed—still needed—such strong measures to save it. But what would Thorne say today? Would he simply say now—as he had then—that there was never a *last* chance?

But Thorne's time had passed, and the corruption that had seemed so shocking two decades ago had become just another acceptable loss of innocence. Thorne was dead, and Colin would never know how his story might have ended.

Thoroughly chilled, he retreated to his car and drove back toward the Taconic Parkway, heading north.

TWENTY-TWO

ARKHAM, MASSACHUSETTS, MARCH 1990

I am become a name;
For always roaming with a hungry heart
Much have I seen and known; cities of men
And manners, climates, councils, governments,
Myself not least, but honour'd of them all . . .
ALFRED, LORD TENNYSON

THE TOWN OF ARKHAM IN MASSACHUSETTS WAS, LIKE THE TAGHKANIC campus in New York, a tiny pocket of the nineteenth century marooned in the depths of the twentieth. The ivy-covered Miskatonic campus was surrounded by ancient New England mansions that had been moldering in earnest since the end of the first World War, and only a few touches of the twentieth century—a supermarket; a steakhouse along the main road that took most of its business from through traffic; a line of tourist cabins for a clientele that had never really materialized—invaded the comalike slumber of the town.

Arkham, like the people of the rural communities which surrounded it— Innsmouth, Whateley's Crossing, Madison Corners—was content to have things so. The people who had fled to this haunted wild land three centuries before asked little more of their neighbors than to be left alone to do as they always had, and to a great extent the modern world had continued to respect their wishes.

The first time Colin had come here, Sara Latimer had been dead for two years.

Miskatonic University was nobody's notion of a first-rank college; it graduated farmers, public health workers, accountants, and homemakers from its two- and four-year programs, and those who asked for more from the halls of academe usually sought it at Harvard, MIT, or Brown University in Rhode Island. Miskatonic offered only one graduate-level program, but those few dedicated souls who wished to take Miskatonic's degree in Esoteric Ethnography came from all over the world.

Colin had lectured here on the Folklore of New England every summer for the last five years, and few suspected his real reason for returning over and over to the Arkham countryside. Now, unfortunately, it seemed that the time was nearing for action. It was 1990, and Sara Latimer had been dead for seven years.

The locals had called her a witch.

They were right. Old Sara Latimer—known as Witch-Sara through most of the surrounding farms—had been the High Priestess of something called the Church of the Antique Rite.

Coincidentally, Colin had known several of old Sara's descendants for years. Paul Latimer, a professor at Columbia, was a tenant in Colin's building in New York. Colin doubted that any of the Latimers knew of their illustrious New England bloodline, or of the fact that there had been Latimers in this part of Massachussets since the 1600s—all tainted by accusations of a witchcraft far less benign than the modern Wiccan sort.

Years ago, Nathaniel Atheling had given Colin what they'd used to call a "watching brief." It was light work, but no sinecure, and it had come to him because Colin had already been familiar with the Church of the Antique Rite. Hunter Greyson had done a research paper on it during his years at Taghkanic.

The Antique Rite had flourished in the New World atmosphere of religious autonomy—if not precisely tolerance—which characterized the pre-Revolutionary period, when almost anyone who could charter a ship could found a settlement in which to practice his own particular variety of religion with minimal hindrance from Church and Crown. As late as the turn of the century its rites had been actively practiced all across old New England.

As far as most people knew, World War I had brought an end to the cult, as it had to so many other things. A new generation, dazzled by hot jazz, strong drink, and the lure of city lights, had little time for the cumbersome paraphernalia of the past, and so the Antique Rite had simply died out.

In most places.

On Colin's first visit, it had taken him less than a week to discover that a coven of the Antique Right was still meeting out near Madison Corners.

It engaged in the same sort of activities that witches had been accused of for centuries: drinking, drugs, gluttony, orgies, ill-wishing their neighbors, petty theft. But none of these acts was the sort of crime that fell within Colin's purview—the coven's magick was weak, and its members seemed to meet more for recreation than for any other purpose.

But perhaps all that would change in the seventh year since Sara Latimer's death.

This year, as usual, Colin spent the first few days settling into the tourist cabin on the outskirts of Arkham and renewing his friendships among members of the Miskatonic Ethnography Department. He found himself out of breath more than usual, and marked it down to the sedentary life he'd fallen into in San Francisco. He promised himself that he'd take more exercise while

he was here, and even make a date to see his doctor when he got home. Fortunately Colin had given up smoking years before. But there was no point in
taking up the time of the local GP—even if the boy did have a bright shiny
new diploma from Johns Hopkins. All a doctor would do was tell Colin
things he already knew: eat right and exercise, take aspirin and hope that another "cardiac event" did not lie in his future.

And meanwhile, there was too much to do to let a little fatigue stand in
his way. Claire would be coming in a few weeks to pay a first visit to her
cousins in nearby Madison Corners.

Colin had been a little disturbed to find that the Moorcock family lived so
near the trouble spot that Nathaniel had set him to watch over, but Claire's
instincts were sound as always, and if she had taken to Rowan Moorcock and
her family there was no possibility that they could be tainted.

Claire had always been so cool and unflappable, an oasis of cheerful common sense no matter the chaos that surrounded her, that to see her at her
mother's funeral, transfixed not by grief but by rage, had been a painful sight.
Colin was pleased to think that Claire could make peace with some portion
of her past. Her friendship with her young cousin Rowan seemed to have
done her a world of good—Colin thought that Rowan replaced, at least in
part, the family that she had hoped for with Peter and never had.

She and Rowan had written back and forth for over a year before this visit,
and Colin had to admit to himself that he had particularly encouraged her to
visit this summer, as it would be useful to him to have Claire on the spot to
function as his Sensitive, should it be necessary.

Privately, he hoped it would not be.

At the beginning of April Colin settled in to his series of lectures. Miskatonic
had an excellent library; the special collection was closed to undergraduate
use, but Colin was able to put his time there to good use, refreshing his
memory about *Les Cultes des Goules,* the sourcebook for the Church of the Antique Rite. The Cults of the Ghouls had been called "a nasty little grimoire"
over two centuries ago by one of the more decadent French ecclesiastics—and
perfectly deserved the title, in Colin's opinion.

Among other things, the cult believed in *metempsychosis*—that the souls of
dedicated cult members were freed by death to be reborn into new bodies,
which would be "awakened" into the memory of their previous lives by exposure to the cult's practices.

After seven years had passed.

The Food King in Arkham was the largest supermarket in thirty miles, but
it was still tiny by modern standards: a relic of days gone by, when the "su-
per" market was only just coming into being. The refrigerator in Colin's
cabin was highly eccentric, but fortunately, the Food King was conveniently
located between his cabin and the college, so that he could buy his eggs by
the half-dozen and his milk by the pint. His mind was on what he should buy
to cook for dinner when he ran into an old friend.

Or to be more precise, an old friend ran into him.

He looked up, startled, at the impact of the other cart crashing into his, and his instant pleasure at the sight of a familiar face turned to a feeling of rue when he realized who it was.

I would have sworn that Paul didn't know about his Latimer heritage—and if he did, that he would have kept it from his wife and children, especially his daughter. . . .

"Why, it's Sally Latimer, isn't it?" Colin said aloud.

Colin had not seen her for at least a year; Sally looked thin and pale, with new lines etched in her face as of grief or illness. She was with a young man who looked vaguely familiar, though Colin couldn't place him.

"Colin!" Sally said, and the young man—obviously *her* young man, in the quaint old phrase—said quickly:

"I didn't think you knew anyone in this part of the country, Sara."

"I don't," Sally protested, and introductions were quickly made. The young man was Brian Standish, the new GP, here helping out his cousin James with the rigors of a rural practice.

With a faint sense of inevitability, Colin heard the rest of Sally's news: the tragic death of her younger brother that triggered her mother's death in turn, the freak accident that claimed her father's life only a few days later.

As if there were something winnowing away the unwanted ones, cutting Sally loose from anything that might anchor her to sanity, reality. And then bringing her here.

He searched her face as she spoke, but could see no trace in those wide green eyes of the ancient malignant soul of Witch-Sara, seven years dead and ripe for her rebirth (so the cult believed) in the body of a family member. He'd never really noticed before, not having seen her for some time, but Sally was the exact image of the pictures of the Latimer witches that Miskatonic kept in the closed stacks: red hair, pale skin, tilted green eyes, and even the small mole at the right corner of her mouth. He listened with a sinking heart as Sally innocently told him about her Great-Aunt Sara's legacy, the house on Witch Hill Road—and about the Church of the Antique Rite, to which, apparently, she'd already been introduced . . . and invited.

Poor child; it was obvious from what she'd left unsaid that Sally really had no other place to go now but to her ancestral home, and to scare her with tales of backwoods demons might simply drive her further into the "Reverend" Matthew Hay's clutches.

It was easy enough for Colin to maneuver her into extending him an invitation to visit the house at Witch Hill soon; he salved his conscience for the duplicity by inviting her and Brian to dinner as his guests. And he tried not to worry about what might happen to Sally, here where the witch-blood ran close to the surface and an ancient decadence seemed to seep from the very bedrock of the land.

It was fairly late when Colin got back to his cabin, but he phoned Claire anyway. It only took a ring or two for the phone to be answered.

"Moorcock residence."

"Is that you, Claire? It's Colin."

Claire had arrived in Madison Corners at the end of April and settled quickly into the Moorcock household. Colin had warned her that they might be called upon to act, and now he was glad he had.

"You're lucky you got through," Claire said. "Rowan's been on the phone most of the evening. I gather the upcoming senior prom is a matter of the keenest interest locally." She sounded amused.

"I don't doubt it," Colin said. "And to think I wondered if I was calling too late. Speaking of interesting, you'll never guess who I ran into down at the supermarket today."

They would have to be circumspect in their conversation: one of the country customs Arkham preserved was that of the operator-assisted party line, and no telephone conversation was ever really private.

"Who?" Claire asked dutifully.

"Sally Latimer. You remember her—her father was one of my tenants back in New York?"

"Of course I do," Claire said, and Colin could tell from the change in her voice that she had picked up the implications of that "was" easily. "But I'm glad you called. Uncle Clarence has been demanding that we have you to dinner ever since he found out you were here. How about tomorrow?"

"I'll be there," Colin promised. "Good night, Claire."

The Moorcocks occupied a rambling old white farmhouse about a mile from the old graveyard on Witch Hill, but the house seemed almost to belong to a different world.

The three generations of Moorcocks were a nineties-style family; Rowan's father Justin was Clarence Moorcock's grandson. Justin's father, like so many men of that generation, had died in Vietnam, leaving his son to grow up fatherless—and, sometimes, motherless. In the wake of his divorce, Justin, a professional software designer, and his then fourteen-year-old daughter Rowan had moved from Boston's Back Bay back to Madison Corners.

Colin parked his rented Chevy in the driveway beside Clarence's old Ford pickup, Justin's sleek BMW, and eighteen-year-old Rowan's practical Toyota. Rowan was already waiting in the open doorway for him, wearing the universal teenage uniform of ragged jeans and rock-band T-shirt.

"Good evening, Mr. MacLaren," Rowan said dutifully. There were dark circles under her eyes, as if she hadn't been sleeping well.

She had earphones slung around her neck, and a Walkman in her back pocket. It was the first time he had seen her since the funeral of her great-aunt, and for a moment Colin wondered how the girl managed to look so much like every other teenager when the nearest shopping mall was no closer than Boston.

"Good evening, Rowan," Colin said. Odd to think that many of his students had been near her age.

He stepped inside the door of the old farmhouse and felt a faint frisson of tension. There was trouble here, and whatever it was, Claire had not felt comfortable mentioning it over the phone.

"Pot roast tonight," Rowan said, as if changing a painful subject. "Claire's cooking. Right through there. 'Scuze me—gotta go change." She turned and galloped up the stairs, fitting the headphones back on her head as she went.

Colin stared after her for a moment, wondering what the problem was—intergenerational tension, or something darker?

Whatever it was, he'd know soon enough. Colin headed in the direction Rowan had indicated.

In the kitchen Claire was making last-minute preparations for dinner. Clarence sat at the kitchen table, overseeing the proceedings with satisfaction.

"Colin," he said, getting to his feet. The hand he offered was still heavily callused from decades of farmwork, and even at eighty-something, his grip was strong. "Good to see you again. Where did Rowan get to? Did she let you in?"

"I think she had to go and change," Colin said diplomatically.

Clarence grinned. "I'm too old and too crotchety to see girls come to the dinner table wearing pants. As Claire here will tell you."

"Oh, yes. Uncle Clarence is quite a tyrant," Claire agreed easily, sliding a tray of biscuits into the oven.

"When the biscuits are ready, we eat," she said, taking the lid off the roasting pan and expertly levering the roast out onto a platter.

"I don't need this at all," Justin complained good-naturedly, ladling gravy over his potatoes and carrots. "It isn't as if I were doing anything more strenuous than sitting at a computer all day."

Rowan had reappeared, wearing a denim skirt and plain white blouse, to fetch Justin from the converted shed that served him as his workroom.

"Rowan and I cooked it," Claire said with joking menace. "You'd *better* eat it."

Colin gathered that usually Rowan and the housekeeper shared the cooking chores: from what Claire said, Rowan had made the scratch-biscuits and the pies for dessert, and Claire had contributed the Moffat family's recipe for pot roast.

Conversation at dinner was general.

The land was no longer a working farm, but Clarence still kept up with the farm news, and Claire had been helping out Joann Winters, the district nurse, and so had some harmless snippets of local gossip to contribute. There was still another week of school to run, but by now the minds of the graduating class were firmly fixed on the senior prom and the class trip to the "big city": Boston, Massachusetts.

And Clarence, it seemed, was far from reconciled to Rowan's decision about college, especially since it seemed her choice had fallen to an out-of-state school.

Taghkanic.

"If you must go, what's wrong with Miskatonic, grandchild? Martha and I both went there. It's a good school—and you could live at home."

"Well," Rowan began. Her father darted a minatory glance at her, and the girl changed her mind about what she'd been going to say. "I guess I'd just like to go somewhere else," she muttered, staring down at her napkin.

"I ran into an old friend yesterday in the Food King," Colin said, to change the subject. "You remember that I mentioned I'd met Sally Latimer yesterday, don't you, Claire?"

Colin quickly related Sally's dismal news, drawing exclamations of sympathy from Claire and the Moorcocks. "So she's staying at the old family house until she figures out what she's going to do."

"Witch Hill? Brrr—! I'd rather bunk in at the Bates Motel," Claire said honestly. "Well, she's dumped that little twerp Roderick, at any rate. I never could stand him—one of those nitpicking managing sorts who can only feel safe so long as he's feeling superior."

"The young man I met last night seems to be rather nice," Colin said. "Local, too—Brian Standish?"

"Knew the mother—a Phillips she was. Town girl," Clarence said, and the temporary awkwardness passed off.

Clarence departed to his bed immediately after supper, claiming the privilege of age and wishing Colin a very good evening. Justin had lingered to make a bit of polite conversation, before admitting that there really were one or two things he needed to finish up before FedEx came tomorrow morning to pick up the code.

Rowan stayed as long as her father did, but as soon as Justin had left, Rowan swore she wanted to do the dishes before finishing up her homework and retreated quickly to the kitchen, leaving Colin and Claire alone in the parlor, where a potbellied stove took the edge off the chill.

"When I was her age, I'd do anything rather than the dishes," Colin said.

"Me, too," Claire agreed. "Rowan's a good kid. She just hasn't been feeling herself lately."

"So I gathered. What was all that at dinner about? It seems like an argument that's been going on for a while."

"Oh, it isn't really that much of anything. Of course Clarence wants Rowan to go to Miskatonic, but both she and Justin are dead set against the idea. Last week Rowan told Uncle Clarence that she didn't want to go to Miskatonic because she didn't want to be either a housewife or a necromancer, and I'm afraid things were a bit strained after that. Clarence is fond of her, but she's his great-granddaughter, and in his day women didn't have that many choices. Not that even Clarence wants her to marry any of the local product, of course. I gather things have gone downhill around here in the last sixty years or so."

"I'm not surprised," Colin said. "I didn't want to go into it at the table, but there's just something a little too pat about the way Sally's family died. She got the letter about Witch Hill the day she buried Paul, poor girl. Worse, she seems to have met Matthew Hay, and that puts her up to her eyebrows in the Church of the Antique Rite, whether she knows it or not."

"Auditioning her for the part of the next High Priestess—or the last one?"

Claire guessed, and shuddered. "Wasn't she a Sara, too? Poor Sally! She must think she stepped into a time machine, coming here. I've only been here a few weeks, and I've already heard more than enough Old Lady Latimer stories— the woman seems to have been a cross between Morgan LeFay and Cruella DeVille!"

Colin stared broodingly into the flames visible through the door of the stove. "I only wish I knew how much Hay knows—or believes. The likeness is devilishly close; there are some drawings in the Special Collection that might almost be photographs of Sally. . . . But I've known that girl since she was eight years old; I can't imagine her going along with the Antique Rite's nasty nonsense."

Not, at least, of her own free will . . . But whose will was it that had engineered the death of Sally's parents?

Nathaniel had been right to send him here. Petty and local though they were, there were dark forces at work here in the New England countryside, and destroying those forces without destroying Sally Latimer as well would require the most careful calculation.

"Do you want me to go sniff around, Colin?" Claire asked, rousing him from his reverie.

"I'd appreciate it. Last night at dinner, Sally sounded as if she could use a few friendly faces around, and I'd like to know just what it is that we're up against. If that old house is psychically active, for example . . ."

"If it is, she can't possibly stay there," Claire agreed. "I wonder if Uncle Clarence would welcome another houseguest?" She hesitated. "But I think we may have another problem as well: Rowan."

Colin cocked his head, listening for the clatter of dishes in the kitchen. The girl was thoroughly occupied and unlikely to overhear. "Tell me," he said quietly.

"You said things seemed a little strained tonight—well, it wasn't all about Rowan's choice of college. About a month ago—around the last full moon— she started sleepwalking."

Colin sat forward, suddenly alert.

"Justin was working late and saw her go out. He took her back to the house and tucked her in—she didn't even wake up—and after that we started locking the house at night. But she didn't stop sleepwalking."

"Did Rowan remember anything about the episodes?" Colin asked. ·

Claire shrugged. "She wasn't even aware of them at first. And for a while the locked doors seemed to stop her, at least from getting out of the house. She'd rattle the knob for a while, wake up, and go back to bed. Of course most people sleepwalk at some point in their lives, and most of the time it's harmless, but lately she's been unlocking the door and . . . well, going out," Claire said feebly.

"After the first time we found her gone and the back door wide open, Justin set up an infrared alarm to wake him, and he goes and gets her, but this has him worried sick. It's pretty clear this has something to do with the fact that Rowan's a Sensitive, but Justin doesn't really want to acknowledge something that seems so irrational to him."

Claire sighed, and shook her head wearily. "He may not want to admit it, but he knows, believe me. And that's the real problem."

"Problem?" Colin asked.

"Oh, you know, Colin—people can't really tell the difference between 'psychic' and 'Satanic,' and Justin spent enough summers here as a boy to pick up the local superstitions about the Antique Rite, even if he won't admit *that* either. He doesn't know whether to call an exorcist or a doctor—not that either one would do him any good. And lately I think the, well, I'd have to call it the weirdness factor is getting to Rowan, too. I think she's keeping herself awake all night so she won't sleepwalk, and that can't last."

"Any notion where she's going?" Colin asked. "That might give us a clue as to the cause."

Claire's face was grim. "Oh, we all know where she's going. That's the problem. Every time she gets out, she makes a beeline due east—right for the old burying-ground   and the Church of the Antique Rite."

It wasn't until Friday that Claire was able to make her promised visit to Sally Latimer.

Up until Colin's visit she'd been sleeping in one of the spare bedrooms—the house had been built for a large farm family, and there was no shortage of guest rooms—but after what Colin had told her about Sally, Claire realized that she couldn't just wait around and hope things would get better. She told Rowan that she was going to move in with her, and was not surprised when Rowan accepted gratefully.

Most of Thursday was taken up with moving furniture to make room for a second twin bed in Rowan's room and then moving Claire's things in. Fortunately, Rowan was already packing her things away in anticipation of going to Taghkanic that fall; the room with the faded white rose wallpaper had even looked a little barren until Claire moved in.

"I'm glad you're here, Claire," Rowan said simply. She was dressed for sleep, sitting cross-legged on her bed in a Miskatonic T-shirt and a pair of plaid flannel boxer shorts, hugging a large stuffed dragon. Its name, so Claire was given to understand, was Lockheed.

"So am I," Claire said. She folded her sensible dark blue wool bathrobe—too warm for the California climate at any season, but the perfect thing for spring in New England—at the foot of the bed and turned back the coverlet. The bed was heaped with hand-pieced quilts that had been handed down through the generations of Moorcock women.

"Claire—" Rowan said.

Here it comes. Of course, Rowan was worried about the sleepwalking—and she would have sensed something out of the ordinary about Colin at dinner last night. Mentally, Claire braced herself for the question she dreaded. But when it came, it wasn't precisely what she expected.

"Do you think it's possible to be a *hereditary* witch?" Rowan asked.

"I'm not sure I understand," Claire temporized. "Where did you hear that?"

"At school." Rowan shrugged, as if dismissing the whole matter. "Laney was talking all this nonsense about the great hereditary witch families of the Wicca, and about how they could all trace their lineages back to Morgan LeFay and the coven of Camelot. But Laney's such a dip . . . stick, that I didn't think she knew what she was talking about. Only she said that everybody born with red hair was secretly a witch," Rowan added, wrapping one of her bright chestnut braids around and around her wrist.

"Well, she doesn't and they aren't," Claire said flatly. "Most of the Wiccans I know are perfectly sensible people who believe that they are *reconstructing* ancient Pagan practices, not carrying them on in an unbroken line. I imagine that every Wiccan—or white witch, if you like—knows perfectly well that she is one, even if she doesn't tell anybody. As for all redheads secretly being witches, well, that's an old piece of English folklore that I'm surprised to see still kicking around."

"I'm not a witch," Rowan said positively, as if that settled the matter of Laney. She gazed at Claire for a moment, her grey eyes disconcertingly direct. "But there *are* witches, Claire, and they aren't all white ones."

Claire wasn't sure what to say. It almost seemed as if Rowan was warning her.

"Well, g'night," Rowan said after a moment, yawning and clutching her dragon tighter.

"Sleep well, dear," Claire said. She waited until Rowan had burrowed under the covers, then turned out the light.

But it was a long time before she could make herself fall asleep.

Somewhere in the deepest part of the night, Claire came abruptly awake. The full moon was shining in through the open windows, and in its ghostly blue light, Claire could see that Rowan's bed was empty.

"Rowan!" Claire said in a half-whisper.

"I'm right here." The girl's voice was curiously remote. Claire thought she sounded tired. She moved, and now Claire could see her standing by the window, wrapped in one of the quilts.

"Come back to bed. You'll freeze," Claire said.

"They're out there," Rowan said. "I can feel it—can't you? They're calling us."

A shimmering darkness; a heart-deep drumbeat calling something older, more primal, than man. Something hideous, but somehow seductive as well, a longing bred into humankind in the interminable night before the dawn of time. . . .

Claire shook her head sharply, and the *call* withdrew, though Claire knew it was still out there. *And Sally is out there, too. Heaven help her.*

"Come back to bed, Rowan," Claire said, a bit more sharply than she'd intended.

"I can't sleep," Rowan said frankly. "And . . . I don't think I should, really. Do you, Claire?"

"No," Claire admitted, giving up with a sigh. "You're probably right. But you mustn't go out to them, Rowan, no matter how much you feel you ought." Even as she spoke, Claire could hear how patronizing and foolish the words sounded. What would she do if Rowan disobeyed?

"I won't," Rowan said, and now Claire could hear reluctance in her voice. She saw the shadow as Rowan put a hand on the cold glass of the uncovered windowpane, as though the gesture could make what lay outside clearer. "I didn't used to hear it. I was too young. Now I can hear it, but I'm not strong enough yet. But I will be." Claire could hear the quiet promise in the young girl's voice.

Rowan decided she wanted some tea, and Claire went down to the kitchen with her. Through the window over the sink Claire could see the light in Justin's backyard workroom.

"Daddy's pulling an all-nighter," Rowan said matter-of-factly, filling the kettle at the tap and setting it on the stove. "Want some cake? There's some left over from dinner."

"No, thanks." Rowan's appetite was a tribute to the legendary all-consuming hunger of the teenager. "But I will take a cup of tea," Claire said.

Rowan went to get the canister down from the cupboard and stopped, looking wistfully toward the workroom light. "He can't hear anything at all," Rowan said, almost to herself. "Tonight's just another night for him." After a moment she moved on, taking down an old brown teapot and filling it from the loose tea in the canister.

"What do *you* hear, Rowan?" Claire asked quietly. Though Claire had known Rowan had the Gift the moment she'd first laid eyes on her, she hadn't been sure whether the girl herself knew—or how much credence Rowan placed in her own abilities.

"Just . . . stuff," the girl said vaguely. Claire had the sense that Rowan's inarticulateness was not so much due to obstinacy as simply to the inability to describe those things that other people had no words for. "Them," she said, gesturing vaguely eastward. "It's like . . . like a sore tooth."

The kettle whistled and Rowan broke off to pounce upon it and pour the boiling water into the old Rockingham pot. While she waited for it to steep, Rowan brought out the cake and cut herself a generous slice, adding a plate and fork out of respect for the delicate sensibilities of her elders.

She carried the pot over to the kitchen table along with two hand-painted china mugs—souvenirs of some long-forgotten country fair—the sugar bowl, and a bottle of unpasteurized cream from one of the local farms. Rowan poured for both of them, and then liberally doctored her own tea with several spoonsful of sugar and a generous dollop of cream that threatened to overfill the cup.

"And what else do you see?" Claire asked her, when it became apparent that Rowan did not intend to volunteer anything more.

"Things," Rowan said, and this time Claire could tell the vagueness was deliberate. "Poor Sara. But I guess sometimes things have to go bad so they

can be good later. God! That sounds like one of Laney's stupid New Age say-
ings," she added in a more normal voice.

"*Poor Sara.*" Claire shuddered inwardly at the remote sound of pity that
had been in Rowan's voice. In the back of her own mind she, too, could feel
the terror tangled up in the sound of drums, but Claire dared not go in search
of Sally Latimer. She would be almost certain to get lost on the back roads in
the dark, and if she went, it would leave the Moorcocks undefended against
whatever might come searching for them—and Rowan, in particular, was
very vulnerable.

But it still seemed like a very long time until dawn.

At about 4:30 Justin came in from his workroom and chased Rowan off to
bed—tomorrow was a school day, as he reminded her, and she'd have to be up
by seven to get there on time. Rowan assured him that she'd be fine—and at
her age, she probably would be, Claire reflected enviously—and skipped off
out of the room after a good-night peck on the cheek.

"Is she all right?" Justin asked Claire, after Rowan had left. "Really?"

"She'll be all right," Claire temporized, not wanting to lie. Whatever had
been calling from the old church on the hill had stopped a few minutes ago,
and Rowan was in no further danger.

Not tonight, anyway.

Claire took the cups and Rowan's plate over to the sink and set them carefully in the dishpan for later washing. "Especially once she goes away to
school. You *know* that, Justin," she added.

Justin Moorcock sighed, running a hand through his thick auburn hair.
"Sometimes I wish I hadn't brought her back here at all, but she was so broken up when Merilee walked out, and I'd always been happy here. Besides,
Granddad isn't getting any younger. . . ." He wouldn't meet her eyes, as if he
were afraid of hearing things that he would have to deny.

"Don't beat yourself up over this, Justin," Claire said firmly. "Rowan's going to be fine. She's a very sensible girl."

"I suppose you're right," Justin said with reluctant relief. "Well, good-
night, Claire."

"Goodnight, Justin."

By the time Claire returned to the bedroom, Rowan was soundly asleep beneath a pile of quilts, tightly clutching her stuffed dragon. Claire only wished
she could set aside her own problems as easily. She had the terrible feeling she
would have to choose between the safety of her cousin and her young
friend . . . and Claire was not sure she had it in her to make such a choice.

It was a long time before she managed to sleep.

It was after nine o'clock when Claire awoke again, this time to the ringing of
the telephone. Clarence was hard of hearing and would just let it ring, and if
Justin was in his workroom he wouldn't hear it either. Fortunately there was
an extension upstairs in the hall; Claire struggled into her bathrobe and lifted
the receiver.

"Hello?" she said groggily.

"Claire?" Colin's voice. "You sound a little ragged."

And he, like Justin, wouldn't have heard a thing even if he'd been right here all night. There are times when I'm downright jealous. . . .

"I had a bad night. Never mind. What can I do for you?" she asked.

"Sally doesn't have a phone and I'm tied up all day, but Brian Standish phoned me about seven this morning; his answering service gave him a message that she'd tried to reach him yesterday, but by the time he got it, it was too late for him to call. He's probably asleep now, but I was hoping you could find the time to run past Sally's place."

"I was planning to do that today anyway," Claire said, mentally arranging her schedule. "I'll give you a call later, okay?"

"I'll be at the college until five or six," Colin said. "You can reach me there."

Hanging up the phone, Claire tottered back into the bedroom. Clouds had rolled in overnight, and the day was drizzly and bleak. She shivered as she tucked her feet into her fleece slippers and padded over to the window. Rowan's bedroom overlooked the driveway; looking out, Claire could see that both Rowan and Justin's cars were gone. Something must have gone wrong with the FedEx pickup—he would have driven Rowan to school otherwise, Claire was sure.

I guess I'll have to see if I can borrow the truck, Claire thought resignedly. She hadn't bothered to rent a car of her own, since it had been easy enough so far to borrow Rowan or Justin's car whenever she needed transportation—and the nearest place to rent one was in Boston in any event. Normally she would have just waited for Justin to get back.

But her errand to Sally couldn't wait.

Uncle Clarence was willing to loan Claire the old truck—if a bit dubious about her ability to drive it—so after a scratch breakfast of coffee and toast, which barely made up for her broken night, Claire was on her way. The raw day did much to clear her head of the lingering cobwebs of the night, and by the time Claire reached Witch Hill at eleven o'clock, she was ready for anything . . . so she thought.

Some lingering intuition—or impulse—had led her to put together a "care package" of coffee and an old drip coffeemaker that no one would miss. Whatever might be going on at the old Latimer house, Claire thought strong coffee would be needed and she wasn't sure Sally would have the makings.

As she nursed the old truck up the hill, Claire could hardly believe her first sight of the old Latimer place—if there were ever a horror beyond imagining, this was it. It looked like one of those old houses in a Stephen King novel, the kind that had rooms leading off into alternate dimensions. Every possible piece of ornamental woodworking that could ever have been added to the house had been added at some time in its life, and towers, dormers, and bay windows seemed to jut from it in a fearful asymmetry. The weathercock at the highest point of the roof was a rather ominous-looking black bird, and as it followed the shifting wind, it made a faint, tooth-hurting screeking.

Claire pulled her uncle's truck up under the porte cochere and shut off the ignition. For a moment she couldn't quite figure out where the front door was—there was something so *wrong* with the design of the Latimer place that it was difficult for the eye to really focus on any part of it—but then she located it and strode briskly toward it.

If just looking at this place gives me the willies, how much worse must it be to live here? Poor Sally! I can at least bring her home with me for a decent meal and a few hours away from this horror.

Her worry about Sally increased when there was no answer to her knocking—though she'd seen a white face peer out through one of the upstairs windows—but finally Claire heard the sound of the bolt being dragged back, and a moment later the door opened.

Sally Latimer stood in the doorway, wearing nothing but a heavy flannel bathrobe. Claire tried not to let her shock show on her face—Sally's glorious red hair was a tangled mess, and her eyes seemed sunken deep in their sockets. Her pupils were enormous; she winced as if the daylight hurt her eyes, staring at Claire as if she might burst into tears at any moment. The girl was bird-thin; what had been coltish slenderness the last time Claire had seen her had now crossed the line into haggardness.

Belladonna would account for the dilation of the eyes, and nightshade was a traditional component of the flying ointment that diabolic witches wore to the Sabbat—or Esbat.

Colin must be told. Things are far worse than we'd thought. But the best thing for Sally just now is the illusion of normalcy, Claire told herself firmly.

"Did I come at a bad time?" she asked, schooling her voice to conventional brightness. "Colin said you were staying here, and I don't know another soul from here to Innsmouth—" Claire chattered on until she saw the first trapped terrified expression on Sally's face fade and thought she might risk a direct question. "Are you sick, Sally?"

"Not exactly," the girl answered. Her voice was rough and slurred, bolstering Claire's impression that she'd been drugged, and finally she seemed to realize that she was keeping her guest standing outside in the rain. "Come in, Claire," Sally Latimer said, stepping back.

Claire stepped inside and hugged Sally impulsively. She felt the girl flinch away from her touch, and felt a warm wave of pity. *Poor child! She shouldn't have had to face last night all alone. . . .*

"I'll just go put on some clothes," Sally said slowly.

"Don't think you need to get dressed up just for me," Claire said reassuringly. "I've brought some coffee—do you mind if I make some up while you dress?"

"Please do," Sally said hesitantly. She wandered out of the kitchen, the robe slipping unheeded from her shoulders as she went.

When she was gone, Claire took a deep breath and, bracing herself, opened her senses to the old house.

There was nothing here—nothing at all.

She realized that she'd expected Witch Hill to be reeking with malignant psychic energy, with the kind of taint that accrued from the practices of something like the Church of the Antique Rite. But there was nothing here of the sort—the place was as neutral and impersonal as a paper cup or a modern city apartment.

Claire shrugged and went to make the coffee. Experience with Cousin Clarence's kitchen enabled her to negotiate the cranky propane stove easily, and soon she had the coffee perking, sending its rich fragrance through the kitchen. As she hunted about for cups and spoons, a magnificent ginger tomcat appeared.

"Hello, sweetie," Claire said, bending down and extending her fingers for it to sniff. Seeing him made her realize how much she missed having cats of her own—Monsignor had died several years before, old and fat and full of years, and then Poltergeist had joined her playmate last fall, leaving Ancient Mysteries—and Claire—catless for the first time in many years. Claire had been thinking about getting another kitten, or even two, but had not wanted to do so while the memory of her dear friends was still fresh. Still, she missed feline company.

The animal butted his head against her hand, and Claire could feel the drops of rain on his fur. So he'd come in from outside . . . but how?

Maybe a window was open somewhere.

About then, Sally returned. She was wearing a powder blue corduroy skirt that looked as if it had been slept in, and a shetland pullover in the same color. Around her neck she'd tied a paisley scarf in a clashing shade of orange—Claire wondered why a flaming redhead had ever bought such an item—and her mouth was smeared where she'd first applied, then wiped off, lipstick in an unfortunate shade of coral. Her hair was still uncombed and hung around her face like a madwoman's.

Don't react, Claire told herself firmly. Her instincts told her that Sally Latimer wasn't ready to be confronted with anything that might frighten her. Something had already done that job too well.

"He's beautiful," she said instead, still stroking the cat. "Did you find him here?" Some perverse reality-testing impulse impelled her to add: "Was he your Aunt Sara's cat?"

"Heaven knows," Sally said dully, slumping into a chair. She laughed unsteadily. "Some of the locals have some theories about that. I call him Barnabas, after that old TV show." She ran her fingers through her hair, pushing it back from her face. There were dark bruises beneath her eyes, more evidence of some sort of drug.

"Have you eaten anything?" Claire asked, and, receiving the reply she expected, began to bully Sally into eating. As she did, she took a good look around the kitchen for the first time.

It looked as if both the Jukes and the Kallikaks had been living here. Dishes and garbage were piled in the sink, and it was plain that no one had cleaned the kitchen since the death of that other Sara, seven years before.

Claire's face must have given her away despite all her good intentions, because Sally, watching her, suddenly began to cry.

"I know—I know—it's all horrible! But it's because of Matthew—he said that I was Aunt Sara and I had to attend the Esbat, and I told him he was crazy—I tried to get away—I called Brian—but Tibby had a pet jackdaw and I kept getting lost—I couldn't get to the bus stop—and then the bus left without me—and I went home and locked the door, but then Matthew came with Judith—and she had a strawberry shortcake—I didn't eat it, but there was unguent on the plate and she drugged me, and then—and then—"

For a moment Sally broke down completely, then finished her story in a wavering ragged voice: how she'd fallen down in a swoon with the witches' unguent on her hands—the Esbat afterward that seemed half dream, half nightmarish reality—how she'd awakened, naked, in the graveyard at dawn. Clare listened to it all impassively, pouring Sally a cup of strong black coffee and setting it in front of her.

"Do you think I'm crazy?" Sally demanded. "Do you believe me, Claire?"

"I don't know what to think," Claire said cautiously. She had the evidence of her own senses that *something* terrible had happened here last night, but Sally's story of her experience was almost too pat to be possible—it contained all the elements of the classic European witch-cult tales, and those tales had been created by the persecutors, not the practitioners, of the Old Religion. It was hard for Claire to believe that any Wiccan coven—or even any Satanist Temple—practiced rituals such as Sally had described.

But then, the Church of the Antique Rite wasn't either Wiccan or Satanic, although its tangled roots might lie somewhere in the pre-Christian folk worship that the missionaries from Rome had never entirely eradicated.

"I believe that you believe it. And I must admit, I knew you were in some kind of trouble. That's why I came."

"You knew—what?" Sally demanded with sudden suspicion.

"That you were in trouble," Claire repeated slowly. For a moment, something unlike the sunny young artist Claire knew had stared out through Sally Latimer's eyes, and Claire felt a faint thrill of unease. "But right now you need food," she said firmly, and turned to making the best she could of Sally's meager supplies.

Claire felt very much out of her depth—how much of what Sally had told her had a basis in objective fact? She wished that Colin were here. He knew more about the Church of the Antique Rite than she did, and would be able to untangle fact from drug-induced hallucination. But Colin wasn't here, and Sally needed answers—and reassurance—*now.*

"All right," Claire said, as they ate. "Let's assume that some of what you experienced was real. Why do you think it might have happened?"

Sally's mouth twisted in a sketchy parody of a smile. "I thought . . . a sick practical joke."

"To be that sick, a man would have to be a basket case," Claire said roundly.

"You don't think Matthew Hay is capable of it?" Sally asked, again with that strange undertone in her voice that put Claire's every instinct on guard.

But what danger could *Sally* be to her? Sally had been the victim, not the instigator, of whatever had happened last night.

Unless, of course, this wasn't Sally at all. . . .

She must not suspect you, Claire thought urgently, and did not question the rightness of that instinct. She had Rowan to protect as well as herself.

"I think Matthew Hay is capable of anything," Claire said. She felt very much as if she were playing a part—the dim but goodhearted friend of the heroine in a creaky Gothic novel, there to offer pretend-sensible explanations for a battery of occult phenomena. She had the strong sensation that if she seemed to know too much—or too little—she would give the game away, and alert the not-Sally that she was watching from behind Sally Latimer's frightened green eyes.

So Claire prattled on as if she had no idea of Matthew Hay's true motives for drugging Sally, and pointed out the evidence that she *had* been drugged (it would have been obvious to anyone with any medical training, and Sally knew she'd been a nurse), and counseled Sally about how hard it would be for her to *prove* anything that had happened the night before.

"I just want to know that I'm not losing my mind," the girl repeated, and Claire heard the plea for help concealed beneath those words. If she could just get Sally to come away with her, she'd drive her straight to Colin. Colin could certainly handle anything Sally—or her unwelcome guest—could throw at him.

"Look here, Sar— Sally. Do you want to go to the hospital? The emergency room's sure to be open—you could have a toxicology screening; I'm sure Brian would order one. At least they could treat your physical symptoms."

She saw Sally hesitate, looking at her like a prisoner gazing at freedom through the bars of her cell. Just as the girl drew breath to answer, the moment was shattered by the clang of the doorbell.

Both women jumped. Sally quivered as if beset by a sudden chill; the coffee in the cup she held between her hands slopped over the sides.

Claire got to her feet and glanced out the window that overlooked the kitchen steps.

"Matthew Hay," she said disgustedly. Claire had run into him once or twice at the general store in Madison Corners—a tall, gangly man with a face like a cold straight-razor and the pale blue eyes and washed-out mouse-colored hair that came with generations of inbreeding. Yet despite the fact that he looked like an unholy combination of Arnold Schwarzenegger and Ichabod Crane, there was a sort of compelling power about him. "I suppose he's come to check on your story."

"Stay out of sight, Claire," Sally said quickly.

Claire looked at her in surprise.

"I mean . . . maybe if he thinks I'm alone he'll say something to prove my story one way or the other," she added. "At least then I'll *know.*"

"I don't like to leave you alone with him." *And why do you want to be alone with him, Sally—if everything you've told me so far today is true?*

"You think I want to be alone with him?" Sally protested unconvincingly. She got to her feet, shooing Claire toward the back pantry with quick motions of her hands. "But you'll be there if I need you."

Some inner warning prompted Claire to withdraw. This was her young friend—and yet it wasn't. There was something else here, just beneath the surface of Sally's normal personality.

Disassociation, rape trauma, schizophrenia, multiple personality disorder . . . Claire ran through the psychological buzzwords she'd learned in her college courses, and none of them seemed to fit. Only the older, darker term seemed right.

Possession. . . .

From her vantage point in the pantry, Claire could only see Hay, and not Sally. She didn't dare move to a better position, lest she draw attention to herself. She listened as Sally and Hay bickered—there really wasn't any other word for it—as if they both shared some peculiar assumption. The conversation even veered momentarily to the young woman whom Sally said had kept her from fleeing the day before—Tabitha Whitfield.

"I notice you didn't think twice about my being poisoned," Sally drawled. Her voice was different; hard, somehow older, and there was a mocking note in her voice that Claire couldn't remember ever having heard before.

"Can't make omelettes without breaking eggs," Hay said, shrugging. The door behind him was still open, filling the kitchen with dank cold, but he didn't seem to notice. "You're alive, so why are you complaining?" He took a step toward her, and Claire felt a sudden rush of Power in the room.

That's quite enough.

"So you admit it, Mr. Hay? You tried to poison Sally? Did you rape her, too?" Claire asked.

Hay seemed taken aback by her sudden appearance—*probably thought his occult powers should have warned him of my presence*—and stared from her to Sally in shock. Claire was chilled to see the taunting smile on Sally's face as she savored his discomfiture.

"Rape? Is that what she told you?" Hay said, sounding like any man the morning after trying to soft-pedal an assault. "All right, Sara, you've had your joke and your revenge," he added, turning away from Claire. "Now get this old hag out of here so we can get down to serious matters."

"I'll go when Sally asks me to," Claire said boldly. "My own impulse is to just throw you out."

Hay's smile widened to a sneer. "Sara, this has gone too far for a joke."

Claire was watching Sally's face. Whatever was going on here, Hay was making it worse. The girl she had known was almost gone, submerged in the dark *awareness* that was growing in Sally's very bearing.

Because Hay was here?

"Now, damn you—*out,*" Claire snapped. Hay stepped toward her, and she shoved him—hard.

The technique she used borrowed a little from every martial art. It was called *victim-proofing,* and Claire had taken the courses along with the women she counseled back in San Francisco.

"I warn you—" Hay said. When he reached for her again, she grabbed his wrist and twisted it up behind him.

"Go to hell. Go directly to hell. Do not pass 'Go.' Do not collect two hundred dollars," Claire said. As he staggered off balance, she pitched him out through the door.

Hay sprawled in the muddy yard, and for a moment Claire feared that she'd really hurt him, but then he got to his feet and glared murderously at her. Claire gripped the edge of the kitchen door, ready to slam it in his face if he charged.

"You'll regret this, Sara," Hay shouted. "I can be your most loyal supporter—*and priest*—or your worst enemy! It's up to you!"

He shook his fist in the air, as if summoning down the wrath of the heavens, and right on cue it began to rain harder. The theatrical absurdity of the gesture was too much for Claire; she began to laugh, closing the kitchen door and leaning against it.

Sally was staring at her, a strange expression of her old-young face. Under that eldritch gaze, Claire sobered quickly. There was something inhuman about that steady, green-eyed regard.

"Let's see about getting you to that hospital," Claire said, trying to regain control of the situation. "And on the way, we can swing by the state police barracks—I can make a report, or you can, and—"

"No," Sally said quickly.

Claire stared at her in worried surprise. *Hay seemed pretty sure you'd be on his side. You aren't—are you?*

"Claire, I—" It was Sally's voice—and it wasn't. As if something inside her skin were playing the *part* of Sally Latimer, feeling out the reactions a young woman would have to the scene she had just witnessed.

"Are you all right, Sally?"

"Oh. Yes. But . . . you'd better go now. I need to rest. Matt won't try anything else now; let's forget him."

She knows I know. The conviction was enough to paralyze Claire for a moment; and suddenly the only important thing seemed to be that she get away and warn Colin what was going on here. Whatever transformation had begun last night was complete now, and Claire had no power to undo it.

"After all . . . there's no law against practicing witchcraft, is there?" Sally said, but it was not Sally who gazed out through those cat-green eyes. It was *Sara*—Witch-Sara, High Priestess of the Church of the Antique Rite, and Matthew Hay's partner in damnation.

"We're too late," Claire told Colin simply as they sat drinking coffee at the only diner in Arkham. "Whatever it is, it's got her—and I'm afraid that Rowan may be next."

She'd come straight to Arkham after leaving the Latimer house, hurrying to find Colin and tell him the evil news. Only Colin stood between the Antique Rite and the destruction of those whom Claire held dear; though Colin had never confided in her completely, Claire *knew* this as surely as she knew her own name.

To protect and to serve: that was Colin's burden in this life, just as it was her own, but Colin's power had been secured with oaths and promises that

Claire had not made. Often before she had blessed the freedom that this gave her simply to meddle, knowing that whatever she did it was a part of that Great Design mandated by the Architects of that Path which they all walked.

Colin did not have the same freedom. He had taken full responsibility for each of his actions in this life, and that promise bound him not to meddle in the affairs of those he called the Unawakened except by their own request. At the moment she wished that were not so: she could not remember ever before feeling quite so helpless as she did in the face of the sheer nastiness going on out at Witch Hill.

"It's never too late, Claire," Colin told her firmly. "I know that sounds like the worst sort of cliché, but it's true. While this isn't at all pleasant for Sally, she isn't in any real danger yet."

"How can you *say* that?" Claire burst out, frightened and troubled. "She told me what happened last night—while she still could—and Rowan's being drawn into it as well! And if you'd only seen Matthew Hay up there, strutting and gloating like a randy he-goat!"

Colin raised his hand to silence her. "I didn't say that Sally—or Sara, I suppose we should call her now—was *enjoying* this. But if we can drive Witch-Sara back where she came from—I suppose psychologists would call it the collective unconscious, or some such idiocy—she'll leave no lasting marks on Sally. And after a while, Sally won't even remember what she did while she was overshadowed."

"But others will—and she'll have to live her life with that. And what if we can't drive her out?" Claire demanded. "What then?"

"Claire, even if Sara's managed to take over Sally, her grip on existence won't be secure until she's been reunited with the Antique Rite as well. That involves a special ceremony, and they won't be doing that until the next of their Greater Sabbats, August first."

"And until then?" Claire snapped. "Even if Sally isn't responsible—"

"In some sense she *is* responsible," Colin said austerely, "and if this is the path she has chosen to expiation, neither you nor I have the right to take her penance from her. If we move against the cult at the right moment, we can destroy them with one stroke. Fail now—out of misplaced compassion for Sally—and who knows when the next opportunity might be? That's worth the risk."

Claire stared at Colin. Though he'd killed men before her very eyes, she could not remember ever hearing him sound so ruthless before.

"And Rowan?" she said evenly.

"No harm will come to Rowan, Claire—I swear it. I don't think Hay has any immediate interest in anything beyond getting Sara back, but I'll go and pay a call on him just to be sure. I need to get myself invited to his Lammas Sabbat, anyway—not that it should be particularly difficult."

"You're going to *go?*" Claire said in disbelief.

Colin smiled grimly. "I wouldn't miss it for the world."

TWENTY-THREE

WITCH HILL, MASSACHUSETTS, SATURDAY, MAY 19, 1990

And thou—what needest with thy tribe's black tents
Who hast the red pavilion of my heart?
— FRANCIS THOMPSON

THOUGH MADISON CORNERS WAS ONLY ABOUT ELEVEN MILES FROM Arkham as the crow flew, it was a thirty- to forty-five-minute drive along the rutted, twisting, one-and-a-half-lane road which was the only route through this lost corner of Eastern Massachusetts. Colin babied his Chevrolet Citation carefully along the crown of the road wherever possible; he had no desire to end up in a ditch and have to be towed out by a local farmer and his team.

To Colin's great relief, Claire had reported that Rowan's sleepwalking had stopped with the Esbat. He did not think there would be any more trouble until Lammastide. And on that night, one way or another, the problem of Matthew Hay and his loathsome church would be settled, once and for all.

Ten years ago—or even five—Colin might have chosen another method of battle than this cat-and-mouse waiting that distressed Claire so. But the power that such an action would require was no longer Colin's to wield. His share of that power and glory had been expended in the struggle which had reclaimed Simon Anstey's soul for the Light, and he was beginning to worry that he might lack the physical stamina needed to carry out even the subtler plan he had devised. He never felt as if he could quite catch his breath these days, though so far he had kept anyone from noticing.

But Nathaniel had sent him after the Antique Rite precisely because mere strength would not serve to win this battle. More than scattering the coven— which any Lightworker might have done at any time—Colin must discover what ties they had to others who worked in the shadow.

What was that bumper sticker he'd seen? *"Old age and treachery will overcome youth and skill."* Colin supposed that on this occasion it was entirely apposite, but somehow knowing that didn't make him feel any better. Today's activities would not tax him, though; they were no more than the opening clash of sabers in a duel to the death—a reconnaissance of sorts.

For matters were often not what they seemed. . . .

Madison Corners, while technically a town, was actually a widespread farm community clustered loosely around the old Latimer place up at the top of Witch Hill Road. Colin drove by the turnoff, past the Whitfield farm and down to the crossroads, where he turned left and drove until he picked up Witch Hill Road at the other end.

It was barely a lane here, unpaved and deeply rutted. Colin drove slowly up the hill, past the Hay house—an ornate Gothic monstrosity, relic of better days in this part of Massachusetts—and on to the graveyard and the ruined church beyond. Parking his car carefully on the driest patch of ground he could find, Colin climbed out and looked around.

Both the graveyard and the church had already been forgotten by any respectable denomination in the days when Massachusetts was still a colony of the English crown. But whatever congregation had built this structure had built it to last, and the stones still endured.

Colin moved slowly into the old graveyard. Rag-poppets hung from the trees, and food offerings were placed on the ancient graves, indications of a wholesome paganism which had long since mutated into something darker, a sick and inbred obsession with sex and death rather than the benevolent celebration of life and love perpetuated by the Hidden Children of the Wicca. Colin stretched forth his Adept's senses, seeking for those traces of that which even Claire's Gift would not be able to uncover: the architecture of sorcery.

Despite the warmth of the spring sunshine, Colin shivered. Yes . . . it was here. The layers of intention reverberated like the echoes of martial music from the bronze lych-gate outside the church, indication enough that the structure was still in use. Cautiously, Colin touched the time-corroded bronze—odd, that the archway should be made of metal, instead of the more common wood or stone—and drew back quickly. It was not that the power of this place was so very great, but what there was, was *unclean.* . . .

"Can I help you?" a voice called from behind him.

Colin smiled to himself, turning away from the gate. As he'd hoped and expected, Matthew Hay was striding across the graveyard toward him, his long black frock coat flapping around him like a crow's wings. Hay looked like an Angel of Judgment from an avant-garde Western.

"Perhaps," Colin said. "I'm interested in certain . . . antiquities."

Hay stopped in front of him. Colin was not a short man by any reckoning, but even he had to look up into Hay's china-pale eyes.

"If you're looking for antique stores," Hay said, "you'll find more of what you're looking for back to Arkham. This is private property, and I'm sorry, but we don't allow rubbings to be taken of the gravestones."

Considering what's carved on some of them, I'm not surprised, Colin thought to himself. "Am I addressing Matthew Hay?" Colin asked, "direct descendant of the Reverend Lemuel Hay?"

Hay looked suspicious, as anyone might. "And who are you?" he demanded ungraciously, not answering Colin's question.

"One who has traveled far," Colin answered cryptically. If he was going to convince Matthew Hay that he was a visiting Adept of his own black stripe without Hay detecting the charade, he would have to use all the finesse learned in decades of deception.

Hay looked sharply at Colin when he gave that oblique answer, and when he spoke again his words were freighted with intent.

"And what is it that you seek, traveling so far?"

"Some travel East, seeking Light. Others do not," Colin answered. It was no lie—he had not said which he sought. But as he had hoped, Hay took his words at face value.

"Welcome—brother," Hay said formally. "What makes you seek us out?"

"I do not come at my own bidding," Colin answered, taking the high-flown tack that Hay seemed to expect, "but have been sent by another, to whom word has come of you."

"And your name?" Hay asked, his natural suspicion reasserting itself. "You already seem to know mine."

"Colin MacLaren."

"I know you." Hay's eyes narrowed. "You're that lecturer fella they've got down at Miskatonic. You're here talking about folklore."

The way Matthew Hay pronounced the word, it was synonymous with "nonsense."

"Some call it folklore," Colin agreed. "But others know that many forgotten truths live on as folklore. 'That is not dead which can eternal lie . . . and with strange eons, even Death may die.' *Af baraldim Azathoth! Ad baraldim asdo galoth Azathoth! Iä Cthulhu fthagn!*"

"Aye," said Matthew, grudgingly impressed. "Go on."

"It's well known in certain circles that the worship of Great Cthulhu and the gods of antediluvian days was preserved here by families who sailed to the New World with certain books in their possession—books like the *Necronomicon, Die Vermis Mysteriis, Les Cultes des Goules* . . . all wellsprings of the elder knowledge handed down by the great Adepts," Colin said.

Hay did not even blink at the intermingling of real and imaginary texts, bolstering Colin's initial guess that the Antique Rite, though still dangerous, was far from being the threat it once had been. Generations of transmission through unsophisticated farm folk had done their work, and Hay and his coven no longer precisely understood what it was they did here at the old church . . . dangerous though their actions remained.

"And you've come to learn from us?" Hay asked, half disbelieving.

"I have come a long way to learn what you are," Colin answered truthfully.

* * *

After he left Hay—it had been easy enough to gain the invitation he sought, along with confirmation of the time and date of the Sabbat—Colin drove slowly back down Witch Hill Road.

His chest ached, and there was a coppery taste in his mouth. Hay's church was a dedicated place of power whose orientation made Colin physically ill, and Claire, he suspected, would not be able to pass the threshold of the building at all. Fortunately, Colin was no psychic. All his plans hinged on that fact.

As he drove past the Latimer House, Colin decided, almost on an impulse, to stop there. *I need to see what Sally knows—and see if Claire was right in her interpretation of what she saw. If Witch-Sara is indeed back for good—or maybe I should say "for ill"?*

And if she is, will she betray us to Hay? It's a long way to August—almost six weeks. He might buy my story that we shouldn't be seen together until the date of the Sabbat itself, but that's still a lot of time in which to keep this masquerade in one piece. Especially if Witch-Sara tells him what Sally knows. . . .

Colin was prepared for anything but the sight that greeted him. Claire had been both clinical and specific in her description of Sally's raddled appearance the day after the Esbat, but the young woman standing in the doorway looked sleek and almost pampered. Her wavy red hair was pinned up in a neat bun with a set of silver-headed pins, and a pair of antique earrings Colin had never seen before glittered in her ears. She was dressed in a time-softened chambray shirt and overalls, and the dirt-smudged knees of the overalls testified that she'd been working out in the herb garden.

But Sally Latimer was—had been—a proper urban child, and Colin had never suspected her of the least interest in gardening.

"Dr. MacLaren!" Sally said cheerfully. "Won't you come in?"

And she had never called him "Dr. MacLaren" in her life.

"You're looking well, Sally," Colin said, stepping over the threshold into the kitchen. A large ginger-colored tomcat followed him inside.

"And this is Barnabas, I see," Colin said, stooping to extend a hand toward the cat.

"*That* is Ginger Tom," Sally corrected him crisply, and then, in an obvious attempt to be more . . . welcoming? said: "I've been working in the garden all morning and I was just about to put on the kettle. Would you care to join me in a cup?"

"I'd be delighted," Colin said, straightening.

Sally waved him over to the table; Colin sat down and looked around.

Claire had said the kitchen was filthy, but everything that Colin could see gleamed with rigorous cleaning. Several batches of herbs were hung from the rafters, suspended upside-down to dry. All in all, it looked as if Sally had made herself quite at home here.

Only I don't think it's Sally, somehow.

"How's the painting going?" he asked.

"Oh, I haven't had much time for that," Sally said airily. "Plenty of work to do in the garden, and spring all but flown. T'will be many a long year before t'is back in good order, I fear me."

No, this proud woman with the poise and carriage of a queen was not the young girl he knew, but an adversary far more potentially dangerous. Witch-Sara of Witch Hill, through life after life for more than three centuries, High Priestess of the Church of the Antique Rite.

It was only a few minutes before the tea was ready. Sally brought the old stoneware pot to a table already set with cups and a large plate of homemade sugar cookies.

"Let me pour," Colin said, filling both their cups.

"What brings you all the way out here?" Sally asked. "This is pretty far from Arkham—I'm surprised you didn't end up in a ditch."

"Oh, I've been paying a social call on Matthew Hay," Colin said lightly.

Sally's eyes flashed green as she looked up quickly. "Why?" she demanded sharply.

"Now, Sally, you know I'm interested in folklore . . . and your Mr. Hay seems to be a goldmine of it. In fact, I've gotten myself invited to your local Sabbat," he added.

While he must walk softly, it was also important to discover where her loyalties lay . . . if anywhere but with herself. He took a cookie and bit into it fearlessly; whatever else might happen in this house, he didn't think Witch-Sara would poison him. A dead body—or a disappearance—would bring far too much attention down on Madison Corners.

"So you'll be at his Sabbat?" she asked. He could tell that the woman opposite him was startled, in a way that Sally Latimer would not have been.

"I wouldn't miss it for anything," Colin said equitably.

He watched with great—though concealed—interest as the woman he knew as Sally Latimer struggled with herself for several seconds.

"Don't underestimate Matthew Hay, Dr. MacLaren," she said in a low voice. He thought he could see Sally Latimer, drowning there in the depths of Witch-Sara's green eyes, and his heart ached for the struggle she faced. It was a struggle she had chosen before this life, but one she was doomed to lose—unless he could help her.

"Believe me, Sally, I don't underestimate him," Colin said grimly. He could tell that she was anxious for him to be gone, and Colin felt he'd learned all he could at Witch Hill this day. After a few minutes more he took his leave.

But he'd be back.

June vanished in a haze of summer heat, and July followed after. Colin finished up his lecture term but stayed on, poking into odd archives here and there or simply keeping up his voluminous correspondence. He was a frequent guest at the Moorcock Farm, but despite the fact that he came to know both Clarence and Justin Moorcock well, Rowan remained curiously elusive.

She was close to the age his own students had been, and Colin had always prided himself on his rapport with the young. It was not that the girl was in the throes of one of those adolescent nervestorms in which every adult was the enemy—in fact, it was impossible to associate such a mood with Rowan, who approached every person and situation with the bumptious effusiveness of a Saint Bernard puppy. It was something more, something that Colin only noticed because he was watching her so carefully for any sign that she had become entangled with the Church of the Antique Rite. She seemed indifferent where she ought to be curious, serene where she ought to be concerned. But if she were acting a part to mislead him, Rowan Moorcock was the best actress Colin had ever seen.

No, he could not impute any corrupt impetus to her behavior, and Colin finally decided that if there were a mystery here, it was not one he was meant to unravel. But he still wondered about it in idle moments, and so was more than happy to accept Claire's invitation to drive down to Glastonbury with her and Rowan.

Rowan would be starting school here in September, and with the worsening situation in Madison Corners, Claire and Justin had decided that she should come early. Claire had friends that Rowan could stay with until the dorms opened.

If Rowan had objections to being swept out of the way in this fashion, Colin had not been privy to them. He thought the relocation was an elegant solution. And in any event, it was an excuse for Colin to check a few things at the Taghkanic library.

And to visit old friends.

Though it was almost ten years since he'd last been here, the Taghkanic campus seemed untouched by the passage of time. Colin felt a pang of homesickness for the place that held so many happy memories.

He dropped Claire and Rowan off at Administration—Claire intended to introduce Rowan to a few of her old friends on the faculty and give her an early tour of the campus before settling in—and took a moment to stop in and say hello to Eden. Taghkanic's distinguished president also seemed unchanged by the passage of time; she greeted Colin warmly, and for a moment or two they talked about old times.

"So what brings you back to us, especially at this time of year? I suppose it's too much to hope that you're staying long enough to take a few lectures?" Eden asked hopefully.

"Not this year," Colin said with regret. "I actually came to have a look over the library. I'm lecturing up at Miskatonic, and they had a break-in last month and are missing several books from the locked shelves, including one I need to consult."

"I'm sorry to hear that," Eden said. "Book thieves are a major problem for libraries, especially those with rare book collections—as we know to our cost. But please, make yourself at home. And of course you'll stop by the institute—Miles would never forgive you if you didn't stop in and see him."

* * *

"Colin! You old fraud," Viv Aillard said. "Come back to see how the inmates are doing?"

Now well into her fifties, Vivianne Aillard's once-flaming red hair had turned the color of cinnamon-sugar. She took Colin's arm and walked with him back into the office area of the institute.

"I thought I might—since I was in the area," Colin answered, smiling.

"After the way you deserted us, I wonder that you had the nerve," she shot back teasingly. "But you left us some good people—Dylan! Come see Colin!"

Dylan Palmer leaned out of his office, his boyish open face breaking into a grin as he saw Colin. "Professor MacLaren!" he said.

"Please," Colin said. "I'm a private citizen, now. Hello, Dylan. How do you find life after grad school?"

"I'm enjoying it," Dylan admitted. "And I think my students are surviving my efforts."

Dylan Palmer had been heading toward a career in parapsychology when Colin had been director of the Bidney Institute—he'd been a classmate of Hunter Greyson's—and Colin was glad to see that the young man had pursued his dream.

"Colin!" Miles said, coming out of his office. "Eden just called. What brings you eastward? I hope you're planning to come back to us."

"'Fraid not. I'm up at Miskatonic doing a series of lectures on folklore. I'm pretty well fixed out in SF, but sometimes a change of scene is nice," Colin said. Miles Godwin had been his handpicked successor, and seeing the institute flourishing under his guidance eased any lingering sense of guilt Colin might have had—and it was very small—about leaving the institute to devote his time to Simon Anstey and the Bay Area occult community.

"You ought to come to some place that *has* scenery, then," Miles said jokingly.

"Miskatonic?" Viv Aillard asked. "Isn't that the little cow-college in Arkham? That whole area's haunted," she added with envious relish.

"That's part of the reason I'm there," Colin said. "Most ghost tales are just campfire yarns, but here and there there's a grain of truth that's worth pursuing. Besides, Claire's got relatives in Madison Corners that she hasn't seen in years—she has a young cousin making the rounds here today."

"Well, we'll look forward to seeing her around the institute," Miles said, making the obvious assumption.

The impromptu visit soon degenerated into a sort of a party. Everyone was eager to tell Colin all the campus gossip, not that it had changed much.

"Betram had his eyes on the prize last week—he really thought his TK was going to be able to cut it," someone said.

"With Bertie around, who needs a fifth column?" someone else replied, in reference to the one-million-dollar prize that still remained unclaimed more than half a century since the institute's founding.

"Well, Devant and Lovelock nailed him good—he's had to take a week of vacation to recover."

There was general laughter. Colin raised his eyebrows interrogatively at Miles. He was glad to see that Miles had such a good working relationship with his staff, since parapsychologists, Colin knew from experience, were inclined to be as temperamental as opera singers.

"Kit Lovelock, one of our researchers," Miles explained.

"I can't stand her," Viv said scornfully. "We might as well have the Amazing Randi on the payroll!"

"We *do* have the Amazing Randi on the payroll," Dylan pointed out amiably. "Only his name's Mask Devant."

"Sneaking a—a—a *magician* in when Bertie was working with Hans—it's a complete violation of trust!" Viv went on.

"Considering that Hans was as bogus as a three-dollar bill," a new voice said coldly, "I think it was just as well that we nailed him now, instead of after several hundred expensive hours of test runs."

Colin turned toward the woman who had spoken. She was standing beside the coffee urn, her cup in her hand. Despite the fact that he was certain he'd never laid eyes on her before, she seemed oddly familiar.

She had dark hair—cut barely long enough to keep from looking mannish—and was severely dressed in a navy pinstripe "dress for success" suit that made her look older than her years. Though Colin knew little about fashion, he felt that this might have been the effect she was striving for, since she looked quite young—probably fresh out of college.

"Colin, you haven't met the newest member of the institute," Miles said. "She's a rather solitary soul, but her work is excellent. Came to us directly from Harvard, and we're lucky to have her. Truth, this is Dr. Colin MacLaren, the former director of the institute. Colin, this is Truth Jourdemayne, our statistical parapsychologist."

Truth smiled—with much the wary expression that one might expect from one who was being introduced by her employer to an illustrious stranger.

So that was the reason for that haunting familiarity! Colin got to his feet.

"Truth Jourdemayne," he said warmly. "I knew your parents. Your father would be proud to see that you've chosen to follow in the family tradition."

Suddenly Colin had the sense that he'd said something terribly wrong. Out of the corner of his eye he saw Dylan wince and cover his face.

Colin had respected Caroline Jourdemayne's wishes that all of Thorne Blackburn's friends and associates stay clear of her and her niece, but it had never occurred to him until this moment that she might not have told Truth who Truth's father was.

"Thorne Blackburn," Truth said, in a voice like breaking glass. "I'm afraid you've been misinformed, Dr. MacLaren. Thorne Blackburn has been dead since 1969. He couldn't possibly have anything to do with my life or my choices."

There was a pause, as if Truth was aware that she'd backed herself into an undiplomatic corner but wasn't sure how to get out. "It was very nice to meet you, but I'm afraid I'm swamped with work." She turned and walked off, her empty cup still in her hand, and a few seconds later Colin heard a door shut firmly.

"Truth is . . . a little sensitive on the subject of Thorne Blackburn," Miles said into the silence.

"'A little' doesn't begin to cover it," Colin heard Dylan mutter.

"I'm sorry to have raised such a painful subject, in that case," Colin said, and the moment passed off.

But despite the leisurely air of things at the institute it was still a work day for the staff, and soon they drifted away—Dylan to teach an afternoon class, Viv to get her notes in order for her trip to the institute's sister organization on the Isle of Man, and the others to pursuits of their own.

Miles walked Colin to his car.

"I'd like to apologize again for saying the wrong thing to Ms. Jourde-mayne," Colin said, opening the door of his little rental coupe. "It only occurred to me after I'd spoken that Caro might not have told her much about her father."

Miles waved the apology aside.

"Apparently she didn't know much about Blackburn when she decided to become a parapsychologist, and of course, as his daughter she attracts the usual lunatic fringe; Blackburn *was* an important figure in twentieth-century occultism, and separating occultism and parapsychology in the public mind is difficult at the best of times. It's a bit of an awkward situation for her."

"I understand," Colin said. "Best of luck to her, then."

"And to you," Miles said. "Don't wait so long to visit next time—and perhaps we can snag you for a lecture series sometime."

"I'll look forward to it," Colin promised. "Why don't I give you a call in a few months, once I'm back in the Bay Area?"

"I'll be expecting it," Miles promised.

The meeting with Truth was an unsettlingly tangible reminder of how time was passing. That terrible night at Shadow's Gate did not seem that long ago, yet Thorne's daughter had been barely two years old then and she was a grown woman now. A generation had passed; time enough for men and women to grow to adulthood for whom the decade of the sixties belonged to that vast prehistory of the time before their birth.

The sense that time was passing—was running out, leaving him with many things undone—stayed with Colin even after he and Claire took the train back to Massachusetts. The days were dwindling toward the Sabbat, and soon the Antique Rite would act to anchor the ancient soul of Witch-Sara in the body of her descendant once and for all.

But Colin and Claire had, themselves, been far from idle.

It was just before dawn on the last day of July when Colin and Claire came walking up the hill toward the graveyard. Over his shoulder Colin carried an old battered canvas bag, grey with age and use; a bag such as plumbers carried their tools in. Claire carried nothing at all. They had left the Chevy parked at the edge of the road a mile away, not wanting to awaken either Sara or Matthew with the sound of the car's engine. But tonight was the night of the Great Sabbat, and there were many things Colin needed to do before then.

"Pheugh," Claire said softly, as they reached the edge of the graveyard. The tumuli and broken stones were barely visible in the cold predawn light. "This stinks."

She looked down at her stout walking shoes, as if expecting to see them covered in garbage.

"I'm afraid it only gets worse before it gets better."

Colin sketched a quick Sign in the air—his fingers tingled numbly—and they went on, picking their way carefully in the dark. Colin paused at each of the trees and gravestones they passed to Seal them, and as he did, he became aware of an increasing dull ache in his chest that tingled down his arm. He put it down to exhaustion, but he could not stop now. They must be done and gone from here before it was full day.

"Won't Hay notice what you've done?" Claire asked. "I've been watching the rest of the coven members, and they don't seem to have the power among them to light a candle with a box of kitchen matches, but Hay's got something."

"Agreed. But it isn't as much as he thinks it is," Colin said. "I'd say that the Antique Rite's been riding on its reputation since his grandfather's time, at least. And my bet is, Hay's going to be focusing on Sally and Brian tonight, rather than on the magic."

Brian Standish was the weak link in the resurrection of Witch-Sara. Brian was Sally Latimer's lover, not Sara's, and Sally's anchor to the human world of light and sanity. Colin had always known that the coven would need to destroy Brian in order to ensure Witch-Sara's ascendancy, and in fact—so Claire had heard from her uncle—there had even been a suspicious "accident" involving the brakes on Brian's car. But for the last several weeks it seemed that Sally had been protecting him from Hay and the coven, finally even going to the extent of driving Brian away by allowing him to catch her in bed with Matthew Hay and Tabitha Whitfield. The young doctor had been heartbroken—country gossip was both far-reaching and precise—but though Brian had avoided her since then, Colin had known that Hay's monstrous ego would not allow Brian to escape that easily.

And he had not.

"Wouldn't just arresting all of them do as much good as seeing this through to the ritual? They kidnapped Brian—he can swear to that," Claire said, glancing up toward the Hay house. There was a light on in the kitchen—country people kept country hours.

"Swearing's one thing, but proof is quite another," Colin reminded her. "It would be his word against Hay's, and I'm sure Hay has a lot of people who would be happy to swear that Brian came to his house perfectly freely. Besides, stopping the coven's Lammas ritual won't do a lot to help Sally—or Brian."

"I'm not sure I like Brian being dragged into all this, though," Claire grumbled.

"I'm not wild about it myself. Undoubtedly Sally bargained with Hay to leave Brian alone in exchange for renouncing him. But Hay can't afford to leave Brian alive if he's to get Sara back."

"So Hay goes back on his bargain and Brian becomes the human sacrifice *du jour*," Claire muttered.

"I doubt Sally knows about that—that's the point. And at any rate, Hay's plans for him will ensure that Brian remains alive and well—if not very comfortable—until tonight. We don't dare tip our hand by rescuing him, not if we're to save Sally too. Now, here's the lychgate. It made *me* uneasy, so be careful."

Claire stopped a few feet short of the corroded bronze archway—no more than a dark shape in the dimness—and closed her eyes to concentrate. Almost at once she winced and staggered back, throwing up a hand to protect herself. The tiny gold cross at her throat glinted.

"Yes," she said unsteadily. "It's bad. You'll need to haul out the big guns."

Colin set down his bag and withdrew a pyx and a small vial of anointing oil. Murmuring prayers, he anointed the bronze gateway at several places. The metal was unpleasantly warm, though the sun was no more than a line of gold upon the horizon.

Though Colin was not himself a Catholic, these objects had been symbols of the Light for almost two millennia and were still the object of reverence for the peoples of half the world. He had a dispensation to possess and to use them, ensuring that these tokens were at their most potent.

Corrosion seemed to spread through the metal at the points Colin had touched with the holy oil. Opening the pyx, he removed a Consecrated Host and touched it to the four places on the archway he had previously anointed before breaking it in half and burying the pieces at the base of the archway. There was a sharp break in the atmosphere of the place, as though the air pressure had suddenly dropped.

"Better now?" Colin asked.

"Yes," Claire answered wanly. "But I'm not looking forward to the church."

It was bad, as Claire had predicted. Using Claire as a spotter, Colin soon ringed the inside of the building with fragments of the Consecrated Host, making a holy barrier against the Shadow.

The stone floor had once been carefully inlaid in a chessboard pattern, just as the floor of all Templar churches were, though time had faded the blocks to only vaguely dissimilar greys instead of their original stark black and white. The walls were carved with the cryptic symbols of a faith far older than Christianity. Fortunately the ornate carving inside the ancient church made it possible to conceal their meddling, and inside the building they could risk using the lantern.

"Anything else?" Colin asked, after the circuit was complete.

"That," Claire said, pointing toward the Black Altar.

Colin advanced upon it, walking warily. It was about three feet high and looked almost like an altar in a conventional church. That similarity was only illusion. The Black Altar was a shaped outcropping of the native bedrock, and in fact the whole church had been built around it.

Though he could anoint it, there was no place near it to conceal any of the more potent items in his arsenal. But as Colin looked closely, he could see that one of the paving stones around the back was loose; the mortar that held it flush with the altar eaten away by time.

"Claire, give me a hand with this. There's a crowbar in the bag."

Working together, they managed to lever the stone halfway out of its bed. Colin was gasping for breath when they were done, and his pulse was a thunderous redness behind his eyes.

"Colin—are you all right?" Claire asked, worried.

"Yes, of course. Never mind me now, we have work to do," he answered shortly.

As Claire kept the tension on the bar, Colin scraped a small hole in the aged dirt beneath the stone and placed an unbroken Host there. Then he reached into his bag and removed one last item: a delicate gold rosary that Father Adalhard Godwin had given him just before he died.

"Save it for a real emergency, Colin, my boy. I'll trust you to know one," the old priest had said.

Colin kissed the symbol of the One whom his Order revered as a fellow Master of their Craft, and placed the rosary against the ground as well. Then he and Claire lowered the stone back into place, and Claire brushed dirt over it until the evidence of their tampering was hidden. Colin knelt beside her, struggling to regain his breath. His chest felt as if there were an iron band about it, crushing away his strength. He wasn't looking forward to the hike back to the car.

Not as young as I used to be, I suppose. But young enough.

"I'd offer to call a doctor, but the only good one in fifty miles is tied up in Matthew Hay's basement," Claire said, covering her worry with a joke. "Colin, are you *sure* you're all right?"

"We can hardly call the whole thing off if I'm not, can we?" Colin said snappishly. He pulled a handkerchief and mopped his face, wiping away the sweat that beaded there. "I'm sorry, Claire. I'm just not feeling quite myself. Tension, I suppose."

"I've never known *you* to get stage fright," Claire said. She bit her lip nervously, obviously deeply concerned.

Well, neither have I, come to that. But we can't *just pack it in and come back later, and this isn't something Claire can handle alone. Thank God Rowan's out of it, at least.*

The first rays of the sun were shining down through the chinks in the old slate roof, and enough light streamed through the open door to make the electric lantern unnecessary. Colin reached out and shut it off.

"How is it now?" he asked Claire, partly to distract her from his distress.

Claire sat back on her heels and closed her eyes. She looked as drawn and weary as he did; the work of both Sensitive and magician exacted its subtle toll from the practitioner.

"Clear," she said at last. "At least I'm pretty sure it is. No longer consecrated by intention, at any rate. When Hay comes here planning to raise up his Dark Forces, he's due for a big surprise." She forced a smile.

"And a bigger one, I hope, than just finding out that his dark gods have deserted him," Colin said. The pain in his chest was finally easing and he could draw a full breath again. He smiled encouragingly at Claire. "C'mon, old girl. Let's get moving before anyone finds we've been meddling here."

Sunset. The ancient church was filled with the twelve men and women who made up the members of the coven itself and the eight who were their acolytes and associates.

How can they not know? How can they not care? Claire wondered in despair as she gazed toward the bound figure upon the Black Altar. She'd told Uncle Clarence nothing more than that she would be staying with friends overnight. He'd been worried enough about her going out on August Eve in the first place to accept her vague tale without comment. Fortunately, neither he nor Justin was in danger, since the family Gift had bypassed both of them. Thank God for Taghkanic College—she did not know what she would have done if she'd had Rowan to protect tonight as well.

From where she stood, Claire could see Brian Standish's eyes glitter with fear and fury, but there was nothing she dared do to let him know that help was near. Twenty men and women had gathered here tonight expecting to see the murder of a human being. This was twentieth-century America, yet they treated tonight's event as though they were going to the movies.

She crowded closer to Colin, trying not to let her distress show. She was huddled inside a too-hot hooded robe borrowed from the Miskatonic Drama department and still felt horribly exposed. When she'd been introduced tonight as Colin's acolyte, she'd been careful to keep her hood well forward, lest Hay recognize her as the woman who'd thrown him out of Sally's house in May. But Hay was far too excited by tonight's ritual to be paying close attention to an insignificant hooded figure accompanying a man he trusted.

Colin stood rock-steady beside her, as impassive as a statue, waiting for the moment to strike. Claire envied him his calm—although perhaps the gun he was carrying had a little to do with it.

It took almost an hour before Hay began the ritual by lighting the incense, adding to the choking summer heat in the crowded space. Sally was not present; she would come later, after the ceremony had begun.

Claire squinted her eyes, trying not to look as Matthew Hay—naked, painted, and masked—made his obeisances to the Great Horned One and the Black Virgin and their lesser devils amid clouds of acrid smoke. After what she and Colin had done this morning, all this was now mere playacting. They had banished the echoes of the Evil that had been done in this place, leaving it inert, bereft of influence. In fact, Hay's posturings would even have been funny, if Hay weren't intending to kill Brian Standish.

Claire did her best not to flinch when Hay lifted a squirming kitten from a basket behind the altar and gutted it as carelessly as another man might open a can of beer. In the dead animal's blood he anointed Brian at the Five Points, and then marked a smeared cross over his heart—no Christian cross this, but a sign of sacrifice, showing the High Priestess where to strike. Claire felt tears gather in her eyes, and took as much comfort as she could from the fact that the poor animal was the last thing that would die at the hands of the Church of the Antique Rite.

Now the congregation began to chant and sway, working themselves into a trance state—not that this was difficult. Claire could smell cannabis mixed with the incense and see smears of grease on several foreheads. She remembered that Sally had mentioned an unguent that the coven members anointed themselves with. Everybody here was already as high as the proverbial kite, and the contact high began to make Claire uncertain of her own perceptions.

At an unspoken signal, the congregation fell silent and began to shuffle backward, opening up a corridor between the altar and the door.

Sally Latimer appeared in the doorway.

No, not Sally. This was Witch-Sara, three hundred years a Priestess and Witch. She stalked—there was no other word for it—slowly toward the Black Altar, wearing a long loose gown of embroidered silk. Hay slipped a black iron knife into her hand, and Sara raised it high over her head.

Claire waited for Colin to produce his gun and stop the ritual, but he did not. She was about to cry out, when the knife came down—but not to kill.

"Run, Brian!" Sally screamed, sounding like herself at last. "Call the cops!"

With a cry, she cut through the single rope that was looped around Brian's body in an elaborate cable-tow. Once the cord was broken, he began struggling free. Sally flung the knife as far from her as she could; Claire heard it ring out as it struck the rock.

Claire wasn't sure what good Sally thought Madison Corners police would be—ten to one, there were a few of them already here—but it was a brave gesture.

"Kill them both!" Hay roared.

Claire could feel his fury, and such was the power of the coven's Horned One over them that his congregation was ready to do murder without a single qualm. But in the moments it took them to rally themselves to do his bidding, Colin stepped forward, drawing his gun at last. As they surged toward the Black Altar, he fired toward the roof.

"Back!" he shouted.

They stopped where they stood, temporarily startled by the gun, and Claire saw Colin reach up to clutch at his chest with his free hand. She started toward him, then stopped as she heard a hideous howling from behind her. She turned, to see Hay advancing upon Brian menacingly, the Black Beast glaring out of the smoke-reddened eyes visible beneath the mask he wore.

But Brian was too furious to reckon the difference in their sizes—he grabbed the heavy carved mask of the Horned One and ripped it from Hay's face . . .

And hit him with it.

The whole thing took only seconds. Hay fell backward, his mouth spraying blood, and hit the corner of the altar with an awful, final sound. By the time he stopped moving, no one in that room had any doubt that he was dead.

Someone screamed. Panic ripped through the room, borne on a wave of psychoactive drugs. Ritual ecstacy was transmuted into the mother of all bad trips in less than a heartbeat. People turned on—or *to*—one another blindly. Brian grabbed Sally in his arms, and Colin turned slowly toward them, gesturing with his gun. His face was grey with pain.

"Come on!" he shouted hoarsely, and began to push through the mob.

I spend too much time in sickrooms, Claire thought sourly. *Thank God it wasn't a stroke—thank God Brian's a doctor—or Colin would be dead now.*

Arkham General Hospital was a small rural hospital without a cardiac care wing; the doctors there had freely confessed that Colin would receive better care in Boston, and plans were being made now to fly him out.

They'd been at the police station, making their statements—carefully edited of anything that would sound impossible to mundane ears—when Colin had fainted. She'd known all day that he was in pain, and the diagnosis, from the symptoms, was pretty obvious. But there had been nothing they could do until Brian and Sally were free, and Claire hadn't realized just how serious Colin's illness was until he collapsed. The first thing Claire had feared was some kind of magickal backlash from the Antique Rite; a simple heart attack seemed wholesome and innocent next to the corruption they had faced together earlier that night. Fortunately he recovered enough to tell Brian his symptoms—and Brian had taken the trouble to retrieve his medical bag on the way to the police station.

"You've got to be on the lookout for this sort of thing when you get to be his age," one of the interns had said offhandedly when they got to the hospital. Colin had been admitted over his protests—Brian had been fiercely insistent—and Claire had stayed with him, watching over him as he slept.

By the next morning, the previous night seemed as much like a dream to Claire as it must to the surviving members of the coven—who were, reasonably enough, also at Arkham General. Matthew Hay was dead, and a woman named Tabitha Whitfield was under heavy sedation, but everyone else would recover in a day or so with no particular ill effects. Sally and Brian had shrugged the whole experience off with surprising speed, but Claire had seen behavior like that before. It was the mind's attempt to cope with something it couldn't understand by simply sweeping it aside. The two of them were already talking about getting married—but it was tacitly understood that Brian would have his rural medical practice somewhere else.

And now I've got to figure out some tactful way to tell Justin that he has nothing more to fear from the local coven.

"Can I come in?"

Claire jerked awake and realized she'd been dozing. Justin Moorcock stood in the doorway.

"Maybe I'd better come out," she answered, and tiptoed past Colin's bed out into the hall.

"It's over, isn't it?" Justin said simply.

"Yes," Claire answered. "I don't think there'll be any more trouble now." She could feel it in the air—though that might be no more than summer sunlight and wishful thinking. "What are you doing here, Justin?"

"Well, Rowan called last night to tell me she thought you were in trouble. You'll say it's silly, but her hunches always seem to be right. I phoned the sheriff's station and the hospital, and figured I was just going to have to drive around until I found you, when the sheriff called back to say that Colin was in the hospital and you were staying with him. So I guess Rowan was wrong, for once."

"Yes and no," Claire said evasively. *There are no secrets in the country,* she reflected. She wondered what story was going around about last night's events, or if everyone would decide simply to pretend nothing had happened. Nearly everyone in this part of the county was related to someone in the coven, after all.

"Is Colin all right? I figured it was better to wait until something closer to visiting hours to stop by, and I didn't want to leave Grandpa alone in the house at night."

Especially considering what might be trying to get in, Claire thought. "I'm glad you came, Justin. Colin . . . well, all the signs have been there for months, and like an utter fool I missed them all. Brian wants to transfer him to a hospital in Boston as soon as possible."

"So you'll be leaving then," Justin said. "We'll miss you. I'll miss you." He hesitated. "Are they all dead? Matthew Hay, and Witch-Sara and all?"

His tone was grave and serious. In his heart, Justin Moorcock believed in monsters. He'd grown up in Madison Corners, after all. He knew that shadows were more tenacious than light.

"Matthew Hay is dead, and I don't think Sally Latimer is going to stay in this part of the country." *Not if she's smart.* "But I'd rather tell the story only once; I'll need to pack up Colin's things and then I'll drive out to the farm and give you both the whole story."

"You'd probably better call Rowan, too," Justin said. "And I wish . . . well, I wish you'd had a better time here."

"Oh, it had its moments," Claire said, smiling.

INTERLUDE #8

AUGUST 1990

COLIN WAS IN THE HOSPITAL FOR SOME MONTHS AFTER THAT—FIRST AT Arkham General, then in Boston, and finally he was allowed to return home to a strict regimen of diet, medicine, and exercise. It seemed only reasonable that he should confine himself now more to the role of consultant, letting younger men and women bear the stress of confrontation with the Unseen.

But the doctors had called him, in simple obliviousness, something I had never before thought of him as being: an old man.

Yes, Colin was not young. He was seventy the year we smashed the Church of the Antique Rite, and had reached his biblical allotment of threescore and ten. But his life had never seemed to me to have anything of a completed quality. Somehow I imagined him still on the threshold of it, his greatest tasks unbegun.

That Colin felt something of the same sense I knew. Even at the end of this long career of service to the Light there was something more he needed to do, and as the shadows of his life's twilight deepened, that undone task preyed upon his mind more and more.

TWENTY-FOUR

SAN FRANCISCO, CALIFORNIA, FRIDAY, OCTOBER 21, 1998

Tears from the depth of some divine despair
Rise in the heart, and gather to the eyes,
In looking on the happy Autumn-fields,
And thinking of the days that are no more.
—ALFRED, LORD TENNYSON

THE YEARS PASS SO QUICKLY NOW, COLIN MACLAREN THOUGHT TO HIMSELF. the October sun warmed his spirit, if not his bones, and though he was expecting company, he lingered on the terrace, unwilling to forsake the sun and the sky so soon.

He was nearly eighty, and even by the most generous possible estimate had already lived far more years than he had left to live. The ebb and flow of world events took on a certain remoteness and inevitability from Colin's hard-won new perspective. The time remaining to him was short, and more and more these days he realized how much he did not wish to leave behind him unfinished business when he left this life: to be called back to the Light with the weight of tasks undone and penances unpaid weighing him down.

Sometimes he wondered how a life could just rush past—it seemed as if he'd only paused for a moment to look back on what he'd already accomplished, and suddenly all his allotted years had fled. Time, as the cliché put it, marched on, and life turned out to be something lived in moments of inattention, while one's thoughts were elsewhere.

The last decade had been filled with milestones, as if even history knew that the Western world was approaching the millennium and wished to get its housekeeping done. Sometimes he wondered what his younger self, unburdened by the weight of experience, would have thought of them. Things he would once have raged against he now accepted as being beyond his power to affect.

Two more wars—they didn't even call them that anymore—and the two Germanies were reunited at last. The war Colin still thought of as "his" war was half a century in the past now, but the peace that should have been established through the Allied victory had never really come—the *Pax Americana* had been a cruel fraud, the full extent of its dishonesty slowly unfolding as the postwar decades passed. And now events had buried even those grave betrayals—and the shining moments of triumph—beneath the weight of sheer incident.

The Soviet Union had dissolved, seventy-five years after its birth, in a move almost completely unexpected by Cold Warriors and Soviet analysts in the West. There'd been new race riots here at home, as terrifying in their way as the Watts riots had been, and this time their violence was broadcast live, thanks to the new flexibility of television. In New York and Oklahoma City, the terrorist bombings that had been a feature of European life for so long finally reached American shores, and television had been there too, broadcasting pictures of the carnage before the first dust had settled.

When he'd made this last relocation—to what the younger generation called a "planned community"—Colin had gotten rid of his television set. He had always mistrusted its false intimacy, and what he saw through its medium had come to sadden him in a deep and inarticulate way. His generation had hoped for so much from television—the electronic global village—and instead television had become an ever-flowing conduit of inanity, of trivial concocted details that Colin found less and less important with each passing day.

Old friends had left him and new friendships were formed. Cassie Chandler had died tragically two years ago in a fire that had gutted the Ancient Mysteries Bookshop. The disaster had somehow seemed to sever Claire's ties to the Bay Area for good. Over the years, her visits back East to her cousin's farm in Massachusetts had slowly become more frequent, and lasted longer, until now her time was divided equally between Glastonbury and Madison Corners, with occasional trips back to the Bay Area. She wrote frequently, always urging Colin to visit the farm, but Colin doubted he would. For now, his work was here.

Caroline Jourdemayne had died in 1995, three years ago this month. A letter had come a few weeks later—written long before her death and left with her lawyer for just this event. She'd asked him to keep watch over her niece, but by the time Colin received Caroline's letter, Truth was far beyond the help that Caroline had intended.

Truth had come to visit him a few months after the letter had reached him. Since he had last seen her, eight years before, she had embraced her father's Path—there was so much of him in her now that it had been quite a wrench to see her again. It was almost as if Thorne Blackburn stood before him once more, with all their old quarrels about Light and Darkness unresolved.

But Colin was no longer the Sword of the Order and had not been for many years. And there must always be change. There must always be someone willing to try that which was perilous, that which had once been forbidden.

Someone to venture into the lands beyond what was known to bring back information from the numinous place where imagination faltered. He was an old man—let him be the one to take the dangerous chance.

When Truth had asked if she could call on him, Colin had welcomed her—even though the life that he had spent in the service of the Light had been spent learning over and over again the harsh and bitter lesson of the dangers of the path of compromise. The worlds he and Truth had been born into were unimaginably different, but their fealty was to Knowledge and Service, however differently defined.

He had been able to do his small part to help Truth Jourdemayne along her path to understanding, but they both knew that her path was not his, nor could it ever be, so long as she held true to the oaths she had sworn. Much of what he had in him to tell was not for her to know, and Colin thought with grave serenity of the disciple to whom he must impart all that he had learned, the disciple he had not found in a lifetime of searching. Colin only hoped the Lords of Light would send someone to him soon, because there was much he must do to prepare for his own final exit.

He felt no fear of that inevitable future day—only a mild curiosity as to the mechanics of the event itself, and the anticipation of meeting old friends once more. But whatever the spirit in which he contemplated it, preparation for his own departure was sometimes a wearying task. There was a lifetime's worth of research and memories to organize; he had donated many of his books and personal papers to the Bidney Institute before his last move, and more were earmarked to go there upon his death.

There would be time enough for that much. He knew it. But why did he feel there was so little time left for what mattered more?

"Colin! I rang the bell but there wasn't any answer, so I thought I'd see if you were around back."

Hunter Greyson pushed through the garden gate, his walking stick in his hand and his laptop slung over his shoulder. He didn't need the cane as much these days—not after nearly two years of rigorous physical therapy—but the fearless recklessness of youth was gone in the accident that had claimed so many years of his life, replaced by the prudence of maturity.

Colin got to his feet and shook Grey's hand. Grey's reentry into Colin's life was one of time's great gifts; the chance to repair, or at least understand, the negligence and missteps of his younger days.

"I was just woolgathering. We'll call it a privilege of age," Colin said, smiling. "How are Winter and the baby?"

"Fine, both of them; Winter says you have to come to dinner again soon, but you already know that. And you've got to see Colleen—you won't believe how she's grown. I can't believe it's only been a year since she was born; she's just so amazing."

"A year—that means Truth and Dylan will be coming up on their first anniversary soon," Colin said.

"December twenty-first," Grey said promptly. "Have to send them a card or something. It's a wonder they haven't killed each other yet, the way they knock heads."

Colin and Grey had both attended the wedding held at Shadow's Gate—Thorne's estate was still a tangled mess, but Truth had finally begun to take steps to be legally declared Thorne Blackburn's daughter. It was at her wedding that Colin had met Grey once more.

"Have you heard from her lately? Is she having any luck with the search?" Colin asked.

At the same time she had taken steps to declare her own legitimacy, Truth had begun to search for her other half-siblings, but the quest for Thorne Blackburn's missing children was a slow business, even in the modern cyberspace world where physical boundaries meant almost as little as they did in the Overlight.

"Not yet," Grey said, shrugging. "Those records are buried pretty deep. Circle of Fire's giving her all the help we can, of course, and so are the other Circles, but . . ." He sighed.

Colin knew—though they rarely discussed it these days—that Grey was still active in the Blackburn Work, doing his best to carry on Thorne's willfully fragmented legacy. It was easier now that cyberspace had become the newest Aquarian frontier; the seekers who had once hunted in vain for their kindred now could form closely-knit communities bound together by phone lines and technology.

"It's just so hard these days," Grey said, sitting down. "Everybody wants a quick fix—become a master shaman in ten easy lessons, that sort of thing. It's hard to find people willing to dedicate themselves to the Work—hell, I hear that even Holy Mother Church is having trouble getting enough nuns for the penguin suits. It's not like it was in the olden days."

"Times change," Colin said. "I know it's the custom now to romanticize the sixties, but they weren't romantic while you were there, believe me. Most of my generation thought that the Communists were going to bomb us back into the Stone Age, and the kids on the streets thought their parents had all become Nazis."

"Yeah, maybe," Grey said, unconvinced. "But at least your generation worried about its problems. Nobody cares about much of anything today except getting by. At least in the sixties everyone knew where the boundaries were."

"Even if they weren't really there," Colin said. "Come on, Grey—there's no use putting it off much longer. The papers will still be there waiting for us, no matter what happens to the world."

They went inside to Colin's office, and for several hours the conversation was entirely about absent correspondents, missing letters, and all the exoteric paraphernalia of a life spent in exploration of the Unseen World. Grey had the training and background to make the work easy, knowing from his own experience what material could go to public collections, what could be donated but must still be restricted, and what should best be destroyed in the absence of a disciple to whom Colin could entrust it.

"That's enough for today," Colin said firmly as the light began to fail. "And Winter will have my head if I tire you out." He sat back on the couch, sighing.

Grey got up and stretched, turning on the lights, and looked down at the day's work.

"Now this deserves a special glass case at the institute," Grey said, picking up the paperweight Alison had given Colin so long ago. "'Whosoever draws this sword is rightwise king of all England' and all that." He slipped the little silver letter opener from its place in the anvil and brandished it a moment before sliding it back and placing the paperweight on the windowsill.

"Not me, though. I'm busy enough as it is. In fact, I meant to tell you, I'm going to have to miss next week," Grey said. "Circle of Fire's getting ready for Samhain; we're going to throw a big whoop-de-do with a bunch of the other Circles, and there's so much work to get done. Permits, licenses, all that kind of thing."

"I hope you have better luck with them than Thorne ever did," Colin answered, and for the first time in many years, the old memories did not bring pain.

Grey only laughed.

Grey had been gone less than ten minutes when the phone rang. Colin picked it up, cutting the answering machine off in midmessage; it was probably just Winter calling, wondering where her husband was.

"Hello?"

"Colin? It's Dylan."

"Dylan," Colin said, glancing at the clock on the sill next to Alison's paperweight. Five o'clock—that meant eight P.M. back in New York; Dylan should be at home. "What can I do for you?"

"Oh, nothing really," Dylan said, so off-handedly that Colin became instantly alert. "I was just . . . you remember Rowan Moorcock, don't you?"

Yes, he remembered Rowan. Claire's cousin had been at Truth's wedding. She'd changed since Colin had first met her, and now seemed to represent the worst of the "bubble-gum occultism" that had come out of the Aquarian Age: the frivolous, superficial approach to the ancient mysteries that Grey had been bemoaning earlier.

"Yes . . ." Colin said slowly. "Is something wrong?"

"Yes. No. That is, I'm not really certain myself," Dylan said slowly.

"That seems to just about cover everything," Colin said, the cold certainty of trouble growing in his stomach with every word Dylan spoke. "But I'm sure you didn't call at this hour just to discuss one of your students." Surely Rowan would have finished at Taghkanic by now? But it was hard to tell with postgraduate studies.

"Well, Rowan's doing her doctoral work here . . ." Dylan said. His very unwillingness to put his fears into words somehow made them seem all the more real. "And with one thing and another, I don't see as much of her now as I used to. I've been pretty busy this summer, what with working on that mess up at Frosthythe and getting Truth off to England to meet the Thornes, and I suppose I just lost track of what she was doing. Rowan, I mean."

Colin waited, half-expecting Dylan to simply hang up; he sounded that much like a man distracted past all sense.

"She's disappeared," Dylan finally said. "I don't know where she is and I think she's in over her head."

"You've mentioned this to her father?" Colin asked.

"What could I do except worry him?" Dylan demanded in frustrated tones. "She hasn't been back to her apartment in a month, she hasn't checked her e-mail . . . what am I supposed to do, Colin?"

"You could start," Colin said, as quietly as possible, "with telling me why you've called me instead of the police."

There was a long silence at the other end of the line.

"Because they won't understand," Dylan said, an impatience like anger in his voice. "I know she's in trouble, but there's no way I could explain it to someone who . . ."

There was another pause; Colin heard Dylan sigh.

"I'd hoped . . . I hope you can tell me where to start looking," he said. "I'm not sure where to begin. Have you ever heard of something called the Thule Group?"

The room grew dim as Dylan spoke. "It was supposed to be a historical research project. In the simplest terms, the Thule Group's supposed to be a German secret society founded in the early twentieth century by Guido von List; Thule is supposed to be the ancient German homeland, and all that. Under Lanz von Liebenfels, von List's successor, there's some evidence that the Thule Group—or *Armanenschaft,* as a number of scholars use the terms almost interchangeably—formed a second order which became the Brownshirts who were instrumental in Hitler's rise to power.

"After the war, of course, all sorts of rumors grew up around it, including the urban folklore that Hitler had himself been a member of one of the Thule Lodges, and that the entire Holocaust had been planned and performed under orders from his occult superiors. Of course, if it ever had existed, it must have been destroyed by Hitler's own purges of the occult Lodges in the thirties and forties," Dylan said.

"I think you know that isn't true, Dylan," Colin said, rousing himself to speech with an effort. There was no point in letting Dylan go on telling him things he already knew far too well out of sheer nerves. "Whatever the Thule Group originally was, it later became a part of the *Ahnenerße,* and it survived the fall of Berlin essentially intact, just as so much of the Nazi power structure did."

Through the connection Colin could almost hear the disbelief, the resistance to what he said.

"That's over fifty years ago. Even if some of them survived, surely they simply disbanded. What was there left for them to work for? They'd lost the war. . . ."

"Sometimes I wonder if that war ever really ended," Colin said, half to himself. "Believe me, Dylan: the Lodge—the original Lodge, the one directly descended from the one List founded—survives today. And it's still fighting for the goals of the Third Reich. Now tell me—how is Rowan involved?"

"Her dissertation topic was *'The Evolution of Trance Mediumship as an Instrument of Nazi Theocracy.'*" Dylan took a deep breath, as if wondering how best to go on.

Colin waited, gripping the phone tightly, as if he thought it might try to get away.

"Well, almost immediately she turned up the contemporary would-be Thulists—the groups that date back to the sixties and later—the mystical branch of the Klan; various kinds of back-engineered neo-Nazi nonsense. And I told her to stay completely away from them. They're nothing but bad news—and more to the point for Rowan's purposes, they're *neo*-Nazi, and have nothing to do with the Third Reich. . . ."

Get on with it, Colin urged mentally, but he could sense that there was information that Dylan could simply not bring himself to reveal over the phone.

"So you told her to drop it. And naturally she did what you said," Colin said neutrally.

But if she had, why would you have called me?

Dylan met him at the small local airport. The drive back to Glastonbury passed in uncharacteristic silence; Colin was occupied with his own thoughts. It was impossible to reconcile the sassy, bouncy, young woman he'd seen at Dylan's wedding last year with someone motivated and willing to go into battle against monsters whose supposed defeat lay half a century in her past.

If, in fact, that had been what she was doing. If she'd taken her work seriously enough to know how dangerous—how real—those monsters could be.

Colin prayed that she understood the stakes of the game she'd been playing. For her own sake.

The apartment was located over a shop in downtown Glastonbury, only a block or two away from Inquire Within. While he was opening the door, Dylan explained—again—that Rowan had left her keys with a student named Val Graves whom she'd hired to look after her plants and bring in her mail. Rowan had paid Val for three months—in advance.

So she intended to disappear. Is that a good sign? I hope to Heaven it is.

Colin looked around the apartment, hoping to find some clue that Dylan had missed. It was a typical student apartment, though Rowan had long since moved out of student housing; the only item that looked as if it had been bought new was the stereo.

The uncurtained window overlooking the street was filled with plants; some hanging, some on shelves. All looked lush and cared-for. Framed posters covered the walls—most of them in the wearily realistic style of modern fantasy art: dragons, knights, tough-looking young women in tattoos and leather. There was a bowlful of multisided dice on the bookcase next to the stereo; Rowan Moorcock, it appeared, was an aficionado of the dice-driven role-playing games that had become most people's modern metaphor for magick and the Unseen World.

Despite the messy disorder of the living room, it did not seem to have been searched. *They haven't backtracked her here, then,* Colin thought. *Or perhaps they didn't need to.*

Dylan was leafing through the pile of unopened mail on the corner of the couch, oblivious to Colin.

"Let's go over it again, Dylan," Colin said. "You told me that Rowan had chosen the *Thule Gesellschaft* for her dissertation topic. Now she's gone. And she didn't say where she was going?" Colin asked. "You've checked with her friends?"

"Nobody knows where she is," Dylan repeated doggedly. "She didn't say anything to Val—the kid she asked to take care of her apartment. Just handed over the money and said she might be in and out."

"What did Truth make of all this?" Colin asked. Though her path was not quite his own, Truth was a magician of considerable power, and her insight would be helpful.

"I haven't told her," Dylan admitted reluctantly. "She's still in England— I don't know what she can do from there and I didn't want to call her back. . . ." Dylan hesitated, his unspoken dilemma plain. Truth might be able to help, but to call her back would be inevitably to involve her in the same danger he feared Rowan had fallen into. But not to call her would be to do less than was possible to save Rowan. He understood Dylan's reluctance far better than Dylan might ever realize—either course of action led to jeopardy, not for himself, but for someone he loved. How could an ethical man choose who to risk?

"Bills . . . checks—she wouldn't have just gone off and left all this stuff." Dylan ran a hand distractedly through his hair. There were dark smudges of sleeplessness beneath his blue eyes.

"Dylan," Colin said, a slight edge to his voice.

Dylan looked up at him, his expression that of a man fighting—and failing—to disbelieve in the fact that something had gone horribly wrong. His shoulders slumped as he surrendered.

"This spring—May? June?—Miles got a string of odd phone calls: people asking questions about Rowan and being very mysterious when he asked questions back. Not just one person, either, but several different people over a period of weeks. He talked to me about it—I even called one of them. He said he was doing a background check on Rowan in connection with an employment interview." Dylan grimaced. If he'd ever believed the unknown man's explanation, he no longer did.

"Do you remember any names?" Colin asked.

Dylan shrugged. "I think I made notes; I'll see if I can dig them up. Of course neither Miles nor I gave out any information, but the whole thing was just weird enough that I braced Rowan with it. She got very upset and admitted that she'd been getting involved with what I gathered at the time were some of the less-savory modern secret societies." Dylan closed his eyes for a moment, and tossed the envelopes back on the couch as if they no longer mattered.

"Colin, I could have strangled her on the spot, I swear it. I demanded that she ditch the Thulists and choose a new topic for her thesis—I swore I'd kick her out of the program, get her blacklisted in the field if she went on meddling with that stuff. She told me she'd gotten in over her head and all that and had learned better. She picked a new subject for her thesis—that's what I thought she'd sent in—but when I read it, it wasn't about trance psychism in nineteenth-century America. It was this."

Dylan opened his briefcase and dropped a thick spiral-bound manuscript onto the couch. This, then, was what Dylan had not been able to bring himself to talk about on the phone, the thing that had frightened him enough to call Colin in.

Colin picked it up. The pages inside the cardboard covers crackled mutely in his hands as if they were erasable bond. Colin opened the front cover and flipped to the first page. The surface was faintly wavy, as if the paper had been damp at some point, and here and there the letters were blurred.

Ultima Thule: The Thousand-Year Reich and the Corruption of the American Dream.

She knows. The cold pain in his chest had nothing to do with physical weakness and everything to do with fear. It was as if his deepest nightmares had been placed into print—and another innocent was poised for sacrifice.

"Not trance psychism," Colin observed evenly.

"I saw that title, and that was when I went looking for Rowan—and didn't find her," Dylan said. "Though I suppose it's just as well—I don't know what I would have done, I was so worried about what she'd gotten into. But I kept looking, and after a while I realized that nobody had seen her for weeks. And then I sat down and read what she'd written—and at that point I panicked and called you."

"Not an unreasonable reaction, all things considered," Colin said. "You're one of the few people alive who know something of the work I did in the forties."

"This is . . . bad," Dylan said inadequately, sitting down on the couch and putting his head in his hands.

Colin looked down at him pityingly for a moment before walking into the tiny kitchen alcove. Something was nagging at the back of his mind; best to try to ignore it and let it surface as it would. Rowan had found her way into the shadow-world of Nazi occultism—and had developed, Colin was starting to believe, a healthy fear of her subject. But she'd persisted in her investigations, and now she was gone.

Where? And was she still alive?

He poked around the kitchen absently. The refrigerator was empty of perishables—a lonely bottle of lemon juice shared the shelves with a jar of pickles and a box of Parmesan cheese. The note from Rowan instructing her apartment-sitter to take the other things away was still stuck to the freezer with a magnet in the shape of a wizard-costumed teddy bear.

She'd had the time to make arrangements to disappear, but the fact that the apartment had not been ransacked worried Colin. If the people she feared were still looking for her, surely they would have come here to try to pick up leads, just as Colin had?

Or was it no longer necessary for them to do so?

Colin opened the freezer, and found it stocked with the usual things one might expect to find in a freezer—no meat, but a wide array of frozen vegetables and grains and a half-finished carton of Breyer's ice cream.

"What are you doing? She isn't hiding in the refrigerator," Dylan said, following him into the kitchen.

"You called me because you wanted my help," Colin said shortly, closing the freezer. "Now let me work."

He sifted the known facts through his mind once more, as if they could produce new information. *She found what she was looking for—the Thule Group. And they found her—checked up on her, either following references she'd given them or backtracking her themselves. She knew they were after her when she decided to disappear. Did she realize how far they were willing to go?*

He had to assume so—and assume, too, that she had not simply fled to the imagined safety of home. The care she had taken to keep her departure a mystery encouraged Colin to believe she had. For if she had not, Claire and Justin were in deadly danger as well.

A cursory examination of the kitchen shelves revealed nothing out of the ordinary, and the bathroom contained nothing that a healthy young woman might not own. Nothing in either room had been disturbed, so far as Colin could tell.

He walked into the bedroom.

The first thing he saw was Rowan's altar in the corner of the room. Four items lay on a white cloth. The water in the offering bowl was long evaporated, the rose petals that had floated on its surface dried to a brown film at the bottom. The matching dish still contained a mixture of rock salt and quartz pebbles, representing alchemical Earth. The only other items on the small table were a covered incense burner and an oil lamp. Hanging over the altar in the aspect of an icon was a framed print of one of the Hubble photos: a glorious nebula, tinged with shades of gold, fuchsia, and vermilion. There was nothing else on, around, or under the altar.

The books in this room were far less innocuous than those in the living room. Colin recognized several titles from his own library: the *Kybalion,* the *Arbatel,* an edition of the *Tesoraria d'Oro.*

A copy of *Mein Kampf.* Colin picked it up, paging through it. The book had been heavily underlined and annotated.

"Is this her handwriting?" Colin asked, handing it to Dylan.

"Yes," Dylan said, barely looking. "Look, Colin, I know I shouldn't have called you. You've got to take it easy these days—Claire would kill me if anything happened to you. But if you have any idea of where I can start look-ing—"

"Not yet," Colin said shortly. The comment about his health—justified as it was—irritated him. His life was not so precious to him that he would choose to preserve it rather than to help where help was needed. All men died in their time.

He sat down on the bed and pulled out the drawer of the file cabinet that served Rowan as a bedside table. The bottom drawer was filled with folders that had names like "World Church of the Creator" and "White Aryan Re-sistance"—all of which apparently indicated dead ends in her research. A folder marked "Thule Society" contained only the familiar—and scanty—historical references from the standard texts, copied and heavily underlined and annotated with Rowan's cryptic marginal notes.

Colin glanced over them. *"Hess a member?"; "Spandau Lodge"; "Templar link—extermination of Freemasons."* He riffled through the rest of the folders in her files, but found nothing that looked useful.

Sanitized. Nothing here, not even the notes for the dissertation she sent Dylan.

Colin sighed, getting to his feet. "You're just lucky she . . ." He stopped as a sudden thought struck him. *You're just lucky she mailed you a copy before it dis-appeared, too. But . . .*

"Dylan, *when* did you get Rowan's dissertation?"

Dylan stared at him as if he were mad, then went back to the living room and brought back the binder. "September fourteenth. I made a note on the ti-tle page."

Colin took the dissertation from him. September 14. Over a month ago. But Dylan, like any other harried professor with too much paperwork, had not thought a dissertation could be such an urgent matter.

Until now.

"And when was the last time anyone saw her?" he asked.

"August," Dylan said slowly. "As far as I can be sure. Between the end of the summer session and the start of Freshmen Orientation."

"So she mailed this a fortnight after she disappeared," Colin said. "About six weeks ago, now." Another thought struck him. "Did you spill anything on it?" He rubbed the title page between his thumb and forefinger, listening to it crackle.

"No. It was like that when it came. It must have gotten damp in the mail. She was lucky I could read it at all; ink-jet printing dissolves when you get it wet. . . ."

Colin walked back into the living room, riffling the pages in his hand. There was something nagging at the back of his mind.

It was only reasonable that Rowan had destroyed her notes and drafts—or hidden them elsewhere—if she'd thought her apartment might be searched. It would keep her hunters guessing about how much, precisely, she knew. But why mail Dylan a copy of her dissertation after she'd already "disappeared"? She had to assume that Dylan was under surveillance as well—in fact, she knew he was, after he'd told her about those phone calls he'd received. But she'd taken the risk anyway. Why? To send him a message?

Old customs, old habits half a century abandoned began to stir in the back of Colin's mind. Tricks of tradecraft that had been carefully instilled in one generation through careful training had become the prime-time entertainment of the next. How many of them had Rowan known, and how many had she used?

"There was no note or anything with it?" Colin asked.

"No," Dylan said slowly. "I was surprised that she'd mailed it instead of dropping it off, of course, but when I saw what it was about I figured she was just trying to stay out of my way until I'd calmed down. By the time I thought to check the postmark or anything like that, the envelope was long gone."

Colin opened the manuscript and turned back the covers. He held up the title page, peering through it toward the light of the living room window. There were lighter marks on the paper, almost like a watermark—but who used erasable, watermarked paper to computer-print a manuscript on?

Dylan watched him uncertainly.

"What is it?"

"I'm not sure yet." Colin sniffed at the page. Did it smell faintly of lemon?

There was a floor lamp standing by the couch; Colin removed the shade and switched it on.

"Oh, come on, Colin, that's a copy of her dissertation!" Dylan burst out. "What are you looking for—secret messages in invisible ink?"

"That's exactly what I'm looking for," Colin told him grimly. Invisible messages, written in an ink any agent—any *person*—could easily buy and legitimately possess: lemon juice. The stuff of old-time spy stories, long since passed into common currency.

Under the heat of the lamp, straggly lines of brown text slowly appeared under the heat of the bulb. They covered the title page, written between the lines of printed text.

"*Dear Dylan. Hope you figure this out. Attached are transcripts and notes. I'm copying everything here and stashing the originals in a safe place—Nin can find the key if he looks around the place and the rest should be obvious. Somebody has to do something, and I guess it's me. I hope you aren't too mad*" the words stopped abruptly, as if she'd meant to write more, and hadn't.

Dylan's face was a study, caught halfway between a sense of the ridiculousness of the situation and real worry at the fear that had caused Rowan to stoop to such a method of sending her message.

"Who's 'Nin'?" Colin asked, handing the page to Dylan. Bringing up the writing on the rest of the manuscript was going to be a long and tedious task; it would be faster to find the originals Rowan mentioned.

"That would be Ninian Bellamy, I guess," Dylan said. "They've worked together on several occasions—they were in the graduate program together—but I wouldn't have said they were close. I suppose I'd better call him. He's still in the area."

Dylan picked up Rowan's phone and dialed a number. It seemed a tacit agreement between them that even if the police were sometime to be called in on this case, there was nothing to find here, no forensic evidence that they could disturb.

From eavesdropping on Dylan's side of the conversation, Colin gathered that Ninian was surprised to hear from Dylan and hadn't known that Rowan was missing.

"He'll be here in about forty minutes," Dylan said, hanging up.

After that, there was nothing to do but wait. Colin was tempted to work on the manuscript, but restrained himself. The writing was safe for now—invisible. There'd be time enough later. Colin leaned back on the couch, closing his eyes. He had not slept well last night, and most of today had been spent traveling. The merciless inelasticity of age reminded him that he did not have the reserves of youth to draw upon; all strength was gone, taken by time, leaving only the skill behind.

But sometimes skill alone was enough, if the skill were great enough. . . .

He must have dozed off, because it seemed to Colin, with the reasonable illogic of dreams, that he was reading Rowan Moorcock's dissertation, and that it held the answers to questions he had puzzled over in vain all through this life. *So this is what it was all for. How simple—and how tragic. . . .*

He was jarred awake by the sound of the doorbell ringing. Colin got slowly to his feet, shaking off the veils of sleep.

"I'll get it," Dylan said, and a moment later, "Hi, Nin."

Ninian Bellamy looked like a tubercular Victorian poet translated into the modern age. He had long straight black hair pulled back into a ponytail, and his skin was the milk-pale color of the Black Celt. His eyes were pale grey under straight black brows, and he wore a dark tweed jacket with a black band-collar shirt buttoned all the way to the throat. As an eccentric touch to his somewhat formal outfit, he wore high-topped Converse sneakers instead of dress shoes.

"Glad you could make it," Dylan said. "How's the dowsing business going?"

"Well enough," Ninian said, shrugging with awkward embarrassment. He did not seem so much hostile as simply confused about the reason for his presence.

"You remember Dr. MacLaren," Dylan said. "Colin, this is Ninian Bellamy, a former student of mine."

"Pleased to meet you," Ninian said formally, though he kept his hands in his pockets.

Colin nodded to himself. If Ninian was making a living as a water-witch—an ancient profession that modern business was willing to employ without understanding it—he undoubtedly had a fairly high degree of psychic potential, and most psychics didn't like to be touched.

"I attended a lecture series of yours a couple of years ago, though you probably won't remember," Ninian said.

"And stayed awake? I'm flattered," Colin said, making a small joke to defuse the gravity of the situation.

"It was interesting," Ninian said, as if by way of explanation. He looked back at Dylan. "You want to tell me why the police aren't here if Ro's been missing for a month?" he asked.

"Because"—Colin answered for Dylan—"we can't prove that anything's happened to her. I think she's in trouble—she left some information about it cached and a note saying you'd have the key to the depository."

"Me?" The young man was obviously startled. "I haven't seen Ro in over a year. *I* wasn't the one who went for a doctorate in forensic psychometry that'd take two extra years."

Colin picked up the bound manuscript containing Rowan's invisible ink message and passed it to Ninian. Ninian stared at it and shook his head, then looked at the other side of the page.

"Thanks a lot, Ro," he muttered, closing the manuscript and handing it back to Colin. "Look, do you mind if I make myself some coffee before I try to figure out what she was thinking—and I use the word in the loosest possible manner. I was up all night trying to find an old sewer line about ninety miles north of here, and I'm sort of bushed. I hate looking for water—it feels like banging on a sore tooth," he added, half to himself.

"The deli's around the corner," Dylan said, but Ninian shook his head.

"I might as well make it here. She owes me coffee, for dragging me out like this."

"You'll have to take it black," Dylan warned. "Val's cleaned out the refrigerator."

Ninian shrugged and walked off into the kitchen, still carrying the sheet of paper. He might not be Rowan's closest friend, but he seemed to know his way around her apartment.

Colin sat down on the couch, prepared to be patient. Ninian wasn't one of his own people; he might not be used to working with the quick decision that Colin preferred. But on this occasion Colin had no choice: he needed everything that Ninian could tell them, however little that might be.

But Rowan must know as well as anyone the strange limitations that bound the use of the psychic gift. How could she expect Ninian to find what an ordinary search could not?

"Yuck," Ninian said comprehensively from the other room.

"What's wrong?" Dylan demanded apprehensively.

"I don't know who put *this* in the freezer, but it's time to throw it out. Ro'd never eat something like that, and it's already melted anyway—see?"

Ninian walked back into the living room, opening the carton of ice cream that Colin had noticed earlier. There was a thick fuzz of ice crystals atop a smooth white surface two inches below the top of the carton—it was as if the ice cream had melted into liquid and then been refrozen.

"Well, toss it, then," Dylan said. "Or put it back in the fridge—we can take it out with us when we leave."

Ninian went back into the kitchen, and the other two heard clattering as he looked around for coffee and sugar.

Invisible ink, Colin thought, still half-drowsy. Boys' Own Paper *cloak and dagger stuff. Why not believe in a literal key as well, hidden somewhere that Ninian would find, once he started looking for it? But he wouldn't come here unless someone found the note and called him—he said himself that he hadn't seen Rowan since he graduated. So someone would have to call him. But if it wasn't someone he trusted, he wouldn't be rummaging around the kitchen. . . .*

Colin got up and walked quickly into the kitchen, an odd expression on his face. Ninian was leaning against the wall, apparently intent on disproving the adage that a watched pot never boils.

"Why wouldn't she eat the ice cream?" Colin asked. "Doesn't she eat ice cream?"

"Not that brand," Ninian said absently. "It's full of additives. She always buys Häagen-Dazs or something like that. That's why I was looking in the freezer. I hate black coffee."

"And you were going to use ice cream in it," Colin said, half to himself, "but only if it was a premium brand. Which is all Rowan Moorcock ever bought."

"That's right." Ninian was watching Colin, an odd expression on his face.

Colin opened the freezer and took out the carton, hefting it in his hands.

"Heavy," he said. Oddly heavy, for a half-full carton of air-puffed ice cream.

. . . but if Dylan found the message, he'd call Ninian, and the first thing Ninian would do would be to make himself coffee. But there wouldn't be any milk, because Rowan told Val to take the milk away. So he'd use the ice cream, the way he often did. . . .

Colin opened the carton, picking up the spoon that Ninian had laid out, and began digging into the ice cream. The spoon penetrated only an inch or so before hitting something hard.

"There's something in here," Colin said aloud, setting the carton into the sink. Reaching for the faucet taps, he turned the hot water on full strength.

The ice cream melted quickly away to reveal a slab of solid ice with something frozen inside, trapped like a fly in amber. Colin levered the ice out of the carton—wincing at the cold—and set it in the sink.

A block of ice, sandwiched between two slabs of ice cream. A ruse that would fool almost any searcher—even one who was tearing the house apart—but not someone who knew Rowan well.

But why such a large slab of ice, if all she needed to hide was a key?

The streaming water slowly melted through the cloudy ice. By now Dylan had come into the kitchen as well, watching the frozen contents of the block slowly appear. When the kettle boiled, Ninian poured the water over the ice, and then rinsed the objects with the tap to cool them.

"A necklace?" Dylan was baffled.

Lying in the sink were a small silver key and a heavy gold chain as thick as a pencil, made of squared-off links that looked vaguely similar to an anchor chain. It held a large pendant, roughly three inches long. Colin picked it up and laid it, faceup, on a square of paper towel to dry.

"It's a crucifix," Dylan said.

"It's broken," Ninian said, reaching out and trying to turn the carved ivory figure right side up. Colin stopped him before he touched it.

"No," Colin said. "Leave it alone. That's the way it was meant to be."

He gazed down at the red-haired, one-eyed figure hanging inverted from an upright cross, the body marked all over its surface with the bleeding rune-symbols.

The three of them returned to the Bidney Institute after that. Ninian had come along. Though Colin really didn't want him involved, there didn't seem to be any real way to discourage the boy.

"This should take care of our secret writing," Dylan said, laying the stack of papers—Rowan's unbound dissertation—on a long table in the lab. "I suppose running the pages through a laser printer might have the same effect, but it'd be a little riskier."

Reaching up, he pulled a rack of lamps into position over it, and switched them on. The table was suddenly bathed in hot orange light.

"Infrared," Dylan said. "From what you've said, this should make Rowan's notes become visible." He took a paper from the top of the pile and lowered the lamps over it. After a few seconds, faint brown writing began to appear.

"Okay," Ninian said, watching the writing darken. "I'd kind of like an explanation. If Ro's fallen into the clutches of the Committee to Reelect the President or some other bizarro cult, I want to know what we're supposed to do about it."

Dylan looked expectantly toward Colin.

Toller Hasloch was dead. He had been dead for more than two decades—since Christmas Day 1972, over a quarter of a century ago. That his perverse, twisted doctrine was still alive was something Colin had never doubted—why, then, was seeing this symbol again such a profound and unwelcome surprise? It did not mean he was alive, Colin told himself, but the certainty he fought felt very much like fear. He took a deep breath.

"I'm going to make a long string of assumptions, which might change once we've read Rowan's dissertation and the notes she concealed in it—and Dylan, if you can remember any of the names of the people who talked to you about her, that would be a great help."

Colin walked over to the table and reluctantly picked up the rune-cross again. It was heavy, ceremonial, made of gold and enameled ivory—an expensive piece of custom jewelry at the very least. The back was plain smooth gold, decorated with a series of shallow holes like a pattern of buckshot or a fragment of a star map.

Who had it belonged to? How had Rowan come to have it, and why had she kept it? Colin turned it over in his hands, but the tiny, tortured figure gave him no answers.

"Rowan began by investigating the historical Thule Group. Somewhere along the way, her investigation shifted to its modern descendant, which to my certain knowledge is still active in this country. As she became aware of the *Thule Gesellschaft,* it also became aware of her, and began investigating her in turn. She's been missing now for about six weeks." The vast empty space of the Bidney Institute's main laboratory seemed to take the words as he spoke them and blot them out, even from memory. Most of the light came from the heat lamps, and their furnace-mouth illumination made the three men look like demons on holiday from Hell.

"We have every reason to believe she's the one who mailed the annotated copy of the dissertation to Dylan a month ago, indicating she was free then."

Ninian shifted uneasily at Colin's choice of words, running a hand over his hair. In the orange light, his expression was difficult to read.

"We have three possibilities open to us. She may still be hiding, she may be a prisoner of the Thulists, or she may already be dead. In any of these scenarios, the police—or, I suppose, the FBI, since this is a kidnapping—will be of no help."

Colin did not mention his conviction, evolved slowly over the decades, that the higher one went in the ranks of the government intelligence community, the more likely it was that any inquiry about the Thule Group would be reported directly to the people Rowan had been investigating—the Thulists themselves. To say such a thing aloud still seemed tantamount to irresponsible paranoia in his mind.

"I can't find her," Ninian said, a little desperately. "You know that, Dylan. That isn't what I do." He covered his eyes with his hand, as if he wanted to blot out everything he was hearing—and thinking.

"For my part—and, I know, for Dylan's—we'd prefer that you simply forgot all about this and went back to your own life," Colin said, though he doubted his words would have any force.

"No," Ninian said reluctantly. "Not if Rowan asked for my help. Space-Nazis from Hell . . . with all due respect, Professor MacLaren." The young man sounded frazzled, as anyone might, having been suddenly presented with such a ludicrous and horrible idea. "It's just . . . There must be something I can do to help besides defrost her freezer."

"There has to be something we can *both* do," Dylan said urgently. "You said you're familiar with the modern group, Colin—how do we find her?"

"I've run into them before," Colin said, staring down at the pendant in his hand. "But I don't want to see any amateurs—any more amateurs—put at risk. If I can find out who to approach—if Rowan is still alive—I think I may be able to arrange for her freedom."

"You?" Dylan said, and Colin could see all his objections as though they were written on his face: *You're a frail old man, Colin, and World War II was a long time ago. She's my student—this is my responsibility—*

"It has to be me," Colin said firmly. "You'll have to agree to that now, Dylan, or I won't help you any further. I've been involved with these people for over fifty years and I can assure you: they have the inclination and the resources to kill for very little reason or none at all with no expectation of discovery. I won't be responsible for feeding any more helpless innocents to that evil."

"I'm hardly a helpless innocent—" Dylan began, but Ninian stopped him, putting a restraining hand on Dylan's arm.

"Let him, Dylan. This is a kind of . . . negotiation, isn't it, Dr. MacLaren? You're saying that they know you. And they don't know Dylan. Right?" Ninian said.

"Something like that," Colin said, grateful for the support, even if it came from such an unexpected source. "Dylan, if you start trying to find Rowan— If they've got her, and you spook them, they might kill her on the spot."

"You said she might already be dead," Dylan said tightly.

"I don't really think so. She would have talked before she died, and they would have come after you," Colin said matter-of-factly. He spoke without realizing how the words sounded, but Dylan's face went white. "See if you can find your notes," Colin told him gently. "Ninian and I will finish developing these pages. Maybe they'll tell us something."

When Dylan was out of earshot, Ninian turned to Colin.

"Do you really think she's still alive?" he asked.

"I think that if she isn't, she died very recently," Colin said. "Because I can't imagine them leaving these things"—he indicated the key and the necklace—"in our hands."

Near midnight local time—but only nine P.M. by Colin's internal clock, still set to West Coast time—he sat in the spare bedroom of the house Dylan and Truth shared, going over the pages of the unbound dissertation. One side of the pages was covered with neat laser-printing, the other in straggly brown handwriting. Colin read both carefully.

Rowan's dissertation was solid, cautious stuff, but the lemon-juice notes were far less so. In them, she covered names, dates, places, that Colin had thought hidden or lost forever—documenting the failed occult ritual that had stranded Hess in England; the secret talks with Dulles that began in Switzerland under the guise of meetings of the BIS, the Bank for International Settlements; the Thule Group's transfer to America. She went on to document ties between the Peronistas, *Colonia Dignitad,* and important members of both American political parties—if even half of what Rowan had written here were published, she'd be defending against libel actions well into the next century, whether it was true or not.

And the picture she painted with her collage of names and dates was worthy of the wildest conspiracy theory.

But haven't conspiracy theories been discounted lately? As if someone—or something—wants to make the whole idea of conspiracies into a joke? So that any conspiracy, no matter how real, is automatically questionable at the moment of its disclosure. . . . Between Watergate and Roswell, nobody even cares what the truth is, anymore. Reflexively, Colin groped for his pipe before remembering—as he always did—that he didn't have it. He'd given it up years ago, at the combined nagging of Claire and his doctor—a pity, as this was what the great detective Sherlock Holmes would certainly have called a "three-pipe problem."

He took off his glasses and fussed with them, polishing the lenses and then settling them back on his nose. Sometimes they proved to be an adequate substitute, giving him something to fiddle with while he gathered his thoughts. He put them back on his nose and peered at the pages on the desk. Not tonight, though. Tonight nothing would help.

His watch beeped, reminding him it was time for his pills. Colin sighed, and rummaged through his bag until he found the bottle. His life was circumscribed by medical advice—the alchemy of Time making him no longer Roland but Don Quixote.

For a moment Colin thought of calling Claire now instead of tomorrow. At least Colin could share his thoughts with someone who could understand the horror and the powerlessness he felt. It was something he would have to do soon—if Rowan had been seized, her family would also be at risk. But Colin dreaded having to tell her—as if ignorance alone could be a shield against whatever evil had taken Rowan.

Evil.

There. He'd said the word, if only to himself. *Evil.*

It was not a fashionable word these days. In a world where children were slaughtered in the dozens, the thousands, by gun and bomb and knife, the word "atrocity" came glibly to people's lips, but somehow the recognition of evil had fallen out of fashion. The horrors of the modern world were bad luck, business as usual, "age-old racial tension," political terrorism, crime . . . but never Evil. It was as if one color in the palette of human understanding had been excised, lest . . . what?

Lest there be hope?

To accept the existence of Evil was to believe in its opposite—to hope, to believe that the Evil could be fought.

As Colin must fight now, though his years were like a persistent weight, and his own destroying angel beat within his chest, always ready to betray him. People spoke of the burden of age without understanding where the cliché had come from. Colin knew age as a thing apart: a constant heaviness sapping the vitality of the man he remembered being. Now the time had come when—though, even with his heart condition, in good health "for his age"—he must plan his days like a master strategist; husbanding his resources, committing his forces with caution, lest he be left, aching and exhausted, his work undone.

He could not afford to leave this work undone.

Colin removed his glasses and rubbed his weary eyes. He didn't doubt any of what Rowan had written in these pages. That was the worst of it. To believe, and to know that honest men did nothing, was an agony greater than any defeat. . . .

He set the manuscript aside and picked up the notes that Dylan had found for him. There wasn't much here, only a name—Caradoc Buckland—and jotted reminders of the questions he'd asked. Good student? Good work record?

Drug use? Hospitalization? Arrests or convictions? Close friends? Family? Outstanding loans? Buckland had said he was calling from Washington D.C., but the location—like the name the man had given—might well be fictitious. It wasn't much to go on.

Deep inside Colin, some fearful part cried out that he was old, he was tired. That he had done enough for any lifetime—won enough victories, made enough sacrifices. That he should be permitted to pass this battle on to a younger man.

One phone call would do it. He would call Nathaniel, tell him what he knew, pass on the blasphemous crucifix, the key, and Rowan's paper. Nathaniel would act. Colin would have done what Dylan needed.

But he would not have done what Dylan had asked of him—or what he knew he must do, even if he were to die in the attempt.

He had been summoned to battle one last time, and though his esoteric armor was gone, he had been armed with a mighty weapon: the knowledge of a secular crime. Properly handled, Rowan's abduction could be used to expose and destroy the exoteric components of this Shadow Lodge—if through nothing more than the credence it lent to her dissertation. Though such an exposure would not be a conclusive victory for the Light, it would be a significant one. And knowing what he knew, Colin might be able to use it to win Rowan's life—if she were still alive.

Nathaniel could not—but Colin might. His enemies knew him of old, and their memories were long.

He sighed, and prepared himself for the battle that would be fought not with strength but with cunning, and with luck. He must check every clue that Rowan had left behind, looking for a place to start. And his soul told him that he must check, as well, to see if —beyond expectation, beyond sense—Toller Hasloch had somehow survived.

Perhaps, in an odd way, the thought gave Colin hope. If Hasloch were somehow alive after what he had done, then Colin was spared the guilt of the deed, if not of the intention.

But that hope, unworthy and conflicted as it was, paled beside the honest fear of what Hasloch could have become in the intervening years—of what the Thule Group certainly had become—if Colin had too easily assumed victory over its brightest fallen star.

TWENTY-FIVE

WASHINGTON, D.C., WEDNESDAY, OCTOBER 26, 1998

O villains, vipers, damn'd without redemption!
Dogs, easily won to fawn on any man!
Snakes, in my heart-blood warm'd, that sting my heart!
Three Judases, each one thrice worse than Judas!
—WILLIAM SHAKESPEARE, *Richard II,* III.II.129

IT TOOK NINIAN APPROXIMATELY A DAY AND A HALF WITH A PENDULUM and maps on a gradually increasing scale to link the key with a safe-deposit box in a bank in Manhattan. The key had a relationship to its lock: by the logic that drove Ninian's gift, psychometry, the two were still connected.

By that time Claire and Justin had arrived in Glastonbury—Colin could not, in good conscience, leave either unwarned.

Justin took the news of Rowan's disappearance very badly. If Claire had not been there to calm him down, he would certainly have gone to the police. *"How could you have let her do it? Why doesn't someone do something?"* The outcry of any anguished parent whose child had gone astray.

Dylan's attempts to reassure him—to explain—were useless.

"Let them do their work!" Claire rapped out sharply.

Justin, who had been pacing the floor of Dylan's living room, rounded on her in surprise. "Give me one good reason that I should! Palmer here didn't even have the common decency to tell me she'd disappeared; I should—"

"If you interfere, she will die," Claire said flatly.

Justin Moorcock stared at her. Claire took a deep breath and continued.

"Justin, you've known me for years. I've known Rowan since she was a little girl, and I love her as much as you do. I know these people, Justin—they tried to kill me when I was about Rowan's age, and Colin saved me then. Let him save Rowan now."

"Why doesn't someone do something?" Justin demanded. But the fury was gone from his voice now. He sat down on the couch. Claire put an arm around his shoulders and looked at Colin pleadingly.

"We are doing all we can," Colin told him gently. There was no need to tax Justin with the fuller explanation of the powerful political protection the Thulists could summon, of their expertise in hiding the proof of the cult's existence.

"What can I do?" Justin asked. "If money will help— "

"I won't hesitate to ask for it," Colin told him firmly. "But right now we need to get into Rowan's safe-deposit box in New York and find out what she's left there for us—"

Claire was watching him with an odd expression on her face.

"I think I can help you out there, Colin."

All five of them went down to New York to open the box, though only Colin and Claire went to the bank itself. Claire was cosignatory on the box; Rowan had rented it two years ago, something Claire had long since forgotten about.

"She fooled me completely," Claire said, a little bitterly. "I had no idea she wanted it for something like this."

"Probably she didn't know either, then," Colin said. "Two years ago would have been before she started investigating the Thulists."

Or would it? he wondered, gazing down at the open box on the table between them. Its contents were heartbreakingly pragmatic: another copy of her dissertation, letters for Justin and Claire, a copy of her will. Rowan's notes and correspondence were there as well, but, as Colin had expected, they did not constitute anything that might interest the police, or comprise proof of a kidnapping. The documents were only ominous if one understood what they represented.

Caradoc Buckland's signature was on a number of otherwise-innocuous letters bearing the name of the Cincinnatus Group and an address in Washington, D.C.

"Now what?" Claire said, when Colin had read everything over twice and taken a few notes.

"Now comes the hard part. You stay here and keep Justin and Dylan out of trouble—Ninian may be of help there, he seems like a sensible young man— and I go pay a call on some old friends."

"God be with you," Claire said solemnly, her face grave.

Colin took the shuttle from JFK on Wednesday morning. National Airport had been renamed for Ronald Reagan last February, but the name change stuck about as well as changing Sixth Avenue in Manhattan to Avenue of the Americas. People used the old familiar names in defiance of signage.

Washington was just as he remembered it: a city that seemed at times to be no more than a stage set, a backdrop for implausible events. It was raining when he arrived, and that, too, matched his memories. Washington, like Berlin, was a city best understood in the rain. He took a taxi directly to his

Georgetown destination, giving, out of old habit, an intersection and not an address. The past seemed present once more, and habits abandoned for decades had gained new currency. Once again, Colin became the man he had abandoned, the one for whom he'd thought he had no further use, once upon a time.

But once upon a time could not last forever, and even the loveliest fairy tale had to end.

With the legendary city traffic, the ride took over an hour, even though Colin had used the closer airport. The neighborhood slowly changed, becoming more moneyed, until the street where the driver stopped at last was filled with brass-plaqued brownstones whose tenants were wealthy and reclusive organizations: law firms, consultants, other groups with less specific purposes. Though long absent from the political chessboard, Colin recognized this shadowland well: this was the intersection of wealth and power, a realm where corruption flourished.

The taxi stopped. Colin paid it off and watched it drive away before turning to locate his destination. Some part of his mind insisted that it would have been better to give an address several blocks away, to make the determination of his destination even more difficult for the hunters, but he knew that was pointless. No one was hunting him—yet. That would come only after he stepped into the arena.

He walked up the street and located his destination: a brownstone indistinguishable from the others. The Cincinnatus Group was the only tenant.

Colin had done his homework. The Cincinnatus Group was an advisory think-tank of the sort frequently retained by the Administration to do in-depth research on various unspecified issues. It was named for the legendary Roman general who had been admired by George Washington—the one who had saved the city, then returned to his plow. The civilian soldier had been an American ideal, once upon a time.

When there had still been American ideals.

Colin mounted the steps. There was an engraved brass nameplate beside the door. The door was locked; he pressed the bell beside it. To his mild surprise, the door opened.

There was one last moment when he could have turned and run. It was surprising how strong the impulse was; as if he shared his body with a pragmatic animal interested only in its own survival, a creature who knew that only danger lay ahead.

But he was not an animal. He was a man. Colin shrugged off the sensation of dread and stepped over the threshold. The reception area was directly to his right.

Colin walked through the archway under the politely inquiring gaze of a receptionist who looked faintly disconcerted to see an unfamiliar face. The desk was bare of anything that might suggest that she worked for a living; there was a telephone, a Tiffany lamp, and a Georgian silver card receiver, nothing more. The woman behind the desk was blond, fine-boned, and patrician, and looked as if she'd be more at home on the runways of Milan than she was here. Her pageboy bob almost—but not quite—concealed the but-

ton in her ear and the wire that ran from it to a transceiver somewhere beneath her jacket; a crack in the amiable facade, and proof that someone, somewhere, was watching.

"May I help you?" she asked. One hand was out of sight beneath the desk-
top—hovering, Colin had no doubt, over a security alarm.

"I'm here to see Mr. Buckland," Colin said.

"Yes, of course, sir," she said, relieved. Both hands appeared on top of the
desk. "Who may I say is calling?"

"Colin MacLaren."

She spoke quietly into the telephone for a few seconds; Colin heard his own
name spoken. The receptionist hung up the phone and brightly invited Colin
to take off his coat and have a seat.

Colin thought he preferred to stand, and to keep his coat. The blasphemous crucifix was a cold weight in his jacket pocket— bringing it here had
been a risk, but leaving it elsewhere would have been as much of one.

He heard the rumble of an elevator through the walls of the old house, and a
few moments later, a young man—presumably Caradoc Buckland—appeared.

He was not precisely what Colin had expected. Buckland was somewhere
in his early thirties, sleek and model-handsome, with dark brown hair cut
fashionably short and hazel eyes. He was dressed in the Washington uniform:
a dark blue blazer, maroon rep tie, and grey flannel slacks. Despite such
scrupulous conservativism, he wore a heavy gold hoop in his left ear and a
massive gold signet ring on his right hand.

"Dr. MacLaren? I'm Caradoc Buckland." He held out his hand and Colin
shook it.

The next thing—the reasonable thing—would have been for Buckland to
ask Colin's business here, but he did not. He gestured for Colin to accompany
him, and led Colin toward the back of the house, where the elevator Colin
had heard before was waiting.

"Did you have any trouble finding us?" Buckland asked politely, sliding
the bronze gates of the elevator shut.

They know. The intuition brought with it an almost overwhelming urge for
flight. But Colin had known they would know who he was—if not at the moment he entered the building, then very soon thereafter. The Thule Group
never closed its books on an opponent until it had buried him itself.

"Oh, no particular trouble," Colin answered easily, the first rush of dread
fading into the prickle of anticipation along his nerves. The urge to play the
Great Game never died, even after half a century.

The elevator stopped on the third floor. "If you'll come this way, Dr. Mac-
Laren," Buckland said. His voice gave no hint that anything out of the ordinary was occurring.

The hallway was carpeted in vivid scarlet, with padding so deep that Colin
was conscious of his feet sinking into the surface. The rug seemed to swallow
sound, giving the hall the same dense hush as a cathedral. With a small part
of his consciousness, Colin wondered how the confrontation was to be staged,
and who the players were to be.

The door at the end of the hall was a single slab of carved rosewood, the grain brought out through generations of hand-polishing. Buckland swung it open and gestured for Colin to precede him. The office walls were paneled in oak, and in its way this room was as much of a stage-set as the reception area downstairs had been.

The desk stood isolated in the middle of the room, an immense ornate carven antique.

"Hello, Colin," the man behind the desk said.

It was Toller Hasloch.

His bright hair had softened with time to the color of old ivory, and his body had thickened with age, but he was unquestionably the same man Colin had last seen a quarter of a century ago. Colin felt the shock of that surprise like a hammer blow to the chest, making him want to gasp for breath.

"Do sit down, Colin," Hasloch said, rising to his feet like any good host. "Doc, please get our visitor a drink."

Colin sank into the offered chair, unable to take his eyes from Hasloch's face. He barely noticed when Buckland set a glass on the table at his elbow. Age was an anchor, slowing his reflexes, sapping his resiliency, and Colin set himself against it as if were a living enemy. Hasloch had meant to stagger him with the revelation that he was alive, and Colin could not afford to let him have his way. After a moment the first paralyzing surprise faded, and he could think again.

"What are you doing here?" Colin asked bluntly, although it was the question Hasloch himself should have asked.

How had Hasloch survived? Though in the final analysis the question was irrelevant to the problem at hand, it still deviled Colin's thoughts. If only he'd stayed in New York—if Simon hadn't been injured almost at that same moment, drawing Colin's attention away to the West Coast. By the time he'd returned to the East to helm the Bidney Institute, checking to see that Hasloch was actually dead had been the furthest thing from his mind.

They always say that it's the details that will get you in the end. . . .

"I'm living my life," Hasloch said, with too much innocence. Buckland had taken up a sentry position by the door, and Colin felt a momentary pang of smugness—all this fuss over one old man!

"While it's true that I prefer to keep a lower profile these days," Hasloch said, still smirking, "I'm hardly a hermit. I have wealth, power, influence, material possessions, pleasant company. . . ."

Hasloch had always been high-strung, and even now, his nerves betrayed him. He could not keep his hands still; they roved across the littered surface of his desk like independent entities, plucking up first one item then another to toy with. Colin watched his hands moving over the objects. Most of them were perfectly mundane, but in the middle of them, gaudy and out of place, were five small clear candy-colored pieces of plastic. A cube, a triangle, a diamond, and two that had so many facets they might as well be round. Gaming dice, such as Colin had seen in Rowan's living room.

Only the fact that he had steeled himself not to betray anything kept Colin from showing his surprise now. This could be coincidence, but Colin thought it was proof, instead.

And the approach he'd planned to take with a stranger named Caradoc Buckland would not work, Colin realized, now that he knew Toller Hasloch was—against all expectation—involved.

"Forgive me," Colin said politely. "I'm just wondering why you're telling me all this?" He'd learn more by being irritating than through conciliation—Hasloch had always had a tendency to make speeches.

"Because," Hasloch growled, placing his hands flat on the desk and leaning up out of his chair across it, "*I want you to know how thoroughly you failed, you son-of-a-bitch.*"

He'd hoped to irritate Hasloch, and it seemed he had. Behind him, Colin felt Buckland straighten to even greater attention.

"So I did," Colin agreed, still calmly. "I suppose I should say I'm happy to see you're looking well?"

"Because it gets you off the guilt-ridden White Light hook?" Hasloch snapped. "Does it, Colin? Does it really?"

He got to his feet and began to pace, but Colin's answer seemed to restore his good spirits. "You tried to kill me—I suppose your Masters gave you hell for that. Did they throw you out? Or did you remain upon sufferance, atoning through good works? Tell me all about it, Colin. Tell me about all the 'good' you've done in the world—is it any match for what I have done?

"Remember our first conversation, all those years ago? I told you then what I intended to do, and I've done it: my patrons ripped America's heart out with the Kennedy assassination, destroyed its soul with Vietnam, and shattered its mind with Nixon's betrayal of trust."

Hasloch must be both secure and confident to speak so freely in front of Buckland . . . or else have an unimaginably strong hold over the younger man. At the moment, it didn't matter which.

"And we haven't been idle since: read the newspapers, Cold Warrior—this is the eve of our triumph! Your American Eagle is dead and the White Eagle of Thule will triumph in my lifetime. What can you possibly set against that?" Hasloch demanded.

"Walls," Colin MacLaren answered. Hasloch's rhetoric was only the expression of his own bleakest fears, and he'd had decades to come to terms with them, and find what comfort he could. "The Berlin Wall is down—and as for Vietnam, you should visit more of your hometown landmarks. The Memorial is supreme proof that hearts can heal and minds can mend—and souls can be redeemed. Even yours, Toller."

Hasloch stopped his pacing and laughed harshly. "Not by a tired old man who refuses to face the darkness in his own soul!" He returned to his desk and lowered himself into his chair, regaining his composure with a visible effort. "But I've been indulging myself at your expense. You had some business with my aide, and I haven't allowed you to conduct it. Please, feel free." He gestured toward Caradoc.

This conversation was not going as it would have if Hasloch had really known the business that brought him here. Was it possible that Hasloch did not connect him with Rowan Moorcock? There was no reason he should. Even if she had been questioned, they were as unlikely to have questioned her about him as she would be to volunteer the information that she knew him. Hasloch knew him in another connection entirely.

Colin said nothing, playing for time.

Hasloch raised his brows inquiringly at Buckland. Colin saw the young man frown, thinking hard.

"I suppose it's about Julian—ah, Pilgrim, I suppose I should say. But I'm not sure why Jourdemayne didn't come herself," Buckland said. "I was looking forward to seeing her again, actually."

Pilgrim? What business did the Thule Group have with Truth's half-brother? He'd been institutionalized since shortly before Truth had come to see Colin for the first time, and Colin was pretty sure he still was. From what little she'd told him, it was for the best. The child Colin had known had grown into a monster—the faint shadow of malice that had marred Thorne's essentially sunny nature reaching full unchecked flower in his son. What business could the Cincinnatus Group have with Pilgrim?

"I'm sure you can think of a number of reasons she wouldn't want to see you," Colin said, getting to his feet. He blessed the assumption that he was here on Truth's business, as it concealed so neatly his own purposes. All that remained was for him to get out of here before they realized they'd been hooked by a red herring.

"She can hardly have thought it would be more impressive," Hasloch said mockingly. "Sending you, I mean. Not that you're not impressive in your way, of course," he added. "A triumph of superannuation, if nothing else."

Both he and Buckland seemed to know what Hasloch was talking about, but that wouldn't last long. "Spare me the trite insults," Colin said. "I'd worry more about my own plans than Truth's if I were you, Toller—at least based on past performance. I suppose you don't need me to spell out the message? And now, I'll bid both of you fascinating gentlemen adieu. Don't trouble yourselves to escort me. I can find my own way out."

Colin was a little surprised to reach the street unmolested, and a few blocks' walk brought him to the attention of a cruising cab. He took it downtown and picked another cab at random from a queue before heading for his final destination. Even his exhaustion could not tempt him to forgo such elementary precautions, though he doubted that Hasloch would bother to have him followed. Both of them knew there was a second act to come—and if Hasloch were very clever, he would realize what it was. Rowan was a student at Taghkanic, after all.

And Hasloch was clever.

The Airport Holiday Inn was a soulless cracker box, set along a roadway named for a famous American traitor. Its accommodations were duplicated in a thousand locations in half a dozen countries, as anonymous as a phone booth. Colin threw his coat over a chair and sat down on the bed, kicking off his shoes. He slipped the pendant between the mattress and the box spring; the concealment would delay a cursory search, though not a professional one.

What came now? If Toller were interested in Pilgrim, Colin owed Truth a warning—but Colin had gained Dylan's promise to stay out of things through the simple threat of involving Truth, who, though in England, was only a phone call away. He knew that wouldn't hold Dylan back for long, but if Colin called Truth now, Colin knew Dylan would consider himself absolved of his promise immediately. And with Toller Hasloch involved, that was far too dangerous.

Colin frowned, pondering. Pilgrim had been transferred to Fall River last year, after Truth had met Nathaniel. He picked up the telephone and dialed.

"Atheling."

"Nathaniel, it's Colin." He thought of telling Nathaniel that Hasloch was alive, then realized that Nathaniel must already know—that he would have kept track of matters involving Hasloch when Colin had not. Nathaniel had certainly known Hasloch was alive down all the long years when the belief in his own guilt had tormented Colin.

But such was my penance, and in the turning of the Wheel all things are understood. So mote it be.

Colin bowed his head, schooling his rebellious spirit to acceptance. It was a moment before he could go on.

"I have some information for you, Nathaniel. You'll remember Toller Hasloch?"

There was a moment of electric silence before Nathaniel answered. "Yes, Colin," he said gently.

"When I spoke to him today—" Colin found himself pausing, and forced himself to go on. "When I spoke to him, he made the assumption that I was acting on Truth Palmer's behalf. He mentioned Pilgrim—in the vaguest possible way, of course. I don't want to sound a false alarm, but—"

"Better a thousand false alarms than no true warning," Nathaniel said somberly. "Pilgrim is here, safe in my care. He has no visitors and would not know them if he did. What is Hasloch's interest?"

"Unfortunately, he didn't tell me. I'll have to ask him the next time I see him," Colin said. There was a silence.

"Is there anything else I need to know?" Nathaniel asked.

Colin debated. But if he did not want to involve Truth, someone must know. "Claire's cousin, Rowan Moorcock, disappeared while investigating the Thulists, and the trail leads right to Toller Hasloch and something called the Cincinnatus Group."

"Ah." There was no inflection in Nathaniel's voice. "Good hunting, then, Colin. And take care."

"As much as I can, old friend," Colin answered. "Walk in the Light, Nathaniel."

"And you, Colin. Always."

*   *   *

When Colin hung up the phone, his duty discharged, he felt a great wave of weariness sweep over him, taking his strength as the riptide takes the unwary swimmer. He'd lived a quarter of a century wishing his murder of Hasloch undone, and when, in one searing moment, he found that it had been, Colin's guilt had been transformed as well. Hasloch was evil, a creature forged out of the dark heart of creation for only one task, just as Colin had been forged as a sword and shield to defy him. Colin could no more avoid his destiny than Hasloch could. They had been fated to be enemies before either of them had been born.

What might the world have been like if Hasloch had not been born into it? If the men and women trusted by a nation had been trustworthy in truth, and had destroyed what they had been sent to destroy? Instead, blinded by petty fears, dazzled by the hope of money, of power, the defenders of the West had betrayed the Light for a thousand base and unworthy reasons, many of them without even knowing the true nature of the war they fought.

Colin lay down on top of the bedspread, a part of him expecting to be able to feel the necklace even through the mattress, like the princess in the fairy tale. A part of his mind expected the phone to ring, though even Nathaniel did not know where he was.

But it didn't, and he slept.

The Adept stood on a green hillside covered with tiny blue flowers whose scent was like homecoming and the morning. He had always come back here, in the interregnums between a thousand lives, seeking his absolution, the sign that he had been forgiven at last. In the distance, he could see the golden towers of the great Temple in which he had died, given the Cup of Nepenthe to expiate his crime. Life after life he had been bound to the Wheel—arrogance was always his besetting sin: pride, curiosity, and a belief that Power was above the Law.

Power. What his soul craved. Power, always power, and mastery over the world that held him. . . .

Colin awoke with a start, wisps of the dream still echoing through his consciousness. He had been taught that the gates of Time opened to the Adept in the shadows of Death, so that in one brief moment the pattern that stretched back through more lives than this could be glimpsed in its entirety. For the first time in his existence, Colin looked toward that moment with dread—what would he see, when he looked back across the gulf of Time that stretched back before his birth?

He sat up, running his hand through his hair. It was dusk: the service-strip signs made a garish multicolored jumble in the road below his window. The memory that was almost a fantasy dispelled like smoke, leaving behind it only a terrible sense of responsibility.

Sleeping in the middle of the day. They say that's a sign of age. But the nap had not refreshed him. Colin sat on the edge of the hotel bed and gazed out the window at the airport sprawl, his mind as intractable as a rebellious beast of burden. He shook his head, half-dazed with lingering exhaustion. He didn't have time for this. He had to make some kind of a plan to deal with Hasloch.

He knew now that Rowan was a prisoner of what lurked behind the facade of the Cincinnatus Group. It was only a matter of time until Hasloch discovered that Colin had come to Washington looking for her. Hasloch would never believe in a deal that traded Rowan's liberty for silence, and, more, he would not accept it. There was too much history between Hasloch and Colin, too much anger.

A lifetime's bitter dealing in the art of the possible made Colin consider the other thing he might trade: Claire for Rowan. Claire would consent to it, Colin was certain, and somewhere in the mechanics of the switch it should be possible to win both women's freedom.

But if he could plan a double cross, Hasloch could plan one too. Reluctantly, Colin rejected the idea. There was too little chance that it would succeed. He did not even know if Rowan was still alive to barter for.

Wearily, Colin rubbed at his eyes. The wisps of his dream lingered, tormenting him with a faint bewildering guilt and a sense of corruption, liabilities he could not afford. He could not proceed in the task before him without a pure heart and very clean hands.

But what was his task? To save Rowan Moorcock, or to destroy Toller Hasloch? Colin rubbed at his temples. So little to choose between the two goals in one sense—and in another, the whole gulf of damnation lay between them.

Where was the utility in saving one life while the Shadow took thousands?

Where was the triumph in letting the Shadow seize a thousand single lives while saying no single life was worth saving?

Who saveth one life, it is as if he has saved the whole world. Out of the stillness of Colin's heart the answer came, and with that answer, the perfection of his life's work. The nagging sense of unkept promises faded, leaving clarity in its wake. This was the path that had been set out for him, a thousand lives ago.

At last Colin picked up the phone and dialed a number he had held unused in memory for more than forty years.

Xavier's was a trendy District "drinkeateria" located near Capitol Hill. As such, it was well supplied with pseudo-Victorian stained glass, blond oak veneer, and even a few ferns. It was the sort of place to which the tragically hip repaired to meet and mate, as anonymous and impersonal as a paper cup.

The message had been left at the desk of Colin's hotel sometime during the night: spuriously intimate and relentlessly cheerful, suggesting that old friends meet for a drink at Xavier's that evening. Almost out of simple curiosity, Colin had come, though the message was from no one he'd ever heard of, and certainly not from an old friend. But that really didn't matter. He had not called that number to play things safe, but to redeem an old promise.

The evening was rainy. The faceted windowpanes of the bar were sequined with raindrops, and cars passing through the streets made hissing sounds like downhill skiers. The man who sat down opposite him at the table near the window was a stranger.

The stranger's dark blue trenchcoat was dark with rain over the shoulders, and rain had managed to get past the shield of his umbrella to star the surface of his long, sleeked-back red hair with droplets. He was a young man, less than half Colin's age, and wore a grey three-piece suit as if it were an unfamiliar uniform. He did not take off his gloves.

"Professor MacLaren—it's been quite a while since I had the privilege of sitting in on one of your lectures," the young man said with careful cheer.

Though Colin did not remember every pupil he'd ever had—no teacher could—in that moment he was certain that this young man had never been one of them. Perhaps it was the amusement with which he watched Colin through fox-bright pale eyes, as if this were all some sort of elaborate prank.

But in that case, who was the victim?

"I know you were sure I'd never amount to much—oh, don't try to deny it—but I have made something of a success of myself. You see, here's my card."

It appeared between his gloved fingers as if through a magician's trick. He held it out and Colin took it.

"Hereward Farrar. Consulting." No address or telephone number, I notice.

The waitress approached. Farrar ordered a Kaliber; Colin was still nursing his double Scotch.

It was nearing seven o'clock, and workaholic Washington was starting to trickle in for a drink before a working dinner or a late-evening meeting. The noise level rose proportionately.

"And what do you consult on these days, Mr. Farrar?" Colin asked.

"This and that," Farrar said, smiling. "And you're wondering who sent me, and what I'm up to, and no matter what I say you'll still wonder if you can trust me."

The waitress returned with a bottle and a glass and left again. Farrar seemed to concentrate on pouring his drink to the exclusion of all else.

"Now that we've gotten all that out of the way," Colin commented dryly, "it seems we've reached an impasse." Perhaps it was the effect of age, but he realized that he no longer had the taste for this sort of cloak-and-dagger feint and double-feint, necessary though it might sometimes be.

"Maybe." Farrar did not sound particularly convinced of it. "I must say, we were awfully surprised when you walked into Hasloch's office yesterday morning—and when you called last night."

"So was I," Colin said blandly.

The voice at the other end of the line rattled back the number he had just dialed with a robot's perfection. And waited.

Forty years. An eternity in Washington politics. Colin had not been certain the number would still be good at all. But this was the response he'd been trained to expect, a long time ago in a world now dead. How long had this number been kept active, a listening-post on the frontier of a war that had never ended?

"This is Stormcrow. I have a message for Kestrel. Tell him the dragon awakes."
"Thank you for calling, Stormcrow," the voice responded. Then the line went dead.

So this was the sort of person who worked for Department 23 these days—assuming he had come in response to Colin's call at all. Department 23 had been an outlaw operation set up by the OSS as a counter-*Ahnenerße* to fight Black Magick with White. It had bound together occultists from a dozen different traditions in the Free World's hour of greatest need, but now the days when the West had been desperate enough to try such things were long past, and other forces were ascendant in today's intelligence community. Farrar's presence might simply be another kind of trap. He'd given Colin none of the half a dozen safewords and countersigns that Colin remembered from the war; possibly he did not know them.

"Question one: Why help me at all?" Colin asked.

Farrar seemed to think about that for a moment, carefully choosing his words before he spoke.

"I'm here because you called me. Some jobs just need a lot of doing, don't they?"

Colin was still unconvinced, but part of him was wondering if Farrar's bona fides were really important, in the long run. If Farrar were acting under Toller Hasloch's orders, then anything he did to Colin would generate information for whomever must next follow Colin into the serpent's nest. If Colin disappeared, Nathaniel would know what he had been hunting when he vanished. Dylan would certainly investigate--and more to the point in this particular instance, so would his wife. Truth was ferocious where her family was concerned, and Hasloch had threatened Pilgrim.

In short, Colin's disappearance would cause a lot of fuss, both mundane and occult, and Hasloch would be subjected to the sort of fifteen-minute notoriety that could destroy years of careful planning . . . or even drive him underground once more. If Farrar were his agent.

Still, Farrar might really be working for the modern incarnation of Department 23. He was precisely the sort of person whom Colin's old allies might have sent—someone low enough in the hierarchy of things to be immune to the Thule Group's infiltration of high office.

"Let's come to the point, young man. This isn't Berlin in the forties, and the Cold War is over. You haven't told me who you are, or why you're here, or given me a good reason why I should listen to anything you say. Undoubtedly you already know anything I could tell you about Toller Hasloch--"

"If you keep up with your old students it won't surprise you to hear that Toller Hasloch is one of our inside-the-Beltway kingmakers," Farrar said, his tone as chatty as if he were doing nothing more than passing on gossip. "The Cincinnatus Group is an important power here on the Hill—a lot of people get their appointments in line with its recommendations. A number of people owe its chairman favors—and the type of people to whom Mr.

Hasloch owes favors in turn tends to disturb some people. People who still remember who you used to be."

Who I used to be. . . . Farrar spun a pretty story calculated to fan the embers of an old man's ego and convince him to go charging off into battle one last time—to use him, as ruthlessly as Colin had once used others, to win a battle, if not the war.

"So your friends don't like Mr. Hasloch," Colin said. "Well, I don't like him much myself. But I've learned to live with things I don't like, Mr. Farrar. I'm here for another reason. If your intelligence is as good as you'd like to imply that it is, you'll know that I called at the Cincinnatus Group yesterday to speak to Caradoc Buckland, not Toller Hasloch."

There was a flicker in Farrar's pale eyes. "Mr. Buckland's not a very nice man. A friend of his shot me once, so I'm in a position to judge. He's very good at doing what he's told, though. I'd forget about all this and go home, if I were you," he added seriously.

"I'm afraid I can't do that," Colin said, and waited.

The silence stretched for several moments, until finally Farrar broke it.

"All right," Farrar admitted. "You've a right to be suspicious of me. For what it's worth, my name really is Hereward Farrar. Who'd make something like that up?" He smiled encouragingly, but Colin refused to be influenced. He continued to wait.

"What can I tell you that will convince you I'm on the side of the angels? I could swear—"

There was a candle on the table, burning deep inside a plastic-wrapped glass chimney. Farrar cupped his left hand around it. His voice became deeper and more solemn, and for a moment it seemed to Colin that the light filled his hand like a solid thing.

"—I could swear by the Light that if I am other than what I seem, I am not heir to the Dragon. Would that help?" he added in his normal voice, and the momentary summoning of Power Colin had sensed was gone.

"All right," Colin said. It was confirmation of a sort: Department 23's code name for the Thule Group had been the Dragon. And more important, no matter how good an actor he was, no matter how diminished Colin's own powers were, Colin knew that someone tainted by the Shadow could not summon Power in that fashion without revealing his true nature.

Whoever Hereward Farrar was, he was of the Light.

"If you're proposing to help me, Mr. Farrar, I have a small shopping list. . . ."

TWENTY-SIX

FAUQUIER COUNTY, VIRGINIA, MONDAY, OCTOBER 31, 1998

If I do prove her haggard,
Though that her jesses were my dear heart-strings,
I'd whistle her off and let her down the wind,
To prey at fortune.
—WILLIAM SHAKESPEARE, *Othello*, III.iii.260

THE VIRGINIA COUNTRYSIDE WAS STILL BRIGHT WITH AUTUMN—THE RICH-est colors were past, but the landscape had not yet softened into the dun-browns of winter. Tonight was All Hallows Eve, the night on which the Wild Hunt roamed the earth, free either from Hell itself or from some harsh Celtic underworld. All Hallows Eve wasn't truly a festival of Hasloch's cult—but Christian or pagan, the spirits that would roam this night brought only danger and death—someone would die tonight.

And if the one who died were Colin, then ten days from now, on the anniversary of *Krystallnacht*, Rowan Moorcock would also die.

Farrar had been true to his promise of help. Colin had told him little enough—not even Rowan's name—but Farrar was able to supply the information Colin needed: the location of Hasloch's temple.

Or so Colin believed. Colin was gambling that Hasloch was important enough in the American branch of the *Thule Gesellschaft* to have its inevitable unholy place under his direct control. If he did, it would almost certainly be located somewhere in his house, just as it had been thirty years before. He glanced down at the dossier that lay on the car seat beside him.

Toller Christian Hasloch, born November 9, 1938, in Baltimore, Maryland. Educated at the University of California at Berkeley and at Harvard. Traveled extensively through Europe. Law practice in New York 1966–1972. Served in an advisory capacity on a number of obscure committees. Attached to Berlin Embassy 1973–1975. Joined the Cincinnatus Group in 1975. Appointed chairman in 1986. Never married, never arrested, no children, pets, or longtime girlfriends.

Residences: a permanent apartment at the Watergate Hotel, and a country house, The Hallows, somewhere off Route 66 between Manassas and Front Royal. That was where Colin was heading now, in an anonymous sedan that could be any of a hundred government cars. Farrar was driving. Cars with drivers were a common sight in this affluent Washington exurb. A driver could answer questions, divert suspicion, raise the alarm if needed. And Colin must husband all his strength for the battle ahead.

The Hallows was a rambling brick house that dated back to the turn of the century. They cruised slowly past it and made a series of turns down winding country lanes.

"It's through that hedge," Farrar said, as if he were announcing the weather. The sedan rolled to a stop at the side of the road. There was no other traffic. The area's inhabitants had already left for their public and private sector jobs—and Colin expected Hasloch to be safely at his Georgetown desk as well.

"How long do you think you'll need?"

"Not long."

Colin suspected that it would not be hard to get into the house. He had not told Farrar about the crucifix, but even now it was a cold weight in the breast pocket of Colin's jacket. It must be some sort of key—there was no other reason for Rowan to have kept it, when keeping it was so dangerous in both the magickal and mundane worlds.

"Good hunting, then," Farrar said, as if Colin had given him a definite answer. He picked up the newspaper that lay beside him on the bench seat of the sedan, seeming to become as engrossed in it as any hired driver awaiting his master's pleasure.

Colin stepped out of the car. There was a break in the hedge, and he passed through it, walking through the yard and across the terrace of The Hallows.

The house, like the house of any rich man, was safeguarded in a number of ways, from dead bolts and double-locked windows to an electronic link to a security company and the police station. A cleaning service came twice a week, and a cook–housekeeper and butler were here on weekends, but on a Monday morning Colin could expect The Hallows to be deserted. He did not worry about discovery in any event. An arrest would serve his purposes far better than it would Hasloch's, and if an embarrassing scene ensued, well, Colin no longer had anyone's honor to look to save his own.

Though he would have liked to have a Sensitive with him, Colin could think of no one whose safety he would hazard by bringing them here. As he had told Dylan, people who pried into affairs of this nature had a way of simply . . . disappearing. At least he would make a more disagreeable mouthful than most.

The attached garage had a door which opened easily to Colin's skeleton key—there was no alarm, and if necessary he could have broken a pane in its window and gotten through that way. It was a loophole that many home-owners left in their security, and apparently Hasloch was no exception.

A moment later Colin was inside the garage, safe from prying eyes. It was a two-car garage, but both sides were empty. The back was piled with the usual mundane clutter that any homeowner accumulates: lawn mower, snow blower, bags of salt and mulch. Colin glanced at his watch. 9:45.

The door that led through into the house itself was far more secure: steel-core, from the look of it, with both a key-bolt and an electronic touchpad. But the LEDs on the touchpad were dark, as were the lights on the alarm box mounted high on the wall beside the door.

Farrar's doing? It was better not to stand around wondering about it, at any rate. The fifth skeleton key that Colin tried dragged back the dead bolt, and the door was open.

Pantry . . . kitchen . . . dining room . . . each room he passed through was perfect and deserted, like a museum exhibit. Despite the fact that the sentry system was down, no one seemed to have come in answer to the alarm that must have been sent. Colin passed quickly through the ground-floor rooms. None of them, even the library, gave a hint of the person Hasloch truly was, the new-minted creature of Evil called out of the stuff of the Shadow by those who trusted their creation to see their plan through to its ultimate culmina-tion.

A wave of giddiness passed over Colin, so that he had to clutch at the door-frame to retain his balance. He felt lightheaded, disconnected by a combina-tion of too much stress and adrenaline, and unequal to the task before him. It was as if there were something here he did not want to face, some darkness. Suddenly he was cold—cold as if he did not stand in a suburban living room but instead within a crypt, a dark shrine cut into the living stone hundreds of meters below the surface of the sun-kissed earth, before an idol that was the mask of a god as yet unrevealed. . . .

He dragged a handkerchief from his pocket, and with a trembling hand wiped cold sweat from his face. In his chest he could feel his heart clenching and unclenching, its blows as hard and distinct as if it were a prisoner pound-ing against the wall of his chest for release.

He fumbled in his jacket for his pillbox, placed a pill beneath his tongue, and felt the painful hammering slowly ease. It came to Colin that all it would take for Hasloch to win was for him to die, and that he might well die here, from nothing more malignant than the inevitable failure of that balky beast, the body.

It was over half a century since he had last faced the united forces of the Shadow in pitched battle. He remembered the date exactly: October 31, 1945, and each Halloween thereafter had carried with it some threat, some echo of that eternal battle.

Old ghosts surrounded him now: dead comrades, summoned once more into battle by the force of memory. Michael Jaeger—who had been reborn into Colin's life once more—Marian Shipton, David Fouquet, Dame Ellen,

Alison Margrave, Father Godwin, Nigel St. Clare, and others he had known only by their codenames: Kestrel, Peregrine, Shrike. Lamplighter. The Roman. Fellow soldiers in the Light, each of whom, in a sense, had given his or her life so that Colin could stand here today and strike in their name.

He would not fail them.

Colin concentrated on his breathing, willing his senses to steady. After a few moments he took a deep breath and focused once more on his task, his hand clenched around the black talisman in his pocket. Hasloch's Temple was here, and Colin was gambling that Rowan was being held somewhere within it. Fortunately he had the advantage of being able to count on Hasloch's colossal ego: it was unlikely that he would leave the prize in anyone else's hands.

Now all he had to do was find his way in. . . .

The cellar steps were behind a door in the back hall. No one would see a light from the road. Colin flipped the wall-switch and made his way down the stairs. He looked at his watch. 9:55. He wondered if Farrar were still waiting—and if so, how much longer he would wait. At the bottom of the stairs, he shone his light around the space, his mind straying to that other cellar, that other desperate search, so long ago. Somehow it seemed as if they were both one moment, and all the years between them an illusion.

There was a locked door in the back wall of the cellar. Once he would have kicked it down. Now he spent precious moments trying passkeys, infuriated by the tremor in his hands, until he found one that would fit.

Beyond the open door, darkness—and then slow illumination as the lights came up. There was a faint smell of burnt charcoal, a whiff of incense. And beyond the door, another door. An elevator, its door open, waiting.

It made a certain ironic sense. The rich and powerful—and venerable—who were Hasloch's clients and patrons would expect the most modern conveniences in their debaucheries. But still, Colin hesitated to enter the elevator. It seemed too much like a killing box.

There was no choice. There might be another way in to what lay beneath the house, but Colin did not have the time to find it. Steeling his resolve, he stepped inside the cabin of the elevator and pressed the single button.

The doors closed. The elevator began to descend. The drop seemed to go on for a very long time; guessing, Colin would estimate the descent at as much as thirty feet, implying a substantial underground structure tunneled out of the raw earth by some unknown feat of clandestine engineering.

The doors opened. He was in a broad antechamber, with paneled walls and indirect lighting. The carpet beneath his feet was the same deep scarlet as the one at the Cincinnatus Group, with the addition of a heraldic phoenix woven into its center in vermilion and gold. Directly ahead were a set of massive metal doors, their brushed bronze surfaces gleaming in the soft light.

The doors were ornate and cyclopean, in such mad contrast to the house above that for a moment Colin's senses reeled. On their surface, armed and armored knights stood facing each other in alert ranks beneath a swastika sun, raising their arms in stiff salute to the dawning of a new day. The rays of the sun spread from it like the wings of an eagle, and the bird-shape was visible behind the burning disk of the sun.

The money it must have cost to do all this. And all in secret, Colin found himself marveling. *It's like something out of a James Bond film.* The thought had a certain dreadful wonder to it. How many people besides Colin had ever seen these doors?

How many had passed through them never to return again?

With something approaching reluctance, Colin pushed at one of the doors. It did not move.

Colin looked around. There was no place else to go: at one end of the room was the elevator, at the other, the doors. Forward or back.

He felt over the whole surface of the doors, looking for something that would show him the way in. He found it at last in the shield of one of the knights: its shape was raised higher from the surface than any other shape on either door, and its edge was sharp. Colin tugged at it, and the shield swung up like a box lid.

I don't see why I ought to be surprised. Our German friends were great ones for silly gadgets.

Beneath the shield lay a smooth black circle, obviously a lock. In the center was a hole in the shape of a cross. Colin took out his pocket flashlight and shone it into the opening. Tiny pin-shapes gleamed in the depths—the mechanism of a lock that could not be picked.

He took the crucifix from his pocket, holding it by the chain. He looked again at the pattern of holes on the back, the reason for them suddenly plain. This was why Rowan had kept it—because it, too, was a key.

The cross fitted perfectly into the cavity, as if they had been made for each other. He pushed, and felt the whole mechanism sink into the door a fraction of an inch. There was an audible click. Beneath his fingers, Colin could feel the door mechanism waken into life. The doors swung inward. The pendant pulled free, swinging like a pendulum at the end of its chain. He put it back into his pocket, wrapping it fastidiously in his handkerchief first.

There was darkness beyond. And suddenly, with a hiss and an uprush of interrupted sound, the lights went on. Colin caught his breath, staring out into something he had never expected to see again in this life.

A round chamber, its size impossible to calculate, its domed ceiling echoing the groined vaulting of gothic cathedrals. In the center, a circular firepit, dug deep into the rock. Surrounding the firepit were twelve High Seats, each with the device of a medieval hero carved into its back, and hanging over each, its battle banner.

But the devices were the wrong ones—not the ones he'd been taught—and the illusion of Wewelsburg, of Wolf's Lair, faded. The illumination here came from hidden lightbulbs, false as a stage-set. This was not one of the Nazi Order Castles, where the mad religion that Hitler and Himmler had fostered between them had been forced to malignant flower. This was some inexact recreation, built by men who had never seen the original. Whatever crimes had been done here, Black Magick was not among them. Feeling vaguely cheated, Colin stepped inside and walked down the steps.

The room was not as big as it first appeared—its grand dimensions were a trick of lighting and forced perspective. His gaze swept over the glittering suits of armor that lined the walls of the room. Behind a drapery depicting more racially-pure rural glories, Colin found a door marked PRIVATE in consciously-quaint gothic lettering. It was locked, but yielded quickly to one of Colin's skeleton keys. He opened it and went inside.

It was a den, an obvious retreat for Hasloch and his particular cronies. The walls were lined with books of a far less benign sort than had graced the library upstairs. A door led out of the library off to the left; this one was not locked. Colin opened it and found himself in a small office containing a desk and file cabinet. There was a woman's purse on the desk.

Colin opened it, searching quickly through it to find the wallet. He opened it.

Rowan's. Here was hard proof at last that Rowan was here—or had been here, alive, recently enough for whoever had taken her purse to have left it lying here on the desk. But where was she? This office was a dead end.

Conscientiously, Colin searched through the desk—the file cabinet was locked and would take him too long to force. The desk contained a number of interesting items: a .45 automatic, a block of hashish, several thousand dollars in cash, and a manila folder filled with glossy professional pornographic photos that contained certain famous faces.

By now Colin had a certain idea of what went on here at The Hallows. The old soul-sickness of the *Armanenschaft,* certainly, but something more cynical and modern as well. This was a safe house for the indulgence of terrible appetites of all sorts, all carefully recorded and noted by its master, Toller Hasloch.

And that would explain the curiously theatrical look of the Temple: it was, as its appearance had suggested to him at first, a stage-set. Nothing real at all.

But no matter what else Hasloch was, in his own monstrous fashion he was sincerely devout. There was—there must be—a second Temple.

He went back to the study, still carrying Rowan's purse. A little experimentation located the secret panel that let a section of the bookcase swing out. *Boys and their toys,* Colin thought sourly. He dragged a chair over to prop the bookcase open and went down the short narrow passage, caught halfway between hope and dread of what he would find.

Another room, this one very modern but a dead end all the same. It contained a console with a bank of screens showing the elevator, the Temple through which Colin had entered, the driveway—empty, not that he had expected anything else—and what looked like a couple of opulent party rooms. There was a slot beneath each screen for a videotape; it wasn't hard to guess what they were used for, nor what use was made of the tapes of the activities there.

Exhaustion pulled at him like a subtle poison, telling him he was reaching the end of his strength. If it had been at all possible, he would have left and returned another day, but there was no prospect of that. His entrance had probably been recorded on one of the cameras that Hasloch seemed so fond of; alerted to Colin's presence, Hasloch would easily guess his purpose and move Rowan.

Or kill her.

Colin was not certain where the conviction that Rowan was still alive came from: stubborn perversity, perhaps. But he knew as well as he knew the Light Itself that to abandon the search without absolute certainty—to leave a fellow soldier in enemy hands—would be a treason he could not live with. Better to die here, today, than to survive on those terms.

Die on your feet or live on your knees? There's only one true answer to that, unpopular though it's become. . . .

The entrance to the second Temple was in the show-temple itself, behind a sliding panel opened by a mechanism hidden in the back of Hasloch's marble throne. Colin hammered the golden crucifix between the door and its track to jam the mechanism open, then started on his way into the dark.

The passageway went from finished stone, to brick, to raw bedrock with wires and pipes running along its surface. The corridor narrowed, and the roof sloped until it was only scant inches above Colin's head. When he opened the plain wooden door at the end of it and saw the Rune-Christ hanging on a floating panel suspended before the wall, he was overcome with a feeling of nausea and relief combined. His intuition had not failed him.

Unwilling to enter the room unless he must, Colin glanced around from the doorway. Indirect lighting washed over the ceiling from some concealed source. The twisted tortured figure—perhaps the same one that had hung in the basement in Berkeley all those years ago—hung upon its ashwood cross above a black stone altar, surrounded by the paraphernalia of High Magick. The walls and floor were simple slabs of concrete, not gilded marble, but the chamber had a power that the finished, theatrical stage-set Colin had left behind lacked. The stench of what was done here was almost palpable, as much an assault upon the senses as the discovery of a mass grave.

There were rings—iron rings, cast in the shapes of serpents—set into the head and foot of the black altar, and its surface was marred as though something had spilled there and then dried. Three walls were solid. The fourth was covered by a long red velvet curtain. *Up to his old tricks,* Colin thought to himself. Gritting his teeth, he walked across the chamber to the curtain and yanked it back.

Open, the curtain nearly doubled the size of the room. Colin saw a light switch set into the wall just beyond the curtain, looking strangely prosaic and homely in this unnatural place. Colin flicked the light on, and stepped back, wincing at the sudden dazzle of illumination as overhead fluorescents stuttered into life.

In the center of the room stood a long surgical table with thick leather straps, with a cart of gleaming instruments beside it. There was a drain set in the middle of the floor, its bright metal discolored just as the altar had been. This was a clinic where only the blackest medicine was performed.

Everything on this side of the curtain was bright and clinical, with racks of metal shelving ranged along the concrete walls, yet it was also a seamless continuation of the medieval cruelty of the altar with its tortured image. The walls were lined with shelving that held the tools of the trade: there was a battery with cables, lengths of rubber hose; incense and oils shelved beside syringes and bottles of drugs. In the unforgiving light Colin could see everything here clearly: the implements of sorcery racked beside those of destruction.

There were knives of gold and silver and stone—whips braided of a curious fragile leather with small triangles of lead tied into the thongs—a refrigerator and sink—a small alcohol lamp, waiting ready for use beside boxes filled with hand-cast candles—an acetylene torch—a cabinet that looked mundane enough to hold vestments, and probably did. Bile rose up in the back of Colin's throat. The enormity of what he saw crushed the breath from his lungs. *Everyone talks,* Colin had told Dylan, and it was true. Once someone entered this room, all choice would be gone. You would talk, and then you would die, for the greater glory of Hasloch's Luciferian dream. A dream that was stronger than any one man's ability to oppose it.

The faint flicker of movement—the gentle movement of breath—finally caught his attention. In one corner of the room there was a cell, perhaps four feet deep. It was made of heavy diamond-paned steel mesh, painted institutional green. Colin had nearly missed it; the room was so full of things he did not wish to see clearly. Even the slenderest prisoner could not fit more than a fingertip through its holes; there was no lock, only a simple drop-latch on the outside to keep the door shut. Whoever was held here would have nothing to do except contemplate the equipment in that room and think about its purpose. The ghastly refinement of cruelty was like the signature of a familiar artist.

Numbly, exhausted by the strength of his revulsion, Colin walked over to see who—or what—was inside. He swung the simple latch up and slid the door back on its tracks.

Rowan Moorcock lay on the floor of the cell, one arm flung up to cover her face. She was wearing a long-sleeved white turtleneck and jeans. If not for that, Colin might not have seen her at all, might have mistaken the mesh for the door of another storage cabinet. Stiffly, he knelt beside her, dreading what he would find, and pulled her arm away from her face.

But she had not been harmed—at least not in any physical fashion that Colin would see. Her long red hair was still neatly braided. The white shirt was grey now with dust along the cuffs and elbows, but she was still fully dressed, down to her scuffed white sneakers. There was no blood on anything.

But Colin could not wake her.

She did not have the reflexes even the sick or the drugged would possess.

Her pupils did not contract when Colin shone his pocket flash into them, and when he took her pulse he could feel her heart beat with the slow, measured regularity of one in deep trance. She breathed as if she were asleep—or as if her body, alone, were present.

Colin knew already that Rowan was a strong Sensitive, and that made her vulnerable in ways that an ordinary person, or even a trained Adept, was not. If she had unwarily opened herself to the taint of this shrine, the shock might have blasted her spirit free from her body and doomed it to wander the Overlight until her body died—the same fate Colin had once attempted to engineer for Hasloch.

But if this were indeed merely the insensate animal shell left behind after an accident—or deliberate destruction—of that sort, Colin did not think Hasloch would have bothered to keep it. If Colin knew his old enemy at all, Hasloch still had plans for Rowan, and that meant that Rowan was here.

Somewhere.

If it had been possible, Colin would simply have carried her out of here and worried about trying to summon back her wandering spirit later. But he could not lift her, much less carry her down that long shaft to the elevator and the surface. And there was no help he could summon—Farrar would certainly be gone by now, even if Colin were willing to risk retracing his steps to go in search of him.

The police? It was all-too-possible that if he called them, Colin would be merely summoning Hasloch's allies. His only real chance to get Rowan out of here was if she could move under her own power.

There was a way.

The powers for which Colin's Order stood guardian were the secrets of Life Itself—those powers that welled up from the dark heart of Nature, carrying such risk to their user. Colin MacLaren was both Magician and Priest, and none knew better than he of the dark temptation of Power unfettered by Duty. Here in the enemy's stronghold, tempted to despair and hatred, there was an immense temptation to use the forces he could summon to blast the Evil out of existence—but to do such a thing was to invite the corruption of those Secrets entrusted to him, which would mean ultimate ruin in a future Colin must take on trust.

Could he take up the Power—and then set it aside, even in the face of defeat, death, and ruin?

Was he as strong as that?

Colin drew a deep breath. *Not my will*, he prayed. *Not my will. I resign all my will, in perfect love and perfect trust. No matter how absolute defeat looks, I will not doubt Your ultimate and unknowable goodness. . . .*

He took Rowan's hand in his, his long fingers closing over her wrist, measuring the slow pulse. With his free hand he sketched a Sign upon her forehead—a Sign of such Power that it would summon back the soul to the body that was dead, not merely to one that slept. He felt her pulse flutter as her heart began to beat to a faster rhythm.

But she still resisted, unwilling to be called back to that excruciating reality from which she must have tried so desperately to escape. What he had dared so far had not been enough.

There were stronger magicks in his arsenal, but to wield them would be to incur a debt that not he, but Rowan, must repay. To force her into such an unbreakable obligation without her will or consent would be Black Magick indeed, leading to nothing but evil. As he had promised, he must be willing to fail.

Or he must have her consent. . . .

"Rowan," Colin said aloud. "Rowan Moorcock. Do you hear me?"

Hear me, Child of the Light, by the Light that is in you . . . Colin said silently. He closed his eyes—

And he was home, once more.

The Field of Stars lay outside the City of the Sun, outside the Temple precinct that a thousand generations of exiled Adepts had recreated in the Overlight in memory of their lost homeland. The soft swell of its hillside was covered with the tiny blue flowers that gave the place its name.

Why was he here? This was not the place he had expected to find Rowan. Hurt, in shock, she would have retreated to whatever place her deepest mind considered safe: a childhood playground, perhaps, or some image gleaned from movies or TV.

Had the magicks of Hasloch's temple led Colin astray—or was this a summoning from a Higher Power, bidding him to attend?

Colin looked around himself carefully, trying to gather the meaning of what he saw. Where was the one who had summoned him? Why—if he had been called—did he not now stand without the great gate of the Temple of the Sun?

As he gazed out across the field, toward the desert and the distant mountains beyond, he saw that a cowled figure stood waiting among the flowers. The maiden wore the simple white robe of the Scribe, that caste from which the Priests and Adepts of the City of the Sun took their disciples.

She was waiting for him.

For him.

Waiting for her master, for the Adept who would set her feet upon the Path. Waiting for the one who would entrust to her his deepest secrets, his power, who would trust her absolutely. . . .

A woman—! Colin felt a sense of profound shock, even as he recognized the penetrating peal of the Astral Bell. And not just any woman, but one who was already known to him.

Rowan Moorcock.

Her? How could it be her? How could I have known *of* her for so many years and not known *her* at all? But it is said "when the student is ready, the Teacher will appear." Have I been waiting all these years for her to be ready? HER? *It was not, he told himself as he sternly mastered his shock and amazement, unheard of for a woman to become an Adept. The man who was in this life known as Colin MacLaren had known many such through his lives; there were women even in his own Order. But he had never thought that the disciple he had sought through all his own long years might be a woman. And Rowan, of all women, was the one he would least have sought: facile and frivolous, glib and superficial—*

Blindness. And arrogance. My besetting sins, in more lives than this, *the Adept remembered sadly. Here and now, in this moment of greatest peril, the Great Book of Life was open to him, the pages stark and clear for him to read.*

"Choose now, Riveda." *The deep and awesome voice seemed to come from everywhere at once, its tone as deep and penetrating as that of a bell.* "For this moment the Book is open for you to read, that you may know how the Black can become Grey, and the Grey become White at last."

And Colin saw all the lives he had lived before this—the lives lived beneath the Adept's great burden: of Knowledge dedicated to Service alone. And he saw the karmic burden that had bound him to the Wheel for a thousand lifetimes. . . .

In the Great Hall of the Temple of Light, a man stood in chains—a tall man, with grey hair and piercing rain-grey eyes. He had been condemned to death by those who had once been his peers, condemned for black transgressions against the Law. Healer and Priest he had been, but for him, that had not been enough. In his arrogance, he had done first good work—returning the Grey-robes to their rightful path as scholars and healers—but in his unwillingness to relinquish the completed task, Riveda had gone too far, had reached for the power of the very Gods, meddling in the blackest mysteries of blind Nature. He had bowed his head to no Law save that of his own devising, and now in punishment he must bow down to the greatest Law of all: Death.

Through the Mercy Cup he would go unrepentant into the Night, and the harm he had done in his life would continue on, until it had destroyed the very physical fabric of the Temple and the City beyond, scattering its priests into the young kingdoms that lay beyond the City's gates.

Here in the Field of Stars, Colin came back to himself, shaken to the core of his being by what he had learned. Truly, the forgetfulness those on the Path brought with them into Life was a great mercy—how could he ever have lived with the intimate knowledge of that great crime? He had labored a thousand lifetimes since to atone for what he had done . . . his lives expended in Service and acceptance, but at that moment, Colin did not feel it was enough.

"Yet know this, Son of the Sun—*that all Paths are spokes of the Wheel, leading but to one Center. And that the greatest of the Mysteries is that Life proceeds from the very hand of Death. . . .*"

Was it all for this? *The man who was known in this life as Colin MacLaren asked.* Was it all for You—the betrayal and the rebirth—the pain, the shame, the lives wasted?

"All," *said the tolling voice within Colin's own heart.* "For this is the center of My Mystery: and all Life is Mine, I waste none. . . ."

And now it was for him to choose again, as he had chosen a thousand times in a thousand lives, so that Perfect Freedom and the Divine Will were as one force.

The man once called Riveda walked across the Field of Stars, and he could smell the perfume of the flowers he crushed beneath his sandaled feet. The young woman looked up as he approached, and as he looked into her eyes he saw the face of the daughter he had never seen—the child that ancient magician had died without knowing. And he knew by this sign that the vast debt was repaid at last, and he was to be free at last of the Great Wheel that bound souls into matter.

He reached out and took her hand. She startled as if awakening from a deep sleep, staring at him in surprise.

"Eilantha," the once-Lord of the Grey-robes said. "I call you to awaken into Life. Come with me."

The feel of Rowan pulling her hand from his roused Colin to consciousness again. He opened his eyes.

Rowan was propped up on one elbow, regarding him warily, as if she were not quite certain who he was. "Dr. MacLaren," she said blankly.

"Do you know who I am?" Colin asked her. He felt as if he had simply dozed, although he knew in his heart that what had transpired was much greater than that, though the memory of all but the glory of the Presence was fast fading. But he must know what she remembered—if anything—from her time in the Overlight.

"You're—" She stopped. "You know, I had this completely bizarre dream, where . . ." Her voice trailed off as she got a good look at her surroundings. "It wasn't a dream. I was there—on that hill where the Secret School meets. And so were you."

The Secret School. The name given by many who visited it only in dream and spirit to the Temple of the Sun. It seemed his original instinct had played him false: if Rowan knew of that place, she was no superficial participant or dilettante of the obscure.

"No. It was no dream, Rowan," Colin said, even while a part of him wondered: *This woman? This girl?* SHE is to be my *chela?* How could he teach her? What did he have to say to her?

What I must. What we have chosen together, she and I.

Her memory of the experience she'd had in the Overlight was fading quickly—Colin could see that in her eyes—to be replaced by the awareness of this place and its attendant horrors. She sat up, groaning with the stiffness of long-unused muscles.

"What happened? The door's open—did Dylan get the message? I've been hiding out for months, trying to get somebody to just *listen,* but it sounds just too *X-Files* for anyone to take seriously—there's a man named Toller Hasloch. He's a big-shot Washington lawyer, and he's murdered at least eight people that I know of. He's got a whole Nazi temple down here, and there's this presidential candidate. . . ."

"There isn't much time," Colin said, interrupting her. "We've got to get you out of here, but there's one thing you must do first, for your protection. You must take the Oath on the physical plane that you have already taken on the Astral, and place yourself beyond Hasloch's power to harm you in any way that matters. By the Power I bear, I seal and sign you to the Power, to Serve the Light until Time itself should end. Is this your True Will?" Colin asked as he raised his hand in the Sign. Irrelevant to Rowan or not, the question must be asked—and answered.

"Yeah, okay, right, I'm there," Rowan said, waving her hands in agitation. "Skip all the Ancient Atlantis stuff, Dr. MacLaren. I've got it. I believe you. I'm in."

Colin winced inwardly. This was going to be just as difficult as he'd imagined it would. Paradoxically, the thought made him smile.

"Where do we go from here?"

Rowan lurched to her feet and leaned against the mesh, reaching out a hand to help Colin up. He could tell she was weaker than she would have liked him to know—he did not know, and suspected that Rowan didn't either, how many days she'd lain unconscious on the floor of that cell. Fortunately, she did not have to walk far—once they were back in the house upstairs, Colin would happily call the police himself.

"We leave," Colin said, steadying himself against the steel mesh of the cage. "Come on." Rowan was safe. All the rest could wait.

Rowan drew breath to argue, and shook her head, giving in instead. She picked up her purse from where Colin had set it on the floor of the cell and slung it over her shoulder, staggering as it pulled her off balance. Colin could see the lines of pain and strain etch themselves into her face as she settled deeper into the awareness of her physical body.

"You're the boss," she said gamely.

Colin pushed through the half-open draperies. The figure on the cross gleamed in the dimness, its carven wounds seeming to shed fresh blood. Colin forced himself to take that first step forward, into the space before the altar.

"Sick," Rowan commented from behind him, though whether it was an announcement or a judgment Colin wasn't sure.

Glancing back, he saw her shake her head, as balked by the atmosphere of the temple as a non-Sensitive would be by a brick wall. He wondered if all those who so blithely claimed great psychic power would as happily embrace its dark side: the vulnerability to invisible forces to which the non-Sensitive was immune. It was this vulnerability and the misunderstandings it engendered which led to the persecution and madness of so many with the Gift. Colin heard her draw a shaky breath, gathering her strength to face that thing.

"Come on," Colin said, encouragingly. He held out his hand. "It isn't far."

"But farther, I think, than you're ever going to go."

Toller Hasloch stepped through the door.

He was dressed for the office—one more note of incongruity in this peculiar place. A mate to the pendant Colin had found in Rowan's kitchen gleamed against his silk tie, an archaicism that had no place in the modern world.

"Oh, Colin," Hasloch said chidingly. "You're far too predictable. As soon as I realized why you'd come to visit me, I also realized that of course you would try to rescue the fair maiden—and of course I would be right here to stop you. I even turned the alarm system off so we wouldn't be interrupted—

I would have left the doors unlocked if I'd known you were coming today, but I'm glad to see you didn't have any trouble."

There was a gun in his hand: in some sense, Colin would have been disappointed if there were not.

"The only thing I'm wondering now is whether you'd like to live a little longer, and see what's going to happen to the girl, or if I should just indulge myself and shoot you now? What do you think? It might be worth it to you—a bit more life, and the hope I'll make a mistake you can use?" Hasloch's voice was genial. Playful.

Behind him, Colin heard Rowan's whimper of disappointment and felt her begin to move away from him.

"You can't shoot us both at the same time," Rowan said gamely. She had edged away from Colin, inching toward the door.

"Don't move, my little *Mischling,*" Hasloch snapped. "I'll shoot you first, if I must—and I can't miss at this distance."

"Stay where you are, Rowan," Colin told her, and once more, through the invisible current of their mutually binding Oath, he felt her reluctant obedience.

"What is it you want, Toller? You must want something, or you'd have shot us both by now," Colin said. Every moment he kept Hasloch's attention on him gave Rowan more chance to recover. If she could gather the strength to run, there was a slim chance she might make it—and even a slim chance was better than what she faced down here.

"While a bullet is an effective way of ending debate, I admit it lacks elegance," Hasloch said graciously. "Just once before you die, you belligerent old fossil, I'd like you to admit that I'm right."

Colin nearly laughed aloud, then his eyes narrowed. *"The thing to remember about Fritz is that he wants to be loved. The Germans are notoriously sentimental and self-pitying for a bunch of murderers. If you're caught, you might be able to play on that to buy yourself some time."*

The words of a long-ago trainer were as clear in Colin's mind as if they had just been spoken. And though Hasloch had been born and bred an American, he, too, possessed that same fatal, self-indulgent flaw. He didn't just want to win: he wanted everyone to recognize that he *deserved* to win.

"You're holding us both here at gunpoint, intending to torture us to death at your convenience, and you want to hold a debate? Fine with me, sonny boy," Colin said, manufacturing a sneer. Hasloch had always liked to make speeches. Perhaps he'd make one now.

"Oh, come now," Hasloch said, coaxingly. "You've chosen our last two battlefields—let me choose this one. A last passage at arms with a worthy—or at least persistent—adversary. Admit your defeat—your failure—and I'll even let you go: you'll live out your days knowing that you gave your whole life to a lie, and served something that you ought, by your own code, to have loathed."

"Maybe," Colin said. "Why don't you just give it your best shot and we'll see?"

His back and chest ached with weariness, and the air seemed stifling, as if he could feel all the weight of the earth above pressing down on him. A few feet away, Rowan was swaying with sickness and fatigue, her face as white as scraped bone.

"Colin MacLaren, champion of Truth, Justice, and all the rest." Hasloch bowed mockingly. The gun did not waver.

"In the name of the holy cause of Liberty you champion the American Eagle against overwhelming odds . . . but how can she be worthy of you, Warrior of the Light? America is a country built upon the principle of intolerance, whose Puritan settlers massacred the trusting aboriginals and their fellow settlers with equal abandon. She is a nation which has pried its great storehouses of wealth from the dead fingers of this land's first inhabitants—whose citizens have slaughtered more animals than the coliseums of ancient Rome—whose founders enslaved a continent and exploited its labor for more than half a century after civilized men had declared slavery an abomination: upstanding American patriots who clutched this peculiar institution to its bosom because it made its wealthy landowners so very rich."

He held up his hand as though Colin might be about to interrupt. Rowan was staring at Hasloch in frank disbelief, but Colin knew better than to think the situation was any less dangerous just because it now verged on the ludicrous. It might seem as if Hasloch's speech was empty words, such as the nation's enemies had flung at her for well over a century, but here, in this time and place, they were not mere words. The Great Book was open, recording all that was said, and what it recorded would have the compelling force of reality.

Hasloch continued.

"And then, when industry had allowed the North to supersede the South, the Northerners slaughtered their brethren using ignorant foreign mercenaries as cannon fodder. The Industrial North freed the slaves, and then attempted to starve them to death.

"*This* is the crucible in which your America, your eternal Champion of Liberty was forged, old man! She moved fast enough to betray her allies, though—you remember Hungary in '56, don't you, Colin? For seven days they begged the West to honor its treaties, until the Russians rolled in and shot them all. Where was the honor of the Eagle then?"

The gauntlet that Colin had taken up for no more reason than to give Rowan a chance to survive was suddenly a far more profound and eternal battle, and one that Colin dared not lose. If Hasloch's arguments could not be refuted, he would have won a true and real victory.

This was a war waged at the heart of Colin's own weakness: his faith. And if he failed—if he *believed*, even for a moment, in the truth of Hasloch's words—then the Shadow could claim a terrible victory.

Hasloch smiled: gleeful, confident.

"Perhaps you've wondered why people seem so tired these days? Why there is such apathy about the wondrous process of democracy? Your beloved citizen-philosophers don't want to take responsibility for this 'political arena' you've bequeathed to them: a responsibility they never asked for, and one they are unequipped to wield. And you know why *that* is, as well.

"It's interesting, I find, that you left the military so conveniently. You never got the opportunity to meet your former foes as they took their new U.S. government posts. The execrated butchers who built German's V-2 program at Dora—who destroyed London—created America's own National Air and Space Administration . . . space for purely peaceful uses, of course. The West's so-called intelligence community, here and abroad, was populated with men who wore the double-lightning rune tattooed upon their bodies. Men in the pay of America, but in the service of the Reich . . . the true Reich: the invisible and undefeated Reich that has always existed—that was a dream in the hearts of men, that was the spirit of an age before ever Hitler was born to incarnate it.

"It is these visionaries who have toiled patiently through the decades, discrediting the weary jejune ideals of the so-called Founding Fathers and replacing them with their own. Your blood-soaked eagle is tired, Professor— her citizens are tired even of bread and circuses. The American Dream is over, and the Racial Destiny of the Superman shall take its place." Hasloch smiled, a predator secure in his ultimate victory.

"No," Colin said. "You're wrong." Empty words would not serve him here, only Truth. His own truth, sought out and tested over a lifetime of doubt and despair—a truth stronger than that of Toller Hasloch.

"There were times when I used to think you might be right, Sunny Jim. It's a persuasive argument. But despair is a sin—and a lie, as well. I don't have any more time for lies, including this one. So let me give you a bulletin fresh from the front lines: The dream is alive, Toller."

He felt Rowan straighten, as if drawing new strength from an unexpected source. Hasloch watched him with glittering-eyed alertness.

"It lives in the hearts and minds of every man and woman across the world who believes in the 'American Dream'—in everyone who fights and dies to reach a thing that they only know by faith. You say you've destroyed us, but a nation isn't only flesh and stone and land—it's built first in the heart and then in the mind. You haven't won. You've lost. Every Chinese dissident— every Hungarian freedom-fighter—is my countryman. You cannot defeat us all."

From the corner of his eye, Colin saw Rowan's head turn slowly toward him, as if she'd only just begun to listen. In a private chamber of his heart he mourned for all that she would lose if they died here.

But even her death would not be a lasting defeat. Colin realized that at last.

"Empty words, Colin; the fantasies of slaves. Your 'dream' is dead—and in fact, it never existed. Our victory parade is no farther away than the next election. A new Pax Americana will sweep across the globe—but I'm afraid you won't like it very much." The smile of triumph on Hasloch's face was fixed. The gun in his hand gleamed silvery in the dim light.

"America doesn't matter, Toller. Are you listening? It doesn't matter. That's what your kind has never gotten straight. We've been aiming toward this Celestial City—a City of the Light—for thousands of years. America is not the point—it's only the closest approach we have yet to an ideal. Smash it, subvert it, we will rebuild the dream from the ashes a thousand times, and each time we'll build it closer to the perfection that the Light has placed in our hearts."

A joy he had not realized that he possessed transfigured Colin. This was the answer he had prayed for, the refutation of the evil and despair he saw around him, the rebuttal to the fear he'd felt in a thousand sleepless nights that Hasloch had won.

"Two thousand years ago, the Church was incarnated as a vehicle of the Light, to make men free and happy—"

"A failure!" Toller sneered, back on secure ideological ground.

"Granted," Colin said easily. "It got bogged down in local customs and trying to legislate morality. The Church failed at what it was designed to do, but it passed the torch: to the Renaissance; to the Reformation; to the Industrial Revolution. None of them was perfect—each advance was bought at the price of blood and sorrow and injustice and thousands of lives—but each was a step closer to the dream we were made for. And that's the bottom line: things get better."

Hasloch sneered, but there was something halfhearted in the gesture. As if, deep within his withered soul, something that hungered to hear this was listening.

"We're smarter, we're healthier, we know better than any time since the Fall of Man who we are and where we're going," Colin said with fierce urgency. "There's one for you—the Fall of Man. It's one of our greatest triumphs—your Serpent won that round, and it took us ten thousand years to work our way back from the bottom of the Pit, but we did it. And we'll keep right on doing it. Until you've killed every last one of us, your Shadow cannot claim victory—and at that, your victory will last exactly until a new Champion of the Light is born."

The Shadow had not won, and it never would. No matter what happened. No matter how long and twisted and weary the road.

Rowan took a step toward him, smiling. There were tears in her eyes, but her face was radiant with an incandescent, impassioned Joy. She held out her hand to Colin, and he took it.

"Go ahead," Rowan urged Hasloch generously. "Kill both of us. But y'know, it isn't going to do you any good. We'll be back. We'll always be back." Her voice vibrated with that promise, bright as a sword blade.

"Give up, Hasloch. You haven't won. And you never will," Colin said quietly.

For the first time since he'd confronted them, real uncertainty crossed Hasloch's face. "You are defeated," he said plaintively. "You know you are. Why won't you lie down and die?"

"It's the American spirit," Colin said with a tight grin. "Never say die."

Rowan giggled, a shocking triumphant sound in this place of horror. "'Do you feel lucky, punk?'" she quoted softly. "'Well? Do ya?'"

"Then die anyway," Hasloch said, raising his pistol and taking aim. "Not elegant, but effective."

The roar of a shot filled the room.

In that confined space the sound was deafening. Rowan screamed at the shock of it. There was a flash, and the stink of burnt gunpowder; instinctively Colin flinched back and covered his eyes, pulling Rowan against him in a futile gesture of protection.

But he was not the target, and neither was Rowan.

Hereward Farrar stood in the doorway in a gunsmoke haze, a double-barreled shotgun cradled in one arm.

Toller Hasloch lay arched back across his own altar, clutching at it for support. For whatever reason, Hereward had aimed low, and most of the load of shot had missed Hasloch's heart and lungs; he was still alive.

His mouth worked, shaping parting words he would never get to say. His feet slipped in his own blood, and he slid wetly down into a sitting position on the floor. Colin imagined he could almost feel the moment that the spirit sprang free of its mortal vessel to return once more to the Wheel that turned for both Dark and Light.

"He's getting away," Rowan said, in a dull, disbelieving voice. "Shouldn't we . . . ?"

"No," Colin said. He squeezed her shoulder reassuringly. "Let him go. He'll be back. But maybe, in time, he'll begin to learn. Remember that when you see him again."

And reverberating through the chamber, Colin heard the soft sound of a Book closing.

But not forever.

"Isn't it time for you two to get moving?" Farrar said. He held out his key ring toward Colin. "I called the sheriff's department before I came down here—I had to leave the car in the driveway, but it ought to be okay there for a few minutes at least. Just leave the keys in it when you're done with it. Park it anywhere."

"Who the hell are you?" Rowan demanded with dazed bemusement. She pushed herself away from Colin and glared at Farrar, holding herself upright now by sheer force of will.

"Nobody in particular," Farrar said, smiling faintly. "Just somebody who was in the right place at the right time—finally."

"What will you do?" Colin asked him.

"Oh, I imagine I'm probably going to jail," Farrar said. "I just killed a man. Hasloch certainly needed killing, but you don't evade the consequences afterward. You take the hit—you don't make things worse. That's the rule."

And then, someday, your atonement is complete. . . .

"You weren't sent by the department," Colin said.

"No," Farrar said simply. He stepped out of the doorway and carefully broke the shotgun open. "Go ahead. I've got a few things to do here before I go." He gestured, "Right down that hall."

"And straight on till morning," Rowan muttered, taking a hesitant step toward the door.

The return down that endless passageway was worse than the first journey had been. The secret door still stood open, and the two of them passed through it hand in hand.

Rowan was staggering blindly, exhausted by her ordeal and the psychic agony of the Temple, and Colin felt the full weight of every moment of his years. But both of them were moved by the same driving motivation: the desire not to spend a moment more than they had to in this unspeakable place.

For one horrible moment Colin thought that the Temple doors would not open without their key, but on this side all that was needed was the simple push of a button. The doors swung inward, and across the antechamber they could see the lights of the elevator, standing with its doors open.

"We should wait here for him," Rowan said, collapsing against the inside wall of the elevator. "Right?"

"I don't think so," Colin said. "We have to get you out of here and safe. You're the best witness if this mess ever goes to court. Toller wasn't working alone. We'll only have leverage if we have something to expose."

"Like an underground Satanist Temple in Virginia?" Rowan said with weary humor. She pushed herself away from the wall and pushed the button. "Geraldo Rivera, here I come."

The elevator doors opened into darkness. The door at the end of the short hallway was closed.

"Come on," Colin said to Rowan. His voice sounded hoarse and strange to him—like a parody of age. But the old man had won one for the home team. "Just a flight of stairs and we're home free."

Rowan was reaching for the knob when the door was jerked open from the outside. She yelped, jumping backward into Colin and nearly knocking them both over.

A Fauquier County sheriff's deputy stared back at her, gun drawn.

TWENTY-SEVEN

GLASTONBURY, NEW YORK,
FRIDAY, DECEMBER 31, 1999

Ring in the thousand years of peace.
Ring in the valiant man and free,
The larger heart, the kindlier hand;
Ring out the darkness of the land;
Ring in the Christ that is to be.
—ALFRED, LORD TENNYSON

TOLLER HASLOCH HAD BOASTED OF THE FRIENDS HE'D HAD IN HIGH places, but apparently he'd had nearly as many enemies there. The deputies who had arrested Rowan and Colin took them to the nearest hospital, and while they waited for treatment—Rowan for dehydration and shock, Colin for the supposed frailty of his advanced age—the uniformed deputies had been replaced by sleek civilians who discouraged questions of any sort.

For a while Colin wondered if he had defeated Hasloch only to fall prey to the rest of Hasloch's monstrous network, but after the hospital released them, their keepers simply drove them to a Washington hotel just off the Mall, where the two of them spent three days locked incommunicado in a suite on the eighteenth floor before they were driven to the airport and released.

No one ever asked either of them any questions, and Colin was content to have it so. He had done what he had come to do. And more—he had found the last work of his life.

"I hope Claire and Daddy are having fun," Rowan said, looking into the fire.

"Probably they're having as much fun as it is possible to have in Rhinebeck," Colin assured her gravely.

Last spring, Claire had finally succumbed to Justin's persuasions and moved permanently to the old farm in Madison Corners. The countryside was much changed from the days when the Church of the Antique Rite had held sway there: though still suffering from the same economic depression that gripped other agriculturally-dependent parts of the U.S., it was a more wholesome sort of stagnation than before, if such a thing were possible. Claire had found a great deal of use for all the skills she'd acquired in the course of a long life, from nursing to crisis intervention, and from what Colin had seen when they came for Christmas, she and Justin were very happy.

It was his second winter in the old farmhouse on Greyangels Road. The house had welcomed him back last fall as if he had never left; Winter Greyson (née Musgrave) was its current owner, and the Greysons had been pleased to find so congenial a tenant. Grey had taken a particular delight in shipping Colin's pack-rat collection of books and papers to him; though Rowan was not as capable a secretary as Grey had been, she had learned quickly. Much of Colin's collection would pass directly to her use in the years to come.

"They'll be staying until Monday," Colin reminded her. "But they do have a home of their own to go to. And an old house needs looking after, especially during a New England winter."

"Yes, but . . ." Rowan said, and let the sentence drop.

Colin knew what she was thinking. While Claire and Justin were here, Rowan was able to maintain the pretence of a normal life. The furnishings of the Sanctuary—which normally occupied the second upstairs bedroom—were tucked away, and the regime of meditation and spiritual exercises that occupied Rowan's time—outside of her mundane studies—was suspended.

"It's New Year's Eve," Colin said. "I've seen too many of them to care, but you ought to be out celebrating, not staying here keeping me company."

Rowan made a rude graphic noise. "And who am I supposed to go out *with*? Ninian? And do what? People—ordinary people—just seem so . . . oblivious. I know it's wrong, but I don't have anything to say to them, and what could they say to me? I feel like we're on different planets."

The path of the disciple had not been—and still was not—an easy path for either of them. The passage to membership in Colin's Order was long and arduous, and many of its time-worn practices seemed meaninglessly archaic to Rowan, who rebelled strenuously against them. For all her manifest dedication to the Light, Colin still sometimes felt that Rowan took the Great Secrets of Initiation far too lightly.

But the past year had taught them much about each other. In the spring Rowan would be finished here at Taghkanic, and Colin would take Dr. Rowan Moorcock to visit Nathaniel, and then—with his permission—would take her on to London, for formal initiation into the Order.

"Well, just as you like," Colin said. "Next year is the real turning of the Millennium, anyway—not that it's anything but an arbitrary benchmark. Just as long as you don't feel you're missing anything."

Rowan shook her head, not looking at him. In some ways her path was harder than his own had been: it was far easier to endure secrecy and isolation than the knowledge that what you were doing would be a source of incredulous mockery if it was ever revealed. Colin was not sure he could have faced what Rowan faced every day with mindfulness and a still heart.

But she has been born for her own age, as I was born for mine. In each lifetime we are given the Tools we need to perform the Great Work, though in every century they are different.

At Midsummer the newest Daughter of the Sun would be received into the Temple of Light as it existed on the Outer Plane, and she would become heir to all of Colin's power and the wisdom of more lives than this. His heritage would pass safely into the hands of his disciple for safekeeping into the third millennium.

"Oh, that reminds me," Colin said. "I have a present for you." He'd meant to give it to her next June, but it seemed right that she should have it now.

"A New Year's present?" Rowan said, getting to her feet as Colin levered himself out of the chair in front of the fire.

"Of a sort. Wait here."

Colin went through the kitchen to his bedroom and took an object off his desk. Carrying it carefully in both hands, he came back into the living room and held it out to Rowan.

"Many years ago, a friend gave this to me. It's served me well all these years—as a sort of reminder, you might say. Now I'm passing it on to you. Call it a legacy."

"It's beautiful," Rowan said.

She held the paperweight up so that it caught the firelight: a sterling sword, its surface soft with the patina of age, pierced an anvil set into a block of white stone.

AND KING HEREAFTER

I have owed to them,
In hours of weariness, sensations sweet,
Felt in the blood, and felt along the heart;
And passing even into my purer mind,
With tranquil restoration:
— WILLIAM WORDSWORTH

IT WAS SOMETHING OF A SURPRISE TO FIND MYSELF LIVING AT MOORCOCK farm once more. When Uncle Clarence died, the farm passed to Justin, with the caveat that I should always be welcome to make my home there if I wished to. It took Justin some years to persuade me that I should really be happy there, but it is a good feeling to have family around me once more. Rowan can share something with Colin that I never could, for all the years of our friendship. It is strange what contentment I find in knowing that he has found it at last.

And so we pass from darkness to darkness, rejoicing at our little time in the Light. All is a sleep and a forgetting, save for those few walking among us who have chosen to shoulder the burden of awareness from Life to Life. As the years pass, the darkness that someday claims each of us becomes more real to me, and more and more I think on what Colin said to me when he first set my feet upon the path I was to follow all my life:

"The great mass of humanity neither knows nor cares about magick and they have the right to keep things that way—to not be troubled by forces outside the scope of their daily lives, or manipulated by forces they have no way of resisting. When I find someone interfering in people's lives with magick in that fashion, it's my duty to stop them if I can—for their own sake, as well as for the sake of the lives they may harm."

It is as good a summation as any, for a life's work and a dear friend. Walk in the Light, Colin MacLaren. I know we will meet again.

> *Enough of science and of art;*
> *Close up these barren leaves.*
> *Come forth, and bring with you a heart*
> *That watches and receives.*
>   —WILLIAM WORDSWORTH